THE
GOLDEN
PINNACLE

ROBERT GORE

ISBN: 1478267186

ISBN-13: 9781478267188

Library of Congress Control Number: 2012913047

CreateSpace Independent Publishing Platform

North Charleston, South Carolina

To all those "yearning to breathe free," including my wife, Roberta; my son, Austin; my mother, Ella Mae Warner; my sister, Judi Voelz, her husband, David, and their children Alex, Katie, and Brian; my brother, Jim, and his wife, Cyndie; my friend David Bird; and to the memories of my father, Raymond Gore, and Charley Warner.

Contents

Acknowledgements

I gratefully acknowledge the assistance of my writing group: Marilyn Lowery, Harriet Trueblood, Cindy Gleason, and the late Ann Shaftel. They are responsible for many improvements and none of the flaws. I also thank Tod Post, the Latin teacher at Crespi Carmelite High School in Encino, California, for his help in translating English phrases into Latin; Ralph MacMillan, a Civil War buff who helped me with the Civil War chapters; and my wife, Roberta, and friend, Susan Largent, for their help with the cover design.

PART ONE THE WAR

Chapter 1

A Place of Peace

Forty-five thousand troops sat around small fires eating breakfast, smoking, arguing, joking, insulting, bragging, scratching, spitting, swearing, burping, farting, and everything else men do amongst themselves when unconstrained by civilizing influences—that is, women. Campfires and tents dotted nine square miles of fields and forests west of Pittsburg Landing on the Tennessee River.

Two privates, Daniel Durand, tall and dark, and Will Farrows, shorter and fair, sat with their backs against a stump, several paces away from a group, smoking cigars, sharing the same amused expression as they listened to their comrades in arms.

"Where's Jake? Where's Charley?" Frank Needham said.

"Jake's at a service with the preacher from the 70th. Charley's got the quickstep—he's in the woods doing God's work." Corporal Mike Riley spit a long strand of tobacco juice into the fire and gulped his coffee. "Do you want to go help him?"

Needham smiled weakly. "No, sir. I wish I had known about that service, though."

"The Cincinnati papers are calling Sherman insane, and everybody knows that Grant's a drunk," Bart Landers said.

"Landers," Riley said, "for a kid who's been in the army one month and who's never fired a shot at anything more dangerous than a rabbit, you sure are a damn know-it-all."

"What makes you such an expert?" Landers scratched his right underarm. His body held a special attraction for lice, fleas, and every other creature that made a soldier itch.

"Grant took Fort Henry and Fort Donelson—that's better than anyone in Virginia."

"Sherman nearly got you all drowned."

"We came back to the landing when the rain got too fierce. Shut your trap and get me some more coffee."

Daniel and Will grinned. Nobody got the better of Riley, who had a quick tongue and was the biggest man in the company.

Landers slid the tin pot over the pole suspended above the fire and poured viscous black remnants into Riley's cup.

"Make another pot," Riley instructed, sipping the sludge.

"Drill, drill, drill," Steve Culpepper said, his words whistling through a gap in his front teeth. "I'm as bored as the buzzards waiting on Methuselah. Is today the fifth?"

"April the sixth, year of our Lord 1862," Needham said.

"I know the damn month and year. We've been here almost a month. Where the hell is Buell? Let's get going. I'm ready to fight."

"You may get your wish. Someone in the 72nd said the prisoners at the chapel were saying they're going to attack."

"Secesh hogwash." Landers dropped a chunk of hardtack in his coffee. "If they were going to attack, do you think they'd tell us about it?" He spooned out a worm oozing from the hardtack and tossed it in the dirt.

"That wouldn't be a very good tactic, now would it?" said Lieutenant Pomeroy, who had quietly approached the group. His kepi was straight, the golden bars on his shoulder, brass belt buckle, and black leather boots gleamed, and his blue, four-button blouse and trousers looked new. The points of his luxuriant blond mustache met the bottoms of his bushy sideburns.

"Do you think they'll attack, sir?" Needham said. "Colonel Sullivan thinks they might."

Pomeroy stroked his mustache. "The esteemed colonel may be overly nervous, although I believe Colonel Buckland shares his fear. That's an unfortunate tendency among militia officers. I understand that General Sherman reprimanded Buckland. The Secessionists are almost defeated, although they'll probably put up a fight at Corinth. Of course they're going to send out some sort of reconnaissance in force to see what we're doing—that's why our pickets keep running into them. But an attack? I don't think so. If it were a possibility, we would have prepared for it."

"Who is he to condescend about tendencies among militia officers?" Daniel said to Will. "His father bought his commission when Sullivan put together this regiment."

Perhaps he had been too loud. Pomeroy glanced at him and opened his mouth, but was cut short by the sound of rifles to the southeast. He turned towards the sound. "More pickets."

Artillery thundered and the long drumroll sounded—the call to battle. The men jumped to their feet, kicked sand on the fire, gulped their coffee, and scrambled for weapons and ammunition. Charley, the unfortunate with the quickstep, ran up from the woods, tugging on his trousers. Pomeroy mumbled something about a skirmish and left.

"The esteemed lieutenant has his esteemed head up his esteemed arse," Daniel muttered, stomping out his cigar. He stared at his pack, wondering what to take and what to leave. These seemingly simple decisions required an unusually long time. His rifle, bayonet, scabbard, cartridge and cap boxes, and canteen would go. His bulky pack, with blankets, extra clothing, and an overcoat, would stay. Food, a metal plate, and utensils could be stored in the haversack, but the haversack itself would be a nuisance. He'd leave it.

"Fall in!" Colonel Sullivan shouted. "Your first fight—time to meet the elephant!"

As a volunteer regiment, the 48th Ohio had received only limited instruction and drill. Private Durand suddenly appreciated the tedium of the drill they had received as the regiment quickly formed a long double line.

"Forward march!"

They marched south towards a small creek, the Shiloh branch of the Tennessee River, brogans squishing in the mud from yesterday's rain. Today had dawned chilly and clear, warming as the sun rose. Wisps of steam carried the smells of mud, flowers, wild grass, and trees. Little conversation interrupted the cadence of the march. They were brought up short two hundred yards from the creek. Across the creek, a mass of Confederates in butternut uniforms emerged from the woody hollow and scraggly underbrush.

The other two regiments in Colonel Buckland's Fourth Brigade—the 70th Ohio and the 72nd Ohio—joined the 48th. Two thousand soldiers formed a two-deep line, the 48th in the middle, the 72nd on the right, and the 70th on the left, on top of a bushy rise that sloped down to the creek. The Confederate regiments methodically fell into line.

"I'd rather have the Secesh come at us here than try to cross that creek and fight them in those woods," Will whispered to Daniel, who nodded. "We do what we're supposed to do, and we'll be chasing them back over the creek into the woods."

Daniel waved towards a sergeant leading a horse towing a caisson. The sergeant stopped and opened a large metal chest containing paper cartridges and firing caps. He counted out forty of each to Daniel and Will and continued down the line.

Colonel Sullivan stepped to the front of his regiment. "Gentlemen, a few reminders. Please wait until the order is issued to fire—there's no use wasting time and ammunition on long shots. Aim low, fire deliberately. Ignore the wounded—they will be attended to by the medical detail. Their best hope is for you to proceed forward and drive the enemy back. Do not fear that you will be unable to do your duty—you will. May God be with us."

"Amen," Riley said. "Look at Landers and Culpepper. They don't look too cocky now, do they?" The two stood side by side, looking younger than their eighteen years, eyes wide, fixed on the Confederates.

Lieutenant Pomeroy stepped to the front of the regiment. "Men, let us not forget the sacred cause of Union. If we fail to squelch this rebellion, we bring dishonor to our country and ourselves. We shall triumph! It is an honor to be one of the officers leading you."

"The only place that lad will lead us is to the grave," Riley whispered.

Daniel stood his Springfield rifle upright to load it. He hadn't shot a rifle until he joined the army. He had been issued a musket, an old-style smooth bore. Jake Blanchard, who had shot many a meal on his family's farm in eastern Ohio, told him that anything with a smooth bore would be useless at distances greater than a hundred yards. A bullet emerging from a smooth bore had no spin, and a spinning bullet was more accurate for a longer range. Although it took most of his meager savings, Daniel had bought the Springfield. Its rifled barrel had spiral grooves, which imparted the desired spin. The first time the regiment took target practice, Daniel had shot passably well despite his lack of experience.

The Fourth Brigade settled into an eternity-long hour's wait. The Rebs continued to mass on the other side of the creek, preparing to attack, preparing to kill. Aside from scattered recitations of the Lord's Prayer and the Twenty-Third Psalm, the men were silent. They heard rifles and artillery in the distance. The quickstep was widespread and many of the sufferers found themselves in a painful predicament. There was an immediate need, but no one wanted to be caught with his pants down when the shooting started. Some of them relieved themselves where they stood, the pungency the smell of fear itself.

The sun peeked through the clouds but didn't vanquish the early morning chill and dampness. Sweat ran down Daniel's neck, back, and underarms. He repeatedly sighted down his rifle at the Confederates behind the creek, two hundred yards away. His mouth was parched, but it would stay that way even if he drained his canteen, so he conserved his water. He exchanged an occasional glance with Will. There was nothing to say.

"Yea, though I walk through the valley of the shadow of death, I will fear no evil," a soldier to his left murmured.

"Forward, march!" Colonel Sullivan shouted.

"Here we come, you Secesh sons of bitches!"

"Look lively, men!"

"Traitors!"

"Here's for Ohio!"

"Here's for Abe!"

"A bullet between your eyes, Jeff Davis!"

"The devil take you bastards!"

"Huzzah!"

"Huzzah!"

This grew into a thunderous, unified cheer that was met by a high, piercing yowl, like a pack of crazed wolves, from the other side of the creek. The Confederates slogged through the water, re-formed their line, fired, and charged.

Frank Needham was the first to die of enemy gunfire. Daniel and Will, stunned, stared at his body on the ground as blood gushed from a hole that had formerly been his nose.

"What are you looking at?" shouted a sergeant. "Return fire, fire at will!"

Daniel aimed at a kneeling Reb, fired, and missed. More Confederates crossed the creek and the whiz of their minié balls grew more constant. Daniel tore open a cartridge, poured the powder down the barrel, rammed the bullet, cocked the hammer, placed a cap on the nipple, stood, and put in his rifle sight an artilleryman helping unlimber a howitzer. Aim low. He pulled the trigger. The artilleryman grabbed his shoulder.

"There's more where that came from, you Secesh son of a bitch!"

A Confederate artillery battery crossed the creek and began firing its six- and twelve-pounder guns—throwing shells, shrapnel, shot, and twelve-pound iron balls that bounced along the ground and bowled over men as if they were ninepins. Union artillery responded with deafening blasts. Two soldiers fell near Daniel and another staggered, his nearly severed arm flapping from his shoulder. Several men ran.

"Get back here, you damn cowards!" Daniel screamed. They kept running.

He reloaded his rifle. Will grinned at him weirdly through a circle of black powder covering his lips and teeth. It grew harder to see as acrid black smoke filled the air. Each reload became more difficult as powder residues built up in the barrel. The end of the ramrod rubbed his palm raw as he forced it down. Every fifth or sixth shot, he cleaned the barrel with a wet rag.

After an hour and a half, he ran out of cartridges and caps. Crouching, he ran behind the line searching for ammunition among the wounded and dead, the battlefield now enshrouded in thick smoke. The shrieks of the wounded cut through the artillery thunder, rifle fire, and minié whiz.

"My leg is gone! My damn leg is gone!"

"I can't see."

"Susannah…Susannah."

Daniel came upon a soldier lying on the ground, his arms and legs splayed, abdomen ripped open. He almost turned away from the blood and stench of perforated guts, but removed the bloody cartridge and cap boxes from the soldier's belt. They were nearly full. The man nodded feebly, mouthing the word "water." Removing the cap on the man's canteen, Daniel cradled his head in one arm and let a small trickle splash over his lips. The life went out of him. Daniel gathered the cartridges and caps, drank from the dead man's canteen, and took it and his rifle.

He crawled behind the line. It was holding, but there were gaps where men had skulked or gone down. A soldier dropped before him, blood spraying from a minié that had ripped through his throat. The writhing soldier's mouth was open as if he were screaming, but he made no sound save a macabre gurgling as he drowned in his own blood. Daniel turned away—the sight was unbearable and there was nothing he could do. As he reached his original position he saw Culpepper, the earlier proclaimer of his impatience for battle, crawling away from the line.

Will shouted in his ear, "Did you get rounds and caps? I'm out."

Daniel tossed the two boxes on the ground between them. He checked the rifle he had taken from the dead soldier. The man might not have died if he had remembered to fit a firing cap to the nipple. There was no cap although the hammer was down—the unfired powder and a bullet were still in the barrel. Daniel rectified the fatal error, putting a cap on the nipple, and fired into the smoky pall. He preferred the action of his own rifle.

For three hours Buckland's brigade held, aided by its position above the Confederates and the creek and dense underbrush. Wounded and dead men and horses and bombed-out artillery littered the area in front of the creek. Unfortunately, to the left, Colonel Hildebrand's Third Brigade began to retreat under heavy fire. Buckland had to retreat or risk his left flank.

"Retreat," the officers shouted, "retreat! To the road past the Shiloh chapel. Fall back!"

They retreated slowly under fire, through thick woods broken occasionally by cleared fields. As they fell back behind their camp, Confederate fire diminished. The Rebs had stopped, apparently lured by uneaten Union breakfasts and the chance to collect war booty and souvenirs. The 48th Ohio regrouped at a road running through a large field. Daniel saw Union soldiers drifting north, quitting after the first battle.

Brigadier General Sherman rode up on a large black horse. He was tall and gaunt, with red hair and a cropped red beard, sunken temples, and eyes that had the preternaturally alert expression of a wild animal that could become another animal's meal at any time.

Daniel, Will, Riley, and Landers watched him survey the scene. Landers whispered, "Look at him, those crazy eyes. The papers were right. No wonder the army relieved him of command. He said he needed two hundred thousand men to put down a rebellion in Kentucky!"

"You were flat on your back with fever, lad, when he took us up the river into northern Mississippi," Riley said. "You've never seen such a fearsome rain. We got off the transports, but we couldn't go anywhere. Our maps and guides were worthless and the streams and bayous were flowing over. We went a couple miles, but when we got to a bayou that only Jesus could have crossed, the general turned around and we came back to camp. He was sane enough that day."

"I don't believe he's crazy, just cut from different cloth than most folks," Will said. "Don't believe everything you read."

Sherman prodded his horse towards the men. He removed a cigar from his breast pocket with a hand wrapped in bloodstained bandages. Daniel had seen Sherman at a distance several times, but had never heard him speak.

"Anybody have a lucifer?"

Will proffered a match and lit Sherman's cigar. Sherman puffed away, surveying the scene.

"This road is where you'll make your stand. They'll come out from those trees." He pointed towards the woods to the south with his cigar. "You'll get a good look at 'em in this field. We'll hold 'em here and drive 'em back towards the Shiloh chapel." He turned his horse and rode away, heading east.

"You know what Shiloh means?" Will said. Daniel shook his head. "A Jew told me it's Hebrew for 'a place of peace.'"

After the soldiers had fallen into battle formation at the road, they received fresh ammunition. The Fourth Brigade had fewer men than it had earlier that morning. The sun had reached its midday peak. No breeze mitigated the still, oppressive heat that had replaced the early morning chill. Flying grasshoppers collided with the men and tiny, maddening gnats filled the air, landing on eyes, ears, nostrils, mouths, and other exposed flesh, drinking from beads of sweat. Thousands of birds contributed a raucous cacophony of chirps, trills, whoops, and riffs

Daniel had been parsimonious with his water, using it to wet the rag to clean his rifle barrel, and had the canteen he had taken from the dying soldier. He was one of the few who had water, but he limited himself to tiny sips, despite overwhelming thirst, and allowed Will a meager swallow. Like Daniel, most of the soldiers, expecting a skirmish, had left their food, so it would be a hungry force that attempted to repel the Confederate advance. The Confederates, replenished on Union breakfasts, would have another ally as well—the charge that sweeps through an army on the move.

They poured from the woods, screaming their high-pitched cry, bayonets flashing. The Union opened fire, but they kept coming, thick and mad as hornets driven from their nest. Shells and shot boomed from guns hidden in the trees, a shell exploding close to Daniel and Will, spraying them with dust and clods. The din was more deafening than before—more artillery, more miniés, and more screaming, wounded soldiers. The Union line crumbled.

Will yanked Daniel savagely on his shoulder. "Skedaddle, Danny!"

The brigade scampered towards the woods north, Daniel and Will joining the chaotic exodus. A minié removed Daniel's cap. In front of him, a shell removed a soldier's head. Daniel tripped over fallen soldiers and scrambled back up. One grabbed him by the ankle, desperately seeking help. Daniel wrenched from his grasp and kept running. As he neared a heavily wooded thicket, fire came from both sides and he dropped to the ground. If the Secesh continued driving north and east, they would trap thousands at the Tennessee River. Union soldiers were making a stand in the woods. Daniel crawled under both sides' bullets. He made it to the thicket and found a tree to hide behind.

He reloaded his rifle and waited for a clear shot. The thicket rang with the sounds of rifle fire and bullets hitting trees, and Daniel saw flashes of both Confederate and Union uniforms. There were no orders or battle line. He didn't see anybody in his regiment. But there was a butternut, crouched and creeping towards him! The Reb reached his tree. Daniel lunged and bashed him in the head with his rifle stock. The soldier screamed once before he fell to the ground, alerting a group nearby who saw Daniel and gave chase. He ran as fast as he could. A minié hit a branch above his head and he ran faster. The underbrush ripped his clothes, body, and face. Low-hanging branches whacked his head. More shots rang out, hitting branches around him. He got away as the Rebs reloaded.

His chest heaved, sweat poured down his face, he bled from the slashing underbrush, his head was bruised, and his ears rang as he came upon a broad, deep ravine. Sunlight flashed off a creek below. Water! Forget Rebs, forget danger, forget the scattered regiment—get to the bottom of that ravine! He half ran, half slid on his butt through the trees and down the escarpment. He plunged his head into a pool, greedily guzzling the cool water, and filled his canteen. Downstream, the body of a Union soldier spun on a bloody whirlpool behind a large rock. Rifle fire rang out above him from both sides of the ravine. The water was a relief, but this place was dangerous. Dark clouds rolled over the western ridge of the ravine, blocking the late afternoon sun. He hopped on rocks across the creek, then jogged north, hiding in the trees, until he came upon a large group of Union troops in a field.

Daniel heard fear as he searched the field for his regiment. The Union was cornered, and the soldiers' hunger, thirst, and weariness magnified their fears.

"They must have a hundred thousand soldiers."

"Those were fresh troops they sent at us at that road."

"How could you tell?"

"Well, you couldn't really, but they sure fought like they were fresh."

"Did you see Sherman prancing around on that damn horse? What's Grant doing? Is he even here, or is he on a bender somewhere?"

"They sure got caught napping."

"Someone said we're getting reinforcements."

"They'd better get here soon or they won't do us any good."

Daniel felt a tap on his shoulder. He turned to see a short, portly lieutenant with a bushy mustache, wearing the red trim of an artillery officer.

"Come with me."

"I'm not with your unit."

"Don't argue. I've got three men down on my gun and I need somebody."

"Yes, sir." Daniel swallowed hard. Batteries inflicted significant damage and were the targets of choice for Confederate marksmen. The soldiers manning them were sitting ducks.

The lieutenant led him to a twelve-pounder Napoleon, manned by six soldiers.

"Soldier, deliver rounds from the caisson to Private Bowles." The lieutenant pointed at a man standing by the muzzle. "Stand back from the wheel when the gun is fired. It bucks like a colt with a bee up its ass and you don't want that wheel landing on your foot."

"Yes, sir."

The lieutenant walked away. Daniel turned to the soldier at the caisson. "What unit is this?"

"Captain Bouton's Battery One, First Illinois Light Artillery. We've been dispatched by General Sherman to support the defense of Perry field. We've been told to hold this position until nightfall, at all costs."

"Where did you come from?"

"Pittsburg Landing. We caught some action on the way."

"What's happening at Pittsburg Landing? Are men skulking?"

"It's a disgrace. Thousands of 'em cowering and wailing at the water, trying to cross. They float on logs or try to swim the river. Some of 'em drown—serves 'em right."

Daniel shook his head. "Are we getting reinforcements?"

"Buell has come up from the east, but his troops haven't crossed the river yet. Nobody knows where Wallace is—he's supposed to be en route from the north."

Confederate infantry flags and the guidons of artillery batteries appeared across Perry field. Soldiers and field guns formed into a line about a third of a mile away. From the field guns came puffs of smoke, followed by the sound of the explosions, the whiz of shells through the air, and the screams of wounded men and horses.

Bouton's howitzers boomed. The roar blew into Daniel's head and shook the contents. His ears rang and he felt a dizzying, nauseating disequilibrium. A cannoneer immediately stepped in front of the gun and rammed a rod and sponge down the muzzle. Daniel took a shell from the soldier at the caisson and delivered it to Bowles, who rammed the round down the muzzle.

"Trail left!" The lieutenant shouted. The cannoneer adjusted the gun.

"Stop. Fire!"

The cannoneer pulled the lanyard and there was another deafening boom. The gun jumped. Daniel concentrated on his task, ignoring the heavy fire directed at the battery and the pings of miniés hitting the field piece. The soldier at the caisson was hit in the leg. Blood flowed from his wound, but he continued to feed rounds to Daniel.

Bouton's battery and the Rebs threw shot and shells at each other for over an hour. Neither side could advance to control Perry field. At sundown, the Confederates withdrew from the field. "Cease fire! Cease fire!" the officers shouted as the Rebs disappeared. Daniel tore a strip from his shirt and wrapped it around the soldier at the caisson's wounded leg.

"Thanks," the soldier said. "Other men are down. Help them."

Daniel went to where a group of soldiers stood over fallen comrades.

"Bill took it in the eye; I knew he was a goner," one said. "I thought there might be hope for Joe and Zeke, but they're gone, too."

The lieutenant approached Daniel. "What's your name, Private?"

"Daniel Durand, sir."

"Did you have any experience with artillery?"

"No, sir."

"You did a good job. What regiment are you with?"

"48th Ohio, under Colonel Sullivan"

"I'll commend you to him, Private Durand. You may return to your regiment."

"Thank you, sir."

Now that the guns were silent, tension gave way to fatigue, thirst, and hunger. Daniel's ears rang and his head ached. He was parched and bone-tired, his belly quaked. Why had he left his food at camp? Because he thought the day's fight would be a skirmish and he didn't want to bother carrying it. Fool, fool, fool! He joined a group of soldiers shuffling across the field towards the stream in the ravine. If he'd had any illusions about battle when he volunteered, they had been shattered by exploding shells, deadly miniés that found their mark, blood spraying from gaping holes, mayhem and retreat, the wailing wounded, and the silent dead. Maybe there was a queer breed—officers, probably—that gloried in all this, but he felt neither glory nor pride.

At the stream, he refilled his canteen, drank, and refilled it again. He dunked his head in the cold water. Dusk would soon give way to darkness. He sat at the bank and leaned against a rock, not noticing the soldiers around him. Sleep beckoned, but it occurred to him that he should find his regiment—it would be his only chance of eating.

He trudged to the road at the end of the field. Amid the dead, the wounded screamed and moaned. He was too tired to stop, too numb to be horrified, too consumed with visions of the day's terrors to offer comfort, and with no food or bandages, too bereft to help. Most of them would die and there was nothing anyone could do about it.

He dragged himself into the woods beyond the road to a small campfire. Four men huddled around it, their faces masks of dirt and powder.

"Who you with?" said one, his hands spread to catch the fire's warmth.

"48th Ohio. You know where they are?"

"No, and it's getting too dark to find them. Set a spell with us. We're from the 49th Illinois. God only knows where the rest of our regiment might be. You need water?" Daniel shook his head. "Sure wish we could offer you food, but we ain't got any."

Daniel sat by the fire, grateful for the warmth. The Tennessee night carried a spring chill and his uniform was damp from sweat. Listening to the campfire chatter, he soon succumbed to his weariness. He crawled away and lay beside a tree, resting his head next to a gnarled root. He had no dinner in his belly and no blanket, but was soon asleep.

The boy knew they would come that night, after what he had done that day. He did not sleep. He waited, listening to the gently rhythmic breathing of the two boys with whom he shared a bed at the orphanage. He pulled a thin blanket up around his face, protecting himself from the Cleveland winter cold. The door at the bottom of the stairs squeaked. They were coming.

Boom!

Daniel awoke from his dream with a start. He shook his head. He was in Tennessee, not Cleveland. A huge explosion came from the east, followed by another and another. They were so loud they had to be from gunboats at Pittsburg Landing. Shells screamed on their way to the Rebs. The salvo stopped, and Daniel went back to sleep. But only for ten minutes, as another round of shelling boomed.

"Damn it!" one of the Illinois soldiers shouted, lurching about. "Did it occur to those bastards that we might need some sleep tonight? They can't see—if those shells hit anything it will be pure luck."

"I'd sit through a month of sermons for a bottle of whiskey right now," another soldier said, rubbing his hand against his beard. "Ain't going to sleep; might as well start another fire." He stumbled through the trees in search of kindling.

Daniel relieved himself against a tree. He gathered some loose branches and underbrush for the fire. He returned to the campsite and dropped his load.

"This your first battle, Ohio?" one of the soldiers asked as they huddled around the flames.

"Yes, call me Danny."

"Ours too. We ran off with no food, no supplies, no nothing but our rifles and ammo."

"Same here. Where are you from?"

"Southern Illinois—Abe Lincoln country. I'm Jed, that's Paul, Hank, and Bill. You?"

"Cleveland."

"Listen to those poor bastards," Paul said. The wounded shrieked and howled.

"I don't think I saw a medic all day," Hank said. "Their only hope is that we get back what we gave up. They're in Reb territory now—ain't nobody going to rescue 'em."

They talked for over an hour, interrupted every ten minutes by shelling from the gunboats. The fire popped and Daniel felt a drop of water on his neck.

"Botheration, just what we need—rain," Hank said. "We'd better get under the trees."

They gathered their rifles and cartridge and cap boxes and ran toward the nearest stand of trees, which provided little cover against the downpour that followed. Daniel stood, hands in pockets, head bowed, his hat back on the battlefield. Water drizzled from above and streamed over his boots. Soon soaked, he shivered uncontrollably and his teeth chattered. His raincoat was in the pack he had left in camp that morning. It was no consolation that his misery had company, including the Rebs. He'd just as soon that both sides stayed dry. He wiped flowing snot on his soggy sleeve. The gunboats continued their salvo.

Finally the downpour stopped.

"Damn, it was raining pitchforks," Bill said. "Can't build a fire—no dry kindling. I guess we clear away the mud and try to get some sleep." He scooped the muck under a tree.

Daniel found a tree and did the same until he reached merely damp dirt. He sat and leaned against the tree, feeling sorry for any creature, including himself, that was outdoors that night. Despite dripping water and intermittent shelling, he settled into a shivering doze.

He was half asleep, his eyes still closed, as the sun rose. He heard a familiar brogue.

"Danny?" Riley and Jed stood over him. "I was looking for some kindling when I ran into Jed. He said a forlorn soul from Ohio had wandered into his camp last night. I'm sure you've enjoyed their hospitality, but would you like to return to our regiment?"

Daniel smiled weakly as he stood up. "G-g-good morning," he shivered. "Let's go." He was tired, hungry, cold…and angry. "L-l-look at this damn uniform—it's falling apart after one rain. Some s-s-son of a bitch made a lot of money selling these shoddy rags to the government." He picked up his cartridges, caps, and rifle.

"Jed," Riley said, pointing towards the sunrise. "We're just through the trees. There are several regiments from the First Division. That's probably where you are."

"Probably. Hey boys, let's get going."

They walked through the muddy thicket to a clearing. Soldiers milled about small campfires, trying to dry out wet uniforms and capture some warmth. They approached a campfire where several men from the 48th Ohio were huddled.

"Danny," Will Farrows said with a smile, "good to see you." His golden hair and beard were damply limp. "Landers thought you ske-daddled."

Daniel glanced at Landers, who looked away. "Thanks for a splendid evening, Jed."

Jed laughed. "Our pleasure." The four soldiers from Illinois left to find their regiment.

Daniel squeezed in between Will and Jake Blanchard. "Are we going to get some food?"

"Soon," Will said. "The wagons are working their way toward us."

"How many soldiers remain from our brigade?"

"Not many, a few hundred. The other brigades in the Fifth Division aren't in much better shape, but Wallace's Third Division to the west is reinforcing us, and there's a rumor that Buell's army made it over the river last night. Word has it that we'll counterattack this morning."

"I'm not counterattacking anybody if I don't get some breakfast."

"Amen."

The food wagon finally arrived. The soldiers rejoiced until they received their rations—salt pork, hardtack biscuits, and coffee. A few of the famished couldn't wait and ate their fat, greasy, rancid pork raw, between two pieces of hardtack. The rest threw their meat into a frying pan.

"Sowbelly stew, gentlemen," Riley said, holding the pan. "No complaining now, looks like they've thoughtfully issued us extra rations." Worms and maggots wiggled in the pan. "I wish we had some potatoes."

"I'm surprised we got our meat. You'd have thought those skippers would have carried it off," Will said.

"Don't cook it too long; that pork will shrink down to nothing," Blanchard said.

Riley's sowbelly stew sizzled and popped as he dished it out to those men who had plates or tin cups. The rest waited until they could borrow a cup or plate. In this group were Daniel and Will, hungry enough to chew on their own arms. They finally got their breakfasts.

Landers poured coffee into Daniel's canteen while his free hand roamed his body in one continuous scratch. Daniel sipped his coffee. "This stuff would knock the rust off a nail, Landers." He choked down the pork and Riley's "extra rations" and wiped his plate with hardtack. He saved two biscuits in his pocket. Rumor had it they would deflect Reb bullets.

Shortly after breakfast, Pomeroy approached their campfire. Yesterday the pompous lieutenant looked like he had just stepped off a parade ground. Today he was as soaked and bedraggled as everybody else.

"Good morning, men. The Rebels withdrew at sundown, but we are not sure how far they pulled back. The general order will be to advance in a southwesterly direction until we encounter resistance. Major General Lew Wallace's Third Division has arrived and is on our right flank."

That news perked up the men, and within an hour they received fresh cartridges and caps. To the south they heard intermittent artillery fire. The Ohio regiments fell in together as Buckland's Fourth

Brigade regrouped. Daniel saw Colonel Sullivan, a bloodstained bandage across his chest and right shoulder. The Fourth Brigade marched through Perry Field, scene of the previous day's artillery duel. Daniel stepped over Union corpses at one end and Confederate corpses at the other, indifferent to the sight of death after one day of battle.

The brigade marched through woods to the middle of a field. Confederates were forming a line in the trees at the southern edge of the field. To the right of the Fourth Brigade, infantry from Wallace's Third Division stretched to the woods west of the field. To the left, Colonel Stuart's Second Brigade completed the line.

"Prepare to attack!" the officers shouted.

"We've received word that Buell's on the field, ready to do battle," a lieutenant yelled.

Notwithstanding his weariness and the havoc his breakfast was wreaking on his stomach, Daniel's spirits soared with everyone else's on the news about Buell. The surge of energy was almost tangible.

"We got Buell and Wallace! We'll lick 'em now!"

"They thought they had us whipped yesterday. They got another think coming today!"

"About time the Secesh went backwards. Let's move!"

"For—ward, march!"

The soldiers ran, screaming and hollering. Some of the Confederates managed to fire, but they were outmanned and overrun before they could reload. Daniel reached the woods and stabbed a Reb repeatedly with his bayonet until he didn't move. He looked around for more fighting and was disappointed that the Confederate force was fleeing en masse. The Union soldiers gave chase, emerging from the woods to a field of about three hundred yards with a pond at the opposite end. They were brought up short. Behind the pond, in a thicket of oaks, a much larger force of Rebs massed. The officers shouted orders for the Union troops to stop and form a line.

"Better than yesterday, eh, Danny boy?" Will said, grinning.

Daniel nodded. "This one will be tougher."

"Anybody need cartridges?" Riley said. A wagon made its way behind the line.

Will shook his head. "Fired one shot back there."

The Union line went quiet as the Confederates advanced. Some waded through the pond at the end of the field, led by an officer waving his sword. Confederate artillery fired and puffs of white smoke floated from the oak thicket. Canister shot cut a swath through the Union line and wounded soldiers screamed.

"For—ward, march!"

The Union advanced, but enfilading fire, supported by extensive artillery, stopped them. They dug in and returned fire. For an hour neither side moved. At about noon, the Confederates received reinforcements. A Confederate officer rallied his troops, riding up and down the line waving a battle flag. The Rebs surged.

Today there was no Union retreat. They backed up, but gave ground grudgingly. At mid-afternoon, they began a grinding counter-advance under heavy fire. The 48th Ohio joined in the advance, but a hole had opened to their right.

"Durand, Farrows, Riley, come with me." Lieutenant Pomeroy walked down the line, tapping men and motioning them to follow. He led a group of soldiers behind the line, towards the gap.

"We're pinned down here by heavy fire coming from that rise," Pomeroy shouted, pointing at a sloping hill about 150 yards away. "If we can attack and take that position, we free up our right flank to advance. Everyone to the left here," he motioned with his hand, "will be in the first group. Everyone to the right will be in the second group. The first group will charge, followed closely by the second."

Daniel, Will, and Riley were in the second group. They exchanged nervous glances. Daniel said, "Sir, is this order coming from Colonel Sullivan?"

"What difference does it make, Private? An order is an order."

"Yes, sir." They loaded their rifles and fixed bayonets.

"Charge!"

The first group had charged no more than fifty yards before a spray of enemy fire from the rise cut them down. The few who survived were hit as they tried to scramble back.

"Now, while they're reloading—charge!" Pomeroy shouted.

Daniel, in the lead, broke from the trees. "Damn if this coward's going to get me killed!" he yelled. He ran to the right, away from the Rebs' fire. The other men followed. They found a scraggly stand of trees that afforded some cover.

A volley of Union fire came from the left. "That may divert 'em. Let's move!" Riley shouted. "Don't fire until you see them!"

Riley, Daniel, and Will were the first to emerge, running as fast as they could. They were half way up the hill before the Confederates started firing at them.

A minié whizzed by Daniel's head. *Faster, damn it, faster!* He stopped, took aim at a soldier taking aim at him, and fired. The Reb went down! They reached the crest and Daniel plunged his bayonet in a Confederate chest. Will jammed the stock of his rifle in a Reb's face. He went down and stayed down as Will pounded his head. Daniel kicked one in the groin. He doubled over and Daniel bayoneted him in the back. He lunged at another, who threw his hands up in surrender before Daniel could plunge a bayonet into his belly.

"You're the damn devil himself!" the Reb shouted. The few Rebs that hadn't skedaddled were surrendering. Union soldiers took their guns and huddled them into a group.

Daniel felt disappointed again. Hand-to-hand combat sent a jolting surge through him that shooting at the enemy at a distance didn't. Kill-or-be-killed was much higher stakes than fistfights back in Cleveland. Fighting fueled bloodlust, and coming down from his deadly elation was wrenching. There was something fearsome about that elation.

After the Confederate position had been taken, Lieutenant Pomeroy emerged from the smoky haze, over the crest of the hill, waving his sword. Staring straight ahead, he shouted, "No quarter for the Rebels. Continue the advance!" Daniel could see from the looks on other soldiers' faces that they shared his disgust.

From the east came heavy artillery fire. For the first time, the volunteer 48th Ohio regiment encountered professional Union soldiers as they met up with General Buell's army. His troops held a tight line. When a soldier fell, another took his place. Round after round of artillery fire blew holes in the Confederate line. They advanced with the steady inevitability of a river rising during a heavy rain. When the Confederate line broke, there were no savage screams or pell-mell rushes, just a steady flow of blue, breaching the banks, inundating enemy positions.

The Rebs' retreat was orderly; defilade fire slowed pursuit, but it was a retreat. The Confederates, attacking, had to win, while the Union, defending, only had to draw. At frightful cost the Union reclaimed territory ceded the previous day, but no more. Late that afternoon, Sherman's tattered division stopped at the area south of Shiloh chapel where it had camped the day before. Daniel was beyond relieved at being alive and whole amidst the thousands of wounded and dead, and beyond wonder that he had been spared.

The campsite was smoking rubble, a few forlorn sticks waving canvas remnants of tents. Vultures and flies, drawn by a retch-provoking death stench that would only get worse, feasted on corpses. Daniel, Will, and Riley surveyed the carnage.

"It'll take us weeks to get the men and horses buried," Will said grimly.

"If we're lucky we'll draw burial detail," Riley said. "If we're not, it'll be medical detail. Holding some poor bastard down for the medics to saw off his arm or leg will make fighting seem like a Sunday stroll."

"I never felt like skulking during the battle, but I feel like it now." Daniel shook his head. "Shiloh—a place of peace."

Chapter 2

The Golden Bull

The soldier with the classically chiseled features and the blond—most of the girls would call it golden—hair and beard had them enthralled. He sat on the couch in the middle of the sitting room with Nellie—the prettiest—telling stories, making everyone laugh. But the most interesting soldier was the tall, dark-haired one, his face all hard angles, standing by himself in the corner, smoking a cigar, watching the proceedings with a smile, as if he was enjoying his own private joke. She had a chance with him. At twenty-eight, Tess was the oldest of the women. Her auburn hair in ringlets framed a broad, rather ordinary face, and she was farm-girl stocky with broad shoulders and muscular arms. She was also the smartest and liked smart men. This one looked smart. The few girls that had approached him hadn't stayed for long. A challenge.

"Now what are you doing over here, all by your lonesome?" she asked, smiling as she approached him.

"I'm enjoying the spectacle."

"Your friend draws quite a crowd."

"As soon as he walks into a room. That's Will."

"How come you're not over there with them?"

"I don't like crowds."

"What brings you to Memphis, soldier?"

"It's Daniel. We fought at Shiloh, but not since, and now we're out at Fort Pickering. Sherman's had us drilling all day, every day this summer. After two months, he's taken pity and let us come into town for a night. And you are?"

"Tess. Paul was telling me you're with an Ohio regiment. Are you from Cincinnati, too?"

"The opposite corner of the state—Cleveland."

She held his dark eyes. Most men liked to talk about themselves, but she'd have to peel this one back layer by layer. "How old are you?"

"Eighteen."

"You look older. You act older. Grew up in a hurry, didn't you?"

"You could say that." He smiled and the joke was no longer private: she was in on it, too.

They talked. Across the room, she saw the big, red-haired corporal—she had been with enough Union soldiers to recognize badges of rank—approach Miss Celeste, the madam, and give her his three dollars. He took Molly's hand and they went through the door to the rooms. That appeared to be the signal the soldiers were waiting for, and everyone quickly paired off. Nellie put her arm around Will, claiming her prize.

"If you'll excuse me for a moment," Daniel said. He made his way over to Miss Celeste to pay his three dollars. When he returned, Tess took his hand and they went down a hall to the room she used for business.

She closed the door. The small room had a large four-poster bed with a canopy. A simple four-candle chandelier hung from the ceiling, casting enough light to see what you were doing, but not enough to be unflattering. Next to an overstuffed red chair was a table with a glass and a bottle of whiskey. There was a large brass spittoon below the table. Above the table hung a circular mirror. Along a wall stood a tall armoire, and a hat and clothes stand. The room smelled of cigars. Tess walked over by a window on the wall opposite the bed.

"Are you going to smoke, Daniel? If you are, I'll open the window, if you don't mind."

He walked over to the window, opened it, reached out the window with his cigar, snuffed it against the wall, and let it fall to the ground below. "No use stinking up your room. It's warm, though. Let's leave it open."

She had a standard little speech she used to get things rolling. "Now Daniel, there's no hurry. We can take all the time we need, so you can just re—" She stopped short. He had taken off his coat, put it on the peg on the stand, turned, and looked at her. He stood tall and straight and proud, as a soldier should. The younger ones were usually nervous, but not him. His eyes crinkled in an amused way and there was a twist at the corner of his mouth.

"Would you like some whiskey?" She gestured towards the table with the bottle and glass.

"No."

He moved toward her, not warily, not hurriedly, just the even movement of a man who knew what he wanted. She felt her breathing quicken as he stood before her. He put his hand on her shoulder, then moved his index finger slowly up her shoulder to her neck to a spot just below her ear. He traced the same route back down. His other hand was on her waist and he bent down, kissing her on the neck. Her body was starting to respond and she kissed the top of his head. He looked up at her with his dark, dark eyes and her lips met his. He tasted of tobacco and beer. He kissed her, softly, and then again, not so softly, and again—passion. Her breathing was quick and heavy and she noted with professional satisfaction that his was as well. He lifted her to the bed. She had learned the hard way that trying to take off each other's clothes, especially hers, with their buttons, ties, stays, hoops, and hooks, could kill blossoming ardor. She quickly removed her dainty high-heeled slippers, dress, and chemise while he slipped out of his shirt and pants. Only with the corset did she need help. He untied the lacing in the back. She removed her petticoat and bloomers. They slid under the covers.

She was very good at arousing a man, even when she did not share his lust. Usually that was how it had to be. This time was different. She wanted him—the dark eyes, the lean, hard body, the intensity and concentrated force when he talked, or when he did anything at all, even something as simple as opening a window, a will that suggested that nothing came between him and his desires, and underneath it, something dangerous, beyond that he killed other men. In bed a man was stripped of everything but his passion. He couldn't hide behind money, or position, or words, or friends, or lies, or boasts—he was what he was, and she knew his essence. The man on top of her was a force that she wanted inside her. She wanted to return the pleasure he would give her.

The pleasure he would almost give her. She laughed, not cruelly, but in a way that said it had happened before, that she understood. There was a moment of silence.

"It's been a long time, hasn't it Daniel?"

He surprised her. He looked directly at her, raised his eyebrows, laughed with no embarrassment, and said, "Yes, it has."

"I've sometimes wondered if soldiers ever take matters into their own hands when they're away for so long."

"There's not much privacy—we share tents. Sometimes you wake up to a sticky situation."

She laughed again. "A man your age has a lot of sap. Let me get cleaned up and we'll try again. I won't tell Miss Celeste, so you won't have to pay twice." She slipped out of bed, took a robe from the armoire, and went down the hall to a washroom.

She returned in a few minutes and slipped into bed, nestling under his arm. "Do you have a sweetheart?"

"No."

"Daniel, men are simple, although they try so hard to pretend they're not. There's no pretending with you. Do you ever lie?"

"No, there's no reason for it. Why do you think men are simple?"

"Oh, I don't know about soldiering and politics and all that, but when they're with women, they're simple. They want one thing."

"What's that?"

"This." She made a gesture that encompassed her body and the bed.

"What do women want?"

"You're not old enough to hear that." She smiled—he was old enough to hear anything. "Women want men's souls, but once they have what they want, they're not happy. Nobody admits what they want, so it's all a lie. When a man comes here and pays for his pleasure, it's more honest than most things that go on between men and women. Daniel, if you ever find a woman who doesn't want your soul, I don't care if she has a harelip and horns—marry her. You'll be happier with her than most men are with their women."

He laughed and looked into her eyes. "The sparkle's gone out of those beautiful green eyes. You believe that, don't you, Tess?"

"I've been doing this for longer than I care to think about, and I know some things. The only reason I say anything to you is because you listen…and you might remember."

They continued talking until she suddenly cupped his head in her hands, pulled his lips to hers, and kissed him. His body stirred and one hand moved over her breast and the other stroked the inside of her leg. She wanted it…now! They were kissing passionately and then he was inside her and their bodies pulsated to an undulating rhythm of unbearable pleasure. He gasped and she cried out as they brought each other to an all too brief peak. They panted wordlessly for several minutes. Temporarily spent, he rolled over on his back. She glanced at the open window and wondered if anybody had heard them. Men always got cold afterwards. She went to the window and closed it.

When she came back, his eyes were closed. She got into bed, propped herself on her elbow, and examined him. He was not a peaceful sleeper. The tension in his face suggested loss and pain. She thought of her own harsh past and nonexistent childhood. She brushed a lock from his forehead and whispered, "Poor Daniel. I'll bet you never had a mother."

She let him sleep for several minutes while she put her clothes on, but then she had to wake him. He stared at her groggily. He said nothing as he dressed. He put his hand in his pocket, withdrew it, and took her hand. He gave her real money, a gold coin, not a greenback, and said, "Thank you, Tess. You're sweet."

She kissed him lightly. "Thank you, Daniel."

They stepped into the hall. He cast her one last glance, walked down the hall, opened the door to the sitting room, and softly closed it behind him. His life would be dangerous. She half envied, half pitied the woman who would share it with him.

Daniel was the last to return to the table in the Golden Bull Tavern, where the soldiers had earlier eaten their dinners of thick steaks, baked potatoes with savory trimmings, and fried onions.

"Looks like Mr. Durand got his money's worth," Paul Mannis said with a salacious leer. He was a big man with an incongruously high voice. The other men laughed and Daniel sat down. Somebody poured him a glass of beer.

"Me and Miss Lizzy had a fine time," Culpepper said, smiling. His missing front tooth made him look like a bumpkin. "But I'll be damned, when we was finished, she took out a pouch of tobacco and put a big plug in her mouth. I've never seen a woman chaw tobacco before, but this gal was an expert. She hit the spittoon every time. Lizzy says lots of gals in the South chaw, and smoke pipes, too."

"Good thing she indulged after your session and not before," Will said. "Is it any wonder why the Rebels are so anxious to protect their treasured womenfolk—these delicate flowers—from Northern invaders?" Everyone laughed. They were ready to laugh and drink and tell stories.

Daniel quickly grew bored. It was past the dinner hour, but the Golden Bull was still crowded, filled with the smell and haze of smoke that rose and enshrouded several enormous chandeliers and their many candles. A pianist banged out a gay tune on his piano near a long bar of dark, richly burnished wood with a brass foot rail. Men knotted in groups around it, drinking, talking and laughing loudly, smoking cigars, and spitting into brass spittoons on the floor. Spectators clustered around three tables, watching poker games. Toward the back of the room, hazily visible through the smoke, a flight of stairs ran up to the girls' sitting room.

Daniel stood up and walked to the one poker table where there were only five players, waited until a hand was finished, slid through the onlookers, and took a seat. He was the youngest at the table, but there was another soldier, a tall, bulky sergeant with red hair, bushy red sideburns, and a red mustache whose ends had been carefully waxed into curlicues. The sergeant glanced at him and looked away.

"Can I buy in?" Daniel said, addressing the player with the most chips, sitting on the opposite side of the table.

"Twenty gold or twenty-five greenbacks gets you twenty worth of chips."

The discount for greenbacks wasn't unusual—Lincoln was print-ing them as fast he could—but it was stiffer than usual. Daniel slid two twenty-dollar gold pieces across the table. The player with the chips functioned as the game's banker and counted out his chips. Daniel checked out the players. Two looked like freebooters, drawn to Memphis by sundry get-rich-quick opportunities presented by the war and Sherman's occupation. Their suits were too new and their vests and ties too colorful for anyone to mistake them for solid citizens. One player looked like a local, a solid citizen wearing a nondescript brown suite and pince-nez glasses. Daniel would have guessed the banker was the best player, even if he hadn't had the largest pile of chips. His black, austere suit, vest, and cravat, with a high-collared white shirt, were probably tailored in New York or London. A gold watch fob stretched across his vest. He was in his late fifties, with gray and black hair swept up off his high forehead, a full mustache, and intently focused dark brown eyes. Everything about him suggested quiet, confident wealth.

"What regiment you with, Private?" the sergeant said.

"It's Private Durand, sir. I'm with the 48th Ohio."

"My cousin is with that regiment. Lieutenant Pomeroy. You know him, Private?"

"I do. What regiment are you with, sir?"

"The 70th."

The banker slid chips towards Daniel. "We play five-card draw and five- or seven-card stud, Mr. Durand." He motioned towards the freebooters. "To my right are Mr. Morris and Mr. Longfellow. You've met Sergeant Pomeroy, and next to him is Mr. Barnes. I'm Deacon Bainbridge." He motioned for a waiter. "Would you like anything?"

"A cigar and glass of water."

Bainbridge handed a deck to Sergeant Pomeroy. "Your deal."

Daniel folded after the draw in the first game. A queen high wouldn't stand up and it was too early to bluff. He played cautiously for several hands, getting a feel for the other players. He won a small pot, but he wasn't getting strong hands. One of the freebooters, Mr. Morris, won three hands in a row.

The name Pomeroy prejudiced Daniel, but he sensed that none of the other players liked him either. However, they hid their distaste—Pomeroy was a stupid player with a lot of money. His face gave away his hands, he bluffed at the wrong times, and he frequently drained his whiskey. Bainbridge sucked him in during a game of seven-card stud. Pomeroy, banking on a straight, bet heavily, oblivious to Bainbridge's three spades showing. Pomeroy got his straight, but two spades in the hole gave Bainbridge a flush and he won the pot.

After patiently enduring weak hands, cautiously betting, and breaking even for two hours, the cards started to come Daniel's way. He won several medium-sized pots.

Will came over to the table to watch him play. He sat behind Daniel, next to a short, fat man with a bushy mustache, ruddy complexion, and small eyes. Will stared at Bainbridge. "Excuse me," he whispered to the fat man. "Do you know that player in the black suit?"

"The one who looks like an undertaker?" The man smiled at his own joke. Will nodded and the man drew up closer. Will got a blast of whiskey breath. "He's the deacon—Deacon Bainbridge. Some of these gentlemen are going to think he really is an undertaker after he gets through with 'em." He again smiled at his own wit.

"Is he a deacon?"

"No more so than you or I. He doesn't have a religious bone in his body. He does, however, have a religious devotion to making money." At this, the man chortled loud enough to draw stares from two of the players. He lowered his voice. "Say, you wouldn't happen to have another one of those cigars?"

Will took a cigar from his pocket and gave it to the man, who lit it and puffed happily away.

"Thank you kindly. By the way, my name is Hamm, Amos Hamm."

Will couldn't suppress his smile.

"I know what you're smiling at. I don't mind. They've been poking fun at my name since I was a child. What's your moniker, soldier?"

"Will Farrows."

"Where you from?"

"Columbus, Ohio. How does the deacon make his money?"

"He's an agent for cotton buyers and a speculator. Makes a fortune trading. Don't ever cheat him—rumor has it he killed a man who tried. He's got a mansion outside of town, and his wife, Hanna, was the prettiest belle in Alabama. She died about five years ago. You don't want to sit down at a poker table with him. I found out the hard way. Do you know those soldiers?" Hamm pointed at the table with his cigar.

"The private."

"The deacon will take that young man's money."

"Don't bet on it. Danny's cleaned out the regiment. Smart as a whip—can cipher anything. He multiplies two four-digit numbers in his head."

"We'll see." Hamm took a tug from his whiskey, puffed his cigar, and turned his attention to the poker game.

"Seven-card stud," Mr. Longfellow said as he began his deal, sliding two cards down and one up. Daniel turned up his two hole cards carefully at the corners—he had seen Pomeroy trying to peek. A pair of threes to go along with a face-up king. Longfellow and Morris had twice bought more chips from Bainbridge. They were running low and courting hope, a player's worst enemy. They stayed in too long with weak hands, hoping lightning would strike, but it struck too infrequently to make them anything but losers. Barnes, the solid citizen, played a cautious game and appeared to be breaking even. Pomeroy had endless cash, most of which flowed into Daniel's and Bainbridge's ever-increasing piles.

Daniel slid fifty cents into the pot and everyone called his bet. His next card was a seven. Morris, with an ace up, bet fifty cents. Barnes raised another fifty cents and everyone called the bet except Bainbridge, who folded—he never courted hope. Barnes had two hearts showing, perhaps working on a flush. Bainbridge was too rich to be bluffed, Pomeroy too drunk, and the freebooters too reckless, but Barnes could be bluffed. Daniel raised him a dollar. Longfellow folded, but Barnes, Morris, and Pomeroy called the bet.

Longfellow slid Daniel another face-up king. With two pair, two cards to go, working a potential full house, he might not need to bluff. Bainbridge watched him. Daniel kept his face an impassive mask. He wouldn't scare away the other players just yet. He bet a dollar. Barnes, who now had three hearts showing, raised a dollar, and Daniel turned up the heat with a two-dollar raise. Barnes stared at Daniel's cards before he called the bet. He didn't raise, perhaps realizing that his flush, assuming that was what he had, might not guarantee him the hand. Morris folded and Pomeroy stayed. Daniel glanced at Pomeroy's cards. It was possible that the sergeant had a pair of something down and a matcher face-up, but he was obvious—he would have bet strong if he had a strong hand. He was just making another contribution to the other players.

Daniel's up card was a useless jack and Barnes' was the eight of spades. This was the tricky part. He could bet modestly and try to keep Barnes and Pomeroy in the game for the last card. If Barnes stayed for the last card, having made it that far he might not fold no matter how heavily Daniel bet. Daniel would then have to get a three or a king to beat him, assuming Barnes had his flush. Barnes looked nervous. Not chicken-with-a-fox-outside-the-coop nervous, but nervous. Better not to draw things out. Greed might be costly—now was the time to squeeze.

Daniel bet three dollars. Barnes looked down at his own pile of chips and rolled one in his hand. He stared at Daniel's cards. Finally he called Daniel's bet. Inexplicably, Pomeroy raised a dollar. Thank you, Sergeant Fool! Pomeroy had nothing—the dollar raise was a feeble attempt to bluff—but it gave Daniel an opportunity to finish off Barnes. He raised the bet another three dollars. Barnes looked like a dog trying to pass a peach pit. Four dollars was a lot of money with one more round of betting to go. What if Pomeroy raised the bet again? Barnes turned his cards over, folding.

Pomeroy stared at Daniel's cards as if he were seeing them for the first time. Something registered through his whiskey haze. "You've got a full house." He turned his cards over.

"You'll never know." Daniel turned his up cards face-down and slid them into the pile of other cards. He gathered the chips in the pot. Everyone save Bainbridge looked tapped out, and trying to take Bainbridge's money would be a fool's errand. "That's it for me. Please cash me out, Mr. Bainbridge."

Bainbridge cashed out the players. As Daniel got up to leave with Will, Bainbridge said, "Mr. Durand, if you'd be so kind, I'd like to have a few words with you."

"I'll see you back at the table, Will," Daniel said. He sat down.

Bainbridge motioned to a waiter. "Henry, I'll have the usual. Mr. Durand?"

"A beer."

"They keep a special bottle of whiskey behind the counter for me. May I offer you a cigar? I think you will find these are of a better quality than what you were smoking." His voice was deep but forceful, with a Southern accent, and his words were measured.

Daniel lit the cigar and puffed. It was much better than what he was used to. The waiter brought him his beer and Bainbridge his whiskey.

"You didn't have that full house."

"No."

"But you knew the sergeant had nothing and you figured that even though Barnes had his flush, he would wilt in the heat. You were quite right."

Daniel nodded.

"You played it well. What impressed me, Mr. Durand, was not so much the play, but that you quit after you won. Most players would have kept playing until they gave it all back. Where are you from?"

"Cleveland."

"What did you do in Cleveland?"

"Shoveled coal for a boiler. Shoveled horseshit for a stable. Worked at the docks, on a barge, and in a foundry. Many different jobs."

"I would think that you're too smart for that kind of work."

"Business was bad in Cleveland. I took what I could get."

"Why, in the name of creation, did you enlist? You're much too smart for the army."

Daniel smiled. "It's regular work, thirteen dollars a month."

"And a not inconsequential risk that you'll get yourself killed."

"That didn't sink in until Shiloh, after the first man went down with a hole in his face where his nose used to be. What do you do?"

Bainbridge sipped his whiskey. "Well, Mr. Durand, where there is war, there is government, and where there is government there is stupidity and corruption, and where there is stupidity and corruption, there is opportunity. Now the Legal Tender law says we all must accept greenbacks, but that law doesn't apply to the United States' foreign creditors. The English and French know a fraud when they see one. If our government borrows from them, it has to repay with gold or silver, or something convertible to gold or silver—in this case, cotton—not flimsy green pieces of paper. Historically, you've been able to tell everything you need to know about a government by the quality of its money. The Secretary of the Treasury has sent revenue agents to Memphis to procure as much cotton as they can. They pay their greenbacks and ship cotton to London, where each bale commands three hundred dollars' gold. All variety of vermin are operating here, but I honor my commitments, deal at fair prices, arrange shipping, and find London buyers, so the Yankees prefer doing business with me."

"You have a Southern accent, but your sympathies are with the Union?"

"My sympathies are with the soldiers. Wars are never about the reasons they gin up to hornswoggle men into dying. Wars are about three things: power, territory, and treasure. The North needs the South to pay for Northern manufactured goods, the prices of which are kept high by the tariff. Mr. Lincoln wants to triple the tariff, so the North fights to keep states in a Union they want to leave. Picturesque plantations, King Cotton, and slavery can't compete with railroads, factories, and free men to work them, so the South is fighting for a doomed way of life."

Daniel puffed his cigar. His decision to volunteer had been rash. By Bainbridge's reckoning, he had been played for a fool.

"Who did you see upstairs?" Bainbridge said.

"Tess."

"The finest filly in the stable. I own part of this establishment. Allow me an observation. Supposedly honorable men rail in statehouses and from pulpits against speculators and prostitutes. I speculate with my own money. Mr. Lincoln speculates with public money on a transcontinental railroad that any fool can see the country will be unable to support for years. The ladies upstairs sell their own favors. Politicians sell what the public has entrusted to them." Bainbridge smiled, puffed his cigar, and jabbed it for emphasis. "Tell me, sir, why it is wrong to speculate with or sell that which is yours, but it is not wrong to speculate with or sell that which is someone else's—the tax-paying public's?"

Daniel laughed. "I never thought about it that way. I don't have an answer."

"Nobody does. The crowd never thinks. People are only comfortable in a pack, and they're most comfortable in one that's racing off a cliff."

Miss Celeste, the madam for the women upstairs, approached the table.

"If you'll excuse me, Mr. Durand," Bainbridge said as both men stood. "I have some matters to discuss with my business partner. I would say contact me after your enlistment is up—I might be able to offer you a job—but you'll be better off back in Cleveland."

"Why?"

"The South will fight like rabid dogs, but those railroads and factories will win this war. Afterwards, the North will boom and Cleveland will boom with it. Memphis won't fare as well. Hard times follow defeat."

They stood and shook hands. "Thank you, Mr. Bainbridge."

"My pleasure, Mr. Durand."

Daniel fell in with Will on the march back to Fort Pickering. "How much did you win?" Will said.

"Fifty-seven dollars."

"Who gets the envelopes filled with greenbacks?"

"An old Jew in Cleveland."

"What does he do with them?"

"Exchanges them for gold."

"You ought to be a banker. Money sticks to your fingers."

"Maybe I'll consider it."

Sergeant Pomeroy approached them. "Excuse me, Private."

"Sir?" Daniel said.

"That poker game left me a little short. May I borrow five dollars until the first, Private…?"

"Durand." Daniel reached into his pocket, pulled out several greenbacks, and handed Pomeroy a five-dollar bill. He wasn't going to give him silver or gold. Pomeroy walked away.

"You'll never see that fiver again, Danny."

"I know, but his cousin, Lieutenant Jackass, already dislikes me, and between the two of them they could make my life miserable."

Chapter 3

Ben

Daniel felt as if he were stepping onto an adhesive sponge. The muddy ground was saturated with accumulated moisture from the winter wet season. He slogged through ankle-to-knee-deep muck. As he pulled his boots from it, they produced a "thwop-thwop" sound of breaking suction. His legs ached and the skin was rubbing away on his heels. Beards of Spanish moss dangled from the trees; when they brushed against his shoulders, neck, or head, it felt like spider-creep. His uniform was soaked after a few minutes of walking around the desolate bog. "This damn swamp is worth ten thousand men to the Confederates," he muttered.

"According to the maps, we've landed at Johnson's Plantation, which is surrounded by the Yazoo and bayous." Lieutenant Pomeroy withdrew his sword from its saber and pointed towards the southeast. "In that direction lies Vicksburg, which stands above the Chickasaw Bluffs of the Walnut Hills. It's the linchpin—take it and we control the Mississippi; it would break the South in two. The Rebels have fortified those bluffs with men and artillery. The entire area, from here to the bluffs, is crisscrossed with bayous and sloughs. It's the rainy season, so all these waterways are filled to overflowing. How we plan to mount an offensive through this inhospitable terrain remains to be seen."

"If this is a plantation, where are the house and the other buildings?" Will pointed to a dilapidated storage shack, the only structure. A thick forest surrounded an empty clearing.

"I don't know," Pomeroy said.

Riley, Will, and Daniel separated from the rest of the soldiers. After several attempts, they were able to light their soggy cigars.

"Pomeroy's a fool," Riley said, "but his drift about trying to fight here is right. Hell, it'll take us days just to figure our way across this damn bog, and then the Rebs will be sitting up in those hills, waiting to pick us off."

"I don't like this one damn bit." Will bit off a loose end to his cigar wrapper and spit it on the ground. "Somebody said Yazoo is the Indian word for death."

Daniel shared their strategic misgivings, but Will's last comment added to a deeper foreboding. Most of the men hadn't fought anything but skirmishes since Shiloh, eight months ago. The Union was stymied in both the west and east. Sherman's troops had spent several weeks and a joyless Christmas on cramped transports; cooped below decks breathing foul, stagnant air; listening to each other cough, sniffle, hack, and moan; arguing and throwing fists over trifles. Disease had taken its toll. Every time they went ashore the chaplains performed short services and they buried those who had succumbed. Now, something ominous had rolled in with the fog and the early winter night. Daniel shuddered.

Camping that evening was misery. The men gave up trying to ignite the loose pieces of water-soaked wood. The few fires they managed to start threw off a pittance of heat, scarcely enough to warm them or to cook their food. They ate maggot-infested hardtack and salt pork rations and slept on soaked ground, the water soon seeping through their blankets and uniforms.

The next day, fog prevented reconnaissance until it cleared at midmorning. The soldiers discovered that their maps of the area were worse than useless, directing patrols to trails, roads, and bridges that didn't exist, but providing no warnings of the waterways that turned the bog into a maze. The swampy terrain all looked the same, and only occasionally were the men able to catch a glimpse of the Chickasaw Bluffs through the foliage and dangling Spanish moss.

On the morning of the third day, Colonel Sullivan addressed the 48th Ohio, standing at attention, enshrouded in fog. He removed his kepi and ran his hands through his hair and over a bald spot. "Gentlemen, there is a road that leads from our present encampment to Vicksburg. Tomorrow, we will proceed up that road to engage the Confederates. We will not advance on Vicksburg, but rather divert enemy firepower from the primary attack force in the middle. Although we don't have exact estimates as to Confederate troop strength, we believe it is not great. The Confederates should have their hands full with our flanks, allowing the Second and Third Division to proceed up the middle. Today, we reconnoiter the road to Vicksburg, performing any repairs that might be necessary to prepare it for tomorrow's advance. At ease."

Will, Riley, and Daniel walked away from the rest of the regiment. Riley spit a long stream of tobacco juice at the trunk of a tree. "We're sending thirty thousand soldiers across this godforsaken bog. You can't see through the fog until midmorning. When you can see you can't march more than fifty paces without running into a damn swamp. Once we've made it through, the Confederates will be waiting for us in the hills, behind fortifications with heavy artillery. Our division is being sent as decoys, we're not really fighting.

And I'm sure that road into Vicksburg won't be protected at all—the Rebs will probably post a big welcome sign."

"Maybe if we let 'em know we're not really fighting, they won't really fire at us," Daniel said.

"Maybe Sherman's crazy after all." Will scratched his beard.

The "road" into Vicksburg was more a path, barely wide enough for a caisson or field gun. It had to be widened and at many places, trees had to be chopped and laid corduroy style, for soldiers and artillery to pass over the watery muck. More trees fell for temporary bridges where the swamp was too deep. By the end of the day, Daniel's company was exhausted, soaked, cold, muddy, and convinced to a man that annihilation lay ahead.

That night, Daniel and Will, unable to sleep, sat by a pile of soggy, smoldering kindling that was more glow than fire.

"Why are you here, Will?"

"To preserve the Union, of course, and now that Mr. Lincoln has made his proclamation, to rid the land of the scourge of slavery."

"Ah, what's the real reason? You don't have any truck with political nonsense."

Will pulled two cigars from a coat pocket, handed one to Daniel, and bent over the fire to light his. He puffed a thick plume of smoke. "I'm here because my father's in jail."

Daniel tilted his head quizzically.

"He owns a newspaper in Columbus and wrote an editorial arguing that since the Constitution treats slaves as property, the North should have to buy the slaves' freedom, to compensate the South for its loss of property. His argument was that in the long run, it would be less costly than waging war. My father's from Virginia and he was branded a Confederate sympathizer. Secretary of State Seward's policemen arrested him at his newspaper. They haven't charged him, there's been no trial, but he's still in jail and they shut down the newspaper. They've shut down many papers. Father said Lincoln would rob us of our liberties, and so he has."

"So why are you fighting in his army?"

"Because I won't have my father and our family tagged as Confederate sympathizers when we're not. After the war that could stay with us for a long time. My father hates slavery—it's why he left Virginia."

"So you agree with Lincoln's proclamation?"

"I'd rather fight to end slavery than to keep the South in a Union it doesn't want to be in. It's all politics—the war isn't going well so Lincoln changes the subject. It's made the men mad. You've heard them: 'We ain't fighting to free the niggers.' But it's a smart move. It fires up the abolitionists and makes it tougher for Britain and France to recognize the Confederacy."

"And all the soldiers can do is grumble."

"We're fodder, Danny. We're going into a battle tomorrow with impossibly long odds. Do you think Sherman, Grant, or Lincoln care? They never would have made it to where they are if they did. Their appreciation for what we face, for risking our lives, goes no further than their pompous speeches. Everything is for fame and reputation, for appearances."

"Death is not an appearance."

"You're damn right it's not."

Three days before the arrival of New Year's, 1863, four thousand soldiers lined up in a long, four-abreast column to march up the road to Vicksburg. The fog cleared early and the march started at nine o'clock. No essential supplies were left behind, a lesson from Shiloh.

Daniel was miserable—chilled inside his soaked uniform, his nose raining snot, coughing incessantly, his boots dripping mud. Every step irritated his bleeding blisters. Fighting to retain his balance through the slippery swamp and slimy vegetation, holding his rifle over his head, drained his energy quickly. Horses pulling wagons and field pieces had the same tough slog as the men; wheels frequently stuck in the mud. Daniel helped push the wagons free, only to have to do it again a few yards up the road.

After two hours they reached a clearing. Above the three-hundred-foot high Chickasaw Bluffs of the Walnut Hills that loomed in front of them they saw white church steeples and rooftops of Vicksburg's buildings. Reaching this citadel on the Mississippi was about as likely as the Confederates voluntarily laying down arms and surrendering. An abatis, a huge pile of tangled trees stripped of branches and given sharp points, barred further progress up the road. Behind the abatis, two hundred yards away, a bayou lay before the bluffs. Atop the bluffs were parapets, walls of earth and logs roughly seven feet high, with embrasures, openings through which marksmen could shoot. Interspersed among the parapets were platforms, supported by planking, for artillery pieces and cannoneers. The soldiers formed into a two-deep line of battle. The artillery units rolled the field guns up front.

"What the hell are we supposed to shoot at?" Daniel said. "You can see a few of 'em running around, but most of 'em are behind those parapets."

"Look at their damn artillery! They've got us outgunned four- or five-to-one, and that's if our field pieces work after being dragged through the mud." Riley pointed towards the bluff. "Hell, with that firepower, from higher ground, they're not going to have to call in reinforcements. If General Sherman is counting on our flank to draw fire from the middle for the real attack, he's got a heap of disappointment coming."

"Prepare to attack! After the artillery! Double time!" the officers shouted.

Two six-gun batteries simultaneously opened the battle with their deafening roar. An eruption from the bluff answered. Soldiers ran a few steps before falling to an unremitting rain of shells and shot that left the line with gaping holes. The Union batteries tried to respond in kind, but Rebel marksmen had drawn a bead on the cannoneers.

Daniel, Will, and Riley were at the front of a group trying to advance towards the bluffs. Murderous Rebel enfilade stopped them. Miniés whined and shells threw sprays of dirt and mud. Men fell, wounded and screaming.

Culpepper went down, holding his bleeding leg. Another soldier writhed on the ground, hands on his gut, not stopping the flow of blood and innards. The Rebel guns boomed and it was soon too smoky to return fire. The Rebs knew where to shoot and Union gunners didn't. Daniel had only one open shot, a Reb running between parapets, and missed. Soldiers were going down everywhere—it was retreat or die. Daniel pulled up Culpepper, who had taken a bullet through his thigh. They had to get back to the road.

Boom! Boom! Boom! Boom!

Shells and shot exploded among the soldiers retreating up the road and they scattered. Swamp water flooded shell craters, rendering the road impassable. Daniel was almost carrying Culpepper. Will and Landers, up ahead, followed Pomeroy. A shell exploded in the middle of a group trailing behind Daniel and Culpepper, knocking them down. Scrambling to his feet, Daniel looked back for the trailing group and saw only random torsos and limbs. Daniel put himself under Culpepper's shoulder and hoisted him to his feet. They hobbled to where the other three men had stopped on top of a steep bank above a bayou. Daniel's chest heaved and his lungs burned. To the left the heavy Confederate fire continued. Moving right would take them away from the road back to camp.

"Farrows, slide down the bank and see if we can ford this bayou," Pomeroy said.

Will removed his pack, put his musket on the ground, and stripped off his cartridge and cap belts. He inched down the steep, slippery bank on his butt. He grasped ground-covering vines and swamp plants, but his handholds came up by the roots and he slid into the water and disappeared. His head bobbed back up. "There's no way we can ford here, sir. I'll swim upstream until I can find a place to climb out."

"Landers, bring Farrows' gear and rifle," Pomeroy said. He turned right and walked along the bank, hacking at low-hanging vines and tree limbs with his sword. He reached Will on the bank, wet and shivering. Will took off his shirt and put on a dry one from his pack.

As the group walked on the bank above the bayou, the sound of artillery fire in back of them receded, but grew louder in front. The bayou widened, rising up the slope and eventually swallowing the bank. They had no choice but to ford.

"Sir," Will said, "with Culpepper's wound, someone's going to have to support him across this swamp, and the rest of us will have to carry his gear."

"All right, Farrows, you help him," Pomeroy said. "I'll take his rifle, and Landers and Durand can carry his pack and belts."

Daniel carried Culpepper's pack. Added to his own pack and rifle, it created a heavy, awkward load. The water came to the middle of his stomach. In front, Will and Culpepper almost fell several times. The deep part of the bayou was not wide and they continued for some distance in knee-deep water. By the time they reached dry ground, an afternoon fog had rolled in.

Daniel, soaked and exhausted, fell to the ground. "Where the hell are we?" He knew where they were—lost. Not since the night it rained at Shiloh had he been this miserable.

The men sat silently, shivering, their energy sapped. Culpepper's teeth audibly banged together. The light was already fading with the early onset of December evening.

"Let's keep moving, men," Pomeroy said, pointing his sword.

Will and Landers helped Culpepper up, and Landers supported the injured soldier as they walked. Will followed and Daniel brought up the rear. The artillery had gone quiet; they didn't have its sound as a guidepost to where the bluffs were. They thrashed through the foliage, occasionally sinking, mud and swamp water filling their brogans. In the gathering dusk, they would have to stop soon and make camp for the night. Daniel was about to shout up to Pomeroy that perhaps they should find a dry spot to stop.

A hand clamped down tightly on his mouth and he couldn't say anything at all. It was a brown hand, at the end of a powerful Negro arm. The man behind him was strong, and he sensed the futility of trying to struggle. The man's smell was as powerful as his physical strength.

"You's a Yankee?" The voice was low and deep.

Daniel nodded.

"Don't be making a sound or you die." No doubt the man could make good on his threat. "You's lost. I can get you back to the road and I can help the one with the hurt leg. But y'all gotta help me. You gotta put me on a boat up the river. If I take my hand away, you gonna holler?"

Daniel shook his head. The man removed his hand from Daniel's mouth. "Turn round."

Standing impassively before Daniel was a tall, muscular Negro in his mid-twenties. A large scar stretched across his left cheek and his right ear was notched with a triangular cut. The whites of his eyes contrasted with his dark skin. He wore baggy pants and a rag loosely draped across his torso.

"You get me on a boat north?" Some of his teeth were missing.

"I have to ask Lieutenant Pomeroy. He's up ahead."

"The one with the sword?"

"Yes, I have to catch him before he gets too far in front of us."

"He be back. There's a bayou—they ain't going nowhere."

"I'll ask Lieutenant Pomeroy to accept your offer. Until he does, stay out of sight."

"When I want to get lost, you never find me. I's watching. Raise your arm if he say yes." He stepped away from Daniel and disappeared.

Daniel went after the group, but the Negro was right. They had turned around and were walking toward him.

"Lieutenant Pomeroy, did you find a bayou? Is that why you turned around?"

"Yes, Durand. How did you know that? Why did you trail away from us?"

"A Negro came up from behind me and grabbed me. He's not hostile and he's offered to help us. He'll guide us back to the road if we'll put him on a boat up the Mississippi. He said you would run into a bayou."

"How do we know we can trust this nigger? What if he leads us back to the Rebels?"

"Sir, he's an escaping slave, and the last place an escaping slave would lead us would be to the Rebs. This man seems to know the area. We should accept his offer."

Pomeroy looked at the men uneasily. His mustache drooped in the damp air. "Sometimes circumstances dictate our decisions. Do you have a way of summoning this nigger?"

"Yes, sir."

"Do so. We'll accept his bargain."

Daniel raised his arm and the Negro emerged. He walked towards the group. Pomeroy turned and slowly looked him up and down. "Now listen, nigger—"

"Name's Ben."

Pomeroy and Ben stared at each other for a long time, until Pomeroy averted his eyes. "Ben…I understand that you'll lead us back to the road if we will secure passage on a transport up the Mississippi. Is that what you propose?"

"Yes, sir."

"I promise, as an officer and a gentleman, that if you do so, I will get you on a transport."

"Thank you, sir. Too dark to keep walking. The one with the hurt leg—he been in the water?" Ben pointed at Culpepper.

"Yes," Will said. "That's Steve. I'm Will."

"Mr. Steve, I's gonna put on rub, else your leg will puff up like a bullfrog. Pus will eat your skin, get in your blood, and run up to your brain. You be getting a fierce fever and maybe die."

"What kind of rub?" Culpepper said.

"It's Mammy's rub, stops the swamp rot. It burns—you gonna holler like thunder—but your leg be better."

"We can't have him yelling," Pomeroy said. "There may be Confederate patrols."

"Then hold him. I be putting my hand on his mouth." Ben walked away from the group, to where he had been hiding. He reemerged with a small canvas sack. He fished into the sack, withdrew a small tin, and removed its lid. Culpepper's eyes widened when he caught a whiff from the tin. The greenish, pasty substance threw off a smell that was a cross between a hateful patent medicine and a stinkbug fending off its enemies. Ben sat cross-legged on the ground.

"Put your head here, Mr. Steve." Ben motioned towards his chest. Culpepper looked suspiciously at Ben. "If I don't put it on, only the good Lord can save your leg. Lie down." Culpepper complied. Ben pointed at Landers. "You—hold a leg. And you"—he pointed at Daniel— "hold a leg. Hold 'em high, cause he's gonna kick. Grab his arms." He pointed at Will and Pomeroy. He took a rag from his bag and wiped the rub onto it. Clamping his hand tightly over Culpepper's mouth, he wiped the leg wound.

Daniel had never seen or felt anything like the spasm that jolted Culpepper. He writhed and screamed through Ben's hands. He had the strength of several men and it was all they could do to control his flaying limbs. Sweat and tears poured down his face. The screams Ben muffled with his hands seemed to push out Culpepper's bulging eyes. Eventually, the writhing and screaming subsided, but Ben waited before he removed his hand.

"What in the hell is that stuff?" Culpepper's words whistled through the gap in his teeth.

"Don't know. That's Mammy's secret. Hot peppers, salt water, roots, pitch, and bark, crushed weevils, and vinegar. She boils it all day. Smells so bad nobody can be around."

"You were wiggling like a snake with its belly nailed to the ground," Will said. "I almost couldn't hold you." He turned to Ben. "Should we set up camp tonight here?"

"Not here." Ben sniffed the air. "Gonna rain. Them trees yonder."

They walked in the near darkness until they came upon a thick cluster of trees on an indented knoll that would afford some cover in a rain.

"We could get a fire going," Will said, "if we could find some dry kindling."

"A fire might be visible to Rebel patrols," Pomeroy said.

Landers kneeled down and started scooping up the muddy ground with his hands. "Sir, we could dig out a pit here that would hide a small fire. Besides, the fog's rolled in."

"Very well, but I doubt we'll find anything dry enough to start it."

"There's always dry wood." Ben walked away. In ten minutes he returned with an armload full of sticks and swamp rubbish. Daniel, Will, and Landers had scooped out a shallow pit. Ben arranged sticks and leaves, Will struck a match, and they had their fire. It cast only a faint glow, but it threw off enough heat for Landers to cook salt pork, beans, and hardtack. They devoured the salty, greasy gruel.

Ben ate little. "I's fixin' something better come morning."

The exhausted men took blankets and rubber rain slickers from their packs. Daniel's eyes were half closed as he dropped down to his knees, ready to wrap himself in his blanket under the indention in the knoll.

"Durand, you'll stand the first watch, then Farrows, then Landers. We must remain alert for Confederate patrols." Pomeroy stirred the fire with his sword.

"Yes, sir." Yes, sir, Lieutenant Bastard, sir. There would be plenty of Confederates stumbling around this damn swamp in the dead of night! He sat by the fire and wrapped himself in his blanket. A bullfrog croaked, and occasionally he heard small splashes in the swamp. Ben was awake, but the soldiers fell asleep almost instantly, even Culpepper. A wound as severe as Culpepper's would usually keep a man up with pain and fever. The rub had worked. The army's medical corps could use Ben's mother.

"Were you at the plantation?" Daniel whispered to Ben. "How do you know this area?"

"My master's family, the Shupes, they's friends with the Johnsons. The Johnsons, they moved after their big house burned and the war started. Me and Jasper and Lucius—they's my brothers—we come up here fishin'. When I left the Shupes, I hide here."

"You left your family?"

"I got no woman, but Mammy and my brothers and sisters. I gotta go north."

"Were you mistreated?"

He pointed to the triangular notch in his ear. "Master Shupe put that cut on all of us, to brand us." Ben removed his rag and turned his back towards Daniel. The slave's back was crisscrossed with long welts. "Master don't like me—he whip me. Master's son— that's Henry—he cane a nigger so hard he up and died. He's a bad one. Sometimes he take sister Jessica...I gotta go north, Mr. Daniel. You make me one promise?"

"What?"

"If soldiers find us, shoot me dead 'fore we get caught out. The Lord will take care of me. I ain't gonna be no slave no more."

Daniel stared at Ben. The stories about suffering and cruelty weren't just abolitionist puff. Will was probably right when he said that Lincoln had issued the Emancipation Proclamation for political effect. However, if the rivers of blood spilled succeeded in eliminating slavery, then some good would come from this awful war. Nobody had the right to keep slaves.

"Promise?"

"I promise."

"Go to sleep. I can watch. Ain't no soldiers out there."

Daniel trudged to the hollow in the knoll. It took him longer to fall asleep than he thought it would—he kept seeing the crisscrossed welts on Ben's back. Finally he slept.

He heard them stepping up the stairs. One heavy clomp-clomp, one lighter step. He wondered if they would wake up any of the other

boys. If they did, the other boys would not let on. They knew some-
thing evil was about to happen. They would pretend to sleep. Could
his bedmates hear his heart pounding? The evil ones were in the hall
outside the bedroom.

His feet were wet. He opened his eyes and shook his head. He had been having his nightmare. He remembered where he was—he was still having one. Ben had been right; it was raining. At least Daniel had some protection. He reached for his rain slicker. Ben sat under the knoll with his arms around his legs, shielded from the rain. Daniel spread his slicker over his feet and legs, wrapped his blanket more tightly around his shoulders, and went back to sleep.

Pomeroy woke him the next morning, shaking him hard. "Durand, the nigger's gone."

A heavy fog enshrouded the swamp. Daniel glanced over to where Ben had been sitting during the night. "He'll be back. His sack is still here. He wouldn't have left without it."

"You'd better be right, Durand."

Ben returned after about a half-hour, carrying a crude fishing pole, a huge gutted fish hanging from a stick inserted through its gills, and more kindling. "Told y'all we be eatin better breakfast. Gonna fry up this catfish. Got mud bugs in the swamp, if y'all got a pot to boil 'em."

"We can use the coffee pot," Landers said. "I'll cut up your fish."

"What's a mud bug?" Will said.

"Show you soon." Ben built and ignited a fire. The smell of fried catfish rose from the pan. Ben occasionally turned the filets with a stick. Landers poured the men steaming, fragrantly strong coffee.

Daniel's stomach roared when he smelled the catfish. The men crowded around the fire. Ben had caught a good-sized catfish; there was more than enough to go around. Daniel ripped the first chunk from the slab on his plate. The firm, white meat was quite possibly the best food he had ever eaten. He wolfed it down and felt slightly crazed waiting for Ben to finish the next batch. He had several helpings.

"That was great, Ben."

"Time for the mud bugs. Mr. Bart, boil up some water." Ben walked away from the fire towards the swamp. Landers followed to rinse the coffee pot and fill it with water.

Ben returned carrying a sack filled with some sort of wriggling creatures. He pulled one from the sack and showed it to Will. "That's a mud bug, sir." It looked like a tiny lobster.

"Oh, a crawfish, a freshwater crustacean. I didn't know people ate 'em."

"Never heard 'em called that. They's mud bugs." After Landers had brought the water to a boil, Ben took a couple of dried peppers from his sack and dropped them in the pot. Then he dumped in the mud bugs. They thrashed wildly until they died. Ben cooked them for a few minutes and put several on each man's plate. "Here's how you eat 'em. Don't eat 'em if the tail ain't curled—they's bad. Split the tail and eat the meat. Best part's the brains. Bite the head and suck 'em out." Ben demonstrated on several mud bugs.

Daniel glanced at the other men and laughed. They looked as if they were about to eat a plate full of maggot-infested meat. Daniel picked up a mud bug, ate a tiny morsel, and sucked out yellow brain sludge. It had a peppery hot taste that was good, but the amount of food was so small that it scarcely seemed worth the effort.

Only Pomeroy refused to try the crawfish, his expression one of sour disgust. He stood up, rinsed his eating gear in the swamp, and stowed it in his pack. "Enough of this, men, it's time to get moving."

Ben tossed water on the fire and covered it with dirt, threw the remaining catfish and crawfish in the swamp, rinsed off the coffee pot and frying pan, and picked up his sack. "We gotta go this way." He pointed away from the swamp. "Water's high from the rain—can't be walking through swamps with Mr. Steve's leg. We's gonna wander, but we be back at the road come afternoon."

"Proceed," Pomeroy said. "You men take turns helping Culpepper."

Ben started walking, followed by Pomeroy, Landers, Will, Daniel, and Culpepper, who moved slowly but under his own power. Ben's route meandered, but they avoided bayous and deep swamp water. When the fog burned off at midmorning, Daniel could tell from the position of the sun that they were moving northwest. His blisters flashed a sharp pain with every step. The trees and bayous all looked alike to him, but Ben appeared to know exactly where he was going. It was another muggy slog and Daniel sweated profusely, although it was not warm. Culpepper slowed them down. He had to stop frequently and rest. They occasionally heard rifle and artillery fire towards the south, but not yesterday's sounds of sustained battle.

Around midday, Ben brought the men to a stop before a swamp. "Mr. Pomeroy, this water ain't deep. It come to our bellies. We cut through, there's a path to the road. We go round, it takes an hour. Mr. Steve can't get his leg wet, but I can carry him on my shoulders."

Pomeroy had stayed by Ben, appeared exasperated at any delay, and cut Culpepper's rest breaks short. "We'll cross here."

Ben squatted and Culpepper climbed on his shoulders. Ben started across the swamp, carrying his load as easily as a horse bears its rider. The other men followed. The going was not difficult, compared to yesterday's fording. They were almost through the swamp when Ben stumbled. He righted himself with difficulty and turned towards the soldiers behind him, clearly in pain. He steadied himself and hobbled through the swamp. After he set Culpepper down, he pulled up his pants to examine his swelling right knee. "Mr. Pomeroy, sir, I ain't walking by myself—I's needing help." He pointed at an open-ing in the foliage. "There's the path."

"I'll help him, sir." Daniel said

Pow! Pow! Pow! Pow!

Rifles fired from the south, much closer than other battle sounds they had heard that morning. Pomeroy paced back and forth, pulling his beard and mustache. "We're already slowed up with Culpepper, and now we've got a crippled nigger. Those are probably Confederate patrols on the road." His voice was higher than usual, his speech faster. He stopped and turned towards Daniel. "Durand, we can find our way to the road, but I can't risk all of our lives by bringing the nigger along. We'll have to leave him here."

Daniel stared at the lieutenant. A few shots and he was panicking. "Sir, we can't do that. You go on ahead. I'll help Ben."

"No, I won't allow that. We can't take the chance that you'll be captured by the Rebels. You wouldn't say anything, but he might." He pointed at Ben.

Ben looked at Daniel. "Mr. Daniel, remember what I say last night."

"Sir, I won't leave Ben here."

Pomeroy's jaw tightened and he clenched and unclenched his fists. "You gutless gelding! You nigger-loving, insubordinate ass! You're a damn pathetic excuse for a soldier! Are you disobeying an order again?"

"Yes, sir."

"Well, I guess you're right, Durand. We can't leave the nigger here." Pomeroy's voice was soft, but his eyes had a sinister gleam. "By God, we'll shoot him! That's what you do with horses and nig-gers when they pull up lame, you shoot 'em! I order you to shoot the nigger, and if you don't, I'll have you brought up on charges. Do you hear me, Durand?" He was shouting, shaking with rage, his lips quivering.

Daniel put his finger on the trigger and cupped his left hand under the barrel, but he didn't aim his gun at Ben. "I hear you, and I won't do it." Will's, Culpepper's, and Lander's eyes were big and they wore sucked-in expressions, as if they were holding their breaths.

"Then I will, Durand. You'll regret tangling with me, you pissant cur!" Pomeroy swung his rifle towards Ben, who stared directly down the barrel.

The shot exploded, filling heads, jolting nerves, reverberating. The echoes died and the soldiers gathered around the corpse. The body had been knocked backwards several feet and there was only half a skull. Fragments had been blown everywhere by the point-blank minié. Blood gushed from the hole, forming a gigantic pool.

"You couldn't have done anything else, Danny." Will put his hand on Daniel's shoulder.

"I've hated that pompous son of a bitch since Ohio." Culpepper almost spat the words out. Landers nodded in agreement.

Will took Daniel's rifle, still smoking, from his hands. Daniel shook his head, too numb to speak. Ben raised himself from the ground, and with a painful effort on his injured leg, hobbled toward Daniel. "Thank you, Mr. Daniel." His eyes glistened.

"Throw the body in the swamp," Will said. "Pomeroy got what he deserved. Scoop the bloody mud in with him. Anybody who finds him will think he lost his way and got shot in a skirmish."

Daniel moved in a dazed trance, saying little. He gradually realized what Will had grasped immediately—the truth had to stay submerged in this Mississippi bog. Military justice was quick and dirty. An enlisted man who killed a commissioned officer would find himself on the gallows or in front of a firing squad, to hell with extenuating circumstances.

Will tossed Pomeroy's rifle on top of his sunken corpse, where the water was about three feet deep, and the men were done. Landers got under one of Ben's arms and Daniel got under the other. The threesome hobbled up the path to the road, followed by Will and Culpepper. The rifle fire had stopped. If there had been a skirmish, it was over. They reached the road.

Daniel's initial shock wore off, replaced by torment. He would have to lie, and lie well. He would be plagued by worry, and only time would allow the incident to recede to more remote reaches of his mind. Either the lieutenant or Ben was going to die. He had made the right choice, but everyone had to keep quiet and he had to rely on them to maintain the lie.

"Before we get to camp, let's get our story straight." Will said, stopping. "We never saw Pomeroy, we have no idea what happened to him. Everything else stays the same. We got lost and Ben found us and led us back to the road. Stay hazy on what route we took back, just say we wandered. Danny did what's right and now we have to protect him—and ourselves. The less said, the better." The other four men murmured in agreement.

"They're back!" Riley cried when they arrived at camp later that afternoon. He threw his arms around Will and then Daniel, while looking askance at Ben. "We feared the worst. Damn, it's good to see you! What happened?"

"We got lost after the shelling," Will said. "Steve took a bullet through the leg, so we had to go slow. Then Ben here found us, and he knows the lay of the land. He's got some home remedy that stopped Steve's wound from getting worse, and he guided us through this godforsaken swamp, back to the road. Now we're going to get him on a boat up the river. Steve needs the medics."

"We'll find a bandage for Culpepper. The only thing the medics would do for his leg is saw it off. We're fixing dinner, come join us."

"Where's Pomeroy?" Mannis said. "Somebody said he might have been with you."

"Never saw him," Will said.

After dinner, Riley produced cigars and a bottle of whiskey and the men sat around a small fire. They smoked cigars and everyone but Daniel drank whiskey. Will recounted their adventure, edited. Ben sat quietly nearby.

"Vicksburg's a tough nut to crack," Will said. "Any word on where we go from here?"

"Some of the transports are pulling out tonight and will take a division and a brigade up the Yazoo to a place in the hills that's supposedly not as well fortified," Riley said. "If it works and draws off defenders from the bluff in front of us, we'll attack."

Daniel dreaded the thought of again attacking the impenetrable bluffs. He heard someone treading through the woods and underbrush, coming towards the group. His stomach coiled into a tight knot. It was the dead man's cousin, Sergeant Pomeroy.

"Durand…Durand, and Farrows. Which one of you is Farrows?"

"I am."

Pomeroy looked at Will and then Daniel. "My cousin, Lieutenant Pomeroy, hasn't come back. I heard he was with you two when everybody scattered. Is that true?"

Daniel looked directly into the lout's eyes. To lie, and lie well. "Never saw him."

"Just as we were pulling out, a group behind us got hit by a big shell. Maybe he was with them," Will said

Pomeroy looked hard at Daniel. "I don't trust you, Durand. You cheated that night at cards—that's how you won. If there's more to this than you're letting on, I guarantee I'll find out about it. Better men than you have found out the hard way—don't trifle with the Pomeroys." He walked away.

"Sergeant Pomeroy," Daniel shouted. Pomeroy turned. "You owe me five dollars."

The big man stomped through the woods.

Daniel stood on the top deck of a troop transport, at the back rail. An impenetrable fog had prevented further maneuvers by Sherman's troops and they were pulling out. He watched the boat's wake in the Yazoo as it pulled away from the bank. Yazoo—the Indian word for death. He took one last look back at the bog, Lieutenant Pomeroy's grave. He couldn't remember what Pomeroy looked like. Every time he tried to summon up his face, all he saw was half a skull, the other half blown away. Between a runaway slave who had kept his end of a bargain and a vain, contemptibly deceitful officer who had gone back on his word at the first sign of trouble, he had made a split-second choice of who would live and who would die. He had made the correct decision, and Ben would be on a transport north. As for Pomeroy, his body—and Daniel's secret—had to stay forever buried in that sinister swamp.

Chapter 4

The Citadel

Four companies of Union soldiers followed a wide dirt road to a gleaming white wooden gate. They were from a much larger force that had avoided Vicksburg's batteries via a circuitous path through eastern Louisiana, crossed back over the Mississippi River south of Vicksburg, and were now marching through southwestern Mississippi. On the gate was a sign in black script letters: *Meriwether Oaks*. The road, framed in magnolias and oaks, looped around a well-tended lawn in front of a stately mansion. Through the trees the men saw slaves working the fields. Paths led off the road to stables and outbuildings. In the middle of the loop stood a bronze statue on a marble pedestal—a man dressed in a military uniform, holding a flintlock musket. The mansion, a traditional two-story affair with four columns on the portico, looked as if it had just received a fresh coat of white paint. Smoke rose from three chimneys.

A middle-aged woman dressed in a white bonnet and light blue dress came through the front door, followed by two pretty young women, more fashionably dressed in colorful blouses with low-cut bodices and hoop skirts. The older woman carried a rifle. She approached the mounted cavalry major leading the foraging party. The young women stood near the porch.

"Good day, to you, sir. Why are you and your men trespassing on our property?"

"She's a saucy one," Will whispered to Daniel.

The major removed his hat. "We've come for supplies, ma'am. We'll take what we need, then we'll be on our way."

The woman pointed at the statute with her musket. "My husband's grandfather, Captain Horace Meriwether, fought in the Revolutionary War. He would have starved rather than steal from innocent women and children. I'm quite a good shot, and I assure you that I will shoot one of you dead before I allow such a despicable act."

"Ma'am, take aim at me if you like, but I assure you that if you fire, it will be the ruination of Meriwether Oaks. There will be nobody left to run it and nothing left to run. If this were a Rebel force, you would consider it your duty to render assistance, so perhaps you could come down from your high horse about the innocence of civilians in military affairs. The choice is yours, but any hostile acts towards the Union soldiers currently on your plantation would be futile. Our retribution will be far greater than whatever act that provokes it."

The woman stood staring at the major, saying nothing. She turned and walked slowly back into the mansion, taking the two younger women with her.

"Spread out with the wagons," the major said to the men. "Find the smokehouses and the storehouses, but don't enter the mansion. I'll stay here with a guard detail. We're low on salt and coffee—take all you can find. Meet back here at sundown."

Daniel and Will's company and a company from the 77th Illinois took several wagons and went down a path leading from the road that went behind the mansion. They found a smokehouse stocked with bacon, ham, and beef. They formed a line and loaded the meat onto the wagons.

"Where are they going?" Daniel said, pointing to two soldiers drifting away from the line.

"I don't know," Riley said. "There's been a few headed that direction."

"Let's see what transpires," Second Lieutenant Cordell LeMasters said. He was Lieutenant Pomeroy's replacement, a West Point graduate. In his mid-twenties, he was tall and trim, stood ramrod straight, and had cropped brown hair. He was by-the-book Army, but he was respected, a welcome contrast to Pomeroy.

He led a small group on a path to a storage shed, where a larger group of men were talking loudly and laughing. The shed contained cases of whiskey and rum, some of which the men had broken open. LeMasters jumped in front of Riley, barring his way.

"Sir, please," Riley said.

"I'll allow you to remove some of this liquor, but drink it back at camp. I fear what could happen if all the men get drunk. That's an order."

"Yes, sir."

Daniel didn't drink hard liquor. He wandered through the surrounding woods as the other men carried away their booty, but was brought up short at the sound of screaming and wailing. He returned to the shed to retrieve Will and Riley. Motioning for them to follow, he led them through the woods in the direction of the screams. The sound grew louder. They crept up on a clearing with several rude huts, staying hidden in the trees. Soldiers stood outside the huts, holding their rifles at the ready, acting as sentries. The wails and the screams came from within the huts, the cries of girls and women, slaves tormented by white men sent to free them.

"Somebody's having their way with the nigger gals," Riley said.

"We've got to do something," Daniel said.

"What do you propose, Danny boy? There's three of us. There's seven or eight of 'em outside and who knows how many inside. We'd have to find LeMasters and come back with enough men to stop this. If there's a captain or a major inside there, we'd all be in a heap of trouble, never mind your good intentions."

Daniel said nothing. He had no argument against Riley's brutal logic. They were startled by an anguished scream, cut short by raucous laughter.

"Danny, you led that charge at Shiloh and you did us all a favor getting rid of Pomeroy, but you can't be a damn hero every time," Riley said. "Forget about this and let's get out of here." He turned and walked back through the woods.

The screaming Negro women and Riley's mention of Pomeroy felt like hard kicks to Daniel's stomach. What did Riley know, and how did he know it? Anxious and bewildered, Daniel followed the other two back to the liquor shed, screams still echoing in his ears.

"We'll have Vicksburg inside of a week," Culpepper said cheerily.

Although the 48th Ohio had done little fighting, the men shared Culpepper's enthusiasm. They had foraged their way through southwestern Mississippi. To the east, General Sherman had defeated a Confederate force at Jackson, severed all its rail lines, and burned any building of military or commercial significance. To the west, they had the Rebs and their general, Pemberton, on the run to Vicksburg. They were a few miles from the linchpin of the South and had executed General Grant's plan to perfection. What could go wrong?

The morning of May 19, Colonel Sullivan addressed his regiment. The hot sun glared through the trees, the usual cacophony of chirping birds filled the air, and the standard hordes of gnats, mosquitoes, and flies flitted about, finding their way into the soldier's eyes, ears, noses, and mouths. The men scratched and whacked their tiny tormentors, mostly in vain.

"This afternoon the 13th, 15th, and 17th Corps will commence a coordinated attack on the Vicksburg fortifications. The grounds around the fortifications are barren and the terrain is up and down. Our attack must be quick and fierce. General Grant has emphasized that once we capture the fortifications, there is to be no straggling, and he has ordered division commanders to post guards to prevent it. Gentlemen, the objective we have striven for these many months is within our grasp, God willing. Dismissed."

"Huzzah! Huzzah! Huzzah!" Men thrust their fists into the air and bounced up and down.

"They're acting like this damn battle is already won," Will said. "If the fortifications are anything like what they had at Walnut Hills, it's not going to be as easy as these fools seem to think." Riley and Daniel nodded, but Will's words were lost in the noise.

By noon, some of the excitement had given way to more sober appraisal as they came in sight of the Vicksburg fortifications. Confederate regimental flags marked built-up parapets that commanded clear lines of fire of the ground before them. There were 1,500 yards between the Union line and the Rebel breastworks, with steep irregular gullies and ravines that would make it difficult for men and artillery to advance. The undulating terrain itself would have to serve as cover—there were only a few scraggly trees.

Daniel half ran, half slipped down a sandy, gravelly slope as they advanced towards a Confederate redoubt near a rail line that extended from Vicksburg to Jackson. Riley was up ahead and Daniel was trying to catch up. He had wanted to question Riley away from the other men since the incident at the plantation, but hadn't had a chance to do so.

"Riley, what do you know about Pomeroy?" he said as he reached him.

"You shot him in the swamp. Don't ask the next question. You did what you had to do." Riley rubbed several days' beard growth with his hand. "Neither one of us is wet behind the ears. Things happen that you don't talk about, ever."

Who had talked? He would get no answer from Riley.

They marched over the hilly terrain until they were about a quarter of a mile—just out of rifle range—of the Confederate redoubt. It stood at the apex of a long, triangular gully. Although most of the fortification was dug in, they could see the top of a log parapet, about twenty yards wide, with embrasures through which Confederate marksmen would shoot. It was part of an elaborate system of fortifications stretching as far as they could see, north and south. Two flags flew above it, a regimental flag and an Alabama state flag.

Riley pointed at the parapet. "Behind that they got plenty of sharpshooters and artillery. We got our work cut out for us."

LeMasters addressed the soldiers. "At two o'clock, three rounds of artillery from the plateau behind us will signal the commencement of our attack on the Rebel fortifications. After the third round, charge. Speed and overwhelming force should enable us to carry the battle."

"Let's get to it!" a soldier shouted.

"Dinner in Vicksburg, boys!"

"Let's all throw in a dollar for the man who tears down those Secesh flags!" This last proposition met with a chorus of approval. They were ready for a fight, ready for a victory.

"Remember Walnut Hills, damn it!" Riley's harsh brogue cut through the clamor. "Will, Bart, Steve—listen to me! The Rebs can't lose here—they're going to hit us with everything they've got. Lct some other idiots try to capture those damn flags! Stay back!"

Will and Daniel looked at each other. The fiery Irishman had his peaks and valleys, but they had never seen Riley this worked up. Daniel remembered Deacon Bainbridge's words: "People are only comfortable in a pack, and they're most comfortable in one that's racing off a cliff."

At two o'clock, Union artillery from divisions north to south and all points in between simultaneously fired three rounds at the Confederate fortifications protecting their citadel on the Mississippi. The battle of Vicksburg had begun.

Daniel watched the soldiers around him charge. Every soldier running in front went down before a Rebel fusillade and Daniel silently thanked Riley. Standing on their platforms, safely behind thick parapets, firing through embrasures that afforded a sweeping view of the exposed Union infantry but protected them from counter-fire, the Confederate marksmen fired volley after volley. Artillery boomed, and shells screamed, exploded, and blew holes in the Union lines. Daniel and Will fell to the ground. The bodies of soldiers offered the only protection against the Rebel firestorm. Keeping as low as they could, they crept along as bullets hit the ground around them, kicking up sprays of dirt. Several times the earth rumbled beneath them as shells fell nearby. They found a large rock in a shallow depression that provided some cover.

"I've never seen it this heavy," Daniel shouted over the din. "Where's Riley? I'd like to shake his hand."

"I'd like to give him a big kiss," Will shouted. "No use wasting bullets here—can't see what we're firing at."

They waited silently behind the rock. After a couple of hours, the noise subsided. Will stuck his hat on the bayonet at the end of his rifle and poked it above the rock. Two miniés ripped through it, knocking it off the bayonet. Daniel and Will looked at each other— they'd stay put until nightfall allowed them to retreat.

After the sun had sunk well below the horizon and they were cloaked in the invisibility of darkness, Daniel and Will slithered on their bellies back down the gully to their camp. Culpepper and Landers were waiting for them.

"I feel like a dog who chases a rabbit into a bush and runs into a skunk," Culpepper said. "What happened to dinner in Vicksburg?"

"The Rebs had other ideas," Will said. "When did you make it back?"

"Not too long ago," Landers said. "When everybody dropped to the ground on the first charge, we dropped with 'em. I must have said the Lord's Prayer two thousand times. When it got dark we crawled back here. By the dirt on your uniforms, you did the same thing."

"Where are Riley and Mannis?" Daniel asked.

"Don't know, haven't seen 'em."

"What about LeMasters?"

"He's been by. Told us not to light any fires. Not that we could, anyway. No kindling in this stretch of country."

Fortunately for the men, foraging had provided better rations than the usual salt pork and hardtack. They ate smoked turkey and cold corn—filling, if not completely satisfying. Will produced cigars. They sat with their backs towards the redoubt on the chance that the Rebs might see the lit ends of their cigars. They were worried about Riley and Mannis, but smoked in silence. With each minute the likelihood that the two men would return unharmed diminished. The wails of the untended wounded and an occasional rifle shot were the only sounds.

It was getting late and Daniel's eyes were only half-open when he saw two bloody apparitions staggering toward him. "Mike! Paul! They've been hit!" He jumped to his feet and rushed to his friends. Both men's uniforms were covered in blood.

"We're okay, Danny," Riley said wearily. "Get us some water."

They thrust their canteens towards the two men. Riley and Mannis drank greedily, water running down their chins and necks. They dropped to the ground, exhausted, and ripped into the turkey that was offered to them.

"What happened?" Daniel said.

"Remember Corporal Hanson?" Riley said. "He played poker with you one night, Danny. They called him Stoneface."

"Yeah, I remember. He was a good player."

"When the Rebs started firing, we hit the ground, looking for something to hide behind. Stoneface turned out to be that something. We thought he was dead at first, when we crawled up behind him for cover. He was bleeding, but he was awake. He'd been hit in the back and said he couldn't feel his legs. We stayed behind him for hours. When nightfall came we couldn't leave the poor soul there to die, though he said we could. He couldn't move his legs and we had to stay on our knees. We took turns. One of us would cradle his body and the other would pull him by his arms. A race between a slug and a snail moves quicker than we did." Riley took a long drink from his canteen. When he resumed talking, his eyes glistened.

"I've never seen anybody like Stoneface. We dragged him along, jolting him every inch of the way, and he never yelled. He didn't want the Rebs taking shots at us. You could see the pain on his face. The only time he talked was at the very end. He murmured something about his father, then he died." There was a long pause. "He…he lost too much blood." Riley stopped talking as tears rolled down his cheeks.

"Perhaps it's for the better, Mike," Culpepper said. He put a hand on Riley's shoulder. "If he couldn't feel his legs, they would have cut 'em off." Riley nodded. Culpepper pointed at holes in Mannis' pants. "Your knees must be rubbed raw."

"They are. The bleeding's mostly stopped, though."

"I've got whiskey," Landers said. "Let's have a pull and maybe it'll help us sleep."

Daniel took a sip before he rolled up in his blanket. He had trouble getting to sleep. The cries of the wounded grew louder. He drifted in and out of a dream in which he saw heads—Will's, Paul's, Riley's, LeMasters', his own—stuck on bayonets, hit by bullets, exploding. A shriek woke him and he stared into the blackness. A dazzling shooting star streaked across the night sky, but instead of giving off a brilliant last flash, it just faded out.

"We attack at ten," Lieutenant LeMasters said. It was the morning of May 22, three days after the failed first attack. Daniel and the other men were stowing their gear in their packs.

"Sir, we'll be stepping over bodies of men killed the other day," Will said. "Why does anybody think the result will be different this time? The Rebs are dug in."

"We control the river north and south of Vicksburg," Riley said. "The Secesh can't get any food or ammunition—we're shelling them continuously. Why don't we wait 'em out?"

"I don't know General Grant's thinking. Perhaps he's afraid of an attack from the east to relieve Vicksburg. He intends to mount a heavier offensive, to hit them with everything we've got. He wants to take Vicksburg sooner rather than later. Those are our orders."

Daniel told himself not to blame the messenger, but he sure as hell didn't like LeMasters' message. After the lieutenant left, he said, "What attack from the east? Sherman tore up all the rail lines at Jackson. The Rebs can't move enough men and supplies to relieve the troops here. We've got sixty thousand men, plus artillery and gunboats down on the river. They don't have anything that can match that."

"I heard we had almost a thousand wounded and killed the other day," Riley said, spitting a stream of tobacco juice. "We barely scratched the Rebs. We might lose ten thousand trying to take this place. Starving 'em out may be slow, but it's sure and we'd lose a lot fewer men."

"Lincoln and Grant need a victory, as Lieutenant LeMasters said, 'sooner rather than later,'" Will said. "They're getting crucified for how slow this war is going. It might take a month or two to starve the Rebels out. What's another month or two? This war is two years old. A siege would save thousands of soldiers' lives, but a camel passes through the eye of a needle before Lincoln and Grant do the right thing by their soldiers. They pay more attention to the editorials in the New York papers than to whether any of us live or die."

From the discomfited looks of some of the soldiers and the awkward silence, Daniel could tell that Will's words had hit home. Daniel's enlistment was up in a month and he would not reenlist. Everyone made mistakes; fools repeated theirs. Bainbridge had been right. The high and mighty filled the heads of boys with glorious abstractions when they marched them off to kill each other—abstractions that had nothing to do with why the war was being fought or the actual horrors of war. Ben had said, "I ain't gonna be no slave no more." Daniel Durand wasn't gonna be no fodder no more.

By ten, four regiments had formed a line at the top of a slope four hundred yards from the railroad redoubt. The 48th Ohio was between the 77th Illinois on the right and the 19th Kentucky on the left, with the 130th Illinois in support. At ten, Union artillery and gunboats on the Mississippi let loose a synchronized fusillade.

There was no pell-mell rush down the slope. Union artillery fire was heavier that it had been three days ago. They were going to soften up the Confederate fortifications before they attacked. A vanguard advanced cautiously until it met with Rebel rifle and artillery fire at the bottom of the slope. The first Union soldiers fell. Daniel's stomach tightened.

The 48th Ohio followed the 77th Illinois down the slope. Smoke and the thunder of artillery fire filled the air. After a while Rebel artillery fire diminished—some of the Union shells must have found their marks beyond the Confederate parapets.

Daniel and Will inched up the hill before the redoubt, crawling from one body to another for cover. A screaming Union shell scored a spectacular hit on the parapet, blasting two Confederates high up in the air and breaching a gap on the right side of the wooden wall. Rebels filled the breach, but the Union soldiers finally had targets they could see. Daniel and Will crept right, towards the breach, firing at the Rebs. To the left, the regimental flags of the 130th Illinois and the 19th Kentucky moved up the slope, their forward soldiers about fifty yards from the redoubt. The wounded and dead littered the gully. Daniel stared at one grotesquely mangled body, wondering what combination of forces could have produced such carnage.

"Damn Secesh have been told to hold this ground at all costs, they ain't giving us nothing," Landers yelled between shots.

"Keep moving forward! We're almost there!" LeMasters shouted. A Confederate shell whistled overhead, exploding behind them. A Union shell passed over in the other direction.

Boom! Boom! Boom! The series of explosions came from within the redoubt.

"That shell hit a magazine!" LeMasters shouted. "Forward!"

Daniel crawled over a face down body with a yawning hole in the back. Preparing for his next shot, he pushed the ramrod down the powder-clogged barrel and tore the flesh on his palm. He would have to clean the barrel before his next shot. He knelt, sighted down the barrel at a Reb in the breach of the parapet, and fired. The Reb went down.

"Huzzah! Huzzah!"

The Rebs were giving ground in front of the redoubt. A group hoisted a soldier carrying a regimental flag up the wooden wall. At the top he tore down a Confederate regimental flag and replaced it with the 77th Illinois flag to thunderous cheers. There were more cheers as the flag of the 130th Illinois went up on a mound in front of the parapet.

The 77th Illinois swarmed into the hole in the parapet and hoisted soldiers to the top of the wall. Several were shot when they reached the top, toppling into the ditch below. The Rebs were trying to brush ants off an apple, but they weren't going to hand over the redoubt without a fight. They reestablished their position in trenches at the rear of the fortification.

"Fix bayonets!" LeMasters shouted. The 48th Ohio was a few yards in front of a ditch before the parapet.

They inched their way down the ditch, held up by the mass of Union soldiers in front of them. Daniel stepped on a fallen Union soldier, the front edge of a three-toned patchwork, butternut and blue oozing red. Three men hoisted a soldier chosen to bear the 48th Ohio's flag to the top of the parapet. He planted the pennant then jolted like a scarecrow blown from his stake, catching a minié in his head, cutting the cheers short.

Daniel and Will crept to the bottleneck at the breach in the parapet and squeezed through. Rifles roared, bullets flew, and men screamed. A haze of smoke hung over the redoubt. Soldiers rolled on the ground locked in hand-to-hand death matches, using rifle stocks, bayonets, fists, knees, elbows, feet, heads, and teeth as close-order weapons. On the firing steps, Reb marksmen fought Union soldiers coming over the parapet and clawing at them from below, swinging their rifles from the barrels or stabbing their bayonets.

Daniel tackled a Reb fighting a Union soldier. He got under his arms and took him to the ground. *Choke the bastard—break his neck!* Thump! Jammed in the back with a rifle butt, Daniel couldn't breathe. *Roll over—get away!* The bastard was on top, punching. *Punch back, bite his ear!* Blood—not his own—filled his mouth. Whack! *An elbow to the bastard's face! And another!* He sprung up and kicked the Reb in the head twice. The Reb stopped moving. *That devil on top of Mannis—whack his head with the rifle!*

Daniel was knocked off balance by a body rolling toward a trench. Someone had his ankles and was pulling him in. He felt a hot flash of stabbing pain in his leg. There was too much dust, he couldn't see. He kicked his attacker in the head and gut. The Reb fell back and Daniel scrambled out of the trench. He looked down. His leg was bleeding.

From the back of the redoubt, behind the trenches, came the piercing Rebel yell. Daniel saw a Texas regimental flag, one star—Reb reinforcements. They were pouring out of the trenches. Somebody had Daniel by the shoulder, pulling him away. Daniel turned to see Will. A sprinkle of Reb bullets was turning into a downpour. They wanted their redoubt back. "Over there," Will shouted. "Get on that firing step and drop over the wall."

They scuttled toward a firing step. Men were shot as they pulled themselves up. It was the only way out.

"Go, Will, go!" Daniel shouted.

Will leapt over a trench, threw his rifle on the firing step, grabbed a plank, pulled himself up, swung his leg over, stood on the step as bullets hit the parapet, grabbed his rifle, hoisted himself to the top of the wall, and rolled to the other side. Daniel followed. *Hurry!* At the top he rolled and fell hard to the ground. *Son of a bitch, that hurt!* Knocked the wind out of him, but he had made it. *Breathe. Breathe. There's Will. Get going.*

They scrambled up the ditch in front of the redoubt. At the top, they dropped to the ground to avoid Union fire from troops regrouping further down the gully. They crawled down the slope, joining a makeshift line.

Daniel opened his canteen and took a long drink. He pulled a rag from a pocket and wet it to clean the barrel of his rifle. A bloodstain had spread out on his pants. His leg hurt. So damn tired. He pitched forward to the ground, head face down on his folded arms. He'd get up in a second. He couldn't go anymore.

"Danny!" Will was screaming at him. "Danny, they're coming. We gotta move!"

He looked up blearily. They had retaken their redoubt. They were dropping down the wall. He'd better get his rifle. Had he cleaned the barrel? Had he loaded it? *Cock it, put on the cap, pull the trigger.* Click. Nothing.

"Damn it, Danny, pull back!" Will grabbed him and forcibly dragged him backwards.

His leg burned every time it jolted on the ground. He wrenched away from Will. "I'm all right, Will, I can make it."

Boom! Boom! Boom! Three Union artillery pieces fired, spraying shot at the Rebels in front of the redoubt.

"That'll slow 'em down." Will pointed to a line of Union soldiers. "Let's go."

They crawled towards the retreating line, Will behind Daniel. The Rebels were holding their position at the redoubt, directing heavy fire at the Union troops. Three bullets kicked up a spray in front of Daniel. He had just about made it to the line, slithering like a snake to keep under his own side's bullets. He turned around to see how Will was doing.

He wasn't there! Where was he? That wasn't him, face-down. Was it? He couldn't leave him there. *Please don't be Will.* He crawled toward the body as fast as he could, pulling his rifle with one hand, scraping his other hand and knees on the dirt. *Please don't be Will.* He reached the body and turned him over. Will. Blood gushed from a hole in the side of his chest. Daniel held his dying friend in his arms.

Will's eyes were glazed. He looked up, trying to see who was holding him. A tear trickled down Daniel's cheek.

"My friend...Danny." Will's body trembled. He hiccoughed. Blood and frothy spittle trickled down his chin. Daniel took his hand, already cold. "I...ro, I...ro."

He was trying too hard to talk. "Be quiet, Will."

Will whispered. Daniel put his ear close to his mouth.

"Make...something...of...yourself...Danny."

Daniel stared into Will's eyes until the light went out. Damn heaven and earth, he was dead! Daniel bowed his head, tears falling on Will. *God damn you, Mr. Lincoln, for putting Will's father in jail. Will this sacrifice be enough for you to let him out? And God damn you, General Grant, for making the same mistake twice, trying to take Vicksburg this way. And God damn war, and killing, and soldiers, and blood, and powder, and the terrible noise.* Bullets kicked up spray nearby. A shell from the redoubt whistled overhead and exploded.

And God damn the Reb bastards that had killed his best friend. *You want a fight, you Secesh scat?* He stood, wobbled on his right leg, and picked up his rifle. Damn it, he'd get something going. Charge, the others would follow. Grant wanted this redoubt—Daniel would give it to him. Charge!

A bullet hit him in the shoulder. He spun backwards and staggered down the slope, dropping his rifle. *Move, keep moving.* Everything was going dark—he couldn't see. *Crawl. Pull. Can't pull, can't pull. Not going to make it.* He slumped to the ground and didn't get up.

The next days occurred only on the edge of Daniel's consciousness, not even as if he were dreaming, but once removed. He was aware of his own immobility. The scorching sun passed across the sky and faded into night, several times. He smelled the death stench, heard the cries of the wounded, felt throbbing pain in his shoulder and leg and the crawling and flying things, feasting on his wounds. Later, he recalled a floating sensation. Only the torture of a blade slicing into his shoulder was real. After that, he passed into unconsciousness.

A semblance of awareness returned long before he opened his eyes. He was in a bed. Men groaned and called, "Nurse!" Pounding pain in his head; a fever cooking him from the inside. Thirst. He opened his eyes.

It took several minutes for the blur to clear and his eyes to focus. He saw a head and a face, the face of an old woman. Wrinkles extended from her hazel eyes and mouth. Black hairs sprouted from warts on her chin and her nose, oversize on her thin, wizened face. Her upper lip was covered with a grayish down. White hair flowed wildly from beneath a blue bonnet. Her thin lips parted in a smile, revealing more gum than teeth.

"Praise the Lord," she said. "Don't tell me there's no such thing as miracles!"

"Water," Daniel croaked.

The old woman poured water from a white pitcher on a table in front of the bed into a metal cup and handed it to Daniel. With an immense effort, he raised himself and leaned against the wall behind the bed. He gulped the water, but it came up as fast as it went down, along with yellow bile, making a mess on the sheet. She wiped his face with a rag and removed the sheet.

"Slowly," the woman said. "Try a sip. You haven't had anything in your stomach for a week."

Daniel sipped the water and it stayed down. "Where am I?"

"Memphis, in an army hospital." She took a washrag from a pan and wiped his sweaty forehead, the cool wetness a blessed relief. "Now lie back down. You're weak and you need to sleep. I'll get you a new sheet." By the time she returned, Daniel was asleep.

He felt her presence rather than saw her when he next awoke, in darkness. He pulled himself up against the wall and she handed him the cup. He remembered to sip. Feeling dizzy, he slid back into bed and a fitful sleep.

She was not at his bedside the next morning, but came by shortly after he awoke. He didn't feel as hot as he had before. She handed him a cup and he was able to drink. She held up a metal bowl filled with some sort of mush. "Would you like to try to eat something, Daniel?"

"How do you know my name?"

"It's on your paper. Private Daniel Durand." She offered a spoonful of the pale white mush.

He carefully sucked a small measure from the spoon. It was bland and tasteless, with a grainy texture. He let it slide down his throat, waited, and sucked the rest from the spoon.

"Good, you're eating. A stiff breeze would blow you away. Would you like more?"

Daniel shook his head. Although the mush was staying down, he felt nauseated. The odor of the convalescent ward made it worse. Crushed sprigs of mint, leaves, and herbs placed in bowls around the ward couldn't mask the smells of diseased and dying flesh, excrement, and urine. "I need to relieve myself, ma'am."

"My name is Mrs. Fulmer." She motioned to two younger nurses, who came to Daniel's bed. He rested an arm on each of them. When he tried to stand his legs gave way and the nurses supported him. They led him across the large room, between two rows of beds against opposite walls, down a hall, to a foul-smelling little room with two chamber pots. He pissed, staggered back to bed with his arms around the nurses, and fell asleep.

Every day Daniel felt stronger and ate more than the previous day. Soon he was eating what passed for meat and vegetables. Hospital food was no better than regular army food. He had a lot of time to mentally sort through the war—Shiloh, Walnut Hills, the Vicksburg campaign, Riley, Landers, Culpepper, Mannis, Ben, Pomeroy, and Will. Especially Will. He'd been one of the few friends Daniel had ever had. The grief was more keenly felt because he would not talk of it. He ignored Mrs. Fulmer's occasional comments on his morose silences—invitations to ease his pain. He was fearful of dormant emotions from well before the war, from his brief and wretched childhood, best left undisturbed.

One day Mrs. Fulmer removed the bandage on his leg. The wound, inflicted by a bayonet or knife, had healed cleanly, leaving a small, straight scar about two inches above his right knee. He limped a little when he walked, but hoped that with time the muscle and sinew would heal.

The condition of his shoulder was more severe. He had difficulty opening and closing his left hand and he couldn't raise his arm above the horizontal plane of his shoulder. Several days after she removed the leg dressing, Mrs. Fulmer gingerly pulled the bandages from his shoulder. Daniel winced as she tugged them from the dried blood and scabbed-over skin. Blood trickled down his chest. Daniel stared at the hole in his shoulder and the raw red flesh around it, repulsed by the thought of the deep, ugly pit of a scar he would have for the rest of his life.

Mrs. Fulmer put her nose close to the wound and sniffed.

"Why are you doing that?"

"To see if your wound is diseased. When it's rotting, it smells powerfully bad. When that happens, the doctor has to cut more, maybe your arm or further into your chest. Your wound don't smell bad. You were lucky Doctor Gaines took the bullet out of your shoulder."

"Why?" Daniel remembered the searing pain that had cut through his delirium and could see nothing fortunate in the experience.

"He's cleaner than the other doctors. He washes his knives and saw every time and he uses fresh bandages. He won't cut off arms and legs unless there's no other choice. He's a young man and he's got his own ideas about doctoring. The other doctors, they don't like him, but the boys he operates on do better." She sponged the blood off Daniel's chest and dressed his shoulder.

The next day, Mrs. Fulmer came by after he had finished his breakfast. "You stare out the window all day, and you don't talk much to the other men. Do you have any family?"

"No, I never had any family—orphaned at birth."

"I'm worried about you, Daniel."

"Don't worry about me." He smiled, perhaps for the first time since he had been in the hospital. "I've been thinking about a suggestion from a friend. Might as well do something useful while I recover. Can you get me books on bookkeeping and accounting? Don't go to a library, because I'll want to keep them. Get my wallet from safekeeping and I'll give you money to buy them."

"Why do want those books?"

"I'm thinking about a career in banking."

PART TWO ENTERPRISE

Chapter 5

Millionaires' Row

Where was he?

The old man sat on a frayed brown couch, sipping his tea. The couch sat against one wall of the apartment. On the opposite wall were his bed and a chest of drawers. His kaftan hung from a peg on a stand in one corner, next to a wardrobe. On top of the wardrobe sat a tall black hat. In another corner, by the room's one window, stood a small circular table with two chairs. Books in English and Hebrew filled the bookcase next to the door. A partition separated the room from the kitchen, with its Franklin stove, teakettle on the burner, icebox, sink, two cabinets—one with a water pitcher on top, the other a samovar—and pans hanging from hooks on the wall.

A visitor would have been hard pressed to find a speck of dust, a crumb, or a stain, although the tenant had lived here for many years. The old man was fastidious, and every week his niece came to clean. The smell of dinner—boiled beef and potatoes—lingered over this spotless perfection.

Where was he?

The old man put his teacup and saucer on a stand by the couch, stood, walked to the table, pulled a paper from his pants pocket, and reread the note as he stroked his long gray beard.

Mr. Gottman,

I have completed my military duty and shall be returning to Cleveland. I will arrive by railroad on Thursday, July 12, and I will see you at your apartment then.

Daniel

Daniel's communications to Abram Gottman were always brief. Envelopes would arrive filled with the new money—greenbacks— and one sentence on a scrap of paper, thanking him for exchanging the paper for gold. Abram was not offended by Daniel's laconic "letters"—quite the contrary. Daniel trusted him with his money and respected his intelligence such that detailed instructions were unnecessary. There was little that Daniel either trusted or respected.

Isaac, Abram's brother, said Daniel would never amount to anything. Isaac was too full of himself—his store, his carriage, his fine house, his *kinderlach*, his *shiksa* wife—to judge anybody else fairly. People tolerated Isaac, but they didn't like or respect him. Their mother, *oleho hasholem*, had said about their older brother, Solomon, *olov hasholem*, that he had been born an old man. Solomon had been more like a father than a brother. It had killed him. Responsibility for his family and making a new life in America had been too much.

Daniel was born an old man, too. He'd part with a *pfennig* before he'd part with an opinion, but he didn't like Isaac, and that was why Isaac didn't like him. One was supposed to respectfully listen when Isaac favored you with his story or his opinion. Daniel didn't suffer fools because he didn't tolerate either suffering or foolishness. He would cut Isaac off in mid-sentence and walk away.

Daniel was rude, but did Isaac deserve better? From that first day, when Daniel had fought the *yungatsh* who were teasing him and pulling his beard, Abram knew he was a *mensch*. Abram had hurried away, avoiding *goyim*, as was his habit, although this *goy* had helped him. Proud, tough, serious, wise beyond his eleven years, it had been Daniel who had sparked their initial friendship, tracking Abram down one afternoon outside the synagogue. Only later did Abram understand that Daniel's poverty went deeper than long hours at menial jobs, pittance pay, and life on the streets. His face was streaked with soot, his shoes had holes, and his clothes were nothing more than smelly rags, but he was also impoverished in his soul, and he seemed to sense it. No loving parents to guide him; no friends, only *yungatsh*, already discovering Cleveland's seamier sides; no God or temple for comfort and inspiration; no learning or books to fuel his curiosity and dreams. That was why he had sought out Abram.

Where was he?

Abram walked to the window. He stood with a slight stoop, his shoulders hunched, and looked at a similar tenement building across the way. He wore a white shirt over his *leibtzudekel*, a sleeveless shirt with fringes, and black trousers and sturdy black shoes. The dying sunlight glinted off his black yarmulke, highlighting the few dark streaks left against the predominate gray in his hair, beard, and bushy eyebrows, deepening the contours of his corrugated face and illuminating his brown eyes, restlessly alive despite his age, inquisitive, probing. Soon he would have to light a candle, which he did not like to do. Candles were expensive. He glanced at a leather pouch on the circular table. Daniel would come. Maybe not for Abram, but certainly for his *geld*.

A soft knock came from the door. He hurried across the room and opened it. There stood Daniel, although Abram could not see him well in the dying light.

"You had other appointments?" Abram spoke with a thick, guttural German accent.

Daniel smiled. "I'm sorry it's so late. I wandered around town and lost track of time, then I had to get a room. But I brought you something." He extended his hand and Abram took a short, waxy, cylinder—a candle.

"Aha!" Abram smiled. "Tonight you pay for the light. Come in, my friend, come in. Would you like some tea, or something to eat?"

"No thanks."

"Come here by the window and let me take a look at you. You're thinner—you didn't eat well in the army. You're older. You were never a boy, but you're a man now. Sit down and tell me about the war. Your last—I can't call two sentences a letter—your last note, then, came from Memphis. Why were you in Memphis? There was no fighting there." Abram put his gift on a plate, struck a match, lit it, and sat beside Daniel on the couch.

"I was in a hospital. I took a bullet in my shoulder and was stabbed in my leg at Vicksburg."

"You were wounded! You might have mentioned that in your note."

"What good would it have done? You would have worried, and I was recovering."

Abram stroked his beard. Daniel was right, he would have worried—like a father worries for a son. That was Daniel, not wanting him to worry. "Vicksburg. A great battle…a great victory for the Union."

"There are no great battles. It's not like what you read in the newspaper." Daniel shook his head. Abram wanted to hear more, but Daniel probably wouldn't say more. He kept his sorrows and struggles to himself. The war had not changed that. Daniel was silent until Abram took up another topic.

For the next hour, their conversation reverted to a familiar pattern—Abram did most of the talking, Daniel did most of the listening. He answered the few questions Abram asked about the war, but it was clear that he wanted to talk of other things.

Abram placed his hand on Daniel's shoulder. "You said you got a room. Where?"

"In a boarding house on Cedar Street. Eight dollars a month, plus five for breakfast and dinner. It's a small room, but it's clean, and Mr. and Mrs. Somerset seem respectable. They have six boarders, and a daughter and a son. I ate dinner there tonight. The food was fine." He smiled. "Better than the army."

It was good to see Daniel smile. "Now you need a job. Are you going to look for something at the docks, or maybe the Flats?"

Daniel looked directly into his eyes with an expression of the utmost seriousness. "I'm going to be a banker."

Abram could not have been more shocked if he had witnessed the parting of the Red Sea, but he would not betray his reaction with any kind of sarcasm, not even a smile. Daniel was telling him his dream. For Daniel to tell him this dream required more trust than sending him his *geld*. "That's an excellent choice. Have you thought about how you will secure a position?"

Daniel brought his hands together and leaned forward on the couch. "I taught myself the basics of bookkeeping at the hospital. I'll start with the banks on Main Street. They may turn me down at first, but if I'm persistent, they'll see that I'm serious and I'll get a trial as a clerk. Perhaps you or your brother knows somebody who works at one of those banks."

Now Abram could laugh, a long hearty laugh that came from deep in the belly and was met by a smile from Daniel, although he could not know what Abram was laughing at. For years, Abram had assumed that his advice to Daniel had fallen on deaf ears. *Adoshen* moved in mysterious ways. Abram felt a pride that could only be described as paternal.

"You would think two Jews would know a moneychanger, but we never borrowed. We financed our expansion from profits. The *goy* banks wouldn't have lent us a *pfennig*. But I can help you in another way. I know a tailor, Moses Minzter. You'll have to see him before you go to the banks. He'll measure you for a suit in the morning." Here was confirmation of Abram's belief in Daniel's dream—he would help him buy his first suit. He stood, walked over to the table, picked up the leather pouch, and handed it to Daniel.

Daniel did not count his money, but withdrew a ten-dollar gold piece from the pouch and handed it to Abram. "Thank you."

"*A lebn af dayn kop!*" He slipped the gold piece into his pocket.

"*Mazel tov*! That's probably not the right response."

"It'll do. Soldiers don't make this kind of *geld*. What accounts for your good fortune?"

Daniel smiled. "Poker." Abram looked confused. "Card games. Gambling."

Abram raised his bushy eyebrows, but Daniel made no further comment. "With all that, did you find time to read the books I sent you?"

"I read them all, at least two times. I liked Franklin's autobiography the best." He stood. "I'm tired from the train ride and walking around town. I'll come by tomorrow morning, early, before you go to the store, and we can go to the tailor."

Abram stood and they walked to the door. "Where did you walk to this day, Daniel?"

"Euclid Avenue."

"Ah, Millionaires' Row."

"One day I'll live there." He did not smile.

Abram put a hand on Daniel's shoulder. "*Mazel tov.*" He opened the door. "I'll see you in the morning."

Daniel disappeared into the darkness of the hallway and Abram closed the door. *A lebn af dayn kop*, Daniel, "life on your head"—his mother's favorite blessing.

Daniel stood at the bottom of a long set of granite stairs leading up to the Cleveland Banking and Trust Company, almost wishing he was back on the battlefield facing enemy fire. It was a sweltering, humid summer morning. Rivers of sweat ran down his back and underarms, under his starched white shirt, black vest, and black topcoat. He wiped his forehead with his fancy handkerchief, tugged his high, stiff collar, and adjusted his simple black ribbon of a tie for perhaps the thirtieth time that morning. Daniel had bought two suits and four white shirts, but he would have preferred standing naked on Main Street rather than in these hot, unfamiliar, uncomfortable clothes. He swallowed hard and marched up the stairs.

Although every window was open, it was hotter and muggier inside the bank, with its high, vaulted ceiling, than outside. Daniel approached a young clerk behind a tall desk.

"Excuse me. To whom should I talk about a job? I'm interested in a position."

The clerk, a pimply-faced young man who was no older than Daniel, peered down at him through his spectacles, his lips pursed. "That would be Mr. Eames, at the desk towards the back. His name is on a sign on his desk. But I don't believe we have anything to offer."

"Thank you." He walked to Mr. Eames' desk despite the clerk's discouraging words. Eames was copying figures from a sheet of paper into a ledger book. He looked up at Daniel. He was in his mid-to-late fifties, thin, with a salt-and-pepper mustache and sparse gray hair around a bald spot. His face had a kindly expression, as if everyone he met were one of his grandchildren, asking for a piece of candy.

"May I help you?"

"My name is Daniel Durand. I'm looking for a position as a clerk."

"Do you have any prior experience, Mr. Durand?"

"No, but I can do bookkeeping. I would require some training, but I'm a quick learner."

"What line of work were you in?"

"I was in the army. I was wounded at Vicksburg and taught myself bookkeeping while I recovered at the hospital."

"That's very admirable, Mr. Durand, but I'm afraid we have no openings now. If you'll leave your name and place of residence, perhaps I can notify you if something comes up."

Daniel thought that he had steeled himself for rejection, but he felt a stabbing disappointment. "Thank you, sir. I'd appreciate it if you would keep me in mind." He wrote out his name and address on a piece of paper, handed it to Eames, and walked out of the bank.

Over the next three weeks, Daniel's entrances and exits became a familiar sight to Cleveland's banks' lower-level employees. He grew inured to the rejections. Most of them weren't as cordial as that of Mr. Eames. On his fourth round of inquiries, even Eames was testy.

"Mr. Durand, there are no positions. I have your address, and I assure you that I will contact you and you shall receive every consideration should we have a suitable position. Thank you." Eames had looked down and examined his ledger, a final dismissal.

That night, Daniel had dinner with Abram Gottman. He was a good cook, ladling out steaming soup with potatoes, onion, and meaty chunks of chicken into an earthenware bowl and placing a thick slice of dark pumpernickel on a plate.

"Daniel, you said you would have to be persistent. It's always difficult to find a job."

"I know. I know." He tried sipping the broth, but it was too hot. He chewed on the pumpernickel, fresh from the baker, its crust still soft. "I just didn't think it would take this long."

"Perhaps you should look somewhere else—the railroads, or the merchants at the port."

"But I want to be a banker. A friend said I should be a banker. He was joking, but I think I'll like it. Numbers make sense to me. Double-entry bookkeeping makes sense to me—everything fits together. Most things aren't like that. Money and banks are at the center of business. I want to know everything I can about all of it." He dipped his bread in the soup.

"Aha! You're curious about the world. That's a fine thing. What is your friend's name?"

"His name was Will Farrows. He was killed at Vicksburg." Daniel offered no elaboration. One day he would tell Mr. Gottman about Will and the war, but not now.

"I was about your age when I first heard of America." Daniel liked the way "America" sounded through Mr. Gottman's thick German accent—"Amereeka." "It seemed too good to be true. In Bavaria, Jews couldn't enter the trades or professions. We even had to buy a certificate from the government to get married. Nobody helps the Jews, but in America we work hard and keep what we earn. An honest man can ask for no more. Nobody's going to give you anything, Daniel, but you keep knocking on those banks' doors until one of them opens."

Perhaps it was Gottman's words, or a good night's sleep, or Mrs. Somerset's delicious griddle cakes for breakfast at the boarding house, or the beautiful late summer morning, but when Daniel set off on his daily trek to the financial district, he felt unusually optimistic. He decided to start his day with his fifth visit to Mr. Keane, who had not expressed even the slightest interest in hiring Daniel. He hadn't been annoyed by Daniel's inquiries, had listened attentively, asked the usual questions, then told Daniel that the Bank of Commerce had no positions available.

The Bank of Commerce building fell somewhere in the middle of the scale of banking grandiosity. It had a short flight of steps before a classical facade, with Doric columns topped by simple capitals, and unadorned bronze doors that opened on a room that seemed like a well-designed financial factory. The windows that stretched to the high ceiling provided ample light. Wall sconces with candles and the oil lamps on desks suggested that men worked there at night, too. Before the tellers' counter stood two empty desks and chairs for customers to sit and write. Behind the tellers' counter were the desks for clerks and loan officers, and to the sides of those were offices with windows for the managers. At the back was an office next to the giant black door to the vault. The place had the musty smell of old documents. Everyone was busy, but there was no wasted motion, no hurrying. Although Daniel couldn't hear the conversations, their muted tone sounded reasonable and serious.

He walked to a half-door to the right of the tellers' counter. A teller glanced at him.

"You're here to see Mr. Keane again?"

"Yes."

"I'll let him know you're here." The teller went to one of the windowed offices, knocked on the door, entered, emerged, and opened the half-door. "Mr. Keane will see you."

"Thank you." Daniel went to Keane's office and opened the door.

"Mr. Durand." Keane motioned towards a chair in front of his desk. "Please sit down." He stared intently at Daniel for a long moment, saying nothing. Daniel stared back. Keane's face appeared sculpted in granite. He was in his mid-forties. His coal-black hair was parted in the middle, emphasizing his high, narrow forehead. He had a touch of frost in his closely cropped sideburns. His skin stretched taut over his high cheekbones, across his cheeks, to a Roman nose, down to an angled chin. His eyes, under thin, black eyebrows, were the blue-gray color of Lake Erie and were as placid as the lake on a windless day.

Keane took a ledger from the top of his desk, flipped through the pages, and stopped at two pages full of entries. "Mr. Durand, there are several errors here. Can you find them?" He handed Daniel the open ledger, several sheets of paper, and a pencil. "Take your time."

Daniel examined the ledger. He tallied several columns of numbers and then crosschecked entries to see that every debit had a matching credit. After about twenty minutes, Daniel looked up at Mr. Keane, who was poring over another ledger. "Mr. Keane?"

"Yes, Mr. Durand."

"The addition for the entries for Mr. Roberts's loan payments is incorrect, so the amount listed here for the principal outstanding is also incorrect. The computation of interest for Mr. Billingham's loan is incorrect in favor of Mr. Billingham by four dollars and eleven cents. Also, a payment was noted from Kramer's Paper Goods, but there is no debiting entry."

"That's correct. This is Mr. Collins' ledger. As you can see, his work is unacceptably sloppy. More's the pity that I hired him—it casts doubt on my competence." It sounded wry, but Keane's expression didn't change. Daniel didn't smile. "Mr. Durand, I'll offer you a trial as a clerk for a month without pay. If your performance proves satisfactory, I'll offer you a position at twenty dollars a month, plus pay you for the month you worked."

"That's acceptable."

"Good. Come with me." Keane took him to an empty desk among a group of clerks and placed the ledger Daniel had examined on the desk. "Go through the entire ledger and note every error. Mr. Collins is late again. I informed him the last time that his employment here would be terminated if it happened again. I'm hoping when he arrives he'll see you in his desk and leave, so that I won't have to waste time firing him."

Overjoyed, Daniel sat at the desk. It was a simple affair—one drawer for writing implements and paper, and a set of empty pigeonholes. There was little conversation among the clerks, just the scratching sound of pens and pencils. Shortly after he began his task, Daniel saw a young man approach the half-door by the tellers' counter. He stopped, saw Daniel, clapped his hand to his forehead, turned, and left the bank. Mr. Keane wouldn't have to waste his time.

For the first time in his life, Daniel had found a job he could love. Each error he discovered as he went through Collins' ledger gave him a quiet thrill. He raced over columns of numbers and totaled sums correctly. Sleuthing through a trail of mistakes, one error leading to another, balancing the entries, was a joy. At noon the other men ate their lunches at their desks. Daniel had brought nothing, so he continued to work. By the end of the day he had finished correcting the ledger. He gave it to Keane, who said, "Thank you," but did not look up from his writing. Daniel left the bank with the other clerks. After introductions, they went their separate ways.

That night, Daniel told Abram about his trial as a clerk. Abram was happy and proud—he served strudel to celebrate—but he frowned when Daniel told him about the end of the workday.

"You should leave after the other clerks and arrive before they do."

The next morning, Daniel was at the bank at 6:20, ten minutes before Keane unlocked the bronze doors. Keane said nothing as they entered the bank, but motioned for Daniel to follow him to his office. He handed a stack of drafts to Daniel and a tall, thick ledger book. "Mr. Durand, these are drafts, or checks, drawn upon this bank and presented for payment over the last two weeks to the Merchants' Bank of Ohio. Do you know what a draft is?"

"Yes, it instructs the bank to pay the person to whom it's made out."

"That's correct, but a draft is also a negotiable instrument. It's drawn by the maker and instructs the bank to pay to the order of the person to whom the draft is drawn. An endorsement on the back of the draft makes it negotiable. It can be endorsed to subsequent holders, and allows the ultimate bearer to receive money from the account of the maker."

"The bearer of a draft also has to endorse it?"

"Correct. Merchants' Bank pays those presenting these drafts and endorses them. We clear the drafts, crediting Merchants' Bank's correspondent account. They credit our correspondent account for the drafts we hold from them. The two correspondent accounts are then netted out. Check to see that all the endorsements are in order. Check the balances of the makers in this ledger and debit their accounts. Total the sum of the drafts. I'll check it against the figure given to us by Merchants' Bank. If the figures are identical, I'll credit Merchants' Bank's account."

Daniel went to his desk. The other clerks came in just before seven o'clock. One named Charles looked askance at him, but Daniel kept working. He was there to make money, not friends. Charley and the boys were going to have to work harder if they wanted to keep up with him.

Later, a tall, stout gentleman entered the bank. He carried a stovepipe silk hat and wore a black frock coat, a blue-and-gray-striped tie tucked under a black vest, and gleaming black patent leather shoes with white spats. He walked through the clerks' area, cast a disinterested glance, entered the office at the back of the bank, and closed the door.

"Who was that?" Daniel asked Jack, the clerk next to him.

"Mr. Haverford, the president of the bank."

Daniel finished five stacks of drafts before he left the bank that evening with Keane, an hour after the other clerks.

"Mr. Durand, I customarily return to the bank after I dine," Keane said. He stood with Daniel on Main Street in front of the bank, the setting sun casting long shadows. The street was filled with bankers heading home from the financial district.

"I'll see you in an hour, sir."

After his dinner at the boarding house, Daniel returned to the bank. He completed another stack of Keane's drafts, working past nine o'clock. He and Keane left the bank together.

Daniel walked to the boarding house, tired but excited, occasionally gazing at the stars shining brightly in the clear night sky. From 6:30 in the morning to 9:30 at night—if that's what it was going to take, that's what he was going to do. This was what he wanted. He had his foot in the door and he damn well wasn't going to let anybody close it on him.

Two weeks after Daniel started, Keane summoned him to his office at the end of the day.

"Mr. Durand, I'd like to cut short your trial and offer you a regular position on the terms we previously discussed. Will that be satisfactory?"

"Quite satisfactory, sir."

"Very good. When we return after dinner, you can work through these accounts payable and prepare drafts for my signature. Reading the law, especially the law of contracts and property, would not be an unwise move to further your career."

"Thank you, sir. Does the library have law books?"

"It has Fleming's *Contracts* and Willingham's *Property*. Those would be a good start."

When Daniel left the bank with Keane, the thought of returning to his boarding house seemed disappointingly anticlimactic. He wanted to celebrate the beginning of his future. Every day he passed an inviting tavern near the bank, but had never entered. Tonight he went in, greeted by a mixture of pleasingly pungent smells. A short, fat man with a bushy beard and wild mustache huffed and puffed from the kitchen and bustled up to Daniel.

"Good evening, sir."

"I wanted to have dinner, but it looks like you have a full house."

"There's room at the bar, if you don't wish to wait." He spoke with an accent that came from the British Isles, but wasn't British, perhaps Scottish or Welsh. "Emma's made a fine stew and she's got chicken pies in the oven. Our potatoes and turnips are up from the cellar this morning."

Daniel sat at the bar and had a pie, a bounty of chicken chunks and vegetables floating in a pool of rich gravy, spiced with parsnip and thyme, in a flaky pastry shell. He was tempted by the bartender's offer of a schooner of ale, but didn't want to return to work with the smell of beer on his breath. Mr. Keane didn't miss much. Daniel drank water instead.

As he cleaned his plate with a chunk of hot bread, he thought of the day's date, September 4, the day he secured his first real job. It would be a day he would commemorate every year, like most people celebrated their birthdays. He had been left on the doorstep of a charity hospital after he was born and didn't even know his birthday. "Sometime around Easter of '44," a priest at the orphanage had told him. Everybody had a birthday; there was nothing special about it. Today was something much more important—the start of his productive life. Happy Job Day! He drained his water, settled up with the proprietor, and went back to work.

A bitterly cold, lengthy winter dovetailed with Daniel's ambitions. There was no place to be other than indoors and nothing to do but work. He thrived on long hours and increasingly difficult assignments. Mr. Keane tolerated no apple-polishing or infighting among his clerks, a hard-working, competent group. Whatever resentment they might have felt towards Daniel gave way to begrudging acceptance, then respect. Quiet and unflappable, everything he said and did seemed to embody the principle that the shortest distance between two points was a straight line. When they were stuck on a knotty problem, they went to him for help. He had the answers and the patience to explain.

One day after winter had finally given way to blustery spring, Mr. Keane approached Daniel at his desk. "Mr. Durand, please come with me."

Daniel followed Keane to Mr. Haverford's office at the back of the bank. Keane opened the door to an anteroom. In the corner, behind a rolltop desk, sat a man in his mid-twenties, wearing a black suit with a dark blue tie. He was writing, but looked up when Keane and Daniel entered.

"Mr. Tinsdale, we're here to see Mr. Haverford," Keane said.

"Yes, he's expecting you. Go right in."

The office smelled of cigars. Mr. Haverford sat behind a large desk of burnished mahogany, an aristocratic heirloom befitting a bank president. Two chairs, burgundy leather with gleaming brass studs, faced the desk. Four more chairs around a darkly varnished circular table sat in the center of the room. Above the table hung an ornate chandelier. Behind Haverford a white marble mantel framed a substantial fireplace. On the right wall were several bookcases and a short stepladder, and above the bookcases, a large map of the United States, with red and blue lines and stars that marked battle sites—Haverford was tracking the war. Daniel hadn't seen anything as fancy as this office since the whorehouse in Memphis.

"Come in, gentlemen, and sit down." Haverford sat in a black leather chair with a high back, puffing on a cigar. He glanced at Daniel. "You must be Mr. Durand."

"Yes, sir."

"Pleased to meet you." Haverford remained seated, silently puffing his cigar. He wore a silk tie of gray and black diagonal stripes, tucked into his black vest. He was in his mid-forties, a big man, but not fat, with a ruddy face, square jaw, reddish blond hair, thick eyebrows, and long side-whiskers. His blue eyes had a remote, veiled quality. His nose and ears both seemed too small for his large face. The sardonic twist of his thick lips suggested something unsettling, perhaps dangerous. Daniel guessed that he could be charming, if need be, but that he was used to getting his way. Not a man to be crossed.

"Mr. Durand, Mr. Keane has given me excellent reports about you," Haverford said, his voice flat. "He also tells me you were in the army. Which regiment were you with?"

"The 48th Ohio Volunteer Infantry."

"Ah, Grant's western campaign. Where did you fight?"

"Shiloh, Walnut Hills, and Vicksburg. That was my last battle. I was wounded."

"Magnificent! I would have pursued a career in the military, but of course I had to take over the bank. I paid to outfit a company in the 72nd Ohio—they were with you at Shiloh. As you can see, I follow the war closely." He gestured towards the map on the wall. "General Grant, in Virginia, has coordinated with Sherman in Georgia, so that the Rebels are everywhere engaged and can't shift reinforcements. Why none of President Lincoln's previous generals adopted this strategy, I don't know. What do you think?"

"I haven't followed the war that closely, sir. I've been busy learning the banking business."

Haverford nodded and flashed a perfunctory smile. "Well, well, learning the banking business…and quite properly so. Mr. Keane tells me that you're a quick learner. Our bank's deposits and our ability to lend are expanding. We need another loan officer, and Mr. Keane has suggested training you for the position." He rolled his cigar between his fingers, inhaled, and blew a long stream of smoke into the air. "Mr. Keane will explain your training, but starting next Monday, you'll be earning twenty-five dollars a month. Congratulations."

"Thank you, sir." His first promotion! He couldn't wait to tell Mr. Gottman.

"Congratulations, Daniel," Keane said. It was the first time he had used Daniel's given name. "Your training will begin in what might appear to be a backwards fashion. I hope you've been reading contract law, as I suggested." Daniel nodded. "Particularly the body of contract law dealing with remedies in case of breach. You're going to deal with those accounts that are in arrears, where our debtors have failed to make payments. This work is invaluable preparation for learning how to prudently lend the bank's money. The foundation of lending is the character of the borrower, and one discovers a great deal about character dealing with those who don't pay."

Daniel glanced at Haverford, who had picked up the newspaper on his desk.

"Most of our lending is to businesses," Keane said. "Although we will occasionally offer a mortgage of up to twenty-five percent of the value of a residence. Anyway, there's time enough to go into all this later. Mr. Haverford, Daniel and I will take our leave now."

The two men stood. Haverford looked up. "Very good, Mr. Keane. And again, congratulations, Mr. Durand." He resumed reading.

Throughout that summer, Daniel worked to unravel a Gordian knot of delinquent accounts. Some loans had not been paid for months. A few of these were easily disposed of—the borrowers had left town. They had to be written off, and Daniel wondered why it hadn't already been done. In other cases, business reversals accounted for the inability to pay. Daniel would begin with letters, generally unanswered, and then visit the establishment itself. These visits were an education, for there was much to learn from poorly run businesses.

Unprofitable concerns had an entirely different feel than those that made money. The employees were inattentive, unoccupied except for conversations amongst themselves, and often rude. The premises were disorganized and unkempt and the bookkeeping was sloppy, riddled with errors. Daniel stared with incredulous disgust when one man, the owner of a trading company, assured him that he kept all his figures in his head. Regardless of the type of unsuccessful business, the proprietors had one trait in common: their inability to pay was never their fault. Daniel heard about adverse conditions, unforeseen circumstances, unfair competitors, disloyal employees, and ungrateful customers. He would cut the excuses short and inform the delinquent debtor that further failure to pay would result in a referral of the loan to the bank's lawyers and immediate legal action, including attachment of assets.

"The devil take you, Mr. Durand, you'll get your damn money when hell freezes over." Mr. Poulter, the owner of a struggling clothing store, had just received the standard threat of legal action. He stood in front of his ramshackle store, shaking his fist at Daniel. He was a short man, with a gray, unkempt mustache, and dark hair combed back, roots extending halfway down his forehead, close to his bushy brows.

"If that's your choice, Mr. Poulter, we shall repossess your store. Nobody forced you to borrow money, and comparing the present state of your store to your loan papers, I would guess that you made certain misrepresentations to get the loan."

"It just isn't right! It isn't fair, damn you! You'll take my family's livelihood from us."

"Mr. Poulter, someone who breaks his promise to pay back the money lent to him isn't in a position to talk about what's right and fair. How is it fair to take money that was entrusted to you and not return it? How is it right for you to deprive the bank of the profit it could have made by lending that money to a responsible borrower? Your loan came from depositors—the bank's creditors—and your failure to repay puts their deposits at risk."

"You're not getting my store!" Poulter shouted. He turned and went back inside, slamming the door behind him.

Poulter lost his store in a foreclosure sale. The price was a third of what he had paid for it, but was 70 percent of the balance of his delinquent loan. The other 30 percent was written off. The buyer was an Irish immigrant with a large family who already owned a profitable store. With hard work and the help of his sons, he would enjoy a similar success with this one. Daniel wondered how Poulter had obtained his loan.

The Honorable Donald Gallsworthy, distinguished member of the Ohio legislature, heir to a shipping fortune, lived in a mansion on Millionaires' Row. He had set up his son, Donald Gallsworthy, Jr., in a business that, according to its articles of incorporation, would engage in "the business of trading grains, salt, coal, lumber, and other essential commodities." The limited liability corporation was a new form of business organization. It allowed an investor to limit his liability to the amount of his investment. Unlike partners in a partnership, the owners of a corporation had no obligation to satisfy the debts of the corporation from their personal assets. The Bank of Commerce had lent the Gallsworthy Trading Company a thousand dollars, but Junior had made only two interest payments. The loan was over a year in arrears when Daniel wrote his first letter, threatening legal action. After that letter went unanswered, he investigated and found the concern's only asset was a lease, also in arrears, on an office at the port.

Daniel had written one more letter to Gallsworthy, Jr., and two to Gallsworthy, Sr., imploring them to honor a moral obligation and repay the loan. All three letters were returned unopened. Daniel went to the Gallsworthy manse on Euclid, where father and son both lived, but was refused entrance at the front gate by the footman. He stood outside the estate as the footman opened the gates for the exit of a fine six-horse carriage, its curtains drawn. Daniel smiled.

"I do not see the humor here, sir," the footman said.

"No, you wouldn't." Theft had been a way of life among Daniel's compatriots when he was growing up on the streets, but there was residual shame among the thieves—they rationalized their crimes. Often it was a choice between theft and starvation. Daniel stared at the Gallsworthy mansion. Here was theft without shame, theft that gave itself airs, rode in fancy carriages, threw itself parties, and got itself elected to the legislature.

Several weeks later, Keane approached his desk. "Mr. Durand, come with me to Mr. Haverford's office. We're having a meeting about the Gallsworthys." They entered the anteroom and Tinsdale ushered them into Haverford's office. Haverford was standing on the stepladder, extending General Sherman's march through Georgia on the map on the wall. He stepped down, took his seat behind his desk, reached over to a humidor, and lit a cigar.

"Mr. Durand," Keane said, "Donald Gallsworthy, Jr. has asked the bank to lend the Gallsworthy Trading Company one thousand dollars. Would you please detail your efforts to collect the loan of that amount that is currently in arrears?"

Daniel looked first at Keane and then Haverford. This felt as if it was a test, but he had no idea who had devised it or for what purpose. All he could do was tell the truth. "The Gallsworthy Trading Company made two payments on its loan, but it is now a year in arrears. Its only asset is a lease on a small office, also in arrears. I've written letters to Gallsworthys Junior and Senior, but received no response. Apparently they don't recognize an obligation to make payment."

"Thank you, Mr. Durand," Haverford said. "Are you aware that Senator Gallsworthy was instrumental in renewing this bank's charter?"

"No, sir."

"Mr. Keane, please draw up the loan papers for my signature."

"Mr. Haverford," Daniel said. "This loan should be structured so that we have recourse against the Gallsworthys for repayment and don't have to look solely to the trading company."

Haverford glared at Daniel. "Mr. Durand, as long as I'm president of this bank, I shall decide on what terms it lends its money, thank you." He glanced at Keane. "That will be all."

Daniel and Keane left the office and entered the anteroom. Tinsdale was not there.

"Mr. Haverford didn't like my suggestion," Daniel whispered.

"Daniel, you've never trimmed your sails to fit the prevailing wind. Don't start now." Keane's voice was low, but not a whisper. "I will never reprimand you for telling the truth, or for honestly suggesting what you judge to be the best course of action."

"What about Mr. Haverford?"

"I'll worry about Mr. Haverford. His father, the founder of this bank, would never have extended a loan under these—"

The door from the anteroom to the bank opened, and suddenly Daniel was not thinking of recourse loans, Haverford, the Gallsworthys, or anything at all connected with banking. He was sure his breathing stopped and fairly certain his heart did too. Perhaps time itself stopped. The woman walking through the door could not possibly exist—she had to be an apparition from those ancient legends of hopelessly beautiful sirens who lured enchanted sailors to their doom. Tall and slender, she wore a green-and-white dress that, from the high collar to the hem, traced out a line perfect in its form and proportions, a line no artist could envision until he had seen this woman. She stood with a poise that suggested her immediate location was of no moment—she could have been by herself. Golden hair, the color of Will's, cascaded in loose curls to her shoulders. Her face would present an inspiration and a challenge to any artist. Only a great one could have captured the perfection of her features: the high forehead and cheekbones, the flawless, milky smooth skin, the rich, red lips, the porcelain-fine nose and chin. The blue eyes, sparkling with intelligence, curiosity, and wit, would have tested Leonardo. And no artist could have captured her scent: fresh, clean, a hint of honeysuckle.

Keane addressed a woman behind the goddess, whom Daniel had not noticed. "Mrs. Haverford, may I present Mr. Durand?"

"How do you do, Mrs. Haverford?"

"Very well, thank you. I'm pleased to meet you."

"Pleased to meet you."

"Miss Haverford, may I present Mr. Durand?"

He looked into her eyes and realized several things all at once: She knew the effect she had on men but was indifferent to it. She was far more dangerous than her father. And only his best would stand him any chance with her. He would fight Vicksburg again to win such a chance.

"It's a pleasure to meet you, Miss Haverford."

She returned his gaze and smiled. "The pleasure is mine, Mr. Durand." Her voice had a joyous lilt that would intoxicate after a few sentences.

"Are you having lunch with Mr. Haverford?" Keane asked.

"Yes, we are," Mrs. Haverford said.

For the first time, Daniel looked at the mother. She must have been a beauty in her day. She had her daughter's fine features and golden hair, though her figure was running to stout. The two women walked to the door of Haverford's office. Keane opened it, then closed it behind them. And Daniel, who not thirty minutes before had been satisfied with his life and excited by his prospects, now found himself in exquisite misery.

Chapter 6

Mr. Rockefeller

Daniel wrapped his scarf around his neck as he hurried back to the bank after dinner at the boarding house. This winter hadn't been as severe as the previous year's. Daniel pulled up short to avoid a drunk stumbling from a tavern, but the drunk slipped on the ice and bumped into him, bringing them both down. Two other drunks laughed uncontrollably at the pratfall. Daniel stood and offered a hand. The drunk almost pulled him over as he regained his footing.

"Danny, is that you?" A cloud of whiskey and beer vapor filled the air.

Daniel examined the drunk's face. Bruno. His face was bloated, he was fatter, and he had a new scar, the kind a hook would leave on a fish if it was suddenly yanked from the fish's mouth, extending from the corner of his mouth two inches up his cheek to his cheekbone.

"It is you," Bruno said. "Look at you, with the fancy suit and hat, giving yourself airs. What are you doing these days, Danny?"

"I'm a banker."

"A banker, my, my. You can dress up a piece of shit, but it's still a piece of shit." Bruno's friends laughed. "Since you've come up in the world, why don't you buy us a pint?"

"What makes you think I'd buy you anything?"

"Still the same goddamn high-and-mighty arse." Bruno moved towards him.

Hit hard, hit fast, and hit first. Daniel's jab smashed into the center of Bruno's face and blood spurted from his nose. Daniel's left uppercut caught Bruno in the jaw and his mouth crunched shut. Bruno slipped again on the ice and went down. As he tried to scramble up, Daniel kicked him in the side of the head. He didn't get back up.

The other two were coming at Daniel. He slipped a haymaker from one, countering with two quick hits to the stomach and a jab to the head. The other was trying to grab him. He elbowed him in the face. They were hitting his body, but he ducked and weaved, avoiding swings at his head. Their blows lost their force as he hammered away. They scurried back into the tavern.

Daniel picked his hat off the ground. Bruno lay prostrate, moaning. "Did you think I'd forget how to fight?" Daniel said. "Stay the hell away from me." He walked away, leaving Bruno to the mindless tribe of the street that sucked in its losers with a grip stronger than Mississippi mud.

His topcoat and shirt were ripped. Should he return to the boarding house and change clothes? Now he was late to the bank. Mr. Keane might look askance at the clothes, but he would care more about the work they had to do. Nobody else would be at the bank.

"What happened?" Keane said when Daniel arrived.

"I met an old friend on the street."

Keane's face remained expressionless. He went to the washroom and returned with a damp towel. Daniel ran the towel over his face. It stung one spot on the side of his chin and he ran his hand over a small scrape. Various places on his body were starting to throb.

"Come to my office," Keane said.

Daniel followed Keane and settled into a chair in front of his desk.

"This Friday, Daniel, at nine o'clock, you're to meet a Mr. Rockefeller at his office. I've never met him, but I know he's an upstanding Baptist. He was in a partnership with the Clark brothers in a commission merchant house. Last month he and Samuel Andrews bought out the Clarks' interest in Cleveland's largest petroleum refinery. There was some acrimony between them. Mr. Haverford sees the Clarks socially, and he thinks that petroleum is a dirty, unpredictable business, filled with unscrupulous characters."

"In other words, there's no chance that the bank will extend a loan to Mr. Rockefeller, but you're sending the newest loan officer to meet him as a courtesy?"

"You're a quick study, Daniel." One corner of Keane's mouth turned up in something that looked like a half-smile.

"Thank you for joining me for lunch." Mr. Haverford said to his wife and daughter.

"It's our pleasure, dear. It's been months since we've done this." Laura Haverford smiled.

"Thank you, Father," Eleanor said.

Haverford opened the door of his office anteroom and watched them walk through the bank. They passed the loan officers and Durand followed them with his eyes. He sure as hell wasn't watching Laura. What presumption! Eleanor turned, looked directly at Durand, and bestowed her most radiant smile. *Don't think of it, dearest Eleanor, don't think of it at all!* She'd damn well better not think of it, or the bank's newest loan officer would never work in Cleveland again.

A clerk ushered Daniel into Mr. Rockefeller's office and closed the door. Rockefeller, seated behind his desk, rose and approached Daniel, his hand extended. They shook.

"I'm John Rockefeller. How do you do?"

"Very well, thank you. I'm Daniel Durand, from the Bank of Commerce."

The only similarity between Rockefeller's office and Mr. Haverford's was the United States map on the wall. The hand-drawn lines on Rockefeller's map tracked railway routes and waterways as well as campaigns and battles. Two chairs before the desk, a window that looked out on the barge traffic moving up and down the nearby Cuyahoga River, a simple fireplace, shelves with ledgers and orderly stacks of papers, and a rack of cubbyholes stuffed with telegraph dispatches were the office's only adornments. A ledger and a stack of papers sat on Rockefeller's desk. Kerosene lamps and light from the window and the fireplace lit the office. Daniel sat in an uncomfortable wooden chair.

"Mr. Durand, Rockefeller & Andrews owns the Excelsior Works refinery, at the Kingsbury Run, which feeds into the river. We purchase oil from western Pennsylvania drillers. It's either shipped across Lake Erie or transported by rail, depending on what affords the lowest cost, to our refinery. A refinery is essentially a still. Crude is heated, which separates its components. The component of most interest is kerosene. Once separated, kerosene is cleaned, or refined, with a sulfuric acid wash. My partner, Mr. Andrews, developed that process." Rockefeller pointed at a lamp. "Kerosene is far cleaner, brighter, and cheaper than whale oil, cottonseed oil, lard, or tallow or wax candles. Someday every home and business establishment in the land will use it. We're shipping it to every state in the Union and to our armies in the Confederacy as well."

Rockefeller paused. He had to give himself a break—he spoke in complete paragraphs. The owner of Cleveland's largest refinery was no more than twenty-five. He had a clean-shaven face, short reddish gold hair combed back and above his high forehead, a small, prim mouth, and wide-open blue eyes that suggested youth. The way he spoke—measured, thoughtful—belied his age. By Daniel's estimation, he took himself, and everything he did and said, with the utmost seriousness.

"Does refining protect you from the price fluctuations of crude oil, since you can adjust the price of kerosene?" Daniel asked.

"For the most part. The keys to this industry are size and proficiency in cutting costs. We're going to control Cleveland's oil refining and distribution. Because we have the largest refinery, we negotiate the lowest prices for crude and the best rates from the railroads and shippers. We're building another refinery and we'll acquire more. We'll buy out our competitors, if they're lucky, or drive them out of business if they're not. All this will take money. Please have a look at our books, Mr. Durand." Rockefeller took three ledgers from a shelf and placed them on the desk.

Daniel examined the ledgers for an hour. Excelsior Works was a mint. Its profit margins were more than 40 percent, even after funding capital improvements. He kept his face impassive as he closed the last ledger. "This is impressive, Mr. Rockefeller. Your business has expanded while you've steadily lowered your costs of refining. It appears that the industry holds outstanding potential and your firm is in a position to capitalize on that opportunity."

"Let's ride out to the refinery." Rockefeller led Daniel out of his office, through a room where a group of clerks sat hunched over their desks, and down a flight of stairs to the back of the office complex that housed Rockefeller & Andrews. They walked to a carriage shed. A hostler led two horses pulling a buckboard to Rockefeller, who removed a carrot from his topcoat pocket and fed it to a black horse with white markings. "Hello, Shadow," he said. "I can't give you a treat and ignore Dancer here." He fed the other horse, a solid brown mare, a carrot and stroked the animal lovingly on its neck. Dancer responded, nuzzling Rockefeller's pocket, looking for another carrot. Both horses were young and strong. Rockefeller stepped up into the seat and took hold of the reins. Daniel sat next to him.

Shadow, Dancer, and Rockefeller knew only two speeds—fast and faster. Jerked back in his seat, Daniel tightly grasped the iron arm rail. Rockefeller's hands were as loose on the reins as if he were holding a paper he didn't want to wrinkle. A gentle tug left or right and the horses went the desired direction. He didn't shout or curse. Daniel eventually relaxed, putting a rig like Mr. Rockefeller's on the growing list of things he would acquire someday.

On the outskirts of town they continued on a rough road next to the Cuyahoga River. Long before they reached the refinery, Daniel saw, smelled, and tasted a sulfuric pall. His eyes burned and he coughed and gagged.

"I did the same thing my first few times out here," Rockefeller said. "You'll get used to it." He pointed towards a small ramshackle shed belching smoke through a stack. "Anybody with a thousand dollars can set up a still, and virtually everybody has. We're competing with former shopkeepers, preachers' sons, patent medicine salesmen, soldiers back from the war—there must be forty or fifty so-called refiners out here. The industry's ripe for consolidation."

The Excelsior Works were a series of buildings spread out over several acres, much larger than the other refineries. They entered the largest building first. At one end of the building, a tall cylindrical metal structure with pipes attached at various levels stood above a burner emitting smoke. Two men tended the still and its pipes.

Daniel sniffed the air. "That's not coal firing that burner, is it?"

"No, it's gasoline, a byproduct of the refining process. Our foreman, Mr. McGregor, configured our burners to use it. We don't have to buy coal. Our competitors bury gasoline underground or dump it in the river after dark. The steamship captains prohibit their crews from dumping burnt coal into the river because the gasoline floating on top bursts into flames.

"Refineries have been outlawed within Cleveland's city limits. Because of the extreme volatility of oil distillates, any fire could wipe out the city. All the refiners maintain a fire watch and pitch in when one starts, but there is that risk. The other big risk is that western Pennsylvania could run out of oil. The fire risk is more substantial. I don't think western Pennsylvania will run out of oil. Even if it does, there's oil in other places."

Rockefeller's candor was disarming. Daniel had to be careful—the oilman's enthusiasm was contagious. He couldn't get so excited that it clouded his judgment.

Rockefeller pointed towards the pipes running from the tall cylinder. "That pipe takes the kerosene. Distillation separates crude, by weight, into different byproducts. One of these pipes is for gasoline, one for heavier gas oil, the bottom for residual waste products and the top for vapors. We've found uses for some of the distillates—benzene, paraffin, and petroleum jelly."

They left the still. They stopped in front of a large shed, open on one side. In the shed were tall stacks of wooden barrel staves.

"We used to pay two dollars and fifty cents for white oak barrels."

"How large is a barrel?"

"Forty-seven gallons." Rockefeller chuckled, picked up a stave, and slapped it in his open palm. "I discovered a way we could make our own barrels for a little over a dollar. The coopers had green timber shipped to their shops. I took up some timber concessions. Instead of shipping the timber, we cut it into staves and fire it where it's felled. That reduces weight, slices our transportation costs in half, and our barrels are tighter, drier, and lighter than the ones we'd been buying." Rockefeller kept slapping his palm with the stave, each slap harder than the previous one. "Nothing stops our competitors from doing the same thing." Whack! "But they don't, missing a saving of three cents a gallon." Whack! "How can they stay in business?" Whack! "It's not right and we're not going to allow it!" Whack!

There was something evangelical about this scourging and exhortation. Rockefeller would smite the inefficient, banish the uncompetitive, and cast down heathens who didn't understand that oil wasn't a business, it was a calling! Daniel suppressed a smile—it would have been a sacrilege, like laughing during a sermon.

For the rest of the morning, Rockefeller led Daniel around the Excelsior Works. Daniel peppered him with questions that Rockefeller took an owner's delight in answering. He knew his employees' names and asked about their work and their families. By the time they left, Daniel was convinced that the future of petroleum refining belonged to Rockefeller.

As he pulled up his buckboard in front of the Bank of Commerce to drop Daniel off, Rockefeller said, "I hope your bank will review my request with favor."

"We'll notify you of our decision promptly."

Daniel bounded up the stairs, through the bank, and forgot to knock on Keane's door before he burst into his office. Keane looked up. "How did your meeting go with Mr. Rockefeller?"

"That man is going to make a fortune in the refinery business. I'd bet the damn bank on it!"

Keane smiled. "Sit down and tell me how you arrived at this conclusion."

For the next half-hour, Daniel recounted his visit with Rockefeller.

"Daniel, I can certainly understand your enthusiasm for Mr. Rockefeller's prospects, but Mr. Haverford will never approve a loan." Daniel's face registered his disappointment. "Problem is just another word for opportunity. It's not cast in stone that either you or I will spend our careers working for Mr. Haverford. But this isn't the time or place to discuss that prospect. It's our duty to present this opportunity to Mr. Haverford. Draft an outline of what you want to say to him. Don't betray your excitement—it will work against you. Haverford regards it as his duty to douse honest interest and enthusiasm. There's an extra warm place in hell reserved for such people."

Daniel had never heard this kind of language from Keane. Still waters ran deep—churning beneath that placid surface were all sorts of interesting emotions. And there was that comment about their careers. Daniel returned to his desk and prepared his presentation.

"They say the Confederates are ready to surrender," Haverford said as Keane and Daniel entered his office. He stood in front of his map of the war, puffing his cigar. "Perhaps inside a fortnight. Won't that be glorious!" He went to his desk and sat down.

Daniel kept his presentation dry and logical. Haverford actually listened, for the better part of twenty minutes, to what he had to say. "And so, Mr. Haverford," he concluded, "Mr. Rockefeller's business prospects merit further investigation and consideration by our bank, and if everything is in order, they may justify an extension of credit."

"Mr. Durand, have you ever been to western Pennsylvania?" Haverford's tone was that of an indulgent parent addressing an errant child.

"No, sir."

"The oil region is somebody's nightmare. Acres of beautiful forests have been ripped up, trees replaced with those damned derricks. You can't walk for slipping on the oil that covers the ground, and all the rivers and streams are choked with black sludge." Mr. Haverford took a long puff on his cigar and watched the smoke contemplatively.

"Say a dreamer is fortunate enough to drill into oil. First he has to deal with the local landowners, mostly farmers. I heard a story of one who wouldn't accept a quarter royalty for his oil, he held out for an eighth. Even if our dreamer can buy his concession, nothing stops someone else from stealing his oil by coming at it from a different angle. It will cost two dollars a barrel to take up the oil, the teamsters will charge two dollars to haul it, and the market price may be a dollar. Of course, somebody's making money—the taverns and the brothels are doing a great business. But it's not an industry where the bank should be risking its money."

"Mr. Rockefeller has no investment in oil drilling. The crucial link in the industry is refining, and he's going to control that link."

"He paid a king's ransom, over seventy thousand dollars, to acquire the Clark's share of that Kingsbury Run refinery you so admire. He overpaid and now he's trying to borrow money to bail himself out."

"Sir, I've seen his books. The profits from that refinery justify the price he paid for it."

"Maybe so, maybe so, but sometimes there's more to business than business. This bank has been lending money to the Clarks since my father was its president. Their commission business, while not without its risks, has produced a steady stream of profits to them and loan repayments to us. They say that Rockefeller has no skill beyond that of a good clerk. I would hate to jeopardize our standing with the Clarks by lending to this young upstart who recently ended his partnership with them. That is my decision, Mr. Durand."

"Thank you, sir, for your consideration."

"Please convey our rejection to Mr. Rockefeller tomorrow morning at his offices. Express our desire to nevertheless remain on good terms with him."

"Certainly, sir."

Back in his office, Keane said, "You handled that perfectly, Daniel, you passed the test. Especially after Mr. Haverford turned you down."

"What do you mean?"

"I had to see how you handled him. I'm working on a business proposition, something you may be interested in. It's too early to reveal the details. Until it comes to fruition, it's essential that we both stay on good terms with Mr. Haverford."

Daniel held his tongue. Keane could clap up tighter than a Scot's purse.

Daniel sat outside Rockefeller's office, reflecting on Haverford. There was no reason the hereditary president of a bank would be immune to stupidity. However, sending him, Rockefeller's advocate, to convey the bank's rejection was beyond stupidity, it was spite. How did this fool expect to retain competent employees if he treated so rudely any hireling who suggested ways to make money? It looked like he wasn't going to retain Keane.

"Mr. Durand, Mr. Rockefeller will see you now." Rockefeller's secretary opened the door.

Daniel sat in the uncomfortable chair. "Mr. Rockefeller, although the Bank of Commerce wishes you success in all your endeavors, we cannot offer you a line of credit."

"It wasn't necessary for you to convey your bank's decision. A note would have sufficed."

"I know, sir."

"Then that was not your decision?"

"No."

"And neither was the decision not to grant our firm credit?"

"No."

"Mr. Haverford is not the man his father was. You're bright and energetic—the kind of fellow I'm always looking for. How would you like a job with Rockefeller & Andrews?"

Daniel was stunned. His answer would be important. He was flattered that a man of Rockefeller's caliber would offer him a job. Rockefeller would achieve his goal of dominating the refinery business. Daniel could negotiate a significant increase over his current salary, and working at Rockefeller's firm would offer him an opportunity to accumulate substantial wealth. But this would always be Rockefeller's firm.

"Mr. Rockefeller, I'm honored that you would offer me a job, but I want to be a banker. I love banking; I'm not sure I'd feel the same about your business. I would rather work for you than Mr. Haverford, but I don't think I'll be working for Mr. Haverford that much longer. I'm going to own a bank, and when I do, you can be sure you'll get credit on the most favorable terms. If I lend you money, or invest in your company, you'll be working for me, and I'd rather have you working for me than me working for you."

Rockefeller burst into long, uncontrollable laughter. He attempted to speak, but each time dissolved into frantic paroxysms of mirth. Daniel had never heard such a convulsive mix of cackles, shrieks, whoops, and snorts, far disproportionate to that which elicited it. Rockefeller wiped a tear from his cheek as he finally regained control of himself. "Mr. Durand," he gasped, "you turned down my job offer with considerably more flair than you denied my loan. When you're ready to start your bank, I'd like an opportunity to invest. I guess that's the only way I'm ever going to have you working for me." He surrendered to more laughter. "Thank you very much, Mr. Durand—for everything. I'm sure we'll get together again soon."

"Thank you, Mr. Rockefeller. I'm sure we shall."

Back at the bank, Daniel went straight to Keane's office, remembering to knock this time.

"How did Mr. Rockefeller react?"

Daniel smiled, closed the door, and sat down. "He offered me a job."

"Smart man."

"When I told him I wanted to one day own my own bank, he said he wanted to invest."

Keane said nothing for several moments, staring off into space, performing some sort of private calculation. He nodded his head several times and a smile spread across his face, as if the last piece of a puzzle had fallen into place. "So you'd like to own your own bank, Mr. Durand. Would you want a partner, a man with some experience in banking?"

"Of course. Is that the business proposition you mentioned yesterday?"

"Yes, and it's important what you just told me. Very important."

"Why?"

"Because only a lack of capital prevents the establishment of the Keane and Durand bank, or the Durand and Keane bank if you prefer. I'm not particular about the name. Our bank needs capital, investors. It's a problem, but problem is just another word for opportunity."

Daniel and Abram Gottman stood in a long line, waiting to view Mr. Lincoln's casket in a specially constructed mortuary pavilion.

Cleveland was one stop of many the funeral train would make on its journey from Washington to its final destination of Springfield, Illinois. Most of Cleveland's businesses, including the Bank of Commerce, had closed for the day.

The casket rested on a bier, with three large, colorful bouquets at the foot of the casket. Soldiers in dress uniforms, three each from artillery, cavalry, and infantry units, stood at attention. A long red rope kept the mourners from approaching the coffin. A women's chorus, dressed in white robes, stood on a raised platform and sang dirges.

Daniel was surprised at the emptiness of his own reaction to the display. President Lincoln, the commander in chief, had met the same fate as thousands of men he had ordered into battle in the just concluded war. Daniel had cried as his best friend died in his arms. Was he going to waste tears for the man who had thrown his friend's father in jail for exercising his Constitutional right to disagree? For a man whose unnecessary war had killed his friend, fighting for a cause in which he didn't believe? Dry-eyed, Daniel followed Abram from the pavilion.

There were few carriages and pedestrians on the streets, and commercial establishments were closed. A church bell rang mournfully. The skies were overcast and the air had the smell of impending rain. Even the birds seemed subdued, only occasionally chirping.

"He was a great man, Daniel," Abram said.

"It was a great deed, eliminating slavery, but he wasn't a great man. A great man would have figured out how to do so without resorting to war. Other countries did."

"Aha! How would you have ended this evil, my friend?"

"The Constitution treats slaves as property of the slave owners. That's wrong, but since it's the law, Lincoln should have proposed compensation to the owners for their slaves. The Fifth Amendment requires the government to pay property owners when it takes their property. The costs would have been nothing compared to what this nation just endured."

Abram chuckled. "So now you're a *lamden* of the law."

"What's a *lamden*?"

"A learned man. A scholar."

"I almost got killed in that cursed war. Lincoln and his generals didn't give a damn about the men who died for them. I laid there for three days at Vicksburg before they came for me. I'll never forget that burning sun, my thirst. It was the Reb commander, not Grant, who proposed a truce so both sides could gather up their wounded and dead—by then it was mostly dead. Don't tell me about great men or great wars or great deeds. Everybody's already forgotten that this war didn't start out as a war against slavery, it was to stop states from exercising their right to leave the damn union." Daniel was shouting, shaking.

Gottman's eyes were wide. "*Oy, a lebn af dayn kop*, Daniel. I meant no offense. Perhaps we should set aside the questions raised by this war for now. I'm sorry."

"I don't know how history will judge Lincoln, but he was no damn saint."

They walked up a maple-lined avenue, silent for some time. As they turned a corner, Mr. Gottman said, "How is your work at the bank?"

Daniel smiled. "Mr. Keane wants to leave and start a new bank."

"Would you go with him? What about Mr. Haverford? Starting a bank sounds risky."

"It depends on how you look at risk. Haverford is a fool and Mr. Keane is a great banker. Isn't it riskier to stay with the fool, especially if Mr. Keane won't be there to clean up his mistakes?"

Abram ran his fingers through his long beard and nodded. "Yes, when you say it that way, it would be better to go with Mr. Keane. When will you start your new bank?"

"We need to find investors. Mr. Keane has been talking to some people with money."

"I might invest in your bank, Daniel, if I had a chance to look things over. So might Isaac."

Daniel was surprised. Mr. Gottman lived so simply, Daniel had never imagined that he had any money, but of course he did; he was the co-owner of a thriving store and had no family.

"We would welcome your investment, Mr. Gottman, and your brother's too."

"Isaac never scoffs at a chance to make money. Your bank will make money. Just remember one thing, or you'll never be happy with your riches: wisdom is far more precious than *geld*."

One day Mrs. Somerset rushed up to Daniel as he entered the boardinghouse parlor, a cozy room with a small couch and several wooden chairs around a worn, circular rug, facing a fireplace. The smells of many meals were part of the furniture, wallpaper, and curtains. Mrs. Somerset carried an envelope. "Mr. Durand, Mr. Durand," she said, excited, "you received this fancy envelope today in the mail. I've never seen anything like it, sir." She was a short, thin woman in her early forties, with brown hair pulled back in a bun and nervous, darting eyes.

She handed him the cream-colored envelope. His name and address were in gold embossed letters and the return address read *HAVERFORD, 377 EUCLID AVENUE, CLEVELAND, OHIO*. She peered over the envelope as Daniel started to open it.

He handed her the envelope. "Why don't you open it?"

Mrs. Somerset blushed. "Oh, I couldn't do that."

"Sure you could, go ahead."

Mrs. Somerset ripped open the envelope. "This is hard to read. It's in that fancy writing. It says, '*Mr. and Mrs. Phillip Haverford request the honor and pleasure of your company to commemorate the twenty-fifth anniversary of the Cleveland Bank of Commerce, and to honor the sacrifices of those who were wounded and killed in service to the United States. Saturday, July 8. Festivities commence at 8:30 p.m. at the Haverford estate, three seventy-seven Euclid Avenue.*' There's foreign words—I think they're French—and Mrs. Phillip Haverford's name."

Eleanor Haverford would be there! He had never attended a party, had never wanted to. Nothing would stop him from attending this one.

"You'll be needing a new suit, Mr. Durand. You don't have a carriage. Perhaps you can use Mr. Somerset's buckboard. I don't mean to criticize, sir, but you may need to learn some of the finer points of manners. Do you know how to dance? There'll be some pretty young ladies at this reception, and you're such a handsome young man, you should be dancing with them. We need to write a nice note to Mrs. Haverford...." Mrs. Somerset's voice trailed off as she left the room, beginning her preparations for Daniel's party a month hence.

He laughed a long, hearty laugh. So this was what it was like to have a mother!

Chapter 7

Eleanor

Eleanor Haverford yawned. The prospect of her father's party that evening left her tired before it began. Not that this was just another party, her father had boasted. He had spared no expense, engaging an orchestra, placing huge orders for food and beverages, hiring an army of attendants, decorating the mansion, and notifying Cleveland's newspapers, which would dutifully report the festivities and the dignitaries in attendance. Downstairs, Eleanor heard him shouting at workers executing last-minute arrangements. He had mostly shouted for the past two weeks.

She looked at herself in the mirror above her dressing table, gazing at her reflection in the same way she would an exquisite painting of some other beautiful young woman—appreciating the artistry, but without vanity. Her bedroom was severe for a woman of her age and station. A canopied bed, done in shades of green, stood against one wall, opposite a wall with a small fireplace. Green curtains framed a large window with a sweeping view of the front grounds. Opposite the window was a painting of a distinguished older gentleman. Her wardrobe stood in a corner. There were a multitude of books in a bookcase on one wall, a handcrafted oak desk in the corner closest to the fireplace, and an intricately patterned rug of brown and gold against green.

Eleanor's mother entered the room, wearing a yellow dress with a close-fitting bodice, cinched waist, and multiple flounces cascading over a skirt with wide hoops.

"Mother, you look so young in that dress. It's lovely."

"Thank you. I'm looking forward to an enjoyable evening, but you don't seem very excited."

"I'm not."

"Any number of young women in Cleveland would be delighted to be here tonight."

"One of them can have my place." Eleanor smiled.

Mrs. Haverford moved to the window and gazed at the front grounds. "Why must you be so difficult?" She turned towards her daughter. "Most of this effort is for you. Your father is doing everything he can to secure a beneficial union."

"Beneficial for me or beneficial for Father?"

"Why, beneficial for you and for him. For all of us. You've had your choice of young men with prospects from substantial families. Yet you take a perverse delight in disappointing their affections."

"Mother, how many of those young men would have prospects if they weren't from substantial families? I prefer visiting with their fathers. At least most of them have done something on their own."

"You don't give the sons any chance at all. You're quiet as they squirm and try to say something to interest or amuse you. They need some assistance, Eleanor."

"I want to meet a man who doesn't need my assistance."

Mrs. Haverford sighed, walked over to Eleanor, looked at herself in the mirror, and moved a strand of hair back into place. "Archer Winfield must be different. You like talking with him."

"He ridicules the ridiculous. We'll wager tonight how many times Stanley Billings tells me I'm beautiful."

"Oh, how vulgar. I hope you have the proper attitude towards Mr. Winfield. He's handsome, and there are undoubtedly many prominent young women who would happily marry him."

"Undoubtedly."

"I wish I understood you. You act as if you have no desire to get married."

Eleanor took one of several bottles on her dressing table, tipped it against her finger, and rubbed it on her neck. "If grandfather hadn't been the founder of a bank, if father had no prospects other than those his own capabilities presented, would you have married him?"

"What a foolish question! Of course not."

"Thank you for your honesty, Mother."

Her mother retreated from the room. Eleanor shook her head. Mother didn't have the necessary weaponry for their long-running battle.

She stared at the painting of the distinguished older gentleman. She wished her grandfather, Alexander Haverford, could be at this reception. Five years after his death, she still couldn't think of him without a tinge of sorrow. She had adored him. He would never have given such a grand party, although he would have been proud of his bank's twenty-fifth anniversary. He would have loved seeing her in her deep blue dress with its simple ruffled bodice trimmed with white lace, and two flounces over hoops that were just wide enough to be considered fashionable. Grandfather had hated frills.

She would talk with Mr. Keane tonight, and his lovely wife, Abigail. Grandfather had hired Mr. Keane and credited him with much of his own success. Perhaps she would also visit with Mr. Keane's protégé, Mr. Durand, if he was there. Her father had scowled at every mention of his name since the last time she had been at the bank and she didn't know if he was invited. Was he as interesting as he looked? She walked out of her bedroom and down the staircase to the ballroom. Negro servants scrubbed the gleaming marble floor. She sat at the keyboard of a grand piano and played her grandfather's favorite Chopin nocturne.

Mrs. Somerset straightened Daniel's black silk tie, took a step back, and inspected her handiwork—black hair slicked back, starched collar and tie, black vest and coat with tails, white, fresh-from-the-tailor shirt, black pants with black stripes down each side that made his long legs look even longer, gleaming spats—every inch the perfect gentleman. He had been just as finicky about his appearance as she, spending a small fortune on his suit and shoes and visiting the bathhouse and barbershop that afternoon.

"Daniel, you look so handsome, and even younger now that your hair's been cut."

"Thank you, Mrs. Somerset. Would you hand me my hat and gloves?"

She took a tall black hat and white gloves from a table in the boardinghouse parlor and handed them to him. She opened a window to rid the room of the smells from dinner.

They walked out the front door, to where Mr. Somerset waited as if he were going to the party. He wore his best black suit, the one with the fewest shiny spots. He was short, with a wiry build. A number of boarders and people from the neighborhood milled about. Mrs. Somerset had proudly mentioned Daniel's big reception to a "few" friends.

A carriage drove up the little elm-lined street, driven by a man sporting the same black-and-white perfection as Daniel, with a lovely woman in a green dress sitting next to him. The man had a severe face and black hair combed back. That would be Mr. Keane. Bringing his carriage to a stop in front of the boardinghouse, he stepped down and looked Daniel over.

"Most impressive. Abigail, may I present Mr. Durand? Daniel, my wife Abigail."

"A pleasure to meet you, Mrs. Keane."

"A pleasure to meet you, Mr. Durand. Please, call me Abigail."

"And call me Daniel."

She smiled. Mrs. Somerset liked that smile and the way her green eyes twinkled.

"Mr. Keane and Abigail, may I present Mr. and Mrs. Somerset?"

There were a chorus of "pleased to meet you" and other pleasantries. Daniel and Keane stepped up on the carriage and sat down. It pulled away, followed by a multitude of curious eyes.

Mrs. Somerset stood with her husband outside the boardinghouse. Daniel had allowed himself to be tutored on the intricacies of etiquette with quiet attentiveness and an occasional flash of humor. To the amusement of the boarders and her children, she had taught him rudimentary dance steps in the parlor as one of the boarders, Mr. Thurman, played a violin. In the two years Daniel had lived at the boardinghouse, he had been unfailingly polite, a model of restraint and reserve. Everyone marveled at the hours he worked at the bank. Such a quiet, ambitious, industrious young man. Yet she never shook the feeling that a powerful force lurked beneath the pleasant surface. There was something unpredictable, probably dangerous, about him, and she prayed that he would be long gone from the boardinghouse when it burst forth.

The Keanes' simple carriage was dwarfed in size and grandeur by elegant broughams and coaches at the Haverford mansion. Some had six horses and a driver. A liveried Negro wearing white gloves took the reins of the Keanes' carriage as it reached the head of a long line waiting on the driveway in front of the Haverford mansion. Keane took off his driving gloves and said, "Thank you." The Negro looked surprised.

Daniel stepped down, slipped on his hat and white gloves, and looked at the Haverford mansion, a three-story box with smaller boxes on either side. A semicircular portico with columns marked the front door. All three gray granite boxes had mansard roofs with protruding dormer windows, numerous chimneys, square windows on the lower floors, and stringcourses with classical figures in bas-relief. This was easily the ugliest residence he had ever seen. Only the grounds broke the ugliness. A majestic maple stood in the center of the expansive front lawn. Projecting in all four directions were long rows of pansies, roses, gladioli, calla lilies, and other flowers, dappled in the fading sunlight, their mingled scent carried on the summer breeze.

Daniel and the Keanes walked between the columns of the portico through the tall front doors. Inside, white-gloved hands reached toward them and the men handed over their hats and cards.

"Mr. and Mrs. Keane, and Mr. Durand," the doorman announced.

Mr. Haverford was at the head of a receiving line in a grand marble entryway. On both sides of the entryway curved staircases with red carpets led to a landing. A classical statute, a winged goddess with a flowing robe, stood beneath the landing at the opposite end of the entryway. Mrs. Keane extended her hand and Haverford clasped it. "You look lovely, tonight, Abigail."

"Thank you, Phillip."

Haverford shook Keane's hand warmly and greeted him, then, less effusively, Daniel.

"Congratulations on the bank's twenty-fifth anniversary, sir," Daniel said.

"Thank you, thank you," Haverford said, looking at the person behind Daniel.

"Laura, Mr. Durand is one of those you're honoring tonight," Mrs. Keane said. "He fought in the western campaign and was wounded at Vicksburg."

"Imagine that," Mrs. Haverford responded, her voice flat. She extended her hand and Daniel briefly clasped it. "We're honored by your presence, Mr. Durand. We met once before."

"Yes, we did, at the bank."

"It's a pleasure to renew your acquaintance. I hope you enjoy the reception." She smiled a correct smile, one that could be endlessly repeated without undue strain on her facial muscles.

Daniel smelled honeysuckle. Eleanor was standing next to her mother. She wore a deep blue dress, simpler than her mother's, which highlighted her blonde hair and fair features and stressed her youthful figure and the vitality of her body. He clasped her extended hand.

"It's a pleasure to see you again, Mr. Durand."

"The pleasure is mine, Miss Haverford."

"Please, it's Eleanor."

"I'm Daniel."

"I hope we'll be able to spend some time together this evening, Daniel." She smiled.

"I certainly hope so, Eleanor." The line of guests was backing up; he had to move on. He met Haverford's oldest son, Steven, and his two oldest daughters and their husbands. At the end of the line, a servant directed him through open doors to the ballroom, already crowded and noisy.

It was grander than anything Daniel had ever seen. Music from the orchestra at the opposite end floated up towards eight massive chandeliers, gaily lit with hundreds of candles. A balcony, its marble railing decked out in red, white, and blue bunting, extended above and around the perimeter. By the orchestra, in the corner, stood a grand piano and bench. French doors on either side of the room opened out to the grounds. Women in plumage of every color, featuring all manner of materials—satin, silk, muslin, taffeta, and tulle, and all manner of decoration—lace, ruffles, ribbons, feathers, flounces, flowers, fans, brocades, beads, and pearls, seemed to float on the gleaming floor in their bell-shaped hoop skirts, jewelry sparkling. Except for the few military men, all officers, the men's clothes were more uniform—black coats with tails, black vests, high white collars and shirts, and black pants. Only the ties, some black, some white, some colored, provided variation. Couples were already dancing, but many guests were socializing.

"Daniel," Mrs. Keane said, "you may want to meet some of the other young people. Perhaps get your name on some dance cards."

Daniel wanted his name on only one dance card and he wasn't about to approach insular groups of well-bred strangers and try to socialize. He shook his head.

Mrs. Keane smiled kindly, her green eyes sparkling. "My card isn't filled yet. Maybe we could dance later on." She was one of those women who became prettier the longer one knew her. A warm smile, a fine figure, auburn hair in ringlets and curls, and those sparkling green eyes…Mr. Keane had to count himself fortunate.

"Thank you, I'd like that."

Keane led them to Mr. Gainesville and Mr. Albright, fellow loan officers, and their wives. After initial introductions and pleasantries, the men drifted into a discussion about bank business, while the women talked of their children. Daniel kept his eyes on the entrance to the ballroom, for Eleanor after she had finished her receiving line duties.

He noticed that a man holding forth in the center of a large group of young people also kept glancing towards the door. He was tall but stood with a slight slouch. He had a large, square head, wavy brown hair swept back, still blue eyes, a patrician nose, dimpled chin, and full, almost feminine red lips. In a room full of expensive suits, he had the fanciest coat and the longest tails, with a wide, colorful striped tie tucked into his vest. When Eleanor entered the ballroom, the cluster of people around the tall man seemed to gravitate over to the group that formed around her. The two met, she smiled, and they briefly shook hands and stood together. He liked to show off his teeth, smiling often. His smile carried a hint of mocking condescension. Who was this bastard?

"Mr. Keane, who's that man standing next to Miss Haverford?"

"That's Archer Winfield, from New York. His immensely wealthy family owns railroads, banks, land, and who knows what else. He's courting Miss Haverford."

That phony swell? That pompous dandy?

"Miss Haverford has rejected other prominent suitors," Mr. Keane said.

"She said 'no' to a Vanderbilt," Mrs. Keane said. "Her father was heartbroken." Everyone in the group laughed.

The ever-expanding swarm of men around Eleanor was a pack of mongrels, except dogs didn't have a genteel system of social pretense to disguise what they were after. Daniel took a deep breath. He was going to have to take on the pack if he wanted to spend time with Eleanor that evening. Bark! Bark! "Excuse me. I believe I should meet some of the other guests."

"Certainly," said Keane.

Daniel stepped towards Eleanor's group. Gradually, he maneuvered through the dense cluster around Eleanor. Progress was slow and he engaged in conversations with other hopefuls. Finally he was close enough to hear several men near Eleanor in a discussion about tactics in the war. He caught her eyes. She looked fabulous in that blue dress.

"Excuse me," Eleanor said, "but I see Mr. Durand. He actually fought in the war. He was under General Grant—perhaps he could contribute his insights. Won't you join us, Mr. Durand?"

The throng parted. Daniel made his way to where Eleanor was standing with Archer Winfield.

"Mr. Daniel Durand," Eleanor said, "may I present Mr. Archer Winfield?"

The two men shook hands. Winfield flashed a correct, artificial smile. "Durand...Durand...There's a prominent attorney in Philadelphia, Junius Durand. Are you any relation?"

"No."

"Well, Mr. Durand, you can tell us, what was General Grant like? One reads the newspapers, but they don't give a sense of what he's about as a person. Is it true that he drinks to excess?"

Will Farrows had once said, "Don't be haughty to the humble or humble to the haughty."

"I was a private in the infantry, Mr. Winfield," Daniel said. "Privates don't generally associate with generals. I saw General Sherman once, at Shiloh, but I never met General Grant. So I don't know what he's like as a person."

"I see, I see." There was nothing congenial about Winfield's ice-cold blue eyes. Daniel was in a pissing contest "Well, perhaps you could offer an opinion about his tactics and strategies. In which battles, besides Shiloh, did you engage?"

"Walnut Hills and Vicksburg. General Grant's defensive preparations at Shiloh were inadequate—we would have lost if General Buell hadn't arrived with reinforcements. Walnut Hills was General Sherman's affair. The strategy was inept and we had to retreat. The

Vicksburg campaign was well designed and executed by General Grant, although he misjudged the extent of Confederate fortifications outside Vicksburg. We attempted two attacks that were repelled. His decision to lay siege to Vicksburg, though he was criticized at the time, was the correct one."

"Daniel, was Vicksburg your last battle?" Eleanor said.

"Yes, I was wounded there, and taken to a hospital in Memphis to recover."

A blonde woman in a light green dress spoke. "Eleanor and I volunteer at the hospital for the war wounded. It's terribly sad, but also inspiring. Many of the men are in good spirits despite their injuries."

"Miss Constance Walter, allow me to present Mr. Daniel Durand," Eleanor said.

"A pleasure to meet you, Miss Walter." She extended her hand and he clasped it.

"Eleanor, you never told me that you volunteered at the hospital," Winfield said. He placed his hand on Eleanor's sleeve and interposed his body between her and Daniel. With a smile, he threw his arm around Steven Haverford, standing nearby. "Who would have guessed that your sister would be ministering to our brave soldiers? I'm surprised, and filled with admiration." The group seemed to move with a unity of purpose against Daniel, the interloper. Two other men and a woman stepped in front of him as Winfield steered Eleanor away. The group, chatting gaily, closed ranks, leaving Daniel behind.

Phillip Haverford poured two cognacs from a crystal decanter and placed it on a silver tray on a mahogany table in his study. He took two cigars and turned towards his guest, seated on a black leather sofa. "I picked these up in New York, Archer. You won't find better this side of the Atlantic. The cognac was bottled before Napoleon invaded Russia."

Winfield took a cigar and a snifter from Haverford, twirled the cognac, sniffed, took a sip, and tilted his head towards his host in appreciation of the rare liqueur. A lively quadrille floated up from the ballroom downstairs. Tall bookcases on three walls ran from floor to ceiling. He'd wager he could count on one hand the number of books in this room the banker had actually read. For a year Winfield had attended Haverford's social functions, gotten to know Cleveland's prominent people, and assumed a leading position among the town's privileged youth by virtue of his distinguished New York lineage and immense wealth. Cleveland was a backwater, but that was the price he had paid in his campaign for Eleanor; a campaign that had been as meticulously planned and executed as any of the war just ended.

Haverford lit their cigars, placed his snifter on a table, and sat on a black leather sofa, facing Winfield. "You said you had a matter of importance to discuss with me. What's on your mind?"

"Thank you for seeing me privately, sir. I know this party demands your attention. I'll get right to the point. Eleanor is the most beautiful, captivating woman I've ever met. I don't think my feelings towards her are any secret." Archer smiled his warmest smile. Like everyone except his own father, this pompous banker could be charmed. "While I would not be so presumptuous as to state that these feelings are mutual, I believe that Eleanor may favor me. With your blessing, I would like to ask your daughter for her hand in marriage. I can offer her my affection and all the advantages in life she deserves."

A smile spread across Haverford's flushed face. "Archer, your intentions towards Eleanor are honorable, and you're a fine young man from an outstanding family. Of course I consent to your request to ask her for her hand. Eleanor must regard herself as quite fortunate. When do you propose to propose?"

Winfield emitted a respectful chuckle. "Mrs. Haverford has invited me to your picnic in the countryside tomorrow afternoon. Perhaps if you and Mrs. Haverford could arrange for Eleanor and me to have some time alone, I could ask her then."

"Splendid! I wish you the best of luck. We'll welcome you into our family."

You should, you small-time fool, Winfield thought. You certainly should.

Daniel stood on a balcony above the portico for the back doors to the ballroom. The orchestra was taking a break. He watched the guests mingle on the expansive back lawn. He'd had his chance with Eleanor and Winfield had pushed him aside. After the snub, Daniel had watched her dance with him and several other men. He had forced himself to remember names and ask questions as Mr. Keane had introduced him to customers of the bank. Now alone, he felt for the first time the full weight of his disappointment. Were his hopes for Eleanor to be dashed by that swell? No, he'd give it another try. When the music started again, Winfield or no Winfield, he would dance with her.

"Yon Cassius has a lean and hungry look."

That enchanting, musical voice! Daniel turned and there she was, her head and the shape of her beautiful blue dress silhouetted in the light from the ballroom.

"Julius Caesar. Why that quote?" She stepped towards him. He smelled honeysuckle.

"That's the way my father sees you, Mr. Daniel Durand. Like Mr. Keane, he admires your industry and ability, but perhaps you pose a danger to him."

"Perhaps I do." Daniel smiled.

Eleanor felt a nervous flutter across her stomach. What a gem of a smile. Here was a man who didn't require her assistance. "Father thinks you're an upstart—that you don't know your place."

"Perhaps I don't. Those people down there, do they know theirs?"

"They most certainly do. It's their birthrights. What's your birthright?"

"I don't have one." Another smile. "Not a family or a name. I don't even know my own birthday."

She felt gloriously, recklessly alive. For once she was free to speak without measuring her words, free to match his candor with her own. "Were you an orphan?"

"They found me on the doorstep of a charity hospital. One of the nurses who cared for me liked the story of Daniel in the lion's den. I can't tell you where the Durand comes from."

Whatever their virtues, the men she knew always mentioned their wealth and their families' prominence, as if those accidents of birth gave them some special value. Even Archer, notwithstanding his sardonic disdain and mocking jokes, made it clear that he belonged to the privileged class. Without a trace of embarrassment Daniel said that he came from nowhere, had started with nothing. Where you started from wasn't important, it was where you ended up—and how you got there. "Tell me, Daniel-in-the-lion's-den, when does a foundling banker who arrives early and stays late every single working day find time for Shakespeare?"

He stared into her wide-open, inquisitive, sparkling-with-mischief, beautiful blue eyes. "I read at nights and my days off. I haven't read all his plays, but I've read the tragedies and histories."

"Which play do you like the most?"

She made it extremely difficult to concentrate on literary criticism. "*Macbeth*."

"Why?" She took a few steps away from him, to draw him away from the balcony railing into the shadows. If they were spotted the horde would quickly put an end to this intimate scene.

He stepped towards her. "It's the most believable of the tragedies. There's no depravity or evil that men won't commit to gain power."

Not only does he read, he thinks. "Are there any you don't like?"

"*Hamlet*. A man shouldn't have so much trouble killing the man who murdered his father and married his mother. If he can't do that, he's not much of a man."

"Did you like *King Lear*?" She smiled. "Can daughters drive their father mad?"

He nodded. A half-smile played across his face. "A certain kind of daughter could visit all sorts of vexations upon her father. Perhaps even drive him mad."

She laughed. "What about *Othello*? Could a man kill his wife out of jealous love?"

He moved closer to her. Disjointed notes came from the orchestra as the musicians, returning from their break, tuned their instruments. They gazed into each other's eyes a long time before he murmured, "Definitely."

A pulsating tremor ran up and down her body. Breathing seemed more difficult and the breaths she drew came short and shallow. He was so handsome, so strong. The desire to reach out to him, to place his hand against her face, to have him pull her to him, to kiss him, to feel his body against hers, to match her strength and will against his, to offer everything to him, was unprecedented, primal, overwhelming.

Daniel knew that the slightest indiscretion, if discovered, would doom any chance of their being together, or he would have done what she wanted him to do. Somewhere on this earth, life had grandeur. People of noble ambitions and unbroken spirits surmounted towering challenges, living in beauty and splendor of their own creation. The way her shining eyes looked at him...did she share this vision? Great attainments required consuming passion...and iron self-restraint. "Eleanor, the music is starting. You have to get back. Before you go, may I have a dance, a waltz?"

She opened her dance card. "I've already written you in, Daniel. Dance number fourteen."

He saw his name on the card. "Mr. Winfield has several dances."

"Well, he is going to ask me to marry him tomorrow. Go down the main stairs into the ballroom. I'll go another way, after you."

He kissed her, quickly but full on the lips, turned, and was gone.

She felt disappointed, wanting more. He hadn't asked how she would answer Archer.

Daniel hurried down the stairs, smiling. She wouldn't have told him of the proposal if she intended to say "yes."

"Daniel, you look like you just found the philosopher's stone," Keane said as he and Abigail left the dance floor. He wiped his forehead with a handkerchief.

"What's the philosopher's stone?"

"Legend says that it could transform base substances into gold."

"Well, in a way, maybe I have. Abigail, if Mr. Keane doesn't mind, do you still have an opening on your dance card?"

"Certainly, Daniel. Thomas?"

"Enjoy yourself. I'll get you some punch."

"And a piece of cake, too, please. Thank you, dear."

Keane walked away.

"Abigail, I need to dance a waltz. I don't know how to dance very well. Mrs. Somerset taught me how to waltz, but I need to practice."

"Because you're waltzing with Eleanor later on?"

Daniel looked astonished and Mrs. Keane laughed. "Oh, you're just like Thomas. You think you're hiding your thoughts from the world. I wouldn't want to play cards or negotiate a loan from either one of you, but you can't keep your heart's yearnings from a woman. It's as obvious as the nose on your face that you're sweet on Eleanor. She's such a lovely young woman." She opened her dance card and glanced at the list of dances. "The next dance, number eleven, is a waltz. So is number fourteen. Would that be the one you're dancing with Eleanor?"

Daniel nodded, smiling. Normally it would have galled him that someone could read him so easily.

The last notes of a quadrille died and it was time for Daniel to dance with Abigail. They stepped on to the dance floor and he placed his hands on her as the orchestra began playing a waltz.

"You're holding a woman, Daniel, not a glass figurine. I won't break."

He held her more firmly and started to dance, trying to remember what Mrs. Somerset had taught him. He felt awkward, but she smiled and eventually the movements came more easily.

"That's it. Just concentrate on the music and the steps will follow. If you're wrong, it's better to be strong and wrong."

Soon they were twirling with the other couples. There might be something to this dancing—he was starting to enjoy himself. He accidentally brushed against other dancers, but he didn't knock anybody over. Although Abigail let him lead, she had a knack for anticipating his movements and subtly correcting his missteps. She smiled her radiant smile the entire dance. Daniel was surprised when the waltz ended; it seemed like it had just started.

"You danced splendidly, Daniel."

Keane approached them. "Excuse me, sir, I believe I have this one." Daniel made a mock half bow. Keane escorted his wife back out to the dance floor for a Spanish Dance.

Daniel watched Eleanor dance with Archer Winfield, wishing he were in Winfield's place. He had no idea why a Vanderbilt, and now a Winfield, would think that their proposals would be accepted. There was nothing flighty or ambiguous about Eleanor. She had let Daniel know how she felt in a space of minutes. Her rejected suitors must have been deluded by her beauty, their own hopes, or exaggerated estimates of their worth—she couldn't have led them on.

Daniel anxiously watched dance thirteen. The Opera Reel finally ended and he approached Eleanor and Winfield. "Excuse me, but I believe I have this dance."

He got Winfield's ice-cold stare and artificial smile. "Certainly, Mr. Durand."

He was finally alone on the dance floor with her. How could one woman be so beautiful, so self-possessed, so witty, so charming, so independent, so vivaciously alive? She glided across the floor in a way that rendered his occasional missteps irrelevant. They ascended with the strains from the orchestra, floating above the crowd and its pretensions. There was nothing but each other. With the last notes of the all too brief waltz, they descended.

"That was wonderful, Daniel," she murmured.

"Yes, it was. I haven't had much occasion to dance, so I'm not as skillful as I'd like."

"You danced very well." She smiled. "We'll just have to keep after it until we're perfect. Besides, there are much more important things about a man than his skill as a dancer." Her smile vanished as she looked past him. "Write your address on a small slip of paper and discreetly give it to me when you take your leave tonight. You'll receive a note from me."

Winfield approached them with unseemly haste, an anxious look furrowing his patrician brow. "Eleanor, my dear, I thought we could sit this one out. Perhaps get some punch and cake."

"Certainly, Archer." Her voice was flat. She turned towards Daniel and offered her hand. "Thank you very much for the dance, Mr. Durand." Her eyes sparkled.

He clasped her hand. "My pleasure, Miss Haverford."

For the rest of the party, Eleanor danced with the men who filled her dance card, but she was conscious of the man she did not dance with again. He talked with people and she was jealous—they got to visit with him and she didn't. She marveled at her proprietary attitude and her hope that he felt the same way towards her. She had wondered what if would be like to love a man. Now she was beginning to feel it, an incessant yearning and diminished interest in anything else. It was not pure joy. She mentally drafted and re-drafted the note that she would send to him. That one brief moment when they would take leave of each other became a preoccupation. Finally the last dance ended and after the usual pleasantries, Eleanor stood with her family in the entryway as the guests departed. Daniel approached her.

"I had a lovely time this evening, Eleanor."

"I'm so glad, Daniel." She extended her hand and he took it. The slip of paper transferred smoothly from his gloved hand to hers, unnoticed by anyone else. She smiled her most radiant smile. "I hope to see you again soon."

"Yes, I'd enjoy that." He turned to her father and mother, standing next to her. "Thank you for inviting me, Mr. and Mrs. Haverford. It was a marvelous reception."

"Thank you for attending." Mrs. Haverford said. Her husband shook Daniel's hand.

Early evening of the day after the party, a six-horse coach pulled up before the front door to the Haverford estate. It had been a lovely day for a picnic, the cloud cover robbing the sun of its usual summer sting. The coachman stepped down from his perch and placed a footstool before the coach door. Steven Haverford helped his mother and Eleanor step down. Mr. Haverford brushed away his son's outstretched hand and leaped straight to the ground.

"Eleanor, I'll see you in my study right now."

"Phillip, your temper," his wife said. He glared at her.

Eleanor followed her father to his study. She sat on a black leather sofa, and after he had hung his coat on a corner stand, he sat opposite her on the other.

"Last night, Archer Winfield asked me for permission to ask you for your hand in marriage. He's courted you for a year and appeared to enjoy your favor. I felt confident that you would assent to his proposal, but I know from Winfield's abrupt leave-taking this afternoon that you declined. Pray tell me why, Eleanor?"

"I thought I loved him, Father, I really did. But at last night's party, I realized that although I'm fond of Archer, I don't love him. Not in the way one should be in love to spend the rest of one's life with someone."

"Did you know Mr. Winfield would propose today?"

"I suspected it. He dropped several hints last night."

He slammed his open hand on the coffee table and Eleanor jumped. "Then why," he shouted, "didn't you tell me that you intended to decline, so that I could have discreetly got word to Mr.

Winfield and prevented this afternoon's fiasco? I look like an idiot to him—and his family. I do business with his father!"

She stood, walked over to a window by his desk, and opened it. He didn't know if she wished to clear out the smell of last night's cigars or to prevent him from shouting. If the latter were her motive, it would do no good. He didn't give a damn who heard them.

She paced back and forth as she spoke. "I'm sorry, Father, it wasn't my intention to embarrass either you or Archer. Perhaps I wasn't thinking as clearly as I should have been." She spoke slowly. "I thought, since he's courted me for a year, that I owed him an explanation. If I had done what you suggest, I would have been hiding behind you."

He rose from the couch, walked over to the table with the crystal decanters, and poured himself a brandy. He swirled the liqueur in a large snifter and sniffed it. Let her stew. He had a surprise for her. "This change of heart you had last night wouldn't have anything to do with the man Mrs. Biddle saw you with on the back balcony?"

The color drained from her face, her eyes widened, and she grasped one of the shelves, seemingly for support. There was a long silence before she responded to the accusation.

"I was with a man on the back balcony."

"With whom?" he said. A mistake—he shouldn't have let her know that he didn't know the identity of the man. She looked like a fox that had won a reprieve from the hounds.

"Father, if I tell you whom I was with, will you promise not to direct any reprisals against him?"

"Reprisals? Reprisals? Who is he that I could direct a reprisal against him?"

"Do you promise?"

"Oh for God's sake, I'll never understand you. Yes, you have my word."

"I was with Daniel Durand."

"Daniel Durand!" he screamed. "Daniel Durand! He's an employee in my bank. I'd force you to marry Winfield before I'd let you receive Mr. Durand's attentions."

"You could force me to walk down the aisle, but if you found this afternoon embarrassing, imagine how you'd feel if I was to say 'I do not' instead of 'I do' in front of hundreds of people." Her voice was cold and her eyes hard. She stepped towards him.

"What do you know about Daniel Durand? What do you know about his family?"

"I know he doesn't have a family. He fought and was wounded in the war you bought Steven's way out of. Like grandfather, he started with nothing. Mr. Keane says he manifests both ambition and skill as a banker. He's plain-spoken and intelligent."

"Well, my dear, do you love this paragon?"

"I feel differently towards him than I've felt about any other man."

With an audible clink he set his snifter on a bookshelf, turned, and pointed his finger at her. "If it's plain speaking you admire, then listen." His words came staccato, hard as bullets. "Under no circumstances are you to see or communicate with Mr. Durand. If you do, I'll no longer be bound by my promise, and Mr. Durand will be unemployed. As long as you enjoy the wealth and social advantages my position affords you, you will not see anybody of whom I do not approve. If you defy me, you will deprive yourself of my blessing, your dowry, and your inheritance."

She stared directly at him and stood ramrod straight, like her grandfather, with her hands folded before her. He wished she'd speak; there was something unnatural about the silence that filled the room. He wished she'd cry or pout or scream or faint or throw a tantrum or cajole or employ at least one of the many wiles women used to get their way. Her face remained a hard, expressionless mask and she locked him in her unblinking, penetrating gaze. Birds warbled outside and the grandfather clock in the hall ticked. Damn it, why didn't she say something? The still silence left him alone with himself—an oppressive condition.

"Do you understand?" he shouted.

"Oh yes, Father, I understand." She sat on the couch and stared straight ahead, as if he were no longer there. He did not know why he felt he had to leave his own study, why he had to get away from her. He slammed the door as he left.

She was at the bottom of a deep well with no way to pull herself out. How was she to communicate with Daniel without imperiling his position at the bank? Was she willing to give up her wealth and social standing for him? Was he willing to give up her wealth and social standing for her? Did she know him well enough to risk everything? Was there any give in her father's edict? Would her rage, so consuming that she had not trusted herself to speak, ever fade?

Questions, questions, questions…and no answers. She rubbed her temple and looked around at the books on the shelves, many of which she had read. She loved spending quiet, happy hours reading. "I'll miss these books," she whispered.

Monday morning, Haverford strode through the bank, his eyes fixed on a distant point, and walked through the door to the anteroom to his office. Within a minute, Tinsdale came for Daniel. "Mr. Haverford would like to see you immediately, Durand."

Daniel followed Tinsdale back to the anteroom, wondering what was in store for him. Did Haverford know what had happened between him and Eleanor at the party? If he did, then perhaps he was going to fire him. No, it was the same as the streets: the guys who pretended they were tough had nothing inside. Haverford wouldn't fire him face-to-face. He'd have Keane do it.

Tinsdale opened the door to Haverford's office. Haverford glared at him as he entered.

"Mr. Durand, you are never to see my daughter again. If you do, I will terminate your employment and you will never work at any other bank or reputable business in Cleveland. That is all." He took a newspaper, opened it, and began to read.

Daniel kept his face expressionless, said nothing, left the office and returned to his desk. Unable to work, he stifled his churning emotions and analyzed his situation. Eleanor must have rejected Winfield's proposal and Haverford knew of her feelings towards Daniel. Somebody had seen them on the balcony, or Eleanor had revealed herself. Why hadn't Haverford fired him, then? Perhaps he wasn't a complete fool after all. As long as Eleanor lived in his mansion and Daniel worked in his bank, Haverford could keep an eye on both of them. If he fired Daniel, he lost control of half the situation, and there was no telling what his headstrong daughter would do. Daniel remained employed by virtue of the threat he posed to Haverford, but he was on a knife's edge.

He looked around the bank—the foyer, the customers in line before the tellers' counter, the clerks and loan officers behind the counter, the doors to Keane's office, Haverford's anteroom, and the black vault. This was the first job he had ever loved, but it was time for his career to take a different course.

Chapter 8

Departures

As Daniel approached the boarding house the evening of the day after his meeting with Haverford, Mrs. Somerset hurried up to him. Hitched to the post in front of the boarding house was an unfamiliar reddish brown horse with white spots.

"Daniel, there's a young man waiting for you in the parlor. He wouldn't tell me his business, but said he had to speak with you. He looks well-to-do. His name is Jonathan Walter. Do you know him?" She stared at him with wide, inquisitive brown eyes.

"No." He had a feeling the stranger had something to do with Eleanor.

They entered the parlor, where a young man, perhaps a year or two older than Daniel, sat on the frayed couch. He was shorter than Daniel, stocky, muscular, with light brown hair, an open, solid face, serious brown eyes, and a square jaw.

"Mr. Durand?" The man extended his hand. "I'm Jonathan Walter. I was at the Haverfords' party, but I wasn't introduced to you. I believe, however, that you met my sister, Constance."

"Oh, yes, I did."

"Could we step outside?"

"Certainly, gentlemen," Mrs. Somerset said. "I'll leave you to your business."

They stepped into the sweltering, muggy summer heat. Jonathan reached into his coat pocket, removed a cream-colored envelope with Daniel's first name written on it, and handed it to Daniel. "I've been instructed to give this to you. It's from Miss Haverford."

"Thank you, Mr. Walter. You must wonder about these strange circumstances."

"Not really. I've known Eleanor since we were children. I don't think she's capable of surprising me anymore. She's an unusual woman, but I'm quite fond of her—as a friend. I'm happy to assist in any communications between you." He removed a business card from his pocket and handed it to Daniel.

Daniel read: *Mr. Jonathan Walter, Walter & Co., Wholesale Commodities Merchants, 405 Commercial St., Cleveland.*

"If you need to correspond with Eleanor, direct your correspondence to that address."

"Again, thank you."

"You're welcome. I wish you well in your endeavors." He smiled and they shook hands. He mounted his horse and rode away.

Daniel tucked the envelope into his coat pocket, reentered the boardinghouse where Mrs. Somerset was sweeping an already immaculate wood floor, walked past her without satisfying her curiosity, and went to his room. He carefully opened the envelope.

July 10, 1865
My Dearest Daniel:
Saturday night was a special evening, and I will always treasure every fleeting moment we enjoyed together. I long to see you again.

He reread the opening sentences several times, shaking his head in wonderment.

There are, unfortunately, several obstacles in our path. We were seen on the balcony, and my father was informed. I rejected Archer Winfield's proposal of marriage and Father confronted me. I had to tell him that I was with you on the balcony. He has prohibited me from seeing you again. I am terrified by the possibility that I compromised your position at the bank, and beseech your forgiveness if I have.

Father will only allow a suitor for me who is wealthy and comes from a prominent family. While I have every confidence that you will make a great name for yourself, Father cannot see past your present circumstances.

Fathers propose, but daughters dispose. I have one opportunity to see you alone. Every Thursday afternoon I ride down Prospect Street to a meadow on the eastern edge of town. My brother, Steven, usually accompanies me, but he is visiting our relatives in Cincinnati. My only chaperone will be Mr. Stevenson, an older gentleman who tends our horses. He allows me to ride on my own. If you can free yourself from the bank, I will meet you Thursday afternoon. Go east on Prospect Street until it ends at a path and a wooden fence. Bear right on the path until you come to an opening in the fence. Take the path on the right to the large oak tree. I will be there at about three o'clock. Be there earlier so Mr. Stevenson doesn't see you.

I count the hours until I am with you again. Only respond to this letter if you are unable to meet me Thursday. My parents are extremely suspicious of everything I do. We must keep our use of Constance and Jonathan as couriers to a minimum, since my visits with Constance are usually no more than once a week. Until Thursday afternoon.

With affection,
Eleanor

Daniel twice reread the letter. Time would crawl until Thursday. He went to the washroom, returned to his room, took off the black suit he had worn to work, and put on an identical suit. He was dining at the Keanes'. He put the letter in his coat pocket. He didn't know if Mrs. Somerset would "clean" his room while he was at dinner, but why take chances?

After a delicious dinner, Abigail Keane served coffee and peach pie. Mr. Keane proffered cigars. Keane sat on one brown sofa and Daniel sat on the other, a dark table between them. It was too warm for a fire, but several kerosene lamps provided light.

"Would you mind if Abby joined us?" Keane asked.

"Not at all." Daniel lit his cigar. He liked Abigail. She sat down next to her husband.

"Daniel, I hope you marry a woman who gives you the kind of good advice and counsel that I receive from Abby. She's an invaluable business asset and I always confide in her."

Daniel wondered if Eleanor knew anything about business.

"Thomas said that you had a meeting with Mr. Haverford yesterday," Abigail said.

"I'm afraid I have a problem that may complicate our plans to establish a bank. I didn't judge it prudent to tell you at the bank, Mr. Keane, but I believe I'm falling for Eleanor Haverford."

Keane chuckled. "That's no surprise at all, Daniel. Every young man in three states has fallen for Eleanor. The problem is getting her to fall for you."

"Oh, Thomas," Abigail said. "Sometimes I wonder why God gave men eyes—they never use them! When they danced at the party, didn't you see the look on Eleanor's face? She was enraptured;

every woman there could tell. And I think Daniel may have had a little *tête-à-tête* with Miss Haverford on the back balcony."

Daniel stared at her—she missed nothing. "Yes, I saw Eleanor on the balcony. From what transpired there, and from a letter I received from her today, I believe she returns my affection."

Keane stood and paced before the fireplace. "That presents a problem. Is Mr. Haverford aware of the situation?"

"Yes, when he called me into his office yesterday, he told me if I tried to call on Eleanor he would fire me. Eleanor said in her letter that he's prohibited her from receiving me."

"Then how are you going to see her?" Abigail said.

"She said that I could meet her this Thursday afternoon when she goes riding. I'd have to be away from the bank."

"Yes, you sure would." Keane threw his cigar in the fireplace. "Isn't there some way you could delay all this until after we establish our bank?"

"She usually rides with her brother. It's happenstance that he's in Cincinnati, which gives me an opportunity to see her."

"A whirlwind courtship," Abigail said. "How romantic!"

"I hadn't really thought about it in those terms. All I know is that I want to see Eleanor. Her parents are already suspicious. I have a chance to see her now. Who knows if I'd have such a chance after we've left the bank."

Keane stopped pacing. "What if you had to make a choice between our bank and Eleanor?"

He chose his words carefully. "It would be difficult and undoubtedly foolish to forego an opportunity to go into business with you, but I'm twenty-one years old. I'll have another chance to start a bank. I've never felt the way I do about Eleanor. I don't think I'll ever find another like her."

Abigail was smiling. Keane sat on the sofa and sighed. "No, you won't find another like her. Whatever happens with you and Eleanor, your days at the bank are numbered. It's essential for our credibility that you and I resign from the Bank of Commerce. Neither one of us can be fired. Mr. Haverford will spread stories—impugn our integrity—even when we resign, but it casts our departure in a better light if we resign on our own terms."

"What do you think we should do?"

Keane shook his head. "Meet with Eleanor Thursday afternoon. If Mr. Haverford inquires, I'll say you're making a call on a client. I don't like lying, Daniel, especially to him. Make sure you return to the bank Thursday afternoon."

Abigail laughed. "Are you trying to squeeze the most work that you can from poor Daniel?"

"Of course I am, dear, but it will also allay any suspicions Mr. Haverford might have if he sees Daniel returning to the bank"

"Thomas, when do you think you and Daniel can start your bank?"

"If you'll excuse me for a moment." Keane went up the stairs and returned with a stack of papers that he placed on the table before Daniel. "This is my preliminary plan, Daniel. Take these with you and study them. Draft your own comments and suggestions. I've worked on this plan for several years. Our biggest problem is capital. We'll need at least fifty thousand dollars to start, and I'd be more comfortable with seventy-five. I'm prepared to contribute fifteen to twenty-thousand, and among my business acquaintances I can raise a similar amount."

Daniel ran his fingers through his hair. "I could only invest a few thousand without borrowing money. After he offered me a job, Mr. Rockefeller said he'd invest."

"Rockefeller's a devout Baptist. Will he still be interested in investing if your situation with Eleanor leads to some sort of scandal?"

"I don't know what his reaction would be."

"Draft a letter to Rockefeller and show it to me. We won't mention your situation with Eleanor just yet."

"Mr. Gottman and his brother might be interested. I'll ask Mr. Gottman about a meeting tomorrow. I met a man in Memphis during the war—Mr. Bainbridge. He was a great poker player, a very wealthy cotton trader, and an investor. He might want to invest."

"Draft another letter for my review to Mr. Bainbridge."

Abigail sat spellbound, listening to her husband and his protégé. They talked in a language devoid of unessential words. She didn't see Thomas at the bank and had rarely seen this side of him—his mind racing, his speech quick and precise. Daniel seemed to grasp Thomas' answers before they were out of his mouth. She didn't interrupt with questions, but she mostly kept up with the conversation.

After about an hour, Keane said, "Let's call it a night. We'll discuss my plan after you read it."

Daniel stood. "Thank you for a great dinner and a lovely evening. I can't tell you how excited I am about the prospect of our own bank."

"That's obvious, Daniel," Abigail said, smiling. "It's exciting. You and Thomas will make a success of your bank, and I think your meeting with Eleanor will go well."

Keane shook Daniel's hand and opened the door for him. "It's been a pleasure, Daniel." He stood with his wife in the doorway and they watched their dinner guest walk down the street.

Keane closed the door. "I don't like this situation between Daniel and Eleanor. We might be forced to hastily establish a bank and do in a month or two what would normally take closer to a year. If there's any kind of scandal, it will hurt our bank's reputation and prospects."

"It might hurt you with the bluenoses, but they're not going to be your customers. Dynamic men starting or expanding their businesses will be your bank's clientele. They aren't going to care how Daniel Durand marries Eleanor Haverford. And he will marry her—that young man gets what he wants. I see only one problem, and it isn't Eleanor."

"What's that?"

"I don't think Cleveland is going to be big enough for Mr. Daniel Durand's ambitions."

Daniel wiped the sweat from his forehead with his handkerchief. It was the hottest, muggiest day of the summer. The shade from the large oak tree offered little relief from the intense sun. Mr. Somerset's horse, Glory, snorted and twitched his tail. Glory was on her last legs, but Daniel had limited experience with horses and required a slow, gentle ride. He removed his watch from a pocket in his vest—2:55. Rivulets of perspiration streamed down his body. He looked expectantly up the path leading from the oak tree.

Was that a small cloud of dust? Yes, it was! He saw a horse, and there she was, riding sidesaddle, wearing a dark green habit, golden hair bouncing. She smiled when she saw him under the tree and pulled up before him. He took her hand and helped her down from her horse.

"I'm glad to see an infantryman can ride a horse," she said.

"We might not have won the war if they had put me in the cavalry."

She laughed. Still holding hands, they gazed at each other. She motioned towards a narrow path between two trees. They led their horses up the path. After several wordless minutes, Daniel heard the gurgling of a stream. They came to a pool, the waters of the stream falling over a natural dam of stones and a log, perhaps felled by a beaver. They looped the horses' tethers over a branch and the animals drank from the stream. Sycamores and elms formed a shady bower around the pool. Two boulders set back from the water, opposite each other, were a natural pair of chairs. Birds chirped and water bugs scooted between water lilies floating on the pool's surface. Daniel removed his coat, placed it on top of one rock, and motioned for Eleanor to sit on it. He sat on the other. He was surprised at how natural their silent walk had been; he had felt no compulsion to speak.

"How did you get away from the bank?"

Daniel laughed. "You're Ambrose Chandler. That's who Mr. Keane will say I'm with."

"I hope I'm not jeopardizing your position."

"Some risks have to be run. If this is what I have to do to see you, this is what I'll do. But since your father knows what happened at the party, my position is precarious."

"Before I told Father, I made him promise not to take any action against you."

"That explains why I wasn't fired."

"He's not bound if we see each other."

"Then we have to be careful."

"You could get a job at another bank if Father found out and let you go."

Daniel picked up a flat, smooth stone and threw it towards the pool. It skipped twice and landed on the other side. "It's easier to get a job if you already have one. It would be better if the decision for me to leave the bank was made by me, rather than your father."

She stood, walked to the edge of the pool, and turned towards him. "It's so hot today. I like to ride on days like this, to feel the breeze on my face, or go sailing—it's always cooler on the lake. What do you do when it gets hot, Daniel?"

"Mostly I sweat." He smiled as he removed his handkerchief and wiped his forehead. The commoner and the princess lived happily ever after in the stories, but the stories hazed over some essential details. How did the commoner make the princess understand that jobs weren't to be had for the asking, or that he worked too hard to have time to ride and sail? He would make the princess understand, but gently. "The only boats I've ever been on were troop transports on the Mississippi River, not really pleasure trips. I did like going to the bow—feeling the breeze, watching the scenery go by. I loaded coal onto the barges at the docks, but I stayed onshore when they pulled away."

"When did you do that?"

"When I was a boy, at twenty cents a day. I'd pick up the pieces of coal in the bins that the laborers had missed with their shovels." He didn't want to tell her the full story of his early life, but she had to understand that her world was not his.

"Is that what you did before you joined the army?"

"I had a lot of different jobs, all of which made a position as a clerk in a bank seem eminently desirable."

"I can only imagine. But you weren't content to be just a clerk. Now you're a loan officer. Both my father and Mr. Keane have remarked about the hours you keep at the bank. What are your ambitions, Daniel? Why do you work so hard, even after you go home at night?"

He stood, stepped towards her, and took her hand. "When I was working those jobs, I thought that regular meals, a roof over my head, and a few dollars in my pocket would keep me happy. Then I wanted to show people—those who looked down on me as well as my so-called friends who didn't want me to go anywhere—I wanted to show 'em they were wrong. After I started at the bank that became unimportant, because I enjoyed the work. That's why I put in the hours I do now—I enjoy it—I love it."

"You work so hard and take your job so seriously, but your position is tenuous. Meanwhile Father wants my brother Steven to take a position at the bank, and he scorns the opportunity."

"Steven doesn't want to be a banker?"

"He says he isn't ready yet to start his life's work. The truth is, he likes to play. When Father isn't around, he says that he's not sure he wants to be a banker, that it isn't important to him. His favorite expression is 'It's only money.'"

"Only an idiot who's never earned it would say that about money! I wish every fool who says that could spend a few rainy nights in a leaky stable with the horses. You'd see how long he scorned money. Money is survival, it's life!" Eleanor's eyes widened. "I just implied that your brother is an idiot and a fool."

"He's both. Did you spend rainy nights that way, Daniel?"

"Yes."

"Let's walk up the path."

They strolled hand in hand. She talked of her friends and they discussed books they had read. They came to a ten-foot waterfall. The sun created a miniature rainbow in the mist, and the cold, fresh smell of the water spray filled the air.

"Daniel, over there." She pointed towards green, leafy shrubbery, flecked with blue. "Are those blueberries? I love blueberries."

He went to the patch, picked one of the blueberries, bit into it, and picked as many as he could carry in his two hands. He dipped them in the stream to wash them. His hands were still dripping as he held them up to her.

She took one, wet and cold, and ate it. Perfectly ripe, it exploded in her mouth. She took another, and held it up to Daniel's mouth. "A man should enjoy the fruits of his labor." She smiled and laughed as a trickle of juice escaped from the corner of his mouth. She ate a blueberry and fed him one as they both laughed. Occasionally she looked directly into his dark eyes and was met with a steady, confident gaze that amounted to an unspoken claim of possession. There was passion in those eyes…and risk and danger. She took the last blueberry from his hands and he wiped away the juice on his chin with his handkerchief.

He moved very close to her. She was conscious of his driving desire, apiece with his driving intensity and ambition. He took her in his arms and brushed his lips against hers, tasting of blueberries. More vigorously, she pressed her lips against his. She could feel the heat pulsing from his body and the passion rising in hers. She had never felt this way with a man before.

He was surprised and pleased by her ardor. His body ached; every nerve, sinew, and instinct wanted to respond. He allowed himself a few kisses, but pressed her shoulder with his hand. She stopped kissing him, but she was breathing heavily and she remained in his arms. She gazed at him, her eyes shining. Her mouth was open in a way that suggested a scarcely whetted appetite. She slowly nodded, understanding. They stared at each other and Daniel could feel his passion rising again. Somehow he had to break the spell.

"What do you do besides read?" he said as he relaxed his embrace and took her hand.

"Um, I play the piano. I love Chopin," she said, her voice strained.

"I'll bet you're good."

"Yes…yes, I am. I also like art. I draw and paint, but not as well as I play the piano."

"Have you had music and art lessons?"

"Yes, I've been to Europe and I want to go again, to see the art and attend concerts."

"I'd like to visit Europe, too."

She smiled in a way that seemed almost shy. "Do you know what else I like?"

He shook his head.

"I like tools and machines. Sometimes when Mr. Quimby comes to tune the piano, I watch him work. He answers my questions. I wonder about engines on trains and steamships. How do they work? My father's library doesn't have any books on engines."

Suddenly her grip on his hand tightened. "What was that?" she asked, frightened. Something or somebody was snapping twigs, trampling underbrush, coming towards them. "That might be Mr. Stevenson. How long have we been here?" The noise grew louder. An animal emerged from the bushes on the other side of the stream and they both laughed. "That's a beaver, isn't it?" Daniel nodded. "I didn't realize they were so big. It must be thirty or forty pounds."

"Its head looks like that of a gigantic rat."

The creature took no notice of them as it walked along the bank, its flat tail dragging behind. It ambled to the still water behind the waterfall and slipped in. A fish jumped in front of a rock downstream. Before its ripples died down, two more rolled over.

"The fish are rising. The afternoon is getting on," Daniel said.

"Mr. Stevenson will be wondering where I am. We have to go."

"Yes, I have to get back to the bank. Mr. Keane said I should return to alleviate any suspicions your father might have, and he usually leaves at around six."

They walked back up the path at a brisker pace than they had come down it, stopped for one last look at the pool, and returned to their horses. He took her in his arms and they kissed.

She gazed at him. His eyes were too darkly probing, his face too narrow and angular to be considered fine art, but those features made his appearance more interesting, and challenging, than an artist's perfection. His face went with the rough edges of his personality. "Can I see you here again next Thursday?"

"I'll find a way." After one long, last kiss he helped her on to her horse, Zeus, and mounted his own. "Until next Thursday, dearest Eleanor."

"Until next Thursday, dearest Daniel."

He watched as Zeus slowly trotted up the trail until all he could see was a thin cloud of dust. Time would crawl until he saw her again.

He returned to the bank just as Mr. Haverford was leaving.

"Where were you, Mr. Durand?"

"At an appointment with Mr. Chandler."

"Ambrose attends the same church that I do. I'll see him this Sunday."

Daniel felt a sinking sensation in his stomach.

Mr. Keane and Daniel sat in Abram and Isaac Gottman's office above the brothers' dry goods store. It smelled of sweat and spiced meat from the day's lunch. Both brothers sat behind battered old desks. Like his brother, Isaac had a long beard, gray with streaks of black, and wore a black kaftan and yarmulke. He had a large wart over his right eye and his mouth seemed frozen in a permanent frown.

"Thank you, gentleman," Keane said, "for taking the time to read our business proposal." He gestured towards a stack of papers on Isaac's desk.

"Ach, who said I read such a thing!" Isaac said. "When Abram and I started—from a pushcart—we could have put our 'business proposal' on a postage stamp. Money lending is a simple business—you pay your depositors two percent, lend out at three, don't lend to *gonifs*, and your money grows. There must be ten banks on Main Street. Why will anyone come to yours?"

"We're not going to wait for people to come to our bank, Mr. Gottman. The founder of the Bank of Commerce, Alexander Haverford, used to say that the time to lend is when a borrower needs you more than you need him. He made a fortune with that philosophy, but his son, the current president of the bank, pursues established businessmen and politicians who already have access to credit on favorable terms and who are, consequently, less profitable. Mr. Durand and I intend to aggressively pursue business among new firms as Cleveland capitalizes on its position as a center of trade, transportation, and manufacturing."

"That sounds riskier than your usual bank," Abram said.

"A bank that extends credit to a venture before other banks are willing to can bargain for a share of the ownership. Such a position gives the bank interest on its loan and a percentage of the profits as well. While the overall ratio of bad loans may be higher than the traditional experience, it should be more than compensated for by the greater returns from those equity interests."

"What part does Daniel play in all this?" Isaac said. "Abram says he's a *mensch*, but the last time I saw him he was *yungatsh*, living on the streets. Now he wears a suit and fancies himself a banker. Why am I supposed to trust my *geld* to him?"

"Mr. Gottman," Daniel said. "When I lived on the streets, I never took a penny from anybody. Your brother fed me and I spent some nights in his apartment, but I wouldn't let him give me money. If I wouldn't take it when I was cold, wet, and hungry, I won't take it now that my circumstances are better. You may lose your investment because Mr. Keane and I have bitten off more than we can chew, but nobody in our bank will steal your money."

"Aha!" Isaac said. "Would you lend money to an Israelite?"

"Yes, provided his loan was well secured, his reputation was good, and the prospective use of the loan was sound. Those standards would govern all our loans."

"Would you give an Israelite a job in your bank?"

"If he was the best man for the position. If you and your brother invest in our bank, we'll offer you a seat on the board of directors."

Both brothers stroked their long beards, a sight Daniel found almost comical. The sun was going down and a musty gloaming enveloped the shelves behind the two men's desks. Two kerosene lamps hung from opposite corners, but it would probably have to be completely dark before the penny-pinching brothers would light them.

"You want an investment of five to ten thousand dollars," Abram said, "which gives us a percentage of ownership and a share of the profits that matches that percentage?"

"That's correct," Keane said.

"And a seat on your board of directors," Isaac said. Keane nodded. "Perhaps we could also have an option to double our investment on the original terms."

"Now he wants an option!" Abram said. "Such chutzpah."

"You're a *luftmensch*, your head is in the clouds! If their bank is successful, what's to stop them from bringing in new investors and reducing our share?"

Keane frowned. "If we're successful, it would be unfair to our other investors to allow you to invest on the original terms. However, we'll give you a right of first refusal to maintain your percentage of ownership if we solicit additional investment in the future."

Isaac stood. "Perhaps that is an arrangement we can accept, if we decide to invest. On that, we'll let you know." The men shook hands and Abram opened the door.

Daniel and Keane left the store. Daylight was fading. There were no carriages on the narrow street. A few men in black hats and kaftans hurried about.

"Mr. Isaac Gottman is a tough customer," Daniel said.

"He had to be tough to start from a pushcart and build this store."

"I was surprised you gave them the right of first refusal on future investments."

"We're going to be the only bank doing business with the Jews. If the Gottman brothers invest, they'll bring in business and help us separate the *mensches* from the *gonifs*. My concession costs us nothing. We'll give the same right to all of our initial stockholders."

Wednesday night, two days after the meeting with the Gottmans and one day before Daniel's next assignation with Eleanor, the two bankers sat on uncomfortable wooden chairs in Rockefeller's office, which was brightly lit by several lamps burning his own kerosene. Rockefeller sat behind his desk, with a copy of the business plan on top of it.

"How's business, Mr. Rockefeller?" Daniel said.

"Booming! We can't keep up with demand and now we're exporting to Europe. We'll have our second refinery up and running by the end of the year. We're already shipping more kerosene than any other refiner in Cleveland. I need money to expand, gentlemen. I'm very interested in your business plan." He picked up the plan and dropped it on his desk.

"I hope it was sufficiently detailed, sir," Keane said. "However, I'm sure you have questions."

For the next two hours, Mr. Rockefeller questioned them about every conceivable aspect of their business histories and their proposed bank. Each answer elicited more questions—the oilman's curiosity was insatiable. He knew more about banking than most bankers.

"Let me make one thing clear." Rockefeller brought his hands together as if he were praying and moved them back and forth towards Keane and Daniel several times. "I want more than just an ample return on my investment. I would assume that my money also earns favorable consideration on any requests I might make for credit from your bank."

"Of course," Mr. Keane said.

"Will the original shareholders have preemptive rights, to maintain their percentages?"

"Yes, and it's our fervent hope that you'll be able to exercise those rights."

"Will I have a seat on the board of directors?"

"We'd be honored."

"Is there anything else you need to tell me about your plans?"

"A certain attraction has developed between Daniel and Mr. Haverford's daughter. If that were to run its course, it could result in a situation that's somewhat out of the ordinary."

"Mr. Durand, do you intend to marry this woman against her father's wishes?"

"Things haven't reached that point yet, but they could sometime in the future."

Rockefeller chuckled. "Haverford is a fool. What you do with his daughter is your business."

Daniel was relieved. Mr. Rockefeller's religious scruples either didn't encompass a parent's right to choose his child's mate, or if they did, wouldn't overrule a profitable investment.

"We are soliciting an investment from Abram and Isaac Gottman. If they invest, they will have a seat on the board," Keane said.

"The Gottmans of Gottman Brothers' Dry Goods, on St. Clair Street?"

"Yes."

"Cettie buys her thread and fabric there. It's a fine store. Smart move—the Jews, plenty of money. That will be acceptable, gentlemen. I shall invest ten thousand dollars in your bank." He stood and walked from behind his desk to shake Daniel's and Mr. Keane's hands. "The best of luck to you." He went to a shelf, pulled out a ledger, returned to his desk, and opened the ledger.

Daniel and Keane left Rockefeller's office and walked down a flight of stairs to the stables and Keane's carriage. "I didn't realize he was so young," Keane said. "He's only a few years older than you, but he carries himself like a much older gentleman—very serious, always thinking several steps ahead. It was stupid of Mr. Haverford not to do business with him, but it's created an opportunity for us."

Daniel pulled his watch from his vest pocket, checked the time, and stared down the dirt path. She was late! Eleanor was over twenty minutes late. Anxiety was giving way to despair. Eleanor would come if she could. If she didn't, it meant something or somebody had prevented her. If he rode up the path and she had only been delayed, he risked being seen by Mr. Stevenson. He tore the bark on the oak tree, picked up a rock and threw it at nothing in particular. Hope didn't die until he had waited over an hour, leaving an acrid taste in his mouth and his stomach churning. He pulled a small box from his pocket and opened it. Although it had been purchased in haste and he had spent too much—over a hundred dollars—he had found an elegant ring, with one crown-cut diamond set in a gold band. There would be no proposal today. He closed the box and put it back in his pocket.

He jumped on Glory and pressed the plodding nag as fast as she could go. The devil take it, he wasn't giving up without a fight! What had happened to Eleanor? That friend of Eleanor's—Constance Walter—her brother, Jonathan—he'd talk to him. He pulled his wallet from his coat pocket and found Walter's card and address: 405 Commercial St., Cleveland. If anyone could tell him what happened to Eleanor, he could. Why was this horse so damn slow?

He finally reached the address on Commercial Street, a modest, two-storied affair jammed between two larger buildings. He tied Glory's tether to a post and opened the door to Walter's office. Four younger men, including Walter, sat at tall desks in a row, making entries in ledgers. An older gentleman sat behind a more elaborate desk in the corner. The room smelled of the sweat of men who worked long hours in close, poorly ventilated quarters.

"Mr. Durand," Walter said, "I was going to come by your boarding-house this evening." He turned to an older gentleman with stringy white hair and a white mustache and sideburns. "May I present Mr. Durand, of the Bank of Commerce? Mr. Durand, my father, Albert Walter." The man nodded. "Father, could we use the office for a few minutes?" He nodded again. Walter stepped up a short staircase and Daniel followed. They entered a small office. Walter took a seat behind a desk strewn with papers and motioned towards the only chair. Daniel sat down.

"She's gone," Walter said, staring directly at Daniel.

"What do you mean, she's gone?"

"Eleanor, her mother, and two brothers and several servants boarded a train to New York this morning. Mr. Haverford booked passage to London for them, and they'll be touring Europe for an extended time. Constance saw Eleanor yesterday and she didn't know about this trip. Her parents must have surprised her with it this morning. Constance found out from the doorman at the Haverfords' and I saw her at lunch. I was going to tell you after work."

"If I could get the next train, maybe I could catch them in New York."

"They're on the express, and the next train isn't until tomorrow morning. Even if you made it before they boarded for London, I have no idea where they'll be staying in New York and no way to find out. New York is much bigger than Cleveland...."

Walter continued to talk, but Daniel couldn't listen. It was Vicksburg again—holding Will in his arms as his friend breathed his last. Will and Eleanor, torn from his grasp. He blinked to restrain his tears.

"Mr. Durand, perhaps it would be best if I let you gather your thoughts."

Daniel nodded glumly and Walter left the office, closing the door behind him. Daniel removed his handkerchief from his pocket and wiped his eyes. Eleanor didn't like Winfields and Vanderbilts here in America. She'd despise Europe's dukes and counts and earls and lords and other worthless worthies. He smiled grimly. He no longer had a job at the Bank of Commerce, but watch out, Haverford, the genteel world of Cleveland banking was about to get a new competitor. And even if that bastard locked her away in a convent or something when she got back, Daniel Durand would marry his daughter. He'd get her back. Assuredly, he'd get her back.

The boy could hear the whispering of the two men standing outside the bedroom door. A floorboard groaned as one of them came in. The door creaked on its hinges. He could feel his bedmate trembling next to him. Clomp…clomp—the older one was moving across the room. His long, bony fingers ripped the blanket away from the boy's clinging grasp. He barely opened one eye just enough to see the tall figure in the dark robe, his face hidden in the cowl.

"Only the innocent sleep," he hissed through his few remaining teeth.

Daniel awoke from his recurring nightmare bathed in a cold sweat. He was in the Somersets' boarding house. Down the hall, Mr. Poindexter snored. The usually annoying drone was oddly reassuring. Eleanor was gone. He would sleep no more that night.

Haverford strode into the bank the following morning feeling jovial. Eleanor was off to Europe and today he would have the pleasure of firing Durand. Where was Durand? He wasn't at his desk. Keane's door was closed—Durand was probably in a meeting with him. Those two were thick as thieves. Keane would be upset when he fired Durand, but once the situation was made known to him, Keane would understand. Yes, Durand showed promise as a banker, but he was still a presumptuous peasant. That was one of the joys of much more civilized Europe—peasants were kept in their place. Haverford generally delegated employee dismissals to Keane. Today's would be different. He was going to personally give this upstart his comeuppance.

Haverford opened the door to his office anteroom. "Tinsdale, summon Durand to my office."

"Sir, Mr. Durand isn't here today. Neither is Mr. Keane."

"What do you mean, they're not here? Where are they?"

"I don't know. I thought you would know."

"Well, I don't. When Mr. Durand arrives, show him to my office."

"Yes, sir."

He entered his office and noticed a white envelope on his desk. It had his name written in script he recognized as Keane's. He tore it open and read:

July 27, 1865

Mr. Haverford,

Effectively immediately, we hereby resign our positions at the Bank of Commerce.

Thomas W. Keane
Daniel Durand

He stared at the note as a savage would gaze at a talisman believed to hold evil magic. He had been too clever by half. He had thought Keane's loyalty to the Bank of Commerce was a fixed, permanent asset, like the vault, and that Keane would never countenance Durand's impertinent advances towards Eleanor. He had misjudged him. That quiet, temperate demeanor disguised a disloyal schemer, a traitor. Durand was expendable and good riddance, but how the hell was he going to manage his bank without Keane?

Chapter 9

Separation

Eleanor sipped tea by herself in the garden of Pennington Manor. The late summer sun was warm, but not oppressive. A gentle breeze meandered through the meticulously maintained hedges and rows of flowers, giving the air a floral bouquet. Lord Pennington's West Sussex estate was far enough to the south of London to escape its perpetual pall of fog and soot. Pennington, scion of a London banking family, former member of Parliament, and long-time friend of both Alexander and Phillip Haverford, had hosted the Haverfords for a week.

Her mother swept down a path, long skirts fluttering in the breeze. She sat in a chair next to the table, holding two letters. "Our mail has finally caught up with us. This one's from Father." Eleanor said nothing. "Let's see what he has to say." She opened the envelope. Not once had she mentioned her daughter's virtual abduction, maintaining the fiction that they were on a happy grand tour. She unfolded the one-page missive. "Your father never was one for long letters." She smiled weakly. "He hopes we're enjoying our trip. Oh, no…oh, no. Bad news."

"What's wrong, Mother?"

"Mr. Keane and Mr. Durand left the bank. I knew Mr. Durand would leave, but not Mr. Keane."

"How did you know that Mr. Durand would leave?"

Her mother's gaze shifted among the flowers, hedges, trellises, and fountains in the garden, everywhere and anywhere except towards her daughter. There was a long, awkward silence. "I wonder what Phillip will do. Steven may have to return home. He'll let us know."

Her beloved was free—her father's threat had been to no avail. He had left the bank with Mr. Keane. Perhaps they were going into business together. That thought eased her pain. She smiled.

"Does your father's misfortune please you, Eleanor? That's hateful."

"As ye sow, so shall ye reap." She stood and walked away.

Daniel recognized the old gentleman with the ivory-handled cane entering the Industrial Bank of Cleveland, but it took a minute to place him. He wore an expensive Ulster overcoat— long, thick protection against Cleveland's severe winter cold— and a fur hat with earflaps. Once he took off his hat, revealing wispy strands of white hair that matched his white mustache and sideburns, Daniel knew who he was—Jonathan Walter's father, Albert. They had met the fateful day at Walter's office when Daniel had learned that Eleanor had been spirited off to Europe. Mr. Walter approached a teller, who pointed towards Daniel's small office.

"Good day, Mr. Walter," Daniel said, rising and shaking his hand. He motioned to one of the two chairs before his desk. "What can I do for you?"

Walter rested his cane against a chair, removed his black leather gloves, put them in the pocket of his Ulster, took off the overcoat and folded it over, put it on one chair, and sat on the other. "I've been banking with Phil Haverford for over twenty years. We're family friends of the Haverfords, but you'd never know it from my last meeting with Mr. Baldwin, Keane's replacement. I know everybody's trying to borrow money and the interest rate is higher, but this fellow Baldwin is raising it from four to five percent. He wants to change the term from six months to four, and he'll only allow us to finance against sixty percent of our accounts receivable, when it's always been eighty. No negotiation—take it or leave it. I guess they need to pay for that new palace Haverford's building." He glanced out the window of Daniel's office. "I like your bank, Durand—nice and simple, keeps your costs down. You and Keane are making a go of it. Maybe you want my business more than those Main Street humbugs."

"We'll finance against eighty percent of your accounts, for up to six months. The rate would be four and three quarters, subject to annual renegotiation."

"I was hoping for four and a half, and we'd look at it every two years."

Daniel made a few quick calculations on a pad. "How about four and five-eighths? We'll stay at a one-year renegotiation."

"Go eighteen months and you've got yourself a deal, young man."

"Done."

"Do you need approval from Mr. Keane or a loan committee?"

"No. We'll have the papers at your offices by tomorrow afternoon."

"I've met bankers who take all day to sign their own names. You're sure you can get these papers to me tomorrow?"

"Yes, sir."

The two men stood and shook hands. Daniel escorted Walter to the door and opened it. A snow flurry blasted them. "I'm glad your offices are only a few blocks away, sir."

Walter buttoned his Ulster and slipped on his gloves and hat. "I've lived through a few score Cleveland winters," he snorted. "This is a trifle—it's hardly snowing. Good day, Mr. Durand."

Daniel turned and watched three people in line at the tellers' counter, either putting their money in or taking it out of the Industrial Bank of Cleveland. His bank—Mr. Keane's bank—their bank. They couldn't have picked a more auspicious time. The city's economy was booming, the pace of business growing increasingly frenetic. Everyone wanted money to fund expansion or a new venture; to buy a competitor; to produce gadgets and inventions; to speculate in land, timber, and commodities; to bankroll their own dream or to buy into somebody else's. Daniel and Keane could say no with the best of them, but they also said yes more often than the others. Soon they would have to hire another clerk and teller, and a move out of their cramped quarters seemed inevitable. Keane was already talking about raising additional capital.

Lord and Lady Pennington and their son and his wife, Mr. Roger and Mrs. Anne Barksdale, were seated in a drawing room on ornate sofas arranged around a large fireplace. Lord Pennington and Barksdale stood as Mrs. Haverford and Eleanor entered. Everyone exchanged salutations and a servant brought tea. Steven came in a few minutes later. Mrs. Haverford thought he didn't look quite up to snuff. He and Barksdale liked to stay up late, drinking Pennington's fine old port. Perhaps he had overindulged the previous evening, although Barksdale looked none the worse for the experience. Seated by his parents, Barksdale seemed like an anomaly, a commoner.

They had slender frames, fine-boned patrician faces, upright postures, and distinguished countenances made more distinguished by their wispy gray hair. The junior Barksdale had a wide, flat face, a beefy build, and flaming red hair flying off in all directions.

A butler entered the room. "The Viscount Newberry."

The viscount breezed in like a gust of fresh air, with the easy assurance of one born into the most fortunate of circumstances. His dark brown hair was swept casually across his high forehead. His blue eyes scanned the room. The corners of his mouth turned up, a hint of an easy smile. His dark suit and high-collared white shirt were obviously from one of London's better tailors. He greeted Lord and Lady Pennington.

Lord Pennington motioned towards Mrs. Haverford and her son and daughter. "Lord Newberry, may I present our guests from the United States—Mrs. Haverford; her son, Mr. Haverford; and her daughter, Miss Haverford."

"It's a pleasure to meet you," Newberry said as he clasped Mrs. Haverford's hand.

"Lord Newberry," Mrs. Haverford said. The viscount looked directly into her eyes—presumptuous from someone else, flattering from one of his social rank. He shook hands with Steven and Eleanor and sat down in a high-backed chair. A servant brought him tea.

"I've long wanted to visit America," Newberry said. "Since I read Tocqueville. Has anyone else had the pleasure of reading *Democracy in America*?"

"I have," Eleanor said.

Newberry turned towards her and smiled, a brilliant, charming smile. "What was your estimation of those volumes?"

"I thought he demonstrated astonishing insight for a foreigner, and he writes beautifully."

"Yes, he conveys the feeling that there's an unprecedented, exciting experiment taking place in the colonies. He argues that democracy is a source of strength, and that your country has unlimited potential."

Lord Pennington snorted. "Potential, perhaps, but right now it's little more than a vast wilderness, badly weakened by the war. It reminds me of Russia—a wealth of land and resources, with visions of grandeur far outstripping its capabilities."

"It's interesting that you should mention Russia," Newberry said. "Tocqueville argues that the United States and Russia will one day grow into the world's dominant powers."

"That's absurd!" Barksdale said. "Not while the most powerful navy in the world rules the seas for an empire on which the sun never sets."

"England is the most powerful nation on the earth," Eleanor said, setting her cup and saucer on a table. "But history demonstrates that it's easier to acquire an empire than to maintain one."

"Well put!" Newberry said, laughing.

Mrs. Haverford was shocked by her daughter's boldness—women didn't discuss such things, and Lady Pennington and Mrs. Barksdale looked askance—but she was also pleased. Phillip had never acknowledged that his daughter was intelligent, but Mrs. Haverford had realized it when Eleanor was a small child. She could see that an instant rapport had developed between her daughter and Lord Newberry—Eleanor had found a mind on the same plane. Eleanor and the viscount argued as partisans for the United States against the view pressed by Lord Pennington and Barksdale that England would always rule the world. Mrs. Haverford noted the quiet forcefulness of her daughter's arguments, her ability to maintain a calm, reasonable demeanor, and her enjoyment of the conversation. It did her heart good to see Eleanor's spirit and animation revive.

Just when the discussion appeared to have reached the point that its participants were starting to repeat themselves, Newberry said,

"Mr. Haverford, do you and Miss Haverford ride? Perhaps we could show you the English countryside, if you're to remain here this week."

"Of course we ride," Steven answered. "We plan to be here several more days, and I think I can safely speak for Eleanor and say that we'd love to see the countryside."

"Splendid! Let's say the day after tomorrow. We'll have lunch alfresco. I'll come around mid-morning. Will that be acceptable to you, Barksdale?"

Barksdale nodded.

The affair drew to its end with the usual exchange of pleasantries. Mrs. Haverford was in her best mood since arriving in England. Even the dark clouds around Eleanor seemed to clear.

Daniel knew that the man sitting across the rectangular table in the conference room of the new quarters of the Industrial Bank would never receive a loan. Mr. Bisby's handshake had been too strong, too long, and too vigorous; his nervous, darting blue eyes belied his hearty good cheer; his pliable face seemed eager to assume whatever shape he thought people wanted it to; and his whole manner conveyed an easy but unwarranted familiarity. His approach was better suited to a tavern than a bank. He was a big man in his fifties, with heavy jowls, thinning blond hair, and a thick, reddish beard. His suit was of a conservative cut, but there were shiny spots at the elbows on the jacket, and the cuffs of his pants were frayed.

"Mr. Bisby," Keane said. "Your foundry has lost money four of the last five years."

"Yes, sir, it has." Bisby smiled. "We've had to keep repairing our furnace, so we haven't been able to deliver our orders on time. I had a man, Darby, who kept that furnace going, but he went to work for Wiggins. Never did figure out why he wanted to work for that old sourpuss."

"Wiggins' foundry makes money."

"Right you are, Mr. Keane. Right you are. Well, my foundry will make money, too, when I get a loan to replace the furnace."

"Your own figures indicate that your revenues have decreased almost fifty percent, during a period when business conditions have been favorable," Daniel said. "Even with a new furnace, it will be difficult for you to win back the customers you've lost."

Bisby turned towards Keane. "That's a bright young fellow you got there, but let me tell you something: I've got a way with my customers. As long as I can fill their orders, they'll come back. They like doing business with me, even if I'm not always the cheapest."

Daniel thought of Mr. Rockefeller. It was easier to imagine him running naked through a public square than asserting that his customers did business with him because they liked him.

"We don't share your confidence," Keane said.

Bisby's eyes darted from Keane to Daniel and back. He tapped the table with his fat finger. "I need a loan or…or I'm going to have to close my foundry. You can't let the town's oldest foundry go under, gentlemen, you just can't. I need the money."

"Mr. Bisby, we're not going to offer you a loan. Your prospects are tenuous and repayment will be far riskier than we deem prudent. Thank you for your time."

Daniel liked the way Keane turned down loan applicants. He looked them right in the eye, gave them his decision, and stated his reasons in a voice of controlled rationality.

"I heard you were different," Bisby said. His voice rose. "I need that money and I'm running out of options. I need that money!"

"We are different," Keane said. "But this is a bank, not an eleemosynary institution. The Sisters of Charity are down the street. Again, thank you for your time."

With an immense effort and a sigh, Bisby gathered himself up and walked out of the conference room, casting a resentful glance at Keane as he closed the door.

"I detest that word *need*," Keane said. "Need has no place in the discussion of a loan. Charity with one's own money has its place, though one's first duty is to oneself. We won't give a cent of our shareholders and depositors' money to those whose only claim is their *need*. If I want to waste money, I'll buy a bottle of whiskey for a drunk or contribute to a politician."

Daniel watched Keane as he made a notation on Bisby's loan documents. The jet black hair, parted in the middle, tinges of gray at the temples, the narrow, angularly chiseled face, the placid blue-gray eyes, and the impassive competence all suggested a not quite human calculating machine, or, more correctly, a machine that was a final masterpiece, a triumph of human ingenuity. Daniel loved that face. He loved the mind behind that face.

"I've heard that some European aristocrats with more titles than money try to snare rich Americans to replenish their coffers," Steven Haverford said. He, his mother, his younger brother, Michael, and Eleanor were having croissants and coffee in the great hall of an old chateau, now a country inn, about fifty miles north of Paris. "Before Eleanor goes too much farther with this Newberry, we should make inquiries about his family's financial condition."

"You're assuming that there's more between Lord Newberry and me than a pleasant friendship," Eleanor said. "I have no intention or desire to make it any more than that. Besides, if you keep gambling with Barksdale, we won't have the means to replenish anybody's coffers."

"I don't think I pose a threat to the Haverford exchequer, but you're quite right about Lord Newberry, sister. I'm sure he followed us from England and has dogged us every step of our way here in Europe to pursue a 'pleasant friendship.' That's what young, unmarried fellows who shadow beautiful, unmarried women are interested in—pleasant friendships."

"I can't speak for him. Nor can I stop him from going wherever he wants or doing whatever he pleases. But if he has more serious intentions towards me, he'll be disappointed."

Steven put his hand over his heart. "Because your heart is given to Daniel Durand."

"What presumption leads you to mention that name! Silence becomes you, and I think you should maintain it on that particular subject."

"That's enough," Mrs. Haverford said. She tore a piece from her croissant, ate it, and turned towards Eleanor. "Though you know, dear, the viscount is quite a fellow. There's his family and his father, the earl, and like his father, the viscount will be a member of Parliament one day. Oxford-educated, very well-spoken, not at all unpleasant to look at, and that dashing, charming manner…"

"We're not playing that game again. It's never going to be more than a pleasant friendship."

When Eleanor entered the Paris hotel suite, Laura Haverford knew that her hopes for her daughter were not to be realized. Eleanor and Lord Newberry had gone on a stroll by themselves through the gardens of the Tuileries. Two young people happily in love would have spent the entire afternoon together. Eleanor had only been gone about an hour and her face was devoid of expression. Laura had christened the blank look her daughter now wore "the wall"—trying to divine what Eleanor was thinking or feeling at such a time was like banging one's head against a wall. She had been banging her head for years. Now, between her husband's heavy-handed instructions for Eleanor, her son Steven's worrisome patronage of Europe's drinking and gaming establishments, and her ongoing conflict with Eleanor, she was bone weary. She didn't have the strength for another battle with her daughter.

"Would you like some tea, dear?" Laura said.

Eleanor nodded and sat next to her mother on a squat, bench-style, mustard-colored love seat with a low back and curlicue arm-rests, designed for decoration rather than something so mundane as sitting. It was apiece with the rest of the room, crammed bottom to top with several rugs of varying hues and patterns, a sofa of the same design as the love seat, three uncomfortable chairs with foot-stools, a coffee table with tea service, a writing table, two end tables, a massive fireplace, paintings and mirrors in gilded frames, heavy damask drapes around the windows and French doors, a huge chandelier, and, wherever an empty square inch or two threatened the decorative scheme, wall sconces with lamps, or vases stuffed with oversize bouquets.

Laura poured her daughter's tea. "I know you're not going to tell me what I want to hear, but today I'm not going to argue with you, I'm just going to listen."

Eleanor looked surprised. Laura couldn't recall any other time when she had surprised her daughter.

"Mother, I intended to tell Newberry that I thought he had serious intentions towards me, but that I couldn't reciprocate his affections."

Laura nodded and took Eleanor's hand. "I started to tell him, but he was preoccupied with what he wished to say—a declaration that he did indeed have such intentions. I was gentle and he took it well, but I told him that I couldn't encourage his courtship. He has decided to return to England."

Tears trickled down Laura's cheek.

"I'm sorry, Mother. He's a fine man, and I'm sure you feel that with his personality, his wealth, and his position in the English aristocracy, he would have been an ideal husband."

"Dear, dear Eleanor, you have to believe me when I say that's not why I'm upset."

"Then why, Mother?"

Laura let out a long sigh. "Oh, I feel…I feel...." Her voice trembled. "I feel like a piece of metal, a horseshoe perhaps, caught between your father's hammer and your anvil. You're both such strong people and I can no longer withstand the blows. And now with Steven...." The tears flowed freely. Laura held a handkerchief to her eyes and hung her head. Eleanor put her arm around her.

"Eleanor, I can't imagine you as Lady Newberry, with those stuffy English snobs, living in a stuffy old castle, going to stuffy little tea parties. Did you tell Lord Newberry that you belong in the United States, and that your affections belong to a banker in Cleveland, of all places!"

"I did tell him that my heart belonged to another." Eleanor smiled and her eyes glistened. "And I do belong in the United States."

"You once asked me if I would have married your father if his father hadn't been president of a bank. I told you that I wouldn't have, and it was fairly easy for me to admit that, but it's hard to accept that answer, Eleanor, because what does that say about my life? I think, from the first time we met Mr. Durand at the bank, I've secretly envied you. Because I knew there was something between you two that I've never had. A woman must make her way in the world, dear, but usually at a cost to her heart…and her soul. The price can be very high."

"Oh, Mother." Eleanor shook her head.

The ensuing silence was interrupted by a knock on the door. "Who is it?" Laura said, standing and moving towards the door.

"*La femme de ménage,*" answered a young, feminine French voice.

"Come back later, *s'il vous plait.*" Laura turned towards Eleanor. "We have to help each other."

"How?"

"We both want to return to America. I've had misgivings about this trip from the beginning, but I told Phillip that I would try, for a year, to find you a suitable match." Eleanor's eyebrows arched. "It sounds coldhearted and it is, but you can't imagine how angry he was about your trysts with Mr. Durand. So we'll have to stay another couple of months."

"Have you written Father about Newberry?"

"No, I didn't want to get his hopes up. When I inform Phillip that we're coming home, I will say that I've grown tired of Europe and am eager to return to America."

"What if he won't allow us to return, since you haven't found me a suitable match?"

"If he won't allow it…well, his letter will get lost in the mail!"

Eleanor laughed a long, joyous laugh and Laura felt better than she had in months.

"You should also mention Steven, to bolster your case," Eleanor said. "He's run through so much money gambling and drinking."

The mention of her son's debaucheries sent a stab through Laura's stomach. "Yes, I'm quite worried about him and I'll tell Phillip so."

"Mother, what will happen when we return?"

"Eleanor, you're a very intelligent woman, but there is some wisdom that only comes with age and experience. You need to learn, as a woman who has to make her way in the world, that there are questions that shouldn't be asked. Remember, dear, that I will have to continue living with your father, and I want to face him with a clear conscience."

Eleanor nodded. It was a subtle point, but one she apparently understood.

"Although I do think we could relax King Phillip's edict about not allowing you to post any letters. When we're ready to leave Europe, I don't see the harm if you sent a brief missive to Constance Walter. Show it to me before you send it."

Eleanor arose from the love seat, walked over to Laura, took both her hands, and kissed her on the cheek. "Thank you, Mother. Thank you. Now if you don't mind, I'd like to lie down for a while. It's been a long day and I feel drained."

"Certainly, dear." Eleanor left the sitting room and went to her bedroom. Laura shook her head. Yes, her husband was the hammer and Eleanor was the anvil. With what had just transpired, Laura might be putting herself in the way of more blows. The strength of the hammer was different from the strength of the anvil. The hammer was used to shape and alter, just as her husband bent people and events to his will. The anvil withstood the hammer's blows. If it could speak, it would probably ask to be left alone. That was the source of her daughter's strength: her ability to stand alone, to resist the force of those who would choose for her. Who would win this contest of wills? The hammer wore out long before the anvil.

Daniel was startled by a loud knock on the front door of the bank. He was alone; Keane had gone home an hour earlier. He stood and walked to the door and there was another knock. He looked at his watch—almost eleven o'clock. Who would want entrance to the bank this late?

"Who is it?" Daniel said as he reached the front door.

"Jonathan Walter."

Daniel threw open the door for his emissary from Eleanor. "Mr. Walter, come in." Daniel quickly closed the door against the chilly autumn air. "What brings you here? How are you?"

"I'm fine, Mr. Durand. I was working late. On my way home I saw the lights on at your bank. I was going to come by tomorrow, but I'm glad I found you tonight, because I have a letter in which you'll be interested."

"Why don't we go into my office and sit down? I can offer you water."

Walter shook his head. "No thanks." Daniel sat at his desk while Walter settled into a chair in front of the desk. "Constance received a letter from Eleanor in Europe." Walter took a letter from his coat pocket and handed it Daniel.

Daniel eagerly unfolded the letter and began reading.

August 15, 1866
Rouen, France

Dearest Constance,

We have spent the last few months in France. Paris has many attractions, but I prefer the countryside. For the last few weeks we have followed the Seine from Paris to Normandy. It is lovely country, with rolling countryside, quaint farmhouses, well-tended fields and orchards, friendly villages and huge cathedrals that are much bigger than any church I've ever seen in America. We will return to London in another week or two. From there, we will leave for the United States. Mother wants to return to Cleveland before winter.

I can't wait to see you and Jonathan again. My best wishes to you both.

Love, Eleanor

Daniel quickly reread the letter. He leaned back in his chair and stared at the ceiling. She'd be home in a month or two—a damn eternity, but she was coming home. This time, nobody was going to keep her away from him, if he had to put together an armed force and storm that mansion on Millionaires' Row. He looked at the square, open face of Jonathan Walter, framed by light brown hair and prominent sideburns. "Odd that all you got is one page," he said, handing it back to him.

"It's the only news we've received from her. Her mother may have prevented her from writing to us. Perhaps she read this letter, or Eleanor snuck it out. Her parents must suspect that Constance and I played a role in getting you and Eleanor together. I think the letter's noteworthy for what it doesn't say more than for what it does."

"What do you mean?"

"She would have mentioned it if she were betrothed. Since she didn't, we can assume she's still eligible. If she hadn't wanted me to tell you of her arrival, she would have said so."

Daniel had not thought of those aspects of the letter, but he was willing to accept Walter's conjecture. He jumped up, banging his knee on the desk. Walter stood. Oblivious to his pain, Daniel rushed around the desk and threw an arm around Walter's shoulders.

"Easy, Durand," Walter said, laughing. "My interpretation may be wrong."

"I know, I know, but this letter has given me my first hope in a long time. Thank you, Mr. Walter, for coming here this late at night."

"Please, it's Jonathan."

"Okay, Jonathan, and I'm Daniel. I'm sure you'd like to get some sleep tonight." He led Walter to the door and opened it. "Say hello to Miss Walter, and I'd be obliged if you'd let me know if you receive any more letters from Eleanor."

Walter laughed again. "Certainly, Daniel, and good night."

After he shut the door Daniel jumped into the air and clicked his heels in a poor attempt at a jig step. Eleanor was coming home!

Chapter 10

A Golden Pinnacle

Daniel sat on the sofa in the living room of his rented house, empty but for the small gray sofa and two end tables, his bookcase filled with books, two boxes with more books on the floor, a circular table with two chairs by the door to the kitchen, and a stack of firewood in a brass basket next to a small fireplace, where a fire crackled. There was no carpet on the hardwood floors, nothing hanging from the freshly painted white walls, no mementoes or bric-a-brac. He had bargained his landlord, Mr. Redding, down to nineteen dollars' a month rent. It was a good rent, but it more than doubled his monthly housing expense and he needed to build up his savings before he'd buy more furnishings. Two weeks ago he had moved from the boarding house. Mrs. Somerset had cried, saying he was like a son to her, but he had to have his own place.

He picked up the second volume of *The Decline and Fall of the Roman Empire*. He loved reading by the fire on a frigid day. A knock came from his front door, so soft that it seemed to fear being heard. He got up from the sofa and opened the door.

Eleanor! She stood in the doorway, her breath turning to vapor, bundled in a long, heavy coat, hands in a furry muff, eyes shining.

She smiled and he knew he would never forget that smile. His heart pounded. He felt the dizzying sensation he had experienced the first time he had seen her. She was so very, very beautiful. Tentatively, as if she were an apparition that might vanish if he tried to touch her, he reached his hand towards her. She withdrew a hand from her muff. When he touched it he knew she was actually there. He threw his arms around her and she squeezed him. His Eleanor! Their agonizing year of separation was over. He felt overcome by an elated sensation that left him lightheaded and weak-kneed.

"You're back!" he gasped.

"I'm back."

Jonathan and Constance Walter stood behind her, Jonathan carrying a box. "Please, come in. It's cold out there," Daniel said. He escorted Eleanor into the living room and the Walters followed. Jonathan put the box on the table and pulled two chairs up to the fire. They all slipped out of their coats. Daniel sat with Eleanor on the small couch and they held hands. Constance took off her hat and her long, dark blonde hair tumbled out. She was an attractive young woman with an angular face, high cheekbones, serious brown eyes, and a thoughtful demeanor.

Eleanor looked around the room. "This is your house?"

"This is my house."

"It's lovely, Daniel."

"How did you get away from your parents? I thought I was going to have to lay siege to Millionaires' Row."

She laughed—the joyous, intoxicating laugh that Daniel would have given anything to hear even once the past year. "I devised a plan while I was in Europe. When we got back, I told my father that I wanted to see my best friend, Constance. I also let him know that I wanted to see her brother, and not just in the way one wants to see an old friend."

Daniel glanced at Jonathan, who smiled sheepishly.

"Although my father was suspicious at first, he's allowed me to visit with them. I never mentioned your name, dearest Daniel." She squeezed his hand. "I've seen these two almost every day. Father has relaxed his vigilance, and Jonathan has done a respectable job as my suitor."

A year ago, Jonathan, prosperous but not prominent, wouldn't have been an acceptable suitor. Haverford had lowered his sights. "What about your mother?" Daniel said.

"She's looking the other way. I've told her nothing and she hasn't asked."

Constance stood. "We brought an apple pie," she said, pointing toward the box on the table. "Jonathan and I will warm it up and fix some coffee."

"You go ahead," Jonathan said. "I'll stay here and talk."

"Jonathan…"

"Oh, ah, yes, I'll help out." He went into the kitchen with his sister.

A hush fell over the room; even the fire stopped crackling. Daniel and Eleanor gazed into each other's eyes. Their silence said more than words. What they had a year ago had grown. They were as necessary to each other as the food they ate, the water they drank, and the air they breathed. He drew her slowly to him and their lips brushed lightly together. She kissed him and put her hand on his shoulder, pressing him towards her.

Daniel kissed Eleanor and pulled away from her. She looked at him quizzically. "I'll be back, dearest," he whispered. He went into his bedroom, picked up a small box from on top of his wardrobe, and rejoined her. He set beside her on the couch. "Darling, every day you were gone I vowed that if I ever saw you again, I'd never let you go. I love you." He opened the box to reveal the ring, bought a year ago, with a crown-cut diamond in a gold band. "Will you marry me?"

"Yes," Eleanor whispered. "Yes, I will marry you." A tear trickled down her cheeks, still rosy red from the cold. She leaned over and gently kissed Daniel. He took the ring from the box and slid it on her trembling finger. "Daniel, it's meant to be—the ring fits. It's beautiful."

Daniel gazed into her glistening eyes. After all he'd been through, he could scarcely believe that he was now engaged to the only woman he had ever thought of marrying. He could scarcely believe his own soaring joy, so intense that it seemed almost uncontainable, as if it would somehow escape him and become its own unharnessed force, bouncing around his house, wreaking havoc. He put his arm around his fiancé as she stared at her ring.

"Daniel, if every cloud has a silver lining, then the silver lining of my year in Europe is that I realized that my feelings for you were true, that what I felt would last…forever. I thought of you every day, every hour. I thought of you and Mr. Keane in your new bank and I hoped, through it all, that you were thinking of me."

"Of course I was, dearest. The bank's done well, but I had such a lonely, empty feeling. I had to have you back before I could take full satisfaction from work, or anything else. There were times when I despaired of ever seeing you again. I couldn't stand the thought of it."

She cupped her hands on his face and stared into his eyes. "Daniel, promise me one thing. Don't ever, not even for one moment, stop being who you are. Don't ever be ordinary. I'll endure anything with you, but I couldn't endure it if you became ordinary."

He laughed. "I don't know how to be anyone other than who I am."

For the next twenty minutes they talked, embraced, and kissed. She told him about Europe, not omitting Lord Newberry. He told her about the bank and Cleveland. Occasionally they mentioned a topic they had never dared consider before—their future together. They smiled and laughed, intoxicated by the possibilities of tomorrow.

"Constance's apple pie must have been frozen," Eleanor said. "It's taking so long to warm."

Finally brother and sister emerged from the kitchen, bearing plates of pie and cups of coffee, which they set on the end tables. With an exaggerated motion Eleanor picked up her coffee cup with her left hand.

"Is that what I think it is?" Constance gasped.

Eleanor nodded, her eyes shining. "We're engaged!"

Constance emitted a cry of delight and the two friends stood and hugged. Eleanor held out her hand to display her ring and Constance and Jonathan made appropriate exclamations.

Jonathan pumped Daniel's hand. "Congratulations, Daniel. Congratulations. You're a lucky fellow." He smiled. "I was about to ask her father for permission to court her!"

They all laughed. "As I told Jonathan in the kitchen, this is a nice house, but it needs a woman's touch," Constance said. "Now it looks as if it will get it. There's just the small matter of how you two are actually to be wed. I don't suppose you've given any thought to that just yet?"

"Not really," Daniel said. "But I'm not the one with the conspiratorial bent. How about you, dearest, have you given it any consideration?"

Eleanor smiled. "Here's what we can do."

The morning of Saturday, November 10, 1866, dawned cold, crisp, and clear. A storm had dumped over a foot of snow the previous night, leaving piles on streets, tree branches, and rooftops.

The sun shone brightly, but with no warmth on the placid stillness. Bundles of greatcoats, leather boots, hats with fur ear flaps, and woolen mufflers, all emitting puffs of vapor, pushed their way through the drifts or sat on top of sleighs, shaking reigns and guiding horses. All across town smoke poured from chimneys, warming those who stayed indoors.

Eight of the chimneys were so employed at the Haverford mansion. At the breakfast table, Phillip Haverford sat with his wife, who was sipping coffee. He drained his cup and wiped his mouth with a linen napkin. "I'd better get going. Baldwin and I have a meeting."

Eleanor entered the dining room, dressed in a blue flannel nightgown and nightcap.

"What rouses Sleeping Beauty at this early hour?" Haverford said cheerily. "If I could stay in my nice feather bed on such a morning, I would certainly do so."

"I wanted a cup of tea, to take up to my room."

Haverford stood. "What are you doing today?"

"Constance and Jonathan are picking me up and a group of us are going ice skating."

"The pond should be frozen solid, but take lots of dry firewood and keep a fire going."

"Thank you, Father, we will." She walked with him and her mother to the front door. He put on his gloves, muffler, and hat. Eleanor took his gloved hands in hers and gravely kissed him on the cheek. "Goodbye, Father, mind the cold."

"Why thank you, Eleanor." He kissed her on the forehead and kissed his wife. "Have a pleasant day, dear." He opened the door and trudged through the snow to the sleigh.

Laura closed the door. "I suppose you didn't sleep very well, but you are either extraordinarily brave or extraordinarily foolhardy to see your father off to work."

"Both." Eleanor took a small box from a pocket of her nightgown and handed it to her mother. "I wanted you to have this."

Laura opened it to reveal a heart-shaped gold locket on a chain. Her tears flowed freely. "It's not right," she whispered, "that I won't be with you today, of all days." She sniffled, wiped her eyes with a handkerchief, and put on the locket. "I shall treasure it, and wear it when I'm able."

"Thank you, Mother."

"You're leaving a letter?"

"Yes, it will be on my pillow, so you won't 'find' it until later."

"Thank you, dearest Eleanor."

The kitchen at the Keane home was filled with the tantalizing smells of cooked onions and bacon, rosemary, bay leaf, tarragon, and freshly baked bread. "Margaret, keep stirring the stew," Abigail Keane admonished her fourteen-year-old daughter, "or it will stick to the bottom." A knock came from the front door. Abigail hurried out from the kitchen to the living room, where Thomas and the two sons, Benjamin and Joshua, were setting up chairs. "That will be Eleanor and Constance. While I get them ready, Thomas, the boys will have to help Margaret in the kitchen." She opened the door. "The bride and the maid of honor!" she exclaimed with a smile. "I should have you stand out in the cold before the wedding, just to get that lovely red glow in your cheeks. Come in. Thomas will take your coats and hats."

"Hello, Mr. and Mrs. Keane," the two women said in unison.

"Miss Constance Walter," Eleanor said. "May I present Mister Benjamin Keane?"

Benjamin, twelve, clasped Constance's hand. "Pleased to meet you," he stammered. The blush creeping up his face offered a sharp contrast to his dark eyes and hair.

"Pleased to meet you, Mr. Keane."

"And Master Joshua Keane," Eleanor said.

A red-headed ten-year-old stepped towards the two women and took Constance's hand as his brother had done. "Pleased to meet you, Miss Walter."

"And you, also, Master Keane." Constance smiled.

"Thomas," Abigail said. "We'll be in Margaret's room. You and the boys stay away. Margaret may come in, but no one else sees the bride until the wedding." She turned towards the two women. "Let's get started." She led them up the stairs. Benjamin followed them with his eyes.

"My poor son," his father said. "You're at that age where members of the opposite sex cease being minor distractions and annoyances, best ignored, and become major distractions and annoyances, impossible to ignore."

Daniel looked himself up and down, carefully inspecting tailor Moses Minzter's finest handiwork—his high, stiff white collar touching his cheeks as he bowed his head. White cotton shirt; black, six-buttoned silk waistcoat, gold watch fob and cufflinks; black tailcoat, left unbuttoned to show off the waistcoat, split tail to his knees, the shiny black stripe on the side of his pants extending from his gleaming black leather shoes. Everything was in order. Who would have thought the first item he would feel the lack of in his new house would be a mirror? With a woman moving in, one would have to be bought. He'd worry about that later. Today, he'd worry about getting married, about snatching the daughter of one of Cleveland's most powerful men from under his nose. A knock came from the door and Daniel opened it.

Jonathan Walter entered, bundled in an Ulster, fur hat, and red wool muffler. "Thunder, Durand, you would pick the coldest day in a decade to get married. Where's your cravat?"

Daniel's faced reddened as he felt around his neck. He went to his bedroom, returned with a white silk cravat, and carefully tied it into an elaborate bow. Jonathan shook his head and Daniel retied it. Jonathan shook his head and Daniel tried again. Jonathan nodded his approval.

"How do I look?" said Daniel, feeling awkward, asking a question men didn't usually ask of other men.

Jonathan gave Daniel a cursory once over. "Fine. From top to bottom you look the perfect groom. Don't worry about any minor imperfections—everyone will be looking at Eleanor."

Daniel smiled. "Let's go," he said, putting on his own great coat. He wrapped a green muffler around his face, donned a fur hat and his regular gloves, and picked up his top hat, white gloves, and walking stick. An icy wind blasted through them as they hurried out to Jonathan's four-horse sleigh and jumped on the front seat. Daniel directed Jonathan to Abram Gottman's apartment in the Kinsman area, the Jewish district. Some of the drifts came up to the horses' hocks. Daniel wiped icy tears from his eyes as his face grew numb. They finally arrived.

"Ach, Daniel, nobody gets married in such weather," Gottman said as he opened the door. "You always do things the hard way. Let's go, before this Mr. Haverford catches on to things. Oh, I didn't see the young man behind you. My eyes aren't what they used to be."

"Mr. Gottman, may I present Mr. Jonathan Walter?"

"Pleased to meet you, Mr. Gottman."

"Likewise, sir."

They escorted Gottman to the sleigh, each offering an arm for support, and helped him to the seat. Daniel directed Jonathan to Mr. Keane's house, which looked like something out of a fairy tale—blanketed in white, snow clinging even to the steeply pitched roof, lights shining through frosted windows, gray smoke curling from three chimneys.

Benjamin Keane opened the door. "Come in, gentlemen. Joshua will take your things and I'll take your horses to the stable." He disappeared into the wintry cold.

A fire blazed in the living room fireplace. A wreath of pine branches and holly hung on the chimney. Several smaller wreathes adorned the room. Sprigs of holly hung from the ceiling and decorated the staircase. The room had the festive feel and evergreen smell of Christmas. A makeshift podium, perhaps a woodworking project by one of Keane's boys, stood in front of the fireplace. It faced two short rows of seats with an aisle down the middle. A white linen runner with two unlit candles on top was draped over the piano. In the dining room, a white tablecloth covered a long rectangular table set with plates, glasses, cups, napkins, place cards, silverware, and a pine and holly centerpiece.

"If the snow doesn't slow people down too much, the guests should start arriving in about half an hour," Keane said. "The men from the bank will be the last to arrive. I didn't think we could close any earlier than three o'clock without arousing suspicion and comment. If Haverford heard something, he might put two and two together."

"Eleanor and Constance are already here?" Daniel said.

"Yes, they've been getting ready for over two hours now." He rolled his eyes.

Joshua brought three cups of coffee on a tray from the kitchen. Daniel caught a whiff of bread and stew. Underneath his nerves he knew hunger lurked, but he couldn't eat. However, the steam rising from his coffee cup smelled good. He sipped the hot liquid and felt himself thawing from the inside. The feeling painfully returned to his benumbed face, ears, hands, and feet.

Somebody knocked. Daniel stared at the door and nobody opened it. It was too early for guests. What if it was Haverford? Another knock. Keane opened the door.

"Mr. Keane," Mrs. Somerset said cheerfully, "so good to see you again." She bustled into the room with her husband. "My word, Daniel, you look even more handsome than the night of the party." She walked over to him and adjusted his cravat. Daniel, relieved, introduced the Somersets to Gottman and Jonathan.

The requirement for secrecy had allowed Eleanor to invite only a few trusted friends. Two of them, Melissa and Deborah, and Deborah's brother Charles, arrived a quarter of an hour later. As Daniel greeted them, he felt an anxious, plunging sensation in his stomach. The ceremony would start within an hour. He glanced at Keane, who looked just as nervous, repeatedly looking out the front window and pulling his watch from his vest. "What's wrong?"

"I'm worried about who might show up, and who might not. Our justice of the peace, Mr. Bushkin, should be here by now. Most ministers and judges wouldn't think of marrying the daughter of one of the town's leading citizens against his wishes, so I made discreet inquiries among minor functionaries. Most of them scurried like roaches in the light, notwithstanding the prospect of a substantial consideration. Finally I found Bushkin in Brighton. I have to warn you, while he's certainly bold, he's also a bit of a character. I wish he'd get here."

Keane's disclosure increased Daniel's anxiety. It was impossible to either stand still or talk with guests. At each knock, he glanced anxiously at the door. Guests entered, decrying the cold and snow, but there was still no justice of the peace. Finally all the guests had arrived. Five, ten, fifteen, twenty agonizing minutes passed. What if this Bushkin had gotten lost? Or had been overcome by the cold? Or had been waylaid by Haverford? Or? Or? Or? Daniel noticed the guests' chatter fading. They too sensed something amiss.

Finally there was a knock on the door. It opened for a tall, rotund figure with an oversize red mustache resting prominently on top of his muffler. He removed his greatcoat, hat, muffler, and gloves and handed them to Joshua as if the young boy were his butler. He looked around the room, spotted Keane, and approached him. "Sorry I'm late, Keane. Our little storm delayed me." He pointed at Daniel. "You're the one who's decided to foreswear all happiness?" Everyone laughed, but the laughter was out of proportion to the humor, relief from the underlying tension.

Keane waved Daniel over. "Mr. Bushkin, allow me to present Mr. Daniel Durand."

"Pleased to meet you, Mr. Bushkin." Daniel extended his hand, which was engulfed in Bushkin's bear-like paw. He had a large head and a florid face. The tips of his mustache extended below his beefy jowls, which were covered by his sideburns. His red hair tonsured a large bald spot. He wore a black frock coat and a red plaid vest that strained against his girth.

"Likewise, Mr. Durand." Bushkin said, his breath a blast of whiskey. "Shall we proceed?"

Daniel felt a rivulet of sweat running down his back. He was about to get married. He and Jonathan went up the stairs and stood in a hallway, both quiet—Daniel because he was too nervous to talk,

Jonathan because he was usually quiet. The door at the end of the hall was closed. Keane came up the stairs and the piano played.

"That's Margaret," Keane whispered. A hush fell over the guests below. Keane went to the end of the hall and knocked. "Are you ready in there?"

"We have been for quite some time," Abigail said, opening the door.

Jonathan and then Keane stepped down the stairs. Jonathan went up the aisle and stepped to the right at the makeshift podium. Keane stopped at the bottom of the stairs. Daniel came down the stairs and walked slowly up the aisle, conscious that everyone in the room was looking at him. He turned towards the stairs to see the rest of the procession. Abigail wore a yellow dress, a dainty yellow hat, and white gloves. Her bodice had a white placket, trimmed in green lace. Crinoline petticoats rustled as she descended the stairs, went up the aisle, and assumed her place on the left side, opposite the men. Constance followed, similarly attired.

Margaret began playing Wagner's "Bridal Chorus" and there was a murmur of expectation. Slowly and dramatically, Eleanor stepped down the stairs, floating on a small white cloud of satin, lace, crinoline, and gauze, carrying a dried lavender bouquet. As she reached the bottom of the stairs, there were gasps of astonishment. While it may be true that there were no ugly brides, Daniel thought, some were more beautiful than others. His was at the absolute pinnacle—enchanting, entrancing, her resplendent radiance not at all obscured by her gauzy veil. She took Keane's left arm and they came up the aisle, looking directly ahead.

"Ladies and gentlemen," Bushkin said. "Today we join together, in the vows of marriage, Mr. Daniel Durand and Miss Eleanor Haverford. Who is it that gives this woman to this man?"

"I do," Keane said. He released Eleanor from his arm and took his place next to Daniel.

Daniel took Eleanor's gloved hand in his and she cast a quick smile at him. Maybe they would carry this thing off after all. She was the most beautiful, the most extraordinary woman anywhere and he was marrying her. Damn her father, he was about to marry Eleanor!

Bushkin recited the lines of the ceremony with surprising fervor and skill. "…And if anyone knows of any reason why the bride and groom should not be joined in matrimony, speak now or forever hold your peace." Someone coughed, but it was just a cough.

"Mr. Daniel Durand, do you take Miss Eleanor Haverford to be your lawfully wedded wife?"

"I do."

"Do you promise to love, honor, cherish, and protect her, forsaking all others, and holding only unto her?"

"I do."

There was a knock at the front door. Everybody froze. Keane quietly stepped, almost tiptoed, to the front door. Another knock. Daniel wished he had a firearm.

"Who is it?" Keane said, his voice strained, higher than usual.

"Please sir," came a youth's voice, "will you be needing any firewood?"

Keane slowly opened the door a crack, then all the way. A youth about Benjamin's age stood in the doorway. Behind him, a young man sat on a sleigh loaded with stacks of wood. The youth saw what he was interrupting and his eyes widened.

"We don't need any firewood. Thank you."

"Sorry, sir."

Keane nodded and shut the door. Daniel exhaled; he had been holding his breath.

Bushkin picked up where he had left off. "Miss Eleanor Haverford, do you take Mr. Daniel Durand to be your lawfully wedded husband?"

"I do." Her voice was sweetly solemn.

"Do you promise to love, honor, cherish, and obey him, forsaking all others, and holding only unto him?"

"I do."

Bushkin nodded at Daniel. Keane handed him a thin gold wedding band. Eleanor took the glove off her left hand and Daniel slid the ring on her finger.

"Mr. Durand, repeat after me. I, Daniel, take thee, Eleanor, to be my wife, to have and to hold..."

Daniel repeated the vows until the concluding, "With this ring I thee wed."

Constance handed Eleanor a thin gold band. Daniel removed his white glove and Eleanor slid the wedding band onto his finger. She repeated after Bushkin, her voice initially shaky but regaining its usual joyous clarity, until her own: "With this ring I thee wed." There was a loud sob from Mrs. Somerset.

"What God has joined, let no man split asunder. By the powers vested in me by the state of Ohio, I now pronounce you man and wife. Mr. Durand, you may kiss the bride."

They had done it! Nobody, not even the powerful father of the bride, could split them asunder. Their audacious gamble had paid off. They had done it!

"Uh, Mr. Durand, you may kiss the bride."

The guests tittered and chuckled. Daniel lifted Eleanor's veil. Her eyes were shining and she smiled. He smelled her lavender bouquet and her honeysuckle scent. They embraced and he kissed her. He was surprised by the ardor of her response. Margaret played Mendelssohn's "Wedding March." They turned towards the guests and joined white-gloved hands. Keane had instructed him that well-bred couples looked straight ahead. Daniel focused his gaze on the back wall as they walked across the living room. They were married!

Keane escorted Constance and Jonathan escorted Abigail to where Daniel and Eleanor stood, happily holding hands. Everyone approached the wedding party at once, chattering, laughing, and expressing relief that nothing had gone wrong. The customary best wishes were offered to Eleanor, and congratulations to Daniel.

Margaret and Joshua started bringing bowls filled with steaming stew from the kitchen to the table in the adjoining dining room. Benjamin brought several loaves of bread and helped his father carry in the punch bowl. His mother set an apple and a pumpkin dish on the table. Daniel watched these preparations with sharp interest. The rich, hearty vapors stoked his suddenly ravenous hunger. Everyone drifted into the dining room.

"Dinner is served," Abigail said.

They found their places. Daniel and Eleanor were in the middle of the long table, with Mr. and Mrs. Keane on one side and Constance and Jonathan on the other.

Mr. Keane said grace. "Heavenly Father, today we celebrate before you the marriage of Daniel and Eleanor. We beseech your blessing of this union. We offer our thanks for the bounty that blesses this table, and the friendship and affection that bring us together. Amen."

A chorus of "amens" followed and everyone sat down. Daniel almost burned his mouth on the steaming stew. He waited a minute that seemed like ten until the stew had cooled, gingerly began to eat it, and found the first few bites only made him more ravenous. An apple-and-raisin compote, seasoned with cinnamon, and pumpkin with walnuts were just as delicious.

Daniel saw both males and females staring at Eleanor, entranced, seemingly compelled by her beauty. Except for young Joshua Keane, every male in the room had thoughts about what would transpire between bride and groom later that night. Daniel tried not to think about it—it made him painfully anxious.

After multiple helpings of food and drink and much jovial conversation, the guests settled into sated lassitude. Keane stood, a cup of punch in hand. "I'd like to propose a toast. I believe I know Daniel well enough to say that his ambition—driving, but never insensible to the demands of integrity and honor—is the dominant aspect of his character. One day he hopes to achieve great wealth. With his marriage to Eleanor, he is already a very rich man."

"Hear, hear!" came an enthusiastic chorus. "Hear, hear!"

Jonathan stood. "I'd also like to propose a toast. I've known Eleanor since we were children. She rarely does what I, or anybody else, expect her to do. I never thought I would meet someone who could surprise me as much as she has, until I met Daniel. Now these two surprising people have united in marriage." He raised his cup and smiled. "To future surprises!"

"Hear, hear!"

On that happy note, dinner ended. Many of the guests refilled their cups. Daniel saw Bushkin pouring whiskey from a flask into his punch. No surprise there.

"That was a lovely dinner," Eleanor said to Abigail as the Keanes and the Durands moved into the living room. "And a charming toast, Mr. Keane."

"Thank you. You know, when we were planning our bank, Daniel came to dinner one night. He told us that he'd give up the bank before he'd give up his hopes for you. I couldn't believe my ears. Abby said everything would work out for the best, but I thought the train might leave the station without him. I'm quite happy he proved me wrong."

Daniel smiled as Eleanor took his hand. "Tell me," she said, "you two have been happily married for a long time. Are there any words of advice you can offer?"

"Well, dear," Abigail said, "you have to realize that you won't always be in your best form and you're going to have your little tiffs. A sense of humor helps a great deal. I think the most important thing is honesty. You have to be honest with yourselves and with each other."

Daniel felt an anxious stab—a goose running over his grave. There was one truth he had not disclosed to Eleanor, one he could never disclose, not if he wished to stay true to Bart Landers, Steve Culpepper, Ben, and the memory of Will Farrows. That truth had to stay buried in the swamp at Walnut Hills. Keane was staring at him. Had some flicker of apprehension crossed his face? "What about you, Mr. Keane, do you have any words of wisdom?"

"Abby said it well, especially about telling each other the truth. Let's get some punch, dear."

"Darling," Eleanor said, squeezing his hand. "I need to talk with Constance."

Daniel watched her cross the room, still thinking about what he had not told her. He would go to his grave with his secret, stifling whatever niggling qualms he had about the matter.

"Daniel, Daniel, Daniel." Mrs. Somerset approached him, her husband in tow. "She is a vision, an absolute vision...." She gushed at length about Eleanor, the wedding, and the couple's happy prospects, finally stopping to sip her punch.

"Daniel," Mr. Somerset said. "I know this farmer named Donahue, he raises horses and races 'em. A while back, he had this horse named Duchess. First time I laid eyes on Duchess, I knew she was a champion. Everyone did. The way that horse carried herself—she was the center of all of God's creation. Turned out, Duchess was the fastest horse in five counties. When I saw your Eleanor tonight, that's what she made me think of—Duchess."

"Oh, you fool!" Mrs. Somerset said. "You just compared his wife to a horse!"

"No, no, Mrs. Somerset," Daniel said. "I take no offense. Eleanor is a champion, although she may not be the fastest filly in five counties." He smiled.

Abram Gottman approached the threesome and clasped Daniel's hand. "*Mazel tov,* Daniel, *mazel tov.* She's very beautiful. Even an old man with bad eyes can see that." He smiled salaciously. "Although I worry about the sleep you're not going to get." He raised his bushy eyebrows. "There was a miserly old butcher, Mordecai, a real *karger*, who wanted a wife. He hired the best matchmaker, who found him a young girl, beautiful but from a poor family. He left his bride in Bavaria when he came to America—he wanted to establish himself, and sent for her a year later. Five months off the boat, she had a baby, a fat, healthy boy. The poor *schlemiel*! He would *kvetch* that it was harder to have a pretty wife than a fortune, because at least you could lock your fortune away!"

Mrs. Somerset was taken aback, but Mr. Somerset and Daniel laughed. Gottman continued with another in what would be a long string of quips, anecdotes, and stories, drawing a crowd that only broke up when Abigail proclaimed, "It's time to cut the wedding cake!"

The Keanes disappeared into the kitchen. Margaret reappeared with the small white bride's cake and Benjamin held the groom's cake, covered with dark frosting. Mr. and Mrs. Keane carried out the much larger wedding cake. It was a dark, rich fruitcake, smelling of brandy, decorated with white scrolls, and orange and yellow flowers. Abigail handed Eleanor a cake server to cut it, symbolic of her first domestic duty, as the guests crowded around the table. There was a murmur of approval as she placed the pieces in boxes for the guests to take home with them. She cut a large piece for her and Daniel, to be saved until their twenty-fifth anniversary.

The reception drew to a close. Daniel felt dazed as the full reality of what had just occurred sank in. He went with Jonathan to the stable to harness the horses and bring up the sleigh. When he reentered the Keanes' house, he saw Eleanor talking with Abigail. They held each other's hands, their eyes glistening. Abigail had become the substitute for the mother Eleanor had abandoned to marry him. Now both bride and groom were orphans.

"Mr. Keane," Daniel said, shaking his partner's hand. Once, just after they had opened their bank, Keane had told Daniel he could call him Thomas, but Daniel had been unable to do so. He had a respect for him that bordered on awe, and that feeling had only grown as they had done business together. He would always be Mr. Keane. "Thank you for everything you've done. There's no way that I can adequately express my gratitude."

The glistening he saw in Keane's eyes surprised him, and even more so when Keane threw his arms around him. "You're like a son to me, Daniel," he whispered.

Eleanor came over and Daniel took her hand. Margaret Keane approached them.

"Miss Haverford…Mrs. Durand," she stammered. "Your dress, and you…it was all so beautiful. I hope when my day comes it will be like that." She glanced at Daniel and blushed. "And that I'll have such a handsome groom."

"Thank you, Margaret," Eleanor said. She took the girl's hands in hers. "Of course your music made it that much more enchanting, and I hope that someone will play as well for you."

"Oh, thank you, Mrs. Durand."

The couple hurried through a snowy flurry with Mr. Gottman and Constance to the sleigh, where Jonathan waited. Gottman and

Constance sat up front, leaving the back seat for the newlyweds. They waved at the Keanes as the sleigh pulled away. Daniel put his arm around Eleanor and drew her to him. "It's going to be cold at our house, dearest," he whispered.

She slipped her hand under his coat, rested it on his chest, looked up at him, and smiled. "Then we'll just have to keep each other warm, my love."

"It's getting late. Don't you think she should be home by now?" Mr. Haverford said.

"She might stay overnight with the Walters," Laura said.

"How would we know?"

"We won't, perhaps until tomorrow morning. Eleanor's not a child, she can take care of herself. She went with a large group. If anything had happened at the pond, we would have heard about it. Why are you so anxious, Phillip?"

"I don't know…I don't know. I have a feeling of some sort, a bad feeling. Bah! I sound like a damn woman. I'll have a cigar in my study." He said nothing more and went up the stairs.

At eight, Laura went into Eleanor's room. She found her daughter's letter on the pillow on her bed. She had read and reread it that afternoon, crying each time. She read it again. Now it left her with a cold, empty feeling. She intended to bring it to her husband, but she hesitated. If he had been drinking, he would be capable of random, furious violence. Most of the times he had hit her had been after he had been drinking. She slipped the letter under the pillow. Better to give it to him in the morning. He'd be irascible, as he always was after a night of drinking, but he would also be more in control of himself. Tonight, she would avoid contact with him.

She retired to the guest room and tried, without success, to read. She fell into a doze, but was awakened by her husband's bellowing.

"Steven, bring round the sleigh!"

She heard the door to her son's bedroom open. "Father, where are you going at this hour?"

"We're going to find Eleanor. We're going to the Walters'!"

Laura tried to think through her frightened confusion. What was she to do? Constance and Jonathan Walter were in Eleanor's wedding. If Phillip went to their house and they were still in their wedding garments, he would figure out what had happened and there was no telling what he would do. He might become violent. She had to stop him. If she gave him Eleanor's letter, perhaps after an initial outburst he would realize that there was nothing he could do, that in spite of his rage, he had to accept his daughter's marriage. He had been drinking, but revealing the marriage seemed like the better choice than a potentially violent confrontation between Phillip and the Walters. She had to get to Eleanor's room.

"Phillip, if you're going to the Walters', would you take Eleanor her nightgown and a few things for the morning? I'll get them." She hurried into her daughter's room and got the letter. Waving it, she rushed from the room. "Oh, no!" she wailed, hoping her act was convincing. "Look what I found." She ran to her husband and handed him the letter.

Dear Mother and Father,

By the time you read this, I will be married to Mr. Daniel Durand. By marrying against your wishes, I know that I forfeit your goodwill. Grievous as that loss is to me, it cannot compare to what I would have felt were I not to marry Daniel. I cannot accept that one's parents and position must ordain one to a life of misery.

Perhaps in the fullness of time you can be reconciled to Daniel and me, but if not, I am prepared to live with that consequence.

Your loving daughter,
Eleanor

"Durand!" he shouted. "Durand!" He crumpled the letter and threw it the ground. "I'll kill that thieving bastard. Steven, get the sleigh. I'll fetch my rifle."

Steven picked up the letter and read it. "Father, the marriage has occurred. You can't stop it and you can't kill Durand. We don't even know where they are."

"Be silent, Steven! The Walters will know. Now get going!"

"If they do, you'll never get through their gate, Father. Even if you got over the fence, Jonathan Walter's a crack shot with a rifle himself."

Haverford stared at him with a wild, desperate gleam in his eye. "Then Keane...Keane will know. That cheating scoundrel will know. Who says I can't stop the marriage? What hasn't been consummated can be annulled. I will not let my Eleanor stay with Durand, have that bastard's children! Damn it, get that sleigh!"

Steven hurried down the stairs.

Laura felt the blood drain from her face. Stopping a marriage after it had happened seemed ludicrously far-fetched, but she saw the murderous rage contorting her husband's face. He pushed her aside, bounded down the stairs, threw on his coat, hat, gloves, and scarf, went into the den, and a moment later emerged carrying a rifle. "Phillip!" she shouted, but he was out the door.

Steven went to the stables. While he readied the sleigh, he tried to think of some way to stop his father. Other than leaving the stables, hiding somewhere on the estate, and letting his father go alone, no course of action presented itself. His father was drunk and had a rifle—he was not to be trifled with. Better to see things through and hope nothing disastrous happened. He jumped on the sleigh and guided it to the front of the house. His father leapt onto the sleigh, the vapor from his heavy breathing filling the air. Steven pulled away, down a trail of packed snow to the front gate. He opened it and they pulled on to Euclid Avenue. "Where does Keane live?"

His father stared stupidly at him, blinking his eyes slowly, as if he had to think about the effort. "I…I don't know," he mumbled.

Steven hid his opinion of his father from him. However, he had inherited his father's temper and was more than a little hot, forced from a sound sleep on this wild goose chase. He wasn't unhappy his sister had done what she had done—it meant a bigger inheritance for him. "The man worked for you for how many years and you don't know where he lives?"

Haverford landed a hard blow with the back of his gloved hand on his son's mouth. Steven tasted blood and felt a loose tooth with his tongue. He tightened his grip on the reins to stop himself from striking back. He hated his father.

"Go to the bank, damn it! Tinsdale will have records. We'll find Keane."

Steven found it hard to see through the billowing gusts. His father ranted—King Lear howling at the wind. They reached the bank. Haverford jumped off the sleigh and rushed up the stairs, but couldn't get the key in the lock with his intoxicated, numb fingers.

Steven took the key from him and opened the door. It was dark inside.

"Find a lantern, damn it!"

Steven walked across the foyer, trying to navigate from memory. After a couple of painful encounters with the clerks' desks, he found a lantern and lit it. They went into the anteroom where Mr. Tinsdale's desk was located. The wall behind the desk had a large rack of pigeonholes. Steven withdrew several envelopes from one marked E, flipped through them, and saw that none contained employee records. His father paced behind him, snorting and stamping his feet.

Steven looked through envelopes in several other holes, finding nothing. He opened the drawers in Tinsdale's desk until he found one containing alphabetized files. He riffled through the Ks. "There's no file here for Keane. Tinsdale probably threw it away after he left the bank."

"What do you mean, there's no file? There's got to be a name in there, an address." He shoved Steven away from the desk, picked up and looked at a file, and threw it to the floor. He did so with another file, then another. Soon he was standing in a pile of folders and papers. Steven felt like laughing, but the throbbing from inside his mouth warned him not to do so.

"There's nothing here." For the first time, some of the anger had left his father's voice, replaced by something Steven hoped was resignation.

"Let's go home. It's past midnight." Steven stepped back, out of range of the paternal fists.

His father's shoulders slumped and his heavy panting subsided. They stood staring at each other in the eerie orange light of the lantern. "Then it's done?" the elder Haverford said plaintively.

"It's done."

"There's nothing we can do?

"There's nothing we can do."

"Take me home. I've lost my daughter."

If anyone other than his father had said it, Steven would have felt sorry for him.

Daniel turned his key and opened the door to the Durand home. He swept his wife up and carried her over the threshold. She laughed her joyous laugh. Daniel's heart pounded and his stomach fluttered with anticipation. Still in his arms, Eleanor put her hand behind his head and pulled it towards her. They abandoned themselves to a long, passionate kiss. He set her down. "Let me get the fires going."

He went into the bedroom and ignited the coal in the heater. He returned to the living room and kindled a fire in the fireplace as Eleanor sat watching him from the couch. The pitch in the wood popped and crackled as the room filled with the smell of the fire. He stood before her. She looked directly at him, not trying to hide the solitary tear rolling down her cheek. She was remarkably strong, but there were limits to any strength.

"Are you thinking about what you've left behind?"

She nodded. "Poor Mother. Everything will be so much harder for her now."

Daniel bent down and kissed her cheek. "I wish she could have seen the wedding, how beautiful you are." He sat next to her on the couch, taking her hand in his and joining her in silent contemplation of the now roaring fire.

The contemplation did not last. The passion they had suppressed for so long would not allow it. Daniel felt a slight increase in pressure on his hand, a signal. He put his arm around Eleanor and they gazed into each other's eyes. She smiled her sweet, engaging smile. His ardor raged within, but he moved slowly, knowing it was a new experience for her. He kissed her and she responded, tentatively at first, then more ardently. He felt his breath quicken and she gasped. They passionately kissed. The spark started a conflagration that soon engulfed them. He loved her beauty, her eyes, her cascading curls, her scent of honeysuckle, her hunger for him, and his insatiable desire for her. When he momentarily relaxed his embrace, she knew his intention. They stood and she was ready to solve what could only have been, for the well-bred daughter of the Cleveland aristocracy, a complete mystery. They glided arm-in-arm to the bedroom, and Daniel closed the door behind them.

PART THREE DURAND & WOODBURY

Chapter 11

R i s k

Energy. Not, Daniel marveled, causeless or chaotic, like the energy of children, but controlled, purposeful, and productive, the energy of experimentation, improvement, progress, and change.

Opportunity. Manufacturing—everything from the great engines for trains and ships to barely visible watch parts—New York was the manufacturing center of the dynamic American economy. Trade—grain, coal, lumber, gold, tonnage from the heartland, bound for more than 150 ports, its ships returning laden with foreign wares—New York shipped a third of the country's exports and half its imports. Money—the Stock Exchange; the Curb; the country's biggest banks, brokerages, insurance and trust companies; Wall Street—New York was the nation's financial capital. Transportation—three railroads; the Atlantic Ocean; two rivers jammed with packets, steamships, clippers, schooners, yachts, ferries, and barges; hundreds of docks—New York was the heart of American transport. Gotham had more factories, offices, warehouses, publishers, restaurants, stores, sweatshops, telegraph offices, hotels, taverns, theaters, churches, and whorehouses than any other American city.

Excitement. This was where the "new" happened. Ideas, innovation, ingenuity, invention, intelligence, and industry were the lifeblood of New York. They all began with the letter "I." New York was an unabashed monument to "I," the "I" of interest, self-interest. It was as palpably in the air as the soot from the factories; as the shouting in dozens of languages; as the din from hundreds of hacks, carts, and wagons, their iron-rimmed wheels rolling over cobblestone streets; as the stench from the docks, rivers, tanneries, and horse excrement; as the aromas from the pushcarts in the streets, their vendors peddling provender as prosaic as bread or so exotic that Daniel could identify neither the food nor the land from which it had originated. This brutally tough city of sharp elbows mercilessly separated the best from the rest. Daniel's competitive juices, a potent mixture of self-challenge, excitement, ambition, and a bit of anxious tension, were already flowing. His love came as quickly as it had for his first job in banking and for Eleanor. He would live here someday, sooner rather than later. He felt more at home in this magnet for migrants than he ever had in Cleveland. He had been in New York for three hours.

Daniel's train had pulled into the depot at 11th Avenue and 32nd Street earlier that morning. It was a fine early autumn day. Daniel had walked down Broadway to the southern tip of Manhattan, taking in the city. In one hand he carried his satchel, in the other a folio of documents and reports. There couldn't be another plot on the planet where so many people were crammed into such a small area. He was jostled nonstop and if he had expired there on the street, his fellow pedestrians would have stepped over his corpse.

His appointment was at the First National Bank, at Broadway and Wall Street. The intersection was clogged with commercial vehicles, their drivers swearing at each other, the jam extending as far as he could see in all four directions. The bank's quarters belied its grand name, with a discreet nameplate on the roster of a nondescript office building at 2 1/2 Wall Street. Inside he found a closed door with a sign: *George Baker, Cashier.* He knocked. The banker opened the door. "Mr. Durand, how do you do?"

"Fine, thank you." They shook hands.

"Please, sir, sit down."

Baker sat behind a large desk, surrounded by a collection of pigeonhole compartments on the walls and shelves filled with papers and ledgers. There were no windows. He was a standard-issue banker: dark hair, a neat, full beard and mustache, black suit and cravat. He leaned back in his chair, his direct, unblinking gaze conveying confidence bordering on arrogance, as if to say: don't waste my time and don't insult my intelligence.

Daniel set his folio on the desk. "I'm here to discuss the establishment of a correspondence between our bank and the First National Bank. Here are our books of account. We have been successful while remaining within the bounds dictated by prudence and good business. Mr. Keane has a sterling reputation, and I think a relationship would be to our mutual benefit."

Baker took the folio, opened it, and without saying a word inspected the papers and ledgers. He moved quickly from page to page. When he finished, he slid the folio back to Daniel. "We know Mr. Rockefeller in New York. He's your biggest account. I don't share my contemporaries' distaste for the oil business, but are you comfortable with your concentration?"

"We don't like the part of the oil business in Pennsylvania—sticking a drill in the ground and hoping for a gusher—but we like the oil-refining and transport business. Mr. Rockefeller is the biggest refiner in Cleveland. He has the most efficient production, the lowest costs, and an integrated operation. He always makes money, pays on time, and his accounting is impeccable."

Baker stood, moved to a shelf, withdrew a thick burgundy ledger with the words *First National Bank* embossed in black on the cover, and placed it on the desk. "Please don't hesitate to ask questions. Our business is somewhat complicated."

That proved to be an understatement. The First National Bank conducted a thriving business in government bonds, maintained correspondent relationships with banks across the country, extended well-secured business loans, and held an extensive portfolio of corporate bonds. The completely safe bank made no money; the completely reckless bank lost it all. The competent banker found a middle way. Baker had found the profitable Golden Mean.

"Mr. Baker, your accounts verify what we've heard about First National."

"We're solid. We don't discount on as favorable of terms as others, but we'll extend to the Industrial Bank a hundred-thousand-dollar line on the same terms as we do to our other correspondents."

Baker's tone left no doubt—there was no room to bargain. "That will be acceptable," Daniel said.

"How are business conditions in Cleveland?"

"Business is good right now, but frothy. We're cutting back and building reserves."

"You're on the right course. Tough times are coming. You'll receive our contract and counterparts in the mail. Good day, Mr. Durand." They shook hands and the meeting was over.

Daniel left the First National Bank and approached an older gentleman who appeared to be in less of a rush than most of the passersby. "Excuse me, sir, where is the Stock Exchange?"

"Broad Street, just south of here. You'll know you're there when you see fools in the street."

At the corner of Broad and Exchange Place, Daniel understood the "fools in the street" comment. Men in the street, under the lampposts and street signs, gestured, wrote on cards and papers, and shouted a clipped argot. They had papers in their hatbands and were oblivious to the gaping onlookers, or to any considerations but trading and making money.

"Half bid twenty-five."

"Three-quarters asked, fifty."

"Five-eighths asked, twenty-five."

A man raised his hand. "Done here, three-eighths bid, twenty." He wrote on a slip of paper.

"Where is Merchants? Market on Merchants?"

"Quarter, five-eighths, thirty by fifty."

Daniel had heard of the Curb, where stocks not listed on the Stock Exchange traded, but he hadn't known that it was actually outside on the street. It appeared chaotic at first, but as he watched it he discerned order—that of an anthill or a beehive. He stood transfixed as men offered stock, bid for stock, made markets, and traded.

Someone was staring at him. He turned and saw a man his own age, wearing a tall black hat and a black frock coat and vest. Daniel recognized the man behind the stare, pointing at him.

"Cleveland! I know you from infernal Cleveland!" He was almost shouting.

"Mr. Winfield," Daniel said, advancing towards him. He extended his hand. "Perhaps you've forgotten my name. Daniel Durand." Several of the traders on the street were watching.

"Durand," Winfield sputtered. "Durand. Yes, from the party at the Haverfords'." They shook hands perfunctorily. "What brings you to New York, Mr. Durand?"

"A meeting at one of the banks." Daniel waited for the inevitable question, which came with a casual lightness he knew was feigned.

"Say, whatever happened to Miss Haverford? She was quite a beauty."

"She's now Mrs. Durand. We've been married two years. She's expecting our first child in a few months." A broad grin broke out on the face of one of the stock traders.

"You...you...but how...how did you secure her father's consent?"

"I didn't. We married against his wishes."

Winfield hastily tipped his hat. "Well, good day to you, Mr. Durand. I must be on my way." He hurried down the street.

"Splendid! Absolutely splendid!" The trader who had grinned stepped forward. "I'll buy a drink for any man who can get the better of Archer Winfield!" He extended his hand. "Will you join me, Mr. Durand?"

"Uh, certainly. And you are?"

"Woodbury. Call me George. Try not to judge me by the company I keep!" He was about Daniel's age, tall—only an inch shorter than Daniel—but heavier. A shirttail protruded from his green vest, his jaunty green and red-polka-dotted tie was loosened, and the top button of his shirt was unbuttoned. He had light brown hair and a bushy mustache. He turned towards his compatriots. "Gentlemen, I'm done for the day. My account is square. See you tomorrow."

He walked away, Daniel following, somewhat bewildered. They made their way through crooked, narrow streets and entered a tavern with sturdy tables and massive ceiling beams. Smoke from an open stone hearth, pipes, and cigars reduced the already dim light. They sat at a table near a grease-streaked window. A waiter in a stained white apron bustled up.

"Your draft," Woodbury said. "And for my friend Mr. Durand?"

"Call me Daniel. I'll have the same."

The waiter soon returned with two beers, foam overflowing the steins. Daniel took a sip and then a long pull. He liked its mellow creaminess.

Woodbury removed a portable leather case from his coat pocket. "Cigar?" Daniel took one and Woodbury lit both their cigars. "I gather you and Winfield contested for the affection of the same woman, and you won."

"That's right."

"You from Cleveland? The Curb is just scenery to the locals. Nobody watches us as long as you did unless they've never seen it before."

"Yes, I'm a banker. How do you know Winfield?"

"Let's just say that his father and my uncle run in the same circles. I'm a bit of a black sheep, so Winfield didn't deign to recognize me."

"You don't like him?"

"Any more than you do." Woodbury took a long puff from his cigar and rolled his box of matches on the table end over end. "What did you think of our little circus?"

"I was so interested I lost track of time. I had intended to see the Stock Exchange."

"Dull as a sermon—they trade one stock at a time. The members look down their nose at the Curb. As if the Stock Exchange hasn't had its share of rascals and thieves. My father, rest his soul, was a member and I'll join one of these days." He motioned to the waiter. "You hungry?"

"Yes, what's good?"

"Have a steak. The usual, Bill, and one for Mr. Durand." The waiter departed. "Take a man like Jay Gould. He's a swindler's swindler, in a class by himself. Right now he's dangling the Erie Railroad in front of Cornelius Vanderbilt like you dangle a ribbon before a cat. The Commodore needs that railroad worse than a drunk needs his first drink, but every time he thinks he's got control, Gould snatches it away. Vanderbilt makes deals, bribes judges and politicians, and tries to corner the market on Erie stocks and bonds. Gould makes better deals, pays bigger bribes, and offers a few million newly issued Erie shares. Vanderbilt's lost millions with nothing to show for it. Gould will take the game as far as it can go, then walk away with millions."

Daniel puffed his cigar. What to make of this Woodbury? Most players would show you their cards, if you let them. "Why do you do what you do if it's a crooked affair?"

"Well, there's the chaff and there's the wheat. Legitimate business is going to grow faster and get bigger than anyone can imagine. For all the shenanigans, the Curb and the Stock Exchange will be at the heart of it. Trading stocks and bonds here is like having front row seats. We don't just trade pieces of paper—we trade information that you can't get anywhere else."

The waiter brought two large platters with big steaks, still sizzling, and baked potatoes filled with sour cream, grilled onions, and bacon. Daniel pounced on his steak. It cut easily and was cooked to perfection. Evidently Woodbury was just as hungry. There was no conversation until they slowed down for their potatoes.

Woodbury pointed his fork towards Daniel. "There's one thing that can ruin business in this country: politics. When men make money, the rabble want it—never mind that they don't deserve a penny—and there are politicians that'll give it to them, after taking a generous cut for themselves. Not even Gould could steal as much as what got grafted out on Lincoln's transcontinental railroad." He had to raise his voice to be heard; the restaurant had filled with patrons and their noise. "The crooks building it are laying twice as much second-rate track as they need through land that can't support a railroad, and the government pays 'em to do it."

They cleaned their plates. The waiter cleared the table and poured coffee. Woodbury produced two more cigars. He lit his and leaned back in his chair.

"A businessman can cheat you once, unless you're so stupid you can't find the privy, but politicians have the law and the prisons. Businessmen can't legally steal your money or perpetrate a fraud like the transcontinental railroad, but the politicians can."

Daniel lit his cigar and blew out smoke rings as Woodbury favored him with his opinions on a variety of subjects. He would have placed a stout wager that Woodbury got into more than his fair share of arguments, and fistfights as well, but Daniel let him show his cards. Woodbury's saving graces were his humor and that Daniel agreed with most of what he said.

Woodbury abruptly stopped talking and looked at Daniel as if he was evaluating him. "You're a listener, Durand—I like that. If you ever wanted to relocate to New York, perhaps we could pursue business opportunities to our mutual advantage."

"Perhaps." Daniel wasn't sure what to make of the voluble trader and was surprised at his inability to form a firm opinion about him. He usually made quick judgments that experience often confirmed.

Eleanor was awake, although it was well past midnight. All day she had felt as if her body, and the baby inside, were preparing for the baby's departure. She had cleaned the house, compelled by a preparatory instinct. Now she was apprehensive and scared. Childbearing and birth were not subjects of polite conversation, but she had heard enough. Giving birth was painful, and the first time could be excruciating...and dangerous...and heartbreaking. Women died during childbirth; so did their babies. Awake while Daniel slept, separated from her family, confronting this frightening mystery, she had never felt more alone.

She listened to her husband's irregular breathing. He didn't usually snore, but he was not a sound sleeper. Some nights he would wake her, thrashing about and moaning. She wondered if he had nightmares. He wouldn't talk about his childhood. There must have been terror, horror, in those years of deprivation, things she feared even to imagine, but they had not produced bitterness and hatred. Instead, the way he treated her won her enduring love. When she talked, he listened—not out of duty, as her father did when he deigned to pay attention to her mother, but because he was interested. He wanted to know about her adventures, and misadventures, in the kitchen. He laughed when she told stories on herself, about learning to wash clothes, to clean, to sew, to go to market. Although he had hired a maid, Eleanor had learned the duties of a housewife—she wouldn't be an ornament. His passion for her was not a passion that paid no heed to her desires. His strength allowed him to be gentle and loving, and he would be the father their child deserved.

What was that—that tightening, painful sensation? She knew what it was. There had been flutters; this was her first pain. She lay terrified. How long would it take? How much would it hurt? She waited for she did not know how many minutes. There was another one, more painful than the last. She gasped. Their baby was coming! She shook Daniel until his eyes opened. "Daniel, it's time. I'm going to have our baby."

He bolted upright in the bed, fully awake. This was Shiloh, Walnut Hills, and Vicksburg all rolled into one. The battle plan had been devised, reveille had sounded, and there was no time to waste. Any delay and the battle would be lost. *Spring from your bedroll, soldier, and throw on your uniform—the baby's coming!* There was a loud thud.

"Damn!" It was the first time he had sworn in front of her.

"What happened?"

"I stubbed my toe on the bedpost," he muttered, holding his foot, hopping around the bedroom on the other. He hopped over to the closet, took off his nightshirt, and dressed. The baby was coming— he had to think about what he had to do. A light went on; Eleanor had lit the lamp. She shouldn't be doing that, not in her condition, but he had forgotten to. Well, it made it easier to see. *No more foolish mistakes—concentrate—the baby was coming!*

"Oh, Daniel?"

"Yes, dear."

"You've forgotten your coat."

"Uh, right." He grabbed his coat from a stand in the corner.

"Slow down, dearest. First babies take their time. Before you go, would you bring me a glass of water? And light the fire in the stove. The pot of water is already on it."

Daniel went into the kitchen, lit the stove fire, and brought back a pitcher of water and a cup. He still felt agitated. He kissed Eleanor. "I'll be back soon with Mrs. Petersen."

He walked to the neighbors' house, not realizing how loudly he was pounding on the door until Mr. Petersen, an immigrant candle-maker from Sweden, opened it.

"Mr. Durand, you'll wake the dead. It's time for the baby?"

"Yes."

"Go wait with your wife. Ingrid will be there soon."

Daniel returned to his house and sat with Eleanor, silently holding her hand. Once she gasped, her face contorted, and she squeezed his hand hard. He couldn't bear to see her agony and was relieved that Mrs. Petersen, an older woman with six grown children, entered the room before she had another pain. She made a dismissive gesture at Daniel.

"Fetch the ladies, now, Mr. Durand," she said in a thick Swedish accent.

Daniel kissed Eleanor. "I love you."

She gently squeezed his hand. "I love you."

Daniel's two horses, Springer and Midnight, and the buckboard were in a stable behind the house. He secured the harness, climbed on the seat, and gathered the reins in his hands. "Giddyap!" The night air was cold and crisp. His child had picked an auspicious time, in terms of the weather, to make his (her?) appearance in the world. It had not snowed for a month, and most of that had melted. April 10, 1869, would, he hoped, mark the child's entrance. The idea of a birth on April 11 made him shudder, thinking of a full day of labor and what Eleanor would bear. He was surprised at how quickly Mr. Keane, still in his nightclothes, opened the door in response to his soft knock.

"Abigail will be down shortly, Daniel. Benjamin will take Mrs. Obermeyer."

Benjamin came down the stairs and went out the back door to fetch the Keanes' carriage. Abigail came down, wearing a white apron over her dress. Keane put his hand on Daniel's shoulder and said, "Good luck. God be with you and Eleanor."

The next stop was the house of Mrs. Obermeyer, the midwife. Abigail knocked on the door and a light went on inside. Mrs. Obermeyer had many late-night knocks on her door; it opened after a few minutes. Like Abigail, she wore an apron, and carried a black bag. Abigail returned to Daniel's buckboard. Mrs. Obermeyer rode with Benjamin.

When they reached the Durand residence, Daniel handed the reins to Benjamin and rushed to the house with Abigail and Mrs. Obermeyer. They entered the bedroom and saw Eleanor upright against the headboard, her bulging belly protruding under the sheets. Mrs. Petersen brushed a strand of hair from Eleanor's face.

Eleanor smiled wanly when she saw him, but she already appeared stressed and tired. "Abigail and Mrs. Obermeyer, it's so good of you to come at this hour."

Abigail went to the bed and took Eleanor's hand. "Babies know enough to arrive when it's quiet and the rest of the world is sleeping." She turned towards Daniel. "Kiss your wife and wait in the living room. I'll come out if I need anything."

Daniel did as instructed, gently grasping Eleanor's hand. They looked at each other without speaking before he left her and the three women to the mysteries of childbirth. They were wise and experienced, and Daniel hoped, as he had never hoped before, that they would bring his wife and child safely through the coming ordeal. He went outside and lit a cigar, resigning himself to the anxious tedium of the expectant father.

Halfway through the cigar, he heard a groan from the bedroom and a cry of pain. He shivered—the ordeal was beginning. He clenched his teeth on his cigar. The first time he had heard that kind of cry was from a Cleveland tenement as he tried to sleep in another tenement across an alley. He had heard that cry, over and over, all night long and into dawn of the next day. Then the cries had stopped, replaced by a long keening wail. Daniel squeezed in among the slum dwellers who gathered on the stoop. A wizened old woman, carrying a tiny corpse wrapped in a bloody sheet, wordlessly pushed her way through the throng and dumped the bundle in a garbage pail.

Another cry came from the bedroom and Eleanor wailed, "Mother! Mother!" Daniel cringed, both at her pain and her cry for her mother. He threw his cigar butt to the ground and entered the house. "Mother…oh, Mother!" came another cry, followed by a long, raw wail. He heard Abigail's soothing voice. "There, there, that's it."

Another scream and fifteen-year-old Benjamin Keane shuddered. Why had his mother made him come? The screaming and wailing, Mrs. Durand crying for her mother—it was awful. What if something happened to her? Poor Mr. Durand looked like he was in as much pain as his wife. Benjamin had an idea. It might not work, but at least it would get him away from the wailing and pain. He went to the back of the house, where he had left the horses harnessed to his carriage. The sun peeked over the horizon. Wisps of pungent steam rose from fresh manure. He climbed on the carriage, grabbed the reins, and directed the horses on a route away from the house, not wanting to alert anyone inside to what he was doing.

Once he had the carriage on the street, he sped the horses to a gallop and raced through mostly empty streets. He reached Euclid Avenue. His father had once shown him where the Haverfords lived. He had never forgotten the sweeping, immaculately tended grounds or the three imposing gray boxes of the mansion. Jumping down from his wagon, he hailed a man who tended the closed gate. "Sir, I have a message that I've been instructed to deliver to Mrs. Haverford."

The man regarded him suspiciously. "Here, I'll take your message." He reached his hand through the bars of the gate towards Benjamin.

"No, I can't do that. I've been told to deliver it personally to Mrs. Haverford. I think she'll be pretty upset if she doesn't get this message. It's important."

The man opened the gate. "Leave your carriage here, it might wake the family."

Benjamin walked up the long drive to the Haverfords' front door and rapped the brass knocker. A doorman opened the door. He seemed more imposing than the man at the gate, and Benjamin's stomach tightened. "Please, sir, I have a message for Mrs. Haverford, which I must see is delivered personally."

"Who is it, Newman?" A man's voice came from behind and above the doorman.

"A messenger, sir, with a message he says he must personally give to Mrs. Haverford."

"Allow him in."

Benjamin stepped inside. He had never been in a house this fancy. A man he assumed was Mr. Haverford, dressed in a gray and black frock coat, loomed above him on the second floor. A woman, also fully dressed, joined him.

"State your business, young man."

"Are you Mr. and Mrs. Haverford?"

"Yes."

"Your daughter, Eleanor, is having her baby and she's been calling for Mrs. Haverford."

"Who are you?" Haverford shouted.

Benjamin looked directly at Haverford. "Benjamin Keane."

"Leave this instant, before I come down there and show you the door myself!"

Benjamin felt the doorman's hand on his shoulder.

"Not so fast!" Laura said. "I'm going with you, Benjamin. My daughter needs me."

"Laura, I forbid you to leave this house." Mr. Haverford moved in front of his wife.

"Phillip, if you don't get out of my way, you shan't know a moment's peace until the day one of us dies!"

Mr. Haverford stepped aside. Laura came down the staircase and clasped Benjamin's hand. "Take me to my daughter, Mister Keane."

Daniel gasped when he opened the front door.

"Mr. Durand," Laura said with a cursory nod, as she strode into the house. Hearing a scream, she rushed to the bedroom and closed the door behind her. Daniel heard a cry of joy from Eleanor, a welcome contrast to the hours of groans and wails.

The wailing soon resumed. For the fifth time Daniel knocked and asked how things were going. For the fifth time Abigail assured him that everything was fine. He managed a smile when Benjamin returned from tending the horses. "So that's where you went, you rascal."

Benjamin laughed and recounted his adventure at the Haverfords' mansion.

"You know, Benjamin, we've decided to name the baby Laura if it's a girl. That's Mrs. Haverford's first name."

"And if it's a boy?"

"His name will be William, after a friend in the army who was killed at Vicksburg."

Daniel had just stepped outside and lit another cigar when he heard a cry different from those that had tortured him for hours, the cry of a baby. A baby! He threw the cigar to the ground and rushed into the house, running into Laura.

"It's a boy! He's plump and healthy. Let us clean things up and you can see your son." She ducked back into the bedroom.

"It's a boy, Benjamin, a boy!" Daniel shouted.

"Congratulations, Mr. Durand!" Benjamin jumped up from the couch, rushed to Daniel, and threw his arms around him, then, perhaps feeling foolish, stepped away.

Daniel smiled, put his arm around Benjamin's shoulders, and took a cigar from a case. "Now don't tell your parents I gave you one of these, and don't get sick smoking it. Ride to the bank and tell your father we have a son—William Farrows Durand. You both come by later on and you can see the baby. Benjamin...tell your father that I hope my son makes me as proud of him as I know he is of you."

The youth pumped Daniel's hand and took the cigar. "Congratulations again, Mr. Durand. Tell Mrs. Durand congratulations, too. I'll go right now—Father will want to hear the news." He slammed the front door behind him.

For thirty long minutes Daniel could scarcely contain himself. Finally Abigail, Mrs. Petersen, and Mrs. Obermeyer, carrying a pot, emerged from the bedroom. Laura remained with Eleanor and the baby. The women's aprons and dresses were bloodstained.

"You can go in, Daniel," Abigail said.

Eleanor smiled when she saw him, but she was white as the sheets around her and obviously exhausted. She held a tiny bundle, swaddled in blankets. Her mother stood on one side of the bed, her expression alternating between happy pride and distaste. The source of her pride was obvious, and so, Daniel realized, was her distaste— she was less than overjoyed by the modest circumstances into which the baby had been born. Daniel rushed to the other side of the bed and kissed Eleanor. He felt her tears against his cheek.

She kissed him and gently handed him the bundle. "Our son, William."

"Gosh, he's so light. I can hold him in one hand! He's bald! And he's gurgling! Look at those tiny little fingers! Are they all this small? When does he open his eyes?"

Eleanor chuckled weakly, and even Laura smiled at Daniel's wide-eyed wonder. "His eyes will open soon," Laura said.

He was responsible for this helpless little life! To protect, feed, clothe, and shelter him. He felt ten years older. It wasn't just Eleanor and him anymore. Now it was the Durand family, and he was carrying it on his shoulders. The way Eleanor gazed at their son...there was marriage, and there were mother and child. A lioness would sac-rifice her life to protect her cubs, but not her mate. Things would be different now. Will would come first. Daniel kissed him on the fore-head and the infant grabbed his nose. Daniel chuckled and handed him back to Eleanor, smiling at the cooing sounds she made to the son she already loved so deeply.

Daniel sat in his office at the bank and read the telegram, dated September 2, 1869.

FIREWORKS IN GOLD MKT STOP PRICE SHOULD RISE STOP GOULD INVOLVED STOP AM BUYING NOW WILL TRY TO SELL RIGHT TIME STOP SEND AMOUNT WITHIN YOUR MEANS IF YOU WISH TO JOIN
WOODBURY

Daniel had Farnsworth, the cashier, draw a check for $2,000, to the order of George Woodbury. He had to find out if this brash New Yorker was a humbug or the genuine item. "Never bet more than you can afford to lose," Keane had said more than once. If he lost, it would just take a little longer before he could buy a nicer house for Eleanor and Will. What intrigued him as much as the potential profit was the opportunity to test his judgment. He suspected that behind Woodbury's verbosity was a first-rate mind and a tempera-ment keenly attuned to opportunity. If he didn't respond to this in-vitation, there would probably be no other. Two thousand was about right—substantial enough to demonstrate wherewithal, not so much as to suggest imprudence.

After he sent the check, Daniel checked the gold quote daily and watched its price climb from $135 per ounce to $139 to $141. Something was indeed going on, and the newspapers began to whisper of a conspiracy to corner the gold market, led by the nefarious Jay Gould, in league with important officials in Washington. Newspaper editorials denounced the conspiracy and called upon the federal treasury to sell gold and thwart it. The price continued to rise.

Three weeks later, Keane, who stopped by the telegraph office every day before he came in, entered his office, visibly agitated.

"Did you see where gold opened this morning?"

"No."

"One hundred and fifty, with an imbalance of buy orders."

Daniel smiled. "It must be what the papers have been talking about—a conspiracy. Or at least somebody believes there's a conspiracy."

"Congratulations, Daniel, but this is the kind of foolishness that leads to panics. I still have my doubts about you sending your money to a man with whom you've had one dinner. Send a telegram to Mr. Baker, requesting immediate shipment of available cash, to the limit of our credit. If there's a panic we shouldn't have any exposure to it, but extra funds never hurt."

Daniel welcomed the opportunity to send a telegram; it gave him a chance to check the gold price. He inquired of the clerk, a chirpy young man barely past his teens.

"One hundred sixty-five. Up twenty today. Should have bought yesterday."

Or three weeks ago. Daniel floated back to the bank. He did his work with less than his usual concentration. Holding out as long he could, he finally succumbed to his internal agitation and returned to the telegraph office late that afternoon.

"Gold is one-thirty-eight; dropping like a stone. Treasury announced it would sell gold. A lot of them speculators are going to be ruined. Serves 'em right, too—no such thing as easy money."

Daniel took his leave from the Voice of Fiscal Rectitude. One-thirty-eight! His stomach was flip-flopping. Had Woodbury sold? Daniel had already mentally relocated his family's new house to a nicer neighborhood. If Woodbury hadn't sold in time, the house was in jeopardy. He might even be looking at a loss! A loss, after such a huge profit had been within grasp, seemed much more unacceptable now than when he'd sent his money to Woodbury.

The newspaper headlines that evening screamed of "Black Friday," of greedy speculators, ruinous losses, bankruptcies, and the Grant administration's culpability, or its heroic response to the nefarious Jay Gould, depending on the political tilt of the newspaper. Daniel read the stories, went home, told Eleanor of the latest developments, and spent a restless night, worrying about when, and what, he would hear from Woodbury. He rose at 5:30, half an hour earlier than usual, washed and dressed, gulped a cup of coffee, and hurried down to the bank.

For the first time since the Industrial Bank of Cleveland had opened, there was a line of customers at the door, waiting to enter. He went to the front of the line, where a man in his fifties, wearing a frayed black suit and a resolute look on his face, stood. "Excuse me, sir. Why are you here an hour before the bank opens?"

"There's a rumor this bank was involved with them gold speculators. Don't know if it's true, but I'll get my money and ask questions later."

"As the vice-president of the Industrial Bank, I can assure you that the bank has had absolutely no involvement with anything connected with the gold market. The bank is solidly profitable, solvent, and quite liquid. We will of course honor your request to withdraw your funds, but there's no need for you to do so. When this rumor is exposed as the falsehood it is, we hope that you'll return your deposit." Daniel unlocked the front door, entered the bank, relocked the door, and broke into a cold sweat.

This was the beginning of a run on the bank. Where had this rumor come from? Did somebody know about his speculation in the gold market? It wouldn't make sense if that was the basis of the rumor. He had used his own funds, not the bank's. Thank goodness for Keane's caution. Sensing the bust that would inevitably follow Cleveland's boom, he had cut back on their riskier loans, built their reserves, and sent Daniel to New York to set up the line of credit with Baker at the First National Bank. He had the foresight to draw on it yesterday, although the money wouldn't arrive until Monday or Tuesday. They might need every dime to save the bank.

Keane entered the bank ten minutes later and went to Daniel's office, worried crinkles on his forehead. "When Stanton comes in, have him leave out the back door. Tell him he's 'sick' today, although he'll be paid. One less teller will move the line that much more slowly. We'll open at 8:00 and close precisely at 4:00. If it turns into a mob, we'll send for the police and close early. We can't compromise the safety of our employees. Send a telegram to Baker. Find out how much money he's sending and when it will arrive."

Daniel composed a telegram to Baker, went out the back door, and delivered it to the telegraph office. He wondered if he had received anything from Woodbury, but the clerk knew him and would have given him a telegram if one had come in. Daniel returned to the bank. The line had doubled in length since earlier that morning. He waited nervously.

The doors swung open and customers began withdrawing their funds. They were quiet for the most part, although it must have displeased them that the three tellers seemed to be painstakingly slow and methodical in their work.

Mr. Keane made inquiries among several customers. Where had the rumor started of Industrial Bank's involvement with the gold market? They didn't know, they had just heard it somewhere. Did they think that a local bank would be involved with a scheme the newspapers said was based in New York and Washington? They weren't waiting around to find out.

Keane addressed the line. "Ladies and gentlemen, I give you my word as president of this bank that we have had no involvement with the gold market. We accept deposits from thrifty people such as you and lend it to solid, profitable businesses and credit-worthy borrowers here in Cleveland. Our repayment history is the envy of other banks. I don't know how this rumor got started, but I assure you we will demonstrate that it is completely false. We have the resources to honor your withdrawals, but time will prove that course of action unnecessary on your part."

Daniel watched the customers. They politely listened to Keane, but no one left the line. A threat to years of scrimping and saving provoked a fear impervious to truth, logic, and calm entreaty. Daniel followed Keane into his office and sat in a chair in front of his desk. There was a thin line of sweat on Keane's upper lip.

"I knew that speech would be useless," Keane said. "How much have they withdrawn so far?"

"A little over twenty-two thousand. At that rate, we have enough to get through today and part of Monday, but if it lasts longer than that, we're going to need the money from First National."

"Have you received a reply from Baker?"

"Not yet."

"Take a look at this." Keane reached across his desk for a paper, but something odd and frightening occurred. His hand started to shake and he couldn't grasp the paper. Daniel gasped, and Keane looked at his hand as if it were that of someone else. They both stared, speechless, until the tremor stopped. "That's happened several times the last few weeks," Keane said, shaken. "I don't know what it is."

"Perhaps you should see a doctor."

"Perhaps I will. What I wanted to show you are these figures. Forty percent of our depositors are individuals. They're the ones taking their money out. The other sixty percent, businesses, will be much less likely to withdraw. We've lent most of them money. If they take their money out, we'll call their loans."

Daniel nodded, but he was too upset by Keane's shaking hand to say anything. He returned to his office. Keane's health was one more thing to worry about and it moved to the top of the list. He decided to walk over to the telegraph office. He took small hope from the line in front of the bank—it hadn't grown any longer. Also heartening was a telegram the clerk handed him.

HAVE FORWARDED FIFTY THOUSAND STOP MONEY ON TRAIN FRI ARRIVE MON STOP CRISIS PREVENTS SENDING FULL AMOUNT STOP SEND REST NEXT WEEK BAKER

"Are there any other telegrams for me?"

"No, sir."

When, and what, was he going to hear from Woodbury?

The train was late, the bank was down to its last $5,000, another teller had "taken ill," Keane was preparing to call in loans, and

Daniel was reduced to standing on a platform, peering down the tracks, waiting to see the smoke that signaled the bank's salvation. He had given three porters a dollar apiece to find the trunk from the First National Bank when the train arrived and to help him with it to his buckboard. He pulled out his watch from his vest. Two-fifteen— twenty minutes late. Where was that damn train?

He paced across the platform. If Keane ran out of money he would have to close the doors and the bank was finished. Word would spread like wildfire and somebody, probably a commercial deposi- tor, would throw them into bankruptcy. Imagine losing the bank be- cause a train was late! The $50,000 would tide the bank over. What was that? A puff, then a long trail of beautiful white smoke! There it was, a gigantic black locomotive, its cowcatcher sucking up the track before it. The whistle sounded as the train slowed.

The porters jumped aboard the baggage cars. Within fifteen min- utes, two of them, escorted by an armed guard, carried a large black trunk across the platform and set it before him. The words *First National Bank* were embossed in gold on the top. The porters had forgotten the bill of lading and one of them had to fetch it. When he returned, Daniel hurriedly signed for the trunk and directed the porters to his buckboard. They seemed unacquainted with the word "hurry." Finally they reached the buckboard and placed the trunk behind the seat. Daniel covered it with a blanket and felt a drop of rain on his neck. He had not gone far before he found himself in a downpour.

The streets of Cleveland's commercial district were jammed with carts, carriages, wagons, individual riders on horseback, and pedes- trians trying to negotiate the storm. The ride back to the bank was maddeningly slow. Daniel's buckboard stopped behind a snarl of ve- hicles, their drivers screaming and cursing at each other. He shouted at a driver in a cart ahead of him and the man shrugged. The sand was running out of the hourglass—the bank would be lost!

Daniel glanced at the pedestrians. At the rate he was going, he could walk faster to the bank. That was what he'd do! Those two laborers—maybe they could help him. "Gentlemen," Daniel shouted, motioning at two men, one tall and wiry, one short and burly. They squeezed through the traffic to the buckboard. "Could one of you help me carry this trunk to the Industrial Bank and one of you bring up my buckboard? The bank is at Mulberry, just off Main Street. I'll pay you both two dollars now and another three when the job's done."

The two men looked at each other. If this fool was willing to pay them a week's wages for such a simple task, how could they refuse? "Let's see the money, sir," the tall one said.

Daniel removed his wallet from his coat and took out four dollars.

"I'll take your cart. Mack will help you with the trunk." The tall one stepped up on the buckboard and helped Daniel hoist the trunk down to Mack. As they were doing so, the blanket slipped off. "First National Bank," the tall one said. The two laborers looked at each other.

As Daniel jumped down from the buckboard, he hitched his coat behind a pistol in his waistband. He faced the two men so they could see his weapon and then let his coat slip back over it. He put the blanket over the trunk. He looked up at the tall man, who had grabbed the reins. "What's your name?"

"Bill Hobbs."

"Take it to the stables behind the bank, Bill. Come into the bank and I'll give you the rest of your money." Daniel didn't know if he'd see his horses and buckboard again, but it didn't matter. He reached down and grabbed a leather handle at one end of the trunk. "Let's go, Mack."

They hurried as fast as two men carrying a heavy trunk on crowded muddy streets could, bumping and shoving past people. By the time they reached the bank, Daniel's face and suit were soaked with sweat, rain, and mud. A line stretched out the door, down the steps, and onto Mulberry Street, but the doors were still open. He had planned to deliver the trunk to the back door of the bank, but had a sudden inspiration. He motioned for Mack to set the trunk on the ground, removed the blanket covering it, took his handkerchief from his coat, and wiped his face. It would inspire confidence among the people in the line if they saw an officer of the bank carrying in a trunk full of money, even if the officer was a soaking mess. They picked up the trunk and carried it by the line so customers could see the First National Bank insignia.

Keane emerged from his office and casually walked over to the door next to the tellers' counter, as if this bank-saving injection of money was merely a normal commercial deposit. Daniel and Mack lifted the trunk to a table behind the counter. Daniel paid Mack. Keane opened the trunk and started counting stacks of bills in full view of the customers. He made notations on a cash receipt register, took stacks of money and replenished the tellers' depleted cash drawers, including the drawers of the two tellers who were "out sick," and motioned towards Daniel. "We'll be tellers, today, Mr. Durand."

The trunk of money, the replenishment of the cash drawers, and Keane and Daniel working as tellers seemed to reassure the customers. They stayed in line, but there was less agitation in their gestures, less worry on their faces. They didn't know how perilously close the bank had come to shutting its doors, but they were going to get their money, and that was all that mattered. As if to confirm the swing in fortunes, the rain stopped, the sun beamed through the windows at the front of the bank, and Bill Hobbes came to receive his three dollars for delivering Daniel's buckboard. However, just as Daniel was starting to feel, for the first time since Saturday morning, that the bank was going to pull through, Jonathan Walter stepped to his window. Had his friend succumbed to the panic?

Jonathan smiled at him. "I'd like to deposit a thousand dollars, sir," he said, loudly enough for everyone in the bank to hear. He removed a stack of bills from his coat pocket and started counting them aloud. When he was through, he turned around to the people in line. "This is the strongest bank in Cleveland. It would be a travesty if a vicious lie threatened this bank. That lie was started by one of their competitors. I wouldn't feel safe putting my money in any other bank."

Daniel wanted to laugh. There was no way, after Jonathan's vote of confidence, that he was going to follow standard procedure and recount his deposit. He made out a receipt.

"That rumor," Jonathan whispered, "is coming from Haverford. His man Baldwin was even spreading it in church yesterday."

"That's like setting your neighbor's house on fire and hoping it doesn't spread to yours."

"Haverford has received a substantial investment and has ample funds to withstand a run on his bank," Jonathan whispered. "Good day to you, Mr. Durand," he said, his voice again loud and jovial. "Keep up the good work." He walked jauntily out of the bank.

By the end of day the line was gone, every customer had been paid, and the bank still had over $40,000 in cash. After he and Keane had finished the final tally and reconciliation, Daniel wandered back to his office. His stomach was starting to unknot, but it tightened again when he saw the telegram on his desk.

EXCUSE DELAY ALL TRADES NOT SETTLED UNTIL
THIS AM STOP VENTURE A SUCCESS STOP USED
BORROWED FUNDS STOP SOLD ORIG LONG POSITION
ONE SIXTY THREE SHORTED ONE SIXTY SIX COVERED
ONE FORTY ONE STOP YOUR SHARE INCLUDING
ORIG TWO THOUSAND IS EIGHT THOUSAND THREE
HUNDRED TWENTY TWO STOP WILL SEND DRAFT OR
DEPOSIT TO YOUR BANK STOP PLEASE ADVISE
WOODBURY

Daniel's laugh came from deep inside. His speculation with
Woodbury had been successful, and he and Keane had stopped a
run on their bank. He couldn't wait to tell Eleanor. Woodbury could
have cheated him and Daniel never would have known. Instead the
speculator had quadrupled Daniel's original stake. He could have
provided a far lower figure for the total profit and Daniel would
have been delighted. To Daniel's benefit he had augmented their
original stake with borrowed funds and included his share when
he went short. Neither course of action had been specified in the
original communication, but markets required quick decisions, and
Woodbury had made the correct ones.

"Yes, sir, Mr. Woodbury," Daniel said softly to himself. "We will
certainly pursue more 'business opportunities to our mutual advantage.'"

Chapter 12

The Auction

John D. Rockefeller was at least twenty years younger than most of the prominent businessmen assembled in the Standard Oil conference room. Yet he conducted himself with complete assurance and mastery, the equal of every one of them, automatically commanding their respect. When he rose from his chair at the head of the long, black walnut table, their conversation stopped and they moved forward in their chairs, eager to hear what the president of the country's largest oil refiner had to say.

Daniel and Rockefeller's brother, William, were the only men younger than Rockefeller. Daniel looked around the room, trying not to be overawed by the assemblage, trying to regard Cleveland's commercial and financial elite with the same cool detachment as Rockefeller while the oilman reviewed his company's results and financial performance.

"The documents in front of you," Rockefeller said, his voice precise, "are the stock subscriptions that will increase Standard Oil's capitalization from one million to two and a half million dollars. This is the first time that shares have been offered to outside investors. The board has authorized an additional million in capital, three-point-five million total."

Daniel and Keane exchanged quizzical glances. One million dollars had made Standard Oil one of the best-capitalized companies in the country. Why such a substantial increase?

"Present refining overcapacity drove prices down again last year. Standard Oil was profitable and paid a forty percent dividend." There was a general murmur of approval—paying 40 percent under even optimal conditions was no mean trick. "We find it necessary to consolidate the industry, eliminate wasteful overproduction, rationalize pricing, and restore normal profitability. We have allied with those railroads that share our interest in assured, regular shipments at a reasonable price and have thus secured advantageous rates."

He picked up a stack of papers, riffled through it, and set it back down on the table. "Gentlemen, Cleveland Trust holds your payments against receipt of counterparts of these subscriptions. If you would kindly sign the original agreement and the counterparts, we can end this meeting."

Daniel stared at the stack in front of him. After he signed, he would own five hundred shares of Standard Oil, $50,000 stated value. When he and Keane had received letters from Rockefeller, soliciting their investments, Daniel had walked into Keane's office, holding his letter.

"How much will the bank lend me to invest in Standard Oil?"

"You can borrow up to the amount you are putting up, secured by the stock."

"I'll draw up papers for a twenty-five-thousand-dollar loan."

Keane's eyes narrowed. "Fifty thousand is a lot of money, especially when half of it's borrowed. With the loans we've got out to Standard, you'll have a lot of eggs in the Rockefeller basket."

"I can think of no other basket in which I'd rather have my eggs. I don't want to be kicking myself in a few years for not pressing my bet when I had a chance."

"All right. Rockefeller is Rockefeller. I'm in for fifty thousand, too, without a loan."

Now Daniel and Keane took the pens from the inkwells in front of them and started working through the subscription documents. Although Daniel felt honored to be included with this first group of outside investors in Standard Oil, his stomach churned. His investment undoubtedly took a far higher percentage of his net worth than the investments of these other men took of theirs. He wouldn't start to relax until he received his first 40 percent dividend.

He looked over at Keane, still working through his stack. His grip was failing, slowing down his writing. The doctors said Keane was afflicted by some sort of progressive disease of his nerves, for which they could offer no cure. The progression had been slow, and the only overt symptoms were an occasional palsy in his hands or his feet and a diminution of strength in his hands. The tremors usually appeared in times of stress. Keane's first concern had been for his family. Daniel had assured him of his and Eleanor's support. Worried about public manifestations of his disease and their effect on the bank's business, Keane had considered not coming to this meeting, but his absence from such a momentous occasion would provoke unwelcome inquiries. He would risk a shaking hand. Keane painstakingly signed the counterparts with no tremors.

Rockefeller stood. "We'll affix corporate seals and return your counterparts and the papers from Cleveland Trust this week. Thank you very much, gentlemen."

Daniel and Keane left the four-story brick building that housed Standard Oil's offices, bundled in their overcoats, gloves, and hats. The day was overcast and cold, with a chill wind off Lake Erie, but it was not snowing as they walked back to the bank. "Beneath that bland-as-porridge little speech, Mr. Rockefeller has the railroads in his pocket, and he intends to take over the refining industry," Keane said. "He made it sound almost benevolent."

"Yes," Daniel said. "Out of the goodness of his heart he's going to undercut his competitors for the benefit of his customers, and from a spirit of largess he's going to let the railroads give him rock bottom rates, and when his competitors find that they can't match either his costs or his prices, he's going to offer generous terms, kindly allowing them an opportunity to pursue other endeavors or retirement. I thought Rockefeller was something special when we first met, but I didn't recognize how extraordinary he is. He gives no quarter, nor does he ask for it."

"You make it sound like war."

"I didn't mean to. War is stupid and destructive. Rockefeller's a builder, not a destroyer."

Keane chuckled. Rockefeller wasn't the only young man who neither gave nor asked for quarter. "Many see war as noble and business as base."

"They're wrong. Production, exchange, and seeking profits are noble endeavors."

Sometimes Daniel inspired confidence because he didn't seem to care whether he inspired anything at all. Keane loved business, but he would never match Daniel's passion. For him, business was a calling with an immutable code of honor; it was a mistress, demanding his best, but returning his love with wealth and, more importantly, with the joy of challenges mastered and of shaping the world to his purposes; ultimately, business was justice, that paramount function of man's gods—logic, integrity, innovation, and unstinting effort rewarded, and irrationality, fraud, imitation, and sloth cast into the abyss. Keane smiled. "I'll make a deal with you. If anyone is foolish enough to sell Standard shares in the open market, we'll buy all that we can and split them."

Daniel laughed. "Agreed. More eggs in the basket."

Laura Haverford held her namesake granddaughter in her arms, returning the six-month-old baby's smile. Little Laura had her father's looks—dark hair and eyes—while Will had Eleanor's blue eyes and golden hair. Mrs. Haverford glanced around the spacious sitting room at the two couches, several chairs, a piano, a big picture window framing the front yard and flower beds, and a fire crackling in the fireplace, warmth against the early autumn chill. It was a cozy, comfortable room.

"I didn't care for your first house, Eleanor, but I like this one. It's in a much better neighborhood. It's nice you have a maid and a nanny."

Eleanor, sitting in the couch opposite her mother, smiled and sipped her coffee. "Daniel's so proud of this house. You should have seen him when he gave me the piano for my birthday. It's as special to him as it is to me. He wants me to play every night."

"What does he like?"

"Beethoven and Chopin. Will likes the piano, too. The other day he got up on my lap and started banging the keys."

"Will, would you play the piano for Grandma?"

Will was playing with wooden animals in front of the fireplace. He stood and toddled to the piano. Eleanor sat on the bench and hoisted him onto her lap. He pounded on the keys. Laura detected a melody and a future virtuoso. "Oh, that's precious." She gazed at her daughter. "I used to worry about you so, but you're happier than I've ever seen you."

Eleanor nodded, setting Will down and returning to the couch. "There were a few times when I worried about whether we'd make it, but I married the right man."

Laura's brow furrowed as she thought of her own man. "It's getting late. I have to get home before Phillip arrives. I wish I could see you every day." She kissed little Laura, stood, and handed the swaddled baby to Eleanor. She spread her arms wide. "Come here, Will."

He toddled to her, kissing her on the cheek. "Don't go, Grandmom."

She loved the way he called her Grandmom. "I'll be back, Will, I promise." A tear ran down her cheek. She should be able to see Laura and Will every day. Damn Phillip! She hugged Will until he started to squirm and then she hugged his mother. "I'll see you next month, dear."

"Goodbye, Mother." Short farewells were best for both of them.

Eleanor walked her to the door. The coachman waited by the four-horse carriage. Laura turned for a last look at Daniel and Eleanor's house. A fine house, and Daniel was a fine man. The rubbish that people thought was important about other people. Daniel had character and integrity, and those were what mattered. More than money, more than family, more than social standing, more than all that nonsense her husband held so dear.

A week after Laura's visit with Eleanor, Phillip Haverford arrived home from work to find his wife in bed, suffering from a severe headache. She did not come down for dinner, but afterwards Haverford saw one of the maids carrying a bowl of soup on a silver tray up to her room. "Is Mrs. Haverford feeling well enough to eat?" he said.

"She said she'd like to try some soup," the maid said with a deferential smile.

"Good." He retired to the study and his cigars and brandy. As he did most evenings, he drank himself into a haze. He dozed, but at about midnight got up and stumbled to one of the guest rooms where he usually slept. He peered into the master bedroom, checking up on his wife. Good, she was asleep. Why was her mouth open like that? He tiptoed across the room until he was beside the bed. He couldn't hear her breathing and there was a strange, unpleasant smell. He bent over close to her. She didn't stir, and he still couldn't hear her breathe. He shook her.

"Wake up, Laura," he whispered. "Wake up, damn it, wake up!" He shook her harder, but there was no life in his wife's body. "Goddamn, she's dead!" he gasped. "She's dead!" He looked wildly around the bedroom, frightened, alone with death. "Steven!" he screamed. "Steven!"

The pounding on the door was loud, insistent, and unmindful that it was well past midnight. Startled, Daniel jumped from the bed, grabbed his revolver from the closet, threw a robe on over his nightclothes, and went downstairs. "Who is it?"

"Steven Haverford. I must see my sister."

Daniel opened the door on a disheveled man whose resemblance to his father gave him a start. "Come in. I'll get Eleanor." She was already coming down the stairs.

"Sister, you'd better sit down."

"What's wrong?" Eleanor sat on the sofa.

"It was all so sudden…she was in bed when we got home."

"Who, Steven? Mother?"

Steven nodded. "She's…she's…she's dead, Eleanor. Mother is dead." His voice trembled.

Eleanor slumped. "How…?" Her voice wavered. "When…?"

"Father found her tonight in bed. She had a bad headache. The doctor thinks something may have happened with a blood vessel in her head—a blockage, or it burst. She's dead."

Daniel rushed to the couch as Eleanor gasped repeatedly, seemingly unable to draw air. A series of small sobs dissolved into a long, low wail and she cried uncontrollably. Daniel's heart ached as he held her. Tears fell on his hands and sleeves and she trembled with pain. Steven Haverford's eyes glistened. He, his sister, and his mother were all victims of the same bastard.

"I have to go," Steven said.

Daniel showed him to the door and stepped outside with him. "Your father doesn't know you're here?"

"No. I left without saying a word. I have to get back before he notices I'm gone."

"Will you let us know about the funeral?"

"Uh…I'll try."

So Steven was unsure whether his father would allow Eleanor to attend her mother's funeral. The bastard! "Good night, Steven, I hope to hear from you soon."

Daniel paced the floor of the sitting room. He hadn't been this anxious since the run on the bank. Steven Haverford had not contacted him; he'd had to find out the details of the funeral from the newspaper. He had said nothing to Eleanor. She was upset and he hadn't wanted to add to her misery, but he had to tell her so that she wasn't caught unaware if they were prevented from entering the church. He went upstairs to the bedroom. Eleanor sat on the bed, appearing mournfully preoccupied, unable to move.

"Darling, I don't know if your father will allow us in the church. Your brother was unsure the other night. He said he'd let me know, but I've heard nothing."

Eleanor looked at him sadly. "Father wouldn't keep me from Mother's funeral."

"Very well." Daniel went to the children's rooms. They were both taking their afternoon naps. The nanny, Miss Taggert, would take care of them while Daniel and Eleanor went to the funeral. He went back downstairs to the sitting room to wait for Eleanor. She came down dressed in mourning black, her face covered by a black veil. Daniel lifted the veil, remembering with dolorous irony their wedding day, took her hands, and kissed her on the cheek.

She smiled wanly. "I'm glad the children are asleep. The veil would scare them."

Daniel had hired a four-horse coach for the occasion so he could sit with Eleanor and not be distracted by the duty of driving his buckboard. He held his wife's hand as they silently rode to the church. It was a fine early autumn day, the brilliant reds, oranges, and yellows of the turning leaves and the riotous chirping of birds incongruous with the sad occasion. Laura Haverford's funeral was well attended by top-drawer society in elegant conveyances, jamming the streets around the church. Tolling bells sounded their elegiac cadence.

The coach drew up to the front of the church. The coachman helped them out and they started up the long flight of stairs. Daniel felt a knifing tension when he saw Steven Haverford and Micah Baldwin, Phillip Haverford's right-hand man at the bank, coming down the stairs. Steven shook his head. They were not going to be allowed into the church.

"I'm sorry, Mr. Durand," Steven said. "Eleanor may pay her respects, but my father believes that it would be inappropriate for you to attend."

Under different circumstances Daniel would have laughed. Phillip Haverford had allowed the wife he made miserable one visit a month to the Durand home and Daniel had gotten to know her. They had liked each other, and nothing could have been more appropriate than paying his respects. He turned to Eleanor. "You go, darling. I'll wait out here."

Eleanor lifted her veil and stared at her brother, eyes blazing. "I'll not set foot in that church without Daniel. Mother will understand." Her voice was a white-hot dagger. She pointed at Steven. "But she'll not understand why you allowed Father to perpetrate this cruelty. Good day." She whirled and hurried down the steps to the coach, Daniel following.

When they were in the coach, Eleanor grasped Daniel's hand. "Thank you for offering to stay outside, but it would be more disrespectful to Mother to go to the funeral without you than to not go at all. Father tried to keep us apart and she fought him, in her own way. She wouldn't want her funeral to be an occasion that separated us." Her grip on Daniel's hand tightened and her face contorted with rage. "If Father had reconciled to our marriage, I could have forgiven his initial opposition. I could have forgiven him for allowing Mother to only see her grandchildren once a month. At least he let her see them. But I will never, ever forgive him for this." She burst into tears, burying her face in Daniel's chest.

"Later," he said, "we'll take Will and Laura and visit the gravesite."

George Woodbury lit Daniel's cigar, then his, leaned back in his chair, and contemplated the smoke he exhaled. They had returned to the same restaurant near Wall Street where they had first dined almost four years ago and again enjoyed fine steak dinners. "How long did you say you'd be in New York?" Woodbury said.

"The conference runs another day and I'll spend three more with my family."

"Well, I'm sorry that I couldn't get you to take a bigger share of the Union Pacific short. You could have made more money than you did."

"I'm as cynical about politics as they come. But it's still hard to believe it all fell apart—what was it, 1869?—only four years after all that gold spike nonsense."

"The railroad had plenty of help from its political benefactors. The papers said thirty-three million dollars went through Credit Mobilier into political pockets, but I'm hearing it was more like fifty."

"I was convinced the railroad would go bankrupt. I didn't take more because I had most of my money tied up in my bank and in another promising investment and I couldn't have accessed it if the bet went sour. You can never be sure about politicians. I worried about the government stepping in and making UP whole. There were rumors, and if it had happened, the stock would have taken off."

A waiter took their empty steins and brought back full ones. Daniel sipped the beer.

"What's your promising investment? Maybe I want in."

"Rockefeller."

"Rockefeller?"

"Rockefeller. Last year he offered stock for the first time to a small group of outside investors. I bought as much as I could."

"Your man is going to own the refinery business. I'd take a piece of that action if anybody offered stock, but it's never for sale." He looked around the tavern, crowded with stockbrokers and traders. "Let's go outside, I don't want anyone to hear what I'm about to say."

Daniel settled up with the waiter and they left the tavern. The night air was cool but not uncomfortable.

"I've got another railroad short for you," Woodbury said. "Even better than UP. Mr. Jay Cooke is going to get knocked off his pedestal."

"The financial savior of the Union? I've heard rumors. He's in over his head with the Northern Pacific?"

"Big time. The NP makes the UP look like a model of probity and sound business practice. It has the usual land grants and the usual gaggle of politicians in its pockets. It has Jay Cooke peddling its paper. What it doesn't have is anybody who knows anything about railroading. The president was just fired for corruption."

"It must have been especially egregious for anyone to notice."

Woodbury smiled. "Last year a section of track sank into a lake. Cooke's advertisements make it sound like half of Europe and North America has moved to Duluth and points west and is panting for this second transcontinental railroad, but buffaloes outnumber people a thousand to one—it'll be years before there's enough freight to generate profits. The NP is bleeding a million a month and Cooke can't sell bonds fast enough to keep it going. They're paying workers in scrip. Cooke's selling 7.3 percent paper at full price to widows, orphans, and flimflammed Europeans, but money doesn't lie and right now I can buy the same bonds at a 10 percent discount. I'm not interested in buying—I want to sell now and buy back later, at a much lower price. The NP's going bankrupt, just like the UP."

"How much do you want to sell short?"

"Half a million dollars. The bonds are cockroaches—lots of 'em and hard to get rid of. We can sell half a million in the high eighties. You don't have to put up any money, but you're liable for interest payments at 7.3 percent on two hundred fifty thousand until the bonds default."

"Eighteen thousand two-fifty a year."

"Aren't you the dandy? When the NP goes bankrupt, we'll buy the bonds back for pennies on the dollar. At twenty cents we'd make about two hundred thousand apiece. If by some miracle they found a savior, the bonds—at worst—would go to full value, par. You'd lose around thirty thousand plus the interest you pay out. There's only one group of fools we'd have to worry about, the politicians, and they're not going to be there this time. Not after the UP. People are madder than Hades about throwing their taxes away on railroads. They won't give Cooke a dime."

"How long do you think before things fall apart?"

"I'd be surprised if he makes it to the end of the year—eight months."

"Why is anyone bidding for the bonds?"

"Cooke. The man has had a halo since he sold all those bonds for the Union in the war. He's got a fifty-room mansion in Philadelphia and a monopoly on government bond sales, and when he says Northern's bonds are money good, people believe him. I've seen it before—markets turn and yesterday's heroes become today's scoundrels. When Northern goes under, they'll be burning Cooke in effigy."

Daniel puffed his cigar. Woodbury had all the cards against the other side's very weak hand. There was nothing quite like the sensation he felt when confronted with a potentially lucrative speculation, an intoxicating mixture of euphoria and anxious tension. It was time to place a bet—a big bet. "Count me in. I'll give Baker at First

National special instructions allowing you to draw against my account, if necessary."

"Baker's your banker?"

"Yes, he's a good man"

"So I've heard. I know markets and my business has grown, but I need someone with your skills, Daniel—organizing, good with numbers, good at evaluating men and their businesses—as a partner. If you ever want to move to New York..."

"You said the same thing the last time. I won't say it'll never happen. Who knows?"

The conference was finally over. Daniel put the finishing touches on his copious notes as the hotel ballroom emptied. It had been a tedious but necessary conclave on the increasingly intricate task of efficiently clearing checks among banks. The New York bankers, whose banks cleared the most checks, had gotten together and were dictating procedures to their brethren in the hinterlands. Daniel felt tired and drained. He could have sent Galloway or Breedlove to this conference, but it was the perfect excuse for a trip to New York. He had longed to return, but the trip served a more important purpose. He had brought Eleanor, to help her shake the melancholy that had gripped her through the ferocious Cleveland winter.

"Mr. Durand?"

Daniel looked up. The speaker was Micah Baldwin, vice president of the Commerce Bank of Cleveland, Phillip Haverford's bank, who with Steven Haverford had confronted Daniel and Eleanor on the steps of the church at Laura Haverford's funeral. Baldwin was tall and slender, with thinning black hair slicked straight back from his high, wide forehead, the upside-down base of his triangular face, his pointed chin and wisp of a goatee the apex. The thick lenses of his wire-framed glasses magnified his bulging, dark eyes, the eyes of an insect. His skin was stretched tight over his prominent cheekbones and the lines of his narrow face. His finely tailored, black suit emphasized his slender frame. Baldwin had been a partner in the law firm handling the Commerce Bank's legal affairs. When Keane and Daniel quit, Baldwin joined the bank as Keane's replacement. He had a reputation as a shrewd negotiator and master of detail. Daniel had seen Baldwin during the conference, but this approach surprised him.

"Yes?" Daniel said.

"Could we talk?"

Daniel felt as a creature in a forest does when it hears a twig snap. Every nerve in his body jumped to full alert. "Sure."

They went into a café and sat at a table by a window. New Yorkers crowded the streets outside, hurrying home. They both ordered coffee.

Baldwin said nothing as they waited for their coffee, crossing his legs, gazing out the window at the noisy throng. When the waiter set his coffee before him, he spooned a cube of sugar from a bowl and dropped it in the cup. He stirred, slowly and deliberately, then sipped his coffee.

"Members of my profession have been justifiably impugned for verbosity, Mr. Durand," he said, his voice sonorous. "I'll come right to the point. Is your bank for sale?"

Daniel sipped his coffee, giving himself time to think. Baldwin wouldn't ask such a question without authorization from Haverford. Did they know about Keane's illness? Did they know how successful the Industrial Bank had been? Or about its equity holdings in a variety of thriving enterprises? Or about Daniel and Keane's ties to Rockefeller and Standard Oil? How profitable was Haverford's bank, and did it have the wherewithal to buy the Industrial Bank? He stared at Baldwin's impassive face. He would get no information there. The one thing he now knew was that Haverford wanted to buy his and Keane's bank. He had an inspiration.

"Is yours?"

Baldwin's insect eyes widened. "I suppose there's not an asset in this world that's not for sale at the right price, but our interest would be in purchasing the Industrial Bank. You and Keane have done an admirable job and our price would recognize your efforts."

"We're not for sale, but if you think Cleveland isn't big enough for our two banks, I'm sure we'd have an interest in buying the Commerce Bank."

Baldwin smiled. "There's a problem of biting off more than one can chew. Are you sure, Mr. Durand, that your refusal to consider a sale is motivated purely by economic logic and not by animosity toward Mr. Haverford? Your marriage to his daughter left bitter feelings on both sides, but Mr. Haverford is willing to set that aside and make an offer for your bank. Shouldn't you consider that offer in the same spirit? Shouldn't you consult with Mr. Keane?"

Daniel stared at Baldwin. His unctuous manner and honeyed baritone gift-wrapped his condescension, but it was there under the ribbon and tissue. Expressing anger in either business or poker was an unaffordable luxury. If you were unsure of your cards after the initial deal, you didn't fold or raise; you called the bet and saw what the next card brought. "Mr. Baldwin, I won't dismiss the idea out of hand, but neither should you preclude the possibility of a transaction running the other way. Perhaps we can pursue further discussions back in Cleveland."

"I'll look forward to the opportunity, Mr. Durand." He removed a gold watch from his vest and glanced at it. "I'm afraid I have to meet an associate for dinner. It was a pleasure meeting you." His coffee unfinished, he stood and extended his hand.

"Likewise." Baldwin's handshake wasn't even a grip, merely a fleeting pressing of his palm. The attorney turned and exited to the street. Daniel caught a glimpse of him through the window before he disappeared into the crowd. Daniel wanted to find a restroom, to wash his hands.

The one-horse carriage maneuvered through the busy streets of New York until it pulled up before an opulent, three-story, brick and brownstone building with a sign in gold that read *Delmonico's* above dark, burnished doors. White marble steps, flanked by white marble pillars with Corinthian capitals, led up to the entrance, framed by a classical cornice.

"I've heard of Delmonico's, Daniel, it's famous!" Eleanor said, excited, as Daniel paid the driver. He took her hand and led her up the steps as two doormen held open the doors.

Eleanor gasped. She had never seen anything as grand as the dining room at Delmonico's. Huge crystal chandeliers hung overhead, throwing gay light on the multitude of wealthy diners, the women resplendent in their plumage and jewels, the men in their tailcoats. Sparkling light reflected off of every surface—the jewelry, the china, the crystal goblets, wineglasses, and champagne flutes, the silverware, the elegant coffee and tea services, the starched white linen of tablecloths, napkins, and waiters' uniforms, and the inlaid floor.

A maître d'hôtel led them to a choice table. Eleanor was used to men whose salaciousness overcame their breeding and she ignored the male heads that turned in her direction. She was not used to seeing other women staring at her husband, however, and she slid her arm in his. They sat down and she clasped his hand. "Daniel, this is fabulous."

"George Woodbury made the arrangements; he knows Lorenzo Delmonico. There are four Delmonico's. The locals call this one the Citadel."

"Daniel, did you notice what I'm wearing?"

He smiled. The strand of pearls around her neck was a recent birthday present.

Their waiter, a darkly handsome man with Mediterranean features, approached their table and placed a massive volume in front of Eleanor and two in front of Daniel. "Our bill of fare," the waiter said, with a trace of a French accent. "And our wines." He pointed to the larger volume. "Our cellar contains more than sixteen thousand bottles, but if I may, I would recommend the Chateau Margaux. We have a particularly excellent vintage."

"Certainly." The waiter left and Daniel opened the listing. "I've never seen anything like this, dear," he laughed. "It must be forty or fifty pages, in English and French. How do you decide what to eat?" Page after page listed beef, game, poultry, fish, shellfish, fruit and vegetable dishes, appetizers, main courses, salads, side dishes, and desserts, each featuring its own robust price. How could one establishment serve such a bewildering variety of foods? "What's an artichoke?"

"It's like a big flower. You bite off the end of the leaves. The hearts are delicious."

"Here's a salad with hearts of artichoke and crab. I'll try that."

Eleanor was delighted at his adventurousness. "I've had chateaubriand. It's an excellent cut of beef, and it's usually served to two people. Would you want to try that?"

"Sure."

They made their way, eventually deciding on a feast unlike any-thing either of them had ever had. Daniel ordered, the waiter poured the wine, and they soon settled into a fabulous repast. Each dish, artfully arranged on fine china, was presented with a flourish as the waiter removed its gleaming metal, bell-shaped cover. Eleanor knew her corset would cinch extra tight the next morning, but she couldn't resist. Although most of the courses were unfamiliar to Daniel, he matched her bite for bite. However, he had ordered oysters on the half shell. He looked suspiciously at the slimy, blobby mollusks. "People eat these?"

Eleanor nodded, smiling. Daniel squeezed lemon over one. With a tiny silver fork, he speared the oyster and slid it into his mouth. Unappreciative of its distinct texture, his face contorted and his eyes scrunched. "Why?" he gasped and took a long gulp from his water goblet.

For the first time in many months, Eleanor laughed uncontrol-lably. Daniel joined her, unmindful of the stares from other patrons. Every effort to stop evoked more mirth. For several minutes they laughed. Tears rolled down Eleanor's cheeks. Just thinking of the look on Daniel's face when he ate the oyster sent her into fresh par-oxysms. Finally her attack subsided into occasional giggles. "Well," she said, gasping, "it's said that they're an aphrodisiac."

"I'll forego this particular aphrodisiac."

"You don't need one, dearest." She took his hand across the table. As the waiter removed the uneaten oysters, they laughed again.

The feast continued for several more courses. Finally the waiter said to Daniel, "Dessert, sir?"

Daniel smiled. "Bring us your choice for the best dessert and some coffee, please."

Eleanor stared at her husband's face. She loved its honed angular-ity and the dark intensity of his eyes. They were the frontispiece of his mind. That mind had taken him to the top of Cleveland's banking world, but it was voracious, requiring new challenges.

"Daniel, you belong in New York. You can put the pieces of the puzzle together as well as I; indeed, you probably already have. What if Mr. Keane gets worse and can't work at the bank? You have a man here in New York who is capable and trustworthy and wants to go into business with you. Now somebody wants to pay a good price for the bank."

"Yes, but—"

"Yes, but that somebody happens to be my father. Daniel, you've told me, more than once, that 'business is business.'"

He nodded at his own words coming back to him.

"You've also said, 'There's a price for everything.' If Father and this Mr. Baldwin are willing to pay a handsome price, why not sell to them? We both think that business conditions are going to get more difficult. Why not get out at the top? If you've hurt Father's business and he wants you out of the way, perhaps he'll overpay." Her expression hardened. "Just make sure you get cash—up front."

"But what about the men at the bank? They wouldn't want to work for your father."

"Daniel, you've made your men the highest paid bank employees in Cleveland because they're the best and you didn't want them hired away. You've built a great bank, but you're going to need new challenges. You can't continue in a job you've outgrown just because other men like working for you. They're good and they'll find other positions."

"What about you? Could you leave Cleveland?"

She smiled feebly, feeling a touch of the recent melancholia. "Daniel, what's left for me in Cleveland? You and the children are my only family now. I'd miss the Keanes and Constance and

Jonathan, but I'm ready for a change. I like the pace of New York, the excitement."

"Sell to your father," he said, shaking his head.

"You don't have to make a decision tonight, dearest, but think about it."

The waiter set two covered plates before them. "Voilà!" he exclaimed, uncovering first Eleanor's and then Daniel's plate. "This is an *omelette à la norvégienne*. Our sumptuous ice cream, encased in meringue, then baked. It's our most popular dessert. It's said to have been served by Thomas Jefferson in the White House. Enjoy!"

Eleanor tasted the warm, airy billows and the frozen treat within, savoring the contrast. It was delicious, and despite feeling only fifteen minutes ago that she couldn't eat another bite, she made short work of it. Daniel did as well, and they settled back to enjoy their coffee.

"Darling," Daniel said with a playful smile, "you're wearing the same shade of blue you wore the night of your father's party, the night I was first smitten."

There were times when she could not read his mind. This was not one of them. "You know, my love, when we get back, we have that big suite, and Miss Taggert and the children will be fast asleep."

"Yes, they will be."

Keane sat with his hands folded on his desk, contemplating what he had heard, his face giving no clue to his thoughts. Finally he let out a long, audible breath.

"Eleanor's right, Daniel."

"You'd sell the bank to Haverford?"

"At the right price. You might find running this bank without me interesting, for a while. But industrial enterprises and railroads are spanning the country, while the banking laws will limit the bank's growth. Even with national charters, banks are going to remain local businesses. Abby said it when she got to know you—you were meant for bigger and better things."

"Why do you say I would be running the bank without you?"

There was a long silence before Keane spoke. "The doctors now say my shaking palsy is Parkinson's disease, a degenerative brain disease with no cure. If they're correct, it will get progressively worse. At some point, I won't be able to work."

And at some further point he would die? "Mr. Keane..." Daniel stammered. "I'm sorry. I don't know what to say. Does Abigail know?"

"Yes. Aside from what this will do to her and the children, the worst part of what's happened is you and the bank. I dreaded telling you. Our bank has been a singular experience for me, Daniel. Not to be able to work..." Keane's voice trailed off.

Daniel wiped his eyes and stared at Keane. He wanted to reach out, put a consoling hand on Keane's shoulder, and offer his sympathy. Keane's face remained implacably stern. He would not accept the pity from anyone else that he refused to grant himself. Sickness and death, like life, were to be faced with dignity. This was courage that matched anything Daniel had seen during the war. "Then we sell the bank?"

"We sell the bank's tangible assets. We can never sell the bank."

"What do you mean?"

"All profit, all wealth, has one source." Keane pointed at his head. "The mind. Haverford can buy our tangible assets, but he can't buy our minds. He can't buy the industriousness of a Farnsworth, the diligence of a Galloway, or the imagination of a Durand. This bank is the people that comprise it. It walks out the door every night. Our people work on their own terms and Haverford will soon find that his terms are not theirs. He should have learned his lesson from you and me, but apparently he hasn't. He thinks that acquiring a strong competitor and assuming its assets will make his bank more profitable. It reminds me of stories about ancient warriors who thought they acquired their enemy's strength when they killed and ate them."

"So Eleanor will be right—almost by definition, her father will overpay. Because he'll think he's buying something that can't be bought: our bank. I'd never thought of it that way. Then the question becomes, how do we extract top dollar from him?"

"By making him think we want to buy his bank. Your reaction to Micah Baldwin was astute. We should be hearing from him shortly. I have a plan. We're going to skin 'em alive!"

Daniel smiled weakly, wishing he could share Keane's bravado.

The boy felt his bedmate trembling next to him. Clomp...clomp... the older one was moving across the room. His long, bony fingers ripped the blanket away from the boy's grasp. He barely opened one eye, just enough to see the tall figure in the dark robe, his face hidden in the cowl.

"Only the innocent sleep," he hissed through his few remaining teeth.

The boy trembled uncontrollably, from both fear and the frigid winter night.

"Get up, evil boy."

He felt the bony fingers tighten on the back of his neck. He couldn't resist the sinewy force of the arm pulling him from the bed. He stumbled as his feet touched the floor, cold through his thin, hole-riddled socks. The grip tightened around his neck, lifting and pushing him to the door.

The shorter one was waiting, his face also hidden by his cowl. "Satan's child!" he hissed.

"Daniel, wake up."

Eleanor was gently shaking him, waking him from his recurring dream.

"Wake up, dearest. You were having a bad dream. You're upset about Mr. Keane."

Through the summer of 1873, a series of letters between the Industrial and Commerce Banks detailed the framework for a meeting in early August. Daniel was allowed to inspect the Commerce Bank's books and Baldwin conducted a similar inspection of the Industrial Bank's ledgers. By Daniel's estimate, based on tangible assets and liabilities, the values of the banks were roughly equal. He took another trip to New York to plan his venture with George Woodbury.

Keane's tremors were increasingly frequent and severe. He ventured out only to go to the bank. As he and Daniel plotted strategy, they worried that he might have an attack during the negotiations— stressful situations exacerbated his condition. They decided that Daniel would do most of the talking and Keane would keep his hands, particularly susceptible to the tremors, under the table. There was nothing else they could do. Keane had to be at the meeting.

Daniel and Keane arrived early at the agreed-upon neutral site, the Cleveland Savings Bank, whose president knew both Haverford and Keane. Keane didn't want Haverford and Baldwin to see that his gait had slowed and he walked erratically. The bank had a conference room with a smaller adjoining room. They entered the conference room, stuffy and warmer than the late summer heat outside. They sat at one end of a long, gleaming maple table, the end farthest away from the adjoining room, and spread out their papers. Daniel hoped that Haverford and Baldwin would use that room when either side had to confer privately, so that Keane wouldn't have to stand and walk.

Haverford and Baldwin entered about ten minutes later and the four men exchanged handshakes and greetings. Daniel again noted with distaste Baldwin's flaccid handshake. Presumably because of his legal training and the animosity between the other men, Baldwin took it upon himself to act as the meeting's moderator. "Gentlemen, each party has expressed a desire to purchase the other party's bank. Commerce Bank will commence the bidding. All offers to purchase must be in cash, payable within thirty days. The bidding will continue until one party agrees to sell its bank to the other party at the stated offer. If a party refuses to sell at the stated offer, it must submit a higher offer for the other bank, by at least twenty-five thousand."

Haverford looked tired. He had gained weight over the years. Several chins rested above his tie and collar. He cleared his throat. "Mr. Keane, Mr. Durand, we are prepared to offer one hundred seventy-five thousand for the Industrial Bank."

Daniel and Keane kept their faces expressionless. "Gentlemen, if we could discuss your offer," Daniel said. Haverford and Baldwin left the conference room to the adjoining room.

"It's a low bid," Keane said. "After what Baldwin said to you in New York about wanting to pay us a good price, I'm surprised. I suppose we should counter in kind, maybe offer two hundred thousand for Commerce Bank. If that's the way things go, it will be a long afternoon."

Daniel stared at Keane. Had he ever played poker? Had he ever watched a hand? A desultory counteroffer wouldn't suit their purposes at all. "I don't think that's the right move. Let's flush them out. We decided Commerce Bank was worth somewhere in the neighborhood of four hundred thousand. Let's double their offer—three hundred fifty thousand. That'll show them that we're serious about wanting to buy their bank and we're not going to give ours away."

"What if they're trying to do to us what we're trying to do to them? This is going to be your bank, Daniel, so it's your decision. If they sold to us at that price, could you make it work?"

Daniel rubbed his chin with his hand. Could he make it work? It would be a stretch, and he might have to keep Baldwin on for a while, but Commerce Bank had some interesting loans, commercial relationships, and depositors, all of which could be mined for increased business. There were undoubtedly opportunities at Commerce Bank that Haverford was too inept to exploit. "Yes, I can make it work." He knocked on the door of the adjoining room and the two men reentered the conference room. They sat at their places.

"Mr. Haverford, Mr. Baldwin, we will offer three hundred fifty thousand for the Commerce Bank," Keane said.

Baldwin's eyes widened, and Haverford sat straighter in his chair. They did not hide their reactions, and those reactions were exactly what Daniel had hoped they would be.

"Gentlemen," Baldwin said, "if you'll excuse us." They went back to the adjoining room.

"What do you think they'll do?" Keane whispered.

"Now that they know we're serious, they'll come back with a serious offer—three seventy-five or four hundred thousand."

When Baldwin and Haverford finally reappeared, neither one bothered to sit down. "Gentlemen," Haverford said, "we'll offer four hundred fifty thousand for your bank."

"You flushed them out, Daniel," Keane whispered after Baldwin and Haverford left. "Four hundred fifty thousand dollars is a pretty full price for our bank. That's over a hundred fifty thousand and re-tirement for me, about a hundred thousand and a good stake for your business in New York for you, and the Gottmans, Rockefeller, and our other shareholders will be happy."

"They gave away their game, Mr. Keane. It's what we thought all along. They came back too high—they want to buy, not sell. They'll go higher. I say we come back with a five-hundred-thousand-dollar offer."

"Daniel, there is no way on God's green earth that Haverford's bank is worth five hundred thousand. Could we even line up the financing? Would Baker lend us more than he's agreed to already? Or Rockefeller? If not, you're bluffing with money you don't have."

"It wouldn't be the first time. They want our bank, Mr. Keane. Baldwin approached me in New York. They raised our ample first offer by one hundred thousand dollars, not by the twenty-five or fifty thousand they should have. They want our bank. It's not about money with Haverford, it's about pride."

Mr. Keane's foot started to move up and down in an involun-tary tapping motion and he swayed in his seat as if he were having trouble keeping his balance. "This is my retirement, my medical care. You'll have to find the money for this offer and you'll have to cash me out, too."

"I know."

There was a long silence. "You know what you're doing Daniel."

Daniel again summoned Baldwin and Haverford.

"Five hundred thousand," Keane said dryly as they sat down. Haverford appeared annoyed and Baldwin looked askance. They quickly returned to the small room.

They were gone a long time. Each minute took a terrible toll on Keane. His hands trembled. A line of sweat beads formed on his upper lip and his swaying became more pronounced. He closed his eyes and remained silent. Daniel felt responsible for the cruel tricks Keane's body was playing on him. Four hundred fifty thousand dollars would have been a fine price. Why had he wanted more? Bulls made money; bears made money; pigs made nothing. Daniel stood and paced. It seemed hotter in the room than when they had arrived and he could feel rivulets under his arms and down his back. Perhaps Baldwin and Haverford weren't poker players, but they knew something about letting the other guy sweat. What the hell was going on in that room?

Finally Haverford opened the door and he and Baldwin returned to the table. Daniel glanced anxiously at Keane, who fortunately was between tremors. There was a long silence before Baldwin cleared his throat. Daniel felt a knifing pain through his stomach—Haverford had announced their previous offers. Why was Baldwin speaking?

"Gentlemen." The sonorous voice hung in the hot, humid, still air. "We will offer five hundred fifty thousand for the Industrial Bank." His tone was unmistakable—this would be their final offer.

"Gentlemen," Keane said, "you just bought yourselves a bank."

When Daniel entered his house early that evening, Eleanor came rushing down the stairs. "What happened?" she said, excited.

"We did it."

"How much?"

"A little over one hundred twenty-five thousand dollars."

She frowned. "That doesn't sound that good. I thought you'd get more for the bank."

Daniel smiled. "Oh, for the bank? One hundred twenty-five thousand is just my share. We got five-fifty for the bank."

Her eyes widened and she whooped. Daniel had never heard a woman whoop before. Indeed, he hadn't heard anything like it since the war. "You skinned him!"

Chapter 13

The Depression

Will bounced around the platform, unable to stand still. All other excitements for the four-year-old towhead with the winning smile paled in comparison to the railroad. "This is my second train ride to New York. Jimmy has never even been on a train, Papa."

"He'll get his chance someday," Daniel said, wiping Will's face and then his own with his handkerchief. It was impossible to avoid collecting a layer of soot when traveling by train. They stood on the platform of the station while the locomotive took on water and coal. Daniel buttoned his overcoat against the evening's chill. He took Will's hand and walked across the platform to a newsstand. He hadn't read a paper since they left Cleveland. When he saw the headline he felt like jumping out of his shoes.

JAY COOKE BANKRUPT!

The poker player had trained himself to remain impassive when he won a big pot. Although the headlines told him he had just won one of his biggest, he kept his exultation in check. He bought two papers and tore through the stories. Cooke hadn't been able to keep the Northern Pacific on track. The financial hero of the Union had closed the doors to his offices in New York and Philadelphia. The millions of dollars of bonds issued to finance the Northern Pacific were so much wallpaper. The collapse of the railroad had precipitated a stock market crash and bank runs. Daniel checked the date on the papers—September 19, 1873. These were this morning's editions and Cooke had closed his doors the previous day.

Daniel pulled Will across the platform and they returned to their car, where Eleanor sat holding Laura in her arms. He held up one of the papers. "The bonds are virtually worthless."

Her eyes widened. "That's what you were betting on, isn't it? Haven't you made a lot—"

"Yes, we have." He put his finger to his lips. "There were millions of dollars of those bonds issued. There may be people, perhaps on this very car, who bet the other way."

Eleanor nodded.

"Papa, when do we get to New York?" Will said.

"Three or four hours. It'll be late when we get in."

"Can we ride up an elevator tomorrow, Papa? Can we?"

"We just did."

"Daniel, wake up!"

"Huh? What is it?" Daniel opened his eyes. It was dark, not yet morning. Where was he? Oh yes, a suite at the Astor House. Why was Eleanor waking him? "What?"

"The money. Where does the money go?"

"What money?"

"From your speculation with Mr. Woodbury. What does he do with the money?"

"When the trades settle, he deposits the proceeds at the First National Bank."

"That's where you deposited the money from the sale of Industrial Bank?"

"Yes, why?"

"The newspapers said that several banks that were involved with Mr. Cooke were subjected to runs. What if that's happening at the First National?"

"Darling, the First National is the most solid, conservative bank in New York. I can't imagine that George Baker would have anything to do with Jay Cooke."

"Daniel, the Industrial Bank was the most solid, conservative bank in Cleveland, and you had a run. You can't say for sure that it won't happen at the First National."

He felt his stomach plunge to somewhere near his ankles. Of course she was right. How could he be such a fool, such a complete idiot, as to put all their money in one bank? Any bank, even the soundest, could suffer a run. He slid out of bed and began pacing, barely noticing the cold hardwood floor on his bare feet. "I have an appointment this morning with Mr. Baker. Now, we shouldn't panic. The First National is very well run. Woodbury might not have covered our short of the Northern Pacific bonds yet, or the trades might not have settled."

Eleanor turned on a lamp and Daniel could see concern and doubt etched on her face. However, she refrained from saying anything more. She sat up in the bed and let him pace in tortured silence until daybreak. The sun poked through the window and Daniel bathed, shaved, and dressed.

"Shall I wake the children for breakfast?" Eleanor asked as Daniel, standing before a mirror, tied his black cravat around his high, stiff collar.

Daniel glanced at his pocket watch. "I won't have time to eat breakfast." He didn't say that his roiled stomach wouldn't allow him to eat. "Let the children sleep, they got to bed late."

Time crawled. As Eleanor put on her many layers of undergarments and then a stylish green dress, Daniel sat in one of the room's two chairs, jumped up, paced, sat back down, then jumped up again. Eleanor, clearly concerned, occasionally tried to say something soothing. He nodded, conscious she had spoken but not comprehending what she had said, and continued his routine until she gave up talking. He never confided his pain, troubles, or doubts to anyone, displaying them about as frequently as he displayed his money. Feelings, especially those he considered maudlin, weak, peevish, or just plain irrational, remained hidden away in a rarely opened emotional vault. Eleanor understood this about him and allowed him his silences, although she undoubtedly found them frustrating.

The stately elegance of the room's furnishings mocked him as he paced. He had spent more than a laborer made in two weeks to stay in a suite in one of New York's finest hotels, when a drastic reduction in his circumstances might be imminent. Idiot! Finally enough time elapsed—he could flee his gilded cage. "It's time for my appointment."

Eleanor kissed him lightly on the cheek. "Good luck."

Perhaps Daniel was only seeing his own wretched inner state in the faces of others, but it seemed as he stood in front of the Astor House that the passersby no longer wore the eager ambition he associated with the city. They looked tense and frightened, their gaits slower, their movements less purposeful, less confident. He hailed a hansom cab.

"Where to, sir?" the driver said. He was a stocky character in his mid-twenties, dressed in a long, rakish brown coat, green vest, and multihued tie, his foppish hat cocked jauntily askew.

"Ninety-four Broadway, just north of Wall Street—the First National Bank."

"The crowds, sir, I can't take you to the door. I'll go as far as I can, but the streets are packed—men looking for news, worried 'bout their money, trying to get it out. The stock market crashed yesterday. Lot of swells ain't as high and mighty as they thought last week."

Daniel nodded, hoping he was not in that group, and said no more. The cab continued south, its progress slowing as the streets became thick with other cabs and pedestrians. The cab finally had to stop. Daniel paid the driver, stepped onto the packed street, and merged into a noisy, swaying mass of frightened humanity. He heard random bits of conversation over the incessant shouting as he fought his way through the crowds.

"Ten, twelve firms closed yesterday after Fisk & Hatch, maybe more today."

"They might close the Stock Exchange. Too much margin, too much debt."

"Bank of Manhattan had a run. It'll close its doors today."

"Union Trust...anyone heard about Union Trust? Saw a big crowd there yesterday."

The closer Daniel got to the First National Bank, the slower his progress. He finally reached 94 Broadway, but a crowd bordering on anarchy was massed there, confirming his worst fears. Four armed guards at the door kept a semblance of order, allowing a few customers in at a time. Noting with savage irony that he might be the only one in this crowd who had been on both sides of a bank run, Daniel surveyed the mob. He had more money in this bank than they did, he was taller and stronger, and he had to know if his money was safe. Putting his head down and ignoring angry exclamations, he bulled his way to the front. "Excuse me, sir," he panted to one of the guards. "I have an appointment with the cashier, Mr. George Baker. I am Mr. Daniel Durand." He handed the guard his card.

The guard slipped through the door and returned in a few minutes. "Please come in, Mr. Durand." He escorted Daniel to an office with a sign on the door: *Mr. George Baker*.

Baker was not in his office and Daniel waited for twenty minutes before he entered. Absent was the serene imperturbability Daniel remembered from their first meeting. His bloodshot eyes, with purple circles underneath and drooping eyelids, suggested a dawn-to-dusk ordeal. Several buttons on his vest were unbuttoned, and his black tie hung sloppily off his wilted collar.

"Mr. Durand," he said, extending his hand. "So sorry to keep you waiting, but I'm sure, under the circumstances, you'll understand. How can I be of service to you?"

"I was going to inquire about setting up a line of credit for our new firm. However, given the circumstances, I'd first better inquire if a large deposit has been made for me recently."

"I just checked your account." He glanced at a slip of paper. "Per your usual arrangement with Mr. Woodbury, a deposit of $165,759.36 was made two days ago. The balance in your account is $282,855.92."

Daniel's heart jumped. Two hundred and eighty-two thousand— he was rich! Maybe. He tried not to sound anxious. "Can I make withdrawals in immediately available funds?"

Baker stared at Daniel. "That is the question of the day, is it not? The First National Bank had some dealings with Jay Cooke. Not his Philadelphia office, the source of his current difficulties, but the New York office. It has a little over two hundred thousand dollars of the bank's funds. Through an oversight, those funds were not segregated. At a meeting of the bank's officers this morning, we recognized them as impaired. However, we have no exposure to the Northern Pacific bonds."

Were there any other nasty surprises? "Do you have exposure to other firms that have gone bankrupt?"

"It would be impossible to be a Wall Street bank without dealing with Wall Street firms, although we've always insisted on a better grade of stock and bond collateral than most banks. Some of that collateral is not currently marketable, but we maintain higher than average reserves and liquid funds to handle the abnormal volume of withdrawals. Of course, you're not worried about anybody else's funds, you're concerned about your own."

Concerned? Worried sick.

Baker placed his hands flat on his desk. "With a Herculean effort, Mr. Durand, we could give you all your money, but it would strain our resources, perhaps to the breaking point. At our meeting of the bank officers, the president, Sam Thompson, proposed that we close the bank and wind up its affairs. His father, John Thompson, his brother Fred, and I rejected his proposal. We have the controlling block of shares. The Thompsons and I have every penny tied up in this bank. We will weather this storm. If I didn't believe that I wouldn't have voted against Sam Thompson's proposal. We can allow a withdrawal of twenty-five thousand, but I request your forbearance in withdrawing the rest of your funds until more normal conditions prevail."

Twenty-five thousand dollars—less than a tenth of what he had on deposit! He could take the twenty-five thousand and then, like Baker, hang on and hope. Or he could give in to his fears, demand all his money, and perhaps sound the death knell for the First National. Daniel took a deep breath, trying to calm his churning stomach, slow his racing heart, and restore order to his jumbled thoughts.

Baker had been straightforward with Daniel. He had been under no obligation to disclose that closing the bank had been considered, especially not to a large depositor concerned about the safety of his funds. He hadn't mentioned that First National had saved the Industrial Bank from its run four years ago. If Daniel withdrew all his money, he couldn't blame Baker and the Thompsons for thinking they had been subjected to churlish ingratitude, and for refusing to conduct further business with him. Once past the panic, that decision could cost Daniel in a big way—the Thompsons were one of New York's leading banking families. If his assessment of Baker was accurate, he was a man with whom a future association could be quite beneficial.

Daniel took another deep breath. "Send twenty-five thousand dollars to the Astor House."

Baker smiled, perhaps for the first time that morning. "At our meeting, Sam Thompson had an amusing witticism. After we decided not to close, he said, 'We've been cooked by the Cookes and baked by the Bakers.' You will not be baked by this Baker, Mr. Durand."

"No, I don't think I will."

"Thank you. I shall work assiduously to give you no cause to regret your decision." He stood and the two men shook hands. There was a knock on the door. "Come in."

A young clerk entered the office. "The Stock Exchange has been closed until further notice."

George Woodbury's office was apiece with his rumpled appearance. Stale cigar smoke lingered in the stagnant air. Woodbury lit a lamp and Daniel inspected the room. A desk and chair, two chests of drawers, a tall stool, and a bookshelf were buried under drifts of newspapers and documents. Stacks of paper covered most of the floor. Daniel remembered Keane's fastidiousness and wondered if he had made the right decision concerning his new partner. Through a soot-covered window he saw the red brickwork of another building. He tried to open the window to air out the room, but it was stuck shut.

Woodbury removed his overcoat and threw it in the general direction of a stand in the corner. "I'll have to clean things up a bit if we're going to use this office."

"Don't bother," Daniel said dryly. "I'll start looking for a new one. With all the bankrupt firms, space is cheap, but I want a partnership agreement. Do you have a pen and paper?"

"You are the proper banker, aren't you?" Woodbury rummaged through his desk drawers before finding the necessary items. He stacked papers on top of stacks on the floor to clear space on his desk.

Daniel sat in a creaky desk chair and drafted the partnership agreement. He kept the document, dated November 7, 1873, simple. The partnership would be known as Durand & Woodbury, an investment house. Unlike a bank, their business would be subject to almost no regulation and could lend and invest its capital without restriction. Woodbury would run the stock and bond trading operation, while Daniel would be the managing partner and develop investment and underwriting opportunities. Profits and losses would be split equally. Other partners would be invited in when appropriate. Stated capital of the firm would be...?

"I know we had talked about capitalizing at one hundred fifty thousand dollars," Daniel said, "but in view of the present situation, perhaps two hundred would be more appropriate."

"Can you get a hundred thousand from Baker?"

"Yes." The day after his meeting with Baker, Daniel had apprised Woodbury of the seemingly precarious state of his finances. Woodbury's reaction had surprised him—he had been unconcerned, saying that there was no way the First National would fail. Events subsequently confirmed Woodbury's judgment. It was for that judgment that Daniel would overlook its possessor's slovenly ways, but they had to get new quarters—with two separate offices.

"Two hundred thousand is fine by me," Woodbury said. "They reopened the stock market, but money is tight and hard times have arrived. Business will be tough and we should have abundant capital."

Daniel carefully signed and dated the one-page agreement and handed the pen to Woodbury, who scribbled an illegible signature. "Durand & Woodbury is now a partnership," Daniel said. He glanced at a yellowing document next to the agreement. "If you're going to clean, you might want to start with this. It's dated July 16, 1866." He handed it to Woodbury.

"Ah," Woodbury said, as if recalling some fond memory. "Prentice Iron Works. I made plenty of money off of that company and I still follow it. I can't throw this away."

"I see." Daniel had sat in Woodbury's office for as long as he could. "I'll take our agreement to the hotel and make you a copy."

Daniel stood with Eleanor at the bedroom window of a New York brownstone. A solitary carriage made its way along 52nd Street. The street was not yet as built up as the lower numbered streets, with their brownstones and Italianate mansions. Across the way was a small park with a walkway, benches, shrubbery, and trees. Eleanor seemed enchanted by the view and Daniel hoped that they had found, after weeks of searching, a house.

They inspected three smaller bedrooms on the third floor. When they reached the top floor, Daniel was almost sure that they had found their house. Some of the brownstones they had viewed were oppressively dark, squeezed in between identical structures, with small windows, only the lighting indoors providing any real illumination. Whoever had built this brownstone had clearly preferred sunlight—the rooms on the top floor had an abundance of large windows.

As they walked into a corner room with sweeping views both south and west, Daniel said, "This would be a perfect room for you. You've always wanted to set up a study for yourself. You could have a desk and bookshelves and there's still room for a sofa and table."

Eleanor smiled at his salesmanship. "I suppose your study would be in that other corner room, the one with the large fireplace?"

"An excellent suggestion! There are extra rooms for more children, if we're so blessed. That is, of course, if you like the house."

"I like the house. Where's Mr. Pettibone?"

The agent entered the room. Woodbury had said, "You'll detest the bugger, but he's the best residential property agent I know of." It had indeed proved impossible to like this pompous little man with the dapper suits, thin mustache, pince-nez spectacles, and pursed lips, but Pettibone seemed to know every fact about every piece of property on Manhattan.

"Is this one large enough to satisfy your requirements, Mr. and Mrs. Durand?"

"Yes," Daniel said. "How much?"

"Twenty-seven thousand. Now, I think that's high, but not exorbitant. You would certainly be within reason to offer in the low twenties, with the financial crisis and all."

Twenty-seven thousand! That was over three times what they had paid for their house in Cleveland. This house was bigger and New York was New York, but it was still a steep price, especially for a home with a lot only slightly larger than the house. Their house in

Cleveland had front and back yards; this one had only a backyard the size of a postage stamp. It was the highest price quoted for the houses at which they had looked, and it would take more money to furnish the place.

"You must realize that this district, from 30th Street through the 50s, between Third and Sixth Avenue, is the most desirable residential area in New York. It's an enclave. The historical pattern is for the better people to move north, while the southern precincts give way to the lower classes." Pettibone couldn't have said "lower classes" with more dripping disdain if he had been a member of the British nobility. "Not only is 52nd Street not as developed as the lower streets, but it affords a measure of protection against this continuous northern progression. It will be a decade or two before the masses reach you here." He smiled.

Daniel didn't—he had been one of "the masses" most of his life. "Why is the owner selling?"

"The present owner is an estate. The head of the household that lived here is deceased."

"Did he die recently?" Eleanor said.

"About a month ago. He committed suicide."

A shadow passed over Eleanor's face. "Here, in this house?"

"No. He shot himself in City Hall Park. He was a speculator, ruined in the crash."

There was a long, awkward silence. Finally Daniel spoke. "Darling, if this changes your feelings about the house…"

It was impossible to tell what she was thinking. She walked out of the room, down a hall, and stopped at the balustrade overlooking the stairway, looking around the house, apparently trying to make up her mind. "I've never been superstitious. What you just told us is a trifle discomfiting, Mr. Pettibone, but I can live with it. Let's make an offer on this house. Considering the suicide and the current financial situation, we should start low."

Reading the newspapers was a grim exercise that filled more of Daniel's days than he liked. Factories, transport companies, retailers, and financial concerns were closing their doors and sending workers into the ever-expanding army of the unemployed. There were too many such stories, their details sadly uniform. Someday there would be gold in those stories, opportunities to buy assets cheaply, but this depression, as the papers were calling it, was still gathering force. It was too early to scavenge. Securities' trading volume had shrunk to a small fraction of what it had been in the boom, and prices seemed to know only one direction. Dozens of banks and brokerages had closed. Daniel and Woodbury took turns informing the many job seekers who knocked on their door that they had no positions available.

They didn't have enough work for themselves, much less anyone else, but at least their firm had its capital and they both had other funds. The articles that had a particular pull for Daniel—reminding him of his own childhood—were those concerning the burgeoning multitude that had little or nothing at all. He read of families with twelve children, abandoned by fathers unable to provide for them and single mothers turning to prostitution, which every New York paper detailed in lurid exposés. The exposé industry was one of the few that boomed during these hard times. The scandalous state of the water, sanitation, and sewage systems; crime, filth, and disease-ridden tenements, housing two or three immigrant families per single tiny, airless room; saloon drinking and debauchery, boxing, gambling, and whoring; "blue" milk from diseased cows, living in close quarters next to distilleries, fed nothing but liquor byprod-ucts, swill, doctored with magnesia, chalk, and stale eggs, then fed to infants, killing them; the b'hoys, dangerous gangs of outlandishly dressed toughs, congregating in the Bowery, and the politicians, a far more dangerous gang of somberly dressed charlatans, congregat-ing in City Hall—all grist for New York's journalistic swarm.

As Daniel read a newspaper one afternoon, a name caught his attention, seemingly jumping off the page. He walked through the anteroom of Durand & Woodbury's new two-office suite. It was functionally decorated with a table, several nondescript chairs, a small writing desk, racks of files, and walls covered with pigeon-holes for documents and correspondence. He knocked on the closed door of Woodbury's office, heard Woodbury grunt, and entered.

Like Daniel, Woodbury liked to read, but his special love was fi-nancial and legal documents. When Woodbury returned to the office from the Curb, he buried his nose in a bond indenture, a prospectus, an article of incorporation, or a statement of accounts. There was an order to the seeming chaos of his partner's office, already buried in paper. He knew where everything was and seldom had trouble find-ing whatever he needed, even seemingly obscure scraps.

"There's an article about a state senator, Stanton Woodbury," Daniel said. "Any relation?"

Woodbury did not look up from the document he was reading and emitted a puff of smoke from his ever-present cigar. "My uncle, on my father's side."

"Do you know him?"

"Much better than either he or I would like."

"What do you mean?"

Woodbury put his document down and looked up at Daniel. "He's a lying, thieving piece of filth. My mother died when I was two. I'm an only child. My father died when I was twelve. He was a stock trader, a damn good one, but either he wasn't the best judge of character or he had a blind spot for his brother. He left me a substantial inheritance, which was kept in trust, with my uncle as the trustee. I went to live with him. He didn't treat me particularly well, but he gave me the same classical education that he gave his two sons. I enjoyed Latin and Greek, and planned to attend Columbia. I didn't know my uncle was looting my trust fund. By the time I was of age, there was nothing left. My uncle said it was because of bad investments—a lie, but how do you sue your uncle, especially when he's powerful and politically well connected?"

"Is that why you don't like politicians?"

"I hate any man who makes a career of getting others to like him. *Non nascuntur viri cives; excernuntur.*"

"My Latin's a little rusty."

"From Cicero: 'Politicians are not born; they're excreted.'"

"Ah, the classics."

"My uncle confirms my prejudice, but I didn't need his help to arrive at it. There's something else you might want to know about dear Uncle Stanton."

"What's that?"

"He's owned by Curtis Winfield, your friend Archer Winfield's father. Curtis pulls the financial strings for my uncle and a whole pack of political hyenas. Last year Curtis bought a seat in the New York Assembly for his second son, Harrison. Hates publicity—woe to the reporter who puts his name in the paper. For my money he's one of the most powerful men in New York—and one of the most vindictive. Count yourself lucky that you stole Mrs. Durand from Archer Winfield without any reprisals...so far."

"Didn't you worry about that when you signed on to do business with me?"

"I'd rather be in business with someone they don't like than someone they do."

Eleanor handed Daniel an unopened envelope and he could see from her expression that something was wrong. He stared at the name on the return address—Isaac Gottman, Abram's brother. A knot formed in his stomach and he felt an unsteadying, disconcerting sensation. He tore off the end of the envelope and withdrew a solitary sheet of paper.

March 30, 1874

Dear Mr. Durand,

> *I regret to inform you that my brother, Abram, died two nights ago.*

His worst fear confirmed. The old man was his father, a part of him. More than a father, really; Mr. Gottman, a private man, a loner, had chosen to rescue him from the streets, had allowed him into his life. He had seen something in Daniel, something Daniel didn't know he had. Will had seen it, too.

> *He had not been feeling well, but he continued working in the store almost until the end. He died in his sleep. His* levaye *was yesterday at Anshe Chesed.*

He didn't suffer; wouldn't suffer. Life, he'd said, was joy, not pain. Except that there was no way to escape the pain of his death.

> *Perhaps in this time of sorrow you can take some comfort knowing how fond Abram was of you and your family. He said*

more than once that the day you were married was one of the happiest of his life. He enjoyed his visits to your house with your family.

The children's only grandfather. Baby Laura, tugging on his beard as he held her. The time Will had snuck into the kitchen and eaten half a strudel Gottman had brought for dessert—the old man's playful mock anger. Eleanor laughing at his stories. The tears trickled down Daniel's face as he recalled the warm images of Gottman at their home.

Abram was a good man and brother. He offered his assistance to newcomers to the United States and Cleveland. Our family will miss him deeply. We pray the Kadish for his soul, that he may find eternal peace.

If anyone deserved eternal peace, it was Mr. Gottman. He had found peace during his life, and that was what Daniel would miss the most. The gentle wisdom, the way he could see another point of view, understand what someone else was feeling. The hand on Daniel's shoulder when he was distressed, angry, disappointed, saying without words: this too shall pass. His strength had been Daniel's foundation and now it was gone.

Sincerely,
Isaac Gottman

Daniel handed the letter to Eleanor. Isaac Gottman, of limited English proficiency, did not write this simple, eloquent note. It was one of his children, although Isaac probably told the writer what to say. Eleanor read it and started to sob.

What a strange twist that an orphaned street urchin—*yungatsh*—and an old Jew should forge such a bond. He took Eleanor in his arms.

Gottman had not found Daniel's dream to be a banker far-fetched; he had helped it grow. The thought ran through his mind: *I wouldn't be here without him.* That thought would be his father's memorial.

"Remember…" Eleanor sobbed, her voice muffled, her face buried in his chest. "Remember our wedding?" She sniffled. "I've never laughed so hard."

He kissed her on the forehead and she looked up at him. Seeing his tears fueled her outpouring and her weeping intensified. They stood in the entryway of their brownstone for a long time, locked in a quiet, consoling embrace.

Daniel stared at the letter on his desk, perplexed. It was from a job seeker. Unlike most such letters, it couldn't be dismissed with a terse rejection.

February 2, 1875

Dear Mr. Durand,

I am interested in banking and finance. I have achieved excellent marks in school and my strongest subjects are mathematics and English. My father has helped me learn bookkeeping and accounting. If you could use a man with my skills as a clerk or an order runner, I would be interested in talking with you about a job. Please let me know at your earliest convenience.

Respectfully,
Benjamin Keane

Benjamin Keane had to be around twenty-one-years old by now. Why had he only mentioned his father as an accounting tutor, and said nothing of his mother? It seemed odd that he had not even passed along a greeting. Did they know he had written to Daniel? Was the job situation in Cleveland so bleak that Benjamin, in desperation, had turned to his father's former business partner, or did Benjamin sincerely want to live in New York? Benjamin was a bright, resourceful lad. Daniel remembered how he had brought Eleanor's mother to their house for Will's birth, but before he could hire him, he wanted his questions answered. Someone who appeared to be right for a job was usually not if he sought it for the wrong reasons.

Daniel stepped into Woodbury's office and dropped the letter on his desk. Woodbury read it.

"Keane—that was your partner in Cleveland. This is his son?"

Daniel nodded.

"Well, he wrote his own letter, that says something for him. I don't like kids who hide behind their parents." He glanced around his office. "I guess I could use some help getting organized."

"That would be a full-time job right there, but we're not making any money."

"Clerks don't cost much and this depression isn't going to last forever. We need to notch up our efforts." He pointed at a newspaper on his desk. "The bankruptcy and foreclosure notices take up an entire section. Land, buildings, whole companies are selling for a fraction of what they sold for two years ago. We can't snatch the bargains if we don't know where they are. A clerk would free us up for more important things. Is Mr. Keane capable?"

"He's intelligent, and he's certainly intrepid." Daniel told Woodbury the story of Benjamin's ride for Laura Haverford.

Woodbury chuckled. "Sounds like our kind of man. Let's give him a trial."

"I need to get a few questions answered, but I'll send him a letter."

A month later, on a Saturday afternoon, Daniel stood at the recently opened Grand Central Depot, waiting for Benjamin Keane. No, Benjamin had replied to the questions in Daniel's letter, he was not coming to New York because he was unable to secure employment in Cleveland—he had an offer. His parents knew he had written to Daniel, they sent their best wishes, but had told him he would have to get a job through his own efforts. Daniel offered Benjamin a trial on terms similar to those Benjamin's father had once offered him.

Benjamin's train pulled into the station on time. Daniel remembered getting off the train in Cleveland twelve years ago, the war behind him, his future before him. He wondered if Benjamin felt the same exhilaration and ambition he had felt back then. There was no way to tell Benjamin what Daniel knew now—that he should cherish the excitement and tension, chase his dreams, take risks, and give it all he had, that it was the arduous journey that made the destination worthwhile. Those were lessons you learned from experience, on your own.

Daniel was impressed by the way Benjamin carried himself. Though he'd never been in the army, he walked like a soldier. The focused gaze, confident expression, determined set of his jaw, ramrod-straight posture, the effortless way he carried what was probably a heavy bag, and his long, even stride suggested the military. Would Daniel expect any less from the son of Thomas Keane? Daniel waved and Benjamin saw him, breaking into a smile. They shook hands.

"How was your train ride?"

"Fine, although I found it hard to sleep on the train. This is the first time I've been to New York. Thank you, Mr. Durand, for offering me this opportunity."

"With the economic situation, we're not as active as we'd like, but we'll have work for you. We're hoping things get better. How's your father?"

"He's in a wheelchair and has an attendant. You know him. He doesn't let it get him down."

It saddened Daniel that Keane was in a wheelchair. They caught up on news as they walked from the depot out to Lexington Avenue. The street was crowded with people, vendors, wagons, hacks, and hansom cabs.

"Benjamin, we have room at our house until you get settled."

Benjamin's brow furrowed. "No…no, sir. I'd like to find a place right away, so I have everything squared away by Monday. I made some inquiries of people Father knows in Cleveland who have lived in New York, so I know where to look."

Daniel suppressed a smile. "You will come by one night this week for dinner, after you get settled? Eleanor will be disappointed if you don't."

"Certainly, sir. Thank you."

"With the depression, there are thieves, rabble-rousers, and men looking for trouble, especially towards the southern part of Manhattan. Avoid that area, except the financial district." Daniel smiled. "Although there are some rough characters there, too."

Benjamin smiled. They shook hands again. Benjamin hailed a hansom cab, waved at Daniel, and climbed inside. Daniel watched it round a corner. Things had come full circle. He was the mentor of his mentor's son.

Durand & Woodbury detected the first hopeful portents of the end of the depression in 1878, almost five years after it began. The firm began buying assets at knockdown prices. The afternoon of a frigid day in March, Daniel stood in front of a squat commercial building that he had just bought at a foreclosure auction. It was the second commercial building he had bought that year. Barring catastrophe, the buildings would repay the partners' investments by the end of the following year. There were bargains and then there were gifts. They had United Trust and Savings, laden with an inventory of foreclosed properties, to thank for this gift.

Afternoon was giving way to evening. Daniel wouldn't return to the office. Despite the scattered patches of ice and snow on the ground, he decided to walk home. He buttoned up his overcoat and slipped on his gloves. Eleanor liked to cook and had become quite proficient. With winter's physical inactivity, Daniel's trousers cinched uncomfortably around his waist. He saw no reason to satisfy the caricature of the Wall Street fat cat—he liked a leaner look. Brisk walks were a defense to big meals and rich desserts, relieved tension, and helped him sleep better.

As he rounded a corner, he saw a group congregated in front of a fire and a speaker, standing above them on a flight of stairs, shouting and wildly gesticulating. With the depression, rabble-rousers were as plentiful as cockroaches in a dirty kitchen. Daniel had once warned Benjamin Keane about the ugly mood that pervaded the city's poorest districts. He would take his own advice, stick to the opposite side of the street, and hurry by the group.

"Why should some be allowed to live in aristocratic splendor?" The rabble-rouser had wild dark hair and a long black beard flecked with gray and white. He wore a shabby black coat that extended below his knees. "Your misery is planned by the rich and powerful, to keep you oppressed and downtrodden! Their wealth is the wealth of the people! Look at what capitalism has produced! Seize the factories and establish a government of benevolence!"

Daniel had almost passed the group.

"You there! Top Hat, why do you scurry by?"

He ignored the speaker and kept walking. He had gone a couple of blocks when the street came to a dead end at the back of a warehouse. He turned around and saw that the rabble-rouser and his crowd had followed him. He stepped back until he was against the warehouse.

"Looks like you don't know this part of the city too well," a man jeered.

"No, I don't," he said, trying to keep his voice steady.

"That's a mighty fancy coat and hat you got there, mister," another man said.

"Thank you."

"Top Hat," said the rabble-rouser, advancing toward him. "What's your profession?" He had only about half his teeth and they were yellow and crooked. His eyes were mostly red, with deep purple circles underneath.

"I'm a banker."

"A banker, well, well." The rabble-rouser stroked his beard. "A filthy parasite. If we beat you, stole everything you have, and left you here to die, the world would be a better place for it." Several of the men laughed.

Daniel took a deep breath. He put his hand under his coat. Some of the men looked alarmed, probably afraid he would withdraw a gun. He took out his wallet. With his other hand, he took out his coin purse from his front trouser pocket. He held them both out without saying anything.

There was a long silence as they stared at him and he stared at them. They were mostly laborers; he could tell from their clothes—tattered, but not rags. He knew these men. He had grown up with them, worked with them, sweated with them, drunk beer with them, complained about low wages with them, passed the hat when one of them had a sick child or a new baby, and had buried them when they broke down after lives of hard labor. Now he was betting that he knew one thing about these men that the rabble-rouser didn't.

"You can take my money," Daniel said.

A murmur ran through the group, but everyone remained where they were. "Why doesn't anyone take the money?" Daniel looked at a tall, muscular man with unusually wide shoulders who stood in front of him. "Times are hard, there are mouths to feed and rents to pay." He looked at the rabble-rouser. "If they took my money, who would be the parasites?

"They would be taking what it is rightfully theirs."

"They don't seem to think so." Daniel turned and pointed at a short, wiry man with a bushy mustache. "I just told you to take my money. Why didn't you?"

"I don't want your damn money!"

"You want to work and make your own way, as every honest man must. You won't take my money when I offer it and you won't steal it from me." Daniel pointed at the rabble-rouser. "If he held a gun to me, took my money, and offered it to you, would you take it?"

"No!"

"There's nothing benevolent about taking money from me, even if he plans to give it to you, no matter how much you might need it. If a man earns his money honestly, isn't there only one person who has the right to it?"

"The man who earned it," said the man with the wide shoulders.

"You don't earn your money, you fancy-arse banker," shouted a man with a long scar running from his chin to just below his eye. "You profit from other men's sweat and hard work." There were shouts of agreement from some of the other men, including the rabble-rouser.

"Yes, I'm a bank—"

"Your filthy breed will be the first to go!" the rabble-rouser cackled.

"Silence!" a man said sternly. The crowd turned towards him. He was a big man with a barrel chest and massive arms, with dark black hair streaked with gray. He was older than most of the others. Judging by the way they grew quiet, he commanded their respect. "We listened to you—now let us hear what this man has to say." He spoke with a heavy German accent.

The men turned towards Daniel.

"Yes, I'm a banker now. Before that, I was a soldier, until I was wounded at Vicksburg. Before that, I shoveled coal on the docks in Cleveland. I was a hod carrier for a master mason, I cleaned slag in a foundry, and I've done many other jobs. I started when I was eight years old, cleaning stables. I've worked hard, for my own benefit, and I'm damn proud of every penny I've earned, from stable boy to banker. Now people trust me with their money. I have to find solid businesses in which to invest at a time when many businesses are going bankrupt. It's not easy work." Daniel turned towards the rabble-rouser. "What do you do, Mr. Revolutionary?"

"I work for the replacement of present arrangements with a more progressive system."

"So you don't work an honest job. What do you mean by a more progressive system?"

"Everyone's needs would be provided for."

"Who would provide? If a man can't keep what he earns, he's a slave to any incompetent who produces nothing at all, who claims he's needy."

"I'm talking about simple human compassion."

"No, you're not, you humbug. If you give your money to some-one else, freely and on your own terms, that's compassion. If you take it from me and give it to someone else, that's theft."

"I don't use terms like slave and theft."

"Of course not. Our careers have one thing in common, Mr. Revolutionary—we've both shoveled our share of horseshit!"

The men laughed and Daniel knew he had won them over. "Good day, gentlemen. My wife and children are waiting for me." He took a step forward and the man with the large shoulders moved out of his way. Other men stepped aside, and Daniel walked through the group.

He walked quickly, trying to keep warm, and thought about get-ting a hansom cab or a hack. His exercise program could wait a day and he didn't want Eleanor to worry. A few blocks from where the crowd had first gathered, Daniel turned up a narrow street to get to one of the big avenues where there would be more people and a bet-ter chance of hailing a ride. He hadn't gone far when two big men, wearing formless hats and tattered dark coats, jostled their way in front of him. Their pace slowed until they came to a dead stop in front of a crooked alley. Daniel realized what was happening just before the pipe hit the back of his head.

White flashes came from the inside of his head. He staggered and his knees buckled. One of the men punched him below his eye. He tasted blood in his mouth. The man behind him was grabbing him un-der the arms and dragging him into the alley. Everything went black.

When he regained consciousness, he felt cold, nauseated, and disoriented. He crawled several yards, made it to his feet, felt dizzy, and immediately vomited. He leaned against a wall and felt the back of his head. There was a large bump, painful to touch, and blood matted his hair. He ran his hand along the side of his swollen face. He was so cold. His overcoat was gone! And his billfold and pocket watch! His hat wasn't on his head and he didn't see it on the ground.

The only thing the thieves had left him was his wedding band, perhaps because it was difficult to take off. Lucky they hadn't cut off his finger! He staggered back to the street and walked unsteadily north to a wider street. He hailed a hack.

"Excuse me, but I've been robbed and have no money. If you'll take me to my house on 52nd Street, I'll pay you double your usual fare."

The driver stared down at him disdainfully. "You gambled away your money and your coat. You don't live on 52nd Street any more than I do." He pulled away from Daniel.

Daniel trudged several blocks. His head ached and he still felt sick to his stomach.

"Sir, would you be needing a ride?" The voice was an Irish brogue.

Daniel turned to see the speaker—a stocky youth with a pug nose and a black patch over one eye, driving a hansom.

"I've been robbed and I can't pay you until we get to my house. I'll pay you double."

The youth stared at his swollen face. "Get in. Where to?"

"Fifty-second Street," Daniel settled into the seat.

"This isn't the place for a gentleman, sir," the driver said as his horse plodded up the street. "Especially after dark. The b'hoys roam, and with times hard, anyone with money is in danger." He tapped the black patch. "Lost my eye in a fight." He chuckled. "The other sot lost a lot more. No, sir—you come to these parts, you bring your gun."

Daniel didn't feel like talking, so for the next twenty minutes he listened to a merry monologue about Peter Pinch, No Name Doogan, the Blade, Little Nick, and other colorfully named hoodlums and their dangerous gangs; the street hazard of drunken Irishmen and Germans, maimed or killed when they lurched in front of carriages; the Shylock Jews, their usurious interest and brutal methods of collecting debts; and the "hoors," some of them just girls, driven to their profession by destitution and mouths to feed.

"Breaks your heart to see the little colleens," he said, as his hansom turned onto 52nd Street.

"Here we are," Daniel said. "I'll get your money."

The driver whistled at the four-story brownstone. Daniel climbed down from the cab and went to the front door, which opened before he could remove his key from his pocket.

"Daniel!" Eleanor gasped, staring at his face. "What happened?"

"I was beaten and robbed."

She threw an arm around his shoulders. "At least you're alive… and standing. I was so worried." She stepped away from him. "Why is the driver waiting?"

"Because he hasn't been paid. My money was stolen. Would you get some?"

Eleanor fetched some money. Daniel took it to the driver. "Thank you."

"Thank you, sir. Have the missus get something cold on your face."

Daniel entered the house and Eleanor rushed to him. She took his hand and led him to a sofa in the sitting room. A maid, a young, homely woman named Sarah, brought in a towel filled with ice chips and gave it to Eleanor. "This will sting," Eleanor said as she pressed it to Daniel's swollen cheek.

He motioned to the back of his head and Eleanor touched it. "That's nasty, and there's blood. Sarah, get more ice and a wet towel." When Sarah returned, Eleanor cleaned his wound and held an ice-filled towel to the back of his head.

Struggling to talk, his words distorted by his swollen tongue and the ice pack on his face, Daniel gave Eleanor an account of the day's misadventures.

"Maybe you didn't win that crowd over as completely as you thought, dear," Eleanor said.

"I don't think the fellows who robbed me were part of that group. The way they reacted—they gave me some hope. And now this…" His voice trailed off. "Are the children in bed?"

Eleanor stared at him and took his hand. "Darling, it's not weakness to acknowledge that you get discouraged or frustrated or anxious or angry. It's weakness to pretend you don't. No one gets through this life without feeling that way sometimes. Be honest with yourself. If you're not, you won't be honest with others, including me."

Daniel remained silent for a few minutes. He sighed. "Eleanor, this just seems like such a humiliation. I thought we would come to New York and I would conquer the world, like Cleveland. Instead we get a depression and my business hasn't made any money, and now this." He pointed to his swollen face and shook his head. "I do get discouraged…and worried. I've never worked so hard and had so little to show for it. Maybe coming to New York was a mistake. Maybe this city is too much for me."

"You've said that one's doing well just to survive these panics and depressions, to be in a position to take advantage of better times." She pressed the ice to the back of his head. "Anybody can get robbed. These were small time hoodlums. You vanquished the much bigger thief. If his ilk get what they want, they'll be more dangerous and ruinous than any street gang."

It hurt when he tried to smile. "Thanks, dearest."

Woodbury let out a long low whistle when Daniel entered the office the next day. "What happened to you?"

"I walked through the wrong neighborhood. I got robbed and the thieves gave me something to remember them by. Knocked me on the back of the head, too."

Woodbury walked up to Daniel and inspected his face. "There are four distinct colors here, Durand. You'll have this for at least a month. Were you carrying a gun?"

Daniel shook his head.

"You won't make that mistake again. It must hurt like the devil."

"It does, but not as bad as last night. That has to have been the lowest point since I've come to New York. I told Eleanor that maybe it was time to pack it in."

Daniel saw Woodbury and Benjamin smile at each other, as if they were sharing a private joke. "That does it, Keane!" Woodbury exclaimed, and Benjamin chuckled.

"That does what?"

"I told Ben last week that the tallest trees in the forest are always the last to fall. I said that if Durand ever talked about giving up, this depression would be just about over. Call me a stark, raving bull! Today, Ben and I are going over to the Stock Exchange to buy a seat for the illustrious firm of Durand & Woodbury."

"Because I got hit on the head and robbed and got discouraged?"

"That's part of it—you, who wouldn't let a locomotive or an army regiment or a forty-day flood get in your way, saying you're discouraged. And that 99.9 percent of the country feels the same way. And that President Hayes supports restoring the gold standard and a sound currency will draw European capital back that left the country after the panic. Yes, sir, Mr. Durand, this country is about to boom and we're going to make more money than we can count, spend, or give away!"

Chapter 14

Mr. Hill's Railroad

Daniel left work on a cold winter night. Snow swirled from the tops of buildings, blown by a slashing wind off the East River. He made his way to the stable in the back of the building.

The hostler, Mr. Palos, handed Daniel the reins of his four-in-one. "Beg your pardon, sir." Palos was an immigrant from Eastern Europe and spoke with a thick accent. A harried Ellis Island clerk had probably shortened his real last name from some jaw-breaking combination of too many consonants and too few vowels. He was short, thick, and grizzled, in his early fifties, his close-cropped hair already gray. His clothes were old, but not tattered or greasy.

"What is it, Mr. Palos?"

"I have four boys," he said, hesitantly. "I couldn't send them to school. Two work in factory, one at the docks. My youngest, Michael, he's different, very smart boy. He teach himself to read and write. He speak English better than anyone in the family. He work loading lumber, but not use his brain. To make money in America, use your brain. You, Mr. Durand—your brain make you rich. So maybe you want to talk to Michael. He can help you, very smart boy."

"How old is he?"

"Sixteen."

"Have him come by my office tomorrow afternoon."

The next day, Michael Palos entered the offices of Durand & Woodbury, eyes wide, obviously nervous. He was tall, skinny, and gawky, with an unruly mop of brown hair and a face that was all angles. He wore a cheap black suit that was too small, perhaps borrowed from a shorter older brother. Daniel escorted him to his office. Palos sat in a chair in front of Daniel's desk.

"Your father said you might want to work here at Durand & Woodbury."

"Ah, yes, sir. I mean, my father thinks I could work here."

"What do you think?"

"Um, I'm not sure, sir. I mean, I'm not sure what kind of work you do here, sir."

"We're a financial firm, Michael. We raise money for individuals and companies, and we're a dealer in stocks and bonds. Do you know what those are?"

"They're like bank notes?"

"A bank note is a claim against a bank. Stocks and bonds are claims against the company or government that issues them." Daniel's brow furrowed. While ignorance about the world of finance could be remedied, he had to find a way to gauge Palos's intelligence. He remembered his interview with Mr. Keane for his first job and the "test" Keane had given him. Shuffling through a stack of papers on his desk, he found a lease. He handed it to Palos. "Read through this and tell me what it says."

"Yes, sir." Palos began to read.

Daniel was surprised when Palos said, "I'm done, Mr. Durand." It hadn't taken him very long.

"What's your understanding of that document?"

"It's a lease, sir, between Dorchester Dry Goods, the tenant, and your company, as the landlord. It runs for an initial period of thirty-six months at a rent of one hundred twenty dollars a month. At the end of that time, your company has the right to change the rent, and the tenant has the right to either continue renting at the new rent or end the lease."

"Aren't lawyers amazing? It took them four pages to say what you just told me in ten seconds. I'll offer you a two-week trial without pay. You'll work with Mr. Keane. If, at the end of two weeks, we decide that Durand & Woodbury can use your services, we'll offer you a clerkship at thirty-five per month, and we'll pay you for the two weeks as well. Is that fair?"

"Yes, sir. It's more than fair, sir. Thank you very much, sir." They shook hands and Daniel took the candidate to meet Benjamin Keane.

Palos had his two-week trial, and Keane's assessment of Palos said something about both men. "He's smart, Mr. Durand, very smart. He's a bit shy around the other men, but he's able to navigate documents and financial statements. It's more than that. He unravels a whole mass of detail in a short time. I slogged through things when I first started, but he gets right to the heart of a matter. I think you ought to offer him a position."

Michael Palos became Durand & Woodbury's newest clerk. The hostler's son raised a few eyebrows among the other clerks, but none of them were foolish enough to express their doubts. The men whose names were on the door said, "We don't care where you started from, only where you're going and how you get there."

Daniel walked the short distance from the carriage house up 52nd Street to his brownstone. When the Durand family had moved in nine years ago, its four-story expanse had seemed too big, with several rooms empty. However, bounty at work had been matched by bounty at home. Daniel and Eleanor now had five children, with a sixth on the way. The house was filled with the family and its servants. Daniel thought it cozy, but wealthy New Yorkers would have advised him to take up residence in something larger, a mansion. Memories of the depression still lingered, though, and deeper down, ineradicable memories of his childhood poverty did not permit, and might never permit, Daniel to consider that housing option.

Daniel opened the front door and awaited his usual reception. Eight-year-old Alexander was first, as he was most nights. The best adjective for the boy was solid—he was of medium height and stocky build, with Daniel's dark hair and eyes but not his angular face. It was round, cherubic when he was an infant. Painfully earnest, he rarely smiled, rarely frowned, learned new things slowly, but mastered them once he did, and was still young enough to worship his father. Following him was his sister Laura, two years older, of the same dark hair and eyes, strikingly pretty. Of all his children, she had a temperament most like Daniel's. Quiet and serious, she seldom joked, but she enjoyed wit in others, which sealed a special bond with her mother. Constance, almost three years old, brought up the rear.

It was a matter of chance whether either Will or Tommy would join Alexander, Laura, and Constance. Thirteen-year-old Will seemed embarrassed about greeting his father at the door. Five-year-old Tommy, his name a memorial to Thomas Keane, would be there if the course of his perpetual motion happened to career him by the door when his father opened it. Tommy's energy would power a locomotive, if only it could be extracted in a usable form. The earliest talker of the Durand children, he wore both his parents to exhaustion, peppering them with questions—when he slowed down long enough to address them.

Tonight's greeting party was only the regulars—Laura, Alexander, and Constance, followed by Eleanor. Daniel wrapped Laura and Alexander in his arms and kissed them on their foreheads, then picked up Constance. Alexander took his coat and hat and hung them on the stand in the corner of the entryway. Laura smiled the shy, sly smile that was reserved for him. However, when he looked up at Eleanor, he sensed trouble.

He kissed her on the cheek. "What's wrong?"

"Mr. Arnold caught Will cheating on a mathematics test. He sent a note for you to sign."

Daniel's jaw tightened. Will's education was a sore point. He was smart, but an average, indifferent student. Daniel had worked twelve-hour days in his youth and then fought his weariness to read the books recommended to him by Abram Gottman. Why didn't his son cherish his opportunity to learn, free from the necessity of having to earn a living? His fury rapidly building, he went upstairs and found a pocketknife. Eleanor and the children stared at him when he came back downstairs.

"What are you going to do?" Eleanor said.

"I'm going to cut a switch. Will has to be punished."

Eleanor took a deep breath but said nothing. The children's eyes widened. Daniel left the house and walked to the little park across the street. The moon shone weakly through the fog and clouds. He found a sapling with low-hanging branches and bent one towards the tree until it snapped. He cut the branch and stripped it, making a long, smooth switch.

He stared at his handiwork. He had endured the switch as a boy… and the cane, the whip, the coarse hair shirt, and dousing in icy cold water. The men in dark robes hated him more than they did any of the other boys. He didn't know why. They would stand over him as he writhed in pain, smiling. The more he cried, the more they smiled.

Don't go too deep! Down below, molten emotions seethed; memories were dangerous. At a certain depth there was no return.

He slapped his palm with his switch. What the hell was he doing? He sweet-talked his horses and fed them treats; his son he was going to switch. Abram Gottman and Thomas Keane had never raised their voices, rest their souls. Daniel dropped his stick and walked across the street. Eleanor stood in the entryway, looking worried.

"I'm going to talk with him," he said. He went upstairs to Will's room on the third floor and knocked on the door.

"Come in," Will said, his voice subdued.

Daniel entered the room. In the corner stood a plain desk and chair. Two bookcases overflowed with titles like *Ivanhoe* and *King Arthur*. Will loved the Middle Ages. His bed was under the window so he could look at the stars before he went to sleep. On the wall opposite were a fireplace and a shelf for toys.

Will sat on his bed. He had his mother's blond hair, blue eyes and striking good looks. Academically unmotivated, he was clever in the ways of people. Child or adult, male or female, everyone seemed to want to be his friend. Women gushed when he smiled, pompous old men found themselves charmed as he pretended to listen to discourses on subjects in which he had no interest, and friends and siblings made him the leader of their games and escapades. He stared at his father, eyes wide, expression grave.

"What happened today at school?"

"Mr. Arnold caught me cheating on a test, sir. I copied off another boy's test."

"Why did you cheat?"

"Because I wasn't prepared, sir."

It was the right tack—straightforward acknowledgement of the truth. The "sirs" were a little much, though.

"Did the other boy know you were copying?"

"Yes."

"Did he get in trouble?"

"No, sir. I don't squeal on my friends."

Daniel sat beside Will on the bed. "The most important thing I can teach you is to be your own man. If you can't stand alone, you won't have the strength to be honest and do the right thing. To be your own man, you have to do your own work. There are no short-cuts. You'll only be cheating yourself. Do you understand that?"

Will nodded.

"There'll be no trotter races for you this spring or Central Park, not until June when school is out." Will and his friends loved to watch wealthy New Yorkers race their trotters on Harlem Lane. Another favorite amusement was to watch carriages promenade through Central Park. "If your work doesn't improve, or if there are any other problems at school, then you won't see any of that this summer, either."

"Yes, sir."

He seemed to take his punishment like a man. "Good." Daniel stood and walked to the door. "If you're a clerk, you can't look over the shoulder of the fellow next to you and get the right answer. You have to do your own work."

"Who says I'm ever going to be a clerk?"

He should have used the switch. Here was a glimpse into his son's soul. "You're right," Daniel said acidly. "You'd have to work up to a clerkship and you might not get promoted that far. Your edu-cation is a privilege. If you scorn that privilege, that's your choice, but if you think you're going to put on airs and live like royalty without effort or merit, you'd better think again. If you're so damn smart, let's see it in your schoolwork, or you can earn your keep. I'll find you a job that'll make clerking seem like a walk in the park. Do I make myself clear?"

Eyes wide, Will nodded.

Daniel left the room.

Everything about the suite of offices, from the elegant anteroom where Daniel and Benjamin Keane had waited for their appointment, to the high-toned lilt of the secretary, Mr. Dandridge, to the antique furnishings of John S. Kennedy's office, bespoke aristocratic refinement. There was no clutter of objects vulgarly displayed to advertise wealth, but rather a lifetime of selective acquisition to the highest standards of good taste. Kennedy, in his sixties, was a handsome, dignified man who fit the patrician environment.

A week ago, Woodbury had dropped a financial report on Daniel's desk. "This is from the St. Paul, Minneapolis & Manitoba Railway, formerly the St. Paul & Pacific. We should check it out—perhaps you can take a trip to Minnesota."

"Another railroad short?"

"Not this time. James Hill, the chief operating officer, is a damn good businessman. He untangled this railroad from a group of Dutch investors and a bankruptcy. He's building a northern line from Minnesota to the Pacific—no subsidies or land grants from the government. Taking his time, building up the region slowly. Sounds like he knows how to build a profitable railroad and we should get in on it. He's got a man here in New York, Kennedy—the best railroad finance man in the city."

Now Daniel and Benjamin Keane sat in chairs before Kennedy's antique desk.

"How can I help you, gentlemen?" Kennedy said.

"We're interested in the St. Paul, Minneapolis & Manitoba Railway," Daniel said. "Mr. Hill's plans sound promising. He'll need investors and capital. I'd like to see his line under construction and talk with him, preferably this summer, if that's possible."

"It's possible, but allow me a word of caution about Mr. Hill. He's like one of his locomotives. If you're with him, you're in for a grand ride. Get in his way and you'll never know what hit you."

"We went through the bankruptcy materials," Keane said. "What a convoluted case. Mr. Hill must be extraordinarily tenacious and completely indifferent to the opposition he faced."

Kennedy smiled in a way that suggested he was including Daniel and Keane in a private joke. "You mean he's stubborn as a mule and doesn't care a whit what anybody thinks of him?"

"Yes," Keane said.

"Quite true, especially about his indifference to opposition. Another caution: he despises lawyers, politicians, and speculators. You'll have to overcome that last prejudice." Kennedy took a stack of papers from a bureau behind his desk. "These are the railroad's most recent statements. You'll form you own opinion about its financial condition. However, I should tell you a few facts that are not in those statements. Mr. Hill has been successful, but he's never undertaken a project of this magnitude. He's lent a substantial portion of his wealth to the railroad and borrowed heavily. Two of the railroad's founding associates are Canadian investors—Mr. Stephen and Mr. Smith. They are also involved with the Canadian Pacific railroad, which will, when completed, become a competitor with the St. Paul. Rumor has it that they intend to withdraw their support, that a split among the principals of the railroad is imminent."

"My partner, Mr. Woodbury, has mentioned that rumor," Daniel said.

"They're baseless, circulated by speculators conducting a bear raid, shorting our stock to drive down its price. One gossip sheet has been especially scurrilous. Mr. Hill and I, as substantial share-holders, would dearly love to see those short sellers get what they deserve. If you decide to invest with us, Mr. Durand, perhaps we can call on your firm to help us give them a twist."

Daniel smiled. Woodbury already liked what he saw of the St. Paul. If Daniel came back from Minnesota with an enthusiastic re-port, turning the tables on the short sellers would be an assignment he'd relish. "That's certainly a possibility, Mr. Kennedy."

Daniel and Keane left Kennedy's offices. Driving his four-in-one home, Daniel had an inspiration: Will could accompany him to Minnesota. He would be out of school and he had never lost his love of trains and travel. It would be good for both father and son to spend time together. He had been working so hard that he hadn't seen enough of any of his children, and he especially needed to spend time with Will.

Ghastly screams filled the brownstone, reminding Daniel of the cries of wounded soldiers. These weren't the screams of soldiers, they were Eleanor's. Something was dangerously wrong with the birth of their sixth child. Daniel's forebodings had begun that morn-ing, when Eleanor's pains came a month ahead of schedule. He had sent for the doctor and Eleanor's friend Amanda Parsons, and sent the children to Parsons' house to play with her children, attended by nannies.

Amanda came down the stairs, looking worried, and rushed through the sitting room, where Daniel sat on a couch. She went into the kitchen and returned carrying a pot of steaming water with several towels over her shoulders.

"Amanda, what's hap—?"

"Not now." She stepped quickly up the stairs, water sloshing out of the pot.

There was another scream. Daniel jumped up and started up the stairs. He wanted to pound on the bedroom door, see what was happening inside, but Doctor Madden had told him to stay away. He went to his study. A crystal decanter of brandy and a humidor sat on a rosewood bureau. He drank brandy perhaps once a decade. His hands shook as he poured the amber liqueur into a snifter. After several broken matches he lit a cigar. He took an ample sip of his brandy and puffed furiously on his cigar, clenching his teeth on it until he tasted the acrid tobacco juice. He paced, absently running a hand through his hair. Cigar ashes fell on the carpet.

The brandy and cigar were no help; his insides were broken shards of glass. What if something happened to Eleanor? He had always found the pain that she had to bear in childbirth unnerving, but these screams impaled his heart, his gut, his soul. What if the worst happened? Even oblique consideration of that possibility ripped something out of him.

Another long scream froze Daniel in mid-step. He rushed from the study to the birthing room, but fighting himself, stopped. Doctor Madden had two nurses and Amanda Parsons. Daniel's anxious presence would make it harder for them to do their jobs. He returned to his study, gulped his brandy, and paced, teeth clenched on his cigar. His tie and collar felt as if they were choking him. He untied the tie, opened the collar, and dropped them on the sofa.

The screams stopped. Ominous. All Daniel heard was the sound of his own steps and the floor creaking. He repeatedly checked his pocket watch—fifteen, twenty-five, forty, fifty-five minutes. No screams. What if? What if? What if? Doctor Madden stood in the doorway.

"What's wrong? Eleanor, what's happened to Eleanor?"

"She'll probably be fine, but it's too early to tell about your new baby son, Mr. Durand."

"Probably? What happened?"

"The birth was not going well. Mrs. Durand was in tremendous pain and the baby was not making progress. You heard the screams. A surgical procedure, a cesarean section, was necessary. I gave her chloroform, an anesthetic that put her to sleep. Then I made incisions into her abdomen and uterus. The baby was alive but struggling—he was in an odd position and had become entangled in the umbilical cord. He's doing better now, but it's too early to tell about him because he's a month premature and the cord was wrapped around his neck. He was partially strangled. There could be brain damage and it might not be apparent for several years."

"And Eleanor?"

"She's still unconscious, but most women recover from this procedure. However, you won't be having any more children."

Daniel nodded. If childbirth posed a danger to Eleanor, it was time to stop. Six was fine.

The doctor put his hand on Daniel's shoulder. His face was lined with the triumphs and tragedies of several decades of bringing babies, alive and dead, into the world. "I sutured her incisions with a silver thread, recently developed by J. Marion Sims, a famous obstetrician. This reduces the chance of postoperative internal disease. You can see her when she awakens, but I have a fetish about cleanliness. The cleaner the environment is kept around a patient, the less chance there is of disease. Keep your visits to a minimum and keep the other children away for at least a week. Nurse Davenport will change the bedding frequently and keep the room clean. You can see your baby son."

The doctor left the study and a few minutes later Amanda Parsons entered, carrying a bundle of swaddling. She was about Eleanor's age, plump, of medium height, with brown hair pulled back in a bun, a broad open face, dancing green eyes, and a sense of humor that reminded Daniel of Abigail Keane. She handed Daniel the baby. "Good thing you had the best baby doctor in New York. I didn't know if this one was going to make it."

Daniel looked at his fourth son, John Walter Durand. He was named after Jonathan Walter, their friend in Cleveland, but Eleanor preferred John to Jonathan. He was smaller than any of his other siblings had been, pink and wrinkled. Other than his size he looked like a healthy, normal baby, but the doctor had said that something could be wrong with him that wouldn't become apparent until he was older. As if there wasn't enough to worry about with an infant.

"Little John," Daniel whispered. "One of your brother Will's favorite characters, Little John."

The baby gurgled and a bubble of spit formed on his lips.

"You're going to make it, little fella. You're going to make it—you're a Durand."

Doctor Madden reappeared. "Mrs. Durand is awake. She's a little woozy, but you can see her now."

Daniel handed John back to Amanda, hurried down the hall, and opened the door to the room. A nurse stood by the bed and motioned for Daniel to approach. He tiptoed toward the bed. Eleanor was propped up on several pillows. She turned towards him and extended her hand, which he took in his.

"How do you feel, darling?"

She closed her eyes. "It hurts," she whispered. "It hurts."

Even speaking required great effort; Daniel said nothing more and held her hand. Never mind her delicate beauty and aristocratic upbringing—she was as tough, resourceful, and resilient as anyone he had ever known, male or female. The woman who had spurned her family and its fortune to marry him would pull through, he told himself, hopeful but not certain.

Daniel rarely journeyed to the floor of the Stock Exchange, but he needed Woodbury's signature on some documents. They stood at a small outpost just off the floor. Runners conveyed orders to market makers shouting bids and offers. Men talked on telephones, scribbling furiously on their pads. Tickers spewed tapes of transactions and prices.

"Market's running today," Woodbury huffed as he signed a paper. His face glistened with sweat and his mustache drooped. An expanding waistline made it harder for him to keep up with the frenetic physical activity. Woodbury was a different person on the floor of the exchange than the affable fellow Daniel knew back at the office. He was brusque and short-tempered, his tension reflecting the atmosphere of the exchange and the money he had at risk.

"I'll get out of your way," Daniel said. "I just need one more signature."

"Mr. Woodbury!" The shout was an Irish brogue. Daniel thought nothing of it—brogues were a dime a gross in New York, until the speaker approached them. He was short and stocky, with red hair, freckles, and a pug nose, and he wore a black patch over his right eye.

"I know you! Did you drive a hansom cab?"

"Yes, sir, I did, until Mr. Woodbury hired me. Now I'm a trader."

"I was robbed several years ago. You gave me a ride to my house. I didn't have any money."

"Fifty-second Street. Nice brownstone. You still there?"

"Yes, I am. You've got quite a memory."

"Thanks. Mr. Woodbury, Erie's hit twenty-two. Sell two hundred at a quarter?"

"Yes. By the way, Mr. Patrick Dolan, this is Mr. Daniel Durand."

Dolan's eyes widened at the mention of the first name on the firm letterhead. He extended his hand. "It's an honor to meet you again, sir, but if you'll be excusing me, I've got to get Mr. Woodbury filled before the market turns."

"Do your job." Dolan disappeared into the mob. "How did you meet him?"

"At Darby's. After a pint or two we got to talking. I took a shine to him. The kid's a born trader—memory like an elephant, brass balls, and instinct. You can't teach instinct. Everyone calls him 'the pirate' because of the patch. Trades like a pirate—moves quick, swings the big sword. Makes me nervous, sometimes, takes some big hits, but he's had some real winners, too. Already the second most profitable trader in the firm."

"I've seen his name on the payroll, but I had no idea he was the driver who rescued me the night I got robbed. We're getting too big or I'm just too busy. I've got to get down here more often if a new hire becomes the second-ranked trader in the firm before I meet him."

"I have to sit down," Eleanor said, handing baby John to Mrs. Henley. The nanny looked concerned as Eleanor sat on a sofa in the sitting room.

Daniel frowned. It had been over two months since John's birth and Eleanor's surgery. Doctor Madden had said her recovery would be slow, but it seemed too slow. Although he had hired an extra nurse and maid and Eleanor's workload was next to nothing, she often went to bed directly after dinner, exhausted. She had lost weight and color, looking frail and wan.

"Darling," Daniel said, sitting beside her on the sofa and taking her hand. "I'm postponing next week's trip to Minnesota. I can't leave you now."

"When would you go?"

"I couldn't get away for another two months—September."

Eleanor shook her head. "Will couldn't go with you, he'll be back in school by then. He's been talking about this trip for weeks and he's so excited. We can't disappoint him like that, especially after the way he turned things around."

Daniel raised his eyebrows. Will had effected an extraordinary transformation in his schoolwork. It was as if a train going ten miles an hour had instantly accelerated to fifty. The day after Daniel's angry remonstrance, Will became a model student. He brought home his books every night, even on weekends. Soon he was receiving the highest marks in his class.

His father could detect none of the superciliousness that had so provoked his ire. There was never even a momentary breach in his correct respectfulness. However, Will's transformation elicited no delight and only begrudging praise from Daniel—he had seen too much of what Will wanted to hide. To Eleanor's happy exclamations he said little.

Ostensible progress had to be rewarded, even if Daniel distrusted the motives behind it. "You're right; he's done well in school and hasn't complained about his punishment, but I worry about you. You're still not at full strength."

"I'm getting better every day. I'm eating more and I've gained some weight. Daniel, you must make your trip with Will, you must. I'll be fine. Amanda will help out."

There was no mistaking the pleading in Eleanor's voice and eyes, as if she sensed that this trip would be a chance, a rare chance, for father and son to bridge the gulf between them.

"So be it, dearest. The trip is on."

Daniel watched as new passengers boarded the train in Chicago, another stop on his and Will's journey from New York to the Dakota Territory. One passenger stood out—a rotund little man, only a few inches above five feet. He was in his forties, dressed in a gray suit of European cut, a red patterned tie, and white vest. He carried a black top hat, his bald pate ringed by a strip of black and gray hair. His brown eyes—set deep between the chubby cheeks of his rounded face, above his button nose, black mustache, and fleshy chin—were constantly in motion. His gaze rested momentarily on Daniel and Will. He sat in the seat across the aisle.

Will looked up from his newspaper a few minutes later. A young girl about his age, with playful blue eyes and a winsome smile, stepped down the aisle followed by her parents, a severe, unsmiling couple whose black, almost funereal garb was relieved only by the gentleman's white shirt. The girl smiled as her eyes met Will's. The threesome proceeded to the back of the car.

Poor Will had reached the age when the bother with females started. Good luck, son, Daniel thought, you're on your own. How long would it be before Will wandered to the back of the car? Good luck with those parents. They probably attended church six times a week, had the Bible memorized, read *Pilgrim's Progress* as light diversion, considered cities an invention of the devil, never drank, danced, played cards, or smoked—because all human enjoyment was inherently evil—and only procreated because it was their Christian duty.

The whistle sounded and the train pulled out of the station. It steamed through acres of stockyards, the pungency overwhelming. Chicago was the manure capital of the United States, rivaled only by the political capital. Children made noises of disgust and the adults smiled awkwardly. The train emerged from the stockyards, heading northwest through the flat countryside on a hot and humid summer morning. Fields of corn and wheat alternated in a monotonous progression, occasionally interrupted by an empty field or a farmhouse. Daniel opened a book.

"Father, I'm going to walk around a bit," Will said.

Daniel smiled. He settled in with his book as Will went to the back of the car. He had not been reading long when he was tapped on his shoulder by the odd little man, leaning across the aisle.

"Excuse me, sir," the man said, with a French accent, "I couldn't help notice what you are reading—*Democracy in America*. Monsieur Tocqueville was the uncle of my aunt's husband, on my mother's side. I never met him, unfortunately. What do you think of his book?" The man stared at him with wide eyes, as if Daniel's answer was of vital importance.

"He writes elegantly, using an economy of words to reflect a precision of thought."

"He published that first volume when he was thirty-two."

"Unusual insight for someone that young," Daniel said noncommittally, hoping to pursue more of that insight. He tried to resume reading.

"Are you a businessman?"

Daniel looked up from his book. "Yes."

The Frenchman stroked his bushy mustache. "One seldom sees an American businessman with the time or the inclination for serious reading. Most are too preoccupied with augmenting or spending their fortunes. My compliments, Monsieur."

"Uh, thank you. My wife recommended the book."

"Your wife! Rarer still—a woman interested in ideas!"

"I'm sure she'd be flattered, Mr. —?"

"Devereaux, René Devereaux. Pleased to make your acquaintance."

"Likewise. I'm Daniel Durand." They shook hands. Daniel picked up his book and read for three minutes before Devereaux spoke again.

"Businessmen, especially American businessmen, should delve into the realm of ideas. There would be more like you, Monsieur Durand, if they knew what was at stake."

Exasperated, but reluctantly intrigued, Daniel closed his book. Devereaux wanted to talk, and unlike most such people, he might have something to say. "What do you mean?"

"Ah," Devereaux said, lightly clapping his hands. "The best businessmen pursue their work, amass their fortunes, and believe their happy circumstances are the natural order of things—an outcome dictated by God and their own talents. In a country scarcely a century old, such naïve complacency is understandable."

Devereaux leaned back and folded his hands on his bulbous little belly. "Understandable, but woefully ignorant of both history and philosophy. Historically, wealth of any kind has been an anomaly. Virtually everyone since the dawn of humanity has been poor. More anomalous still have been those few times, brief interludes really, when the most competent and industrious have been allowed to harvest the fruits of their own labor. Most of the great European fortunes have been stolen. European nobility rests on a foundation of plunder."

Devereaux sat upright and leaned across the aisle. "You are quite wealthy," he whispered.

Daniel stared at Devereaux.

"Don't ask me how I know this. If you are unaware of this current state of grace, you are, of course, unable to protect yourself from the lurking dangers."

"What dangers?"

"The envy of those aligned against you. Allow me to explain."

As if he could stop him!

Devereaux gestured towards the flat plain rolling by. "An American's prospects appear wide open, limitless to the distant horizon. He's free to progress as far as his ability and industry will take him. He bears no animus towards the successful because he hopes to join them.

"But this American system, by giving opportunity to those who have never had it, displaces those who have enjoyed the highest status in Europe—the nobility, the clergy, and the scholars. The nobility especially scorn the enterprise and industry of those who support it. Capitalism generates its own aristocracy based on productive ability, but it constantly changes—there is no permanent nobility. As for the government, Monsieur Tocqueville noted that its powers are so limited that the wealthy are content to allow it to be filled with men of inferior quality."

"And the clergy?"

"As long as this country maintains a separation of church and state and allows freedom of religion, the clergy is relegated to attending to spiritual needs. The scholars are more important."

"Why?"

"Their commerce is mankind's most important product—ideas. They are already pressing a malignant assault on the ideas that have produced America. Sophistry proclaims capitalism, the only system that gives the masses a chance to escape their poverty, a threat to the poor. We are told that misery and squalor are morally superior to production and wealth, and that revolutionary liberty should surrender to the old forms of slavery. I'm ashamed to say that most of this foolishness emanates from Europe. Americans must never take it seriously."

"It's nonsense!"

"One fights bad ideas with good ideas." Devereaux withdrew his gold watch from his vest pocket. "I assume you are going all the way to St. Paul?"

"Yes."

"It's still many hours until we arrive. We'll talk later on, *après dejeuner*. In the meantime, I'd like to read, *merci*." He buried his nose in his book as if Daniel weren't there.

Daniel, amused, decided to check up on Will. He walked to the back of the car, swaying with the motion of the train. Will was happily ensconced next to the pretty girl who had boarded with her parents in Chicago. Surprisingly, the girl's dour parents were beaming at him.

"Allow me," Will said, "to introduce Mr. and Mrs. Ellis of Elroy, Wisconsin, and their daughter, Penelope. This is my father, Mr. Daniel Durand."

Penelope gazed at Will worshipfully. Daniel shook hands with the couple.

"Mr. Durand," Mr. Ellis said, "your son was saying that although you live in New York, he's always wanted to experience life in a small town in the country."

Daniel raised his eyebrows. As far as he knew, Will had as much affinity for small towns as criminals did for jails. "Perhaps we could arrange for him to spend some time in one."

"If your duties permit it, sir," Mrs. Ellis said. "You must be very busy with your position."

"My position?"

"On the board of directors of Standard Oil."

Daniel owned an ample stake in Standard, which he had mentioned to Will, but he had never said he was on the board. "I'm not on that board."

Will's smile was remarkably unstressed. "Am I mistaken? I just assumed that since you've owned shares in the company for a long time that you were on the board of directors." There was not a trace of guile on his son's face as he stared at Daniel.

"That's not how it works, Will. My shares don't give me a seat on the board."

"We surely have enjoyed visiting with Will, Mr. Durand," said Mr. Ellis, apparently unfazed. "He's a fine young man. You must be proud of him."

"Thank you, Mr. Ellis." The train hit a rough patch of track and Daniel, standing in the aisle, grabbed a seat for support. His stomach was suddenly churning. "It was a pleasure making your acquaintance, but the ride is getting a little bumpy and I think I'll return to my seat."

"A pleasure, sir," Mr. and Mrs. Ellis chirped in unison.

Will stayed with Penelope and her parents until they reached their stop at Elroy. He made a promise to write to Penelope that he knew he wouldn't keep and waved to her as she stepped to the platform. He took an odd pride from the anticipation tinged with sadness radiating from her face. He returned to his seat to find his father fast asleep. Will picked up *The Three Musketeers* and began to read.

He glanced up and saw the short little man across the aisle staring at him with twinkling, friendly eyes. "Do you know this book, sir?" Will whispered.

"I've read it many times. A fine book." The answering whisper had a French accent. "What do you like about it?" Devereaux motioned toward the open seat next to him. "Perhaps you should sit over here, so we don't wake your father."

Will was flattered that this gentleman took an interest in what he read. "I likc the duels. The heroism—it was face-to-face. And I like the kings and queens and dukes and duchesses."

"You are Will?"

Will nodded.

"I am Monsieur Devereaux. There is heroism in every age, Will. Your father was a soldier."

"He never talks about the war; I wish he would. Did he tell you that?"

"No."

How did this man know his father had been a soldier? The Frenchman smiled, as if he knew what Will was thinking.

"Does our age seem too complicated, Will? What would you have been back then?"

"A nobleman, maybe the king, with castles and knights and serfs."

"Perhaps only the nobility saw the charm and romance of that age. Chances are you would have been a serf, working the land, giving your crop to your lord and master."

Will frowned. This little Frenchman had the same annoying habit as his father, sticking an awkward fact into the conversation like that. Will deployed the same strategy he used with his father and changed the subject. "'All for one and one for all'—that's what I admire about *The Three Musketeers*."

Monsieur Devereaux again smiled. "None of this individualism and self-reliance for you? Forget all that life, liberty, and the pursuit of happiness nonsense?"

Was the Frenchman making sport of him? "That's the Declaration of Independence."

"*Oui*, Monsieur. Independence—every man for himself."

He was making sport of him! "Well of course I believe in independence, but I also believe everyone has a duty to everyone else. Men have to consider more than just their own interest."

"Do they?"

"They should! And they would if I were running things!" Will said forcefully. There was something about this Frenchman he didn't like. His eyes had lost their twinkling friendliness and he stared as if he were examining him, judging him. It made him uncomfortable.

"I'm going to return to my seat." He sat down and closed his eyes. His father awoke and began talking with Devereaux. Will hoped to have nothing more to do with the Frenchman.

The train pulled into St. Paul's Union Station a little after nine o'clock. Will, his father, and Devereaux gathered their coats and stepped down from the train. The northern summer sun had not set and the night was warm and humid. Mosquitoes and black flies buzzed through the air.

"Monsieur Devereaux," Daniel said as they walked across the station platform. "Perhaps you could give me your address. I'd like to correspond, if you're amenable."

"Most amenable, but we shall see each other again."

"When we will see each other?"

Devereaux smiled. "Sooner than you think, Monsieur." He shook hands with Will and Daniel, and then pointed at a porter who was pushing a cart loaded with luggage. "There are my bags. *Au revoir.*" He hurried over to the porter and they left the station.

The rising sun was the only lighting adequate to illuminate, in all its grandeur, the Stone Arch Bridge, stretching arch after graceful arch over the mighty Mississippi. The bridge projected west from

St. Paul's Union Station, where Daniel stood with Will on an outside platform, then curved north upriver as it approached the factories, flour mills, and grain elevators of Minneapolis on the west bank. It was nearly complete and would provide a crucial rail link for the burgeoning Twin Cities. The spray, mist, and dawn rainbow of a thundering waterfall were visible further upstream. Daniel stared at Will, wishing he could somehow freeze, in his mind's eye, the expression of unalloyed awe on his son's face. As long as greatness opened a window to the part of Will's soul that felt such reverent wonder, he couldn't judge him too harshly. He put his arm around Will's shoulder.

"The design is Mr. Hill's." The speaker was Mr. Manvel, a vice president for the St. Paul, Minneapolis & Manitoba Railway Company. His trim, dark beard emphasized his deep-set brown eyes, angular nose, and the gaunt hollows of his cheeks. "Twenty-three arches, twenty-one hundred feet long, eighty-two feet high, and twenty-eight feet wide—enough for two tracks. The cost will be about six hundred fifty thousand."

Daniel nodded in admiration. When it was done, when the first train pulled over the bridge, the cynics, the doubters, the worrywarts, the obstructionists—the little people—would fall silent, at least for a moment, overwhelmed by the cheers from those who saw it for what it was: a monument to its builder. And the builder, what would he feel? There had to be a joy, a special moment of heaven on earth—the only heaven—reserved for those who accomplished such deeds.

The group entered the concourse of the station. Light streamed through high windows below the vaulted ceiling. The concourse was already crowded as passengers and porters, pushing carts piled high with baggage, hurried to their gates.

"What is it like to work for Monsieur Hill?" Mr. Devereaux asked. He had been on the viewing platform when Daniel and Will had arrived at the station early that morning. When Daniel pressed him on how he knew they would be continuing their journey together, he had only smiled and said, "In good time, Monsieur, in good time."

Manvel smiled weakly in response to Devereaux's question. "He pays extraordinarily well and he has been quite generous with stock in the company."

Daniel and Devereaux glanced at each other. They could fill in the rest of the response: but he's a taskmaster who drives his men to the breaking point.

When they reached their platform, Daniel saw the uncontainable excitement on his son's face and felt the same. At the head of the train was the largest locomotive he had ever seen. Its cowcatcher looked as if it could sweep aside an entire herd. Smoke curled from a funnel-shaped black smokestack taller than a man. The eight drive wheels were four feet high, connected by steel driving rods. The eight-wheel coal tender was huge. The monster locomotive would be as ravenous as a bear emerging from a winter's hibernation.

Will hurried down the platform to the end of the train. He returned, running. "It's pulling thirteen flat cars loaded with rails and ties, three boxcars, four dump cars full of gravel, a caboose, a passenger car, another locomotive, and its coal tender."

Manvel smiled at Will. "The passenger car is for our group. All aboard."

Their car was more sumptuous than a regular passenger car. There were two tables with kerosene lanterns, heavy green curtains, overstuffed brown leather chairs, an icebox and coal-fired stove attended by a man in a white jacket, a coal-fired heater, a humidor stocked with cigars, and compartments in which the group's luggage was stored.

"Make yourselves comfortable, gentlemen," Manvel said. "It will take the better part of the day to reach the Dakota Territory."

The train's whistle shrilled and the car shuddered as the train started to move. The three men sat at a table and Will took a chair by the window. The big locomotive accelerated and the train chugged northwest along the river.

"This train shakes and sways less than any I've ever ridden," Daniel said.

"It's the rails," Manvel said. "Mr. Hill replaced all the iron rails with the best steel rails from Europe. They cost a lot more, but they last twice as long, and because they ride smoother, they reduce maintenance and repair charges on the locomotives and cars. We recover the additional cost fairly quickly." Manvel glanced toward a shelf jammed with ledgers and documents. "Uh, if you'll excuse me gentleman, I need to get some work done. I've brought copies of our latest financial statements." He walked over to the shelf, picked up two stacks of documents, and placed one each in front of Daniel and Devereaux. He returned to the shelf and picked up several large stacks and took them to the other table. "If you have any questions, please don't hesitate to ask." He started reading through one of his stacks.

Manvel did his work, Will read *The Three Musketeers*, and Daniel and Devereaux settled in with the St. Paul's finances. Daniel occasionally looked out the window. The countryside became a monotonous progression of wheat fields, interrupted occasionally by a stand of forest, a river, or a lake. At a town that Manvel told them was St. Cloud, about eighty miles from St. Paul, they crossed the Mississippi, now a skinny child of a river, not the strapping adolescent that flowed through the Twin Cities or the overgrown brute Daniel had seen farther south during the war.

From its statements the St. Paul was making plenty of money, and every dime was plowed back into the business in capital expenditures. The railroad devoured capital, so the St. Paul not only regurgitated its profits, but went to the financial markets with stock and bond issues. For Daniel, cynical about railroad finance from his two speculative coups shorting railroad securities, it was refreshing to see a well-capitalized, conservatively financed, solidly profitable line.

"Monsieur Manvel," Devereaux said. "I'm impressed by the extraordinary growth of traffic through the Red River Valley. It's been your biggest moneymaker."

Manvel stood, went to the window, and gestured at a wheat field with tall, orderly rows of grain. "This Red River Valley has become a breadbasket, but five years ago it was barely developed. We brought in the immigrants, provided credit, showed them how to farm, and shipped their supplies and grain. Mr. Hill built this valley like he built the Stone Arch Bridge."

The way Manvel spoke of his boss was the verbal equivalent of the way Will had gazed at the Stone Arch Bridge—reverent awe. It gave Daniel an uneasy feeling. Prominent men rarely lived up to their towering reputations. He didn't see how Mr. Hill could match his advance billing from Manvel and Mr. Kennedy.

An hour later the attendant, Mr. Nelson, made them a simple lunch of bread, ham, cheese, apples, walnuts, and beer.

"Can I try the beer, Father?" Will asked.

Daniel smiled. "Sure." Nine-tenths of the attraction of any vice to adolescent boys was that it was forbidden. Will sipped the beer and quickly washed it down with water.

After lunch, Daniel felt himself getting sleepy. The beer and the gentle rhythm of the train were soporific. He fell asleep in his chair.

"Father, look outside!"

It was darker in the car than when Daniel had nodded off, and the train was crawling. Will was beckoning him to the window. Thousands of buffalo filled the landscape ahead of the train. The orderly wheat fields were gone, replaced by the wild grass of the plains—buffalo fodder. Daniel had never seen buffalo, with their massive heads, humped backs, and thick, shaggy coats. Some lumbered away as the fire-breathing monster slowly approached. Most glanced at the train and returned to their grass. One male mounted a female in a comically ungainly coupling.

"Father, what are those two doing?"

Daniel smiled. "They're mating, Will."

"What's that?"

"That's how we get baby buffaloes. Are we in Dakota?"

Will scrunched his forehead, confused. "We have been for about half an hour."

Twenty minutes after the train cleared the buffalo herd, the passengers saw smoke puffing up ahead, above an encampment on the south side of the tracks.

"We'll have to do some walking," Manvel said. "The track ahead of us has been recently laid and is untested. We can't run two big locomotives and twenty-two cars over it."

They stepped down from the car onto the Great Plains. The grass came up to Will's waist.

"Watch where you step, or you're liable to find a prairie dog hole. There are millions of 'em out here—the men shoot 'em for sport."

Daniel saw a group of men on a hand-pumped flatcar coming towards them down the track. The flatcar stopped before the train and eight men jumped off. They began unloading ties and rails. They wore grimy work clothes and formless hats. Daniel took off his coat and slung it over his shoulder.

The air was less humid than it had been in Minnesota and a breeze carried the scent of the prairie grass. The sun appeared directly in front of them, a couple of hours above the horizon, more orange than yellow through the dusty haze. They walked on the railroad ties towards the encampment. Daniel was reminded of his army days. There were about fifty makeshift tents; crude stools; sheds for supplies and food; one large pit, littered with burnt coal, over which was suspended a large iron grate; and another pit for campfires. Down the line a man knelt over the tracks and another man stood with him. Farther down men scythed swaths of prairie grass, shoveled, and swung large hammers.

There was only one man at the encampment, so old, dirty, and grizzled that he might have been mistaken for part of the landscape, except that dirt and grass smelled better.

"Where's Mr. Hill?" Manvel asked.

He pointed his thumb towards the two men down the track.

The foursome approached the two men, who made no indication that they noticed them. One of the men was on his knees on the track, peering at a large level spanning the track. All Daniel could see of his features was the top, bald part of his sunburned head.

"We still need more ballast on the northern side," the kneeling man said.

"Yes, sir, Mr. Hill," said the other man. He carried a tablet and pencil and made notations.

"What's the grade here?"

The man flipped through his tablet. "Point zero zero sixty-eight."

Mr. Hill crawled up the track, followed by the other man, laying the level across the track, asking questions, making comments, and giving instructions, all of which the other man dutifully recorded. The foursome shuffled behind them, ignored. Mr. Hill stood and, shielding his eyes, looked straight west, toward the sun. "I wanted to survey the grade up ahead, but I waited too long. We'd be looking straight into the sun." He turned and saw the three men and Will. He walked up the track. "You must be Mr. Kennedy's investors."

"Mr. James Hill," Manvel said. "This is Mr. Daniel Durand and his son Will, from New York, and Mr. René Devereaux, from France."

Hill looked them in the eye and firmly clasped their hands when he shook them. As he shook Will's hand, he said, "Did you see any buffalo on the way out?" Will nodded. Hill's voice dropped to a stage whisper. "Do you know what to do when buffalo stampede?" Will shook his head. "Get out of their way!" The men laughed and Will grinned.

Hill's appearance suggested a buffalo. His large head was mostly bald, with a shaggy fringe of black hair streaked with gray that hung to the collar of his dirty white shirt. Something was wrong with his eyes—they didn't move together. His mustache and beard were the same black-and-gray patchwork as his hair. His shirtsleeves were rolled and his black pants were covered with dust. In his mid-forties, he was considerably shorter than Daniel, but had a massive torso that rested on short haunches. If New York was the city of sharp elbows, then the Northwest was the land of big shoulders, barrel chests, and thick thighs, a land tamed by men with the strength of Hill, who could survive the unforgiving terrain and brutal winters.

"You gentlemen ever had a buffalo steak?" Hill said after explaining some of the basics of laying track. The visitors shook their heads. "You're going to have one tonight. Old Josh will prepare a real prairie feast. Won't have quite the fancy trimmings you get in New York, but it's good eats."

Daniel felt a sharp stab of hunger as they walked back to camp; the smell of grilling onions, bacon, and buffalo steaks filled the air. The grizzled old man was Josh, the cook. The men lined up at the large iron grill, an inferno underneath belching smoke. Josh stabbed steaks with a long metal fork, put them on metal plates, and ladled gravy thick with potatoes, onions, carrots, and bacon. Daniel was surprised when Will filled his cup with beer. The railroad men sat on stools or blankets spread around the campfire. The visitors and

Manvel dined with Hill at a table made of planks, with railroad ties as legs. Hill pulled a corkscrew, wine glasses, and a bottle of wine from a wicker basket and presented the wine to Devereaux.

"A very good vintage, Monsieur."

Hill uncorked the wine. Will declined when it was offered to him.

For a while there was little conversation—the food and drink were too good. Buffalo meat was leaner than beef, which might have meant a tough, dried-out steak if it had been overcooked. However, Daniel's was done to perfection, and the gravy and vegetables were delicious. As Hill was finishing his dinner, sopping up gravy with a piece of bread, he turned to Daniel. "It's to your credit, Mr. Durand, that you and Mr. Devereaux came out here to see what we're doing before you invested. It's amazing how many people put their money down sight unseen. Our railroad has many investors, but few visitors."

"How far across the Northwest will you extend your line?" Daniel said.

"Do you remember the description of Marias Pass from Lewis and Clark?"

"It was supposedly the lowest pass through the Rocky Mountains."

"Nobody knows where it is, or if it even exists. If we can find it, we'll be able to go all the way to the Pacific."

"What about Villard and the Northern Pacific?" Devereaux asked. "They'll soon have their transcontinental line completed."

"I don't regard—"

"Do you know Henry Villard?" Will said. "He has one of the grandest mansions in New York and the newspapers always have stories about his parties."

Hill turned his off-kilter gaze at Will and regarded him coldly. "And while he's having his parties, young man, I'm out here on the Dakota plains, watching how the track is laid and the money's spent. You know more about running a railroad than Villard does."

Will squirmed, embarrassed.

"To return to your question, Mr. Devereaux," Hill said. "I don't regard the Northern Pacific as any kind of competition. They've been paid by the government to build the longest, most inefficient line possible, and they've fulfilled their end of the bargain admirably. Villard thinks tourists and fancy hotels will support his line. He's wrong—a line has to be built around farming, ranching, mining, and timber, and at the pace of development. The NP will run through a lot of empty, profitless territory. It went bankrupt before and it will go bankrupt again." Hill drained his glass of wine. "And when it does, I'll buy it and turn it into a paying proposition."

"You're not worried about the aid it receives from the government?" Daniel said.

"If you crawl into bed with the government, you're laboring under a delusion as to who's doing the poking and who's getting poked." Hill smiled. The four men laughed as the joke sailed over Will's head.

"We buy our rails—the best available—from Europe. The government-subsidized lines have to buy inferior American rails. Our route map looks like a spider web, with hundreds of spur lines branching off the main line, to bring us closer to our customers. We build a spur wherever it's profitable. The NP has to get an act of Congress every time it wants to build one. If I had to get an act of Congress every time I wanted to build a spur, Will here would be six feet under before the St. Paul reached the West Coast. Not to mention the expense of bribing those rascals!"

"If you're building a better railroad, sir," Will said, "then it doesn't seem fair that the government should help your competitors."

"My competitors are worse off for it, so I don't care. Notwithstanding all the help other railroads have received, we have the lowest freight rates in the country, especially for crops."

"Doesn't stop the farmers from complaining about them," Manvel said.

"Farmers are farmers—they're not happy unless they're complaining about something. But the Northern Pacific has a gaggle of politicians in its pockets, so I've got to bribe at double the going rate if I want to buy a right of way through public or Indian lands. That's an annoyance." He turned towards Will. "You're looking at my eye, aren't you?"

"Y-yes, sir."

"When I was about your age, I made myself a bow and arrow. It must have been made to NP standards, because when I pulled the string it snapped and the arrow stuck in my eye." He pointed at his right eye. "I've been blind in this one ever since. It doesn't move right, does it?"

"No, sir."

"The doctor who treated me saved the eye, but the optic nerve and some of the muscles that hold the eye in place were damaged. Enough about that! MacIntyre, get over here. Let's have a tune." Hill refilled the men's wine glasses.

MacIntyre, a tall, burly man with a coarse, black beard, stood and pulled a hornpipe from his coat. The other men clapped and pulled their stools around the fire. MacIntyre played a tune, Hill sang in a deep, mellow voice, and the others joined in.

"I bought a wife in Edinburgh
For a bawbee
And then I got a farthing back
To buy tobacco wi'!
And wi' you, and wi' you,
And wi' you my Jenny lass
I'll dance the buckles off my shoes
Wi' you my Jenny lass!"

They sang several lusty verses, Daniel, Devereaux, and Will joining in on the chorus.

Hill and MacIntyre ran through a repertoire of Scottish airs. Daniel lost track of how much he had to drink, but he felt a hearty fellowship with Hill's men. He had to stop Will from having a second cup of beer, but Will still had a rollicking good time, joining in on choruses and shouting boisterously with the men.

Hill glanced at him and smiled. "Let's have a song out of you, Master Durand!"

"I…I don't know any of the kind of songs you were singing," Will said.

"Then sing us something you know, lad."

Will stood. His voice was initially soft and wavered a bit, but the men roared their approval.

"Mine eyes have seen the glory of the coming of the Lord;

He is trampling out the vintage where the grapes of wrath are stored…"

Daniel didn't know if Will's choice was inspired or just lucky. It didn't matter; here in the northern most reaches of the country, he could do no better than the Union anthem. Some of the men were probably Union veterans. Daniel marveled at his son's ability to evoke genuine affection from people he had just met.

People found Daniel reserved, even forbidding. Keeping them at arm's length served his purposes. His opinion of them was far more important than what they thought of him. You made a choice, he had concluded, about whether other people's opinion of you would be important. If it wasn't, you were called aloof or arrogant. Were Daniel to be offered Will's gift, if that's what it was, he would reject it. Nothing was free in this world, including affection. He had seen what his son would offer to obtain it, lying to impress that small-town family from Wisconsin. Integrity was the first casualty of popularity.

"Glory! Glory! Hallelujah! Glory! Glory! Hallelujah!

Glory! Glory! Hallelujah! Our God is marching on."

Will beamed when Hill patted him on the back and the men shouted and cheered as the evening drew to a close. Daniel and Will followed Manvel, who led them to a small two-man tent. The ground was covered with hides and warm, luxuriant furs. They crawled under the furs and were asleep within minutes.

Will awoke with a start. He heard a long, high-pitched howl, answered by another howl. Were those wolves or coyotes? He didn't know. He was almost back asleep when his father groaned.

"Stay down in the swamp!" his father hissed. "Stay down in the damn swamp!"

Will bolted upright. His father was apparently asleep, but he was talking.

There was what seemed like a long silence. "Stay in the swamp, Pomeroy!" His father groaned again and lapsed into incoherent mumbling.

"Pomeroy," Will whispered to himself, startled but curious. He had to remember that name. "Pomeroy…Pomeroy…Pomeroy." He repeated it until he was overcome by sleep.

"I'd wager that New York would slide into the East River before I'd bet that Mr. Hill won't run his line to the coast," Daniel said. "I'm ready to invest."

"So am I," Devereaux said.

The two men and Will were returning to St. Paul the day following their rousing evening. The two men sat at one table and Will sat by the window, reading. Manvel had stayed with Hill.

"I should like for your firm to handle our order," Devereaux said.

"Not until you tell me how you know so much about me."

"I represent a group of Europeans interested in American opportunities. I had been doing business with a New York firm, but I am dissatisfied with them. Of course we need expertise in American finance and capital markets, but we need more. Substantial sums of money are involved, so we must work with men who hold themselves to the highest standards of integrity and conduct. And I have my own personal requirement. Americans like Hill—"

"Hill is Canadian."

Devereaux raised his eyebrows. "Ah, Monsieur, men are French, or English, or Spanish by an accident of birth. Men are American because they want to live in freedom and are willing to fight for it. By that standard, Hill is an American."

"By that standard, many Americans aren't American."

"And many people all over the world are."

"Including Monsieur René Devereaux?"

"Yes."

"So how did you find out about me?"

"I first heard about you from Mr. Baker, at the First National Bank. He spoke favorably of your financial ability and the acumen of your partner, Mr. Woodbury. I've known Mr. Kennedy for years. He mentioned that you had become interested in Mr. Hill's railroad and were planning a trip to see it. I decided to make the same trip. I investigated your firm, and I've made up my mind. I'll give your our order for twenty thousand St. Paul shares. We'll also buy bonds."

Daniel nodded and slipped on his poker face. At the current share price, Devereaux's order was worth over two million dollars. His group of European investors must indeed be quite "substantial." Daniel was ready to buy, but his purchase wouldn't be that large.

He extended his hand across the table and the two men shook hands. "You've got yourself a deal."

Will glanced over at his father and Mr. Devereux to make sure their attention was elsewhere. He wrote seven letters with a pen on the inside front cover of his book. Q... P... N... F... S... P... Z. It was the name he had remembered from the previous night— Pomeroy—with each letter advanced one. This simple code would protect him if his father ever saw it.

Daniel sat in his study one night about a month after his visit to the Northwest, reading the newspaper. There was an account of the "Golden Spike" ceremony marking the completion of the Northern Pacific's transcontinental railroad. President Arthur, General Grant, and a host of other dignitaries had attended to see what the tax-payer's money had bought. A thousand feet of track had been left unfinished for a demonstration of rapid track construction. The chief of the Crow Head tribe formally ceded the right of way through the tribe's hunting grounds to Henry Villard. Artillery fired and military music played as Villard hammered down the last spike.

Daniel laughed a bitter, ironic laugh at the last sentence of the story.

The locomotive used for the ceremony was on loan from the St. Paul, Minneapolis & Manitoba Railway.

Chapter 15

Enemies

The patriarch, Curtis Winfield, stared at his four sons from behind the desk in his library. They had their brandy and their cigars, acceptable indulgences during the holiday. Even the patriarch had a brandy with his ever-present cigar, although he would take no more than a couple of sips. The library was more like a great hall, with massive stone fireplaces, large picture windows that looked out on the Hudson River valley but now showed only a flurry of nighttime snow, and overstuffed leather sofas, oak tables and chairs, bearskin rugs, gas lanterns, and shelves filled with musty, unread books that ran to the high ceiling.

The sons made light conversation but the conviviality was artificial. Every so often one would glance nervously at the father. Very few men, and certainly none of his sons, could say they were comfortable in the presence of Curtis Winfield. Only the sixth man in the room, Micah Baldwin, appeared undaunted. He stood at one of the tall windows and watched the snow. He had no brandy or cigar; he neither smoked nor drank. This was the first time an outsider had been invited to the Winfield estate for Christmas and New Year's.

For the sons—Archer, Harrison, Prescott, and Edwin—the supposedly festive holiday visit provoked untoward anxiety. The "old man," as they called him behind his back, always closely questioned them about their affairs, always prodded, and always reproached them for their failures. The unprecedented presence of Micah Baldwin magnified the usual tension. He would only be there because Winfield had some momentous, far-reaching design to announce. The conversation by the fireplace dwindled as the tension mounted and the anxious glances towards the father grew more frequent. Finally, he stood up from his desk, grasped his cane, and hobbled to the front of the massive stone fireplace. The sons sat in two sofas right-angled to each other but facing towards the fireplace. Baldwin pulled up a chair.

"Everything I've built," Winfield said. There were no preambles or pleasantries when he talked; he despised the unessential. His voice was high-pitched and raspy. "And everything you'll continue, rests on friendship. We have our friends in the law and the judiciary, in business, the press, and, most importantly, in politics. There's nothing more important than friendship."

Winfield puffed his cigar and flicked an ash towards the fireplace. Short and thin, the fire roaring behind him made him appear even more diminutive. His wispy white hair receded from his high forehead and was brushed to the side. His eyebrows formed inverted white Vs over his black eyes. The bones of his thin, angular face threatened to poke through his parchment-thin, almost translucent skin. He had no beard, mustache, or sideburns—vanities; his personal barber shaved him clean every morning. His use of the cane was not due to his advancing years, but to an accident on a streetcar.

He had started working in his parents' small shop in Buffalo when he was eight. He taught himself to read, write, and calculate—school would only have slowed him down. Smarter than other children, he made no effort to hide his disdain. He became indispensable at the shop—accounting, taking inventory, placing orders—and threatened to quit if his father didn't pay him more. He got his raise. When he was fifteen, his father died, giving him the opportunity he craved. No longer accountable to a lesser light, he expanded the shop's business and made investments. His mother warned that there were things money couldn't buy. His reply—"I have no use for the things money can't buy"—was to become one of his trademark aphorisms.

He was a millionaire by the time he was twenty-six. When he was twenty-nine an inattentive driver of a horse-drawn streetcar cost him two toes and a mangled foot. For his thirtieth birthday, he bought the streetcar company, fired all the workers, and replaced them.

He didn't believe any drivel about following the dictates of his heart—women were fungible. When it was time to start a family, he selected Gertrude Horst, the daughter of prosperous German immigrants. They were impressed by his wealth; he was impressed by her stout constitution, phlegmatic personality, and good sense. She was breeding stock and gave him what he wanted: four sons to perpetuate his dynasty, four daughters to seal strategic alliances. While he gave her little in the way of romance or affection, she got a full staff of servants, mansions, and finery, and he treated her with a courteous, reserved deference.

"We've always rewarded our friends, but friendship stands on more than mere goodwill. A man who doesn't punish his enemies will have no friends left to reward." His voice dropped. "Our friends are our friends because they respect, they fear us." He cleared his throat and glanced at his youngest son, Edwin, twenty-eight, who did not know as much history of this secretive family as his older brothers. "Eleanor Haverford, of Cleveland, spurned the courtship of Archer in favor of Daniel Durand, a man of no distinction, family, or wealth."

Archer Winfield squirmed. Although he was now married with three children, the memory of Eleanor's rejection still rankled.

"Through Micah, we eventually resumed contact with her father, Phillip Haverford, and bankrolled his purchase of Durand's bank. Haverford was looking for money and a way to get rid of Durand. But he's an idiot and despite Micah's warning, he overpaid for the bank."

The father nodded toward Baldwin and the sons looked at him with a mixture of admiration and jealousy. Their father addressed few men by their first name.

"After a few years we bought him out. Micah took control and made the bank the most profitable in Cleveland, the anchor of our Ohio interests. I thought we'd heard the last of Mr. Daniel Durand, but our paths have crossed again. Two years ago, Harrison became aware of a situation regarding the St. Paul, Minneapolis & Manitoba Railway."

It was Harrison's turn to squirm. Although the family had an intricate web of political connections, he was the only son overtly involved in politics. He was in the New York Assembly and had announced his candidacy for the United States House of Representatives. His father had pulled the necessary strings so that he faced only token opposition. Harrison was portly, which he used to political advantage. People didn't like their politicians to be too smart, and his girth seemed apiece with his affected geniality. The façade masked a shrewd mind and his father's ruthlessness. In his early forties, he had thinning blond hair and a moon-shaped face.

"Micah knows the story, so I'll let him tell it." Winfield sat down.

Baldwin rose and stood before the sons. Tall, thin, dapper, dark hair slicked straight back, his insect eyes behind their thick glasses briefly made contact with each of them before he spoke. The self-possessed lawyer addressed them as he would a courtroom. "It was

Harrison's understanding that two Canadians on the board of directors were leaving. They provided crucial financial and political support. Harrison also learned that James Hill, the president of the company, was overextended. In his effort to expand, the line was competing against the Northern Pacific, which has received thousands of acres of federal land and right of ways through federal and Indian lands, and continues to receive government subsidies.

"Archer and Harrison built a substantial short position in the securities of the St. Paul. Rumors were circulated and stories planted. Through the summer of 1883, the effort appeared successful—prices of the St. Paul's securities declined. However, they reversed, and except for a brief drop during last year's panic, they've continued to rise. The St. Paul has successfully met the competitive threat posed by the Northern Pacific. The short position has been covered at a substantial loss." Baldwin paused, as if to emphasize this ugly fact.

"Unbeknownst to Harrison and Archer, Daniel Durand and a group of European investors using Durand's firm, Durand & Woodbury, as their agent made a substantial investment in the St. Paul in the late summer and early autumn of 1883."

"Harrison and Archer were shorting the best damn railroad in the country," Curtis hissed.

Baldwin continued, unmindful of the interruption. "John Kennedy, formerly the owner of a firm specializing in railroad securities, but now directly involved with the St. Paul, spearheaded an effort to support the firm's stock and bond prices. Durand was part of that effort and now has a large position in the St. Paul."

Curtis rose and stamped his cane on the floor. "That's three times Durand has got the best of us. The Winfields don't lose three times to anyone," he said, almost shouting. "A man who doesn't punish his enemies will have no friends to reward." He jabbed his cane. "I want Durand destroyed. I don't care how long it takes or how much money we have to spend. I want it done carefully—no dirty hands, no tracks, nothing to connect this to the family. Micah and Prescott will make inquiries. Durand must have a few skeletons in his closet."

The other three sons looked at Prescott. That he would be chosen to work with Baldwin on such a matter underscored their father's esteem. Prescott, the third son, was, like Baldwin, an attorney. He had attended Harvard Law School, clerked with a Supreme Court judge, and made partner in a prestigious New York firm. He bore a strong resemblance to Archer, with the same square head, wavy brown hair, blue eyes, and dimpled chin.

"Those skeletons might be difficult to find," Prescott said. "Durand is a Civil War veteran, and his firm is one of the most highly regarded on Wall Street. Along with his holdings in the St. Paul, he has large investments in the First National Bank and Standard Oil. He could sit on all three companies' boards, but he's a loner and hates committees and boards."

"He sounds like a tough nut to crack. What if we can't find anything?" Edwin said.

"There's always something." Curtis scowled. "We just have to dig deep. We'll find it."

The sons glanced at each other uneasily. Edwin shuddered.

"There's one other thing, gentleman," Winfield said. He never called them "boys" or "sons," it was always "gentlemen." "Prescott is quitting his position in New York to devote his full time to our interests. He'll work with Archer and Micah."

Harrison, Edwin, and Baldwin nodded their congratulations to Prescott and avoided looking at Archer. Their father's statement carried momentous implications. He had decided that Archer did not have what it would take to someday run the Winfield empire. None of them was foolish enough to believe that a sentimental attachment to the oldest son would outweigh considerations of ability, but as the oldest son, Archer had been given the first chance to fill his father's shoes. Now power was shifting to Prescott.

Furious and humiliated, Archer smoldered on the sofa as the meeting broke up and the other men left the library. It was Durand's fault, and if Durand was now to be a target of the family's vengeance, he was also going to be the object of Archer's personal vendetta. Yes, he would get Durand. By any means fair or foul, he would get Durand.

The Durands were returning from a birthday party for Peter Groves, Will's classmate, at the Groves' estate. The birthday had been an excuse for Peter's father to show off his new three-story Italianate mansion and its English garden. New York City's elite had been invited to an afternoon "picnic" that had stretched well into the night. The Durand clan, tired but, with one exception, happy, stepped down from the carriage, still chattering noisily about the party. The hostler helped Eleanor, Laura, and Constance step down. The yellow ribbons in Constance's hair matched her yellow party dress, stained where she had spilled ice cream. The seven-year-old was still floating, ecstatic at attending a grown-up party.

Only Will seemed pensive, dissatisfied with the day's festivities. As they entered the house, Eleanor asked, "What's wrong, Will? Didn't you enjoy the party? All your friends were there."

"No, Mother, I'm fine, it was a nice reception," Will said unenthusiastically.

"Will's mad," nine-year-old Tommy said, "because all the girls were sweet on Andrew Elmwood and they ignored him." Still in short pants, black-haired Tommy seemed destined to be both the tallest and thinnest of the Durand children.

"Why you little insolent…I ought to box your ears!" Will snatched his brother by his lapel.

Daniel grabbed Will's arm. "What kind of rot is that—boxing his ears? No one in this family has their ears boxed, and if they do, it will be by me."

Tommy poured it on. "He can't pass a mirror without looking at himself. Too bad the girls don't love him as much as he does!"

Alexander chortled, and Laura and Constance giggled. Will wrenched away from Daniel's grasp and aimed a roundhouse punch at Tommy, who ducked and scampered away.

"Will," Daniel said. "Take another swing at one of your brothers and your next fight will be with me. Get up to your room."

Will tromped up the stairs.

"It's late," Eleanor said. "The rest of you get ready for bed."

The other children went upstairs, leaving Daniel and Eleanor alone in the entryway.

"Are you going to say anything to Tommy, for provoking Will?" Eleanor said.

"If the truth provokes Will, that's his problem, not Tommy's."

One day Daniel came to work earlier than usual to catch up on paperwork and found a young man sitting on the couch in the ante-room outside his office, undoubtedly let in by Michael Palos, always the first to arrive. The young man had brown eyes, a thin long nose that went with his thin long face, and a scraggly beard. Although he wore a suit, not a yarmulke and kaftan, he could have been a rabbinical student, but his restless eyes suggested he wasn't suited for a life of scholarly contemplation.

"May I help you?" Daniel said.

"Are you Mr. Durand?"

"Yes."

"My name is Jakob Gottman. My grandfather, Isaac Gottman, referred you to me. May I have a moment of your time, sir?"

Daniel was delighted to see this young man, a link to memories of Abram Gottman and Cleveland. "Certainly, step into my office."

"How is Isaac?" Daniel asked as they settled into their chairs.

"Well and prosperous, thank you. He retired from the store and turned it over to my father several years ago. He sends his best wishes."

Daniel peppered young Gottman with questions about his family and Cleveland. His answers were brief and to the point. He spoke with no trace of an accent, didn't sprinkle his conversation with Yiddish, and demonstrated none of Abram's gift for telling stories.

"What brings you to New York?"

"I want a job in your firm."

"And what would you have to offer as an employee of Durand & Woodbury?"

"I've gone to school and worked part-time in the store since I was seven. I write well, and do accounting, purchasing, and finance." Gottman leaned forward in his chair. "What I like to do is sell. The store had its best days when I worked. I sold to *goyim*, to Jews, to men, to women, to old people, to children—to everyone. My father is saddened that I've come to New York, but I do so with his blessing. He said I owed myself the opportunity."

"You've got chutzpah."

"I've got chutzpah."

"And what would you sell here?"

"What do you have here? A stock is a stock. A bond is a bond. A deal is a deal. What you peddle has to be sold, doesn't it? Just like dry goods and pots and pans."

"Yes, it all has to be sold," Daniel said. There was the religious issue. Wall Street had divided into *goyim* and Jewish firms. There were a few *goyim* employed at Jewish firms and vice versa, but it wasn't the usual practice. "Why do you come to me? There are a number of respected Jewish firms."

"I want to make it in New York, Mr. Durand, in your world. You're the only banker I know here, but it's not just that. I want to be a successful banker, period, not a successful Jewish banker. Perhaps that's hard for you to understand, but that's my ambition. Grandfather said you didn't let prejudices get in the way of business."

No, he didn't allow any kind of irrationality to get in the way of business. Reaching out to the Jews had been a profitable strategy in Cleveland, and there were a lot more Jews in New York. The firm could use some chutzpah. "We'll put you on a two-week trial."

"You are absolutely despicable!"

Will smiled at his fifteen-year-old sister, Laura, who had just burst into his room and hurled her malediction. With her dark eyes blazing, she reminded him of Father when he was mad.

"How could you do what you did?" she demanded.

"What was that, dearest Laura?"

"You know! You've been flirting with the Harrison twins. I tried to warn them, but they're both sweet on you and they wouldn't listen. Darcy and Candace are so close and you caused a rift between them. They're at odds, and today I find out you've moved on to Priscilla Wilkerson, and Darcy and Candace won't speak to me!"

Will smiled again. "It's a first for me, breaking two hearts at once."

"You're horrid, absolutely horrid. I'm going to tell Mother and Father."

"Are you sure you want to do that, sister? I might be forced to tell Bruce Elway about the warm place he holds in your affections."

"I detest him!"

"I know, but he would need only the slightest encouragement to make himself inseparable from you. That might frighten away shy Holman Stevens, who, if I might venture a guess, is the true recipient of your affection."

"You…you wouldn't."

"I would."

"That's…that's…that's despicable!" Laura slammed the door and left the room

Eleanor remembered the last time she had stepped up the stairs to the church in Cleveland. Her brother Steven and the man named Baldwin had stopped her because her father wouldn't allow Daniel to attend her mother's funeral. That was the final, irrevocable break. She had never forgiven him, but never was too long for the rest of her family. Today, at her father's funeral, she would reconcile with her sisters, Josephine and Rebecca, and her brothers, Steven and Michael.

The autumn sun shone through wispy clouds. Trees rustled and windblown leaves tumbled down the stairs. Bells tolled as Daniel took her hand and the Durand family merged into the crowd filing into the church. Eleanor saw looks of shocked recognition and she returned stares with nods and polite smiles. The church was dimly lit after the outside brightness.

"We'll sit in the section reserved for the family," she said to the usher. Daniel took her arm and they walked down the aisle, Will, Laura, Alexander, and Tommy behind them. John and Constance

were with their nanny at the hotel. Heads turned and there were fur-
tive whispers. Eleanor kept her gaze focused on the closed casket
before the altar. They reached the front rows and the usher removed
a cord across the pews reserved for the family. She saw her brother,
Michael, her sisters, and their families, most of whom she had never
met. Her brother Steven wasn't there.

There was an awkward silence. "Is there enough room?" Eleanor
whispered. Her sister Rebecca smiled, stood, and opened her arms
to Eleanor. They embraced.

"There's room. Delighted to see you and your family." Rebecca
extended her hand towards Daniel. "You must be Mr. Durand. I'm
Eleanor's sister, Rebecca."

Through the murmured pleasantries and expressions of surprise,
Eleanor detected an undercurrent of anxiety. Her sisters and brother
glanced frequently towards the back of the church. The minister had
stepped to the altar before Steven entered. He hurried down the aisle
and squeezed into the pew, next to Eleanor. She was shocked by his
appearance—massively overweight, his body, fingers, hands, and
facial features grotesquely bloated. His tie was askew. Almost lost
amidst the fleshy lumps of his cheeks, his bloodshot eyes registered
surprise verging on fear.

"What are you doing here?" His breath was a blast of liquor.

"We've come to pay our respects," Eleanor said.

Daniel extended his hand. "Steven, good to see you again."

Clumsily reaching over Eleanor, Steven extended his hand.

"A pleasure."

The funeral featured three eulogies, one from the mayor of
Cleveland, but tellingly, none from the Haverford family. The town's
worthies donned their masks of solemn respectfulness. Eleanor
wondered how many of them were glad to see her father go. She felt

unmoved, empty. Except for a few sniffles and tears from those who always cried at funerals, there wasn't a wet eye in the house.

Finally the last "amen" was murmured. The pallbearers, including Eleanor's younger brother, Michael, but not the unreliable Steven, carried the casket down the aisle and out of the church. The rest of the Haverford family filed out of their pews and followed. They stopped on the church stairs and watched the pallbearers load the casket onto the hearse.

"What happens now?" Tommy said. "Where will that wagon go?"

Eleanor smiled. It must have tried her son sorely to sit still through the service without asking a question or starting a conversation. She ran her fingers through his hair, dark like Daniel's, and put her hand on his shoulder. The ten-year-old was rail-thin despite an always hearty appetite. No potential excess ounce could withstand the blast furnace of his irrepressible energy. "That wagon is called a hearse, Tommy. It will take the casket to the cemetery."

Steven put his hand on Rebecca's arm. "I'll see you at the reception. I'm going to skip the cemetery." He waddled away without looking at Eleanor.

"It was quite a privation for him, going the entire funeral without drink," Rebecca said acidly. "There'll be no alcohol at the reception, so he has to get it now."

Eleanor shook her head. "We'll see you at the cemetery," she said, squeezing her sister's hand.

A large, six-horse coach conveyed the family to the cemetery. Only one other carriage had arrived at the gravesite. A low wooden platform stood beside a hole covered with a tarp at the Haverford family plot.

"Darling," Eleanor said to Daniel. "I'd like to be alone at Mother's grave."

Daniel nodded and Eleanor stepped out of the coach, aided by the coachman. She had asked him to find some flowers during the service. He handed her a simple bouquet of freshly cut daffodils and tulips. "Thank you," she said, handing him a coin.

She walked to her mother's grave and laid the bouquet before the granite headstone.

LAURA HAVERFORD
MARCH 18, 1818—SEPTEMBER 20, 1872
MAY HER SOUL KNOW PEACE

The emotions of mourning that she had not felt at the church came now as tears streamed down her cheeks. Mother had defied Father, for Eleanor's sake, and for the sake of her children. If Mother and Father were joined after death, it wouldn't be in heaven. A just God would keep them apart. She stood before the grave, head bowed, for several minutes.

The graveside service for her father was short. The pastor read a few Bible verses and said a prayer. After pleasantries the family climbed back in the coach and Eleanor directed the coachman to her father's mansion on Euclid Avenue.

"Rebecca has been wonderful," Eleanor said. "I wonder if everyone else will be so forgiving. It will be a long afternoon if everyone gives us the cold shoulder."

She needn't have worried. Her family and the guests at the reception accepted them with open arms. From elderly dowagers who were undoubtedly aghast when Eleanor married Daniel, to her young nieces who had heard the stories about their impetuous aunt, female after female took Eleanor's hands, offered condolences, and asked her about life in New York. Her scandalous behavior had been transmuted into an almost Shakespearean romance. Daniel enjoyed a warm reception and Will attracted a crowd of young men and women. The other children disappeared into a horde cavorting on the back lawn of the Haverford mansion.

"My, my, sister, you and yours have certainly been welcomed back to Cleveland," Stephen said, slurring his s's, taking Eleanor's arm while blasting her with one-hundred-proof breath. "If you had married a failure, dearest Eleanor, they would all be the same sanctimonious hypocrites as when you left town, but Durand is the richest bastard here, so all is forgiven. There's not a scruple out there that can't be bought."

"I favor a more charitable explanation for their goodwill."

"Don't be a fool. The last thing any of these people deserve is charity."

Eleanor was exhausted by the time the Durands' coach left the reception to take the family to their hotel. She had seen Abigail Keane, Constance and Jonathan and their families, and reconciled with her own family, her goal in returning to Cleveland, but she had a disquieting feeling. After the children were asleep, she sat with Daniel on a sofa in the suite's sitting room. A fire blazed in the fireplace. "What did you think of the reception?" she said.

"Henry Fielding wrote in *Tom Jones* that among the upper classes, the request is never made to kiss one's posterior, but it's always done, while among the lower classes the request is often made, but it's never done. I've never had my posterior kissed as much as it was today. Everybody has a son, nephew, or grandson who wants a job in New York. Your brother Michael offered to open an office for Durand & Woodbury here in Cleveland."

"What did you say?"

"I said we had no plans to open a Cleveland office."

"He would have regarded it as a social plum, not a job. It was good to see him and his family and my sisters and their families, but—"

"But you were disappointed."

"They've waited too long for this, for their precious inheritances, dancing to my father's tune. They were afraid of him and it's drained the life out of them."

Daniel chuckled. "You heard where some of that inheritance came from?"

"Archer Winfield's family! I can't believe father sold his bank—and your bank—to them."

"When we sold to your father, Mr. Keane predicted our best people would leave for other jobs. He was right, but Micah Baldwin managed to put things back together. Now he's got a high position with the Winfields. I wonder how that family operates. They seem more like a business, but Woodbury says they're very politically connected."

She stared at him. "Stay away from them, Daniel. They play by their own rules."

"I got what I wanted from them—you—and a big price for our bank. I'll stay away."

The Durand family sat around the long dining room table, enjoying a Saturday dinner. Daniel was out of town on business. Will sat in his place at the head of the table. Eleanor presided over the boisterous give-and-take among her five oldest children—even seven-year-old Constance held her own. John sat in a high chair and his nanny fed him porridge.

"Will, I hear you won an election," Laura said.

"Uh, that's right, I did."

"You won an election and you didn't mention it?" Eleanor asked. "That's not like you, Will."

"Uh, yes. I was elected president of the rowing club."

"Whom did you run against, Will?" Laura said.

Will's answer was unintelligible.

"Whom did you beat?" Laura again asked.

"Timothy Dickens" was the mumbled reply.

"Timothy Dickens," Eleanor said. "Didn't he sponsor your membership in the club last year?" She stared at her son, who looked away as he nodded his head. "Oh Will, you're better than that."

Will glared at Laura across the table. She smiled sweetly.

Will sipped his coffee. Daniel knew he wasn't particularly fond of it, but it was the adult thing to do. At seventeen his appearance was closer to that of a man than a youth. About six feet tall, he was shorter than his father, but stouter. His blue eyes, wavy blond hair, and handsome features—strong chin, Roman nose, high cheekbones—favored his mother. The three sat in Daniel's study—Will had requested a private setting—Daniel and Eleanor on one beige plush sofa, Will on the other, the coffee service set on a walnut table between the sofas. Daniel's massive mahogany desk and chair on the back wall dominated the room. Bookcases lined the other three walls. A muted, patterned carpet of grays and greens covered the floor.

Will set his cup and saucer on the table and looked first at Daniel and then his mother. "Mother, Father, I've decided that I want to attend Harvard. I've talked to Mr. Cunningham. He says that with my marks, his position as headmaster, a letter of recommendation, and his influence at Harvard, he can secure a place for me in next year's class."

Both Will and Eleanor stared at Daniel. He didn't share many of his Wall Street contemporaries' disdain for higher education. The books on his bookshelves were dog-eared, with underlined passages and notes in the margins. An autodidact, he would like to have shared his education with teachers and fellow students.

"Why do you want to go to Harvard?"

Will smiled. "Do you remember about a year ago at that reception, the bombastic professor from Columbia? I'll never forget what you muttered to me as he was spewing forth his nonsense: 'It takes years of education to produce such an idiot.'" He smiled again. "While I recognize the danger of idiocy, I think Harvard attracts first-rate students and professors, and presents the best environment for the serious pursuit of scholarship."

Daniel crinkled has forehead. He expected better than this, especially since Will had obviously put a great deal of thought into it, probably rehearsing it before the mirror in his room. "What subject do you intend to seriously pursue?"

Will glanced at Eleanor. "I'm not sure. My interests will develop more fully once I've had the opportunity to see what's available. A Harvard education will serve me well in later life. I'll be associating with men who will be at the heads of their fields—politics, law, science, education, and business."

"I've only met a few Harvard men in my work. These future leaders, they'll help you in your own field, once you decide what that field will be?"

"Of course, Father. I'll be meeting the best people."

"The best people for what?"

"The best people to know, to advance my career."

"Is who you meet at Harvard more important than what you learn there?"

"That doesn't sound right. That's not what I mean."

"What do you mean?"

"I mean...I mean that Harvard offers advantages that aren't available elsewhere."

"We're going around in circles. What are those advantages?"

"Father, I should think the advantages of attending the finest university in the country are self-evident," Will said, obviously exasperated.

"Not to your obtuse father. You want to attend Harvard but you don't know what you want to study. You say you'll meet the best people, whatever that means, but that's not your primary reason for going, either. What do you hope to get from Harvard?"

"Does he have to have all the answers right now?" Eleanor said, evidently sharing Will's exasperation. "Does he have to have *any* answers right now? He wants to go to Harvard because he wants to go to college and Harvard is the best college."

"When you finish Harvard, would you want to work at Durand & Woodbury?" Daniel asked.

"Probably, but I'd like the opportunity to be on my own for a while."

"Let me talk this over with your mother."

"Certainly." Will stood. "Thank you for hearing me out." He left the study.

"What was the point of that little inquisition?" Eleanor said, pique in her voice. "You know why Will wants to go to Harvard. He reads about Mr. Morgan's yacht, the Vanderbilt mansions, Mr. McAllister's Four Hundred, Saratoga Springs, Newport, and so on. He wants a seat at that table."

"Why didn't he just say that?"

Eleanor sipped her coffee. "What do you mean?"

"Beware reasons that don't proclaim themselves. Why does he want to join high society? So he can spend time in clubs, go to operas and fancy balls? That's not his motivation."

"Then what does he want?"

"He gave it away when he talked about leaders in their fields. The first field he mentioned was politics. Will likes people paying attention to him, and he particularly likes telling them what to do. He's after power."

"You make it sound like an indictment."

"It is an indictment. Why do you think Will wouldn't say it? He knows the way I think. It's the love of power, not money, that's the root of evil."

"Do you realize what you're saying about your son?"

"I do. On the surface, Harvard will make him a better man—polished, sophisticated, urbane, and well connected. But he'll emerge with the delusion that he's entitled to run the world. That's what they teach at Harvard and it's what Will wants to hear. His little sneer, the one you don't like—when he's through with Harvard, I wager we'll see a lot more of that sneer."

"But you'll allow him to attend?"

"It's dangerous for him, the worst place he could go, but I won't stop him."

"You mystify me. Why?"

Daniel stood, walked to a bureau, took a cigar from the humidor, and rolled it in his fingers without lighting it.

"Because I love him. If I were to deny him Harvard, it would cause an irreparable rupture. He'd probably find a way to go. I don't like the path he's chosen or the reasons he's chosen it. Nothing good will come of it, but it's his choice and he's too old for me to stop his choices, although I won't always be paying for them. I want to stay close to him, because someday he may discover the truth about himself. When he does, he'll need me."

Eleanor stared at him for a long time. "You're wrong about Will."

"No, I'm not.'"

George Baker, president of the First National Bank, paced on the dock where Pierpont Morgan's *Corsair* was berthed. An accomplished sailor, he admired the massive black yacht looming above him as he waited for Daniel Durand. Yachting had become a mania among New York's aristocracy. At one time the 189-foot-long *Corsair* had been the biggest boat on the pond, but Jay Gould's 230-foot *Atalanta* had supplanted it. Baker didn't doubt that Pierpont would eventually commission a still larger yacht. That was the way he was.

Baker had delayed this first meeting between Morgan and Durand for as long as he could. Morgan was the quintessential insider, Durand the quintessential outsider. Baker suspected they would mix as readily as oil and water. He had offered once to sponsor Daniel's membership to a prestigious club. Daniel's wealth and position virtually guaranteed his acceptance, but Baker had known the answer before he asked.

"No, thank you."

"Why not?"

Daniel smiled. "I like people, at least some of them, well enough by themselves. People change when they get in groups, and not for the better. The group becomes the tool for the strongest people in the group and swallows up the rest. I don't want artificial allegiances—I want to pick the people with whom I associate."

"It would cement your position as a financial leader."

"Cement is the right word. Nothing moves through concrete."

He had not pursued the matter. However, one could only stall Morgan for so long, and he had insisted on meeting the rising star of New York finance.

Baker saw Daniel at the end of the dock and waved. It was the first time he had seen his friend dressed in other than a dark suit and hat. Today he wore a light gray suit with pinstripes and a wide-brimmed white hat that softened his severe features. Clean-shaven, with almost no gray in his dark hair and a still slender frame—had Durand found the fountain of youth? Baker's girth and luxuriant beard, mustache, and sideburns, turning gray, made him look much older than the man extending his hand to him, although the difference in their ages was only a few years.

"Good to see you, George," Daniel said.

Baker waved his hand in invitation towards the gangplank and they walked up to the deck. From the tip of the raised prow that pointed the yacht not towards the water but to the sky above; to the long, sleek wheelhouse; to the three yellow smokestacks, one stout and two thin, raked back as if blown that way by ocean winds; to the massive aft deck and angled American flag fluttering on its stern post, everything done in gleaming dark wood and white trim, the *Corsair* was the embodiment of propulsion and speed. Below decks, the idling steam engines threw off a steady vibration that hinted at their power. Baker had been on the yacht several times and took it in quickly, but Daniel seemed to inspect the vessel foot by foot, as an engineer might.

"Welcome aboard, Mr. Baker." A member of the crew, a tall man dressed in white, approached them. "And you must be Mr. Durand. Everyone's aft."

About fifteen men, all of whom Baker knew, congregated on the deck, smoking cigars and holding drinks. Members of the crew manned a bar and carried trays of hors d'oeuvres. A small group huddled around Morgan. Baker escorted his friend around the deck, making introductions. Daniel already knew some of the men. For someone with his antisocial tendencies he made conversation well, asking questions and listening intently to the answers. He had a good memory for names, never forgetting one after an introduction. Baker began to relax. Maybe the evening wouldn't be as awkward as he had feared.

The engines rumbled as the yacht pulled away from the dock. South down the Hudson River, with Manhattan port and New Jersey starboard, the yacht steamed toward the Atlantic, wending between barges, freighters, clippers, schooners, and pleasure craft. Daniel smiled, apparently enjoying the setting sun on his face and the wind blowing through his hair, the gentle up-down rocking as the big boat flew over small waves, the crisp air, and perhaps the feeling that he had left his cares and troubles back on shore. He had said he had limited experience with boats, but to Baker he seemed more in his element than any of the other men on deck, except for Morgan. The knot around the financier dispersed and Baker made the pivotal introduction.

"Mr. Pierpont Morgan, may I present Mr. Daniel Durand?"

Baker watched the two men shake hands and exchange greetings. The first thing Baker had noticed, the first thing everyone noticed about Pierpont Morgan, was his dark eyes—they held a compelling, hypnotic sway. The Morgan stare had brought captains of industry and titans of finance to their knees, but aboard his yacht, his floating domain, his stare relaxed to intent watchfulness. Daniel had a few inches on him, but Morgan was the stouter, more imposing figure. He wore a dark blue suit and a gold tie with blue anchor decorations. About fifty years old, his hair was thinning, mostly white. A white mustache extended to his chin. His face was square and solid. Only the prominent red and purple veins in his nose marred his otherwise handsome appearance. Morgan liked his drinks and cigars.

"Mr. Durand," Morgan said, "I expected an older man. You've made quite a name for yourself in a short time." This was a host's flattery—Morgan had quizzed Baker about Durand, including his age.

"I admire your yacht, sir. I was hoping I'd have a chance to see the wheelhouse, maybe ask the captain a few questions."

"But of course! Every owner loves to show off his boat, even if it's a tub. Let's refresh our drinks. You don't have a cigar, Mr.

Durand. We'll find one to your liking and then I'll give you the two-dollar tour." Morgan put his hand on Daniel's shoulder and Baker understood that he was not invited. He slid away and joined a conversation with several of his other friends.

As Manhattan faded into the distance off the port stern and the *Corsair* cruised through the Verrazano Narrows between Staten and Long Islands, a bell sounded and Morgan, Daniel, and the other guests converged in the dining room below decks. A long table was set with fine china, crystal, silverware, silver candlesticks, and a starched white linen tablecloth and napkins. Liveried servants filled water goblets and wine glasses. Morgan took his seat at the head of the table and announced that dinner would be a "light" six courses.

It was a convivial meal, the bonhomie increasing with each refill of the wine glasses. At first Morgan dominated the conversation, but a group of six men that Morgan called the Corsair club, who regularly cruised with Morgan, were interspersed around the table. They all had stories to tell. The *Corsair* had, on occasion, served other than business purposes. It seemed that both Mr. and Mrs. Morgan enjoyed lengthy annual vacations to Europe, but not with each other. Several of the guests expressed their envy at this "excellent" state of affairs. Morgan's salacious winks made it clear that he had found ways to assuage any loneliness he might have felt in his wife's absence. Many times the *Corsair*'s passenger roster had included feminine names, some of which also graced the *Social Register*.

Baker, getting a little tight, embraced the spirit of the evening; Daniel, sitting next to him, did not. He sipped his wine and stifled several yawns. This was more what Baker had expected of him—Durand the damn Puritan. Amidst the cornucopia of food and drink, he showed the most enthusiasm when his coffee was poured.

After a two-hour feast, the host and his guests moved to a large salon in the forward bulkhead. It had several quilted plush divans, sofas upholstered in black and gold silk, and mahogany cabinets that matched the paneling. Morgan made a point of motioning Daniel to sit in a chair next to him. Baker sat next to Daniel.

Pierpont slowly performed the ritual of cutting, with a gleaming gold cutter, a fresh cigar and lighting it. Daniel cut his cigar and Morgan lit it. He sipped his brandy and said, "I understand, Mr. Durand, that you have some involvement with Mr. Hill's railroad."

"I'm not on the board, but I have a substantial investment."

"Do you enjoy cordial relations with Mr. Hill?"

"Cordial enough, but I don't know him well."

"Mr. Hill presents a problem. His aggressive tactics and cutthroat rates pose a threat to the stability of the entire Northwestern transportation system. He's failing to recognize the necessary community of interest in the region." Morgan took several long puffs from his cigar. "I'd like you to use your influence with Mr. Hill to see if he won't agree to a more rational rate structure."

Baker noticed that the other conversations in the salon had stopped. Daniel's face remained impassive. When he spoke, his voice was low but firm.

"You mean you want me to see if he'll fix rates with the Northern Pacific?"

Morgan cleared his throat. "Essentially, yes—to keep the peace in the region."

"No."

The answer seemed to hang in the air like something tangible. Baker had seen several businessmen—John D. Rockefeller, steel magnate Andrew Carnegie, and James Stillwell, president of a rival New York bank—use silence to devastating effect. Morgan was a master. His eyebrows arched. Equanimity unbroken, he stared at Daniel as he would a large rut that blocked his carriage—a problem, to be sure, but no cause for alarm. Baker felt anxious, but Daniel appeared equal to the test of wills. He never looked away from Morgan.

"Am I to understand, Mr. Durand," Morgan said calmly, "that you're refusing this request?"

"I am."

"Why?"

"The Northern Pacific is an uncompetitive, second-rate line. As a major shareholder of Mr. Hill's St. Paul line, I don't want to see him offering relief on rates to the Northern Pacific. I'd prefer that he drive it out of business and take it over."

"Are you aware that I'm a director of the Northern Pacific?"

"Yes."

"Young man, you don't appreciate the risks of having only one railroad in the Northwest."

"Were you worried about those risks when the Northern Pacific was the only line?"

Morgan took a long puff from his cigar, emitted a small cloud, turned, and began talking to one of his friends. It was a curt, appallingly rude dismissal. Daniel glanced around the room and Baker saw the other guests avert their eyes. Daniel had been ostracized. "Excuse me," he said, and left the salon. His cigar remained in its ashtray.

Several minutes later Baker slipped out and found Daniel at the stern rail. The *Corsair*'s churning wake and the spray it threw off illuminated a foamy white iridescence against the darkness. Baker rubbed his hands against the cold and stood by Daniel, staring at the wake, not saying anything for some time.

"You could have stalled, put him off somehow."

Daniel looked at Baker as if noticing him for the first time. "What good would that have done? I wasn't going to do what he asked. I've found no more succinct, readily understandable way to say 'no' than to say 'no.'"

"Yes, but it created an awkward situation."

"That couldn't be helped."

"Daniel, you don't want to make an enemy of Pierpont Morgan."

"I believe I already have. Morgan went on quite a bit during our tour. He's all for innovation and progress—on his terms—but he has this sense of propriety, of order and rank. His problem is that he's trying to impose it on capitalism. By his position and sheer force of personality he may be able to hold things together for a time. But capitalism is nonstop change. Nobody will stay on top for more than a few decades—too much is required to keep ahead. Mr. Morgan asks Mr. Hill to preserve the peace as if this were a squabble among feudal barons. How quaint. He's not going to turn business into a gentlemen's club, with everyone observing his rules. Mr. Hill has no truck with such nonsense. Morgan will bend to him or they won't do business."

"Well, this railroad competition is getting out of hand. The interstate commerce act is going to pass."

"That's it, isn't it? If you want to slow down a great railroad, go to the government. It will be the law and it will end up creating a railroad cartel more effective than anything Morgan and the railroad barons could dream up. Some commission will regulate rates, allocate territories, and decide how much money everyone makes. The Northern Pacific will have a leg up on Mr. Hill, who has this odd idea that one competes by building a superior line and setting low rates. Is bribery and wheedling favors out of Washington better than Hill's way?"

"There has to be a middle way…between outright political control and market anarchy."

"Between coerced and free markets? Good luck finding it, George."

Baker had no response. It was cold and he went below decks, leaving Daniel standing at the rail, watching the wake.

PART FOUR THE SECOND GENERATION

Chapter 16

Harvard

L ittle John had assumed his post, sitting on the bottom stair at the end of the entryway. He fit his nickname, small for his four years, a towhead whose round face usually wore an expression of uncomprehending sweetness. It was Friday afternoon. Will was coming home from his boarding school, the Concord Academy, and John would wait, for hours if need be, until Will came through the front door. Eleanor watched him, hands folded in his lap as he patiently sat for his older brother, and marveled at the odd, touching relationship that had developed between them. Will, who generally had no time for anything but his own pursuits, always had time for John, and once he came through the door the two would be inseparable while Will was at home.

Eleanor went into the kitchen to supervise dinner preparations. The front door opened and she peeked through the kitchen door. Will stood in the entryway, a bag in one hand and his overcoat in the other, and grinned at John. His smile was genuine, not the perfect, posed-for-a-photograph article he could summon when necessary. Will dropped the bag and hung his coat on a stand as John righted himself and toddled towards him. "Will, Will," John said.

He stretched out his arms and Will picked him up and hoisted him above his head, the toddler gurgling with delight. Will kissed him on the forehead and embraced him.

"How's Little John?" Will said, heartily. "Did you miss me as much as I missed you?"

Eleanor saw the too rare glimmer of comprehension on John's face. He nodded.

Will put John on his shoulders. "Grab my head." John locked his hands on Will's forehead. Will stooped to pick up his bag. "Let's go upstairs, I've got something for you.

When they got to Will's room, he put John down on his bed and opened the bag. He took out a scuffed baseball. "The other day Harlow hit a ball so far out of the yard that everybody gave up looking for it. After the game I went and found it. Concord's got lots of baseballs—this one will never be missed." He handed the ball to John, who took it and threw it. Will caught the ball, which otherwise would have crashed into a lamp. "You've got a good arm, but don't throw the ball inside the house, or Mother might get upset. Do you understand?"

"Yes, Will."

Will gave him the ball back. John rolled it on the bed, while for the next half hour Will told him about baseball games, rowing, how much he disliked mathematics, and what fun it was to short-sheet that obnoxious little pinhead Elmer Merckle's bed. John was an excellent listener, smiling when Will smiled, frowning when he frowned, and giggling happily when he laughed.

Thaddeus Cunningham, headmaster at the Concord Academy, sipped his coffee and glanced around the Durands' sitting room.

Most of his adult life had been spent in the sometimes enviable, sometimes unenviable position of living in the presence of wealth without having attained it, and he had become an expert appraiser. The sofas and divans of burgundy plush, landscape paintings, maple wood floors, Turkish carpets, and crystal chandeliers were of exquisite quality, chosen certainly by Mrs. Durand, a born aristocrat if he had ever met one. Tonight Cunningham had enjoyed the Durands' hospitality, offered because he was helping their son apply to Harvard. They had set a magnificent table for dinner and now they were in the sitting room for coffee, Cunningham and William on one sofa, Mr. and Mrs. Durand opposite them on the other.

"Does Harvard require students to take Latin and Greek?" Mr. Durand said.

"Yes."

"What about more usef—classes of more immediate applicability?"

Cunningham smiled. Mr. Durand had caught himself and softened his language, diplomacy from an undiplomatic man. He liked Mr. Durand. "Yes, there are science and history classes."

Cunningham was tall and thin, in his mid-fifties, with thinning brown hair, a wispy mustache, pale blue eyes, a narrow face, and prominent Adam's apple. He wore a sturdy black suit and simple black tie. A modest man, he was aware of people's indifferent first impression of him, one that was overcome as they discovered a first-rate mind, steely determination, and a rigid sense of honor. He had transformed the Concord Academy into an elite preparatory school. Mr. and Mrs. Durand, exceptions to the usual prejudgment, had asked all sorts of questions, discovering the person beneath the unprepossessing appearance.

He set his coffee cup and saucer on the table between the two sofas. "After such an excellent meal, a walk would be salutary." He glanced at William. He had taught him for two classes and recognized the look the youth had worn for most of the evening. William had not been particularly interested as his parents had questioned Cunningham, just as he had not been particularly interested in geometry, but he had paid enough attention to carry him through the evening, just as he had paid enough attention to angles, theorems, and proofs to secure an excellent grade. "Perhaps William could show me your neighborhood."

"Mother, Father, would you mind?"

"Not at all," Eleanor said.

Cunningham and Will stepped out into the warm summer twilight. The gas lamps were on and 52nd Street was alive with fashionable people on their evening strolls. Men smoked cigars and expounded; their women pretended to listen while eyeing the other women and comparing plumage.

"Do you have any advice, words of wisdom, for Harvard?" Will said.

"I remember the boy who entered Concord, and I look at you now—you're a man. I think our lessons sank in. If they have, they'll serve you well at Harvard, and if they haven't, nothing I can say now will help you."

"I suppose I'm a little anxious how I'll fit in. Harvard is a blue-blooded lot, especially the men from Boston."

It was disappointing that William's first concern was social, not academic. Disappointing, but not surprising. "The best advice I can give is to be your own man. Anyone who looks so far down his nose that he can't see you for what you are isn't worth your time."

"What about Harvard's final clubs? Should I try to join? Do you have any influence there?"

Of course William would care, perhaps obsessively, about the clubs. Their reputation for exclusivity, and the entrée they provided into the loftiest strata of American business, politics, and society, were legendary. To try to discourage him would be worse than useless. "My influence at Harvard is with the administration and faculty. The clubs are student-run affairs."

"Is lineage crucial? Mother comes from a distinguished Ohio family, but Father was an orphan. He doesn't even know his own birthday."

"That's what makes what he's done all the more remarkable, William," Cunningham said sternly. "Whether your Harvard classmates are impressed or not, you should be proud of him."

"Of course I'm proud! But his background may foreclose worthwhile opportunities."

"There's nothing you can do about that. Pursue your interests and be your own man. Let them come to you. What's important is what you think of them, not what they think of you."

There was something odd about the fleeting expression that flashed across William's face—as if he'd solved a difficult problem. It was odd because Cunningham had never seen that expression in the classroom. His words had had an effect, but he was sure it was not the one he had intended. Some of life's lessons were necessarily harsh; experience, as Benjamin Franklin had said, was "a dear school." William had important lessons to learn in that school. The headmaster was suddenly certain that the best thing that could happen to William would be if he was rejected by every one of the clubs.

The crowd—people rushing, porters pulling overloaded carts of luggage, conductors yelling, the heightened emotions of reunion and farewell, bumping and jostling; the trains—black iron monsters, whistles shrieking, steam hissing, engines chugging, wheels grating on the tracks; Eleanor had always found trains stations disorienting. She stood crammed with her family on the crowded platform at Grand Central Station, by the train that would soon take Will to Harvard. The train that would actually take two Wills to Harvard.

There was the Will she saw now, kneeling before Little John, holding his hands, trying to cheer the crying, disconsolate lad. There was nothing contrived about the way Will treated his little brother. He had forged a bond that no one else in the family, not even Eleanor, had been able to duplicate.

The other Will was the one most often on display. This was the Will who couldn't pass a mirror without looking at himself, delighted in breaking two hearts at once, defeated his sponsor for the rowing club in an election, and would abandon a friend if a more popular one became available. This was the Will that Daniel saw when he had said his son liked people paying attention to him, and that he was after power. Shocked at first, Eleanor later conceded to herself that he might be right, which raised obvious questions. How responsible were she and Daniel for Will's character? Where had they gone wrong? Where did parents' responsibility end and children's begin? She shared her husband's disdain for those who sought power. He regarded it as a pathological addiction, like alcoholism. Her judgment wasn't as severe, but the love of power was a grave weakness. How had Will acquired this ambition his parents loathed?

Will picked up John, hugged him, and kissed him on the forehead. He set him down and tousled his hair. "If you'll stop crying and be brave while I'm gone, I'll send you a letter every week. Constance or Laura can read it to you and they'll help you write letters to me. Do you understand?" Will made a gesture with his hands as if he were writing on a piece of paper.

John sniffled and the flow of tears abated. "Yes, Will."

A promise from Will wasn't money in the bank, but Eleanor was certain he would keep this one. He'd get a letter to his little brother every week, without mentioning his devotion to anyone at Harvard or caring if anyone found out. That was the Will that Eleanor would try to hold on to, but it didn't quell her anxiety.

The train whistle sounded. The crowd on the platform pressed towards the train. Eleanor, apprehensive—people fell from platforms—put her arms protectively around Tommy and Alexander. Will shook their hands. Constance and Laura cried as he hugged them stiffly. Now Will was standing before her and she couldn't hold back the tears. "I'll…I'll miss you, Will."

He embraced her. "I'll miss you, Mother. I'll write as often as I can."

Holding her ground against the teeming masses, roiled by her conflicting emotions towards her son, she wept. The first fledgling was leaving the nest and she hoped he'd fly. Will stepped away and grimaced. She knew her tears embarrassed him.

The conductor shouted, "All aboard!"

Will had to leave. He stepped towards Daniel and extended his hand. "Father."

To Eleanor's surprise, Daniel threw his arms around his son. His words were more in character. "This can be a great experience for you, Will. Make the most of it."

"Thanks, Father. I'll do my best." Will stepped back, tousled John's hair, grabbed his bag, pulled himself upright, squared his shoulders, hurried up the platform, and stepped onto the train. He waved to his family and they waved back. Little John cried. Will turned away before the train left the station—perhaps happy, Eleanor thought, to be rid of his family.

"Durand, if you can remember to start with the salad fork on the outside and work in, you should do just fine." So said Morton Billingsley, one of Will's friends at Harvard and the son of a Pennsylvania coal magnate. His older brother, Chester, a junior, knew the ropes. Will, Morton, and Chester were having a Saturday afternoon bull session in the brothers' apartment on Harvard Yard. A fire burned low on the hearth and a bearskin rug stretched across the floor. Chester's pride and joy, an eight-foot-long stuffed alligator named Overbite that had had the misfortune of wandering onto the Billingsley winter estate in Florida, occupied a place of honor in one corner. Chester sat in a chaise longue. Will and Morton were on a brown leather sofa. The brothers looked nothing alike. Chester was of medium height, stocky, red-haired, with a sprinkling of freckles on his beefy face. Morton was taller and thinner, and had a narrower face, with brown hair swept off his high forehead.

Will crinkled his forehead in mock confusion. "What was that on those forks—start in and work out? If I blow my nose at the table, do I hold the handkerchief in my left or right hand?"

"Either hand is proper if you use the tablecloth," Morton said.

"The Stewarts have hosted this soiree for years," Chester said. "It affords Brahmins with eligible daughters an opportunity to inspect Harvard's newest crop of suitable freshmen. The only thing worse than getting invited is not getting invited. It means you're not worth a glance down those long, snooty noses. When I went, most of the daughters were ugly. You'll meet their ugly sisters. There'll be a faculty member or two, and a few Adamses."

Will raised his eyebrows.

"Yes, *those* Adamses, and they'll ask how many presidents you have on your family tree. Somebody will talk about the *Mayflower* as if he just sailed over on it. If you're going to butter up the hostess, the house is done in Regency style. One poor soul said Georgian and was banished to Yale. Talk about the weather, talk about your classes, talk about old families and how they're the backbone of this great country, but don't, I repeat, don't mention M-O-N-E-Y. Every man there will come from wealth. Believe me, they'll know more about your family's finances than Dun & Bradstreet. If someone asks about your father, Will, he's not a banker, he's 'in banking.'" Chester sprung up from the chaise lounge. "That's the sum of my wisdom. Tonight you're on your own. I'm thirsty. Let's knock a few back."

"A splendid suggestion," Morton said, and they adjourned to their favorite tavern.

Will approached the hostess, Mrs. Stewart. The short, plump matron wore a gray dress and yellow blouse and bonnet, the queen bee in her exquisitely decorated hive. He smiled at her. "I must confess, Mrs. Stewart, home furnishings are not my strong suit, but I've noticed your rooms are done consistently in one style. From what period is that style?" He saw Morton roll his eyes.

"English Regency, Mr. Durand. I'd be delighted to show you our pieces."

"I'd be delighted to see them."

For the next fifteen minutes, Mrs. Stewart enthusiastically tutored Will about the slender, elegant lines of Regency antiques that filled the bottom floor of the three-story gabled manse. Will made appreciative noises. As they returned to the drawing room, Will said, "Your items are of such high quality they could be placed in a museum."

Mrs. Stewart beamed. "As a matter of fact, Mr. Durand, Mr. Stewart has set up a testamentary trust to donate some of our pieces to the Boston Museum."

The drawing room was a portrait gallery; a host of distinguished worthies watched from the walls as small groups stood in conversation. Will's "reward" for buttering up Mrs. Stewart was to have her steer him to one of the more unattractive guests, standing by herself.

"Miss Rebecca Wentworth, may I present Mr. William Durand?"

"A pleasure to meet you," Will said, as they shook hands and Mrs. Stewart slipped away. Rebecca was tall and thin, with a narrow face and long nose, pale green eyes, and dull brown hair with curls that had already gone limp.

"A pleasure. Where are you from, Mr. Durand?"

"New York City."

"Oh, I've been to New York many times. My aunt Priscilla— that's my mother's sister—lives there with Uncle Roger. Perhaps you know him—Roger Boyle? He's in the law."

Will shook his head. There were a few thousand lawyers in New York.

"We visit them every year at least once. I love the theatre. Last year we saw Mr. Gilbert and Mr. Sullivan's play *H. M. S. Pinafore* at the Standard. Have you seen that play? It's wonderful, I do recommend it. And I saw Sarah Bernhardt once, at Booth's Theatre..."

Miss Wentworth droned on. Will's eyes wandered from her unlovely face until they came upon a much fairer one. Across the room, a dark-haired beauty stood with a small group and she was looking in his direction. Her face was impassive and he wondered if she sensed his plight.

Morton rescued him. He tapped Will's shoulder and said, "Durand, Harvard has inexplicably admitted another New Yorker,

Tim Harkness. He's a trump—you'll want to meet him. Miss Wentworth, if I could steal Mr. Durand?"

"But of course."

Out of earshot of Miss Wentworth, Will muttered, "She's got a face a mother couldn't love, a body like my little brother's, and she won't shut up. Ten gets you one—spinsterhood!"

"I'd be taking your money. She has her charms. Her father's bank accounts have many, many digits."

"I see." So he'd be nice to her when they parted…but he'd make sure that was the only damn time he talked to her again.

"You'll want to meet Harkness. Both his father and uncle were Bovinity."

Will nodded. Bovinity, Porcellian, and A.D. were the three leading Harvard clubs. The names of the first two were spoofs of the clubs' cow and pig mascots. Morton's brother, Chester, had received one of Bovinity's prized invitations at the beginning of the school year.

They approached a knot of young men and women. One man, an athletic-looking fellow a head higher than everyone else, seemed to hold the group in his sway. As Will and Morton came up, he smiled, and Will could have sworn he heard a couple of feminine sighs. Truth be told, he did have an engaging smile, and Will could see how the women might be attracted to his muscular build, rugged features, blue eyes, and thick, sandy, wavy hair.

"Billingsley, there you are," the fellow boomed. "And who's this stalwart you managed to pry away from the lovely Miss Wentworth?"

"Tim Harkness, meet Will Durand," Morton said. "You're both New Yorkers."

They shook hands, Will's engulfed in Harkness' oversize mitt.

"Good to meet you, Will. Durand…Durand. Any connection to Durand & Woodbury?"

"My father, Daniel Durand."

"One of the finest banks on Wall Street. If you want to be a banker, Durand, you're set."

Harkness had broken a Chester rule with impunity. Will smiled. A couple of women cast discreet glances his way. "It is a great firm. I only hope I can fill my father's shoes one day."

Will had thought he knew all there was to know about charm, but fifteen minutes with Harkness left him feeling like a rank amateur. There was nothing calculated about his easy, confident affability. He was the center of attention but didn't monopolize the conversation, asking questions and showing a lively interest in what everyone else had to say. The affection that flowed towards him from both males and females seemed almost palpable. Will found himself, like everyone else, liking Harkness, but felt a twinge of jealousy as well.

A bell chimed for dinner and they went into an ornate dining room where three large chandeliers hung over a long table, covered in a white linen tablecloth and elaborately set with silverware, china, and crystal. Serving dishes were set on two sideboards covered with white linen runners. Four servants in burgundy livery stood ready to serve. Will's place card put him in proximity to Morton, Harkness, and two attractive young ladies, Miss Clarisse Fenster and Miss Evelyn Sharp. Only an older gentleman, Mr. Marbury, with pursed lips and a sour expression, appeared unpromising, a stuffed shirt.

The Brahmins carried the conversation, talking at length about the search for a new minister for the local church, making no effort to include the Harvard guests in the conversation. Will's attention wandered. He looked to the opposite end of the long table, where the dark-haired beauty sat, but looked away when she glanced at him. He was startled when a frail, ancient dowager who had not said a word barked, "They should bring back Parson Ames."

Miss Fenster whispered to Will, "That's Aunt Mildred, Mrs. Stewart's sister. She's daft—Parson Ames has been dead twenty years."

As off-beam as the remark had been, it served to loosen things up. The guests broke into a series of smaller conversations. Will found the food mediocre, overcooked, and wondered why his wealthy hosts couldn't have done better, but the talk among the younger people was enjoyable. The stuffed shirt said little.

"Mr. Durand, you and Mr. Harkness are both from New York City?" Miss Sharp said.

The stuffed shirt said, "I don't like New York. Such a dirty, unrefined place."

"Too many Jews. Sneaky people. Greedy," Aunt Mildred said loudly, voicing a widely held but rarely expressed sentiment. There was an uncomfortable silence.

"New York is dirty, and it can certainly be unrefined," Harkness said. "It has more taverns and saloons, more bums, hooligans, and thieves, more tenements and more bro—dance halls than anywhere else. There's plenty to dislike, but there's also plenty to like. New York has its fine old families, its citizens who share patrician Boston's devotion to civic uplift. It also has more churches and charities, more theaters and concert halls, more parks and museums than any other city. New York's too large, too varied, to be pigeonholed. It's what one makes of it."

"I meant no offense," Marbury said.

Harkness spread his arms magnanimously. "None taken, sir."

Will had never seen anyone disagree so agreeably. This was a talent he had to cultivate. The rest of the dinner continued without incident. After coffee and dessert the guests rose from the table and drifted back into the drawing room. The dark-haired beauty was talking to Miss Fenster. Will approached them.

"Miss Arabella Brewster," Miss Fenster said. "Mr. William Durand."

He took her hand. "Pleased to meet you, Miss Brewster."

"Pleased to meet you, Mr. Durand."

The dark ringlets of her hair cascaded down her forehead and framed a wide, rather round face that reminded Will of those portrayed in old Dutch paintings. Her skin was fair and smooth, with a rosy tinge in her cheeks. There was nothing particularly remarkable about her straight nose, strong chin and cheekbones, or placid blue eyes, but the whole was greater than the sum of the parts—her face was undeniably beautiful. She wore a long yellow dress, less elaborate than most of the other young women's, which emphasized the swell of her breasts and her slender waist.

"Weren't there Brewsters on the *Mayflower*?"

"Yes."

Will waited for further response. None was forthcoming. "Would they be your ancestors?"

"No."

No further response. Miss Fenster had slipped away. Was Miss Brewster shy, socially inept, or just trying to make things difficult for him? He wracked his brain for something to say. "Are you enjoying the party?" Clever.

"I enjoy seeing my friends, but we're supposed to be meeting the Harvard men. That part is harder for me."

"Why, are we that frightening?" He beamed his most disarming smile.

"Not frightening, really, but everyone tries to display the best parts of themselves at parties. I find it difficult to determine what's feigned and what's genuine, especially among the men. Who is truly kind—a gentleman—and who is not."

What an odd thing to say. "Have you met any gentlemen tonight?"

"I'm not sure. I thought Mr. Harkness was bold, the way he defended New York, but you probably want to know if I consider you a gentleman."

Will felt his face flush. "No," he stammered, "not at all. You'll make up your mind about me in good time."

"Perhaps, although sometimes I get more confused about people the longer I know them. I think, from the way you talk, that perhaps you're clever, or try to be so. Clever people often aren't very kind, but I can't say that about all clever people."

What could he say to that? "What line of work is your father in, Arabella?"

"He's a judge, a very respected, honest judge. He's not wealthy."

Will laughed. "Only the dishonest judges are."

"Yes, I know," she said softly. "Virtue is often its own, and only, reward."

Their hostess, Mrs. Stewart, fluttered up. Will wasn't sure if he was relieved or disappointed. Two young ladies, an older woman, and a Harvard man joined them, and Will had no more opportunity for private conversation with Arabella Brewster. When the evening drew to a close, Will took his leave of her, said farewell to Miss Wentworth, paid his respects to Mr. and Mrs. Stewart, and left the party with Morton. They walked through the Cambridge streets, their overcoats buttoned against the chill New England night.

"That pretty little flower you were talking with, Arabella Brewster," Morton said. "Her father, Phineas Brewster, is a judge. He wasn't there tonight. I understand he's been ill. By all accounts, he's the sternest judge in town, knows the law better than most people know their names, and loves torturing pompous attorneys. What did you think of Miss Brewster?"

"I don't know."

"What do you mean, you don't know? Did you like her?"

"I'm not sure."

"This is strange. What was she like?"

"I can't say for certain. She's either very simple or very wise."

"But you can't tell which?"

"No."

"Do you think you'll try to see her again?"

"Your guess is as good as mine."

"You need a pint."

His father had written two weeks ago that he had a business meeting and luncheon in Boston, but would have the afternoon free before he returned to New York; could he spend it with Will in Cambridge? Of course he could, Will had replied in a letter. He would give him a tour of Harvard and even arrange for him to sit in on a lecture. Daniel arrived late at night, attended to his business the next morning, and met Will on the campus early in the afternoon. Harvard showed well in its springtime glory, and Daniel asked Will about his classes, teachers, and activities. He listened more attentively to Professor Hippolite's history lecture than most of the students, and Will knew his father would have liked to ask questions. Unfortunately, Hippolite had an appointment after class and only had time for a brief introduction.

As they left the lecture hall, Daniel smiled and said, "All this education is thirsty business. Let's get a beer."

This was a first. Men drank beer together, and now one man would show another to his favorite pub. Already crowded and noisy when they entered, its clientele was mostly Harvard men. Waiters in dirty white shirts maneuvered between the tables, carrying trays laden with mugs of beer and plates of food. They found a small corner table where the din wasn't as loud.

"Well, Father, what do you think of Harvard?"

"I wish I had been able to do something like this." He smiled. "Just to be able to talk with the professors or other students about what you read and learn. That's the big drawback of 'self-taught.'"

This was a significant concession. Father had put Will through the wringer to justify his decision to come to Harvard, but now wished he had been able to attend. "At the beginning of the year, everybody acted as if the last thing they were interested in was learning—that was for the drudges." Will shook his head. "I suppose I was as bad as anybody. That's fading, though. The other night we discussed Tennyson and Yeats until well past midnight."

Daniel's face assumed a look of mock amazement. He had always been an enigma to Will. Impervious to external pressure, he was driven by powerful internal forces, some of which Will guessed, some of which remained a mystery. Will had thought of him as older than his actual age, but today there was something youthful about him. The years had been kinder to him than most men in their mid-forties, but it wasn't that. There had been an ever-present tension in his father's face, a tension of purpose, impatience, and preoccupation, his drum beating at double time to everyone else's. Today that tension wasn't there.

"Father, you seem more relaxed than usual, more easygoing."

He smiled again. Weeks went by when his father didn't smile.

"I've been thinking. Business is going well, you're off to college, the other children are growing up, and your mother is still the most beautiful woman in the world. It's time to step back, enjoy the fruits of my labor a bit, and spend more time with the family."

Too bad he hadn't had this revelation a few years earlier.

"Do you have a group of friends, Will?"

"Some of us—Harvard men, local women—do things together. Skating, ice cream socials, sailing, day trips to the countryside, and the like. My two best friends are Morton and Chester Billingsley, from Pennsylvania."

"Any of those local women strike your fancy?"

Should he say something about Arabella? He wasn't even sure he liked her, but he found her intriguing, or maybe just perplexing. He hadn't been alone with her very much. She acted the same with him—direct, unable to hedge or tack to the prevailing winds, sometimes simple bordering on naïve, other times wise bordering on profound—as she did with everyone else. Guile, pretense, flattery, and sarcasm—she rendered his usual arsenal useless…but once he had told her about Little John. The way she had looked at him then—admiration—had felt good. No, his feelings towards her were too unsettled, and perhaps too special, to reveal to his father, even this "new" Father. "No, not really, although some of them are pretty and nice."

An hour and a half of easy conversation, the easiest Will had ever had with his father, slid by. Daniel was in an expansive mood and Will wanted to listen. He opened up about his past. He told the story of his and Mother's marriage, a story Will had heard before but didn't mind hearing again, and mentioned the war, of which he seldom spoke.

"Why did you go to war?" Will asked.

"I was shoveling coal at the time and being a soldier seemed a more interesting career choice. You don't think about the dangers, don't really believe them, until you're on the battlefield, and the bullets and the shells start whizzing by and the man next to you drops dead."

"Did you fight to stop slavery?"

"No. When the war began, it wasn't about slavery. Lincoln wanted to increase the tariff. Since they paid higher prices for manufactured goods because of the tariff, the Southern states threatened to leave the Union. Lincoln said he'd accept slavery if it kept the Union together. I was young—I got caught up in the fervor with everyone else. That's when I learned something about following the crowd—it can get you killed. We fought to put down the rebellion by the South. Later, when the war wasn't going well, Lincoln turned it into a fight against slavery. Most of his soldiers were damn mad about it—they didn't care about the slaves. I'm happy they were freed, but I didn't go to war to free them."

"Do you regret volunteering?"

"Yes, although I might have been drafted and I didn't have any money to hire a substitute. Some veterans glory in their war experiences and want their sons to follow in their footsteps. I don't. I'm glad you're here."

Will nodded. There was a name he had been curious about since their night together at Mr. Hill's railway outpost on the Dakota plain. An odd coincidence gave him an oblique angle of inquiry and the beer emboldened him. He wanted to see his father's reaction to that name. "Hard to believe we're at the end of the school year. This week I select my classes for next year."

"What are you going to take?"

"I have to take English literature, probably with Mr. Munson. Mr. Cadwiler teaches a great forensics class, and I'd like to get into Mr. Pomeroy's class on political economy."

Sometimes his father's poker face worked against him—reactions were magnified because of their rarity. But there it was—a flinch when Will said "Pomeroy." Nothing most people would detect, just a slight tightening of the jaw, a backward movement of the head, and narrowing of the eyes, but unmistakable to Will.

His father recovered quickly. "Have you thought about what you want to do this summer?"

Will smiled. "I'd like to loaf a few weeks, and after that, I'd like to work at your office."

Daniel raised his eyebrows, evidently surprised. "That can be arranged, but don't think anybody's going to cut you any slack because you're my son. You'll be there to work."

Still the same "old" Father. "I'd expect no less," Will said.

"Good." Daniel withdrew his watch from his vest pocket. "I've got to catch my train." He took some money from his wallet and left it on the table. He picked up his valise and they walked out of the pub to a crowded Cambridge street. Will hailed a hansom cab.

"It was good seeing you, Will. Harvard is agreeing with you." He put his arm around his son.

"It certainly is. Great seeing you, too, Father. Give my love to everybody."

His father stepped into the cab and Will watched as the hack weaved amidst the people, wagons, and carriages on the street. He smiled. He had surprised his father twice in the space of a minute. His father didn't like surprises—they threw him off balance. However, it served Will's purposes to have his father off balance. He whistled as he walked back to his apartment.

Daniel stared into the night from his window seat on the train. Why had that name—Pomeroy—come up in his conversation with Will? Was it just one of those weird coincidences that a professor at Harvard had the same last name as a man Daniel had killed? Was the professor any relation? Daniel had never mentioned Pomeroy's name. Eleanor said Daniel sometimes talked in his sleep, but she had never said anything about that name. He had slept within ear-shot of Will several times—camping trips in the Adirondacks, the trip to Minnesota and Dakota. Had he said something while he slept during one of those trips? No, he was getting carried away with his fear about the deed hidden in his past and suffering from an overac-tive imagination. How had the conversation turned in that direction? Will said he had to pick his classes for next year, a logical topic. After he mentioned this Professor Pomeroy he'd said, in response to Daniel's question, that he wanted to work at the office that summer. Was there some sort of connection? Had Will's expression changed when Daniel said "Pomeroy"? Daniel stared into the night, unable to vanquish the doubt that marred an otherwise enjoyable visit with his son.

Arabella opened a basket, took out a bunch of grapes, a small jug, and a tin cup, poured water into the cup, and handed Will his re-freshment. She looked around Fresh Pond from their vantage point in a row boat at the center. It would be a scene to paint—thick stands of trees with an occasional opening for a path, the maples, birch, and ash, each one's leaves a slightly different shade of green, a few leaves turning red, orange, and gold, couples and families stroll-ing, dogs, a rising bluff, other people in rowboats, fishermen cast-ing their lines, thin clouds scudding across the cerulean sky, darker clouds looming on the horizon, the breeze rippling the water. She had painted a similar picture once, on a riverbank. She felt an anx-ious stab in her stomach. Should she ask her question now? No, bet-ter to wait, to work up to it.

"How was working for your father this summer, Will? Were you a little nervous?"

He smiled in an odd, rueful way. "I was more than a little nervous."

Good. He wouldn't have admitted that when she first met him. It was only logical; he was starting at his father's big firm, who wouldn't be nervous? Why not just admit it?

"I learned a lot about my father this summer, and about Durand & Woodbury. I thought some of the men might resent me, but it wasn't like that at all. They were polite, but they were just too busy to be either hostile or chummy. That's the thing that struck me—how hard they all work, especially my father. If he's taking it easier, he could have fooled me."

A fish splashed, and concentric rings spread out over the water.

She had started liking him the day she saw the part of him he kept hidden. It had been at a party at Mary Shipley's house, not long after Will had seen his father. They were alone in the Shipley's garden.

"Mr. Shipley certainly has his opinions," Will had said, "which he expresses quite forcefully."

It was a true statement, but it was like much of what Will said—cautious, bland. "Yes, that's true," Arabella said flatly.

Perhaps Will sensed something from her tone. He stopped walking and looked directly at her. It was as if he had made some sort of decision.

"Actually, he's a pompous blowhard who hasn't asked anybody else a question about themselves for thirty years. Nobody calls him to account because he owns Boston's largest printing company."

It was such a departure, so unlike anything Will had said before, that it startled her. That's exactly what Mr. Shipley was, a pompous blowhard, and she laughed. He laughed too and they were laughing together. They sat on a bench and talked and laughed for a long time. He said things about people they knew and spoke with no hedging, no restraint, and Arabella listened and marveled. A fissure had opened and the real Will came spilling out.

He saw deeper beneath the surface of people than she did. When she looked at something, she tried to see it exactly as it was. She amazed her father and brother with her detailed descriptions of a scene or a person's face. But what people presented to the world, what one saw, was often pretense. They disguised their true motives and intentions and she usually couldn't discern those. Her instincts were often correct about whether someone was telling the truth or lying, but that's as far as they went. Will dissected people with the precision of a biologist dissecting an organism. He saw them as they were. It was fascinating to hear him unravel the mystery of a personality, because his analyses coincided with what she felt, but couldn't define or articulate.

Now that he wasn't pretending, Will was much more interesting. There might be some dark undertones, but every good painting had dark undertones. Now, as he continued talking about the people in his father's firm, she felt, from the way he described them, as if she knew them, what they were about, and not just their superficial characteristics.

"Do you think you'll go into trading or banking?" she asked.

"Banking. People like me. Trading is solitary and I'm not solitary."

Will understood that about himself. With his insights into people, he could be a writer, but writing, like trading, like art, was solitary, and he was not solitary. And he was right—people liked him. She gazed at his face. She'd like to paint that face—the wavy blond hair sweeping off the high forehead; the well-defined cheekbones; the honed angles of his chin and nose; the expressive blue eyes; the unmarked skin, a darker tint that wasn't quite tan but contrasted well with his light hair; the fine mouth and lips, which weren't too full, like a woman's, but weren't too thin either, like many men's. What would it be like to have those lips on hers? She felt a stirring inside. She had never been kissed that way, although she had wondered about it. She was not embarrassed or shamed by her thoughts, any more so than when she saw a sculpture or painting of a nude male body. Men and women kissed—why act as if it was wrong or unnatural?

Will looked towards the bank where they had had their picnic. Dark clouds were rolling in and some of the rowboats had returned. Several anxious parents of the group they had come with were waving them in. "God and our chaperones are conspiring to prevent us from having any more time together," he said. "Much as it disappoints me to say it, we have to head back."

It was time to ask her question. She felt less nervous than she had earlier, but still nervous. "Will, would you like to come to my house for dinner two weeks from today? You'll meet my father, my brother, Ezekiel, and his wife, Deborah."

Will smiled. "I'd be delighted. I thought you seemed a little anxious, but you had nothing to worry about."

That was easy enough for him to say, but she couldn't know until she'd asked. She was relieved by his acceptance.

Will took the oars and began rowing. The breeze had turned into a wind and the water was choppier, making his job harder. His breathing grew heavier and sweat beads made their way down his forehead, into his eyes. She took a napkin from the basket and wiped his brow. He was working too hard to talk, but every so often he smiled at her. By the time they reached the bank, the sky had grown ominously dark. He jumped out of the rowboat, splashing in the water and getting his feet wet, and pulled the boat further up the bank so she could step to dry land. He took her hand as she stood to get out and they shared smiles that said more than words, but she wondered—what would her father and Will think of each other?

Will stood outside the three-story, red brick townhouse, which was trimmed in white. A maid opened the door and led him into an entryway, where he was greeted by a man his own height, but stockier, with bushy sideburns and the kind of stolid face that he associated with British men.

"Mr. William Durand?" the man said.

"Yes."

"Ezekiel Brewster. How do you do?" He extended his hand. His grip was firm and his direct gaze reminded Will of Arabella's. "May I take your hat and coat?"

Ezekiel put Will's hat and coat on a corner stand and led him to a sitting room, where Arabella, an older man, and a woman about Ezekiel's age, who Will assumed was Ezekiel's wife, sat on overstuffed sofas before a crackling fire in a large stone fireplace. The room had an intimate, roughhewn feel, with a stone floor, partially covered by an old brown rug, small windows, a low wood-beam ceiling, and a little nook with a padded bench under one of the windows—Will imagined Arabella reading there. The older man stood and advanced towards them.

"Mr. William Durand, my father, the Honorable Phineas Brewster."

They shook hands. Will was struck by the resemblance between father and son. The gaze of the father's dark eyes was more penetrating than Ezekiel's, as if he saw more. The face had a quality that reminded him of his own father's—its intent, serious cast suggested formidable intelligence. This would be a challenging evening.

Ezekiel introduced his wife, Mrs. Deborah Brewster, who sat next to Arabella. She was plump, with a round face that had no angles, just fleshy circles and semicircles, merry green eyes, and an easy smile. Will sat with Ezekiel on a sofa opposite Phineas, Arabella, and Deborah. Arabella looked fetching in a blue dress that matched her eyes and seemed to draw out the rosy redness of her cheeks. The maid served eggnog, a fine concoction, rich and creamy with only a hint of rum, not laced with it as it usually was in the taverns.

"Arabella tells us that you've completed your first year at Harvard, Mr. Durand." Judge Brewster's voice was deep and low. "What is your impression after one year?"

"It was everything I thought it was going to be, sir. I found most of the classes interesting, but difficult. The faculty and students are first rate. However, I worked hard and I'm proud to say I held my own. I'm looking forward to this year."

Will tried to answer Phineas and Ezekiel's subsequent questions without appearing either flippant or excessively earnest. The women said little, but Arabella occasionally smiled encouragingly. After a while, Phineas said, "Arabella, perhaps you'd like to show Mr. Durand the house."

Beneath the imposing exterior, maybe the judge had something resembling a heart. He was at least giving Will and Arabella some time together before dinner.

Arabella led him down a hallway into a larger, more formal room, featuring a full-length portrait of a beautiful woman in a flowing white dress against a vague background of a waterfall, stream, and foliage of dappled greens and browns. The woman bore an unmistakable resemblance to Arabella. He looked inquisitively at her.

"My mother. She died when I was five."

"It's a beautiful picture."

She looked thoughtfully at the painting. "No, it's not. Her arms are too long, out of proportion to the rest of her body. The angles of the shadows are inconsistent, as if there are two different light sources. The folds of her dress are wrong and her eyes—those aren't mother's eyes. Hers were alive. Those eyes are flat, like the eyes of a stuffed animal. But father likes the painting."

Will knew Arabella painted, but the critique suggested it was something more than a hobby. "I stand corrected. It's not a beautiful painting, but I didn't see it until you pointed it out." He gazed at the painting and then at Arabella. "It's a beautiful woman, though, like her daughter."

Her smile was wistful and poignant. "Mother was beautiful," she said softly.

He wished he could take her hand. Instead, they silently left the room and continued through the townhouse. It was an odd tour. They didn't stop long at the various rooms—Arabella seemed to have some sort of objective. The house was furnished for the comfort of the occupants; there were no museum pieces to impress visitors. Finally, they stopped in front of a closed door on the first floor at the back of the house.

"When mother was alive, this was her room. It's fairly large and has lovely windows overlooking her garden in the back. She loved to grow things, her vegetables and flowers. Several years ago, my father converted it for me."

"Converted it to what?"

"My studio." She took a key from her dress pocket and unlocked and opened the door. "I have the only key. It's getting too dark, you can't see." Stepping inside, she lit several lamps. "I don't work in this light, but I'll show you some things I've done."

Will had always been indifferent to art and reckoned as phonies those people who stood in seeming awe before paintings or sculptures, claiming to be "transfixed." The gasps he emitted when he saw Arabella's paintings were real. There were about a dozen, some on easels, others hanging on the walls, amid an untidy assemblage of cans, paint tubes, brushes, rags, palettes, knives, a small table, and a chair at an easel. The room reeked of paint and kerosene and Arabella opened two windows, letting in the cool, refreshing air.

Will stood before a painting of a deserted beach, curling waves crashing into a black, rocky outcropping, throwing off white foam and spray, an expanse of overcast gray sky meeting the ocean. It captured the feeling of contemplative, sometimes desolate, solitude he felt when he was alone at the shore. Sitting on the chair next to the easel, Arabella said nothing. She painted what caught her eye, in vibrant, colorful oils with meticulous attention to detail. Will shook his head in wonder at a picture of a nun sitting on a park bench. The lines of care so delicately drawn on the face of the wizened old woman, framed by the stark contrast of black and white, suggested sorrow and suffering, but her eyes had the serenity of quiet acceptance, perhaps a welcoming of the final release from life's woes. He glanced at Arabella.

"I had to paint her face. Her habit framed it perfectly and she let me sketch her."

Not every painting was pleasing to Will's eye. One, of a dog lying in a bloody pool on a cobblestone street, part of its head crushed, life barely flickering in its eyes, only a minute or two from death, he found particularly disturbing. He stood before it for a long time, "transfixed."

"I saw that dog get run over by a coach. I couldn't get it out of my mind until I painted it."

Phineas Brewster's dark eyes stared at Will from an unfinished canvas. Arabella hadn't just caught her father's stern visage—the face of justice; she had caught his soul—implacable rectitude—with prodigious skill.

"I've never…I've never seen anything like it." He stared at her. If she was to remove her clothes, she would be no more naked to him than she was now, sitting on her chair, confident, completely at ease in her studio, her world. She was offering herself to him. He stepped towards her, pushed and pulled by opposing forces, until he was close enough to touch her. His hand alighted on her cheek as if it were the most delicate bubble. He wanted so much to kiss her. Her upturned face and shining eyes said she wanted him to. He hesitated. He couldn't match her offering, couldn't stand naked before her.

He heard footsteps from down the hall. He stepped away from her, disappointed and relieved.

Deborah Brewster appeared. "Time for dinner. Aren't Arabella's pictures pretty, Mr. Durand?"

"Pretty" wasn't the right adjective, but he nodded in agreement as they left her studio.

His mind still full of the images of the studio, and an image of Arabella's upturned face, Will didn't notice the smell of something wonderful until they walked into the dining room. He felt the stab of keen hunger. The dining room was apiece with the rest of the house—eight sturdy chairs around an oak table, matching sideboard, an old-fashioned chandelier, burnished pewter tableware—utilitarian and comfortable. Will sat between Arabella and Deborah. Phineas intoned a solemn and lengthy grace, thanking God for everything from the bounty that found its way to the Brewster table to the weather to the pleasure of entertaining Mr. Durand, and then beseeching the Almighty for wisdom, kindness, and every other biblical virtue. By the time the servant ladled a fragrant stew into his pewter bowl, Will was ready to chew on the tablecloth.

The oyster stew was the best he had tasted. The hearty mixture of fresh oysters and potatoes, creamy broth, piquant onions and shallots, and an enticing blend of seasonings could have graced the tables at a fine New York restaurant. "This is delicious."

Phineas smiled. It was the first time Will had seen him smile. "That's Quadros, our cook. He's from Portugal. I had a bowl of his oyster stew one day at a café by the port and came back every day for a week. Mrs. Brewster had recently passed away, and I had no one to cook for me. I couldn't eat at the café every night—Arabella and Ezekiel needed me. But we needed a cook, so I offered Quadros more than what he was making at the café and he's been here ever since."

"He's a great cook," Will said.

"Tell me, Mr. Durand," Ezekiel said. "What's your opinion of the presidential election?"

"Difficult as it is to unseat a sitting president, I think Harrison stands a chance of defeating Cleveland. I hope he does, although he wasn't my first choice among the Republicans."

Ezekiel nodded. "Who was your first choice?"

"Mr. Sherman." John Sherman, as Secretary of the Treasury, had restored the gold standard in 1879. Brahmin Boston was "hard money," the creditor class that favored the gold standard.

"We favored him, too," Phineas said. "A nation can only be as strong as its money."

Will smiled. "My father says the same thing." He wasn't going to treat his father like a skeleton in the closet, notwithstanding his humble origins and Wall Street ties.

"Your father is in banking, is he not?" Phineas said.

"He is. He's a founding partner of Durand & Woodbury. It's a Wall Street firm, but he has substantial interests here in Boston." Might as well score a point by mentioning those interests.

"What kind of clientele does Durand & Woodbury represent?" Ezekiel asked.

"My father is discreet about that." Better to impress Ezekiel and Phineas with his father's virtues as a banker than to mention his clients. "The better capitalized, more substantial railroads, some of the higher rated industrial concerns."

"How did he make his start in banking?" Ezekiel said.

"He started in banking in Cleveland, after he completed his service in the Civil War."

"Your father fought in the Civil War?" Phineas said.

Arabella had mentioned to Will that Phineas' father had been an ardent abolitionist. "My father saw slavery for what it was—a grave moral wrong. He took up arms against it. He fought in the West until he was seriously injured at Vicksburg."

"My father was an abolitionist! I was fourteen when the war began, but I enlisted in a volunteer regiment in '64. The war ended before we got to fight. I've always regretted not being able to join men like your father on the field of battle!"

Will had put his father on the moral high ground, hopefully eliminating any qualms the Brewsters might have about his background. Phineas and Ezekiel shifted to less monumental topics than elections and war, and Arabella and Deborah joined the conversation. Will found it hard to look directly at Arabella.

"Let's have our coffee and pie in the sitting room," Deborah said as the meal ended.

"An excellent suggestion," Phineas said. "Mr. Durand and I will join you shortly, but I'd like to speak with him privately in my study, if he would so oblige."

"Certainly," Will said apprehensively.

Phineas led Will upstairs to his study, lit two kerosene lamps, and started a fire in the stone fireplace. Two windows looked out on a Boston street below. Every inch of available wall space was taken up with shelves and bookcases. Books and papers were neatly stacked on Phineas' large oak desk and in one corner was a gavel affixed to a polished block of wood. The judge sat in a high-backed black leather chair and motioned for Will to sit in the chair before the desk.

"Mr. Durand, Arabella is fond of you." Phineas' tone was the dry summation of a lawyer. "Only her family and two of her closest friends have seen her studio before today."

"She's marvelous. It's to your credit that you've provided a studio and encouraged her."

"I could no more stop her from painting than I can stop the rain from falling. You need to understand that, you need to understand my daughter, before you contemplate your next step."

"What do you mean, sir?"

"The morning sun illuminating our garden, the different shades of red and orange that maple leaves turn in the autumn, the lines of a bridge—those things are important to her. Lawsuits, business, money, power, and social position—the things that occupy most men's time, attention, and affection—mean nothing at all." Phineas' dark eyes bore in on Will and he tried not to squirm. "The world is a hypocritical and wicked place, but Arabella is oblivious and ill-suited for it. None of it is important to her, because she has her art."

Phineas was disclosing as much about himself as he was about his daughter. The modest townhouse, his career as a lower court judge, preserving his scrupulous honor by remaining away from the fray—was this a man who didn't trust himself, who feared this "hypocritical and wicked" world? Daniel Durand's course had been different—ambition and integrity within the same person guaranteed a life of conflict. Was it better to recognize one's moral frailties, carve out a safe niche, and keep one's honor, or pursue what the world had to offer while fighting to preserve one's honor? It was an interesting but academic question—Will had no intention of following either course.

"I think I understand, sir. It's one of the reasons, I must confess, I am attracted to her."

"Mr. Durand, you're a man of this world. My daughter will require an extraordinary man. I'm not saying you're not that man—I don't know you well enough yet to say. Arabella is an innocent. Only you and God can look into your soul. If you decide now that you and she are not meant for each other, there would be pain but no permanent harm. However, if you take the next step, you run the risk of breaking an innocent heart." Now he sounded like a judge. "God decides our fates, but the hottest spot in hell should be reserved for those who harm innocents."

Phineas stared at Will. He wished he hadn't lied about his father. "I understand, Mr. Brewster, and I'll carefully consider what you've said." His decision was already made. It had been made in Arabella's studio—what he felt, what he knew she felt. Her beauty, his longing…he could no more stop himself than he could "stop the rain from falling."

They rejoined Arabella, Ezekiel, and Deborah in the sitting room. One phrase from Phineas stuck in Will's mind: "Only you and God can look into your soul." It evoked fear, looking into one's own soul—as if there was a room where the door was always kept closed because something ghastly had occurred there. You stared at that closed door, but, too afraid to see what was behind it, you turned away with a shudder. Now Will turned away, as he always did, and thought of something else.

Nobody had told Will that part of his initiation into Harvard's most exclusive, coveted club, Bovinity, would be in a drafty old barn, redolent of cow piss, manure, and tobacco, presided over by a crusty curmudgeon of a farmer emitting a perpetual stream of tobacco juice to the straw-covered dirt. Nobody had told him he would be waiting his turn to milk one of the farmer's cows. Nobody had told him that as a new member, or "neophyte," he would be an object of riotous sport, with bets greater than a workingman's monthly wage made on his ability to extract milk. Nobody had told him because members of Bovinity took a blood oath of secrecy not to reveal its activities or rituals—ever.

"Our next two neophytes are Durand and Harkness!" shouted Maynard Michelson, scion of a Boston banking dynasty, this year's president of Bovinity, and tonight's master of ceremonies. He was a tall, bulky fellow whose snout-like nose had small nostrils. He took a long draught from a stein of beer and favored the noisy assemblage—twenty Bovinians, swilling beer, smoking cigars—with a thunderous belch, to their acclaim and applause. "Place your bets, gentlemen."

"Fifteen here on Durand!"

"You're done, and I've got another ten for Harkness!"

"I'll take that!"

So it went until everybody had a betting interest on who could fill a quarter of a pail with milk the quickest, Durand or Harkness.

"Neophytes, assume your positions!" Michelson shouted.

Morton Billingsley, also a neophyte, clapped Will on the back. Will, apprehensive, sat on a low stool at the side of one of the cows, a brown one with white patches.

"That's Patches," said the farmer, standing between Will's and Harkness' cows.

An imaginative name. Will looked over his shoulder at Harkness. The big man looked even more ridiculous on his tiny stool than Will felt on his.

Harkness smiled. "May the best man win, Durand."

Will grabbed a warm, slippery teat in each hand and squeezed. No milk, and Patches flinched. He tried again. Not a drop. He felt sweat running down his forehead. He tried pulling down on the teats as he squeezed them and Patches let out an annoyed moo. The men howled.

"Watch it, son," the farmer said. He spit a stream of tobacco juice. "She'll kick if you don't handle her right."

Nervous sweat poured down Will's face. How was the competition doing? He glanced at Harkness. Damn, he was making it look easy! Long streams of milk squirted from his cow into the pail. How did he do it? Will studied his technique and tried to imitate it.

Gentle but firm, that seemed to be the trick. Rolling his fingers down the teats, he squeezed one and then the other and a few drops dribbled out. Encouraged, he alternated squeezes and got a gratifying stream, but there was no hurrying the process and Harkness had a head start. What was that rumbling noise from Patches' stomach? No mistaking that noise from Patches' ass. A cow fart! Good God, the smell—Billingsley's ripest couldn't match this! Will's eyes watered and he thought he might toss. He made a face and crossed his eyes, setting off Bovinian paroxysms. As the odor dissipated his urge to gag faded—he'd get to keep the many beers he had drunk that evening. However, he was going to lose to Harkness, who continued to milk.

Harkness held up his pail in triumph. Will hated to lose, but he knew better than to show anything but good sportsmanship. He shook Harkness' hand, wet with milk and sweat like his own. The men who had made winning bets shouted and clapped, the losers groaned. "He's a ringer. A city boy can't milk a cow like that!" one of them yelled.

Will had to pay the loser's penalty. Michelson handed him a stein of beer and the Bovinians shouted, "Drink, neophyte, drink!" He chugged as the men continued their chant. He drained the stein and Billingsley pounded him on the back.

"You drink like a trump, Durand!"

Will basked in the beery good fellowship—laughing, making sport of each other, drinking, smoking cigars, settling bets. Forget classes, professors, and books, this was what Harvard was about—the culmination of two years of effort, the fulfillment of his plan. "Be your own man, let them come to you," Mr. Cunningham had said. Will hadn't mentioned his Bovinity aspiration to anyone; he hadn't been an obvious social climber, like Gossage. Ah, Chester Billingsley's priceless line about Gossage: "He's keenly sympathetic towards those more fortunate than himself." Will had let Chester, who was Bovinity; Harkness, whose father and uncle were alumni; and the current members of Bovinity come to him.

One morning shortly after his junior year began, Will found the envelope that had been slid under the door to his apartment the night before. Although a Bovinity man had once died in prison, it was safely said that if you were Bovinity, you had to strive to fail. A conversation or letter guaranteed an introduction, a position, an investment, an exclusive club membership, and, for Bovinian sons, acceptance into a choice preparatory school or college. Will had his father's wealth and prominence on Wall Street to thank for his Bovinity membership. Now he wouldn't have to struggle like his father had—Bovinity would open his doors.

Only Arabella's reaction had marred Will's triumph. She expressed happiness for him, but it was the I'm-happy-if-you're-happy variety. Will had dismissed her reaction and ridden a wave of euphoria with Morton Billingsley and Harkness—they were three of only ten men chosen, a group that didn't include Gossage—that lasted through a candlelit initiation ritual at Bovinity's clubhouse and tonight's festivities at the barn. Now they stood together, watching two neophytes sweat their way through the cow milking. Morton pointed at the farmer. "That old buzzard's getting more for his milk tonight than he could ever get at the market. The club gave him fifty bucks for the use of his cows and barn."

"Harkness, where did you learn to milk a cow?" Will asked. "It's not fair that I had to go against an expert."

Harkness smiled. "At my grandfather's. He's got an estate bigger than Manhattan, on the Hudson, where he keeps dairy cows. One of his hands showed me how to milk."

An estate bigger than Manhattan? "Who might your grandfather be?"

"Curtis Winfield, my mother's father. Have you heard of him?"

"No."

"I'm not surprised. He's very rich, but he hates publicity."

Chapter 17

Europe

Arabella frowned. She had to get the mouth right. Will sat on a
tall stool in her studio, his face illuminated by the early afternoon springtime light. He had done most of the sitting for his portrait earlier that spring. Arabella had been reluctant to ask him for
this sitting; his final examinations were the following week. However, after examinations he would go to Europe with his family for
the summer and she wouldn't have the opportunity. She stared at
him, not thinking about what he had become to her, only trying to
decide how she would paint his mouth. She had the rest of his face,
but she had to get his mouth. The mouth was the most expressive
part of the human face, but most paintings didn't give it its proper
role. *Mona Lisa* was an exception.

Arabella labored for another forty-five minutes. It was a good
portrait, although she still wasn't sure if she had the mouth. Except
for minor details, the painting was finished.

"We're done, my dearest. What do you think?" She motioned
toward the painting.

Will stepped in front of his portrait and studied it. In Arabella's
experience, no one could look upon his own face in a mirror, or see

a representation of it, indifferently. Will liked to look at himself. He was handsome, why shouldn't he? Arabella liked to look at herself. She liked what she saw, and she studied her face's angles and proportions. There were those who didn't like looking at themselves, sometimes because their faces were unsightly or deformed, but usually because they saw deformity or ugliness in themselves that no one else saw.

"I've never had my portrait painted. Is this really what I look like?" He sounded disappointed.

Arabella examined her portrait. It was right. "We don't see ourselves as other see us."

Will stared at the painting some more. "I guess seeing your own portrait takes some getting used to. It's a fine painting."

"I'd like to keep it through the summer. I always go back and touch up something. Although if I have your portrait, I'll miss you more while you're in Europe."

He took her hands in his. "I'll think of you constantly. I'll write as often as I can."

"Of course I want you to write, but make one promise to me. There's great art in Europe, try to see as much as you can. Go to the galleries and museums."

He smiled. "I promise. When I return, you'll come to New York and meet my family."

She drew close to him and lightly kissed him. He responded with a short kiss, but then looked to the open door of the studio. She understood. Ezekiel or Deborah usually interrupted them at the most inopportune times.

On cue, they heard footsteps from the hallway and there was Ezekiel. "We're having punch in the den and Father wanted to know if you'd like to join us. Oh, are you done with Will's portrait?

May I have a look?" Behind Ezekiel's back, Will smiled ruefully at Arabella.

Eleanor stood alone at the railing of the *City of New York*, refreshed by the North Atlantic spray on her face. The night air was chilly and she had on her wrap. The stars twinkled in the black, cloudless sky. The steam engines droned below as the big liner rode the waves up and down. Blessedly, only Alexander had problems with seasickness. Perhaps it had something to do with his eyes. His vision was the poorest in the family and he required glasses.

She had to have time to herself. Tonight, she had tucked John in and kissed him good night, left ten-year-old Constance and sixteen-year-old Alexander reading in the Durands' cabin, and come to the deck. Laura was playing one of the ship's pianos, undoubtedly to a crowd drawn by her skill on the instrument as well as her dark beauty. She had taken lessons since she was a girl, with her mother's enthusiastic encouragement. Will had befriended a group of Yale men. They were off somewhere doing whatever college men do, the one consistent element in their activities being the intake of alcohol.

Where was Tommy? Who knew? Eleanor was seldom aware of his whereabouts. Trying to get him to stay in one place was like trying to dam a stream one stone at a time. She and Daniel accommodated Tommy's desires to roam, explore, and learn new things. She no longer worried about his wanderings. On board he and Mario, the thirteen-year-old son of one of the Durands' maids, had explored every inch of the ship, somehow persuading a captain's mate to give them a tour of the ship's engine room. Tommy had excitedly told her about the ship's twin propellers and how if the driveshaft of one broke because driveshafts often broke the ship would still have enough power from the other propeller and didn't have to use the provisional sails and the wind to get across the Atlantic so soon steam-powered ships wouldn't have the masts and rigging that the *City of New York* did. Tommy words and sentences ran one into the other—pauses or punctuation couldn't hope to squeeze their way in. She smiled when Tommy told her about the engine room, wishing she could have seen it.

Daniel had wanted the children to see Europe and they were eager. She wished she shared their enthusiasm. There were the memories of her last trip to Europe—banishment, her punishment for falling in love with Daniel. Her brother Steven, obnoxious and drinking heavily. Poor Mother, caught between her husband's demand that she find her daughter a suitable aristocrat and her daughter's determination to spurn whomever she found. Dashing, charming Lord Newberry and his unsuccessful courtship. However, her trepidation came from more than just memories.

A metal door opened behind her. Daniel stepped out and stood next to her at the railing. "You have misgivings," he said, a statement, not a question

She nodded. "The children should see Europe."

"But?"

"It's not just the castles and cathedrals that are old. People still think that old way—masters and serfs. You see it in how they act towards each other—haughtiness and servility. Not like America. They have this feeling towards Americans."

"Are you afraid we'll be snubbed?"

"You're impervious to snubs and our children can withstand them, too, but this is something that will be directed particularly at you. You'll feel it—I know you will. It comes both from those at the top and those at the bottom. I don't completely understand its source. It won't be anything you say or do, but because of what you are: an American, an obviously successful American."

"Another castle! We saw a castle yesterday, why do I have to see a castle today?"

Daniel shared Tommy's feelings—he didn't want to see another damn castle, either, which made it difficult to answer his son's question. Their host, Sir Edwin Compton, had made his fortune as a London merchant and retired to Renwick House, his country estate in Kent, southeast of London. He was devoted to the area and its history, an enthusiastic but long-winded guide. Tommy was crawling out of his skin on the previous day's tour. Compton had been one of several Europeans referred to Daniel by Monsieur Devereaux, the Frenchman he and Will had met on their trip to Minnesota. Compton had half a million pounds invested with Durand & Woodbury, so Daniel would grit his teeth through another castle, but it was a lot to ask of Tommy.

"What would you do if you didn't come with us?"

"I'd stay here with Mario. It would be fun to go exploring."

"You can do that." The pastoral countryside seemed harmless compared to New York.

That afternoon was hot and sunny. Tommy and Mario tramped through the countryside, fascinated by the farmers working the land; thatched little houses and dainty gardens; tiny villages; odd, windy footpaths through hedges and fields; the traffic of people, carts, and livestock on the crude roads; the smells of hay, grass, barley and wheat, dirt, dust and manure, bread baking and meat cooking; the colors, especially the profusion of flowers.

The natives regarded them with curiosity, not responding to their greetings, perhaps put off by their odd accents. The sun was several hours past its midday peak when the boys stopped at a bridge that crossed a wide, gently flowing stream, sat under a massive, shady oak, and ate the last of the food that Mario's mother had packed for them. Mario bit an apple and wiped the juice from his chin with his sleeve. He was a couple of inches shorter than Tommy, with dark hair and eyes, and Mediterranean swarthiness.

"Do you know where we are?" Mario said.

"No."

"Then we're lost."

"No," Tommy said, smiling, "we just don't know where we are."

Mario reached over and removed Tommy's watch from the breast pocket where he kept it. "It's almost four now and we said we'd be back by six. We should go."

"We'll ask someone in the next village the directions to Renwick House."

They had gone about a half-mile when they heard youthful shouts and commotion. They rounded a turn in the road and came upon a playing field where a group of boys were playing soccer. They stopped and watched the game. Someone kicked a ball out of bounds and it rolled towards Tommy and Mario. Mario bent down to pick it up.

"Don't touch that!" A husky boy with red hair and freckles came running up. "New footballs have a way of getting pinched." Several other boys approached.

"I was going to give you the ball," Mario said.

"So you say."

"Why would we try to steal your ball when there are so many of you and only two of us?" Tommy said.

"You're a Yank. A Yank and a Dago," the husky boy said contemptuously.

Tommy knew Mario had heard worse, but it was still an insult. If the odds were better, Mario would have thrown a punch—he was restraining himself with an effort. "Can we join your game?" Tommy said. He didn't play soccer, but Mario did.

"I thought you didn't play football in America," one of the other boys said.

"How hard can it be? You kick a ball and run around."

The redhead smiled menacingly. "You blokes want a game of football, we'll give you a game."

Daniel stood in front of a mirror as he knotted his tie. Tonight Sir Compton was holding a reception in honor of his guests. Tomorrow the Durands would depart for London and then on to France. Sir Compton had cut the day's castle tour short after Daniel had suggested that perhaps they could see other sights. They returned to Renwick House after an alfresco lunch and a pleasant ride through the countryside, much to Daniel's relief.

There was a knock on the bedroom door.

"Come in."

Will entered. "Isabella's worried. Mario and Tommy aren't back." Isabella was the Durands' maid and Mario's mother.

Daniel pulled out his watch. Almost seven. Tommy was rarely late. He frowned. There was at least another hour of daylight left, but once it was dark it would be difficult for the boys to find their way. Of course, anyone who lived in the area could direct them to Renwick House, a local landmark. "Talk to that butler—Mr.

Pembroke. Everyone's busy with party preparations, but see if he could spare a couple of men to go look for them."

Will nodded and left. Daniel knew he had to tell Eleanor about Tommy and Mario and didn't relish doing so. She would worry about Tommy and he would worry about her worrying. He stepped out of the bedroom to go to Laura and Constance's room, where Eleanor was helping them prepare for the party. As he walked above the sweeping entryway to the mansion, he heard a shriek from Isabella, Mario's mother, outside the front door. He hurried down a curving staircase. Outside, Tommy and Mario stood before her, looking as if they had been in a brawl. Their clothes were torn and they were scraped and bruised. Tommy had a black eye. With Tommy and Mario stood two other boys, one a stocky redhead and the other a shorter but thicker blond. Mr. Pembroke, the butler, witnessed the scene with barely concealed distaste.

"What happened?" Daniel said.

"We were playing soccer...uh, football, Father." Tommy said, grinning.

"Old Tommy took everything we dished out," the redheaded boy said, cheerfully diffident. "He's tough as a tanned hide." He put an arm around Mario. "Mario here, he's a bully player!"

"You've been drinking!" Isabella shrieked. She was a short, dark woman in her early forties.

Tommy grinned. "We had a pint or two with our friends Neal and Nigel after the game." He spoke with a mock British accent. "We had a smashing good time!"

"When they said they were at the Renwick House," the other British boy said, "we didn't believe them."

"Since they couldn't remember the way back, we brought 'em here, sir," the redhead said.

Daniel realized he was looking for some sort of recompense. He took the coins from his pocket and gave both boys a few. "Thank you for bringing them back. Neal?"

"That's it, sir. Thank you, sir." Neal shook Tommy's hand. "Too bad you're leaving tomorrow, we could've played again. Cheerio, Tommy…Mario."

"Likewise, blokes!" Tommy said in his mock accent, grinning, pleased with himself.

"Thomas, up to your room and don't come out for the rest of the evening," Daniel said. "You'll have to miss the reception. We'll talk about this in the morning."

Isabella took Mario by an earlobe and administered a hard twist. He let out a startled cry. She unloosed a stream of Italian scolding that needed no interpretation. Daniel glanced at Pembroke. His barely concealed distaste had turned to barely concealed contempt.

"Lord and Lady Mallenbury, may I present Mr. and Mrs. Durand of New York." Sir Compton, standing with Lady Compton, made the introduction. Sir Compton was Daniel's picture of a British aristocrat—tall, slender, impeccably dressed, a distinguished head of white hair and a white mustache, his "Queen's English" spoken in a cultured baritone. He had married well, to a daughter of an earl. She was as distinguished as he, the years enhancing rather than fading her delicate beauty, her wise blue-gray eyes twinkling at the humorous and absurd.

Daniel bowed, Eleanor curtsied, and greetings were exchanged. Daniel soon decided that the couple before him, almost twenty years younger than he and Eleanor, would take the prize as the grandest snobs in the ballroom. The lord was short and fat, the lady tall, thin, and ugly. They tilted their heads—he looked down his snout; she looked down her muzzle. His slouch emphasized his ample belly. Her hunched shoulders suggested that vast wealth, ease, and privilege were heavy loads indeed. A world-weary ennui seemed to run so deep that Daniel wondered how the poor thing rolled out of her eiderdown bed every morning.

"I've never been to New York," Lord Mallenbury said. "Never been to America at all. I've never had any desire to visit, actually."

"A pity," Lady Compton said, sounding like a mother trying to correct a spoiled, obnoxious child. "Such an interesting, dynamic country. The whole of the British Isles would fit into one of their states. The people, even from the humblest ranks, are so spirited. We've enjoyed our visits."

Lady Mallenbury stifled a yawn.

"My lord, yesterday we toured Lynworth castle," Sir Compton said deferentially. Daniel wondered why a man who had built a commercial empire with businesses on five continents, and whose value to England had been recognized by Queen Victoria when she conferred his knighthood, had to show any deference at all to Lord Mallenbury, whose only accomplishment seemed to be the accident of his birth into nobility.

"Of course, Dunlop has it now, my second cousin once removed on Mother's side," Lord Mallenbury said. "Ah, it's an interesting story how the family acquired Lynworth. In 1678…," and he launched into a long narrative, which was anything but an "interesting story."

"Mr. Durand," Mallenbury said as he concluded. "What did you think of Lynworth?" Eleanor's opinion was evidently too unimportant to solicit.

"It's in good shape, considering it's over five hundred years old. Those thick walls could withstand an extended artillery barrage.

The ramparts have been maintained—if properly manned, boiling oil can be poured on any attackers. However, since the possibility of warfare appears remote, I think the place needs to be spruced up a bit. It seemed a bit dreary. With the right work, it would make a dandy hotel!"

Mallenbury's jaw dropped, Sir Compton's eyes widened, Eleanor and Lady Compton smiled, and Lady Mallenbury looked as if she were sucking on a lemon. Daniel said, "It was a pleasure meeting you, your Graces." He took Eleanor's arm and steered her away from the group.

"I believe," Eleanor said, smiling wickedly, "that you only use 'your Grace' with dukes and duchesses, if you're their social inferiors."

"An egregious breach of etiquette. Can you imagine someone using the term 'social inferior' in the United States? There'd be a riot. That Mallenbury is a fat fop. One of those evil kings had his lordship's ancestor murder someone and rewarded him with a title."

"You've read too much Shakespeare."

Outside, on a sweeping veranda overlooking Renwick House's gardens, Will had been talking for almost an hour with Lady Sylvia Barrows, Sir Compton's granddaughter and his guide for the previous three days. She was petite, standing almost a foot shorter than Will's six feet, and pretty, with angular, delicate features, brown eyes that narrowed in a way that gave them an Asian cast, and brunette hair done up in curls and ringlets under her elaborate white hat. She wore a sweeping yellow gown with diamond-and-sapphire jewelry. However, it was neither her looks nor her finery that attracted Will to her, it was her smile. Congenially conspiratorial and mocking, it invited Will to secrets that cut against propriety and convention.

"My interest in politics comes from my father," she said. Her father, the Earl of Chatenham, was a member of Parliament in the

House of Commons. "His allies call him a hard-nosed, practical politician; his enemies say he's a ruthless opportunist. He's certainly tough…and smart. Many of the Peers turn up their noses at the merchants, bankers, and industrialists. Father inherited his title and landed estate, but this rising new class has all the money." She smiled. "So father aligns with Sir Compton by marrying his daughter, a union of wealth and respectability."

"Wedded bliss. You didn't mention if there was any romance involved."

Her smile was her answer. She took several steps away from him and then turned back in a way that was both dainty, like a ballerina's twirl, and decisive. Her movements were lithe, pleasing to the eye. "Do you follow politics?"

"Avidly. Don't tell my father, though, he despises politics and politicians."

"I find America fascinating, I've visited twice. I've often wondered what it would be like to live there." Another smile. "In your country, any man can run for office."

"Yes, any boy can grow up to be president."

"That's a problem. The top reaches of government should be restricted to the upper class. However, the wealthy are the upper class in America, and money would confer a decisive advantage." She stepped towards him, so close that he felt the bottom of her gown brush against his leg. "Have you thought about entering politics?"

"Not really," he said, distracted by her closeness.

"That's rubbish and you know it. The way you talk about your father and his firm—you have no passion for finance and banking. Politics is your passion. Why shouldn't you be the one who grows up to be president? With your father's money, and your natural gifts?"

She had given voice to thoughts that had run through his head for years. "My father's sentiments about politics are not uncommon. Most of my Harvard classmates share them."

"They're fools! Are you supposed to apologize for wanting to be the driver rather than a horse? Let men like your father pull the carriage—you'll hold the reins!"

He liked the imagery. He turned towards the veranda's stone balustrade and placed his white-gloved hands on top of it. She placed her white-gloved hand next to his; they were touching.

There was something intoxicating about Lady Barrows that went beyond her delicate beauty and grace, the heat he could feel from her body, her perfumed scent, and the look in her eyes that conveyed both admiration and a challenge for him to live up to it. The intoxication ran deeper—she encouraged a part of him that Arabella, blinded by her innocent affection, had never seen. The thought of Arabella elicited a twinge of guilt—he hadn't written her since the Durands' arrival at Renwick House—but it was just a twinge. Only propriety stopped him from doing what they both wanted and kissing Lady Barrows—there were others on the veranda and guests in the ballroom could see them through a large picture window. She increased her pressure on his hand. He glanced at her and thought of Arabella. How could he have such different passions for such different women at the same time?

The train from Paris pulled into Rouen, in Normandy, at mid-afternoon. From his window Daniel saw the little Frenchman in a dapper black suit standing on the platform with another man, from his livery a coachman. When the Durands got off the train, Monsieur Devereaux hurried up to them, smiling. His bushy mustache was now the only hair on his head, and he was more rotund, but those were the only concessions his appearance had made to the years.

"Finally I have the pleasure of meeting your family, Monsieur Durand." He shook Daniel's hand.

"Monsieur Devereaux, may I present my wife, Madame Durand?"

Eleanor extended her hand and Devereaux bowed and kissed it. She smiled.

"You remember Will?"

"But of course." They shook hands. "Has it been seven years? Such a fine-looking young man, and I understand you're at Harvard. Your parents must be proud."

"I hope so."

Daniel introduced the rest of the children. Laura blushed and Constance giggled when Devereaux kissed their hands. He shook hands with seven-year-old John.

"We went to the top of the Eiffel Tower," John said. "In Paris."

"Isn't it marvelous? Did you know it's the world's tallest structure?"

John nodded. "Yes, sir, I know that."

The coachman came up with two porters and their carts, laden with the Durands' luggage. Devereaux gave instructions and they departed. Devereaux led the family outside the train station, where two jaunty landau carriages, each drawn by four horses, awaited them. Eleanor, Daniel, Devereaux, Constance, and John got in one, the other four children got in the other.

Eleanor liked Devereaux almost immediately. The Frenchman was, to use an Old World term, gallant. He sprinkled his tour of the sights of Rouen with witticisms and the occasional odd bit of lore. He patiently answered the children's questions. Eleanor felt strongly that adults should listen to children and take their questions seriously.

They left Rouen after stopping at the square where Joan of Arc had met her untimely end. They traveled through countryside less manicured, more natural than the English countryside. At the top of a hill, between the road and the Seine, stood a gabled chateau. The landaus turned from the main road onto a lane that led to the chateau. They made their way by a field with orderly rows of wheat swaying in the breeze, a fenced-in pasture where sheep and cattle grazed, and then up a winding road to the top of the hill and a courtyard, in the middle of which stood a circular fountain. Manicured hedges lined crossing granite walkways. The chateau had two wings on either side of the courtyard and a grand semicircular entryway.

The carriages stopped before imposing front doors. Through the tall windows above the doors a large chandelier was visible. As the family and their host stepped down from the carriages, the doors opened and a woman, two young men, and a girl about Constance's age emerged. The woman caught Eleanor's eye. She wore a light blue dress, simple but appropriate in this pastoral setting, and her only jewelry was her wedding ring. No other adornment was necessary—she was one of the most beautiful women Eleanor had ever seen.

She was about forty, perhaps ten years younger than Devereaux and at least half a foot taller. She bent over to kiss him on the cheek. Her dark hair was done in a casual style above her head that left a few fetching loose strands. She had a high forehead and cheekbones, warm brown eyes, an angular nose, flawless skin, and full red lips. Her body was classically proportioned and she moved with grace and assurance, casting a radiant smile at Eleanor and Daniel.

"Monsieur and Madame Durand, may I present Madame Devereaux?"

"Welcome to our home, you have a lovely family." Her French accent gave an added sensuousness to the low pitch of her voice.

There was nothing incorrect about the way she extended her hand to Daniel. There was nothing improper about the way he took it, but Eleanor felt an uncomfortable twinge at the way she looked at Daniel, a look that seemed to linger too long. Her discomfort increased when she saw Daniel following Madame Devereaux with his eyes as they entered the chateau.

Their hosts made no demands on the Durands during their stay— no banquets or receptions. The Durands did as they pleased, but Eleanor was unable to relax. There was no gainsaying that Madame Devereaux was attracted to Daniel—she smiled every time she saw him and they enjoyed congenial banter. Eleanor could find no fault with her husband's restrained but friendly responses to Madame Devereaux, but she knew he liked her and couldn't help but admire her beauty. Complicating matters was the fact that she liked Madame Devereaux as well. They took their tea every day in the estate's lovely garden.

They visited there the day before the Durands journeyed north to Le Havre for their ship back to New York. There was a slight chill in the damp air. Overcast skies threatened rain. Roses, tulips, larkspur, and irises blended with other flowers around a small pond into a dappled montage, their intermingled scents perfuming the air.

"When I married Monsieur Devereaux, this chateau, which has been in his family for generations, was so dilapidated it was virtually uninhabitable. His family was deeply in debt. His father had suffered ruinous financial losses that I'm certain hastened his death." Madame Devereaux sipped her tea. "Perhaps you are wondering why I married Monsieur. Certainly not for his wealth…or his stature."

Eleanor laughed. One thing she liked about Madame Devereaux was her sense of humor. "So how did Monsieur Devereaux win your hand?"

"He had just started restoring the chateau and farm when we met. My family is old nobility; they considered his courtship preposterous."

Eleanor smiled. Madame Devereaux's story was like her own.

"At first I was amused at the audacity of this little man, but he has such confidence in himself. You Americans have an expression: he was going places—I could see he was going places. Monsieur Devereaux gets what he wants…in every field of endeavor. He has a force that a woman of spirit cannot resist, no? Of course, your husband has it as well, Madame Durand. It's why I find myself attracted to him."

Eleanor was stunned. Why would Madame Devereaux make such a disclosure?

"Are you surprised that I would say this?"

"Yes." Eleanor absently noted a frog emerging from under a water lily on the pond.

"You shouldn't be. Monsieur Durand is handsome and very masculine, but it's his presence, the strength and confidence he radiates, that appeal to me. I can see that makes you uneasy, but I cannot be the first woman other than his wife to wonder what it would be like to be with him."

Eleanor cherished honesty, but she was unprepared for this kind of candor.

"Americans do not discuss such matters?"

"No…no, they don't. Not among my circle of acquaintance."

"Have you never wondered what it would be like to be with a man other your husband?"

"No…I mean yes, I have."

"Madame Durand, you are a beautiful woman. Monsieur Devereaux admires your beauty. He is an extremely passionate man. If he didn't admire you, I would check his pulse, I should think he had taken ill! There is a vast chasm between admiration and deed." Madame Devereaux placed her hand on Eleanor's. "I have nothing to fear from you, and you have nothing to fear from me. Despite my imaginative flights, I am devoted to Monsieur Devereaux and you are my friend. You evoke Monsieur Durand's ardor, his passion. I can see it in the way he looks at you, the way he treats you. I suspect that he had a difficult time winning your hand and regards it as a paramount attainment."

Eleanor stared at the beautiful chatelaine. She usually formed opinions about people quickly. It was disconcerting that she wasn't sure yet what to make of her. One thing she knew—the French were certainly different.

After dinner on the family's last night in Normandy, Daniel and Monsieur Devereaux retreated to the library. The host proffered two choice cigars and a bottle of Calvados, the local apple brandy. They settled into plush couches, sitting opposite each other.

"Which do you think is the most successful nation in Europe?" Monsieur Devereaux asked, picking up the thread of a three-day conversation.

"The obvious answer is England. Pax Britannia, the empire upon which the sun never sets and all that. I suspect that's not the right answer."

"Ah, you don't disappoint, Monsieur. Yes, the English have their empire. Before them we had ours, and before us the Spanish had theirs, and so on back to Alexander. No empire endures. They're expensive to maintain and no matter how benevolent the imperial administration, the subjugated eventually get restless. However, Europeans equate success with empire. It's a disease."

"A disease?"

"In America, ambitious boys want to grow up to be Monsieur Rockefeller. In Europe, they aspire to be Caesar. Our affliction is that we want to rule the world."

Devereaux stood, stepped next to a large globe, and pointed toward the center of Europe with his cigar. "Only the Swiss have resisted. They neither conquer nor submit. Europe's empires come and go; the Swiss prosper and grow rich. The Alps are a natural fortress, and every able-bodied male owns a gun and must defend his country."

"You're telling me this as a prelude to a larger point," Daniel said, curious.

Devereaux spun the globe, stopping it with his finger on the United States. "Look at your country. Less advanced and less populated countries to the north and south. To the east and west, the moats of the Atlantic and Pacific. At least four mountain ranges, some rivaling the Alps, enormous rivers, deserts, swamps, and the Great, difficult-to-traverse Plains. Not to mention natural resources, industry second to none, and widespread possession of firearms. Even the consideration of an invasion would be insanity. The American fortress is impregnable."

"As long as we don't venture from it."

Devereaux clapped his hands. "Wasn't that Monsieur Washington's advice? Trade with all, ally with none, and stay out of Europe's quarrels—but I fear his wisdom will soon be honored only in the breach. Influential people in your country are envious of the British and their empire. They see an American empire as the natural successor, although few will say so publicly."

"I've heard the whispers. What nonsense."

"Empires are the road to ruin. A peaceful, prosperous United States, standing alone like the Swiss, would endure for centuries. Those lusting for empire know that your small, inconsequential government can never amass one. It must be much larger, more powerful. Military forces, foreign adventures, and colonies cost money. Since your Constitution won't let your government steal it through an income tax, it must find other ways to acquire it."

"So it prints it—the Silver Purchase Act."

"That legislation makes me, and those who invest with me, very nervous indeed."

Daniel nodded. The Silver Purchase Act required the Treasury to buy four and a half million ounces of silver a month with newly printed paper currency, supposedly to redress the scarcity of money. "Once every generation, my country revisits the idiocy of leaving the gold standard. Lincoln tried the same trick. It won't work any better now than it did for him. Prices will go up and all those new dollars will buy less and less. Debtors, however, especially farmers, love it—they pay their debts with less valuable dollars."

Devereaux paced and puffed his cigar. "Your country's creditors receive those less valuable dollars. It's intolerable—our pockets are being picked! My group has decided to liquidate, in its entirety, its investment in the United States. Of course, you'll handle the liquidation, but the money is leaving your country. We want our proceeds in gold, shipped to London."

Daniel nodded. Devereaux's investors would be in the vanguard of a flight of capital. Millions of dollars would leave the United States, perhaps never to return. The booming American economy devoured foreign investment. The boom would give way to panic and depression.

"I'm sorry that we must do this, Monsieur Durand."

"I understand. I blame the pickpocket, not the man who hides his wallet."

Will stood alone at the eastern end of the westbound ocean liner. He had to get away from the bar—from the same people he had seen every night, the smoke-filled air, the bartender who had exhausted his store of friendly banter, and the damn piano tinkling out tunes— even the gay ones sounded melancholy. The trip home was torturous compared with the trip to Europe. There were no Yale men to share laughter and beer. He stared down at the churning foam and spray of the wake because when he looked up he saw all those stars and they just made him feel lonelier.

He wished he hadn't seen that damn painting in Paris. He had honored Arabella's entreaty to visit European galleries. It was not a great picture—Arabella would have done it better—but it was bold and erotic, a view from the side of a dark-haired nude lying on a divan, her face turned toward the painter, nothing hiding her full, ample breasts or the cinch of her waist, one bent, obscuring leg the only concession to propriety. An overwhelming physical desire, painful in its intensity, had surged through Will. He had been embarrassed by the bulge in his trousers, thankful that he was by himself. He had wandered about the gallery, but he kept returning to the painting. Finally he had left, but he remained a prisoner of his own lust.

He needed to be with a woman, to release this maddening physical tension that made him irritable, aroused him every time he saw a pretty face or fine figure, and prevented him from sleeping without his cocktail sedatives every night. The tedium of their voyage made things worse—there was nothing else to think about.

What would it be like to see Arabella naked? He felt a biblical "stirring in his loins." He smiled ruefully. Yesterday, desperate for distraction, he had absently opened a Bible, only to read of harlotry, adultery, and fornication—no help.

If Arabella could magically appear, naked, he would have her right there on the deck. If Lady Barrows magically appeared there naked, he would have her, too…or Madame Devereaux. She was old enough to be his mother, but she was still a damn sight of a woman. Father certainly thought so. The way Will felt now overcame any discernment. A woman for hire could douse his ardor. Wanton fornication with a degenerate harlot—he'd pay twice the going rate. He was going to need another drink to sleep. He reluctantly returned to the bar.

A week after his return from Europe, Will went to greet Arabella, visiting from Boston, at Grand Central Station. He saw her before she saw him. Something had changed with her. Not necessarily a bad change, but a change. She was wearing a blue dress with white trim that could have come from a Paris boutique, and wearing it as if she had been born to such finery. She seemed to have shed her discomfort with strangers and unfamiliar places. There was an ease and assurance to her stance that drew lingering glances from both men and women.

She smiled when she saw him and extended her arms to embrace him. They held each other for a long time, unmindful of the people jostling by, of propriety, of anything but each other. Will was conscious of her arms around him, her understated floral scent, the pressure of her body against his and her breathing on his neck and shoulder. He couldn't take his eyes off her face as they separated. "I can't tell you how much I missed you."

"I know," she said, gasping. "The only things I had were your portrait and your letters."

He should have written every day. "Tell me about your summer, dearest." He took her hand. "Did you paint?"

She smiled. "Of course I painted. Perhaps you've read about artists who've been unusually productive for a period. I'm quite certain it's because they were compensating for the absence of someone dear to them. You name it—landscapes, seascapes, portraits, city scenes—I painted it."

They found a porter for her bags, walked through the crowded station, and loaded the chaise carriage. It was as if they had never been apart, chatting, gaily holding hands, gentle squeezes and spontaneous smiles punctuating their conversation.

The streets were jammed with people, carriages, pushcarts, and wagons. The din of iron wheels and horseshoes on cobblestone, drivers shouting their curses, and peddlers hawking their wares made it difficult to speak, so Will said little and occasionally glanced at Arabella, wide-eyed, taking in the sights of the city. Not until they reached the Durands' residential district did the noise diminish. Arabella raised her eyebrows as they rolled down 52nd Street, passing brownstone after brownstone. Will had never spoken of his father's wealth to Arabella, figuring she would be indifferent and think less of him for mentioning it.

They stopped in front of the Durands' brownstone and a hostler for the street's carriage house hurried up and took the reins from Will. "Have Miss Brewster's bags brought up to the guest bedroom," Will said. He helped Arabella down.

Mr. Thomas, the butler, opened the front door. "The family is in the sitting room, sir."

"Thank you. This way, dearest." He took her hand and led her to the sitting room, where his mother and father sat on one couch, Tommy, Constance, and Little John were on another, and Laura and Alexander sat in chairs. Everyone except John had a cup of tea for this very grown-up occasion. Arabella took in the spacious, high-ceilinged room, undoubtedly noting his mother's taste in décor. His father, Alexander, Tommy, and John stood.

"Mother, Father, may I present Miss Brewster?"

"Pleased to meet you," Daniel said, taking Arabella's extended hand.

"A pleasure," Eleanor said.

Will introduced Arabella to his brothers and sisters.

"You're pretty," John said as Arabella took his hand.

Arabella smiled graciously. "Thank you, Master Durand."

Eleanor poured tea as Will and Arabella settled onto a love seat. She asked Arabella the polite questions that were obligatory in such situations. Will was anxious, but not terrified, about this first meeting. His mother, an experienced hostess, could put just about anybody at ease. Beyond her social dexterity, he had a hunch that she, Father, and Arabella would all like each other.

"Will tells us that you're an artist," Daniel said. "What kind of pictures do you paint?"

"All sorts, really. Whatever I find that's interesting. I paint portraits. I did one of Will."

Constance giggled and Arabella smiled at her. "I paint the country and the seashore around Boston. I've painted buildings and scenes from the streets of the city."

"We saw paintings in France from what we were told is a new school—Impressionism," Daniel said. "When you see the paintings from a distance you can tell what they are, but up close they were blurry, fuzzy. Do you paint in that style?"

"No, I try to sharpen details, not obscure them."

Father didn't ask a question unless he was interested in the answer, and the first question was usually followed with a second and a third and so on. Will found sincere interest annoying. Daniel was quizzing Arabella about her art. Eleanor and Laura enthusiastically joined in, and Arabella expounded on her passion.

Initially delighted by the course of the conversation and his family's interest in Arabella, Will began to feel piqued. The conversation had veered from the expected course of banal pleasantries and small witticisms in which he excelled. He had minimal interest in art. Sure, he admired Arabella's paintings, but who the hell cared about the merits of sunlight at dawn versus dusk? He had no passion to match Arabella's for art. He had put his heart and soul into his campaign for an invitation to join Bovinity, but such social machinations didn't rise to the level of her love.

As the conversation continued, Will detected the erection of a subtle barrier. He tried to join in with an occasional witty comment, but his parents, Laura, and Arabella were enjoying a serious discussion and ignored his intrusions. There was probably no intention to exclude on their part, but Will felt excluded, an odd turnabout in his own home with his own family and girlfriend. He must not have hidden his feelings very well. He glanced at Tommy and his younger brother's face assumed a sour expression, mocking Will. The brat should have been locked in his room for the duration of Arabella's visit.

Arabella had not been at the Durand home very long before Daniel concluded that her and Will's relationship, like a dubious income statement, didn't "sum up." Daniel was fond of her and would have been happy if she was to become his daughter-in-law. She was talented, intelligent, gracious, straightforward, and of course beautiful. Beauty was either enhanced or diminished by a woman's personality; Arabella's was enhanced.

Love might not be blind, but it was certainly myopic. Arabella didn't see the Will his family knew. Such myopia could be charming, but to Daniel, schooled to see people and situations unsentimentally, it was dangerous, ultimately disastrous. Someday the fog would clear for Arabella, and he hoped for her sake that it was before any irrevocable decisions had been made. She might accept Will for what he was, but she first ought to know what he was. Not that Daniel felt he could or should do anything to educate her—time and Will would take care of that.

On the third night of Arabella's visit the family and their guest enjoyed, or in the case of the younger Durands endured, a formal dinner in the dining room with the best silver, china, and crystal. At first the evening seemed as stiff as the men's and boys' high collars and Eleanor's insistence on the children's strict observance of the rules of etiquette. Tommy punctured the prevailing sobriety, a role he frequently filled.

"I understand that Mr. Stillwell has retired, Tommy," Eleanor said.

"That doddering old fool should have retired years ago." Tommy smiled mischievously. "Last year, when he was scribbling on the chalkboard and his back was turned, we'd all change seats just to cross him up. Sometimes a boy would hide his lesson book."

"You wouldn't happen to have been that boy?" Daniel said. He knew the family saw only the tip of Tommy's iceberg.

"A time or two, but I wasn't the only one."

After the laughter died down, Eleanor said, "I don't think Mr. Stillwell ever fully recovered from his injuries." She turned to Arabella. "He fought in the Civil War."

"Father was a soldier in the Civil War," John said.

"Yes," Arabella said. "Will told me. Where did you fight, Mr. Durand?"

"In the west, Tennessee and Mississippi. Shiloh was my first battle and Vicksburg was my last. Will is named after a friend, William Farrows, who died at Vicksburg."

"I can't imagine the courage it must take to be soldier," Arabella said. "Even if one's fighting, like you were, for a great cause, to free the slaves."

Daniel generally didn't waste time addressing the rampant distortions, inaccuracies, and outright falsehoods he had heard through the years about the Civil War. However, he didn't want Arabella to think his motivations for going to war were any grander than they had actually been. "Well, the truth about why the North fought is more complicated, and undoubtedly less honorable, than what we now read. As I've told Will, soldiering appeared a good deal more exciting than shoveling coal in Cleveland. I wasn't particularly concerned about the plight of the slaves, although looking back, I'm happy that we freed them."

Daniel could tell by the way Arabella's eyes widened and the way she set her fork on her dish, laden with a morsel of meat, that something was wrong. She stared at Will. Will looked at him and shook his head. His face had turned a bright red. The table went silent; even John seemed to sense something amiss. Tommy, usually eager to capitalize on Will's misfortunes, wore a pained expression.

"So you didn't volunteer to fight slavery?" Arabella said.

"No."

The next quarter-hour seemed as if it were an hour. There was little conversation. Arabella said nothing. Will said nothing.

Eleanor finally ended the ordeal. "Children, you may be excused." Their plates still contained ample amounts of food. "We'll have our dessert and coffee later in the sitting room."

Arabella stared at Will. "I should like to take a walk, Will. Perhaps the park across the street."

"Certainly," he said weakly.

Will and Arabella walked out to the entryway. The butler brought them their coats and Will helped Arabella with hers. As they stepped down the stairs of the brownstone he tried to gently take her arm; she moved it away from him. He felt a plunging sensation in his stomach. An icy foreboding clenched his throat. Saying nothing, they crossed the street and entered the park. She stopped in front of an empty bench.

"You lied to me and you lied to my father, Will. I had told you his family were abolitionists. You said your father joined the army to end slavery, but that's not why he went to war and you knew it." He had never seen her angry. Her words were harsh and distinct, delivered the way her father might condemn a criminal who stood before him. He wished she wouldn't look so directly at him, into his eyes, that she would give him some quarter and glance away, but she didn't.

"I embellished what my father did in the war. I—"

"Why do people call lies other than what they are? It's another lie that makes the first one worse. You embellished! You lied, to impress my father and my family. Do you think we judge you by what your father did or didn't do? You're judged on your own merit, or its lack!"

"Arabella, let's sit down." He motioned towards the bench.

"I don't want to sit down!" They continued to stand. She continued to stare at him.

"Arabella, I guess I was just nervous. I'm so sorry. You meant so much to me, even then, and I wanted to make a good impression on your family…your father."

She looked away from him, towards the ground. "Will…Will." Her voice broke. "I've thought about us…spending our lives together. You've thought about it, too, I know you have, but to lie about something so inconsequential, and for what? To gain some small measure of undeserved favor from my family? Will, you're not who I thought you were." She looked up at him again. Tears rolled down her cheeks. He put his hand up to her face to brush one away.

"Don't." She pushed away his hand. She wiped her tears with a handkerchief.

"Arabella, people don't swear on a Bible and vow to tell the truth every time they open their mouths. That's not the way the world works. It's naïve to think that people don't fudge a bit. I'm afraid it's rather routine, and most of the time no harm comes of it. It's the way things are."

"So I'm naïve? Do you think your father, or mine, routinely lies?"

"I didn't say you were naïve," Will sputtered. "But I'm sure my father has lied at some time or another." Her eyes narrowed. He had again said the wrong thing. "As for your father, I don't know him well enough to say."

"Tell me one time when your father has lied! I think he's an honest man, unlike his son."

Will said nothing. It ran the other way with his father—dinner tonight wasn't the first awkward situation he had created by telling the truth.

"I want to go home. Please take me to the train station tomorrow."

"Arabella, I hardly think that's necessary. Can't we talk this out?"

"So you can 'fudge' a bit more? What else can you say, Will?"

What else could he say? "Nothing…nothing except that I'm sincerely sorry."

"I sincerely accept your apology." Her voice was cold. "But it doesn't change the way I feel. Will you please take me to the train station in the morning?"

Will hung his head and shook it back and forth. He felt desperately like crying, but he wasn't going to let her see that. "Yes, I'll take you the station."

She stepped past him to return to the brownstone. He followed her across the street, feeling embarrassed, foolish, impotent, and angry all at once. The damn butler must have been watching them through the window because the front door opened before she could knock. She removed her coat and handed it to him.

"I'll spend the rest of the evening in my room, Mr. Thomas," she said, and hurried up the stairs to the guest room.

"Have Horton bring around the chaise early tomorrow." Will tossed his coat to the butler.

"Yes, sir."

Eyes brimming with tears, Will went upstairs to his room and slammed the door.

A somber ride to the station the next morning was punctuated only twice by Will's halfhearted attempts to make small talk and Arabella's monosyllabic responses. He found a porter for her bags and walked with her to her platform.

"It's not necessary for you to wait with me," she said coldly.

He stared at her. "Perhaps you'll feel differently after a time."

Her reply was a withering look, a look Will wouldn't have thought her capable of before yesterday. "Please don't try to call on me when you return to Boston."

"Goodbye, Arabella." With her words ringing in his ears as a lashing rebuke, he walked away. He thought he heard her say, "Goodbye, Will," but he wasn't sure. He was sure that his emotions were no longer the jumbled mix of the previous evening. They had melded into a white-hot rage.

When he returned home, his mother and father stood in the entry-way, looking concerned. Will's only communication with either of them since the previous evening was a terse "Arabella is returning to Boston" to his father early that morning. Seeing his father now, Will lost control. "Has it ever occurred to you, you simple-minded fool, that your family is not as proud of your mundane reasons for going to war as you seem to be?"

Daniel stared at Will. When he spoke, his voice was stripped of any vestige of emotion. "You're upset, Will, but don't ever speak to me in that manner again. I'm not the one who lied to Miss Brewster. Don't do yourself or me the dishonor of thinking that I would or should lie for you."

Will opened the front door and stepped outside. "Damn," he whispered as he closed the door. It was still early, but he knew a nearby bar that would be open. He hurried down 52nd Street.

Inside, Daniel said, "I've never felt so bad for him, but he wasn't the right man for her." Eleanor said nothing, her expression impassive.

On the train ride home, Arabella had dabbed her tears and thought of what she would do to Will's portrait. Once she saw her painting, she was unable to administer the slashing attack with her paint knife she had planned. Instead, she repainted Will's mouth. People said her portraits revealed character as well as depicted appearance. No wonder she had had such trouble with Will's mouth. Now she painted it with a slight, upturned corner, the hint of a secret smile. It was perfect—the mouth of a liar. She had been too much in love to see it before.

She stood for a long time before her painting. Her painting. She had saved everything she had ever done—every sketch, study, and painting, including the few she had abandoned before completion. She had saved them because they were her art, they were her. More important than anything else.

Than anything else...including Will. It was his portrait before her, but it was her art and she couldn't desecrate it. She put it in a corner to dry, facing a wall so she wouldn't have to see it.

An acquaintance of her father owned a small gallery. After many requests she had let him see her work. He liked her paintings and offered to show and sell them. She had not responded to his offer. She had planned to talk to Will about it in New York.

She walked around her studio, running her fingers over some of her favorite paintings, tracing out their lines. Placing her work before the public, selling it, letting go of it, would be difficult. But maybe she had the strength to do it. What she didn't have was the strength for marriage to a man like Will.

Money was independence.

She trusted her skill in art, but discerning character was terribly complicated. She had almost made a tragic mistake, one with lifetime consequences, leaving herself dependent on a man she would ultimately come to despise. Why must so much turn on one decision?

Money was freedom.

Maybe she'd meet a man of stainless character. Maybe she wouldn't. Did she have to live her life like everyone else? She smiled. She would show her art.

Chapter 18

Fledglings

The richest man in America had an appointment with Daniel, to ask him for money. Daniel hadn't seen Rockefeller for years, although the oil magnate had relocated to New York. Daniel was a large shareholder in Standard Oil, but had declined an invitation to sit on the company's board of directors. Other bankers talked of beneficial contacts and the rubbing of influential elbows on boards of directors, but Daniel considered them rubber stamps and a waste of time. Rockefeller and other Standard Oil executives had invested with Durand & Woodbury, but their dealings had been conducted through subordinates. When Rockefeller walked into Daniel's office, both men seemed to realize that their separation might have been a mistake. They smiled as they shook hands.

"Daniel, good to see you."

"Likewise, John."

To Daniel, the first names underscored the significance of the reunion—here were two men who could regard each other as equals, and more importantly as friends. The difficulty of finding the former magnified the difficulty of finding the latter.

Rockefeller put his hat on a stand and settled into the chair in front of Daniel's desk. His reddish gold hair, now tinged with gray, had thinned considerably and receded, making his high forehead appear even higher. He was more slender in his early fifties than he had been in his mid-twenties. His blue eyes were still mercilessly direct, probing, but the slight droop of the eyelids above and the sag and darkness below hinted of an unsurprising weariness.

"What can I do for you?" Daniel said. Rockefeller wasn't much for pleasantries.

"I'm helping to start a university in Chicago. Our group intends to build an institution of the first rank, on par with Harvard and Princeton. To that end, Dr. William Rainey Harper, the preeminent educator, has agreed to serve as president of the university. He's already secured commitments from a number of illustrious professors. The university will commence next year."

"Talent isn't cheap," Daniel said, coming to the preordained point.

"No, it isn't. I don't know what your philosophy of giving is, Daniel. I've found that it's best to concentrate my efforts in a few areas—education, medicine and public health, spreading the Gospel. A scattershot approach doesn't yield lasting progress."

"Will this university be a religious institution? I'm not religious."

"The school will be under the auspices of the American Baptist Education Society, but the curriculum will be of the widest liberality, and we intend to draw both our faculty and students from all races and creeds. A great school can't be restricted to a denomination and its teachings."

"From what I read, and from what my son, who attends Harvard, tells me, there's a growing sentiment among professors against the wealthy and our system of free enterprise. You and I have been two of the biggest beneficiaries of that system. Will your university defend the principal of liberty and its natural expression, capitalism?"

"Not explicitly, no."

"Will you exercise any control over what is taught?"

"No, that would be an abridgment of the professors' freedom to teach."

"Then I won't give your university a penny."

Rockefeller straightened up in his chair. "Why?"

"A man can teach whatever he pleases to whomever will listen and I have no right to stop him. But when he says that my wealth and the capitalism that produced it are evil, and that someone has more of a right to my money than I do, I'm not paying his way. Your university will become a prominent institution, but I don't like what I'm hearing from our prominent institutions. Since I have no assurance that I won't hear more of the same from yours, I won't fund it. I won't support my critics."

"Your son attends Harvard."

"Yes, and he receives his dose of nonsense. I've paid his tuition and he's learned some useful things, but I haven't donated any money."

"Have you read Mr. Carnegie's essay?"

"Part of it." Andrew Carnegie's essay, "Wealth," argued that the rich should donate large sums to worthy causes during their lifetimes, to diffuse tension between the rich and poor and spread wealth more widely. "When I came to the sentence 'the man who dies thus rich dies disgraced,' I threw it in the fire. I'll die rich and leave most of it to my family."

"What of the danger Mr. Carnegie warned, that they'll fritter it away?"

"If unearned money presents a danger to my children, I haven't done much of a job rearing them, have I? I have more faith in them than that. I've made it clear that inherited wealth must be used productively."

"For making more money?"

Daniel shook his head, dismayed. Rockefeller had never exploited a worker. He had made them shareholders—many were millionaires. His refineries were among the safest workplaces in the country. By reducing the price of kerosene, he had lit the country. This was the "cutthroat competitor" the editorialists decried, writing their screeds by the light of lamps fueled by Standard kerosene.

"John, you could give away every dime and your critics wouldn't be satisfied. You know that. Service is your touchstone, not mine, but producing wealth does more for society than giving it away. I don't care how many libraries Carnegie slaps his name on or how many universities you found, Carnegie Steel and Standard Oil have benefited far more people than your philanthropies ever will."

"There are people who need help."

"I'll give my money to some of them, but not if they're going to condemn me and the system that produced my donation."

Rockefeller abruptly stood and took his hat from the stand. "Good day, Mr. Durand." He did not extend his hand, but turned and quickly exited Daniel's office.

Daniel sighed. "Good day, Mr. Rockefeller."

One early autumn evening, two months after Daniel's meeting with Rockefeller, Alexander asked to speak with his mother and father about his future. Daniel had never really thought much about his seventeen-year-old son's future, assuming he would either work at Durand & Woodbury or follow his brother to college. Alexander had neither Will's ambition and charming deviousness nor Tommy's erratic brilliance, but he was a diligent student and made good marks. Daniel had to remind himself not to overlook his quiet son.

He suspected that at the core of his character was a tough-minded tenacity, although Alexander had never been put to the test.

He settled into a sofa opposite his parents in Daniel's study. A fire crackled in the fireplace, its light dancing on the bookcases lining the walls. Daniel and Eleanor had coffee; Alexander never partook. He was almost as tall as Daniel, over six feet, but stockier. He had a wide, oval face and brown hair, neatly combed and parted down the middle. He rarely received a second glance. Only the brown eyes behind his wire-rimmed glasses—intent, serious, unyielding—belied his nondescript appearance.

"I've been in New York all my life," Alexander said. "I'd like to try something different. Mr. Rockefeller is founding a new University of Chicago and I've always admired him. He's been successful in everything he's done and he'll build a great university. I want to apply."

"A new institution has growing pains," Eleanor said. Now in her late forties, her face had acquired a patina of experience and wisdom while being spared the ravages of age. She wore an elegant green dress with white lace and yellow trim. "I share your belief in Mr. Rockefeller's abilities, but are you sure you want to attend a school that's just getting started?"

"It's exciting, being part of something new. There's another reason I want to attend. Mr. Rockefeller is a Baptist, and his university will be a Baptist institution."

"Why is that important?" Daniel said.

Alexander looked directly into his father's eyes. "Several months ago I was baptized at Paul Wainwright's church." Paul Wainwright was Alexander's best friend and a devout Baptist.

"You didn't tell us," Eleanor said. Her voice carried a note of disappointed wonder.

"You and Father aren't religious. I didn't think you'd approve, but it was something I was going to do, regardless."

"We're not religious." Eleanor spoke tentatively, as if choosing her words carefully. She glanced at Daniel. "But we respect your decision. You must reach your own conclusion about such matters. Your baptism was an important moment in your life. We would have attended the service—the whole family would have."

"Then you understand my decision to attend the University of Chicago?"

"Yes."

Daniel nodded in agreement. "Though I'm afraid I've made your admittance more difficult than it otherwise would have been." He told Alexander about his meeting with Rockefeller.

"I'm still going to apply," Alexander said.

"Who knows?" Daniel said. "Perhaps Mr. Rockefeller will think it a grand joke to admit you. It would tweak a man, a nonbeliever no less, who wouldn't give money to his university. Or perhaps Rockefeller won't be involved in the admissions process at all."

Alexander stood. "Things will turn out for the best. Thank you for supporting my decision."

After he had left, Eleanor smiled. "It's always the quiet ones who surprise you."

It was one thing, Will thought to himself, to confidently assert to his Bovinity chums at Harvard that one day he would run Durand & Woodbury. After a few months at his father's firm, however, he knew it was going to be quite another to make his assertion reality. He was working harder than he ever had—fourteen-hour days and six-day weeks were the routine. He was expected to think, all the time. "What do we sell?" his father would ask. He would tap his temple with his index finger. Brains, brilliance, creativity—that's what they sold. There was no room for the ordinary, the run of the mill.

Nor was there room for winning smiles, an arm around a shoulder, alcohol-soaked fellowship, or whispered insults—the stratagems that had served him so well at Harvard. Will's charm, his appearance, and even his last name were irrelevant. Had he analyzed the Comstock income statement? How was he coming on the Allied–Eastern Shipping merger agreement? Did the Southern Pennsylvania Railroad's indenture allow its bonds to be called? His answers were the only aspect of his personality in which his coworkers seemed to show any interest.

Will sat with them in Durand & Woodbury's large meeting room on a warm afternoon, late in the summer of 1892. Client presentations were often conducted here, a showcase of the firm's wealth, with Turkish carpets, richly upholstered maroon leather chairs and sofas, original landscapes on the walls, matching furnishings—bookcases, bureaus, stands, humidors, and the table in the center of room—done in rich, dark mahogany. The technological innovations—two ticker machines in opposite corners, covered to muffle their noise, four telephones on slide-out shelves in the bureaus, diffuse electric lights that mimicked the old lamps—were placed in unobtrusive locations so as not to mar the room's traditional elegance.

The partners sat at the table and the associates sat on the chairs and sofas. Cigar smoke hovered above the room. George Woodbury stood and took several puffs. His blond hair, only recently beginning to thin and acquire a few streaks of gray, was uncombed since that morning. One of the buttons on his vest had popped, losing the battle against his girth, but several more would have to go before he would retire the vest. Notwithstanding his disheveled appearance, everyone listened to the cofounder of the firm and head of its trading operations.

"As our friends in Europe warned, gold is leaving the country." Woodbury's voice was a deep, raspy rumble. "We've sold them out and sent them their gold. There have been rallies—we got good prices. Now that that piece of business is done, we're quietly setting up our own short positions. Mr. Dolan's in charge of that." Woodbury took his place at the table.

Will glanced at Mr. Dolan—the "Pirate," former hack, now a Wall Street legend. If he was setting up the short positions, then Durand & Woodbury was positioning itself for an apocalypse. The Pirate didn't make small bets.

Benjamin Keane stood. He was Will's boss, the number two man, behind Daniel, in corporate finance. He was wealthy from his share of the partnership and astute investments. Everything about him—his neatly combed black hair with touches of gray at the temples, the gold-rimmed glasses that intensified the serious, analytical cast of his face, his military-straight posture, his Saville Row suits and shoes—bespoke confidence and competence. Keane had potential clients halfway won over before he shook their hands. He spoke in well-crafted sentences, the modulations of his voice providing subtle, compelling emphasis. Will's father trusted the son of his old business partner implicitly. Keane ran the firm in Daniel's absence.

"My father used to say the time to prepare for a flood is before your toes are wet." Keane smiled and everyone smiled with him. "We are reviewing every one of our commitments—trade financings, merchant banking arrangements, margin credits—and discreetly curtailing those in which we aren't completely sure of the financial soundness of our counterparties…"

Will had been involved with these reviews for weeks and nothing Keane was saying was news to him. His attention wandered and he glanced around the conference room. Michael Palos, a compulsive note-taker, was writing furiously on a tablet. Palos never spoke at these meetings. He hated being away from his office, with its reassuring stacks of contracts, corporate charters, and bond indentures.

Truth be told, the partners preferred he stay there as well, although he would probably be the next associate offered a partnership. He was awkward with clients, but nobody could unravel a financial document or an accounting statement better than he.

His father was listening intently to Keane. He listened intently to everyone. He spoke less than anyone in the firm, except for Palos, but the firm bore the unmistakable stamp of his personality. Woodbury and Keane were delineating their quiet partner's strategy, devised after the Durands' trip to Europe.

Jakob Gottman wore Wall Street's standard sober dark suit and colorful tie, but with his trim black beard, long, narrow face, and deep-set brown eyes, he still looked like a Jew. He too was an intent listener. Gottman had built the firm's relationships with the Jewish investment banks, both sides gaining from the others' prowess in unfamiliar markets. Active in his synagogue, Gottman also benefited from close friendships with many of the city's wealthy Jews. He had become a key asset for Durand & Woodbury and had been invited into the partnership the previous year.

Gottman turned towards Will and met his gaze. Everyone in the firm, even his father, had at one time or another been the object of Gottman's pointed, merciless wit. Will had trained himself to show no pique when the rapier was aimed at him. Anti-Semitism had been as natural at Harvard as club memberships. From the first time they met, Will had sensed suspicion. Perhaps after centuries of persecution Jews had some sort of innate instinct. Nothing had ever been said, but they avoided each other. Now Gottman's dark eyes stayed on Will and his face remained impassive. Will suspected the Jew knew exactly what he was thinking.

The evening had disappointed Lady Sylvia Barrows from the moment that the carriage carrying her, her brother, the Viscount Manford, and her grandparents, Sir and Lady Compton, had turned up the New York street to the Durands' residence. They were hosting a reception for their English hosts of two years ago. Lady Barrows had assumed that Mr. Daniel Durand would have an elaborate mansion that occupied at least half a city block. Instead the carriage stopped before a plain brownstone. Inside, the appointments were of the best quality—she had an expert's eye—but there were no Rubens or Rembrandts, no antiquities' sculptures or vases, no medieval tapestries or other symbols the wealthy used to advertise their wealth. The house had electric lights, an innovation still confined to the dwellings of the elite, but light bulbs were not *objets d'art*. Even the other guests didn't measure up. She had expected a glittering array of plutocrats and socialites, but she had met no Astors or Vanderbilts or Morgans, only some men from Durand & Woodbury and their wives, and the Parsons and the Douds, who had been introduced as friends of the family.

Will saved the evening. He was more subdued, deferential, than he had been in England. She approved. His father had surrounded himself with intelligent, capable men. The Jew was disconcerting, but Mr. Keane was in a class by himself, and Mr. Woodbury, who did not wear the latest men's fashion, the tuxedo, particularly well, made everyone laugh with his scathing comments. Will had to fit into his father's world, and one did not fit in by upstaging his father's partners. That chameleon-like ability was the quality he would have to have. His serious demeanor and sober conversational style would gain the confidence and trust of the men he would somebody command. He was what she wanted, what she loved—America, wealth, and someday, power—and he was still taken with her.

They stood together in the drawing room. She wore a light green dress from Paris. Groups were scattered around the large room, the men drinking whiskey or brandy. Will had whiskey. An occasional laugh floated above the chatter. Lady Barrows smiled. "Your father really is, as you Americans say, 'all business,' isn't he? I see it more in his own realm than I did in England."

Will nodded. "Durand & Woodbury is his life. He loves his work. More, I sometimes think, than his family, maybe even more than Mother."

The sad resignation in Will's voice was disconcerting. "One mustn't get maudlin about that sort of thing."

"No, one mustn't."

"Your parents don't go in for the trappings and frippery."

"Not at all. They deem social prominence and their political position unimportant." Will's eyes narrowed. "Not sentiments I share."

This was what she wanted to hear. She smiled her conspiratorial smile and put her white-gloved hand on his sleeve. "Of course not. I do love America, Mr. Durand. I love this city, so alive with possibilities, so powerful, so rich." She inched toward him; her body touched his. A woman who didn't use that arrow might as well throw away her quiver. He pressed against her; she could feel his heat. They continued their intimate conversation, aware of each other's smallest body shift, gesture, and brush of hand against hand.

A man who had been introduced to her earlier, Mr. Palos, oblivious to their intimacy, approached them, accompanied by Will's younger sister, Laura. Tall and thin, the wild curls of his brown hair appeared as if they had never met a comb or brush. He seemed out of place and ill at ease in the Durands' ornate drawing room.

"Are you enjoying your visit to New York?" Laura said.

"I was just saying how much I love your city. The excitement, the tremendous energy, you can feel it in the air." Laura stared intently at her. Lady Barrows' father, an astute politician, said that one had to be able to divine people within a minute of meeting them. Laura's intense dark eyes and earnest expression suggested she was one of those souls who felt, and bore, the sorrows of the world. It was intuition, but Lady Barrows had gambled on less. "Of course," she said, allowing her voice to trail off slightly, "like London, New York has its poor, its downtrodden. I cannot avert my eyes from them."

Laura nodded in agreement and her face brightened. Lady Barrow's gambit had come a winner. Not that the stakes were high; who would dispute such a sentiment?

"We can't forget those less fortunate than ourselves," Laura said.

"It's not enough, to simply dispense charity to the poor," Mr. Palos said. "They must be taught skills, so that they can acquire jobs and help themselves."

Lady Barrows said, "If you give a man a fish, you must give him another on the morrow, but teach him to fish, and he'll feed himself for his lifetime."

Eleanor approached the group and placed her hand on her daughter's arm. "Excuse me for interrupting, dear, but I was wondering if I could impose upon you to play the piano."

"I'd love to hear you play!" Palos said with too much enthusiasm.

Laura smiled shyly. "Yes, I'll play, Mother." Palos in tow, she went to the grand piano in a corner of the drawing room. Palos sat in the closest chair. Mrs. Durand shepherded the knots of people towards the piano, and Lady Barrows was again alone with Will.

She smiled. "I didn't have an opportunity to finish that old fish adage."

"What's that?"

"Once you've taught that man to fish, he might be better at it than you and drive you out of business. Therefore, it's better to give him his fish a day until his initiative and industry are destroyed and he's dependent upon you. Then you've eliminated the threat."

Will smiled. They understood each other.

"Mr. Palos is quite taken with your sister."

"Something must be done. The man is a peasant—his father was a hostler."

Lady Barrows raised her eyebrows. "Shall we find a place to sit?"

They sat on a sofa together. The strains of Beethoven's "Moonlight Sonata" filled the room. Laura played with precision and passion, but the selection was not one of Lady Barrows' favorites. There was little music that she liked. She glanced towards Mr. Palos. He gazed adoringly at Laura, who glanced at him between movements and smiled sweetly. Lady Barrows looked away. She would never give or receive that kind of devotion—a simple statement of fact, devoid of emotion.

Will stepped into his father's office at the end of a workday. What he had to say was best said here, not at home. He shut the door and sat in one of the chairs before his father's desk.

"Father, are you aware of a warm sentiment between Mr. Palos and Laura?"

Daniel chuckled. "Poor Will. Your family won't follow the script you want to write for us."

"What do you intend to do about it? I'm only thinking of Laura. Mr. Palos has nothing. He comes from nothing. His father was a hostler, for God's sake."

"May he rest in peace. Mr. Palos had a father, that's something," Daniel said softly. "Will, when you say you're thinking of someone else, ten dollars gets you only one that you're thinking of you. Are you worried that if they were to wed, the story might not look so good on the society pages? Or are you concerned that your Harvard buddies might rib you about your brother-in-law, the son of a hostler? Or does it trouble you what Lady Barrows might think of such a union?"

He would get nowhere with his father on preventing this romance. Time to change the subject. "Speaking of Lady Barrows, she's invited me to visit her in England next summer. Would it be possible for me to take off for a month?"

"Are you thinking of marriage somewhere down the road?"

"Yes."

"If she were Sylvia Barrows, not Lady Sylvia Barrows, would you still be interested?"

"Yes." Will hoped his voice conveyed the conviction he didn't have.

"That sprightly little thing eats men for breakfast, but I won't stand in the way of the dictates of your heart. Nor will I stand in the way of the dictates of your sister's heart."

"I've got to hand it to Palos," Will said with a sneer. "Courting the boss's daughter is one way to advance a career."

"It didn't help mine."

No man, by Daniel's lights, ever deserved a celebration and tribute more than James J. Hill. On January 6, 1893, beneath towering pines, boughs laden with snow, on the western slope of the Cascade Mountains at a siding appropriately named Scenic, the last spike on the transcontinental Great Northern Railway, the new corporate parent to the St. Paul, Minneapolis & Manitoba Railway, was driven into the frozen ground. There were no dignitaries giving speeches for the occasion; not even Hill was there, only the workers and a handful of low-level executives who reluctantly left the warming hut to have their commemorative photograph taken.

The Great Northern was the fifth transcontinental railroad spanning the North American continent, but to Daniel it was the only one that counted. The others had been boondoggles of the U.S. or Canadian governments—subsidized, poorly built, corrupt, inefficient, with routes dictated by politics rather than economics, hamstrung by the strings that inevitably came with public money. The first transcontinental, a posthumous monument to the flawed vision of Abraham Lincoln, had been bankrupt two times and was flirting with a third. The finances of the others were almost as shaky. Durand & Woodbury had huge short positions in all of them.

The Great Northern, on the other hand, was a profitable, privately funded venture, financed in part by the Minneapolis and St. Paul citizens who threw a celebration for Mr. Hill on two sunny June days, almost six months after the last spike was driven. Hill, a modest man who often refused to allow news photographers to take his picture, had suggested the money be used for a public library, but they would have none of it. The Emperor of the North, a disdained sobriquet once hung on Hill by a reporter who had never met him, would have his days, and Minneapolis and St. Paul would have theirs. The completion of Hill's railroad marked the Twin Cities' ascendancy into the first rank of American cities.

Daniel's initial reaction when he had received his invitation had been to decline. Financial markets were falling, business was contracting, and he felt he should stay in New York. For reasons he couldn't completely explain to himself, though, he decided to attend. Parades, pomp, and speeches were wastes of time, but he wanted to be there. He would like to have taken Will, reliving their trip to Minnesota ten years ago, but Will was in England, courting Lady Barrows.

When Daniel picked up his copy of the *Pioneer Press* outside the door to his room in St. Paul's Aberdeen Hotel, he had a glimmering of why he had come. From the front page of the newspaper stared a pen-and-ink portrait of Hill. The railroad baron probably winced when he saw it, but it was a good portrait.

That afternoon Daniel watched float after float—commissioned by the fire department, the Historical Society, dozens of local merchants—pass through triumphal arches. Hill's career had been marked by controversy and acrimony, but his critics and enemies must have stayed home. Cheering throngs of people lined the streets. U.S. and Minnesota state flags waved, and several banners of a white mountain goat on a rocky outcropping—the corporate symbol of the Great Northern—hung from balconies and in storefronts. The Twin Cities radiated a joyous innocence, their citizens paying wholehearted, enthusiastic tribute to achievement, without a trace of the resentment and cynicism that oozed from editorial pages and university lecterns in diatribes against the men who were building the nation.

Several of those men were present the following evening in the packed ballroom of the Aberdeen Hotel for a dinner honoring Hill: Marshall Field and George F. Pullman from Chicago, and Sir Donald Smith, one of Hill's original associates, also instrumental in building the Canadian Pacific Railroad, from Montreal. There were Great Northern employees, local businessmen and their wives, and, like moths, only more distasteful, a gaggle of politicians and journalists who flitted in the reflected glow of Hill's glory.

Hill received an ovation as he stepped to the dais. Boisterous "huzzahs" and shouts of "speech, speech" filled the ballroom. He was bulkier, more buffalo-like than when Daniel had first seen him ten years ago. All the hair was gone from the top of his head. The fringe and his beard were shaggier and whiter.

Hill smiled and raised his hand for a silence that did not come until he began speaking. "Ladies and gentlemen, distinguished guests, I'm overwhelmed by the honor you show me tonight." His voice was deep and sonorous, filling the ballroom. The crowd was going to cheer anything he said and there was another ovation. He again raised his hand.

"We encountered a few obstacles in the course of our undertaking."

The crowd roared with laughter at this massive understatement. There had been the lawsuits, filed solely so Hill would pay the litigants to go away. There had been the politicians, some undoubtedly in the ballroom that night, bribed by Hill's competitors to deny charters and right-of-ways to the Great Northern. Hill had paid bigger bribes or outmaneuvered them.

"The financing wasn't always certain..."

In the early days the Great Northern consumed capital like its giant locomotives consumed coal. Hill had plunged into debt, dancing on the precipice of financial ruin. Daniel's ability to raise money, including his personal investment in the railroad's securities, had been one of the company's lifelines. By 1890 the Great Northern was profitable and solidly solvent, but the last nine-hundred-mile push to the Pacific required millions, which was to have been raised in England by the venerable Barings bank. When Barings went bankrupt, Hill's American financiers had to scramble to raise the required funds. Daniel had been part of the group that filled the breech, helping distribute $11 million of bonds. He still owned $500,000 worth of those bonds, now considered good as gold on Wall Street.

"Facing substantial engineering and construction challenges, our men labored under considerable hardship..."

When Daniel met Hill, the railroader had talked of a Marias Pass through the Rockies as Ponce de Leon must have talked of the fountain of youth—unsure of its existence but obsessed with the possibility. After much fruitless exploration, a Great Northern engineer, John F. Stephens, discovered the pass in the winter of 1889. At five thousand feet, a little over half as high as much of the Rockies, the pass was the golden door to the Pacific. It made the seemingly impossible project possible, but it wasn't easy. Streams had to be bridged, chasms spanned, embankments whittled from mountains of hard rock or unstable mud and clay, tunnels bored, with the weather—driving rain, flash floods, blizzards, subzero winters, blazing summer heat and its attendant swarms of black flies and mosquitoes—providing its own obstacles.

"I drove the men hard..."

Hill had gone through executives like other businessmen went through boxes of cigars. Reciting the two tenets of his religion of perfection—"The best possible line, shortest distance, lowest grades, and least curvature" and "Make the work permanent and good in every respect so that it will not have to be done over again"—Hill personally supervised the construction of the line and approved every expenditure. He laid down the law—speculating in land alongside the railway, political monkey business, and less than scrupulous observance of treaties with the Indians and laws regarding removal of sand and gravel from their lands were firing offenses. Hill's chief engineer, E.H. Beckler, repeatedly bore tongue-lashings from his demanding boss, the last when he told Hill that the final link through the Cascades would have to wait until the spring of 1893. Perhaps out of sheer fear, Beckler had proved himself wrong when the last spike was pounded that January. Hill drove himself more mercilessly than his men—twenty-hour days, seven-day weeks, and long absences from his wife and eleven children were routine.

"We paid the monetary costs for our railroad, but we also paid in blood. Please observe a moment of silence for the men who perished in our endeavor."

Men had died during the construction, despite Hill's attention to safety. The Great Northern project had employed thousands of men, drawn by the highest wages available for such work. The risks of working in the far north and building a railway over two towering mountain ranges from remote encampments were obvious and not entirely avoidable.

"Ladies and gentlemen, thank you very much."

As Daniel leapt to his feet to join the thunderous and lengthy ovation, he realized why he had come to St. Paul. You were lucky if you had personally witnessed even a single instance of true greatness—the golden pinnacle—as it happened. James J. Hill stood alone, a hero at the apex of his golden pinnacle, and tonight was an instance rarer even than that attainment—greatness generally recognized. The human spirit craved such moments, needed them as sustenance in its hard, lonely battles. Daniel's spirit needed that sustenance and it had brought him here. He looked around the ballroom at the wildly clapping and cheering crowd. His glistening eyes were the rule, not the exception.

Michael Palos rubbed his face and eyes. It was close to midnight, but he was at work. He had worked past midnight almost every night for several weeks. He worked in the paper-strewn conference room of Durand & Woodbury with an imposing group—partners Daniel Durand, Jakob Gottman, and Benjamin Keane, two other associates, and eight men from prominent Wall Street investment and law firms. He sipped his six or seventh cup of coffee, he had lost track.

Palos unraveled complicated documents and financial statements, but the ways of people and their politicians were a mystery. Durand & Woodbury was working with its competitors in a triage operation, sorting through the wreckage of the American railroad system. The carnage was the predictable consequence of two laws. The Interstate Commerce Act of 1887—the first federal legislation to regulate the railroads—was supposedly intended to help smaller railroads and farmers by outlawing collusive practices and rate discrimination. However, the smaller railroads had been the main beneficiary of pooling—setting rates in conjunction with other lines to offer a guaranteed rate to big shippers who shipped across several regional systems. Now outlawed, the end of pooling sped the consolidation that the law's backers claimed to abhor, the big railroads swallowing the small lines that could no longer guarantee a rate, then raising rates.

When Mr. Durand returned from Europe in 1890, he had warned the partners that the Silver Purchase Act would drive the surest form of money—gold—out of circulation and out of the country. In three years the U.S. government lost half its gold reserves. The resulting contraction in the money supply had precipitated a vicious downturn that had come to a head a week and a half ago, on July 26, with the "Black Wednesday" stock market crash.

A grandfather's clock in the hall outside the conference room tolled twelve times as August 6 became August 7. Today Congress would meet in special session to repeal the Silver Purchase Act. The damage had been done, although the proponents of the act insisted the contraction and crash had nothing to do with their legislation. Thousands of railroads, industrial concerns, and financial firms had gone bankrupt and hundreds of thousands of workers had lost their jobs.

Palos was Durand & Woodbury's indispensable detail man on the railroad reorganizations. He seemed to remember every obscure clause of every pertinent contract, indenture, and charter. The bankers and lawyers decided, usually after hours of negotiation, which creditors would get paid and how much, which strong roads would buy which weak ones at what price, which securities would be issued and how much capital would be raised, and which lines would simply cease operations. Tonight they were mired in a contentious discussion about staggered terms on a board of directors. Finally a settlement was reached; time to call it a night. The men trudged out of the conference room. Palos was exhausted. He walked with Benjamin Keane to his office.

"I suppose you didn't ask him again?" Keane said. Keane, thirty-six—ten years older than Palos—was Palos' mentor and confidant.

"No, I didn't. We're so busy that it never seems like the appropriate time."

"Strike when the iron is hot, or not at all."

"Mr. Durand intimidates me. I don't know how he'll react."

"How he'll react to what?" It was Mr. Durand, who must have heard the conversation as he passed by Keane's office.

"Sir…" Palos stammered. "Sir, could I have a moment of your time?"

"If we can keep it brief. I want to get some sleep tonight."

"Yes, sir, I'll be brief."

They went into Mr. Durand's office. He dropped his hat and briefcase on his desk, sat down, and motioned for Palos to sit. "What's on your mind, Mr. Palos?"

Palos felt trapped. There was only one way out. "Sir, I'd like to ask your permission to court Miss Laura. I know I don't come from much, but I've made something of myself here, and I believe Miss Laura would look upon my courtship with favor."

Mr. Durand seemed incapable of controlling his laughter, which lasted a long time. When he stopped he smiled at Palos. "Excuse me. With the hours we've been working, I don't know when you're going to find time for a courtship." Palos suspected the joke ran deeper than that, but he couldn't guess what it was. "If you can find the time, you have my blessing to call on Laura."

"Thank you, sir. Thank you very much."

Benjamin Keane stood before the assembled partners and associates of Durand & Woodbury, presenting the firm's results for 1893. A howling New York blizzard rattled the windows of the conference room, but the results generated their own warmth—in the midst of a depression the firm had had a good year. Will marveled that Keane spoke with no notes, but concisely summarized the salient points of each department's results.

"Income was down in banking and market making, reflecting our decision to cut our exposure," Keane said. "However, that was offset by the success we enjoyed with railroad securities. The bankruptcies of the Union Pacific, the Northern Pacific, and the Santa Fe validated our skepticism of the government-financed lines and Mr. Woodbury's and Mr. Dolan's short sales of their securities. On the long side, we've just received results from Mr. Hill concerning the Great Northern. With its competitors' bankruptcies it has a seen an increase in traffic. It made over two million last year, almost a ten percent increase. Now Mr. Woodbury will say a few words."

Will was surprised, with such favorable results in a difficult year, at Woodbury's scowl. Dolan, the Pirate, was scowling as well. Woodbury held a newspaper in his hand.

"Let me read an item to you, gentlemen," Woodbury said. "'*In the midst of panic, bankruptcy, and depression, there are a few Wall Street scavengers feasting on the carcasses. Thousands of investors lost their life savings this past year, but Durand & Woodbury, a shadowy firm that, with good reason, shuns publicity, made $1.1*"

*million from those innocents' misbegotten faith in our free enterprise
system. The firm sold railroad securities it did not own, a nefarious
but legal practice known as selling short, to the small investors Wall
Street loves to fleece. Later, when many of the railroads succumbed
to the unexpected downturn in business conditions, the firm bought
back the securities for pennies on the dollar. They are undoubtedly
laughing all the way to one of the few banks that have not failed.'"*

Woodbury rolled the paper and slapped it against his palm. "I
shouldn't have to say what I'm about to say." His voice was low,
but it was loud enough—the room was quiet. "Much of this piece
is garbage. We didn't sell to widows and orphans. We sold to other
traders, big boys. There was nothing 'unexpected' about the downturn. We expected it, planned for it. This writer has no love for Wall
Street; he's probably a socialist. I don't care what anyone who pays
attention to this drivel thinks of our firm as long as we're doing
right by our customers and our own consciences. Somehow this reporter got the correct number for the profits we made on those short
sales. That number was no secret within the firm, but somebody
mentioned it outside the firm.

"Our clients cherish our discretion. We liquidated huge positions
recently and nobody knew what we were doing. What are our clients
to make of a firm that can't keep its profits out of the newspapers?"
Woodbury's voice was rising.

"More important, I care about how we carry on business within
the firm. Mr. Durand and I have always wanted our men to be able to
talk freely, without reservation. If we don't share information, we're
only hurting ourselves. Our accounts, our results, have never been a
secret within the firm. BUT IT'S ALWAYS BEEN UNDERSTOOD
THAT WHAT WE TALK ABOUT HERE STAYS HERE!" He
slammed the paper on the partners' table. "IF I FIND THAT THIS
NUMBER CAME FROM SOMEONE IN THIS FIRM, I DON'T

CARE WHO HE IS, HE'S FIRED! I TRUST I MAKE MYSELF CLEAR!" He seemed to throw himself into his chair as he sat down. It creaked angrily under his bulk.

Confused, anxious conversations broke out around the room. Unless someone stepped forward or an investigation revealed who had talked, everyone was under suspicion.

Will shifted uneasily in his chair. He hadn't been entirely circumspect in talking about the firm's affairs. After work, he would sometimes meet with friends at one of the better Wall Street pubs. There were Tim Harkness and a couple of other Bovinity men, a few from Harvard who had been in different clubs, and a few from Yale, Princeton, and Columbia. Most of them, like Will and Tim Harkness, were working in their families' firms. They were a good group of fellows to drink with and blow off steam. Naturally enough they talked about their jobs, and naturally enough there was some boasting. Will had scored points when he mentioned how the firm had positioned itself for the downturn. He didn't recall saying how much Durand & Woodbury had made on its railroad shorts, but he had known the number and he might have let it slip.

How would a newspaper reporter get the profit number from this group of drinking buddies? Blue bloods, they disdained the press and wouldn't count a reporter among their friends or even acquaintances. They were all imbued in the Wall Street tradition of discretion. It seemed a stretch to say that something he had let slip weeks ago in a pub found its way into a newspaper today. However, the timing of the story was certainly curious. It had run that afternoon, the afternoon of Durand & Woodbury's annual review—quite a coincidence.

Will couldn't banish his uneasy feeling. He glanced towards the partners' table. Woodbury was staring at him.

Chapter 19

Adieu

Eleanor couldn't reconcile herself to Tommy's decision. After a protracted battle of wills she knew she would lose, a battle she nevertheless fought, she couldn't watch her son's train pull away from Grand Central station with the same anxious optimism she had seen off Will and Alexander. She felt nothing but dread. Tommy was more like his father than any of their other children. He and Laura were tall, dark, and slender, favoring Daniel, but Laura never kept her mother up at night, worrying. It had been Daniel's dash, his audacity—risking his job in courting Eleanor—that had attracted her to him, and Tommy was cut from the same cloth. What had been dash and audacity to the smitten young woman was now stubborn independence—outright foolishness—to the mother.

The battle had begun during a family dinner in the Durands' dining room.

"Tommy," Eleanor said, "have you started thinking about college?"

"I'm not going to college."

"You're not going? But…but why? Your academic record is as good as Will's and Alexander's. You could get admitted to Harvard or Yale."

"I don't want to go to Harvard or Yale or the University of Chicago. I want to work."

"Have you thought this through?" It was the wrong thing to say. "There—"

"Yes, I've thought this through," he said testily. "I plan—"

"Perhaps we can discuss this after dinner," Daniel said.

"Aw, we want to hear the argument," Constance whined.

Daniel, Eleanor, and Tommy adjourned to the study after quickly and quietly finishing their meal. "What do you intend to do?" Eleanor asked as she poured the coffee, failing to hide the anxiety in her voice. She and Daniel sat on a sofa opposite their son.

He looked her directly in the eye. Just like Daniel, he met things head on. "I want to learn the railroad business and I want to see the country. This summer, Mario and I are going to go out west and find jobs on a railroad. We've saved some money."

"Does Isabella know about this?"

"Not yet."

"Working on a railroad is hard, dangerous work," Daniel said.

"I know, but you've said the only way to learn a business is from the bottom up."

Daniel nodded, saying nothing.

"Jobs aren't for the asking right now, Tommy," Eleanor said. "The country is in the middle of a depression. There are at least ten men for every open position, what few there are. Father knows Mr. Hill. Perhaps he has something on the Great Northern."

Tommy shook his head. "I don't want to get a job that way. I want to do it on my own."

"We could make arrangements to get you money in an emergency," Daniel said.

"Then I wouldn't really be on my own, would I?"

"I don't like this at all," Eleanor said.

"It's what I'm going to do." After a lengthy silence, Tommy left the study.

Eleanor, shocked, turned to Daniel. "Are you going to allow this?"

"How do you propose that I stop it?"

She had no answer. Her husband's cherished hope was that his favorite son would someday work at Durand & Woodbury, but he would let Tommy have his way.

That didn't stop her from waging her battle. She tried three times to calmly and rationally discuss her son's plans with him, to show him the unwisdom of his course. Tommy answered in kind, but the answer was always the same—he and Mario were headed west. Her disappointment that he wasn't going to college was magnified by anxiety and sleepless nights over the course he had chosen. She had won a single concession, though: Tommy would wait to leave until the following summer, after Laura's wedding to Michael Palos.

Conceding defeat, Eleanor bought him an Ulster overcoat as a going away present. She didn't understand his pained expression when he opened the box. Surely he wasn't going to carry this independence fetish so far that he wouldn't accept her gift? He was stubborn, but he had a good heart. He wouldn't hurt her if he didn't have to.

"What's wrong?" she said. "It's for your trip."

"You worry about thieves. Wouldn't wearing this coat be like hanging a sign on myself: 'I have money'?"

Of course it would. She felt like an idiot. Tears came to her eyes.

"Keep it for me, Mother. It's a fine coat. I'll send for it when I get established."

Now, at Grand Central, he and Mario were boarding the train. Mario, short, swarthy, physically strong, with coal-black hair and brown eyes, looked as determined as Tommy. They waved to Eleanor, Daniel, Constance, John, and Isabella, shaking her head, as the train pulled away.

"Foolishness," the maid muttered.

John and Constance were crying—they adored Tommy—but Eleanor had resolved not to burden him with her tears. At least Tommy wouldn't be alone. Mario was a year older than Tommy and had grown up in rough neighborhoods without a father. He knew how to take care of himself. It was meager consolation. As the train left the station her resolve crumbled—she buried her head in Daniel's shoulder and wept. Tommy could wind up sick or destitute or stranded and he wouldn't ask for help. He was just that stubborn.

They were on their own. Tommy looked out into the darkness from the parlor car as the train rolled through the Illinois countryside, two days out of New York. To hell with the Concord Academy and boys who wanted nothing more than to work in their fathers' firms and spend their fathers' money; he and Mario were on their own. Mario, sitting next to him, gently snored. Mario had been his best friend since he was seven years old. They were inseparable until he went to Concord and Mario left school and found a job as a mechanic's apprentice, working on engines in a metal-stamping factory. He loved steam engines, but the depression shut the factory down. He had jumped at Tommy's railroad idea—a chance to work on locomotive engines.

The hardest part of leaving was saying goodbye to his father. He had put his arm on his son's shoulder and said, "You'll do just fine." That was the only thing he said about Tommy's plan. It was the only thing Tommy needed to hear. He knew his father wanted him to work at Durand & Woodbury, but Will negated whatever desire he might have had to do so. He wasn't going to work with his older brother. Will was a fool when he went away and Harvard had only made him a better-educated fool. He was going to marry that English witch next spring and if he couldn't see what she was all about, he deserved the misery he'd get. Whatever job Tommy found wouldn't, regrettably, permit him the time off to attend the wedding—or so he would say.

He loved riding on the train, seeing the country, talking to other passengers, asking the railroad men questions. What's a switchman? How do switches work? What do the station agents do? What do the brakemen do? How do the steam engines work, and who operates the controls? Do you have to be a fireman before you can be an engineer?

Are there any jobs available? To that question he got the same answer. Maybe out west—lots of empty miles of track that needed to be maintained, fewer men looking for work. Everywhere they saw the unemployed, the dispossessed, risking their lives jumping on and off moving freight cars in the train yards, walking through the open countryside, huddled around tiny fires.

Tommy opened a paper bag and took out a slab of smoked ham, a chunk of cheese, and a hard roll. After he ate, the swaying train and chug-chugging steam engine lulled him to sleep.

He was awakened the next morning by a conductor's not so gentle shaking.

"What is it?" Tommy said groggily. "I have a ticket."

"You have to get off," replied the conductor gruffly. "This train ain't going nowhere."

"Why?"

"The yardmen won't move passenger trains on account of the Pullman strike."

"Where are we?"

"St. Louis."

"How long will the strike last?"

"How would I know?"

"Those bastards at Pullman," Mario growled. "They cut the workers' wages, but not the rents for company housing. The workers got squeezed. They had to strike."

What Tommy and Mario had hoped would be a one- or two-day stay in St. Louis stretched into a week. They took two dirty rooms just bigger than closets in a miserable boarding house near the train station to conserve funds. The floorboards creaked and the walls smelled of cabbage and onions. They read the papers, hoping for progress in ending the strike, wandered about St. Louis, and found the cheapest places for semi-edible food. It rained for two days. They stayed cooped up, reading, playing cards, and getting on each other's nerves, arguing over nothing.

Tommy lay on his cot late one night and pondered their plight. A metal bar ground through the thin mattress and into his back. They were making a total hash of things. It was not to his mother, full of doubt, that he didn't want to make such an admission, although it would prove her right. He would feel worse about proving his father, of the unwavering faith, wrong. Someone next door passed wind. They had to get out of there. The rail companies were firing strikers and boycotters. Perhaps that would open up opportunities.

The next morning he put the idea to Mario as they ate breakfast—apples, past their prime, starting to shrivel, but a penny cheaper than the good ones.

Mario snorted. "You want to be a blackleg?"

"What's a blackleg?"

"A strikebreaker."

"It would be work."

"Not for long. This strike won't last forever. Once it's over, they'll give your job back to the man who had it, if you're lucky. If you're not, they'll let you keep it. The strikers won't be your best friends—blacklegs have a lot of 'accidents.' We're better off waiting out the strike."

"But we're running out of money."

"I know."

Two days later the papers trumpeted the end of the strike. Tommy and Mario had nineteen dollars and change between them. Their last night in St. Louis they saved money and ate the boarding house's indigestible fare. Stomach woes kept them up through the night.

The next morning they went to a Union Pacific office. Tommy asked a clerk about jobs.

"Cheyenne, that's where you boys want to go. It's a junction between a big north-south line and a big east-west line. They got a yard and a repair station that both run two shifts, twenty-four hours. If anywhere's got jobs, Cheyenne's the place."

"How much are tickets?"

"Ten dollars and fifty cents apiece."

They left the office. How the hell were they going to get to Cheyenne?

Mario smiled. "You ever hopped a freight?"

"No."

"Not that hard. I did it in New York. The toughest part is staying out of the way of the yard guards. They carry guns and can arrest you, but it's our only way to Cheyenne."

Nightfall found them hiding in an uncoupled, empty boxcar in the sprawling St. Louis train yard, waiting for Union Pacific 233 on track seven to Kansas City. Other men furtively darted among the cars, hoping to catch a free ride to somewhere. Tommy felt the same anticipation mixed with trepidation he had felt before his exploits in New York.

"That's it," Mario said, pointing at a locomotive rumbling towards them, its light shining.

They waited for the locomotive to pass before they jumped out of the boxcar. The flat cars and cattle cars, mostly empty, passed, then the tank cars. They saw an empty boxcar with an open door. The train was moving at their running speed, but gaining steam. Mario reached the boxcar first, threw his bag inside, grabbed a vertical iron rail by the side of the door, jumped up, swung his leg over, and rolled into the car.

Tommy slipped on loose gravel as he reached for the rail. He went down hard, within an arm's length of the train's crushing wheels. He rolled away and scrambled up. The train was picking up speed. He ran after the boxcar, barely outrunning the train. Mario was hanging out of the boxcar, one hand grabbing the rail, one foot dangling in the air.

"You there, get away from that train!"

A yard guard! If he didn't get on the train he'd be arrested.

"Hurry!" Mario shouted.

Tommy was almost up to him. He reached out to Mario's outstretched hand. Mario locked his wrist in a vise grip. "Drop your bag!" he screamed. "Grab my arm!"

Tommy dropped his bag. His feet left the ground. Mario released his grip on the iron rail, grabbed Tommy's arms, and swung him into the boxcar. Tommy landed with a painful crash on the floor of the boxcar. He looked up, shaken, and saw a man with his arms around Mario's waist, his boot planted against the boxcar wall, stopping Mario from falling out of the boxcar.

"You always find a way to get in trouble!" Mario yelled.

"There's easier ways to hop a freight, lad," the man said. He sounded older than Tommy and Mario. Between the black grease coating his clothes and face and the fading light, it was impossible to make out his features. "Name's Gilbert," he said, extending his hand. "You boys headed anywhere in particular? By the looks of things, you ain't done this much."

"Cheyenne. I'm Mario and he's Tommy."

"The best time to get on a train is when it ain't moving. Every yard guard has his price, usually two bits. That's a bowl of stew, and ain't your life worth more than a bowl of stew?"

They arrived in Cheyenne before sundown of their third day out from St. Louis. The Union Pacific depot was almost as lavish as Grand Central. A porter gave them directions to the hiring office. It wasn't closed, but there was only one clerk, a man in his thirties in a threadbare gray suit, putting papers from his desk in pigeonholes, preparing to leave.

"Excuse me, sir, are there any jobs available?" Tommy asked.

The clerk looked him up and down. "You ever work on a railroad?"

"No, sir, but I learn fast."

"I've worked on steam engines in a factory," Mario said. "I can work in the shop."

"We're always looking for mechanics. Come back tomorrow morning at eight. As for you, I've only got one opening, working with a night brakeman."

The railroad workers Tommy had talked to always described the job of brakeman as dangerous. "What kind of work is it?"

"You help a brakeman in the yard, finding cars and coupling them together, eight at night to eight in the morning, Tuesday through Sunday, twenty cents an hour. You want to give it a try?"

Tommy gulped. "Yes, sir."

The clerk pulled a watch from his vest. "Can you start in an hour and ten minutes?"

He was exhausted and ravenously hungry. He had three dollars and four cents in his pocket and only the clothes he wore, having dropped his bag in the St. Louis yard. "Yes, sir."

"Ask for Mr. Winters, he's the yard supervisor, at 7:45."

They found a café in the depot and spent thirty cents apiece on gristly roast beef, mashed potatoes, and gravy. Tommy choked down two cups of coffee so he could stay awake.

Mario yawned. "I got enough for a room, but it won't be the Waldorf. I'll hunt you up in the morning, before I start work, and give you the key." He wiped his mouth with a napkin. "Are you going to be all right? You don't have to take this job. We'll think of something else."

"I'll get through tonight."

"Good luck, then. I'll see you in the morning."

Tommy watched his friend walk out of the depot. He felt utterly alone.

Mr. Winters, the yard supervisor, was a bulky man with narrow eyes and a perpetual sneer. He led Tommy over empty tracks and in between cars. The huge yard smelled of oil, grease, and burning coal. Kerosene lanterns and a few light bulbs were strung up above, throwing off harsh, glaring light. Locomotives puffed and the iron wheels of slow-moving cars screeched against the rails. Men shouted and cursed. They stopped at an unattached boxcar where a man in greasy overalls and a railroad cap was stooped over a coupling. Winters tapped him on his shoulder and he stood up. He was short and thin, his face so dark and grimy it was difficult to make out his age, although Tommy guessed he was in his fifties.

"Hadley," Winters said. "This is—" Winters hadn't asked his name.

"Tommy—" Tommy was a boy's name. "Tom Durand." "Tom" extended his hand. He sensed something wrong when he shook Hadley's hand. The middle finger was missing.

"This is your new assistant." By the way Winters looked at him, he knew the yard supervisor thought he wouldn't make it through one shift. Winters walked away.

Hadley smiled grimly. He only had about half his teeth. "You ever thread a moving needle?" he said, his breath reeking putrid decay. Tom shook his head. "You find couplings that match. Sometimes you look all over the damn yard. The engineer backs the train. You guide the link into the slot and then slide a metal pin in a hole to secure the coupling. You only got a second, and if you don't get the damn pin in the damn hole, or if you didn't guide right to begin with, you start over."

Hadley held up both his hands in front of Tom's face. Not only did the right hand have a missing middle finger, the pinky and ring fingers on the left hand were gone, too. Hadley stepped uncomfortably close to Tom. "There's a lot of accidents in a yard, boy. Most of 'em happen to brakemen." Tom almost retched from Hadley's breath. "There ain't a brakeman here that's got all his fingers." He waved his left hand. "You only need these three to do the job. I lose one more, I'm out of work. Fingers, hands, arms—they ain't nothing when you're working between these cars. You get an engineer that's dipped into the firewater and brings the train in too fast, you'll lose more than a finger." He grabbed the front of Tom's shirt and pulled him a couple of inches away from his face. "You're too young, you damn wet-behind-the-ears pup, for me to tell you how many men I knowed that got killed here. What do you say to that?"

Tom grabbed the grizzled coot's wrist, wrenched away his hand, and stepped back. He looked him in the eye. "Let's get to work."

Jakob Gottman had seen it before, the self-assurance that comes from being born into immense wealth—*goyim* wealth; the unquestioning acceptance of the beliefs instilled by parents and their exclusive churches (Protestant churches—the Catholics, like the Jews, always had rough edges), preparatory schools, and colleges; the conquer-the-world confidence you got from breathing the sweet air at the top of the heap. It was assurance that never knew the sting of ostracism, of being different, of fighting to break through, to be seen and judged for what you were, not dismissed because of how you worshipped. Many times you didn't break through.

Gottman didn't like the golden *goyim*. They'd never struggled, never been hurt. Alexander Durand, he suspected, might be an exception. He was home for the summer from the University of Chicago, working at Durand & Woodbury. Alexander and Gottman had not said two words to each other since their initial introduction, but Gottman's intuition was there might be something to this quiet young man. He invited him to attend a meeting with Mr. Friedlander, a wealthy client, and Mr. Richmond, who was trying to sell some warehouses in the shipping district. Alexander would have no real function in the meeting—he would observe. Like his father, silence seemed to be a strong suit. The four men sat around a table in a small conference room. Richmond was talking up his warehouses.

"I have a number of interested parties looking at these properties." He was tall and blond, with a neat mustache, in his mid-forties. He wore a conservative black suit, but his shirt cuffs were frayed. "I wanted to give you gentlemen the opportunity."

Gottman soon grew bored. Alexander gave his full attention to Richmond. Judicious—that was a good adjective for Alexander. He wouldn't make snap decisions; he balanced, deliberated, discussed, and reasoned, considering all sides. Of course, it was easier to keep emotion out of your decisions if your placid exterior masked a placid interior, and perhaps that was all there was to him. Why hurry when dinner would be on the table regardless? Gottman, on the move, made quick decisions and most of them were right.

Richmond was little better than a confidence man. Gottman wondered if Alexander had drawn a bead on him—there had been no confidence men in his rarified world. "You have no other 'interested parties,'" Gottman said. "There are warehouses for sale all over the district. You missed a payment on a note. Now, if you want to continue on a more realistic basis, Mr. Friedlander has an interest in your properties. If not, we must say good day."

Richmond's shoulders slumped and he crumbled, as Gottman knew he would. He slowly shook his head. "Perhaps a price adjustment."

Gottman hammered Mr. Richmond until he accepted 15 percent of what he had originally asked—one quarter payable in cash, the balance financed by a non-recourse note, secured only by the warehouse, from Friedlander, who said nothing during the negotiations. After many years of doing business with Gottman, he trusted him implicitly. Everyone shook hands over the agreement and Richmond left, disconsolate. Alexander smiled at Gottman's bare-knuckled negotiating.

Gottman asked him to work on several other projects and took him on client calls. Alexander enjoyed Gottman's humor with his clients—the sarcasm, the "I should live so longs" as his eyes rolled beseechingly heavenward, the barbs, the questions answered with questions—and Gottman liked an audience. Alexander might have the makings of a *mensch*.

His older brother did not. Late one night Gottman was in a negotiating session with Will, Alexander again an observer. Durand & Woodbury had issued bonds for a coal company that was now insolvent. Gottman had sold the securities to his clients and Will had found investors interested in a recapitalization.

"If your group would further reduce their interest," Will said, "I believe that I could effect this recapitalization. But they must reduce their interest beyond what you've proposed."

It was late. Gottman was tired and had a headache. "What language are we speaking here? I've said it four times already, but I'll say it a fifth, slowly, because perhaps you got so much Latin and Greek at Harvard that your English is rusty. My investors will write down their interest fifty percent—that's a five followed by a zero, fifty percent. They will not go beyond fifty percent. Before they will accept less, they will throw Consolidated Coal into bankruptcy and take what they get in the dissolution. Do you understand? Fifty percent, take it or leave it!"

Will's jaw tightened and his fists clenched. "I understand, there's no need to talk to me as if I'm a fool. If I were running Durand & Woodbury, Gottman, you wouldn't be working here!"

These Ivy League swells hated Jews. Gottman said nothing. This was a contest and the Jew was going to win. He stood, gathered his papers, and filed them in his briefcase. He stared at Will. "You're correct, Mr. Durand. If you were running Durand & Woodbury, I would not be working here. Good night." He left the conference room.

Will stared at the papers on the table. After a long silence he looked up at Alexander.

"That was the wrong thing to say, Will."

Hank Suderman, superintendent of the Union Pacific's Cheyenne yard, hesitated before the door of the yardmaster's office, his perch above the yard. Suderman, whose nondescript appearance belied the intelligence and industry that had lifted him from clerk to his present position, was the yardmaster's boss, but Bill James intimidated him, as he did everyone else. He suffered fools and foolishness not at all. Suderman wasn't a fool, but in his position as the intermediary between James and headquarters in Omaha, he had to countenance foolishness. Suderman knocked on the door.

"Come in."

Suderman entered. James stood surveying the yard below—men shoveling away last night's snow, the train cars casting long shadows in the cold morning sun—through a pair of binoculars. The yardmaster had the most challenging job in railroading, and running the huge Cheyenne yard was an especially complicated proposition. Cars had to be routed, transferred, and coupled, track switches thrown, roundtables rotated, and light signals flashed as trains going north, south, east, and west passed through the yard. The yardmaster was the yard's brain. James had unwavering concentration, an infallible memory, and made hundreds of correct decisions quickly. He was the best yardmaster in the Union Pacific system, and was better paid than many of its executives.

James picked up a telephone to the yard. "Switch the three coals on twelve to fourteen for the 9:07 Denver." James never wasted a word. Woe to the man at the other end of the line who wasn't paying attention and called back. A chart of the yard covered most of his desk. The office was Spartan—the desk, a hat and coat stand, two wooden chairs, filing cabinets, and pigeonholes lining three walls, with the fourth given over to route maps. James hated disorganization and clutter. Messy offices led to costly mistakes. He turned towards Suderman. "Yes?"

James looked more like a cowboy than a railroad man—he had grown up on a ranch. The other yardmasters wore suits. James wore a leather vest over a flannel shirt, jeans, a black belt with an oversize silver buckle and black leather boots. His Stetson sat on the stand in the corner. Nobody told Bill James what to wear. His fifty-seven-year-old face looked like a rock formation: lines, planes, and angles chiseled by gritty winds whipping off the prairie. His eyes were the icy gray-blue of a mountain stream at sunup. They could scan the yard in an instant or, so the men in the yard said, bring a liar to his knees. It was his eyes that posed the problem.

"I got word from headquarters this morning," Suderman said. "A new candidate."

"After that last one, why are they trying again? Another nephew?"

Suderman shook his head. "Son of a friend, a powerful friend, a politician. Thinks he might want to get into railroading."

James had a degenerative eye disease. Soon he wouldn't be able to do the job he loved. It was a shame bordering on tragedy. Three years ago his beloved Lucille had died; now he was going to lose his job. What would he have left? Headquarters had insisted that he find and train his replacement. They hadn't even offered him another, less sight-dependent position—he had offended too many executives. A smaller man would have stuck the railroad with the first plausible replacement, but not James. Suderman had lost track of the number of men who had failed to meet James' exacting standards. Some didn't last an hour; only one made it a month. The last had been a nephew of a vice-president. Half a day.

James stared at Suderman. "Do these Omaha puffballs realize how much money an incompetent yardmaster will cost them? If this new boy wants to play choo-choo, give him a free pass and conductor's cap and let him pretend he's doing something useful. I don't care if he's the son of the president of the United States, I'm not interested, not after that last idiot. Besides, I might have found my own man right here."

"Here?"

"Out there on the yard."

"Who? What's his name?"

"Damn Durand."

"That can't be his first name. Damn?"

"I've heard him called that so much you would think it was. This fellow Durand remembers the type of coupling on every car he sees. You know how the brakemen dog it toward the end of their shifts, supposedly 'searching' all over the yard for matching couplings instead of actually coupling cars. They can't do it as much because Durand remembers all the couplings. The supervisors have discovered Durand's memory. Suddenly there's a lot less 'searching' and a lot more coupling, and Mr. Durand has a new first name—'Damn.'"

"What's his real first name?"

"Tom. He works with Hadley."

"That buzzard's breath would stop a locomotive at fifty yards, but he'd give you a fair read."

"He said Durand was the sharpest lad he ever 'knowed.'" James smiled. "Works hard, works steady, pays attention, remembers everything he's told. Keeps to himself. He's from back east. The men don't like him because he shows 'em up, but Hadley says he's a good lad."

"Did he think Durand could be a yardmaster?"

"He said he thought Durand was meant for bigger things than brakeman."

"The other men aren't going to like it. How long has Durand been here?"

"About five months."

"So you're going to promote him over men who've been here for years?"

"Only if he can do the job. If he can't, he's right back to brakeman's assistant. Nobody else out there can do this job. Half of 'em can't read. I need a brain, and brains aren't easy to come by. Even when you find one, it may not be the right type for the job."

"So you want me to tell headquarters that you're turning down their candidate, sight unseen, for a brakeman's assistant?"

"That's what you're going to tell them. If they don't like it, they can have my resignation."

Suderman shook his head. As he had in the past, he found himself between Bill James and headquarters; and as he had in the past, he would risk his job siding with James. Saying no to James meant saying no to the human face of logic and sweet reason. Suderman feared the hard stare of those cold gray-blue eyes more than he feared the wrath of all the executives in Omaha put together. "I'll send a telegram telling them to keep their man." He left the office.

Later, James summoned Tom before his night shift began.

"Sit down, Mr. Durand," James said, motioning towards a chair in front of his desk. "Where are from, son?"

"New York, sir."

"What brings you to Cheyenne?"

"I wanted to work on the railroad and I found a job here."

"Brakeman's assistant. Been here five months and haven't lost any fingers yet."

"No, sir."

"Are you smart?"

"Yes, sir."

"Did you go to school?"

"Yes, sir. The Concord Academy. It's a preparatory school."

"How did you do?"

"Best marks in my class."

"Why didn't you go on to college?"

"I wanted to learn the railroad business."

"There's no better place to learn this business than from the yard-master's perch." James motioned towards the yard below. "How would you like a trial as my assistant? If you work out, you'll make forty cents an hour, double what you're making now."

Tom grinned. "When do I start?"

"Get yourself a good night's sleep. I'll let Hadley know you won't be working with him tonight. I'll see you tomorrow morning at seven-thirty."

They stood and shook hands. Tom left the office and ran out of the station. He had done it! Done it! Done it! There was no way he was going to sleep, not for many hours. He had slept during the day and he was too damn excited. Yardmaster—the best job on the rail-road! Who to tell? He had to tell somebody. Mario was working and his supervisor didn't like outsiders coming into the shop. He'd catch him at the end of his shift, but he wanted to tell somebody now! It was snowing again and he ran into a nearby telegraph office and wrote out a message to his parents.

PROMOTED TO YARDMASTER ASSISTANT DOUBLE THE PAY STOP

Technically not correct, but he knew he could do the job.

REGRET NEW POSITION WILL NOT PERMIT ME TO ATTEND WILLS WEDDING STOP

Ain't that a pity!

COLD OUT HERE SEND ULSTER STOP

Your boy made it, Mother.

LOVE TOM

The Durand-Barrows wedding was more than a wedding, it was a transatlantic union between the American commercial and the British political elites, Wall Street and Parliament, the event of the season, front-page society news in both countries. Beside Will on the altar of Canterbury Cathedral stood five members of what in America constituted the aristocracy—Will's brother Alexander, three Bovinity "brothers," and Benjamin Keane. By Lady Sylvia Barrows stood the corresponding bridesmaids, who like the bride bore the title "Lady."

If at any time during the preceding week Lady Sylvia had experienced any of the roiling emotions that had afflicted Will, she never betrayed them. He had worked hard to memorize the faces, names, and titles that populated her retinue. She effortlessly kept names and associated positions straight, a trick she must have learned from her political father. Both his best man, Morton Billingsley, and Tim Harkness had pulled him aside to tell him how captivating they found her. Of course, she was operating on her home territory and he wasn't, but he found her command of herself in the face of daunting pomp and publicity intimidating.

"Dearly beloved, we are gathered here in the sight of God, and in the face of this company, to join this man and this woman in holy matrimony…"

The archbishop was in his late sixties and his voice was not strong. The archbishop of Canterbury! The bride, resplendent in a white veil and dress with lace, tulle, and pearl trim, high lace collar, billowing leg-of-mutton sleeves, and pleats cascading down her long train, took it as her due. The groom, in a split-tailed black coat with a white vest and cravat, couldn't stifle his giddy pride. If people in America knew only one English religious official, it was the archbishop of Canterbury. Will looked heavenward to the vaulted arches and gilt roof bosses. The sun streamed through the high windows.

"…And, forsaking all others, keep thee only unto her, so long as ye both shall live?"

"I will," Will said.

"Sylvia Penelope Maude Barrows, wilt thou have this man to be thy husband…" Will gazed at his bride. Her brown hair was in elaborate curls and ringlets and her delicate, angular face had never looked lovelier, her dainty nose turned up slightly, her brown eyes intent, captivatingly alive. Beautiful, intelligent, aristocratic—his requirements for the ideal bride. Why had he been so taken with quirky Arabella Brewster?

"…And, forsaking all others, keep thee only unto him, so long as ye both shall live?"

"I will," Lady Sylvia said. Will loved the lilt of her voice, so refined.

"Who giveth this woman to be married to this man?"

The Earl of Chatenham, who had been holding his daughter's white-gloved hand, gave it the archbishop, who then placed it in Will's own white-gloved hand. The earl, a tall, heavyset man with prominent jowls and thinning black hair streaked with gray and combed straight back, sat down next to Lady Chatenham. The London newspapers speculated that he could be the next prime minister. Imagine, son-in-law to a prime minister!

Will tried to keep his voice loud. "…To love, cherish, and worship, till death do us part, according to God's holy ordinance, and thereto I plight thee my troth." His troth plighted, he relaxed his grip on Lady Sylvia's hand.

She said her vow. Her voice was soft but firm, and she looked Will directly in the eyes as she spoke. "…To love, cherish, and obey, till death do us part, according to God's holy ordinance, and thereto I give thee my troth."

Will wondered how the "obey" part would work out. The archbishop handed him the ring. "Bless, oh Lord, this ring," the prelate intoned, "that he who gives it and she who wears it may abide in thy peace and favor, unto their life's end, through Jesus Christ our Lord. Amen."

Lady Sylvia removed her glove and Will slipped the ring on her finger.

The archbishop raised his arms. "With this ring I thee wed: in the name of the Father, and of the Son, and of the Holy Ghost. Amen."

They were married! He had done it! She smiled at him and he smiled back. The congregation stood and repeated the Lord's Prayer and the archbishop said two more prayers. He then joined the couple's hands and looked at them gravely. "Those whom God hath joined together let no man put asunder. Forasmuch as William and

Sylvia have consented together in holy wedlock…" Will felt a giddy rush of wonder and awe. "I pronounce that they are man and wife, in the name of the Father, and of the Son, and of the Holy Ghost. Amen."

Will and Lady Sylvia kneeled before the archbishop. "May the Lord mercifully with his favor look upon you, and fill you with all spiritual benediction and grace, that ye may so live together in this life, that in the world to come ye may have life everlasting. Amen."

They stood, turned, and faced the congregation as man and wife. Mendelssohn's "Wedding March" sounded from the organ. Will glanced at his mother, who was beaming and dabbing her eyes with her handkerchief, and his father, who nodded at him. The packed nave was dauntingly long, the white columns imposingly tall. Lady Sylvia placed her hand on his arm and they stepped down from the altar to the aisle. The eyes gazing at them, gazing at him, were the eyes of nobility, powerful political figures, important men of commerce and finance. He straightened his shoulders and reminded himself to walk slowly.

They emerged from Canterbury Cathedral to a dazzling spring day. The sun shone brightly, there were only a few clouds, and a gentle breeze seemed to carry the mingled scent of every flower populating the Kent countryside. Will glanced at his bride. She was smiling, but not at him. It was as if she had realized some private vision, satisfied a secret calculus. Although the day was quite warm, Will felt a shuddering chill.

The wedding breakfast, an elaborate banquet, had reached the point where Daniel could mentally take his leave. He had done what was required—stood in the receiving line greeting hundreds of guests, made polite talk with those around him at the long table in the formal dining room of the Earl of Chatenham's manor, offered a toast to his son and daughter-in-law—and now he drifted away in his own thoughts. To his right Eleanor was dutifully engaged in conversation with Baron Bumptious. To his left a lady talked with her lord.

After Will had announced his engagement with Lady Sylvia to the family, Daniel had talked with him in his study. "I asked you once before, son, but I'm going to ask you again. If your fiancée wasn't the Lady Sylvia Barrows, would you marry her?"

"I would love this woman regardless of her social rank."

Where had Daniel failed? Will was making perhaps the most important decision of his life as a matter of social advancement. A steppingstone marriage was no marriage, and a life lived for others' approval was no life. If everyone was your mirror, you were just a reflection. Will's only hope was that he wasn't lying to himself, although he was lying to Daniel. If he could occasionally be honest with himself, there was the possibility that someday he'd change— but only after things had gone horribly wrong.

"Mr. Durand?" A servant was holding a small silver tray with an envelope on it.

"Yes?"

"For you, sir. It was posted express with instructions to be delivered immediately."

"Thank you." He opened the envelope.

20 April 1895
Rouen, France

Monsieur Durand,
    Please pardon my family's absence from your son's wedding. As you know, my father is very ill. His condition has deteriorated

and he is not expected to live through the week. I hesitate to convey this request, but he has asked for you repeatedly. I understand the imposition, during your son's wedding festivities, but if you could journey to France before my father dies, you would have my eternal gratitude. Of course I understand if this is not possible. Merci.

Your faithful servant,
Jacques Devereaux

Devereaux was near death. Daniel hadn't known that the illness that had prevented his friend from coming to the wedding was life-threatening. His friend—he had so few—such a loss.

"What is it, Daniel?" Eleanor said. He handed the note to her and she read it. "What are you going to do?"

"I want to see him before he dies. I'll find out how quickly I can get to France."

Eleanor's mouth tightened. There was no denying that there had been a certain spark of attraction between Daniel and Devereaux's beautiful, soon-to-be widow. Sparks sometimes turned into flames, even under inauspicious circumstances. "Perhaps the entire family could go to France," he said.

"How could we, with the social functions we're to attend here over the next week? It would be taken as a colossal snub. It will be awkward enough explaining your departure."

"I have to go, dear. I can't deny the deathbed wish of a friend."

Eleanor remained silent for a painfully long time. "Go, if you must."

Monsieur Devereaux breathed his last six hours before Daniel arrived at the chateau. His eldest son, Jacques, much taller than his father and graced with his mother's angular face and dark hair and eyes, imparted this sad news upon Daniel's arrival. Servants hurried about, beginning preparations for the funeral and reception. For the next two days Daniel was left on his own. He spent his time taking long walks by himself on the grounds of the estate and the surrounding countryside and reading in Devereaux's library. A steady stream of visitors paid their respects to Devereaux's two sons and his daughter. Madame Devereaux remained in seclusion.

Only at the funeral in a stately cathedral in Rouen, when Daniel saw the casket before the altar, did he feel the full emotional force of his friend's death. There were personalities of such immediacy, who stood out so prominently from the crowd, that they made an indelible impression. Devereaux's diminutive stature became a minor, overlooked physical characteristic once one encountered his probing intelligence, wit, and Gallic charm. Daniel had discovered, through a cherished correspondence, Devereaux's commitment to logic, and his admiration, with his forebear Tocqueville, of the American republic, liberty, and limited government. Daniel had kept his letters, minor masterpieces of incisive reasoning and lucid prose. Now he felt sadly empty. There was only one Devereaux. Adieu.

Back at the chateau, Daniel greeted Madame Devereaux in a receiving line. Her black veil did not conceal her beauty.

"My condolences to you and your family."

"Ah, Monsieur Durand," she said with a small smile. "It is good of you to come. I'm so sorry you did not make it before Monsieur Devereaux left us. I've been a poor hostess. Perhaps in the next day or two we can spend some time together. How long do you intend to stay in France?"

"I interrupted my son's wedding proceedings in England. I return tomorrow."

"Oh, that is unfortunate, but I do understand."

Daniel took his leave. He found this social occasion difficult because most of the guests were speaking French. Eventually he started a conversation with two Englishmen.

After the reception, which lasted into the night, Daniel took a walk. The food had been excellent and he had eaten too much. When he returned he settled in the library with a snifter of Calvados and a cigar. It hadn't been necessary to journey to Normandy after all. He would have been better off staying in England and not raising Eleanor's suspicions. She might always wonder about this trip—not that there would be anything to wonder about.

The door to the library opened. Madame Devereaux entered and softly shut the door. Her black mourning attire had been replaced with a simple green dress. Her hair was above her head, in the fetching style that Daniel remembered from the first time they had met. High forehead and cheekbones, milky white skin, angular nose, inviting eyes, and rich, full lips—just as beautiful as he remembered. His pulse quickened.

"Monsieur Durand, may I join you?" The widow smiled.

"Certainly."

She sat beside him on the couch, close enough that he could smell her perfume, some intoxicating mixture, perhaps distilled from the floral scents of the local countryside. "Monsieur Devereaux always spoke of you in the most glowing way." She placed her hand lightly on his sleeve. "He said that you were a businessman, a man of action, but that you were a man of thought as well. That combination is rarer than a fine diamond, and more treasured. He allowed me to read some of your letters, and I could see a mind of the highest order at work."

He suspected Madame Devereaux wasn't there just to praise his prose. How to respond? "Thank you" were the only words that came to mind.

"I am alone now, Monsieur Durand. It will be hard—no, it will be impossible—to replace what we had together. He said, toward the end, when he knew his fate, that I must find someone else." Her smile was sad and wistful. "He said I had too much life to wither on the vine."

Daniel saw no danger of Madame Devereaux withering on the vine.

She stood and walked slowly around the library. "This was his favorite room, his library." She made a sweeping gesture that encompassed the entire collection of books. "He loved to read…and write." She pointed at a large desk in the corner of the room. "I imagine you have a library like this, Monsieur Durand. You love to read. I can tell from your letters."

She probably wasn't interested in a literary discussion, either. "Yes, I do like to read," he said, dazzling again with his conversational brilliance.

She sat down again on the couch, placing her hand on his sleeve. "Monsieur Devereaux was sick for many months; we were not able to be together." Uh oh. "I miss the arms of a strong man." Her face was very close to his, he could feel the warmth of her breath. "He did not see things in a conventional way," she whispered. She kissed Daniel lightly.

"Now wait—"

She put a finger on his lips and stared directly into his eyes. "I know, you are a man of honor, true to your word and your beautiful Eleanor. I do not seek that, Monsieur. Just to be held…consoled, for a night. Monsieur Devereaux would understand. Perhaps so too would Eleanor." She stood before him. He was acutely conscious of the body beneath the green dress. "I will depart now, Monsieur. My room is down the hall from yours. The door will be open to you." She took his hand and squeezed it. "Do not be afraid." She walked slowly across the library, as if to give him time to admire what she was offering, and slipped out the door.

Eleanor had been right, after all. Daniel's thoughts were a confused jumble. Would the deceased have understood if Daniel "consoled" his widow on the night of his funeral? Would Eleanor? Try as he might, he couldn't imagine her saying, "You're a fine man, Daniel Durand, for consoling Madame Devereaux in her time of need," nor a voice from the grave: "Thank you, Monsieur, for consoling her on the day I was laid to rest." Console indeed! He had a better chance of swimming the English Channel than he did of containing the fire that would rage in his loins if he "held" Madame Devereaux. Temptation, temptation, temptation—there was no denying he was tempted. One night and Eleanor would never know, not to a certainty. She already had her suspicions, which he might never completely quell—better to go out a lion than a lamb. His entreaties to his iron will went unanswered. He drained his Calvados in one fiery gulp. Temptation. He went upstairs to his room. She was just a few doors away. He locked the door and laughed bitterly. He couldn't lock the door against himself.

He paced about the room, a caged animal trying to remain caged. He removed his clothes, put on his nightshirt, and climbed into the four-poster bed, knowing sleep would not come. His member sprang into action every time he thought of Madame Devereaux. Yes, he loved his wife, but…but after thirty years, what was once a raging fire had settled to a warm glow. Flesh had begun to sag and spread, and mature beauty was "different" than youthful beauty. Novelty was no longer among the sensations one enjoyed during coupling.

Novelty—the new, the different, the unconquered. It beckoned for every man, no matter how beautiful his wife, no matter how satisfying their times together, no matter how happy their home life.

Just a few doors down waited a dazzlingly beautiful, aristocratic novelty, a woman of breeding and distinction—French, exotic, sensuous. Several times Daniel walked to the door. Once he unlocked it, but then relocked it and stepped back.

There was only one solution. He reached down. If it was a sin—he had never thought it was—it was a sin in prevention of a greater one. For the memory of his friend! For his honor! For Eleanor! For his marriage! For a decent night's sleep!

Number 247 from Ogden was twenty minutes early. If it had been on time Tom would have directed it to track four, but 199, eastbound, was still on that track, picking up cars. There would be no harm in letting the Ogden train wait, since it was early, but wouldn't it be better to keep it moving? He could call Mr. James, who was in a meeting with Mr. Suderman, but after almost four months on the job he knew enough to take some initiative. He picked up the telephone to the yard. "Direct two-forty-seven to track two."

James returned about fifteen minutes later. As usual, the first thing he did was take his binoculars and look over the yard. "Why is two-forty-seven on track two?"

"I directed it there, sir," Tom said.

"You did?" James shook his head. "Two-forty-seven has to take on coal and water, drop two cars, and pick up four. That'll be seventy minutes if things go off without a hitch, which takes you to 4:20, and how often do things go off without a hitch? What were you planning on doing with one-eleven, which is scheduled for track two at 4:05?"

James' face was impassive but his eyes held Tom's in an uncomfortable stare. Tom's stomach tightened as he picked up a clipboard with a schedule of incoming and outgoing trains and their track assignments and scanned it. "We can put one-eleven on track seven."

"One-eleven won't clear for fifty-five minutes. Five-nineteen will need that track before one-eleven's ready."

Tom scanned the schedule again. They could put 111 on track eight—no, they couldn't do that because 624 wouldn't be finished. Track three was no good either. Tom's face flushed. "It doesn't look like we're going to have a track for one-eleven."

"Not with the way you've done it." James picked up the telephone to the yard. "Back up two-forty-seven and reroute it to four." Tom heard an angry exclamation over the phone. "A mistake was made, we have to fix it." There were more angry words from the phone. "Two forty-seven was early, now it'll be late, but if we keep it on two we gum things until early evening. Two forty-seven can make up the time by Greeley, certainly by Denver." James hung up the phone and turned towards Tom. "I'm disappointed, Mr. Durand, but I'm too busy to talk now. We'll talk after work." He turned away and scanned the yard through his binoculars.

His first big mistake! Why hadn't he thought things through? Mr. James was disappointed with him—damn, damn, damn! The rest of the shift would be like waiting for a herd of buffaloes to pass. Mr. James would concentrate on the yard like he always did, say as few words as possible like he always did, calmly issue his instructions and explanations like he always did, all the while Tom feeling like he'd sat in the middle of a cactus patch. Would Mr. James fire him? He wanted things perfect and Tom had just made a damn boneheaded mistake. Maybe he was thinking Tom wasn't smart enough for the job after all. "I'm disappointed, Mr. Durand," felt like a haymaker to the stomach. What would he do if he got fired? What would Mario say? What would his father say? Put that aside or you'll make another mistake, he chided himself. *Think about the job!*

Tom stifled his churning emotions and flip-flopping stomach. James said nothing more about the incident and the rest of the shift passed without mishap. Instead of leaving with Mario as he usually did, Tom followed James through the streets of Cheyenne on a pleasant early summer evening. The air smelled of dust and manure. James greeted several gentlemen who looked like ranchers and doffed his Stetson to their wives, but said nothing to Tom. He was hanging him out to dry. Why were they stopping at the Rusty Nail? Tom didn't go in saloons and he couldn't imagine Mr. James in one.

It was better lit than Tom would have guessed, with two large chandeliers and several lanterns around the room. A group of cowboys sat at the bar in the center of the room. Most of the tables were filled. A poker game was going at one large circular table. In the corner a man played a gay, tinkling tune on a piano. The smells of tobacco and grilled meat filled the air. The bartender, a natty fellow with a handlebar mustache, said, "What'll it be, Mr. James?"

"Two of the usual."

The bartender grabbed two glasses and a pitcher of ice water and escorted them to a table by a window. He poured the water and Tom felt oddly relieved that James wasn't drinking alcohol—it wouldn't have fit his picture of his forbidding boss. He was surprised when Mr. James removed a pipe and tobacco pouch from his coat, filled and tamped the pipe, lit it, and began smoking. Still he said nothing, letting Tom stew in his own juices until he was good and cooked.

A waiter soon placed two plates with sizzling steaks, fried potatoes and onions, and biscuits and gravy before them. Mr. James dug in, but Tom hesitated. How was he going to eat with his stomach all knotted up? The steak, potatoes, and onions smelled good and this was miles better than anything he was going to get at the boarding house. He cut a piece of steak.

James glanced at him. "Eat up, son."

With that encouragement Tom ate, regretting he couldn't enjoy it more, wishing Mr. James would say what he had to say.

"Do you play chess?"

"Yes, sir."

The waiter cleared the table and brought them apple pie and steaming coffee. "Have Frank bring us the board," James said. The waiter went to the bartender, who walked to a back room, disappeared for a moment, and reappeared carrying a chessboard and a black velvet bag. He set the board, a gleaming masterpiece of the woodworker's art, between the two men and removed pieces of beautifully carved and polished wood from the bag.

"Set 'em up. You're white."

What in Sam Hill was his boss doing? Tom arranged the pieces on the board.

"Anything else, Mr. James?" the bartender asked.

"We're fine. Let's get started, Mr. Durand." James relit his pipe.

Tom advanced a pawn two squares and James moved a knight. Tom was soon engrossed in the game. He planned his attacks and tried to figure out his opponent's moves. James anticipated his attacks and took several key pieces. They sipped their coffee and ate their pie, but neither of them talked. Tom finally hit on a plan that might turn things around. He took a pawn with his bishop in a way that left the bishop as bait. He looked up at the hard lines of James' face. James regarded him coldly and Tom knew the moment he had feared was at hand.

"The problem with smart young men is they haven't learned that smart's a train that'll only take 'em so far. They meet up with some success and they start feeling like polecats walking through a yard full of dogs—nobody's going to touch 'em. They got the answers and they don't need any help." James moved his rook, ignoring Tom's bishop. "Check."

The noose was tightening. Tom moved a knight to block the rook.

James looked hard into Tom's eyes. "Running that yard is just like this game—you think your moves in advance. What you do at eight in the morning affects what you do at four in the afternoon. It took me two years to learn how to plan out a day in the yard and a few more before I really knew what I was doing. You're not going to pick it up in four months, I don't care how many brains God gave you or how fancy your school. Smart is as smart does, and smart asks questions when it sees something it's never seen before. You go off on your own and make the wrong decision and it can cost the railroad a lot of money. It can cost you your job." James captured Tom's knight with his queen. "Check."

Tom gulped. Here was a lesson he had to learn. He damn well better ask questions when he didn't know what to do. He stared at the chessboard. No way out—if he blocked the queen with a bishop, James would take the bishop with his knight. "That's checkmate, sir."

James nodded. A loud noise and a burst of laughter came from the bar—a cowboy had fallen off his stool. "I don't give advice—the wise don't need it, fools don't heed it—but stay away from alcohol. I've seen good men ruined. You're better off drinking porcupine piss." He knocked the cinders from his pipe into an ashtray and yawned. "It's time for some shuteye. We'll hit it hard in the morning."

Chapter 20

Politics

Will had concluded that his father disliked Theodore Roosevelt, the assistant secretary of the Navy. Perhaps he didn't like the raspy voice or the self-important, pompous way Roosevelt carried himself or the way his eyes worked—unfocused, flitting from person to person as he performed quick political calculations. Neither the laugh (too booming, too hearty) nor the smile (too automatic, too rehearsed) nor the handshake (too firm, too long) furthered Roosevelt's impression with his father. All were designed to convey his "Man of the West" image, although he was a New York native and a former police commissioner of New York City.

None of these deficiencies bothered Will. You took your politicians as you found them, and none of them were particularly admirable human beings. Yet they had their uses. Roosevelt had signed millions of dollars' worth of contracts with firms to build the ships that would expand the navy, his oft-stated goal. One of those firms was Blinders and Sons' Steel, supplier of the steel hulls that went into the ships built at the Brooklyn Navy Yard. Malcolm Blinders was the biggest client Will had brought to Durand & Woodbury. Blinders hosted a reception at one of New York's better clubs, ostensibly to allow the assistant secretary to detail his plans for the navy, but also to get him in front of potential campaign contributors—everyone knew Roosevelt aspired to higher office. Daniel had expressed reservations about attending, but Will had prevailed upon him, in the interest of not offending a substantial client.

A layer of cigar smoke hovered above a small group of wealthy businessmen as the mingling ended and they sat in overstuffed leather chairs. Roosevelt stood before them and cleared his throat. "Gentlemen, I believe the end of the century finds America's role in the world in transition. Thanks to our industrial might, we've become a wealthy nation, but with that wealth come responsibilities we haven't wholly embraced. American military power must be used in service to those responsibilities, and to project our global political and commercial interests."

Will found the voice grating and the style labored. Roosevelt had been a poor public speaker who, through diligent effort and practice, had made himself a mediocre one. He pressed his case for an expanded navy as the vanguard of an American empire, making his proposition sound like a test of national character. America's martial spirit and strength were already giving way to materialistic indulgence. Anybody unwilling to make the necessary sacrifices lacked "courage," "resolve," and "manliness." Will liked the virile adjectives. There was a smattering of polite applause when Roosevelt finished.

"Thank you, gentlemen, thank you. Perhaps you'd like to ask some questions?"

Daniel held up his hand and Roosevelt nodded towards him.

"Mr. Roosevelt, you envision a navy that's not just defensive, but offensive as well?"

"Yes, I do, Mr. Durand. The days of a purely defensive military are over."

"If we retained a purely defensive philosophy, do you see any threats to the United States proper that would justify your military expansion?"

"Spain is on our doorstep in Cuba. There have been German incursions in Central America."

"Do they constitute a threat to the U.S.?"

"As a businessman, Mr. Durand, you surely can see the advantages of using the military to protect and expand our commercial interests."

"What foreign business I've done has been with the understanding that the rewards and the risks of such ventures were mine. I've never thought it was the responsibility of the government, using my fellow citizens' money and the lives of our sons, to protect my investments."

"How noble of you. Then you don't see the benefits of American expansion…if we were to annex, say, Hawaii or the Philippines?"

"No, and I don't think the Hawaiians and Filipinos do, either!"

There was laughter and Roosevelt's face reddened. "A great imperial power can't be too sensitive to the wishes of inferior peoples. A nation that occupies itself purely with commercial pursuits, with the acquisition and spending of wealth, is marching down the road to—"

"Prosperity and peace," Daniel said.

Roosevelt stared at Daniel. "Is marching down the road to decadence and ruin. I find that most of our business captains, Mr. Durand, having shirked from military service, lack the martial spirit, the appreciation for the glory of war, that is the hallmark of great nations."

"I served with the 48th Ohio Volunteer Infantry of the Fourth Brigade of the Fifth Division of the Army of Tennessee, at Shiloh, Walnut Hills, and Vicksburg. I find that most of the politicians who talk about the 'glory of war' have never been in one."

Will cringed.

"Gentlemen," Roosevelt said, looking away from Daniel, "thank you for this opportunity to meet and speak to you." He pulled a watch from his vest. "Unfortunately, I have another engagement. I look forward to seeing you again." He glanced towards Malcolm Blinders, who stood up from his chair, and the two men exited the room. There was an uneasy stirring among the businessmen, several glancing nervously at Daniel.

Daniel smiled. "Good day, gentlemen." He stood and made his way to the door with Will. In the hall, Daniel said, "That Roosevelt is an idiot. How did he get to be assistant secretary of anything? Standards must be even lower in Washington than I thought."

Will hoped that his father hadn't cost him a client. "My friend Tim Harkness thinks he'll be president someday," he said acerbically.

"Nonsense! Unless people have much less intelligence than I give them credit for, that man will never be president!"

What would Mr. James have done? Tom knew exactly what his retired mentor would have done. Nobody questioned an order from Mr. James. Even Mr. Suderman, Mr. James' boss, had been too intimidated to challenge him. Tom, on the other hand, was only twenty-one years old, an outsider no less, promoted by Mr. James over many older, more experienced men. He had eventually won James' full confidence, but the yardmaster had said, "Don't take this job if you don't like your own company. It's lonely work."

Tom stared through his binoculars at track seven, where the 126 line, bound for Granger, had been switched. It was supposed to be on track eight. Tom turned to Mr. Suderman, who was standing behind him, and pointed at 126. "Caldwell missed the switch again. That's the fourth time this month. We'll lose at least thirty minutes rerouting one-twenty-six and it'll be late."

Suderman nodded, but didn't say anything.

"Don't get mad," Mr. James had told him. "State your case—your facts and your reasons—and don't raise your voice. You aren't going to win every time, that's just the way it'll be, but you should win more than you lose."

"Mr. Suderman, we've been lucky—all Caldwell's mistakes have cost us is time. But one of these days he's going to throw the wrong switch and there'll be a collision, or a brakeman will get hurt or killed. Caldwell's drinking and he's not fit to operate switches."

"I can't fire him. He's a union officer and the men would raise thunder."

"Then I'll start routing trains away from him."

"Make those executives eat their own cooking," Mr. James had said. "Tell 'em what's what and let 'em do what they're paid to do—make a decision."

Suderman grimaced. "If you route trains away from Caldwell, every train will be delayed, and the delay will get longer as the day goes on. We can't have that."

"You want me to take a chance that he might make a more serious mistake?"

"I didn't say that."

Tom didn't like unions—they protected the worst men, like Caldwell, and hindered the best by enforcing the lowest standards—but Suderman was the one who had to deal with them. He paced the floor. Another Mr. James' aphorism: "Don't take this job unless you're prepared to lose it." Tom risked his job every time he challenged his boss. Suderman stopped pacing. "Perhaps I could put Caldwell in a less critical position."

Tom didn't know of any railroad jobs that could be performed half-drunk, but they had to get Caldwell off the yard. "Can you do that, with the union and all?"

"They might file a grievance." Anger flashed across Suderman's face. "But damn—" He rarely swore. "That man shouldn't be out there." Suderman picked up the phone and dialed. "Briggs, have Caldwell report to my office and you cover for him."

Briggs, now a yard supervisor but formerly a switchman, threw the correct switches for the rest of the afternoon. Tom had forced the issue without losing his job. Mr. James had taught him a few things besides how to run a yard.

One day after work, Mario and Tom were walking to their boardinghouse. Although it was late April, snow had recently fallen and they had to make their way around piles that had been cleared from the streets. Mario bought a newspaper from a vendor and stared at the banner headlines. "We're at war."

Tom shook his head. "Over what? Over a battleship that may or may not have been blown up by Spanish agents. The Cuban rebels probably did it, to draw us into their war."

"What if they did—they're fighting for their independence. They deserve our support."

Mario and his mother, Isabella, had the immigrant's unquestioning patriotism. Isabella's husband had died in Italy when Mario, her only child, was six years old. Mother and son had boarded steerage for America. Once Will had said something critical of the United States. "You foolish boy!" Isabella had screeched. "You don't know how lucky you are to live in this country!" Will had looked to his mother for support, but she said, "Don't look at me, she's right." It was one of the few times Tom could remember his mother not coming to Will's aid. After that, Tom never said anything against the red, white, and blue around Isabella…or her son.

"Well, I'm not risking my life in their war," Tom said. "The Cubans have a lot more at stake than the Spaniards. Sooner or later they'll get their independence."

"When you're born in this country, especially when you have a lot, you take it for granted. It's easier to let someone else fight. Where's your patriotism? When your country calls, you go."

"Where's your brain? It's got nothing to do with taking my country for granted or my family's wealth. Politicians and generals dish out bilge to get men to die for them. That's what war is, Mario. Dying for some phony cause—getting shot or blown up or rotting away."

"That's your father talking."

"And he knows. I listen to him."

"I can't believe what you're saying. Do you really love this railroad job so much that twenty years from now you're going to tell your children, 'I didn't fight'?"

"If Spain invades Florida, I'll be the first to sign up. Until then, I'll stay here. Do you want to fight in this phony war so badly that you'll give up your job? It might not be waiting for you when you get back."

"It sure as hell better be. I'll be fighting for my country."

"I'm not going to sign up, Mario."

They walked to the boardinghouse in silence. Unless he could talk him out of it, Mario was making a foolish mistake, perhaps the ultimate mistake. Tom shuddered. Wars were dangerous—his friend might not come back.

Daniel whistled under his breath and put the newspaper down. He sat with Eleanor in his study after dinner one evening. "It's not supposed to happen this way."

Eleanor looked up from her book. "What's not supposed to happen this way?"

"This Roosevelt fellow thinks war is a great thing, so he volunteers to fight in Cuba. Men like that, with no military training, who want to be at the head of the line and lead the charge, are usually the first ones killed, and rightly so, but the Spaniards can't shoot straight and Roosevelt takes San Juan Hill. Now he's a national hero, they're talking about a Medal of Honor, rumor has it he's going to run for governor, and here's an editorial that claims he's 'presidential timber.'"

"This is the man you disagreed with a few months ago, the one you told Will was an idiot?"

"The very same."

Eleanor smiled. "The Winfields, Morgan, Rockefeller, and now Roosevelt…dearest, you have a gift for making enemies in high places."

"We saw battle, all right," said Wiley, a Missouri native and the Mark Twain of Mario's regiment. "We battled mosquitoes the size of sparrows, we battled swamp up to our necks, we battled gnats that make a meal of every man they meet up with. We battled swamp fever, jungle fever, and yellow fever, we battled itches over every inch of our bodies, we battled the sun and heat and humidity—yes, sir, we battled everything except Spaniards."

Mario smiled bitterly and shook his head. He didn't much like Wiley, but Wiley was right. Cuba had been a fool's errand. The beach landing had been inept. Horses from the cavalry units drowned in the surf and washed ashore. Five hundred Spaniards could have halted the invasion, but only sweltering, steaming heat and crawling things the likes of which they had never seen before greeted U.S. soldiers. Then, in the words of Wiley, they "waited, followed by waiting, more waiting, and still more waiting, with an occasional break to wait." It took several days to outfit the soldiers with carbines, ammunition, gear, and rations. Once they started marching, Mario, unaccustomed to the burning sun and drenching humidity, discarded almost everything but his rifle and ammunition. Those proved the most unnecessary items of all. Spain surrendered before Mario's regiment saw a skirmish. The regiment then waited to be evacuated back to the states, and almost half the men contracted yellow fever. Mario had so far escaped the disease, but his stomach hadn't been right for several weeks. His digestive disorder would be all he brought back from his adventure—he had done nothing for his country.

"I signed up to fight," he said to a small group of his comrades in non-arms lounging on their packs under the shade of a palm tree.

"Looks like there'll be some excitement in the Philippines," Wiley said. "Seems the Filipinos don't understand the difference between the Spanish yoke of oppression and American liberation. They want to run their own islands. Might be a battle or two there before we plant Old Glory."

Mario knew two men who were volunteering for the Philippines. It would be a chance to see action. How could he answer his country's call and then not fight?

Eleanor smiled at her first grandchild, six-month-old Gwendolyn, who smiled back. Gwendolyn's brown eyes shifted their wide-eyed gaze to the side of Eleanor's head and she stared with infant intensity at the light playing through diamond earrings. Her eyes had the Asiatic cast of Lady Sylvia's, and her hair was brown like her mother's as well, but Eleanor could see Will in the shape of her face and its features.

She rocked the baby in her arms and cooed as Daniel, sitting next to her, rubbed her little chin with his finger. They sat on a severe, pale gray sofa in the sitting room of Sylvia and Will's brownstone apartment opposite the new parents, an antique silver tea service on the coffee table between them. Sylvia had decided where the couple would live—on 56th Street in the general vicinity of Daniel and Eleanor. She had chosen the brownstone, an elegant three-bedroom affair. She had furnished the apartment with museum-quality imports from England, correctly fashionable but lacking the grace Eleanor had tried to give her home. Photographs, mostly of Sylvia's relatives, were arranged in military formation rows on a table. After running through a dozen or so Americans she found substandard, Sylvia had imported servants from England as if they were furniture and had borne all the expense. At each step she dutifully asked her husband's opinion after she had made up her mind.

Gwendolyn started to cry. Eleanor took her to Sylvia. "Perhaps she's hungry," Eleanor said, handing over the small bundle of baby and blanket.

"Or she's tired or has a full diaper," Sylvia said, regarding her squalling daughter as she would a mildly interesting *objet d'art*. "Margaret, please." She kissed Gwendolyn on her forehead and gave her to the nanny.

"She's beautiful," Daniel said.

"She has her mother's looks," Will said with a smile and a sideways glance at his wife.

Sylvia smiled indulgently. "Mr. Durand, was your firm involved in the formation of this United States Steel Corporation?"

Eleanor had always been interested in her husband's business and encouraged him to talk about his work. However, she couldn't match Sylvia's interest in Durand & Woodbury. Eleanor had thought that with the birth of her baby her focus would shift to her child, as it did with most new mothers. Instead, when Eleanor and Daniel visited, little Gwendolyn was displayed—never long enough for the grandparents—and then dispatched to the nanny. There were few anecdotes from the parents about the cute things their daughter did; rather the conversations inevitably turned to Durand & Woodbury, business, or politics, an obvious passion of Sylvia's.

"Our firm was in a syndicate that distributed some of the securities," Daniel said. The conversation, which Sylvia dominated, took its usual turn. At the end of their visit, Daniel and Eleanor, unaccompanied by the parents, went to the nursery, decorated in pink and yellow, duck and bunny, to see Gwendolyn, asleep. They hovered over her crib, wordlessly gazing at the innocent. Eleanor was sad, as she had been on every visit.

"I know," Daniel whispered.

After they had said their goodbyes and were walking home, Daniel said, "Sylvia takes a lively interest in everything but her baby." Horses clop-clopped and carriage wheels grated on the cobblestone pavement.

"I can almost forgive her that, but Will bothers me more. Is he just following her lead, as he does with everything else, or is he indifferent to his own child?"

"I'm disappointed. I remember how good Will was with John. I thought he might still have some of that for Gwendolyn." Daniel shook his head. "Maybe he would have been better with a son. Sylvia has the typical attitude of the English aristocracy—let the nannies take care of the children until they're packed off to boarding school."

"Then she shouldn't be a mother, regardless of the practices of her class. There are women who shouldn't be mothers and men who shouldn't be fathers. The difference is, if a man is intelligent and ambitious, but indifferent to his children, nobody cares. If a woman has the same qualities, she's condemned as a bad mother, but she can't pursue a career that might fulfill her ambition and challenge her intellect; she can only be a mother. Sylvia could be in business or politics and do as well as many men, but she's denied that opportunity."

"Perhaps that will change someday."

"Not soon enough, dearest."

Cheyenne, Wyoming
September 9, 1898

Dear Father,

> *A new group has taken over the Union Pacific and brought it out of bankruptcy. The Chairman of the executive committee is E.H. Harriman. You might have met him. He started on Wall Street and founded a brokerage firm. He was the director of finance for the Illinois Central Railroad and joined the Union Pacific Board earlier this year.*

> *I met Mr. Harriman this summer in Cheyenne. He toured the UP routs with a group of executives. He asked many questions and*

*listened to the answers. I think he has the right outlook on busi-
ness and the right plan for the railroad. The depression is ending.
Traffic is picking up and the businessmen I talk to are preparing
for better days. Mr. Harriman wants to spend $25 million upgrad-
ing the line, making it more like Mr. Hill's Great Northern, with
the heaviest gauge rails and best laid routes.*

*Now that the UP is free from interference by the government,
the economy is improving, and Mr. Harriman is implementing
his plans, the railroad's stock will be a good investment. Mr.
Harriman is buying. I have bought shares from my savings and
would like to buy more. I propose to borrow as much as you are
willing to extend to me, at a rate of seven and one-half percent. I
recommend that you look into this situation and perhaps make an
investment as well.*

*Please consider this proposal as expeditiously as possible. The
stock has been moving up and if you are not willing to make a
loan, I will try to obtain one elsewhere. Give my best to Mother
and the family.*

Love,
Tom

Daniel smiled as he reread the letter. Tommy was maybe trying a
little too hard to sound like an experienced businessman—the letter
had even been addressed to Daniel at Durand & Woodbury, rather
than home—but the tone was perfect, a marshaling of facts justify-
ing the extension of a loan. Daniel was inclined to take up the proposition. He had met Harriman a couple of times and liked him—a
short, energetic man, brusque, gruff, who ran a conservative, well-
regarded brokerage firm and was involved with the Illinois Central,
a well-regarded railroad. Business was picking up and Harriman
was following the trail Hill had blazed.

Daniel had another reason for striking a deal with his son: he still had hopes that Tommy would one day join Durand & Woodbury. If you wanted to develop a business relationship, you didn't reject the first opportunity to do business. Daniel picked up a pen and wrote a reply on a pad.

WILL EXTEND LOAN UP TO THREE THOU AT SEVEN AND HALF PERCENT STOP WILL ESTABLISH ACCOUNT IN YOUR NAME AT DW TO HOLD SHARES STOP PLEASE ADVISE HOW MUCH YOU WILL TAKE UP STOP BALANCE AVAILABLE FOR FUTURE INVESTMENT STOP WILL INVEST FOR MY ACCOUNT
FATHER

Daniel summoned a clerk and handed him the message. "Send this telegram to Tom Durand, at the Union Pacific station in Cheyenne."

Tom stood outside the Cheyenne courthouse, perplexed. His interest in politics was minimal—he shared his father's disdain—but he was eligible to vote, having turned twenty-one earlier in the year, and he intended to exercise his right. What he couldn't understand was the number of women he saw walking up and down the courthouse steps. Some accompanied their husbands, but some were by themselves. He walked up the steps and into the spacious, high-ceilinged foyer of the courthouse. Men and women stood in lines before tables with ballot boxes on top, behind which sat voting officials.

"Excuse me," Tom said to a pretty young woman in a blue dress. "Why are women standing in the voting line?"

The woman smiled. There was something captivating—an invitation and a challenge—about her smile. "Women can vote in Wyoming. You're not from around here, are you?"

"No, New York, but I live here now. Women don't vote in New York."

"I know that. They only vote in Wyoming."

Tom was embarrassed. "How come you're not voting?"

"Next election. I'm only nineteen."

"Well, now I've seen everything—women voting!"

The young woman's eyes narrowed. "You make it sound odd, like a two-headed calf."

"Uh, no, that's not what I meant. Uh…I just never thought that women had the experience to vote." The interval between when the words left his mouth and his wish that he had them back was a fraction of a second.

"Rearing children and keeping a house don't count as experience?"

"Sure, that's experience, but it's not experience in business or government, the imp—"

"The important things? How do we get experience in government if we can't vote or hold office?"

Talking with this woman was like playing chess with Mr. James—you had to think out your moves beforehand. She stood like she was taking on the world, straight and tall as her medium height would allow, with her head held high, and she looked him right in the eyes, like a man would. Her eyes had an unusual greenish blue cast. She had blonde hair, a high forehead, sharp, angular features, and a narrow face—unconventional, but not unattractive.

"I see your point," Tom said. Time to start crawling out of his hole.

"Women have voted here since 1869. Believe it or not, the state seems to do all right."

"How did women get the vote?"

"Wyoming was a dangerous place—Indians, wild animals, stampeding buffalo. The men were away driving cattle or working on the railroad. They left their women with guns and taught 'em how to shoot." She smiled. "Now how's a man going to tell a woman who shoots better than he does that she can't vote?"

"I guess he doesn't. Do you have a gun?"

She looked at him as if he had a bull's-eye painted on his forehead. "Since my ninth birthday, and I can hit my mark at a hundred paces." She glanced past him. "My parents are finished voting. I have to go. Good day to you, sir." She stepped away.

"Good day to you, Miss—" She was already walking across the foyer. He liked the way she held her head up and squared her shoulders, daring anybody to get in her way. There was the swell of her breasts, the curve of her waist, and the sway of the feminine gait. He drew a short, sharp breath. He didn't like dull women, but damn, the smart ones could tie you up in knots! Handling this one would be like handling a lynx. She was uncommonly pretty. He wished he knew her name.

Chapter 21

Cornered

George Woodbury stood before a map of the United States' railroad routes, which took up a good portion of a wall in the Durand & Woodbury conference room. "The railroad stocks have had a great run from ninety-nine through last year and right into this year." He used his cigar as a pointer, explaining his views to the partners and some of the associates of the firm. "The buying has been steady. The most persistent action is in the Union Pacific, the Milwaukee, and the Northern Pacific."

"Are the newspapers correct? Are Morgan and Vanderbilt buying the UP?" Will asked.

Daniel winced—Woodbury generally despised whatever the newspapers had to say about the stock market—and glanced at Will. The Wall Street watering holes were having their way with him; he was getting fat. The formerly distinct lines of his face were dissolving into rounded bloat. Undoubtedly prompted by Sylvia, he wore boxier suits to hide his steadily advancing girth and larger collars for his multiple chins. He looked older than his thirty-two years. His eyes were red-rimmed, his hairline was receding, and there were already gray interlopers amidst the blond.

"I doubt it. Harriman didn't turn the UP around to have it bought out from under him. He would stop a takeover attempt that's so obvious the papers are talking about it. It's the usual nonsense, and those with the least to say are saying the most, but to me, UP just feels like the speculators buying because it keeps going up."

And up and up. Good for Tom, who had borrowed money from Daniel to buy shares in his employer and had kept buying as Harriman worked a spectacular turnaround. And good for Daniel, who had bought shares with each glowing letter from Tom.

"So what about the Milwaukee?" Benjamin Keane said. "Harriman missed the Burlington, he still needs to shore up his connections to Chicago and the Great Lakes."

"He should have got the Burlington," Woodbury said. "It's a better road than—"

"He had his chance, but he got stubborn on the price," Will interrupted.

Daniel took a deep breath. His son had become cocksure at work and Daniel couldn't understand why. Perhaps he felt invulnerable as the son of a founding partner. Perhaps his sessions with his friends fed his vanity. Perhaps he was compensating for his wife's dominating ways. Whatever the reason, Daniel knew he wasn't the only one who found it annoying.

"It's possible he's buying the Milwaukee," Woodbury said. "It's been moving up steady."

"You mentioned the Northern Pacific," Keane said.

Woodbury puffed his cigar and exhaled a stream of smoke. "That's what I can't figure out. Morgan and Hill have the Great Northern and the NP."

It was perhaps inevitable that Hill, America's best railroad man, would link up with the country's most powerful banker, Morgan, who regarded the railroads as his personal fiefdom. However, it saddened Daniel that a man he admired and respected had aligned with Morgan, whose autocratic imperiousness he despised. At least it had been Morgan who had eventually bent to Hill. Business was business.

"And they bought the Burlington after Harriman missed it," Woodbury said—

"I'm sure he regrets that one," Will said.

"I'm sure he does," Woodbury said testily. "The Burlington is split between NP and Great Northern. With those three, Morgan and Hill have put together the strongest system in the country. They have them locked up, but NP trades like somebody's buying it."

"They don't, technically, have the NP locked up," Michael Palos said.

Everyone turned towards Palos, who rarely spoke at meetings.

"The NP has eighty million dollars in common and seventy-five million in preferred stock. While Hill and Morgan have a majority block in the Great Northern, they only have about forty million dollars worth, between the common and preferred, of NP."

Daniel's son-in-law never got details like that wrong. "This sounds ludicrous," Daniel said. "But perhaps somebody is trying to buy the NP out from under Hill and Morgan."

Woodbury shook his head. "Who's got the balls? Who's got the wallet?" He pointed towards the northern part of the U.S. map with his cigar. The Great Northern and Northern Pacific ran side by side. "If they lost control of the NP, they'd lose half the Burlington. All they'd have outright would be the Great Northern. It would still be a good line, but they wouldn't have the stranglehold they now have. Morgan and Hill aren't exactly wet behind the ears."

"Maybe it's Harriman," Daniel said.

"Harriman?" Woodbury said.

It did seem like a stretch—Harriman buying the Northern Pacific on the sly, hoodwinking Morgan and Hill. The steady ascent of NP could be a manipulation—Wall Street was rife. Daniel had a hunch. If he was right and NP continued its ascent, there was a lot of money to be made. On the other hand, the higher NP's price went, the farther it could fall. If there was a manipulation, NP would drop when whoever was putting up its price started selling. Such vertiginous drops had brought down more than one proud investment house. Daniel felt a shudder of self-doubt. One never knew anything to a certainty until after it happened.

"Harriman lost the Burlington," Daniel said. "He still needs Midwest connections. If he gets the NP, he gets half the Burlington and he sticks it to Morgan and Hill."

"We all know personal factors rarely enter into business decisions." Keane smiled. "But it may be salient that Hill and Morgan despise Harriman, and he feels the same towards them. Buying the NP would be the kind of Napoleonic masterstroke Harriman loves."

"He's also short," Jakob Gottman said. The men laughed.

"Okay, so maybe Harriman's got the balls," Woodbury said. "But where does he get the money? At current prices it would take over seventy-five million to gain control."

"Well, there's that personal element again," Daniel said. "Rockefeller detests Morgan and he certainly has the money to fund Harriman. What a sockdolager that would be—Rockefeller and Harriman versus Morgan and Hill, a battle neither side could afford to lose."

"I smell a trade," said the Pirate, Patrick Dolan. "If Mr. Durand is right and we've got a battle that four of the richest men in the country can't afford to lose, then NP's price has only one way to go. Imagine the payoff on this one!"

"I don't like it-can-only-go-one-way thinking and counting un-hatched chickens," Daniel said. "I think this hunch is an interesting bet, but the dangers are obvious. Buy quietly and watch your downside. Nobody buys for his own account or says a word after this meeting."

"And if NP proves Daniel right and keeps moving up, nobody shorts it unless he's tired of working here," Woodbury said, laughing. Everyone laughed with him.

Will was sitting at a fabulous banquet without being allowed to eat. Every day after the stock market closed during its glorious bull run, he, along with seemingly everyone else on Wall Street, went to the Waldorf Astoria Hotel, drawn by the spectacle of instant wealth on display. In the aptly named Peacock Alley, long-time operators and parvenus who six months ago didn't know the difference between a stock and bond strutted and preened. A rising tide had lifted all yachts and they vied for acknowledgment of their brilliance. The usual trick? Ask about another fellow's superlative speculation as a lead in to boast of one's own. While Will never saw anything as gauche as someone lighting his cigar with a hundred-dollar bill, it wouldn't have surprised him if he had. A fog of expensive cigar smoke hung with the ornate crystal chandeliers above the milling millionaires and soon-to-be millionaires. They talked too loudly and laughed too much, intoxicated by the wealth raining down on Wall Street, far more powerful than mere alcohol, although there was plenty of that as well. Will heard the usual self-laudatory bombast as he made his way to the Men's Café one afternoon.

"You call yourself a trader, Moseby? I bought Consolidated at sixty-three because you said it was going to eighty. Damn if it didn't trade at ninety-two today. What the hell do you know?"

"You jump on a speeding train and hang on—this one won't stop anytime soon!"

"Now that the shares have been absorbed, Steel has nowhere to go but up!"

Speeding trains, nowhere to go but up...Will's thoughts were bitter as the maître d'hôtel of the Men's Café escorted him to his table. The name Men's Café belied its nature. It was essentially a semiprivate club, a luxurious enclave with a four-sided mahogany bar that offered the only respite from the clamoring crowd. Here the boasting was more muted, the laughter less giddy. The really big operators had their own tables—Bet-a-Million Gates, Diamond Jim Brady, Edwin Hawley, and the biggest of them all, James Keene, who had handled the successful flotation of J. P. Morgan's U.S. Steel. They had made fortunes, but had also lost them. Will's friends had secured their table not by dint of speculative success, but because their forebears ranked among the most illustrious of Wall Street names, and presumably the sons would someday follow.

"Why so pensive, Durand?" asked Timothy Harkness, Will's friend from Bovinity, as Will slid into his seat at the table with seven other men, all about his age. Harkness had grown more handsome with the years—he kept himself trim and no gray marred his sandy blond hair—and his personality more magnetic. "You look as if you shorted Standard forty points ago!"

Will smiled automatically. "I took some profits today in Milwaukee, and I'm not quite sure where I want to put them. I'm looking at Atchison." A waiter quickly came up. "The usual," Will said.

"You can't go wrong with Atchison!" Earnest Shockley said. Shockley, an attorney, was the son of a name partner of one of Wall Street's biggest law firms. He had been a bull on the Atchison, Topeka and Santa Fe Railway, and Will assumed he had made a fortune in the stock. It was the group's concession to good taste that although everyone talked about their trades, nobody mentioned the number of shares they had bought or the amount of their profits. Will suspected that everyone at the table had garnered a far larger share of the market's instant wealth than he had. He played the game as well as anyone else, lowering his voice, mentioning his "holdings" in this or that highflying stock. However, those holdings were usually only a few hundred shares, and he was sure the other men's were in the thousands. He was the son of one of the richest men on Wall Street and his wife had an ample trust fund, but he had comparatively few funds with which to speculate. His paycheck was the only money he received from his father and he wouldn't realize his inheritance anytime soon. His father was healthy as a horse, although Will couldn't help but hope on those rare, once-every-other-year days when he missed work due to illness.

Neither his father nor his wife would finance his speculations. He had asked his father for a loan to buy a stock after receiving a can't-miss tip. His father had asked Will what he knew about the company. Will had stammered—other than knowing what the company manufactured he knew nothing at all—and his father refused. Will had been fortunate; the stock had gone down instead of up. He didn't have the courage to ask Sylvia for a loan, to risk her contemptuous sneer and withering glare.

So he sat at the feast chewing on a bread crust. The waiter brought his whiskey and he took a stout pull to steel himself against the chatter of successful trades and immense fortunes growing more immense, while he was left behind for want of a large enough stake.

Someday he would be a partner and his income would increase, but the bull market was now!

"Durand, perhaps you shouldn't reinvest your Milwaukee proceeds," Harkness said. "Perhaps it's time to stand aside, take some more profits."

This cautionary note from the table's unacknowledged leader silenced everyone.

"Are you saying that you think the party's over, Harkness?" asked Don Gaines, son of a wealthy investment banker.

"You never pick the top, but trees don't grow to the sky and we've had a good run in here. The family is liquidating its holdings while prices are strong and sizable lots can be sold. I'd be tempted, after we saw some weakness in the market, to put in some shorts."

Will looked around the table and saw creases in the foreheads of his drinking companions. Here was something they had to consider. Everyone was bullish, but Harkness was sounding bearish. More ominously, the Winfields—and nobody was richer than Harkness' grandfather, Curtis Winfield—were moving money out of the market.

Will had an inspiration as the table debated the heretofore undreamed-of possibility that the ever-rising stock market could go down. He had made chickenfeed money on the way up, but perhaps he could make his mark on the way down, not just with his drinking chums, but within Durand & Woodbury as well. He could seal his partnership. He smiled as he formulated his plan.

"The market's running like a jackrabbit with a firecracker up its ass! We're going to set a record for volume this week!" Woodbury screamed to Daniel over the deafening din of floor traders shouting bids and offers, the exuberant commotion of a fast, rising market. His face streamed with sweat. He had removed his vest, his shirt was drenched, and the end of his unlit cigar was chewed to a pulp.

"Where's NP?" Daniel asked.

"One hundred two and a quarter, up three and a half."

Northern Pacific was up over 20 percent since Woodbury and the Pirate had begun buying. Not bad for a few weeks' work, but Daniel wouldn't offer compliments, advice, instruction, or even questions about the traders' strategy going forward. Woodbury let Daniel talk to him on the floor during trading hours because Daniel let him trade, only interrupting with absolutely essential business. Distractions could be inordinately costly.

Daniel prized Woodbury because his partner could make or lose tens of thousands of dollars in a day, walk past every bar in the financial district, cheerfully kiss his wife when he arrived home, play with his children, eat a hearty meal, rest his head on the pillow, and fall asleep. Daniel didn't have the stomach for trading. He took no joy when the market proved him right, and any loss, no matter how small, tormented him. He had started from Nothing, and Nothing sometimes issued round-trip tickets. Profit or loss, his trades impaired his digestion and his sleep until he closed his position.

However, he was free of other demons, ones that plagued most of Wall Street. When Daniel had first met Rockefeller he knew that he had found the right combination of man, plan, place, and time, not just for the immediate future, but for a span stretching as far as he could see. His success, to Daniel if to no one else, seemed preordained. And you didn't just take a flyer on preordained success, you bought as much stock as you could. You didn't worry about fluctuations in its price, because eventually it would go up. You didn't sell it when it did, you kept buying. You didn't sell it when it went down, you thanked the market for putting your stock on sale and bought more. Daniel had repeated his Rockefeller strategy with Hill, Harriman, and a handful of the thousands of other men and their companies he had evaluated through the years.

Daniel still owned every share he had ever bought of those companies. Great businessmen built great businesses and their efforts had showered Daniel with wealth. However rare and remunerative the gifts of the successful trader, the gifts of the successful investor were even more rare and more remunerative. Daniel could print his investment philosophy on the back of his business card, but he knew very few people who were so constituted that they could practice it. Woodbury and the Pirate had both made fortunes in the course of their careers, but they had also lost them. Like most traders, what they eventually bequeathed would depend on where they were in their cycles. In his entire life Daniel had written a quantity of stock orders that any good trader surpassed on a busy day, but his fortune dwarfed that of anyone else in the firm.

"Will wanted to know if he could watch the 'action,'" Daniel said, knowing the answer.

Woodbury frowned. "Not today. We're too busy and he'd be in the way."

Daniel knew Woodbury and the other traders had made up their minds about Will, though none of them had said a word to Daniel. Traders who always followed the crowd had short careers. Will was a follower, perpetually sacrificing his judgment and independence to the random impulses of the herd. His was the personality of an actor or a politician, not a trader, investor, or most importantly, businessman. The trading partners kept Will off the trading floor and Daniel suspected that eventually they would keep him out of the partnership. Will was Daniel's potential successor and the business couldn't be entrusted to someone so essentially flawed. Daniel didn't look forward to the day when he would have to tell Will.

Thursday, the first of two requirements for Will's plan, hatched at the Men's Cafe, was satisfied. He had run into a smiling Keane in a hallway at Durand & Woodbury.

"You look as if you're on top of a cloud," Will said.

"Woodbury and the Pirate closed out their position in Northern Pacific."

"How much did we make?"

"Two plus," Keane whispered.

Two million was staggering, assuring the partnership a prosperous year, but it wouldn't help Will much, perhaps a slightly larger bonus. "Congratulations," he said with bluff heartiness.

Today, Friday, the second of Will's requirements had been met. Selling was heavy throughout the trading session. Will had occasionally sold short stocks that had run up, betting on a decline in price. Invariably, they kept going up. However, Tim Harkness had said something that made sense. He was going to wait for weakness in the market before he went short, and Will had decided that would be his strategy as well. He would go short after the market started down and established its new trend. Which stock would he short? None other than Northern Pacific's, the stock Woodbury had joked that nobody should short at the risk of his job.

He found his father's hunch—that Harriman was raiding NP under the noses of Morgan and Hill—not just wildly improbable, but absurd. One had to question Harriman's sanity if he thought he could best those titans. NP had gone up because the market had gone up. Now that the market was turning around, it would go down with it. Will would short the stock, demonstrating a faith in his own convictions that couldn't fail to impress his father and that damn Woodbury, who wouldn't let him on the floor. He would short the stock for the account of the firm. It would show that he placed Durand & Woodbury's interest before his own chance for personal gain. The profits would excuse his brashness.

Execution of his plan presented some difficulties, but Will was helped by a move by the Stock Exchange—its building demolished to make way for a larger building—to temporary quarters in the Produce Exchange. Not far from Will's office, on top of a counter, was a basket used for stock orders. Usually these orders were transmitted to the exchange over the telephone. However, there was a shortage of lines to the Produce Exchange, so runners were hand-delivering all but the highest priority orders. Will made out a short-sale order at market for two thousand shares of NP and then scrawled an illegible signature. Peters, the man who called in orders, would have tried to determine who had written it. During the day, Will kept his eye on the order basket and the flow of the runners picking up orders. When it was the turn of the least experienced runner, Timmons, who was no more than eighteen years old, Will slipped his order to the bottom of the stack. Timmons took the stack to the exchange. Will had to hope that neither Woodbury nor the Pirate saw his order—they would question it. If the order bypassed them, whoever executed it would assume that Durand & Woodbury was acting on behalf of a customer.

When it came to light that the firm was short two thousand shares of NP, Will would step forward. He would admit that he had placed the order—not for a customer, but for the firm's account. Of course he hadn't meant for his signature to be illegible. He had thought the firm's liquidation of its long position a prudent move. However, the whole market was overvalued and he had put on a short to capitalize on its inevitable fall. It was admittedly a bold stroke, but one had to go with one's strong hunches. Will could see the looks on Woodbury and the Pirate's faces as they regarded him in a new light, and his father shaking his head, but smiling, as he did when Tommy pulled one of his winningly audacious stunts. And in the improbable event the price of NP went up instead of down? That was why the signature on the ticket was illegible.

Sunday evening, Daniel was in his study, reading and smoking a cigar, when the telephone rang in the hall. Daniel rarely used the telephone at home, so he hadn't installed one in his study. His children had grown up with the telephone and used it far more than he did.

John answered it. "Good evening," he said slowly. "This is the Durand residence. This is John speaking." There was a moment of silence. "He's at home, sir, I'll get him."

John filled the doorway. He was the only one of the Durand children who was fat. His blond hair hung just above wide-open eyes and he looked like an overgrown child, an impression furthered by his slow speech. He had been extensively tutored to about a fourth-grade level. Unfortunately, he was easily distracted, unable to keep his mind on a task for more than a minute or two, so it was hard for him to find work. Some of Daniel's business acquaintances would have given John a no-work job to curry favor with Daniel if he had asked, but Daniel wouldn't ask. Instead, he assigned John chores at home and paid him for doing them. On weekends, he devised some task that he and John could do together.

"Father, Mr. Gottman is on the telephone."

"Thank you." Daniel walked down the hall and picked up the telephone receiver. "Hello."

"Hello, Daniel, this is Jakob Gottman. I'm sorry to call you on a Sunday night, but I've wrestled with this matter for several hours and decided I should call."

"It's not a problem, Jakob. I was just reading."

"Daniel, do you know of a man named Louis Heinsheimer?"

"The name sounds familiar, but I can't recall where I've heard it."

"He's a friend of mine, a junior partner at Kuhn, Loeb. Our families get together socially. This afternoon his family came to our house for dinner. Something was troubling him. When we were alone I asked him about it. Do we have any position at all in NP?"

"No, everything has been closed out."

"Then I feel better about what I'm about to tell you. The firm can't use this information."

"Jakob, everything you tell me will stay with me. We won't use the information."

There was a moment of silence. "Yes, I'm sure we wouldn't. It's just difficult to tell someone's secret. Yesterday, Louis was at his office when he received a call from Harriman. It seemed far-fetched at the time, but your hunch about Harriman trying to buy NP on the sly was correct—that's what he's doing. He's got a lot of stock, a majority of the preferred and almost a majority of the common. He was disturbed that he didn't have a majority of the common, although Louis and the partners at Kuhn, Loeb think he has enough to exercise control of the NP. However, Morgan and Hill and their lawyers might argue things differently."

"If they knew Harriman had as much stock as he does."

"They do know, at least Hill does. He's in town and went to the offices of Kuhn, Loeb on Friday to meet with Mr. Schiff. Mr. Schiff was in tight spot—he's helping Harriman buy Hill's stock and he's got Hill asking him what's going on. Louis says Mr. Schiff can't lie to save his life. He told Hill that Harriman was trying to buy control of the NP."

"Then Morgan must know as well."

"Probably, but Louis says Morgan is in France."

"So Harriman's been buying NP, and now Hill and probably Morgan know about it."

"There's more. When Harriman called Louis Saturday, he told him to buy forty thousand shares of NP common that morning, so he'd have a majority of the common stock. Louis thought he should get approval from Mr. Schiff before he executed an order of that size, so he went to our synagogue, where Mr. Schiff was attending services. Louis doesn't know why, but Mr. Schiff told him not to execute the order. Louis is guessing that Mr. Schiff believes that Harriman already has enough shares, between the common and preferred, to control NP. Louis didn't execute Harriman's order, but he's in a torment because he had to go against either an important customer or the senior partner of his firm. He hasn't told Harriman that he didn't execute the order. He'll be furious when he finds out. Harriman will try to buy the shares Monday, and Louis thinks that Hill and Morgan will be in there trying to buy shares ahead of him, to stop him."

"That means the fireworks aren't over for NP. Too bad we sold our shares." Daniel felt a plunging sensation in his stomach. If Durand & Woodbury had held on to its NP shares, it could have multiplied its two-million-dollar profit. "Thank you for telling me, Jakob. We won't trade in NP tomorrow, although I can't imagine what's going to happen to the price. How high is up?"

"Pity the shorts. Imagine trying to buy shares ahead of Morgan, Hill, and Harriman to cover."

Will stepped into Benjamin Keane's office Monday morning. Keane sat at his desk and smiled ruefully. "Never discount one of your father's hunches, Will."

"What are you talking about?"

"I just got off the phone with George. When the market opened an army of James Keene's brokers—Morgan's men—swarmed onto the floor. Morgan's buying NP shares and it's pandemonium! George said men are getting knocked over and a fellow had his jacket ripped off. Anybody who has NP for sale is taking his life into his hands trying to sell. Your father was right; Harriman has tried to buy NP from under Morgan and Hill!"

"My God!" Will gasped. "What happened to the price of NP?"

"It opened up eighteen points, at 127.50. What is it? You look like you've just seen a ghost!"

"Excuse me." Will had to get to the bathroom—quickly. He ran down the hall, his hand on his mouth, overcome by an intense and immediate sensation from his stomach. Eighteen points on two thousand shares—a thirty-six-thousand-dollar loss and probably more! His head throbbed as if it would explode. He burst into the men's room, empty save for the attendant, hurried to the toilet, retched once, and vomited repeatedly.

The Pirate gingerly felt his swollen upper lip with his tongue and tried to hold his ground against the frantic, jostling swarm of traders on the floor of the Produce Exchange. Yesterday, James Keene's men had fanned out over the floor, buying NP, while the Pirate traded everything but NP. The order had come down from Mr. Durand himself—no trading in NP, which was fine with the Pirate; he had no desire to wade into the dangerous lunacy that had engulfed the stock.

However, all wars had casualties among noncombatants and the Pirate's lip was a casualty of this one, taking a shot from the elbow of a trader short the stock of NP, frantic at the prospect of imminent ruin. The Pirate had thrown a punch that missed, but even if it had landed it would have fazed its target as a stick to its head fazes a rabid dog.

"Mr. Dolan, Mr. Dolan!" A Durand & Woodbury position clerk named Michaels rushed up.

"What is it?"

"Abbot & Tinsley is trying to compare on a trade in NP. They say they bought two thousand shares on a short sale from us Friday. Do you know the trade?"

"No, we sold out last Thursday. I wouldn't have done a short sale and neither would George. Perhaps it's a customer short, although I can't imagine how it would have been approved. Has Abbot & Tinsley shown you a ticket?"

"No, not yet."

NP was up another sixteen points. The realization that NP was moving up because of a contest for control—Mr. Durand's hunch several weeks ago—had finally dawned on the floor traders. Between Hill and Morgan on the one side and Harriman and Schiff on the other, the stock was virtually cornered. Very few shares that could be physically delivered were in any other parties' hands. Nobody on the floor was offering NP for sale.

The Pirate made a flat motion with his hand. "Tell them they've got the wrong counterparty. We didn't do the trade. The last shares we'd short would be NP."

The next day, as Daniel returned from a mid-afternoon meeting, the telephone in his office rang. He picked it up.

"We may be short two thousand shares of NP." It was Woodbury.
"What?"

"Yesterday, Abbott & Tinsley tried to compare on a short sale of two thousand shares of NP. The Pirate declined the trade and told the position clerk to have them show us the ticket. Well, they have the ticket. It's odd—from the number on it, it comes from the office, not from the floor. You can't read the name on the ticket and there's no customer account number, so it's a trade on the firm's account. I talked to Peters. He didn't transmit the order over the telephone. It had to have been run over here. This looks like someone was trying to put it in on the sly."

"We've got to find out where that order came from."

"What about the open short? If the firm's short, we've got to cover and fast. NP is trading in odd lots. There's no stock for sale—the big boys have it cornered."

"What's the price on the ticket?"

"One hundred six and five-eighths."

"Where's it at now?"

"Last trade, twenty shares at one-fifty-seven and a quarter."

Over fifty points on two thousand shares—at least a hundred-thousand-dollar loss. An order for two thousand shares would push the price up more. Daniel felt a cold, plunging sensation of impending disaster. Woodbury's words: "This almost looks like someone was trying to put in the order on the sly." The monetary loss would be substantial, but a more important—the most important—Durand & Woodbury asset was at risk. Daniel pulled his watch from his vest. "The exchange closes in thirty minutes. I'll try to call before then, but I may not be able to."

"I'm going to buy whatever NP I can find. However it happened, it looks like we're on the hook. I won't get two thousand done—there's not enough time or stock for sale." The phone clicked.

Daniel walked into Benjamin Keane's office. Keane looked up from a document.

"I want everyone—partners, employees, no exceptions except for those who absolutely must remain at their posts—in the large conference room. Now. I'll explain there."

Within fifteen minutes the conference room was packed. The urgent summons was unprecedented. and Daniel stood before the anxious group.

"Last Friday a ticket was executed on the floor for a short sale of two thousand shares of Northern Pacific. The ticket came from this office; it wasn't a floor ticket. It had no account number and an illegible signature. Without an account number the trade is for the account of the firm." There were a few gasps and a low whistle from the back of the room.

"Yes, gentlemen, we're looking at quite a hit, but that's not what disturbs me most." Daniel surveyed the room. Gottman shook his head. Alexander stared at him, wide-eyed, as did Palos. Will was writing something on a pad. Keane's eyes had narrowed.

"I hired just about everyone in this room. I thought I was hiring intelligent, capable men, and the success of this firm has borne out those judgments. Before I hired you, I asked myself, 'Can I trust this man?' If the answer had been 'no,' you wouldn't be here, no matter how bright and competent you were. The foundations of Durand & Woodbury are trust and honor. It appears that whoever wrote this ticket did so in a way as to conceal its origin. Our reputation in the marketplace, our effective dealings with each other, rest on our integrity. We can't abide deception. If that's the way we're going to do business, we'll stop doing business. If anyone knows anything about this ticket, I expect him to step forward. I'll be in my office."

Daniel left the men in stunned silence. He sat alone in his office until it was time to go home.

Benjamin Keane stared at the bleary, red-rimmed eyes staring back at him from the mirror of the Durand & Woodbury men's room. It was done in the style of men's rooms at the best clubs, with burnished dark woods and polished brass, toiletries and towels laid out on a marble dressing table, an attendant, and two showers. These were necessities, not luxuries, for men who frequently spent long nights at the office. Keane had not slept the previous night. Did he know, with swear-on-a-stack-of-Bibles certainty, who had written the NP ticket? No, but he had an overwhelming suspicion. He had hoped that the suspect would come forward after the meeting.

It was not his conscience that had kept Keane up. He would disclose his suspicion. What had robbed Keane of sleep was the vision of Daniel Durand's face—the clench of the jaw, the narrowing of the eyes, the slight shake of the head—when he heard the news. He fought pain, had no use for it, but what Keane would tell him would cause pain, unavoidable pain. Keane would be ripping the heart out of a man he loved as he had his own father, a man his father had loved as a son.

Daniel made mistakes and fathers had blind spots concerning their families, especially their sons. Keane wet his hands with cold water and rubbed his face. Daniel could not have refused his first son a place at the firm, but Will would not follow in his father's footsteps. He lacked an intellectual interest in finance and didn't seem to have an avaricious interest in money. Burning interest and avarice were the lifeblood of Wall Street—more the latter than the former, in Keane's estimation.

He dried his face with a starched white linen towel and deposited it in a wicker basket. He stared at his face one last time in the mirror. It looked older than it had yesterday. He took a deep breath.

He could delay no longer; he had to speak with Daniel before the market opened.

Keane walked into Daniel's open office, closed the door, and sat in one of the two maroon leather chairs before Daniel's desk. "I have a strong suspicion about that NP ticket."

"Why didn't you say anything yesterday?"

"I was hoping the person I suspected would step forward."

"Who?"

"Will."

There was a moment of silence. "Why do you suspect him?" Daniel's voice was calm.

"Monday morning he dropped by my office. He seemed chipper enough. I said something to the effect that one shouldn't bet against one of your hunches, and I told him what was happening at the exchange with NP stock. I told him NP was way up and he looked as if he had eaten a bad oyster. His face went white and I thought he was about to get physically ill. He rushed from my office, probably to the men's room."

Daniel leaned back in his chair and stared at some far distant point out a window, as if Keane weren't there. After a protracted silence, he said, "Would you get Mr. Johnson?"

Keane went to the washroom and fetched the attendant, Mr. Johnson, a slim, older black man with mostly white hair who always wore a pressed black three-piece suit and white gloves.

"Mr. Johnson, Mr. Keane, please sit down," Daniel said, and the two men settled into the chairs in front of Daniel's desk. "Mr. Johnson, do you recall anything out of the ordinary that might have happened with Will Durand in the men's room last Monday morning?"

Johnson looked first at Daniel, then at Keane and then back at Daniel. He hesitated.

"Mr. Johnson, we need to know what you saw," Keane said.

"Well, Mr. Durand, Mr. William came in that morning…in a hurry. He rushed into a stall and it sounded like…like he lost his breakfast, sir. I didn't think too much of it, sir, because it's happened before, when Mr. William had too much to drink the night before."

Daniel closed his eyes and slowly shook his head. "Thank you, Mr. Johnson, you may return to your duties." Johnson left the office.

"Benjamin, bring Will to my office when he gets in."

Will entered his office, set his briefcase by his desk, and hung his overcoat on a stand. He had never liked his office. It was too small, too unprepossessing, too much like all the other employees' offices. Not that the partners' offices were lavish—Durand & Woodbury didn't waste money on their decor—but they were of a better grade. To Will's consternation, his brother Alexander's office was slightly closer to those offices, the locus of the firm's power.

Hell, Will thought, it wasn't an office—it was a damn cell! Convicts worked better hours than the firm's partners and employees. That's what he liked the least about his office—you were expected to spend many hours in it, working. Midnights often found the lights on at Durand & Woodbury. And then there was Palos. Nine nights out of ten, Will's brother-in-law turned out the lights and locked the doors. No surprise that he and Laura were still childless.

Will closed his door. He wanted to hide. He sat down at his desk, absently grabbed some papers from a stack, and stared at the top paper as if he were reading it. For as far back as he could remember, he had felt he was hiding a shameful secret he couldn't put to words. He charmed effortlessly, had many friends, was admired and envied, but always felt he was a charade. What truth required hiding? What compelled him to fool people? Did he like himself? Questions welled up that didn't admit of comforting answers, or any answers at all. There were no answers, he often told himself; nobody had the answers.

There was a knock on his door and Will looked out his office window. It was Keane.

"Come in."

Keane opened the door and stepped into the office, his face a blank. Will's stomach tightened.

"Your father wants to see you."

Will stood and his legs trembled. He followed Keane out of the office. Keane opened the door to Daniel's office and Will entered. Will and Keane sat down.

"Did you write that ticket on NP?" Daniel asked.

In all his years, Will had never seen his father's face as implacably stern as it was now. His eyes bored in on him. "No, no, of course not," Will stuttered. "Why would you think I wrote that ticket?"

Daniel glanced at Keane.

"Monday morning, I told you the situation with NP on the floor of the exchange, and you asked me what had happened to the price of the shares. When I told you it was up eighteen, your face went white. You rushed away and I thought you were going to be ill."

Will felt his face flush. He suddenly felt very hot. "I…I didn't do it," he stammered.

"Mr. Johnson said you were in the bathroom, vomiting," Daniel said.

Will's shoulders slumped. The game was up. He couldn't lie to his father. If he'd had a gun he'd have put it to his head and pulled the trigger. He slowly shook his head. "It…was…my …ticket," he whispered. Tears came to his eyes and he hung his head.

"Why?" Daniel said.

"Oh God, I don't know why! I…I wanted to show…that I could trade." Will, overcome, tried to suppress his sobs, but he couldn't.

Neither his father nor Keane said anything. Will's sobs and sniffles eventually subsided, and he blew his nose and wiped his eyes with a handkerchief. He looked at his father, whose unyielding face held no trace of compassion. He glanced at Keane, hoping to see some hint of the Keane who enthusiastically greeted him each morning, who took him under his wing, who liked him. Keane's face was of the same cast as his father's.

Daniel picked up the telephone on his desk and dialed. "George, how many shares of NP are we still short?" Noises came from the telephone. "Twelve hundred? Cover them. The ticket definitely came from Durand & Woodbury. I'll explain later." There were more noises. "George, we can't count on Harriman and Morgan working things out. Those are just rumors. I don't care what we have to pay, if there's any stock for sale, buy it!" Daniel hung up the telephone.

"Will, go to your office and stay there until I send for you."

"Yes, sir." Will stood and hastily left his father's office, feeling as if he were on a rack being pulled apart into a thousand pieces.

Insanity! Madness! The Pirate shook his head. He had bought 950 shares of NP that morning, at prices ranging from $350 to $740, with 250 shares to go. He was battered from battling with other fools who were short and cornered, and the deafening noise had given him a throbbing headache. The air reeked of sweat, suits badly in need of laundering, stale cigar smoke, and an occasional zephyr of flatulence. Rumors flew that Morgan and Harriman would reach some sort of settlement, but if he had a dollar for every false rumor circulated on the floor that week he could have bought a castle somewhere. His trading instincts screamed that he was making a costly mistake, but you didn't question an order from Mr. Woodbury that in turn came from Mr. Durand.

"I sell three hundred at one thousand dollars, all or none," a man with a torn brown coat screamed.

There was a momentary silence as the reality, the absurdity, of buying shares at $1,000 that had closed the previous day at $160 hit the grasping, desperate multitude of traders.

The Pirate broke the silence. "I buy!" He had covered at one thousand dollars a share! The net loss was north of a million. Not only had he wasted all day on this fool's errand, he had closed out his short positions in other stocks because he couldn't devote the necessary attention to them. All those positions would have been profitable because the rest of the market was crashing while NP soared. Whoever was responsible for this damn short should be keelhauled!

He fought his way through the mob. He spotted Woodbury.

"Did you cover?" Woodbury shouted.

"Bought three hundred at one thousand."

"Oh, good God, I've been trying to find you!" Woodbury pulled his watch from his vest. "There's an announcement from Morgan and Harriman at three—five minutes."

When the announcement came, the Pirate felt like jumping off a bridge. Morgan and Harriman were going to allow shorts to settle at $150 and not demand immediate delivery. He glanced at Woodbury, who obviously felt the same way. "I need a drink," the Pirate said.

"Absolutely. We have to be at the office at the close. Daniel's called a partners' meeting."

"Fine. Let's just get out of here. I don't want to know where NP closes today, but it sure as hell won't be at a thousand dollars."

Keane entered Daniel's office. "The partners are in the conference room."

Daniel stood tall and squared his shoulders. A tempest of emotions raged inside, but he'd deal with that later. Now he owed his partners, the men who had built the firm, the men who had their money on the line, an accounting. "Before the meeting starts, would you tell Will that I won't be able to see him today, but to be in my office first thing tomorrow morning."

Keane raised his eyebrows. "He's going to have a rough night."

"That's a damn pity. I can't talk to him until I talk with Eleanor."

Daniel went to the partners' conference room and sat at the head of the table. Except for Keane all the partners were present: Woodbury, the Pirate, Palos, Jakob Gottman. Keane came in a few minutes later, his face grim.

Daniel stood before them. "Gentlemen, you know the situation with the Northern Pacific short sale. Will has admitted that he placed that order. He didn't make his admission after the meeting yesterday afternoon; he did so only after Benjamin and I confronted him this morning. We covered the short at prices as high as one thousand dollars per share. George, what was the loss?"

"One million, one hundred thirty-six thousand dollars. That doesn't include the loss on an additional fifty shares that we're long at one thousand dollars per share. NP closed at three-twenty-five. That loss is thirty-three thousand, seven hundred fifty dollars."

The men around the table shook their heads. The firm had made enough on its initial NP speculation to cover the loss, but the manner of the loss was shocking.

"I'll make good the losses," Daniel said. "They will not be borne by the firm. The question before us: What do we do about Will?"

"What the hell was he thinking?" Woodbury said.

Daniel sighed. "That's not clear. He was very emotional when Benjamin and I talked to him this morning. He wanted to show that he could trade, but that's all we got from him."

"Why didn't he step forward Monday morning?" the Pirate asked. "It would have only cost around thirty points to cover then. That's the first rule of trading—your first loss is your best loss."

"Indeed it is, Mr. Dolan," Daniel said. "Unfortunately, the one thing that's clear in this whole mess is that Will is not a trader."

There was a long silence. Daniel glanced at Keane. Somebody had to address the issue of what to do about Will. One day Keane might run the firm. He needed to show some leadership now.

"I think, at the very least, a severe reprimand is in order," Keane said. "Obviously reimbursement of the loss is beyond Will's means, but there should be no bonus at year's end, and for several years going forward. Consideration for partnership must be delayed indefinitely. An apology to everyone in the firm would be appropriate."

There was another silence. Daniel glanced around the table at his partners, mentally trying Keane's suggestion on for size.

"That won't do. None of it will do."

Daniel stared at the speaker, his son-in-law, Michael Palos, shocked.

"With all due respect, Mr. Durand, you shouldn't have to make up the NP loss. We all want to bring our sons into the business. It sets the wrong precedent if we say it's the father's responsibility to cover the mistakes of the son. It's our responsibility to supervise and train our employees, and it's our responsibility to pay the price when we don't."

Palos took a breath and looked around the table. "I have not yet been blessed, but our sons have to be held to the same standard as everyone else. If the employee in this case were anyone other than the founding partner's son, would there be a question?" Palos looked directly at Daniel. "You said it yesterday, the foundations of Durand & Woodbury are trust and honor. Will has acted dishonorably and we can no longer trust him. He's my brother-in-law, but he has to go. I wouldn't want to work here, to have my money invested, if he was to stay."

The last person Daniel had expected to throw down the gauntlet had just done so.

"I'm afraid there's been a personal animus between William and me for many years," Jakob Gottman said. "However, I want to set that aside and analyze this situation. The ticket was written in such a way that it was impossible to determine who had written it. Why would he do that? There is only one plausible reason. If NP went down and the trade was profitable, he'd step forward to claim credit, but if it went up, he'd say nothing. From the beginning, his intention was to deceive. His father and Mr. Keane had to confront him— he never stepped forward. If he had done so at any time, then Mr. Keane's suggestion would merit consideration, but he didn't, so I must say that I agree with Mr. Palos."

"That's the most important thing to me," the Pirate said. "Anyone can make a mistake, but you own up to it. Will hid his mistake. I don't want to work with someone I can't trust."

"I'm sorry, Daniel," Woodbury said. "I'm of the same mind. Will's got to go."

That left Keane as the sole potential holdout. Daniel turned to him. "What about you, Benjamin? Do you feel the same way?"

Keane let out a long breath. "I suggested a course of action that wouldn't have involved firing Will. Would I have made the suggestion if anyone other than Will were involved? No. Mr. Palos is right—we can't have different standards for different employees. Will can't work here."

Daniel's choice was before him. It would fracture the firm beyond mending if he ignored his partners and allowed Will to stay. But firing Will would shatter their relationship. He was going to lose his firm or his son.

Eleanor knew when her husband was troubled. He spoke less and ate less. Usually a good listener, he would be preoccupied when others talked. It was useless to press him; he would disclose when he was ready. For her, talking was a way of setting things straight in her mind. Daniel had to have things straight in his mind before he talked. He hadn't said a word at dinner. Afterwards, they sat on a plush couch in the sitting room, a fire crackling in the fireplace. Eleanor poured their coffee.

"Have you had a chance to look at the newspaper?" Daniel said.

"Just the headlines. That Northern Pacific situation you've been talking about caused a commotion in the market. It was on the front page."

"We made quite a bit of money on that situation, although we closed out our position last week. Unfortunately, that situation also cost us quite a bit of money."

"How?" There was something unsettling in Daniel's tone.

"We discovered yesterday that we were short two thousand shares that we didn't know about. We had to cover at a loss, over a million dollars."

Something was terribly wrong. "Why would you be short two thousand shares?"

"That's what I wanted to know. We verified the trade ticket, but it was done in such a way that we couldn't tell who wrote it. Yesterday afternoon I had a firm meeting and asked whomever had written the ticket to step forward, but nobody did. Then this morning Benjamin and I discovered who had put in the ticket."

No, no, no, it couldn't be. "Who?"

"Will."

It was hard to breathe. Her arms trembled with the weight of her saucer and cup. She almost dropped them on the table as she set them down. Daniel placed his hand on her shoulder.

"Will?" she gasped. "How? Why?"

"I don't know. Benjamin told me this morning that he suspected Will. We called him into my office and confronted him. He lied at first. Then he admitted putting in the ticket. There was some foolishness about wanting to show that he could trade. He started crying and we got no more from him. I sent him back to his office and haven't talked to him since."

"Do...do the other partners know?"

"We had a meeting this afternoon."

"What's going to happen?"

"What would you do if you were in my shoes, if you were a partner in the firm?"

She wasn't sure what she would do, but she knew what Daniel was going to do. His face and his eyes were set, hard and cold. Her breaths came in short gasps and she couldn't speak.

Mother had said something long ago. She had pointed at Will, waving a toy sword. "The world of men is a terrible thing, Eleanor. Boys learn to fight, to compete. A man's first love is himself because it has to be—no one fights his battles for him. He thrusts himself forward, hard, proud." She held up her index finger at an angle, stiffly rigid, obscenely symbolic. "They don't bend and most of them break. Yet even when they break, we love, because love we must."

Eleanor had known then that her mother would always love her father. Mother had gone on. "A man loves his wife because she's his wife and his children because they're his children. A man is what a man does, not whom he loves. Daniel is a good man. He may even be one who doesn't break, but never forget, my dear, his first love is himself...what he does."

"You're going to fire Will," Eleanor whispered.

"Yes."

Tears streamed down her cheeks. Will tried to be what others wanted him to be, to win their love. Those who needed it most received it least. Will didn't love himself. Tommy did; love flowed towards him like water flows down a hill. Those who needed it least received it most. The tears were falling on her dress. She wiped her eyes with her handkerchief. Will needed a love from Daniel he would never receive—a love that didn't judge. An impossible love.

"You don't know why he did what he did, do you?" Eleanor asked.

"Not really."

"He wants...he's always wanted to be accepted, to belong. He wants to be accepted by you, to belong in your world. The men in your firm put themselves...their jobs...their honor before what anybody else thinks of them. Will needed to show that he could do something they would respect, to measure up."

"That wasn't the way to do it."

"Of course not, Daniel, but that's how he felt. Eighteen-hour days, contracts, trading, finance—that's not Will, it was never Will."

"So he tried a shortcut and he lied about it—that's Will." Daniel didn't hide his contempt.

"Then why did you hire him in the first place?" she said angrily. "You're too smart not to know then that he didn't have what it would take in your firm."

Daniel was rarely challenged or confronted, by her or anyone else. She expected anger, to match hers. Instead he stared into space, his iron self-control clamping down. She wished it wouldn't. Sometimes she stirred the cauldron, but rarely saw what she was stirring—only in oblique glimpses. Mostly she saw what he disclosed.

"You're right. It was a mistake." His voice was unnaturally calm. "In this life, you pay for your mistakes. Tomorrow, I'll pay for mine." There was a slight catch in his voice. This was her oblique glimpse. Tomorrow was going to be terrible for him. He stood. "I'm going for a walk, have a cigar, think about things." He walked slowly to the door.

"Daniel, I'll be thinking of you."

"And Will. A mother thinks of her son." He opened the door and stepped out into the night.

The tears flowed for Daniel, for Will, for her. She wouldn't see little Gwendolyn or the new baby, Roger. If it were up to Will—perhaps, over time, but Sylvia would never allow it. For Sylvia this would be a declaration of war. Eleanor wept as she hadn't wept since her mother's death.

The long, thin fingers tightened on the back of his neck as he was dragged from the bed. The boy trembled from his fright and from the dead-of-winter Cleveland cold. His thin socks were no protection against the frigid floor. He was pushed painfully towards the door.

The short one was waiting, his face hidden by his cowl. "Satan's child!" he hissed. He had a candle and led the way down the narrow corridor. The boy saw their breath in the candlelight. It would be much colder—freezing—outside. The tall one turned towards him. He had an evil face and an evil smile, with dark toothless gaps between his remaining teeth.

They came to a steep, narrow staircase—they were going down. He grabbed the rickety rail. This was the stairway to the back of the orphanage, to the kitchen and the storeroom—always locked against hungry, thieving boys—the stables and the privy, the cleaning of which fell to the ones, like the boy, they hated the most.

They reached the bottom of the stairs and went down the short hallway to the kitchen. It stank of last night's gruel—cabbage, onions, and turnips, not potatoes or meat. As he stumbled past the stoves, he felt a draft of warmth from the precious burning embers of coal. He would have traded his place in bed, with its frayed sheet and thin blanket, to sleep on the floor by the stoves, like a dog. Then the warmth was gone and they were before the door to the back yard. On the floor was a pail of water. He trembled violently.

The short one pushed the door against the snow on the ground outside and opened it. The cold blasted in. A path through the snow, packed down by the procession to the privy, led from the door. Stinging tears came to his eyes. The tall one pushed him roughly out the door and he fell into the snow. The wind off the frozen lake whipped through the yard and the snow swirled. He stood up, but sank into the snow. The short one grabbed the pail of water and came towards him. His teeth chattered and he was shaking so hard his whole body hurt.

"Daniel, wake up! You're trembling." Eleanor was shaking his shoulder.

He opened his eyes, trying to remember where he was. It was warm here. The blankets were thick, but he was scrunched up into a ball as if it were cold. He rolled over. There was Eleanor, reaching out, taking him in her arms. "Bad dream," he gasped. "Sorry I woke you up."

"I was awake."

Daniel had to tell Alexander what he was going to do before he did it. He regretted the times he had overlooked his quiet son. Daniel knew it had hurt him, although he had never said anything. Laura would learn the news from her husband, Michael Palos. Daniel would tell Constance afterwards, but not John. He wouldn't understand why his father had to hurt Will, his long-time favorite. Later, when Will got a new position, Daniel would tell John that he no longer worked at Durand & Woodbury.

Alexander worked hard, with dogged determination. He wasn't the one to call on when bold, innovative thinking was required, but he was proficient at fleshing out the details of someone else's plan. In his five years at the firm, he had won the partners' respect and there was a good chance he would be invited into the partnership in a few years.

Alexander had set his own course, picking his religion, his university, and most recently his fiancée without consultation. He had met Miss Hanna Rosemont at his church. The first time Daniel and Eleanor heard about her was when Alexander asked if he could invite her home to dinner. She was attractive, with green eyes and curly, auburn hair. Reserved and quietly serious at first, as the dinner progressed she displayed a whimsical sense of humor that extracted small absurdities from the commonplace. Not that Alexander asked, but Daniel and Eleanor liked her and told him so when he returned from taking her home.

"I'm going to ask her to marry me next week," Alexander said, his tone matter-of-fact. A month later the announcement made the society page that they would be wed April 12, 1902.

Daniel arrived at work, dropped his overcoat and briefcase in his office, and went to Alexander's. His son kept a neat office—papers labeled and stacked in orderly piles on shelves and a large calendar pad on the desk to keep track of appointments. Daniel settled into a chair.

"Will wrote the ticket. He admitted it to Benjamin and me yesterday," Daniel said.

Alexander shook his head. "What a foolish thing. I can't imagine why he did that, but you're more concerned because he didn't come forward and admit it."

"That's right."

"What are you going to do?"

"We had a partners' meeting. Will has to go."

"And you're the one who has to tell him."

Daniel nodded.

Alexander ran his hand through his hair, an uncharacteristic gesture. "Ah, Father, that will be very hard to do, but I don't see how you could do otherwise."

"You wouldn't give him another chance?"

"No. Will doesn't belong here. He doesn't belong in this business."

How long had Alexander held that opinion? "I'm going to talk to Will as soon as he gets in."

"If you want to get together afterwards, or at the end of the day, let me know."

"Thank you, Alexander. I appreciate that."

"Thank you for telling me what you're going to do."

Daniel left Alexander's office and returned to his own, to wait for Will. His anxiety gnawed a hole through his stomach.

Twenty minutes later, Will came to Daniel's office. "Well, Father, what's to become of me?" he said with a half-smirk and an affected breeziness. His red eyes belied his attitude; he hadn't slept well.

"Close the door and sit down." Will's pose was not the contrition he had expected. The first order of business was to get rid of that damn smirk.

Will sat down and Daniel was further annoyed that he slouched. "Father, I don't know why I did what I did, and I may never know. I understand the loss was in excess of a million dollars, although it ultimately could have been a lot less if we had waited until after the announcement to cover. I obviously don't have the resources to make good on the loss now, but if it takes until the end of my days, I'll pay it back. Every penny, with interest—I swear I will."

Daniel wondered how many times Will had run through this speech in front of the mirror. This was miles wide of appropriate.

"The million dollars is not the partners' main concern. Our main concern is that you deliberately hid that you wrote that ticket. You said nothing for several days as the trade went against you. You said nothing when I asked whomever wrote the ticket to step forward. You didn't step forward, and Benjamin and I had to confront you. Even then, you initially denied it. By not stepping forward, you lied, Will, that's the important thing. You—"

"I understand, Father, that my behavior in this incident was questionable. Whatever judgment and penalty the partners mete out—including, as I've said, restitution—I'm ready to accept."

"I don't think you're ready for their judgment."

"What do you mean?" There was fear in Will's voice—finally.

Daniel let out a long breath. "You're fired."

Will's balled up in his chair, as if he had been punched in the stomach and had the wind knocked out of him. "Fired," he gasped. "You can't fire me…you can't fire your son!"

"Did you think that was a blank check?"

"I was going to run this place! I was born to it!"

"You think this is some sort of birthright? This isn't primogeniture. If you want hereditary kingdoms to the oldest son and the like, go back to England with Lady Sylvia. I made it clear that there were no guarantees. I said it more than once and I meant what I said—nothing in this firm is unearned."

"You're going to fire me over this one mistake?" Will screamed.

"If that bonehead ticket was all there was to it, maybe not, but you lied about it. I can't ask men to let you stay in the firm, much less run it. Don't you realize what you've done?" Daniel's voice grew louder. "You can't stay. You've violated the trust of every man here. That's why you're fired. If you had admitted your mistake and offered to do what you could to make things right, then you might have had a chance of staying, but not after all this."

Daniel had never seen an emotion so completely take control of a person as the anger, the overwhelming fury, that gripped his son.

"I know things!" he shouted wildly. "I do! I hate this place! You can keep your damn firm! Who's going to run it? Alexander is a plodder, Tommy wants nothing to do with it, and Little John is an imbecile! You'd better watch out, Father—don't sleep too soundly, I'll get you! God be damned, I'll get you!" He stood, walked to the door, fumbled with the doorknob, opened the door, and left, slamming the door so hard the wall shook.

Daniel stayed in his office for a long time, staring out the window. He had lost his oldest son. How could he have stopped it? Where had he gone wrong?

"Oh, you fool! You absolute dunce! What on earth possessed you?"

After Will had been fired, he had gone to a tavern for the liquid courage that would allow him to tell Sylvia. Now, at home, her words cut like a lighthouse beam through his self-induced fog.

She jumped from the couch and began pacing back and forth across the den. She said nothing, only paced, for a long time.

Will grew uncomfortable. "Darling, I—"

"Quiet! I'm thinking."

Will dared not speak. The only sounds were the rustle of her green-and-yellow dress and the repetition of her soft steps on the carpet. Finally she spoke. "The most important thing is to control the perception of this affair. We don't want word out that you bungled a trade, weren't forthcoming about it, and were fired. That won't do at all. In England such incompetence from the son of the top man would be ignored and the son would retain his position, but your father is a different man. However, he abhors publicity and he'll want to keep this quiet."

"It might help if I was to offer restitution."

Sylvia stared at him with withering contempt. "Dearest," she said acidly. "Disabuse yourself of two notions. We are not going to use my money to cover your losses, and we are not going hat in hand to your father for anything, ever."

"What are we going to do?"

"My father says that when your opponent lands the first blow, your counterblow must be quick and lethal. Men like your father are a force of nature—he recognizes no authority greater than himself. That's intolerable. The whip is held by those who boldly grasp and use it. Power rests on fear, and the man who refuses to punish his enemies will never be feared. Tomorrow you'll call on your Harvard chum, Mr. Timothy Harkness. The enemy of our enemy is our friend, and we're going to bed down with the Winfields, your father's enemy."

"The Winfields!" Will gasped.

"Yes, the Winfields. I think Mr. Harkness' grandfather, Curtis Winfield, is a man with whom we can do business. Your father defeated his son in an affair of the heart and sold the family his bank for too high a price. He should welcome Daniel Durand's son with open arms."

Will's insides churned as he tried to formulate his thoughts. What a "counterblow" that would be, to go over to the Winfields. If anybody could take his father down a notch, they could. Curtis Winfield had a score to settle. There was something brilliant about the way Sylvia devised the strategy…and frightening.

"I suppose I could ask for a position in one of the Winfield's financial concerns."

"Absolutely not! Curtis Winfield anoints politicians. It's time you followed your destiny. You can be a first-rate politician, a power in your own right, rather than a second-rate businessman. The House of Representatives, the Senate, maybe even the presidency. You'd never have that chance if you stayed with your father. Curtis Winfield could make you, could make *us*."

"A power in your own right." He loved the sound of it! Oh, to be free of his father. Better yet, to grasp the whip and one day lash him. Lash all those damn tycoons, to show them the world didn't dance to their tune, that things wouldn't always go their way.

"I'd sell my soul."

She looked down at him, sitting on the couch. Even at a few inches above five feet she appeared tall and beautiful and terrible. "Of course you would. You want power, Will. You want it more than anything else. How badly do you want it, what would you do for it?" She pursed her delicate lips.

His eyes narrowed.

She bestowed her conspiratorial smile. "Every man," she said, stressing the second word, "who seeks power sells his soul. The trick when one bargains with the devil is to sell dear, and you can sell very dear, indeed…my dear."

"How so?"

"You've known a name since you were a boy. Pomeroy."

Will's eyes widened. "There's something about that name that greatly upsets my father."

"Perhaps the Winfields could find out why."

Chapter 22

Rising and Falling

Tom stared out the window towards the western horizon, lost in black clouds and flashing webs of lightning. Soon the train would roll into the thunderstorm, and it looked like a bone-rattler. He was returning from Alexander's wedding, his first trip to New York since settling in Wyoming in 1894, eight years ago. The wedding had been a beautiful affair, but the absence of Will had been a black cloud. Not because Tom had any great love for his older brother, but because of what it had done to his parents, especially his father.

Daniel Durand's ambitions were starting to ebb. Part of it was age. He was approaching sixty, his hair now more gray than black. Part of it was success. Durand & Woodbury was a prominent investment bank, he was wealthy, and maintaining a financial empire didn't carry the same challenge as building one. Part of it was temperament and interest. Even at his busiest, he had managed to find time to read and to think about issues that transcended commercial concerns. That part of his personality now seemed to be pushing to the forefront. Although he was interested in Tom's work, they had talked less about business than Tom had expected and more about politics, philosophy, and literature.

His father had not wanted to talk about Will, rebuffing Tom when he brought up his older brother. He shook his head, said nothing, and waved his hand in dismissal. Will had taken a toll on his father. Tom didn't know which had hurt him more, having to fire Will, or Will's subsequent break with the family. Worse, there was an undertone of tension between his father and mother over Will.

Raindrops hit the roof of the passenger car. The train had caught up to the storm and its darkness, howling winds, and thunder. The train had been scheduled to arrive at Cheyenne by early evening. Tom wondered how much the storm would slow it up. He had to work tomorrow and he wanted to unpack, put things in order, and get a good night's sleep. The light in the car was too dim for reading. He put his head back and closed his eyes, but the wind and thunder kept him awake.

A wrenching sideways lurch banged his head against the wall and he heard the harsh shriek of metal wheels grating against metal track. The train was slipping backwards. Behind him, men shouted, women screamed, and children cried—something had happened at the back of the train. The car came to a standstill. Tom jumped up, jostled the man in the seat next to his, ran up the aisle to the door of the railcar, and pushed it open. He looked towards the back of the train, not seeing much through the pouring rain, jumped out, and sank into muddy slop. He plowed his way through the mud.

Something was very wrong. One of the cars was at a tilt and the people inside were screaming. Tom kept going and found the next car at a more precarious angle. The following car was off the track, almost perpendicular to it, as if a giant had wreaked the kind of havoc a boy would visit on his toy trains. Most disturbing, there were no cars behind this last one and its coupling was mangled. He heard the roar of rushing water. In front of him loomed the trestles of a bridge.

A section had given way while the train rolled over it, its moorings probably weakened by the rain. Trestles and supporting spans of steel were twisted askew. Only one rail remained connected above the chasm. The river raged below. He gingerly stepped to the edge of a canyon, fearful of losing his footing on the slippery rocks and mud, and peered down, trying to make out the odd, disturbing collection of shapes below.

One passenger car, its roof crushed inwards, partially submerged in the torrent, thrust out of the water and rested against a rocky pile. Tom shuddered—there were people in that car and they couldn't all be alive. They could all be dead. Behind the passenger car was an angular projection from the water that might have been part of the caboose or a rock formation, Tom couldn't tell. Water streamed down his forehead into his eyes.

"Help!" An urgent wail, the high-pitched scream of a woman, rose above the roar of the water and the howl of the wind. Someone was alive in the passenger car!

"Help, oh please, help!"

"Hold on!" Tom yelled, hoping his words could be heard. He ran back towards the train, maddeningly slowed by the mud grabbing his feet. Other people were jumping out of the cars, including a conductor carrying a lantern and an umbrella. Tom ran towards him. "The bridge gave way," he shouted. "The caboose and a passenger car are at the bottom of the canyon. There's a woman in the passenger car—she screamed. Find ropes. Round up every man you can."

"Wait a minute," said the conductor, a white-haired man in his fifties. "You can't be issuing orders like that. You got no authority."

"I'm Tom Durand, the superintendent at Cheyenne. If you want your job tomorrow, do as I say. Move!"

The conductor slogged away. Tom hurried up the steps of his passenger car. Inside, children wailed and passengers huddled in clusters. "You there!" Tom pointed at a man with his arm around a woman. "Come with me!" Tom saw three other men. "And you, and you, and you!" He jumped out of the car, making a splat as he sank into the mud.

He rounded up the men in two other cars and soon there was a group outside, shivering in the rain. The conductor had a long length of rope and they hurried to the edge of the canyon.

"There's a passenger car down there and I heard a scream. You're going to drop me in and we'll try to rescue the woman and anyone else who's alive in that car." Tom pointed at the conductor. "Give me the rope." He looped the rope around his waist and began tying a knot.

"You'll kill yourself with that," a burly man growled in a Boston burr. The man elbowed his way past the other men and untied the knot. Treating Tom like a men's store mannequin, he quickly fashioned the rope into a makeshift harness that looped around his legs and shoulders and was held together by an elaborate knot in the middle of his chest. "You need a knot, you need a sailor." He stepped to the edge and looked over. "Those rocks will slice right through this rope. I'll stand here and hold it out far as I can. You mates hold on to me." He glanced at a man wearing an expensive coat and leather gloves. "Give me those gloves." The man complied.

Three men braced the sailor as he put the rope over his shoulder. Tom winced—the rope would rub his shoulder raw as he fed him down into the canyon. The other men stood in a line, holding the rope. He stepped to the edge. "When I get to the car, play me out a lot of slack," he said to the sailor. "When I tug three times, hard, bring me up."

He dropped over the edge, the rope biting into his legs and shoulders. Foot by foot the men above eased him towards the passenger car. As he was lowered, Tom could make out the scene below. The angular projection was indeed the red caboose—it was wedged into a rock formation. Directly below him was the upright passenger car. If the rope were to break, Tom would drop onto the car or the bed of jagged rocks that surrounded it. Either way he would be dead.

He swayed above the flood-swollen river, roaring as it crashed on the rocks. He swung into the side of the car, smashing his chest and banging his forehead. The windows of the car, which rested upright in the water against a pile of boulders, were broken out. He grabbed a windowsill and rested his feet on a sill below him. A child cried inside. Blood trickled down Tom's forehead. He looked down. He was about ten feet above the river.

"Can anyone hear me?" he shouted.

"Oh, praise God!" a woman screamed. "In here! In here with my little boy!"

"Hold on!"

"Oh, glory be! I was saying my prayers, preparing to meet my Redeemer!"

Tom used the windows as a ladder. He stepped up on a window sill and put his head through the window he had grabbed. His shirt hung up on a shard of jagged glass and ripped. He tore away a swath, wrapped his hand with it, punched out the shards from the shattered window and looked inside. His eyes had to adjust to the dim, gray light and the perspective of the car pitched at a right angle to its normal position.

The plunge into the canyon had ripped seats from the floor—there was a twisted pile of them below him. Among the pile he could make out mangled bodies. Open, vacant eyes stared up from faces frozen in terror. He couldn't take his eyes off a man's head—it didn't appear that it was still attached to a body. Death stench filled the air. A ragged hole opened out onto the river on the opposite side of the car. There was a huge inward dent in a section of the car's roof. He looked up but couldn't see the woman or her son. "Where are you?" he shouted.

"Up here, holding on for dear life!" the woman screamed from above.

Tom grabbed a seat that was askew but still anchored to the floor and pulled himself through the window. Guided by the boy's cries, he used the seats that hadn't been ripped from the floor to climb to the woman and boy. Testing each seat before he placed his full weight on it, he slowly made his way upward, pulling enough rope with him so that it didn't hang up on the seats.

"Someone's here to rescue us, Billy."

Billy continued to cry.

Tom made it to the woman and her son, huddled on the backs of two adjoining seats and clinging to them.

"Oh God, you're an angel!" the woman shrieked.

"First time anyone's called me that. Are you hurt?"

"We're banged up, but nothing's broken. Billy's got a gash on his head."

The woman and child were in a narrow space between their seats and the indented roof of the car—a miraculous indentation, just enough to stop them from falling into the ghastly heap below, but not enough to crush them. The woman's face was bruised and scraped. The boy's head was bleeding from a gash that ran back from his forehead. He was about four years old.

Tom hoisted himself and stood on the back of a seat. He was below the woman and child. "Can you climb down here?"

The woman's eyes widened with fear. "What if I fall?"

"It's the only way out."

"What about Billy?"

"Hand Billy to me, then I'll help you down."

The woman let out a long breath. The sobbing boy was huddled in her arms. "Billy," she said, her voice barely above a whisper. "I'm going to hand you to this man. You've got to be brave and stop crying. He's going to save us."

Billy's crying subsided. The woman lowered him as far as she could without falling from her perch. Tom grabbed him by his thighs and hauled him in. With his arms around Billy he stood the boy up on the back of his seat. "Billy, can you grab this?" Tom pointed at a strut. Billy grabbed it. Tom released his grip on him and turned towards the woman. She had shifted her position so that her legs dangled down.

"I can't reach high enough to get you. You're going to have to drop down and I'll catch you."

She inched over the seat and hesitated, her eyes wide.

"It's the only way."

She dropped and he caught her around the waist. Fortunately, she was a tiny thing. "Now you're going to have to grab my rope, and follow it down to the window I came in. I'll get Billy. When you get to the window, don't look down! Do you understand?"

The woman nodded. Tom grabbed a seat strut, cold and wet, on a chair above him and shook it to test it. It felt solidly anchored. He braced his feet on the seat back. "Go."

"You've got to stay with this man, Billy. He'll bring you down." The woman grabbed Tom's rope and roughly lowered herself to the next row of seats, banging against the floor of the car.

"Are you all right?"

"I'll make it."

For the next several minutes Tom was jerked and yanked as the woman dropped, swayed, and banged against the seats and floor. Finally the rope went slack. "I'm at the window," she shouted.

"Don't look down! Okay, Billy, our turn." Tom reached down and gathered the child in his left arm, keeping his right arm free. The railcar lurched. If Tom hadn't grabbed a seat rail, he and Billy would have been pitched into the gruesome abyss. The woman and Billy both screamed. The car came to rest at an oblique angle.

"Are you all right?" Tom shouted.

"Yes, is Billy all right?"

"Yes, we're coming down." They had to move fast. He lowered his feet to a seat back below and dropped. Following the trail of his rope, he made his way down through the maze of seats still attached to the floor. Billy squalled each time he was jostled. Tom made it to Billy's mother at the window. Outside, the tempest raged.

"I'm going to sit on this window," he shouted. "You're going to sit on my lap, and Billy's going to sit on yours. I'll hold you and you hold him. I'll tug the rope and the men above will pull us up. Do you understand?"

The woman nodded. Tom sat on the windowsill, his feet dangling inside the car. The woman cradled Billy in her arms and lowered herself onto Tom. He put one arm around her waist and gathered the slack in the rope with his other. Once he had it gathered he let it play out the window. He gave three sharp tugs to signal the men above. He clasped his hands, his arms tight around the woman. The rope went taut. His harness jerked and tightened. They were pulled through the window and free of the car. They swung wildly above the river, dangerously close to the canyon wall. The woman screamed and Billy howled. There was a crack of splintering wood and twisting metal below and a thundering crash as the car toppled into the water.

The swinging subsided and they were pulled straight up, foot by foot. Tom's interlocked hands soon went numb. It felt as if his arms would rip from their sockets. He gritted his teeth, desperately wishing the men could pull faster. The rain made his load slippery. He tightened his grip. Mother and child were crying. "Hold on!" he yelled.

Finally they heard the shouts of the men above. He felt a blessed pair of hands under his armpits, pulling him up and back. Whoever was pulling him stumbled. Tom fell into the mud and the woman and child fell on him. Glorious mud! They had made it! Someone picked up Billy and someone extended a hand to the woman. The sailor dropped the rope, grabbed Tom by his numb hand, and yanked him up. The sailor's coat and shirt were ripped and his shoulder was bloody where the rope had run over it.

"Good God, mate! Good God!" The sailor untied his knot. Men cheered and shouted, slapped Tom on the back, and tried to shake his hand. Others tended to the woman and her son.

"Get 'em back in the train before they freeze to death!" someone shouted.

"You've got to get a man across the bridge to warn off any on-coming trains, and another man the other way," Tom said.

"It's been taken care of," the sailor said.

Sobbing with relief, the woman took Billy from the man holding him and cradled him in her arms. Tom put his arm around her as they trudged toward the train, dazed and bedraggled. The conductor held his umbrella over their heads. The derailed cars had been evacuated and decoupled, and the remaining cars were packed with passengers staring out the windows at the group. Tom, the woman, and her son stepped onto a car and a man shouted, "Give 'em a seat!" Two women jumped up and gave their seats to the woman and boy. Tom declined a seat but took the blanket a man handed him, sat down in the jammed aisle, and wrapped up. A woman pressed a damp cloth to the bloody gash on his forehead. Injured passengers groaned.

It was forty-five minutes before the train started to move. Tom huddled in the aisle, wet, shivering, and disoriented. Billy cried and Tom stood unsteadily to see what was wrong. A cloth strip had been wrapped around the boy's head where he had been cut. The woman appeared not to notice her son's cries, staring straight ahead. Tom guessed she was in shock and put his hand on her shoulder. She looked up at him, her eyes wide, frightened.

"I looked down!" she gasped. "You told me not to, but I looked down!"

Tom's knees went weak and he slumped back into the aisle, seeing vacant eyes, faces frozen in terror, and a disembodied head.

The train rolled into Cheyenne station over two hours late. Tom stood unsteadily, feeling woozy and nauseated. His head and chest ached. His clothes were wet, caked with mud. He looked out a window to the lit platform. People undoubtedly annoyed at the delay waited for friends and relatives. The conductors had compiled a list of the passengers on the train. This night would go from annoyance to tragedy for those whose loved ones weren't on the list—the dead, floating down the river.

The train stopped. Tom looked down at Mrs. Sarah Davenport, the woman he had saved, and Billy, asleep with his head on her lap. She took his hand.

"God bless you, Mr. Durand," she whispered.

Tom nodded and squeezed her hand.

A conductor stepped down to the platform. The passengers had been instructed to remain on the train until after he made his announcement. Windows were opened for the passengers to hear his words.

"Ladies and gentlemen, for those waiting for passengers on six-eighty-one from Omaha and points west, I regret to inform you that there has been an accident. A section of a bridge gave out and the caboose and a passenger car fell into a canyon. We were only able to save two passengers from that passenger car. We know that one member of the crew was in the caboose. I have a list of all the passengers currently on the train. If the passengers you are waiting for don't get off the train, please see me. On behalf of the Union Pacific, I want to extend our sincerest apologies for this unfortunate accident and our condolences to those who have lost loved ones."

People murmured in low, anxious voices. As passengers stepped off the train there were shouts and cries, much more intense than the usual platform greetings. Tom stepped down. Several people cast worried glances at him and looked away—he wasn't the one they were looking for. He offered his hand to Mrs. Davenport, carrying Billy, wrapped in a blanket. A man about Tom's age rushed up.

"Sarah!" the man said. Then he noticed her bruises and tattered dress, and the bandage on the boy's head. "Sarah, what happened?"

"We were the two rescued from the car that fell into the canyon," she said, her voice barely above a whisper. "Mr. Durand saved us."

The man turned to Tom, his eyes wide. "You saved my Sarah and Billy?"

"Me and the men who held the rope."

"Is Billy all right?"

"He's got a nasty cut on his head, but he should be fine."

The man threw his arms around his son and wife as she cried. Tom felt lightheaded and dizzy. He had to get to the boarding house and get some sleep. He was forgetting something. His bag, where was it? The conductor who had questioned his authority approached him.

"Mr. Durand, the newspapers have been notified about the accident. Your bravery is the only positive aspect of this tragedy. Can you wait until the reporters arrive and give a statement?"

Tom shook his head. "I can't, I need some sleep. I'll talk to them tomorrow." He went to retrieve his bag, but the platform and the foyer inside had erupted in bedlam. He had not realized how seriously some of the passengers had been injured. Some were laid out on the platform, tended by other passengers and people who had been waiting at the station. Two men carried a man covered in blood on a litter. The sailor was supporting an elderly woman as she walked. Tom couldn't leave just yet.

A young woman in a light blue and white-trimmed blouse and a light blue skirt, her face obscured by the brim of her hat, was stooped over a man writhing on the platform, holding his knee. Tom approached them. "Can I help?"

The woman looked up. "It's his knee—he can't walk. I can't support him on my own, but if we could get him outside, people are bringing their carriages to take the injured to the hospital."

He knew her! She was the one he had met at the courthouse on election day. He had never forgotten her. He'd seen her only once since, in a carriage riding away. The blonde hair, those unusual greenish blue eyes, the sharp, attractive features—a mental photograph of her had stayed with him like no other woman's face ever had. She probably didn't remember him, and even if she did, she wouldn't recognize him now, covered in mud. What a time to meet again! He stooped down and the injured man put his arm on Tom's shoulder. He pulled him up. The man hobbled on his uninjured knee, Tom and the woman supporting him across the foyer of the station.

Outside, a line of buckboards, carriages, and stagecoaches had formed a convoy. A man jumped down from a carriage. Without saying a word he helped Tom and the woman put the injured man into the carriage, where another injured man was already laid out on a seat.

"Thanks," the injured man gasped, his face contorted with pain.

The driver jumped up on his seat, tugged the reins, and two horses pulled the carriage away. The young woman headed back into the station. He couldn't let her get away! She walked quickly, but Tom caught up to her. He thought about introducing himself, but this wasn't the time for pleasantries. They reached the platform without saying a word to each other. She went to a dazed woman sitting on the floor, her back to a wall. Tom helped load an injured man onto a litter and carry him to the front of the station. He helped people to the front of the station until there were no more who needed assistance, his eyes never straying far from the woman. She was standing in the foyer with another woman about her age and an older couple. They all had bloodstains on their clothes. Tom swallowed hard and approached the group.

"Excuse me, miss," he said. "I believe we've met before."

The woman looked at him quizzically. "We have?"

"Several years ago, at the courthouse, on voting day."

She stared at him.

"You were kind enough to explain to me that women can vote in the state of Wyoming."

He saw a flicker of recognition on her face. "Yes, I remember. You were surprised that women could vote."

"Well, I was at the time. Since then I've come around to the idea."

"That's good to hear."

There was a moment of silence. He didn't know what to say. "I'm Tom Durand," he finally blurted. "It's a pleasure to make your acquaintance." He did not extend his filthy hand. "Please excuse me for not shaking hands."

"Tom Durand—you're the one who dropped into the canyon," the older woman said.

"Yes, ma'am."

"Mr. Durand," the older gentleman said. "May I introduce my wife, Mrs. Cooper, our daughter, Miss Jessica Cooper, and my niece, Miss Beth Ryder, of North Platte, Nebraska? I'm Ted Cooper."

"A pleasure to meet you."

"Mr. Durand, do you live here in town?" Mrs. Cooper asked.

"Yes, I work for the railroad."

"Would you do us the kindness of coming out to our ranch, when your schedule permits?"

"Thank you Mrs. Cooper, I'd like that."

"Mr. Cooper can leave directions for you at the station the next time he comes to town. Now I think it's time everybody went home after this terrible night."

Miss Jessica Cooper smiled at him before she walked away with her cousin and parents. Tom left the station and walked to his boarding house. His emotions had run a gamut—shock, fear, and horror at the train accident, soaring relief after the rescue, and now anticipation at the prospect of calling on Jessica Cooper. Then he saw, with terrifying clarity in his mind's eye, the mangled bodies piled at the bottom of the railroad car, a vision he would never forget.

Prescott Winfield wheeled his seventy-six-year-old father's wheelchair into the massive library at the Winfield estate on the Hudson, where Tim Harkness and family attorney Micah Baldwin waited for them. Curtis Winfield had embraced the works of Charles Darwin. Prescott, Tim, and Baldwin, having proved themselves the most cunning and ruthlessly ambitious—the fittest—men in Winfield's sprawling empire, stood just below Curtis at the apex, it being understood that Tim ranked first among them. Prescott and

Baldwin were too rich, too jaded, too many years past youth, and too cynically compromised to assume Curtis's mantle. The energy in the room emanated from two sources: Tim, intelligent, decisive, commanding, and Curtis, his dark eyes ancient but still alert, probing.

When Tim was eight years old, he had made a decision that at the time appeared reckless, but in retrospect had been boldly brilliant. Every year his family joined his aunts, uncles, and cousins at Curtis Winfield's huge estate on the Hudson for the Christmas holiday. These were never joyous affairs and young Harkness figured out why—everyone was afraid of his grandfather. They tiptoed through the holiday, holding their breaths lest they somehow offend the great man. Tim decided he wasn't going to be afraid of Curtis Winfield.

One day he and his cousins were having a snowball fight. Curtis and Prescott walked on a path cleared through the snow-covered grounds. The fight stopped to let them pass, but Tim threw a snowball that knocked off the elder Winfield's hat. Prescott stooped to pick it up.

"Who threw that?" Curtis Winfield said gruffly.

"I did!" Tim chirped. "You should know better than to walk through a battlefield!"

The only sound in the stillness was the wind blowing through snow-covered boughs. Winfield stared at his daughter's offspring, seemingly noticing him for the first time. He handed his cane to Prescott, bent down to the snow, shaped a ball, and threw it stiffly towards Tim. Though wide of the mark, Tim shouted, "Nice try!" Curtis Winfield smiled as he walked away.

From that day on, Tim was Winfield's favorite. Towards most of his grandchildren he manifested no interest—they were annoyances if they were anything at all—but Winfield always wanted to know how Tim was doing in school, what games he played, and what he liked to read. On Christmas mornings Tim received the grandest gift, picked out by Grandfather rather than Grandmother, who bought everyone else's present. An exceptional student, Tim didn't ask for or need his grandfather's help to get into Harvard, but Winfield made sure he met the right people when he got there. He had plans for Tim. His grandson had everything going for him—intelligence, independence, ambition, and looks and charm that made the ladies swoon. He would always have options. Winfield's hope was that he would join the family enterprise, accept his tutelage, and potentially assume control when the time came. However, Winfield knew that Tim had to make that choice; it couldn't be foisted upon him.

Will Durand became the linchpin for Winfield's plans. Winfield had kept a close eye on Daniel Durand and his family for years, waiting for his chance for revenge. When he learned that the oldest son was applying to Harvard, he pulled strings to ensure that Will was accepted. After school began, he summoned Tim from Boston to the Hudson estate. On a glorious autumn afternoon, with the leaves beginning to turn, they sipped lemonade on a veranda with a sweeping view of the river valley. They sat in cushioned wicker chairs at a table shaded by a white umbrella, the pitcher of lemonade on a silver serving platter.

"There's a young man in your class, William Durand. Do you know him?" Winfield said.

"Yes, I know him rather well."

"What do you think of him?"

"Pleasant enough fellow. Tries hard to appear that he's unaffected by the social jostling—who's going to get into what club, that sort of thing—but deep down, it's important to him."

"Good, that's perfect."

"Perfect for what?"

"Do you know who Durand's father is?"

"Daniel Durand, of Durand & Woodbury."

"I have a score to settle with Mr. Durand, or more accurately, three scores."

"What are you going to do?"

Winfield contemplated his grandson, impressed that he had not asked him the particulars of his "scores" with Durand. It was important to know when to ask questions and when to keep one's silence. The moment of truth was at hand. His only question about Tim was whether he had the Winfields' trademark ruthlessness. Today he would find out. If he could enlist Tim in his design, he would seal a tacit bargain with his grandson.

"I intend to ruin Mr. Durand, and I intend to do so in a way that leaves no trace of evidence of our family's involvement."

There was a long silence as Tim mulled over the matter. "What do you want me to do?"

"I want you to be William's good friend. Do you know which club he wants to join?"

"He's been coy, but I would guess it would be Bovinity. He'd want the leading club."

"Of course you'll be invited since your father and Prescott were Bovinity, but Mr. Durand may need a little assistance, which we'll provide. You just make sure he decides on Bovinity."

Tim smiled. "I can do that, Grandfather." With that, he became the heir apparent to the Winfield throne.

Now, Prescott wheeled Curtis to his favorite spot in front of the massive fireplace, where he could feel the warmth. Tim, Prescott, and Baldwin sat on overstuffed brown leather sofas. Tim glanced out a window at the flower-covered meadow and a distant stand of pines.

"Tell Prescott and Micah about Durand," Curtis said, turning towards Tim.

"Will Durand approached me. He said that he had meant to go long the shares of Northern Pacific before its big run up last fall but had mistakenly gone short, costing Durand & Woodbury a great deal of money. He felt the only honorable course was to resign from the firm. I pretended not to be interested in the details, but of course I found out the real story. He had fully intended to go short Northern Pacific, hid that he had written a ticket, then lied about it, and his father fired him." Tim stood, paced to the picture window, looked out at the bucolic summer scene, and turned back towards the men. "Those details aren't particularly important, other than that they reveal Durand to be an incompetent, dishonest fool. I already knew that."

Prescott withdrew a cigar from a jacket pocket, cut the end with a gold cutter, and lit it. "Ah, but he approached us, that's important," he said, blowing a puff of smoke.

"Correct," Tim said. "Durand wants to go into politics. He knows we have political influence. I knew Grandfather would be interested."

Curtis turned towards Prescott. "I saw no reason to involve you or Micah. I discussed it with Tim and we agreed that the best course would be to welcome young Durand. If he wants into politics, let's get him into politics. We can't have too many friends in government."

"When I met again with Durand, I told him that he would need to read law before he ran for office," Tim said. "I put him with Moorhead. He's discreet—nobody will know Durand came from us—and he's introducing Durand to the right men around the state. Calhoun, in Durand's district, will be moving on to bigger things. Durand will take his seat in the assembly. Through Uncle Harrison, I arranged a reception with our friend in the White House. Mr. Roosevelt was most charming—I thought he laid it on a bit thick.

Durand was giddy and he had too many brandies on the train ride back. He mentioned a name he thinks is important, and upsetting, to his father—Pomeroy. We've got to turn over every stone in Durand's past until we find this Pomeroy."

"You'll do that, Micah," Curtis said. "Devote as much time as you can and move quickly. I'm not going to live forever. Prescott will smooth Durand's entry into politics, making sure he gets the right committee assignments and so on. Take the usual steps to ensure his reliability."

"Durand drinks rather heavily," Tim said. "And his marriage isn't the happiest."

Prescott smiled. "As sure as night follows day, a man who drinks will eventually bed down with someone—female or male—other than his wife."

"Good," Curtis said. "The only contact Durand has with the family is through Tim."

Tim felt the anticipation that comes as one nears completion of a complex, difficult task. Slowly, his grandfather was handing him the reins of power, in such a way that Prescott and Micah Baldwin would understand and accept the transition. Tim couldn't claim the throne yet, though. He must never underestimate his grandfather; the old man still thought several moves in advance, still saw around corners. Any manifestation of impatience might ruin Tim's chance of ascension. But his grandfather wasn't "going to live forever." The prize was within sight.

"Follow me!" Jessica Cooper turned her horse and set off at full gallop down a path that emerged from the woods to a pasture. The command was superfluous. Tom was always following Jessica; he had to ride fast just to stay close. In New York women rode daintily sidesaddle through Central Park in long dresses, holding parasols. Jessica rode like a man and dressed like one, too, in denim trousers, chaps, spurs, a green plaid shirt, cowboy boots, a white Stetson, and red neckerchief.

He jumped his horse, a Palomino named Thunder, over a small creek and then a fence into a hayfield. Jessica streaked across the field towards a tall stack of hay bales. He held his breath as she made it over with only inches to spare. She turned back towards him, waiting for him to follow. Thunder picked up speed, galloping towards the haystack, which loomed larger and larger. At the last moment, Tom pulled hard on the reins. "Whoa! Whoa!"

Thunder came to a quick stop.

Jessica rode up. "Why did you pull up? Thunder can take this stack. I've done it with him. He makes it over easier than old Sparky here." She patted Sparky on his neck.

Tom stared at her. There was something about Miss Jessica Cooper that bothered him. There had been moments—a hint of a smile, a knowing look—that suggested intimacy, but she kept her guard up. This was the third time he had visited her at her family's ranch—in the aftermath of the accident he was spending many extra hours at the station, but he had managed to get away—and he felt he was involved not so much in a courtship as a competition. She had shot more bull's-eyes than he, pulled more fish from the ranch's streams, and left him and his horse eating her dust. She needed a "whap upside the head," as they said out here, perhaps with a two-by-four.

"You started riding before you could walk," he said, dismounting from Thunder. "I'm not breaking my neck trying to keep up. You're a better cowboy than I'll ever be, if that's what you want to hear, but I never wanted to be a cowboy."

She jumped down from Sparky and looked at him as if she had never seen him before. "Did you…did you always want to work on a railroad?"

"The first time I saw a locomotive, I was four or five. The whistle blew and the steam billowed out and the wheels made that scraping noise against the rails as this huge train rolled to a stop. I could see the engineer up in the cabin, controlling it all just by flicking levers and switches." He stepped away from the horses, which were munching hay, and she followed. "I was coming out of my skin, I was so excited." He smiled. "I still get a little thrill when I see the locomotives pulling in and out of the station. I'm still amazed at the engineers controlling them, how we control the yard from up above, and how the system meshes together across the whole country. It's funny how some of the things you feel as a kid stay with you. You probably felt like that when you first saw a horse."

"Yes, I know what you mean…"

Then they were talking and strolling across the field, their boots crackling on dried hay, simply talking and strolling, a breeze relieving the summer sun. When she stumbled over a rut and brushed against him, he ran the risk and took her hand in his. She did not withdraw it.

Micah Baldwin turned up the collar on his overcoat against the fog rolling in off Lake Erie. He had been standing under a streetlight in Cleveland, Ohio, of all places, for almost two hours. He would stand there until the man he was waiting for left the saloon across the empty street. Hopefully the man wouldn't be too drunk to talk to him. He crinkled his nose in distaste at fools—like his father—who spent their meager incomes and precious time in saloons.

Without self-control a man couldn't hope to lift himself, and those who lacked it deserved contempt.

The man he had been waiting for emerged from the saloon with two companions. "Don't let the missus box your ears for being out so late!" one said, and the other two laughed. Baldwin's man, wearing a shabby, shapeless coat, started towards him, while the other two went the opposite way. Fortunately he wasn't stumbling.

Baldwin approached him. "Excuse me, sir, are you Mr. Bartholomew Landers?"

The man regarded him suspiciously. He was in his late fifties, with a pockmarked face and strands of greasy black hair poking from under his hat. "Yes, that's me. What's it to you?"

"Do the names Cyrus Pomeroy, or, as you probably knew him, Lieutenant Pomeroy, and Private Daniel Durand mean anything to you?"

Landers stepped back and from the look on his face, Baldwin could see that those names meant a great deal to him. "Why do you want to know? What do you want?"

"I want your time, Mr. Landers, and I want the truth." Baldwin reached into his overcoat and brought out a bulging envelope. "For your time, I'll pay you a thousand dollars." He handed the envelope to Landers.

Landers opened the envelope, riffled through the money, and stared wide-eyed at Baldwin.

"If I get the truth, I'll pay you another thousand."

Landers continued to stare. This was the point in the conversation, two days ago, when Mike Riley had told Baldwin to "go straight to hell, you bug-eyed bastard." Riley, a corporal in Durand's regiment during the Civil War, had been Baldwin's first encounter in his quest for information about the link between Durand and Pomeroy. That had also been outside a saloon, in Cincinnati, where Sergeant Riley of the Cincinnati Police Department had been drinking with his police chums. Riley had shoved the envelope full of money hard into Baldwin's chest and walked away as Baldwin stumbled backwards.

"How will you know if I'm telling the truth?" Landers said.

"I'll know."

Landers squeezed his eyes, as if he were trying to squeeze alcohol out and sobriety back into his clouded mind. He nodded slowly. "I knew Durand, and that jackass Pomeroy. We was in the 48th Ohio, during the war…"

Jessica let Tom ride ahead of her. She wanted the scene at the end of the wooded trail to open up as a surprising panorama, without her in the picture. She hoped he would be as taken with what was coming as she had been when she first saw it.

She smiled. This was the first time she had ever really concerned herself with the feelings of a man other than her father. Not that men hadn't tried to win her attention. Cowboys mostly, so lean you wanted to fix 'em a week's worth of meals, scrubbed several times over to wash off layers of range grime, hair shiny with pomade slicked straight back or parted down the middle, Sunday-best freshly laundered jeans, shirts with mother-of-pearl snaps, Stetsons doffed respectfully to her and her mother.

The problem with cowboys was that they spent most of their time with other cowboys. Around women, they were either awkwardly shy or strutted and preened like bantam roosters. She had been told she was prettier than columbines, Indian paintbrushes, daisies, honeysuckles, or just plain wildflowers, prettier than a summer sunset, prettier than a harvest moon, prettier than a mountain stream, and prettier than a two-pound trout. She had laughed uncontrollably at that last one, leaving a boy named Larry so tongue-tied and embarrassed he slunk away.

Tom wasn't a cowboy or any other kind of boy. He had nothing to prove; he was where he wanted to be and doing what he wanted to do. If you meant something to him, he'd kind of open up to you, like a long book. To get someone itching to enter a room, you kept the door closed. Tom excited her curiosity. Truth be told, that wasn't all he excited. Truth be told, she was as sure as a gal could be that the excitement ran both ways.

Tom emerged from the trees and came to a stop. Jessica pulled up beside him. They were on a rise above a meadow ringed with pine, which abruptly yielded to a jagged range, gray and dark blue in the afternoon light, dotted with stands of white-barked aspens. A sea of pink peonies, purple clematis, white poppies and irises, yellow wild roses, orange Indian paintbrush, and lavender columbines ebbed and flowed in a cooling breeze, multitudes of bees buzzing among them. To the right a pond nestled in a bowl-shaped depression. Cicadas whined. Scents of flowers and pine filled the air.

Tom took in the scene, not saying anything, and turned towards her, looking at her in the same way. She held his gaze until he turned again to the meadow. "Beautiful," he said.

Don't ask. "Let's ride to the pond and water the horses."

At the pond, they dismounted and the horses drank. He took her hand and they strolled on a trail that circled the pond, flowers brushing against their boots. He didn't have the hands of a cowboy—too smooth, no calluses.

Halfway around the pond he stopped, faced her, and squeezed her hand. He wasn't going to compare her to a flower. It was warmer—where had that cooling breeze gone? He wasn't going to cast his eyes bashfully down and kick the ground and tell her how wonderful it would be if she'd let him kiss her, just once. The cicadas' whine was louder, ringing in her ears. He wasn't going to ask. He drew near and her thoughts jumbled up. A locomotive—she had as much chance of stopping him as she would have of stopping a locomotive. His lips met hers. She kissed him and then again, more forcefully. Why would she want to stop a locomotive? Her head tilted back and her Stetson fell to the ground. She knocked his off. Her arms were around him and she could feel the taut muscles below his shoulder blades. She wanted his lean, hard body pressed to hers. His tongue was inside her mouth and she wanted that, too. There was her light-headedness and his irregular breaths and the heat coming from their bodies. He was kissing her neck. A pulse came from deep within and moved out through her whole body. She wanted him, all of him.

"Not now," he gasped. "Not like this." He stopped kissing her.

She realized her hands had moved down to the small of his back and she was pulling him to her. Her body shuddered like a train shudders before it stops. She felt a swaying sensation. Her swirling emotions came in short bursts—the disappointment of an unfulfilled hunger, wonder that he could pull back from the brink, the realization that if he hadn't, she wasn't sure she would have been able to. The swaying and the lightheadedness subsided. "Not now, not like this" meant sometime later, when it was appropriate. She knew when that would be.

Two weeks later, Tom rode out to the Coopers' ranch after his shift, although he usually came on his day off. Jessica could tell he wanted to talk, but he waited until after he had exchanged pleasantries with her mother, father, and two sisters and they were alone, strolling through a pasture. Tom stopped, withdrew a small envelope from his coat pocket and handed it to her. "Read this."

She withdrew a letter from the envelope and unfolded it. It was written on a flimsy piece of unlined paper. The writing was a barely legible, scrawling script, in pencil.

Dear Mister Tommy,

Mario not rite me for six months. Then I got letter. I can tell he is not good in his head. Something very wrong with him. He has moved to Portland. If you go to Portland would you find Mario and help him. Thank you Mister Tommy.

Isabella

"Mario—that was your best friend from New York, the one who came out here with you?"

"Yes, he worked on engines in the shop until the war. He joined the army and went to Cuba, then the Philippines. Isabella is his mother. She was a maid for our family for many years, until she got too old and sick to work."

It was just like Tom that his best friend was the son of the maid.

Tom shook his head. "I've been worried. I knew he had returned from the Philippines. He never wrote to me and he never came back here to get his job back. He could have—he was a good mechanic. I wrote a couple of letters to addresses his mother gave me, but he never answered. He was mad because I wouldn't join the army with him, so I thought maybe that was why he didn't write back, but that's not like him. We've had arguments but he doesn't stay sore for long. Now, with this letter, I'm starting to think something happened to him."

"What are you going to do?"

"I'm going to Portland to see if I can hunt him up."

"How long will you be gone?"

"A week, maybe ten days."

"I'll miss you."

"I'll miss you, too." He nodded absently, preoccupied with the fate of his friend.

The tall, corpulent, middle-aged man with thinning red hair wiped his brow with his already soaked handkerchief for perhaps the hundredth time that day. Richard Pomeroy was too old and too fat for this kind of work, dredging a spider- and snake-infested swamp, but when this job was done he'd never have to work again. Only a large sum of money could have made him return to the Mississippi swamp at the base of the Walnut Hills, where four decades ago the damn Secessionists had sent Sherman's army running with its tail between its legs. That was what Baldwin, of the bulging eyes, had given him—a large sum of money—with a promise of much more if he found a body and other "evidence."

Baldwin had approached him outside the foundry where he worked as a foreman. Pomeroy had disliked the dapper lawyer before he opened his mouth, but the first thing he said got his attention.

"I know how your cousin, Lieutenant Cyrus Pomeroy, died."

"What do you know about Cyrus? Who are you?"

"My name is Micah Baldwin. I'm an attorney. Is there somewhere we can talk privately?"

They had gone to a corner saloon, Baldwin drawing a few glances in the workingman's bar. Pomeroy had a beer and Baldwin a glass of water. Pomeroy distrusted men who didn't drink.

"What do you know about Cyrus?" Pomeroy said gruffly.

"Your cousin was with four other men—Daniel Durand, William Farrows, Bartholomew Landers, and Steven Culpepper—when they were separated from their regiment at the battle of Walnut Hills. As I understand it, the terrain was essentially a swamp. They got lost."

"Yeah, that's the story I heard, but nobody said anything about my cousin being with them."

"He was with them. Private Culpepper was wounded. A runaway slave named Ben helped them find their way through the swamp, but he got hurt. There was an altercation about what do with the slave between your cousin and Private Durand, and Durand shot him in the head, killing him instantly. The men buried him in the swamp and swore out a vow of secrecy. That's why you never found out what happened to him."

"How do you know that?"

Baldwin looked Pomeroy in the eye. Pomeroy shuddered. There was something frightening about this lawyer.

"Landers told me what happened, after I paid him a substantial sum of money. I offered him much more to do the job I'm about to offer you, but he refused. I believe he was having second thoughts about what he had told me."

"What job are you going to offer me?"

"The people I represent want to find your cousin's bones and his personal effects."

Pomeroy snorted. "You're a lunatic. You'll never find 'em in that godforsaken swamp."

"I didn't say it would be easy, Mr. Pomeroy. I'm prepared to offer compensation commensurate with the difficulty of the task."

"How much?"

"Ten thousand dollars, with another twenty upon delivery."

"Why wouldn't Landers do it?"

"Durand is a wealthy, powerful banker in New York and Landers knows it. He fears retribution if his role in this matter was disclosed. Lieutenant Pomeroy was your cousin. I thought you might have a different, a stronger, motivation."

Oh yes, he had a different, a stronger, motivation. He had hated that upstart Durand, and just hearing the name was enough to revive his feelings. Imagine that bastard becoming a rich New York banker! He and Durand had traded places; the Pomeroy fortune had been lost in the 1880s' depression. There was his hatred, and there was the money. Ten thousand dollars was retirement; another twenty was retirement on an estate with servants. Baldwin stared at him. He suspected the lawyer knew his entire story and exactly what he was thinking.

"Why do you want the bones and Cyrus's effects?" Pomeroy asked.

"That's my business." Baldwin withdrew two envelopes from his coat, placed them on the table, and quickly covered them with his gray hat. "There are five thousand dollars in each envelope. They're yours with a handshake. Record your expenses and hire as many men as you need. I'll reimburse you. Take precautions to protect yourself if you find what I've asked you to find, and you'll receive the other twenty upon delivery. Don't get greedy and try to extort more money. My client believes in the sanctity of contract, and the consequences of any attempt to renegotiate would be most unfavorable for you."

That was how Pomeroy found himself in the Mississippi heat and humidity, pouring sweat. He had hired a local of dubious character, Slydell, to oversee the job. Slydell had paid off Vicksburg officials—not that anybody cared what went on in the swamp below the town—and had hired a gang of Negroes from nearby shanties to dig it up. The more they dredged without success, the more Pomeroy became convinced that he was on a fool's errand, but for ten thousand dollars, he owed Baldwin his best effort. Somehow, Baldwin would know if that effort wasn't forthcoming, and he was afraid of the bug-eyed shyster and whoever was behind him.

Slydell emerged from a stand of trees, carrying a sword. "Mr. Pomeroy," he shouted. "One of the boys found something."

"We've found scores of swords. What's so special about this one?"

Slydell sauntered up to him. These damn Southerners never put themselves out, never hurried. The sword was corroded and rusted, but there was an engraved monogram on the hilt. CLP—Cyrus Lawrence Pomeroy!

"Get the men to where this was found. Drain the area and dig up every square foot."

On his third night in Portland on a fruitless search for Mario, Tom stepped into a ramshackle saloon by the Willamette River. Men from the salmon canneries, logging and paper mills, ironworks, and the docks drank their stout beer and harsh whiskey. Smoke, jeering laughter, and the smell of fried onions and sausages filled the air. Nobody cast Tom, dressed in clothes from his brakeman's assistant days, a second glance as he made his way to the bar. He ordered a beer.

"I'm looking for a friend of mine," Tom said as the bartender set the beer on the counter. "Name's Mario Bandolini. Shorter than me, dark hair, dark eyes."

The bartender shook his head.

"Maybe he got shanghaied," a man several stools away said.

"Shanghaied?"

"Maybe your friend got drunk and woke up the next morning on a ship for Shanghai. That's how ship owners around here find their crews. They pay the bartenders. Ain't that right, Pete?"

The bartender shook his head as the men laughed. They were making sport of Tom. It was no use saying anything, he might start a fight. He'd check another saloon.

"Your friend Mario, does he talk like you, like a New Yorker?"

Tom turned towards a short, stout man with a nose that changed course several times and an inch-long scar at the corner of his mouth. "Yes, he's from New York."

"There's a Mario from New York at the sawmill where I work. Your friend spend some time in the Orient?"

"The Philippines."

"He likes the Chinks. Goes to them after work—for the women and the opium."

"Opium?"

"He smokes opium. You can smell it on him."

"Do you know where he goes?"

"There's a place on Ash and Third, in the Chink district."

"Thanks." Tom left the saloon without finishing his beer and walked north on a street parallel to the Willamette. It didn't sound right—Mario smoking opium? Mario had a beer or two once in a while, but that was it. New York had plenty of short, swarthy Marios; more than one could have found their way to Portland. Besides, this Mario was working at a sawmill, and Tom assumed his friend would have a job as a mechanic somewhere. He'd track this Mario down, though. It was the only lead he had.

It was still light outside, another hour before the late summer day gave way to night. Tom reached the Chinese district. Some of the men dressed Western workingman style, but many had long pigtails and wore colorful flowing tunics and skirts. They out-numbered the women, who went in and out of the shops with their children following obediently behind. There were white men as well, probably looking for opium and women. Pushcart vendors peddled their wares, shouting in Chinese and broken English. Rows of plucked ducks and chickens hung in storefront windows. Enticing smells floated from the cafés, but Tom wasn't there to eat.

He found the corner of Ash and Third. There were shops and apartment buildings, but nothing that looked like a brothel or an opium den. "Excuse me," he said, tapping a Chinese man on the shoulder. The man stared at him impassively. What should he say? He didn't even know if the man spoke English. "Opium?"

The man turned and hurried away. Tom tried twice more and met with the same response. He withdrew a coin from his pocket and approached an older man. "Opium?"

The man took the coin and motioned for Tom to follow him. He led Tom to a door at the side of a two-story building with a laundry on the bottom floor. The man knocked hard and the door opened a crack. A conversation in Chinese ensued and the man received another coin from behind the door. Tom caught a distinctive, sweet smell, not unpleasant. A wizened Chinese woman opened the door. Tom's guide left and the women turned and started up a flight of stairs.

"Wait," Tom said. "Do you understand English?"

The woman turned back towards him and nodded.

"I don't want opium. I'm looking for a friend. He goes to places like this. His name is Mario." Tom held his flattened hand at eye level. "This high, black hair, dark eyes. Talks like I do."

She motioned for Tom to follow. They climbed the stairs. She opened the door at the top and he saw his first opium den. There were such places in New York, but he had never been in one. The light was dim, coming from lamps with dark red-and-gold shades fringed with beads. Prone bodies lying on pillows and cushions sucked from long pipes with circular appendages at their ends. An old man plucked exotic notes on a string instrument in the corner. Tom had expected a haze of smoke, but curiously, there was none, just the sweet smell. Men in traditional Chinese tunics, skirts, and slippers weaved about, bringing tea and tending to the pipes. The scene was repellant, fascinating, and ultimately, depressing.

The woman led him across the room and stopped in front of a man and woman lying together on a large pillow. Mario was thinner than he had been in Cheyenne. His face was gaunt and he looked older than his years. His black hair was longer and hung in sweaty strands. What the hell was he doing in this place? He inhaled from a pipe and looked up at Tom.

"Mario?"

Mario had to make an effort to focus his bleary eyes. "Tommy?"

"Yeah, it's me."

"Why are you here?" He handed the pipe towards Tom. "Try it."

"No. When did you start doing this?"

"The Philippines."

"Why didn't you come back to Cheyenne? You could've had your job back."

Mario turned to the woman. "Get us some tea." The woman stood and walked across the room. "Shai Ling's a treasure," he said languidly.

"What happened to you?" Tom said, bewildered and angry. This was far from the reunion he had imagined.

Mario stared at him. "How did you know I was in Portland? Mama Isabella?"

"I got a letter from her. She hadn't heard from you. Did you get any of my letters?"

"I don't remember. I think I did. Sorry for not writing back."

Tom shook his head. This was a completely different Mario. "Were you mad that I didn't go with you?"

"I was mad that I went with me." He smiled bitterly. "It's not good to be mad at yourself." His voice was flat.

"What happened in the Philippines?"

Mario took a long pull from the pipe.

"What happened in the Philippines?"

Mario again seemed to refocus his eyes with an effort. "You don't want to know. Nobody wants to know."

"What happened?"

Mario let out a long, deep breath. "The Philippines are just as bad as Cuba—heat, humidity, jungles, and bugs bigger than your hand. Admiral Dewey took care of the Spaniards, but the Flips didn't like their new masters any more than their old ones. They had this crazy idea that they should run their own country. They had to be pacified."

"Pacified?"

"Pacified and Christianized—those were McKinley's words. Guess he didn't know the Spaniards had already Christianized 'em." Mario picked up his pipe and inhaled deeply. "You can't shoot what you can't see. The Flips would attack and disappear, attack and disappear—into the jungle. You didn't know which ones were for you and which were against you. We were on Samar, that's an island. They killed our men, but we didn't know who did it." He looked away at some distant spot behind Tom. "General Smith ordered us to kill everyone over ten years old."

"Everyone?"

"Everyone."

"Did you do that?"

"They were killing us, one by one. We went monkey hunting. We'd find a Flip who might know where his buddies were hiding. We'd hold him on the ground and force water down him, then pound his yellow belly until he told us where they were. If he didn't tell he'd explode and his guts would be on the ground. The flies would buzz around. We'd laugh while he died."

"Mario—"

"There's worse." Now that he had begun, he wouldn't be silenced. His eyes were wide, haunted. "We torched villages. We found boys, huddled together in a trench under fronds. Some of them weren't even ten."

Shai Ling returned carrying a teapot and porcelain cups. She poured tea. Mario took a cup like a drowning man grabs a lifeline and slurped his tea.

"Remember England?" Mario said. "Remember our soccer game?"

Tom nodded, hoping Mario wouldn't continue his story.

"Not even ten. Screaming, running away from us. We shot 'em. Women ran out from the trees, crying and screaming at us. Mothers. We shot them, too." He shook his head. "How can I go back? McKinley, Roosevelt, Smith, me—we all deserve the hottest fires of hell."

Hell had already arrived.

"Go, Tommy. I won't go with you. There's nothing you can do." He took Shai Ling's hand. "She'll take care of me."

Tom was stunned, speechless. What could he say? Mario's guilt would never fade. How could it? He had killed young boys and their mothers. His escape was the opium and Shai Ling and he was right—there was nothing Tom could do. Tom didn't want to go, but he didn't want to stay, either.

"Don't tell Mother you found me."

Tom shook his head. He wasn't going to lie. He'd tell Isabella, maybe not everything, but something. "Goodbye, Mario," he whispered. He stumbled over a man on a pillow, made it to the door, down the stairs, and into the twilight. Helpless and defeated, he plopped onto a bench, put his elbows on his thighs, and rested his head on his fists.

Mario was a murderer, a killer of women and children. Father said war was a terrible thing and it made men do terrible things, but women and children? Mario was gone, beyond pity or hope, irretrievably lost. He was honest enough with himself to neither forget what he had done nor forgive himself for doing it. Why, if the Filipinos wanted to run their own country, didn't the American government let them do so? Because they were "monkeys," "Flips," little yellow people? That had to be part of it. So kill them until they submit. Murder was murder. To pretend otherwise was a fraud that had cost his best friend his soul.

Father's harsh antipathy towards politicians and government must have started with the Civil War—what he saw, what he had to do. Tom had mostly ignored the government and the people who ran it, but Mario's destruction put things in a new light. Government of the people, by the people, and for the people could be malevolent, evil.

The crowd in the packed hall was on its feet, cheering for William Farrows Durand, winner of his first election, for the New York state assembly. Will stepped to the podium but did not speak, wanting to savor the cheers as long as he could. This was what was important, what he had always wanted. It didn't matter that he owed his victory and his soul to the Winfields. No one in this adoring mob knew who pulled the strings.

He turned to Sylvia, standing behind him, and took her hand. She stepped next to him and Will triumphantly raised their hands together, to a new roar and intensified applause. It didn't matter that she treated him with contempt, that they slept in separate beds and he visited hers infrequently. She was British nobility, she said the right things about the duty of the privileged to serve the public, and the press and voters loved her cultured accent and delicate beauty.

Sylvia released his hand and stepped back dutifully as if to tell him that it was time to begin his speech, before the frenzy died. He raised his hands and the clamor abated.

"My friends," he shouted, straining his voice, already hoarse from campaign speeches. "I owe this victory tonight to you, and I thank you for your support."

This sent the crowd into fresh paroxysms and Will waited for the noise to subside. "I'd like to read a note I received from a man for whom I have the greatest esteem, our president, Mr. Roosevelt!" As he knew it would, this created new pandemonium.

Dear Lady Sylvia and Will,

Congratulations on your stellar campaign and rousing victory for the state assembly. As you may know, the assembly can be a fine place to begin a political career.

The crowd roared with laughter—Mr. Roosevelt had started in the assembly.

I salute both of you, for you have forsaken your birthrights of easy luxury for the hard path of service and sacrifice. I know that you share my commitment to all of the people of this great land, to challenge the wealthy and powerful and to uplift the poor and the downtrodden. I predict an illustrious career for you and I offer my humble support.

Sincerely,
Theodore Roosevelt

Deafeningly, the crowd chanted, "DURAND! DURAND! DURAND!"

It didn't matter that he was estranged from his father and family. It was a great story, this son of a plutocrat devoting his life to public service, willing to start at the bottom in the state assembly rather than at the top of his father's firm, publicly deploring Wall Street's greed and selfishness. President Roosevelt liked that story and so did the people chanting his name. This was the happiest night of his life.

It was cold like only a winter day with a tiny sun high overhead and no clouds can be. Tom and Jessica could see their every labored breath. They had left their horses below and were slowly making their way around and over the boulders. Since last summer, when Jessica had first brought him to this lake they had christened Hidden Lake, Tom had wanted to see it in the winter, after a snowfall, its stark, singular beauty blanketed in snow and winter's silence.

He climbed on a jagged rock and offered his gloved hand to her. She didn't always take his hand, but this time she did—the rock was slippery from the snow. They continued to climb until the lake was before them.

It was better than Tom had imagined. Three snowcapped mountain peaks ringed the lake. Wind rustled through towering pines and aspen, occasionally knocking snow from a bough. To the right a creek ran over rocks worn smooth and under fallen trees with icicles glistening from their branches. An eagle circled overhead and another bird screeched. At the far end of the lake a buck saw them and bounded away.

"It's even better in the winter," Jessica said.

Tom squeezed her hand, but said nothing. He loved Wyoming's scenery—plains stretching under the big sky to the distant horizon, streams rushing through chiseled canyons, pristine lakes, and trees climbing jutting mountains, giving way to massive boulders and snow above the timber line. Hidden Lake was the perfect setting for Jessica—beauty deserved beauty—and for his romantic mission. He gazed into her eyes. He wasn't a poet, given to flowery comparisons, but her eyes reminded him of the lake, clear, greenish blue. He had rehearsed what he was about to say in his mind many times, but that didn't make it any easier. He just had to say what he had to say, as directly as possible. They both deserved that; besides, he was too nervous to deliver anything complicated.

"I love you." He had never said that to her. Her eyes widened. "I love you," he repeated. That hadn't been in the rehearsals. "I want to spend the rest of my life with you. Will you marry me?"

She stared at him and Tom felt a stab of apprehension. The hood of her coat framed the face that had obsessed him for years and her cheeks were rosy from the cold. She'd never looked prettier. Then she broke into a smile. "Yes, I'll marry you." Her eyes glistened and she threw her arms around his neck. "Of course I'll marry you. I love you, Tom Durand."

In his anxiety he had forgotten to present the ring as he proposed. Now he reached into his coat pocket and withdrew a small jeweler's box. He opened it to reveal a ring with a square-cut diamond set between two blue sapphires. She slid it on her finger.

"It's beautiful." She kissed him and they stood locked in passionate embrace, witnessed only by the forest and the mountain creatures making light footfalls over snow-covered ground and the birds circling overhead.

Opium and Shai Ling had stopped chasing away Mario's memories, and now the memories chased away sleep. It had been that way since he had seen Tommy. Every night he saw the boys, huddled in the ditch, eyes wide with terror, screaming, climbing over each other, running away from the soldiers, the murderers. He heard the shots and smelled the powder. He saw the women and heard their wailing. A man didn't kill innocents.

Carrying a leather satchel, he climbed to the top of a snow-covered hillock in the secluded center of the park. He sat in snow under an oak with his back against it, oblivious to the cold wetness soaking his pants. The morning was the time to do this, when he loathed himself and the excess of the previous night and his body felt weak and sick, before it craved the opium. Once the craving began, in the middle of the afternoon, he cared about nothing but satisfying it.

He opened the satchel and took out a revolver, a .45 Long Colt, his sidearm in Cuba and the Philippines. He turned the bag over and five bullets fell into his hand. He opened the loading gate for the bullets on the right side of the gun, behind the cylinder. After a lengthy inspection of one of the bullets, as if the fate of his country rested on the precision of its manufacture and the accuracy of his shot, he halfcocked the hammer and slipped the bullet into a chamber. Performing the same inspection for each bullet, he loaded five of the six chambers in the cylinder, leaving one empty, the army precaution against an accidental blow to the hammer leading to a discharge. An unnecessary precaution. He spun the cylinder to a loaded chamber.

He full-cocked the revolver, placed the barrel to his temple, and pulled the trigger. The snow on the ground and trees dampened the reverberations from the shot.

PART FIVE THE LAST BATTLES

Chapter 23

Inquiry

The Durands' coach rolled up Park Avenue from Grand Central Station. The family was returning from Tom's wedding in Cheyenne.

"You're next," Eleanor said to Constance, seated opposite her. Her daughter, twenty-three, had Eleanor's blonde hair and blue eyes. Neither beautiful nor homely, she was blessed with maturity beyond her years, rejecting matrimonial entrepreneurs who would have tolerated mirror-cracking ugly in favor of her eventual inheritance. Six months ago she had accepted the proposal of Heinrich Larsen, a doctor ten years her senior and scion of a Norwegian industrial dynasty. Larsen was a medical researcher, using his family's money to fund laboratories in Oslo and New Jersey devoted to solving the mysteries of disease.

Constance smiled. "Heinrich would elope in the morning and be back at work in the afternoon if he thought his family and I would put up with it. He can study slides past midnight, but his attention wanders in less than a minute when I try to talk to him about wedding details."

Daniel laughed. "You've found yourself a fine man. I like Heinrich."

"Of course you do—he's cut from the same cloth as you. Mother and I are going to end up planning this entire wedding. We'll just have to hope that he can pull himself away from his microscope long enough to show up at the altar."

"Are Tommy and Jessica in San Francisco on their honeymoon now?" John asked.

"Yes, they are," Eleanor said.

"Tommy is lucky to find her."

"Yes, he is." Eleanor liked Jessica, liked her spirit. Out west, women were less dependent on men. They talked more freely, were less deferential, more self-sufficient, and, unsurprisingly, garnered more genuine male respect. New York's aristocrats piously paid homage to the ideal of the dutiful wife who kept her place, then took mistresses. Daniel had never strayed, not even in France. She had believed him when he told her that he had resisted Madame Devereaux's advances, although he might have left out a detail or two. He was too honest—he never could have hidden an affair from her.

Eleanor trusted Tommy's integrity, but he was a man and even the best men had trouble with their urges. He was moving up the Union Pacific ladder and was now a regional manager, responsible for a five-state territory. Jessica had told her that she thought they'd eventually end up back in New York. If Tommy succumbed to the gentlemen's club ethic, Jessica wouldn't feel trapped, as so many women did—she'd be on the first train back to Wyoming.

"Mario should have been the best man," John said.

Just before the wedding, Tommy had said, "Mario should be here," and that was all he said about him. Jessica told Eleanor that his friend's deterioration and suicide had affected him deeply, but he was determined not to let his death mar the wedding. Mario was in a Brooklyn cemetery. Tom had paid to transport his body cross-country and for the burial.

The big coach stopped in front of the family's brownstone on 52nd Street. Daniel helped Eleanor and Constance down. The butler, Mr. Thomas, helped the driver with the luggage. Inside, Daniel went to a stand at the end of the entryway, flipped through his letters, stopped at an official-looking envelope, quickly opened it, and began to read.

"Father, your face is all white!" John said.

Eleanor looked at Daniel. His face was indeed alarmingly drained of color. She had never seen him so pale, seemingly mortified, as he stared at a letter he held in his hands.

"Father, what is it?" Constance said.

Eyes wide, Daniel said to Eleanor, "I need to talk to you in the study. John and Constance, we'll talk later."

She followed him up the stairs and he closed the door behind her as they entered the study. They sat across from each other on the sofas. Daniel slid the frightening letter across the coffee table. The letterhead was that of the United States Department of the Army.

Mr. Daniel Durand
88 52nd Street
New York City, New York
August 12, 1904

Mr. Durand:

Pursuant to the jurisdiction of the United States Department of the Army Military Court under Article 58 of the Articles of War, you are hereby ordered to appear before the Court of Inquiry concerning the death of Lieutenant Cyrus Lawrence Pomeroy. The Court of Inquiry will convene at 0900, November 8, 1904, at Fort

Hamilton, Brooklyn, New York. It is recommended that you secure legal representation. All materials related to this Court of Inquiry will be made available for inspection at Fort Hamilton.

Lieutenant Colonel Paul S. Flint
United States Army

"Who is Lieutenant Cyrus Lawrence Pomeroy?" Eleanor said, bewildered.

"He was an officer in my regiment during the war." Daniel took a long breath and stared up at the ceiling. "We were in Mississippi, just north of Vicksburg at a place called Walnut Hills. That would be the winter of 1862. The Confederates were up in the hills and Sherman wanted to drive them out, to take Vicksburg. Below the hills—where we were—was a swamp." Daniel clasped his hands together and moved them up and down. "We attacked, but the Rebs chopped us up. Pomeroy, my friend Will Farrows, and two other soldiers, Culpepper and Landers, got separated from our regiment. Culpepper was hit in his leg. Pomeroy was the commanding officer.

"We were lost in the swamp, but we met up with this Negro named Ben. He was a runaway slave. He knew the area and we made a deal with him. He'd get us out of the swamp and Pomeroy would put him on a boat to a Union state up north. Ben had some sort of homemade salve that made Culpepper's leg better and he helped us find our way out of the swamp. We were almost back to camp when he hurt his leg carrying Culpepper. He was going to need help walking the rest of the way."

"What happened?"

"We heard rifle and artillery fire and Pomeroy panicked. He said you shoot horses and niggers when they pull up lame, and he ordered me to shoot Ben."

"What did you do?"

"I said I wouldn't do it. He said he'd have me brought up on charges, but I wouldn't do it. Then he aimed his rifle at Ben and said he'd shoot him." Daniel sighed, the sound of battling emotions. It felt to Eleanor as if her next question would open a door to something frightening, and, once answered, that door would close behind them, forever locked. There would be no turning back.

"Did he shoot him?"

There was a long silence. "No," he whispered. His jaw tightened and he clenched and unclenched his fists. "No," he shouted. "Because I shot that bastard right between the eyes! I killed him before he could kill Ben!"

"What an awful choice!" she gasped. Tears came to her eyes. "My God, what a terrible choice to have to make."

Daniel's lips quivered with long-suppressed rage. This was her Daniel, waging a battle between the knowledge that life wasn't fair and the conviction that it ought to be. Most men would have watched Pomeroy shoot the Negro. Daniel couldn't. She sat next to him and wrapped her arm around his shoulders.

"If you had seen this Pomeroy..." He spat out the name. "Pompous. Incompetent. If I had followed his orders at Shiloh, I would have been killed. He ordered men in my regiment to attack a Reb position and they were mowed down like a row of wheat. Then he ordered us to try the same route! I wasn't going to get shot doing the same damn thing! We went a different way and took the position. Then he marched up the hill waving his sword, like he had led the charge!"

"How can they bring this up now?" she whispered. "It's been over forty years."

"I don't know. In civilian law, there are statutes of limitations for most crimes, but not, I think, for capital offenses."

Eleanor felt an icy sensation in her throat and her eyes went wide. "Capital offenses?"

"Crimes punishable by death. Killing your commanding officer is a capital offense."

It couldn't be possible. It simply couldn't be possible. Would Daniel have to stand trial, a court-martial, for something that happened so long ago? Would he face the death penalty? Why had all this surfaced now?

"Who knew about what happened?"

"There were the men who were with me—Culpepper, Landers, and Will, and Ben. They helped bury Pomeroy's body in the swamp. We all swore out a vow of secrecy."

"Your vow…that's why you never told me?"

"There was the vow, yes, and I could see no reason to burden you. Would you have wanted to spend our years together worrying about it? It was hard enough on me, but after all this time I thought I was safe and I'd go to my grave with it."

It wasn't the time for recrimination; there would never be such a time. The initial shock was giving way to numbness, numbness she'd have to fight. She had to think. This was a most dangerous time. She had to think…for her, for Daniel.

"So those men were the only ones who knew?"

"No. Will and I had a friend, Riley. He said something to me later. He guessed or somebody talked, but he knew I had killed Pomeroy. I think he guessed. He was smart that way."

"We have to find these men, find Riley, if they're still alive. We have to figure out what's happened. Daniel you need an attorney."

He sighed. "Yes, the best money can buy."

Three days later, Daniel and Eleanor sat in the office of the man who was, by the light of Daniel's expedited investigation, the best attorney money could buy. Aldus Manse Kincaid was an alumnus of the Virginia Military Institute, Yale Law School, and the Army's Judge Advocate General's Corps. After his discharge, he'd gone to New York, lured by the challenge. He spent five years in the district attorney's office and then established a criminal defense practice. Selecting his cases carefully—"tough nuts, but ones that can be cracked," as he called them—he won some noteworthy victories and his practice thrived. The contrast between the North Carolina native's soft Southern accent and impeccable manners and his opponents' New York abrasiveness served him well with judges and juries.

Kincaid was in his mid-forties, of medium height and build, with thinning brown hair and a neat mustache, a narrow face, high forehead, and pince-nez glasses on his thin nose. He was an intent listener and his blue eyes were alert. "The first point, Mr. and Mrs. Durand," he said after Daniel had finished his story, "is that this is a court of inquiry, not a court-martial. Three officers from the Judge Advocate General's Corps conduct the court of inquiry to determine if there is sufficient evidence to bring you before a court-martial."

"But how can they do that after all these years?" Eleanor said.

"That's a good question." Kincaid stood, went to one of the bookcases that lined his office's walls, and pulled out a thick volume. He returned to his desk and opened the book. "The governing law is the Articles of War, and the issue is the statute of limitations. Section 103 reads: *No person shall be liable to be tried and punished by a general court-martial for any offense which appears to have been committed more than two years before the issuing of the order for such trial, unless, by reason of having absented himself or of some other manifest impediment, he shall not have been amenable to justice within that period."*

"To bring this case to trial, then," Daniel said, "the prosecution would have to argue that there was a 'manifest impediment' that prevented justice from being served."

"That's correct, sir. The argument would be that you and the other men were involved in a continuing conspiracy to suppress the evidence of Lieutenant Pomeroy's murder."

"Would this court of inquiry accept that argument?" Eleanor said.

"The army will be reluctant to open a case that's over forty years old, and that's a point in our favor. However, somebody went to a great deal of trouble to even get this case this far."

"What do you mean?" Daniel said.

"Somebody, probably outside the army, has uncovered evidence. They've got one of the men involved to talk, or they've found evidence at the scene of the incident. Not only have they obtained evidence, they apparently have enough influence to overcome the army's institutional reluctance to pursue this case. Mr. Durand, do you know of someone with an animus towards you, someone with both resources and influence, who would want to put you in legal jeopardy?"

That was the question—who was pulling the strings? From the moment Daniel had read the summons from the army, he had suspected Will. He hadn't voiced his suspicion to Eleanor. She would resist any conclusion of Will's complicity until it couldn't rationally be denied. Will, the fissure running through their marriage. He had to say something if he expected Kincaid to do his job.

"I fired my son, Will, three years ago. We haven't spoken since."

"Does he have money?"

"Not that I know of, but his wife is wealthy."

"Neither Sylvia nor Will would want a scandal involving Will's father," Eleanor said. "Will is in the state assembly and he wants to run for higher office. His concern for his political career would override whatever desire he has for revenge."

"No, he wouldn't want a scandal," Daniel agreed. "Neither would Sylvia."

"It's been my experience that prominent men acquire enemies, known and unknown. Could there be anyone else with influence and wealth?"

"Eleanor says I have a gift for making enemies in high places. Mr. Morgan isn't fond of me, and I had a falling out with Mr. Rockefeller. The Winfields aren't warm friends."

"He publicly challenged President Roosevelt," Eleanor said.

"That roster will keep you out of our finest gentlemen's clubs," Kincaid said. "But unless I miss my guess, Mr. Durand, you're not particularly interested in gentlemen's clubs."

"No, I'm not," Daniel said, wondering how Kincaid had reached that assessment. "Does that roster make you pause as far as wanting to handle my defense?"

Kincaid stroked his mustache. "It makes your case that much more interesting. Let's assume that whoever put this effort together has been comprehensive. You'll have to fund the necessary investigative and legal work, but I'll leave no stone unturned either. We'll hope for the best, but prepare for the worst."

Daniel glanced at Eleanor. From her expression—perplexity, sadness, anger, and pain—he knew she was thinking of Will. It was best to leave her alone. His attention returned to Kincaid, who was mapping out Daniel's potential defense.

The conference continued for another ten minutes. Daniel wrote a check for Kincaid's retainer and he and Eleanor left the office. When they were alone in the hall outside the office, she turned to him. "Do you actually think your son could initiate something that might lead to your capital punishment?" she asked angrily.

"I don't know. I didn't think he could do what he did three years ago. Now, I don't know what he and that damn wife of his are capable of."

They returned to their carriage and rode home in silence.

Tom read his father's letter for the third time. He was in grave danger, but Tom didn't know exactly why. *An inquiry has been opened into my role in the death of a Lieutenant Pomeroy that could lead to a court-martial. I am blameless in the matter, but I must make my case.* Tom slid the letter across the kitchen table to Jessica.

She gasped several times as she read, once exclaiming "Oh, no!" She set the letter on the table and stared at Tom. "I can't believe it. To have this opened up after all this time…somebody's out after him. What's he going to do?"

"He has to stand for this court of inquiry."

"Tom, this worries me. What if they decide on a court-martial?"

"I wish I had all the details. I want to help him."

"You can help him. You've got to help him. Listen to this. '*I have engaged Mr. Aldus Kincaid for my defense. He has a good reputation and was with the Army's Judge Advocate General. His staff is fully engaged and he has hired private investigators. It would not be proper to ask anyone at the firm to help me on this personal matter, although I have informed Mr. Woodbury and Mr. Keane.*' Your father has never asked anybody for help his entire life. Reading between the lines, this is as close to it as he's ever going to come. He's got the best investigators and attorneys and they'll give him the best money can buy, but that's all they'll give him. This is a dangerous situation.

Money won't take on danger, but love and courage will. He needs you. You're smart and resourceful. You've got to help him."

"I'll need to get some time off from my job."

"Ask the railroad for a leave of absence and if they won't give it to you, quit. You're one of the best railroad men this side of the Mississippi and everyone knows it. We've got savings and your Union Pacific stock and you'd find another job in a week. I'll be fine and if I need anything, I've got my family."

The railroad wouldn't let him leave for an indefinite time. What if he had to quit? It was his job, his career. He could find another job, but Mr. Harriman had turned the Union Pacific into a great railroad and Tom was on the way up. He stared at the letter on the table.

I am blameless in the matter.

Something had happened back in the Civil War, something that didn't happen in the "ordinary" course of a war. This Lieutenant Pomeroy had died and somehow his father was involved. Doing the right thing was often risky, costly—if it weren't, the right thing would get done more often. He loved and respected his father. Tom couldn't refuse to help him, not if he was to be the man his father had taught him to be. "I'll make arrangements."

"My father always spoke highly of your father, Mr. Durand. He called him a moneymaker—his highest compliment. I was distressed when I learned of his difficulties."

"Thank you." Tom sat with Terrance Stoddard, a private investigator from New York, in the Memphis office of Matthew Bainbridge, the son of a man his father had met in a saloon during the Civil War. Deacon Bainbridge had been a poker player and cotton speculator extraordinaire, and through the years he, and then his son, had invested in a number of Durand & Woodbury ventures. He had died twelve years ago and passed on the business to Matthew.

Puffing an expensive cigar, dressed in a dapper white suit, gold watch chain stretched across his vest, speaking softly in an unhurried cadence, stroking his gray-and-white mustache and goatee, his blue eyes behind circular gold-framed spectacles taking their loving sweet time on every detail within view, Matthew Bainbridge seemed to Tom as organic a part of the region as the Mississippi River visible out the window. This man could help him find Ben, a Negro who would help establish the truth about Pomeroy's death.

"Mr. Durand explained what we're looking for?" Stoddard said. If Bainbridge was Tennessee then Stoddard was New York, with a brusque disdain of pleasantries that was considered rude anywhere outside of Gotham. He had been a detective with the police department before going into business on his own. He was in his mid-forties, of medium height, beefy, with a florid face and thinning red hair.

"You're looking for a needle in a haystack," Bainbridge said. "I'm a partner in a concern that owns most of the riverside warehouses. We lease a warehouse to the authorities for records storage for the port. There are boxes stacked to the ceiling, but I have no idea how far they go back. Nobody has gone through them for years, but that's the authorities' business, not mine."

"There's no problem if we have men going through the records?" Tom said.

"I've secured the necessary approval, but please refer any inquiries to me."

"Why?" Stoddard said.

"Mr. Stoddard, you're looking for a record concerning a Negro who was a slave. Mr. Durand evidently helped this Negro to his freedom. When I secured approval I didn't mention certain details.

There's also the fact that you and your men are Yankees. I hope you understand."

"I do. Forty years—damn shame some people can't get past it."

"That's easier to say when your side wins. They don't celebrate the Fourth of July in Vicksburg because that's the day Grant accepted surrender after the siege. Some people in England still resent the Norman Conquest and it's been eight hundred years. There are those who are willing to live and let live, but there are others who haven't forgotten, who will never forget. Be careful."

It was a cloudy night and the twinge of pain in his calf told Mike Riley rain was coming. The twinge was the only souvenir he had kept from the Civil War. He wasn't bitter about the twinge; he was lucky to have it. Lucky the doctor in the field had taken the time to remove the bullet, rather than just saw off the damn leg, and lucky the leg had healed, not rotted away.

He had been lucky about some things, unlucky about others—it evened out. People had only themselves to blame for how their lives went. His mistake had been to join the Cincinnati police. Not that this conclusion would do him any good a year away from retirement. It was a job, and with all the men coming back from war, jobs hadn't been easy to come by. It was supposed to be temporary, but then he had married Colleen, may she rest in peace, and soon there were six hungry mouths to feed. To be honest with himself, there were also the stop-offs after work for a pint and a spot of poteen with the boys. How much time and money had he wasted on the Irish curse?

Sure, he made sergeant, but any cop who showed up every day made sergeant sooner or later. And any cop who knew what was what knew which brass to polish and when to keep his mouth shut.

Riley knew, but there were those times when he hadn't kept his damn mouth shut and it had cost him—sergeant was all the further he had gone. He couldn't polish brass. He should have been his own boss. He wouldn't have been a millionaire, like Durand, but he could have saved his money, opened a store maybe, and been his own boss.

Riley was walking home from work to his daughter's house, where he lived. He was on a street full of warehouses. It was usually deserted this time of night, but there, right under a gas lamp, were two young fools trying to jimmy a lock. There was no such thing as a smart criminal. One of them saw him and motioned to his partner. Riley drew out his nightstick as they ran. No use wasting his breath shouting after them. He'd give chase because he was supposed to give chase, but his sixty-year-old legs were no match for theirs. Unbelievably, they ran into an alley he knew was a dead end. These two were even bigger stiffs than the usual hoods and toughs.

Huffing, Riley turned the corner into the alley. He was met by the barrel of a gun and a flash. He slumped to the pavement. A pool of blood spread out beneath his head.

Tom barely glanced at the two pinpoints of yellowish red reflections from his lantern, gleaming at him—just another rat. He opened the box and riffled through the papers. They were manifests dated 1864—only two more years back in time to go. He picked up the box with his gloved hands and carried it to the front of the warehouse. After one of Stoddard's men was bitten by a black widow, Tom started wearing leather gloves. Rats, spiders, cockroaches that were bigger and crunchier when you stepped on them than the ones in New York, birds, snakes (not necessarily a curse; they kept down the rat, spider and insect populations), disgusting smells, temperatures twenty degrees hotter than outside—it was all in a day's work in the Memphis warehouse.

Tom, private investigator Stoddard, two of his men, and two locals had started four days ago, searching in the warehouse filled with wooden pallets and boxes stacked to the corrugated metal ceiling for a record concerning an escaping slave named Ben, who was put on a Union transport early in 1863. They had worked back from 1903 records at the front of the warehouse. Most of the stacks were jammed against each other and there were only a few rudimentary aisles. The front boxes had to be moved to get to the back boxes. A ladder was required for most of the stacks, making the work slow and tedious. Occasionally a stack would tumble, taking ladder and man with it.

"Here's December, '63!" shouted Harris, a local. "We're getting close."

The other men crowded around Harris. There were a few weeks' worth of papers per box. Tom guessed the box they were looking for was in the stack next to Harris, but the boxes weren't arranged in any logical order. Tom placed a ladder against the stack, climbed to the top, grabbed a box, put it under his arm, climbed down, opened the box, and checked the date on the top paper. May 9, 1863—he was close. He repeated the procedure six more times and opened a box. The top paper was dated January 21, 1863. The record, if it existed, might be in this box.

"Bring that lantern over here," Tom said to the other local as he gingerly began removing curled, yellowed, brittle papers from the box. He could make out the faded writing in the light. The documents were mostly cargo bills of lading and passenger manifests. Fortunately, they covered both military and civilian traffic through the port of Memphis. Towards the bottom of the box he came upon a passenger manifest dated January 13 for *The Henry McAllister*, which, from the designations of rank next to the names of the

passengers, was a troop transport. The last entry on the page, separated by a few lines from the names of the other passengers, read:
Ben, Negro, Sp. Ord. Gen. W. T. Sherman, dest. Quincy, Ill.

The needle in the haystack! Apparently it had taken a special order from General Sherman, but the slave Ben had been put on a boat
north. They had spent precious days—his father's board of inquiry
was in two months, and Tom's leave of absence from the Union
Pacific ran out in less than three weeks. Now they had to find Ben, if
he was still alive. "Where's Quincy, Illinois?" Tom asked of no one
in particular. The men looked at him and shook their heads. The first
order of business would be to find a map.

Only in public did Will's family resemble the one in which he
had grown up. When they promenaded through a park—Will holding seven-year-old Gwendolyn's hand, his four-year-old towhead
son Roger racing ahead as he chased a squirrel, Sylvia pushing their
newborn, Henry, in a stroller—Will remembered similar scenes
from his childhood, his mother and father taking the children to
the park on Sunday afternoons. Those had been fun outings, happy
times...innocent times. Now such outings were exercises in career
advancement. In Albany they might run into a legislator or newspa-
perman—opportunities to politic and burnish Will's image. In New
York City they might see a constituent, or better yet a contributor. In
either locale, Sylvia would put her hand on Will's sleeve and laugh
politely, in that English way, at his small jokes, Gwendolyn would
shyly smile and extend her hand when introduced, Roger might do
something mischievous but adorable, and who could resist a baby?

Will hadn't escaped the hallmarks of dissipation: girth, drooping jowls, red-rimmed eyes, crimson strands traced over the flush

of his cheeks and nose. His wife, on the other hand, hadn't gained a stone since their marriage. Any plump park pigeon ate more, and she yanked her few strands of gray hair. Her quick wit and conspiratorial smile still charmed, although such charms seemed wasted on her bloated husband.

Perhaps power was an aphrodisiac. The newspapers had hailed Will as a "natural" and labeled him the most accomplished first-term New York legislator since President Roosevelt. He railed against popular villains—monopolies and the wealthy—while soliciting contributions from both, shamelessly borrowing both Roosevelt's quotes and his tactics, and became a "reformer" by upsetting a few minor apple carts while cozying up to the old bull committee chairmen and behind-the-scenes string pullers. Whispers around Albany suggested a candidacy for either the House of Representatives in 1906, or perhaps, with a little more seasoning, the governorship in 1908 or 1910. The Winfields would make that decision, but Will did nothing to stop the whispers.

He and his wife sought the spotlight like sleepy cats seek the sunlight, but in private the charades of Happy Couple and Beautiful Family fell away. Only after he had been drinking did he approach Sylvia. He regarded the births of their two younger children as miraculous conceptions. Sometimes he went elsewhere, but sometimes he had to show her, and himself, that she was still his wife. She did her duty. Peel away duty and there was usually fear—Will had reached that conclusion in a moment of alcohol-inspired lucidity. He had the usual male advantage of physical strength and the usual capacity for violence, although he had yet to employ them against Sylvia.

On an autumn Saturday afternoon in Albany, as the family left the park, the passage through the wrought iron gate seemed to mark one of Will and Sylvia's transitions from public to private. They had not seen anybody important, anybody who mattered. Like a farmer who knows rain is coming before the storm clouds appear, Will knew his wife's mood would darken. As they passed a newsstand she picked up an afternoon paper and he gave the vendor a coin. She was even more obsessed with the newspapers than he. An article on one of the back pages grabbed her attention. When she finished it her eyes were wide with surprise and perhaps fear, although Will couldn't imagine what would elicit such a seldom seen emotion.

"Read this," she whispered, handing him the paper.

"Banker Subject of Army Inquiry," read the headline. Will skimmed the short article then reread it more slowly.

Prominent Wall Street banker Daniel Durand, cofounder of the investment firm Durand & Woodbury, has been ordered to appear before an Army Court of Inquiry investigating the death of Lieutenant Cyrus Pomeroy during the Civil War. Mr. Durand and Lieutenant Pomeroy were with the 48th Ohio Regiment. Lieutenant Pomeroy went missing and was presumed killed during the Battle of Walnut Hills, north of Vicksburg, Mississippi, on December 29, 1862. The battle was a defeat for the Union.

The Court of Inquiry was convened in response to the investigative efforts of Mr. Richard Pomeroy, the decedent's cousin and a sergeant in the 70th Ohio Regiment, and a sworn affidavit from Bartholomew Landers, of the 48th Ohio Regiment. Mr. Pomeroy claims that Mr. Durand killed his cousin. This charge implies that Mr. Durand, who was a volunteer and a private, killed his commanding officer, a capital offense under military law. The Court of Inquiry will determine if there are legal grounds and sufficient evidence to conduct a court-martial of Mr. Durand. Proceedings begin November 8. The Army confirmed that there will be a Court of Inquiry, but refused to provide details of its size or composition. Mr. Durand had no comment on the matter.

Mr. Durand is the father of Mr. William Durand, a member of the New York State Assembly.

Will felt as if the wind had been knocked from him. He glanced at the byline; he knew the reporter. "I wonder…I wonder why Matlock didn't contact me about this," he gasped feebly. He knew from the sneering curl of Sylvia's upper lip, the narrowing of her eyes, and the slow shaking of her head that withering contempt was on its way.

"Just once," she said, her voice dripping an acid so corrosive no container could have held it, "try looking beyond the tip of your own nose. The reporter didn't contact you because he was told not to. You've told me that the Winfields secretly have the controlling interest in this newspaper. One would suppose that a story like this would merit front-page coverage in a New York newspaper. Instead, it's buried on page eighteen of an Albany rag. Why do you suppose they did that, dearest?"

She had a way of saying "dearest" that was more hateful than a string of curses. Bewildered, Will shook his head.

"It appears they're lighting a very long fuse. They want the story before the public, but in a manner that draws no attention to its source. You do realize that the Winfields are behind this Pomeroy cousin and Landers?"

Unfortunately, Will hesitated before he said, "Of course."

"Oh, you're obtuse. Do you think it's a coincidence that after forty-two years these two men put together a case plausible enough to persuade the army to conduct this inquiry? And that it happens after you divulge the name Pomeroy to the heir to the Winfield throne? They must be behind this. We'd be fools to assume otherwise."

"But Tim never told me they were doing this."

"Most worrisome. They're sending a message to you: nary a thank you for the name you provided and we'll use it as we please. This should dispel any illusions you might have about your place within the Winfield empire. They'll support you as long as you stay on your leash, but should there be any trouble, well, it's straight off to the kennel for you."

He winced. She attacked his psychic sore points with the unwholesome zest with which children pick scabs. "Then they have us."

"Not completely. We could, if necessary, walk away from your political career. Undoubtedly, the Winfields keep their vassals in line by exploiting their foibles. As far as I know, you've done nothing with which they could blackmail you into complete submission. It's vital you keep your nose clean enough to afford them no such opportunity. Retiring from politics would be one thing. Leaving in disgrace would be an entirely different affair."

He recognized the implicit threat, one that touched upon the evolving bargain in their marriage. She would tolerate his "foibles"—the drinking and the dalliances—perhaps even a discreet mistress. Scandal, however, would be intolerable. The thought floated like a softly lobbed tennis ball: soon all he would have with her was this cold-blooded arrangement.

He swatted it away and pointed to the article. "As this thing blossoms, the newspapermen will be asking for comment." He shook his head. "A capital offense. I can't believe he would kill an officer during the war. If he did, he had a damn good reason for doing so."

"You will say no such thing. The silver lining of your Great Northern speculation is that you've publicly broken with your father. We've assiduously rewritten history about that fiasco; here's our chance to further the edit. Your statement to the press will be that the army's judicial processes must be allowed to run their full course and that your father, like anyone charged with a crime, is entitled to a fair adjudication. Privately, however, there will be hints and insinuations—you'll imply that like so many of the wealthy and powerful, your father has something to hide. 'Why,' you'll ask with a wink, 'do you think I left his firm?'"

"So publicly I'll let my father twist in the wind," Will said, disgusted, "while privately I'll be putting the knife in his back. If I had known it would come to this, I never would have given Harkness that name."

"What's done is done, dearest. Now screw your courage to the sticking place."

He stared at his lady…his Lady Macbeth, for once able to hold her gaze. Alcohol beckoned, a mirage oasis in a barren desert. "Take the children home. I have to meet a friend." Which friend, Mr. Whiskey or Mr. Gin, and at which tavern?

"When will you be home?"

"Late." Without his customary kisses to his children or his wife, he turned and walked away.

"Nominally, Mr. Durand, you have three options," Aldus Kincaid said in his dry Southern accent. Daniel and Eleanor sat with him at a table in a conference room at his office. "But in reality you have only two. You can refuse to testify on Fifth Amendment grounds of self-incrimination, but that's not really an option. Jurors are instructed that they should infer nothing from a defendant's refusal to testify. A court of inquiry has no such constraint. If you refuse to testify, it will conclude there's evidence of culpability and recommend a court-martial."

"What are my two options if I testify?" Daniel said.

"You can deny whatever testimony is presented against you. You can say that whatever the prosecution's witnesses say happened never happened. We don't know what those witnesses are going to say, but we have Pomeroy's and Landers' affidavits, which give us an idea. Landers was present at the time of the incident. Of the other contemporaneous witnesses, William Farrows and Lieutenant Pomeroy are dead, and the whereabouts of Culpepper and Ben are unknown. If all they have are Landers and Pomeroy, denial may be the strategy to pursue."

"But how can Daniel do that?" Eleanor said. She had been with Daniel at every session with Kincaid, asking questions and taking notes. "Some of what Landers said in his affidavit is true. Daniel did shoot Pomeroy."

"Mr. Durand has said nothing publicly or under oath. If he were to testify that Landers' account is a complete lie, it would be the word of one of New York's most prominent citizens against that of Landers, who, according to my men's investigation, is an unimpressive fellow with a drinking problem. Sure, they have what may be Pomeroy's skeletal remains with a hole in the skull, but there are many bodies with holes in their skulls at that site—it was a battlefield.

"Consider something else. Mr. Durand, you told me that a Mike Riley either guessed or was told about the incident in question. Riley was a sergeant with the Cincinnati police department."

"Was?" Eleanor said.

"I'm afraid I have bad news. Somebody put a bullet through his skull last week. They found his body in an alley. There are no suspects. I have trouble believing that his death was just a coincidence. What if whoever is behind this case approached Riley, but he wouldn't cooperate? Mr. Durand, you said he was a friend to you and Mr. Farrows during the war. Maybe he wouldn't get involved in something he regarded as nefarious. Then he'd pose a threat if we contacted him or he contacted us. That's a threat best eliminated, so he was murdered. Perhaps fear is motivating Landers as well."

Eleanor shook her head, shocked. Who could be so ruthless? Why were they after Daniel?

"That's what we're up against. If we can make this what Landers says versus Mr. Durand's denial, that's our best strategy. However, I'm worried that we won't be able to do that."

"Why?" Daniel said.

"If that's all the other side has, they wouldn't have gone to this trouble. It's too weak a case. They have something else, perhaps Culpepper, the man who was shot in the leg. We think Culpepper lives in Cleveland, but our men have been unable to locate him. If he testified, with the same story as Landers, it would be the corroborating stories of two former soldiers against yours. That changes the calculus. We'd have to consider an affirmative defense."

"You mean Daniel would tell the truth?" Eleanor said.

"He'd admit that he shot Pomeroy, but we would argue that the shooting was legally justified. It's a far riskier strategy than denial. If there were two witnesses testifying against him, I wouldn't even consider this strategy without testimony that corroborates Daniel's story. That testimony could only come from the Negro, Ben. People being what they are, even military officers, the testimony of a Negro wouldn't carry the same weight as that of a white man. But we'd have to find this Ben for an affirmative defense to have any chance at all."

Daniel removed a large envelope from his briefcase and handed it to Kincaid. "Here's the record Tommy found in the Memphis warehouse of where Ben went—Quincy, Illinois."

"Your son and Stoddard might find him, but the odds are against it. As a former slave his life would have been very hard. He'd be in his sixties now and I doubt he'd have lived that long."

Eleanor stared out a window. Behind two buildings were the waters of the Hudson River. Mr. Kincaid was telling them that Daniel would have to resort to either a lie or a long shot. She shuddered with a dread that dwarfed fear.

Tom awoke with a start. The same nightmare he had had every night for the last two weeks broke through his sleep, leaving him shaking and sweating in the damp, predawn cold. He coughed, deep and aching from the chest. He had run out of the cough elixir the farmer's wife had given him, not that it had done much good. A horse couldn't carry enough blankets to keep a body warm sleeping out in the Illinois countryside making ready for a harsh winter. Frost coated the prairie grass around him. During the day, the skies occasionally darkened with flocks of birds flying south. Tom, lying in the grass, clutched his blankets around his shoulders, vainly hoping for additional warmth. Soon he'd be compelled to stand and greet the frigid morning.

He heard the piss streaming from his horse and smelled the manure. Strider liked to put some distance between himself and Tom during the night, and then for some reason at dawn move closer to do his business, as if he were bestowing a gift. The power of suggestion was too great—Tom had to bestow his own gift. He shrugged off his blankets, stood, shivered, stepped away from his campsite, faced east where the first sliver of gray light illuminated the horizon, blew out his snot on the prairie, unbuttoned his pants, and relieved himself, steam rising from his stream.

By the time he had eaten some dried meat and two ears of corn he had roasted in their husks the previous evening, it was light enough to ride, once again, in search of Ben. Almost a month ago Tom, Terrance Stoddard, and a six-man team from his firm had arrived in Quincy. The town of around twenty-five thousand people was on the eastern shore of the Mississippi River, the western boundary of Illinois, in the middle of the state. Perhaps Quincy had been chosen because it had been a way station on the Underground Railroad that had secreted freedom-seeking slaves out of the South. Presumably there would have been people in Quincy who could help Ben.

Stoddard tracked down a woman, now in her seventies, who had been a "stationmaster" on the railroad, hiding escaping slaves in her home. Until the war, the Fugitive Slave Law had allowed for the pursuit and return of escaping slaves to their owners, generally by bounty hunters. Stoddard endured several of her lengthy stories about aiding fleeing slaves before she disclosed that she had had no such role during the war. However, she guessed that if a slave had been a field hand, as Ben had been, he would have tried to find work on a nearby farm.

Quincy was surrounded by some of the most fertile farmland in the United States. The eight men fanned out. They agreed to circle back in Springfield, a little over a hundred miles east from Quincy, at noon at the courthouse where Lincoln had once practiced law, on November 1, one week before Daniel's court of inquiry. From there they would return to New York, they hoped with Ben. Just before he left Quincy, Tom received a telegram that should have been joyous, but under the circumstances only increased his anxiety. Jessica was with child. She encouraged him to continue on his quest, but assurances that her mother would help her failed to quell the feeling that he should be back in Wyoming.

Tom had set out east. He soon discovered that hostility against Negroes ran as deep in the Land of Lincoln as it did in New York or Mississippi. On the first day of his search he rode up to a farmer plowing his field.

"Excuse me, sir. I'm looking for a Negro named Ben. He's about sixty."

The farmer had a weather-beaten face and a stolid expression. He let fly a long stream of tobacco juice. "Don't know any old niggers."

"Could you tell me where the Negroes around here live? They'd probably have a better idea."

The farmer said nothing and trudged away behind his horse and plow.

For the next farmer he met, Tom scowled and said, "I'm looking for an old nigger named Ben." The tone of his voice suggested that when he found him he meant to do him harm.

The farmer shook his head. "Can't help you, sir, but there's some nigger shanties up the road."

Tom found the Negroes in a field picking corn, and found that they were even less forthcoming than the farmers. A white man searching for a black one usually meant him no good, and all Tom got was "no, sir, don't know no Ben."

White indifference and black reticence were the standard reactions, but with no alternative, Tom continued on his unpromising mission. One day he rode into a small town and found the town square packed with people. A gallows with a noose stood in the center of the square. He thought he should ride away, thought he had no desire to see a hanging, but found himself in the grip of a morbid fascination. Four police deputies cleared a path through the throng for a tall man in a black hat and suit, followed by a weeping man with his hands handcuffed behind his back, and a preacher reading verses from the Bible. The crowd shouted, hissed, and jeered as the three men stepped up the stairs to the gallows' platform. The din of the crowd grew louder. The tall man in the black suit raised his hand and the noise subsided.

"Jack Trice," the man said in a loud, clear voice. "You have been found guilty by a jury of your peers of the murder of Leonard Mason and the theft of his horse. You have been sentenced to death and the

Supreme Court of Illinois has refused your appeal. Have you anything to say?"

Trice shook his head. Even from a distance Tom could see he was trembling uncontrollably, tears streaming down his face.

The man in black removed his hat. "I commend you to God's hands." He motioned to a deputy, who stepped up to the gallows carrying a black hood. The deputy put the noose around Trice's neck, cinched it, put the black hood over his head, and buckled a thick leather strap around his ankles. He stepped down from the platform, followed by the man in black. The preacher whispered through the hood to Trice, then closed his Bible and stepped down from the platform. Rustles from the crowd were the only audible sounds.

Trice raised his hooded head towards the sky. The man in black nodded toward a deputy who pulled a lever that sprung the trap door. Trice dropped and was yanked violently upward as the rope tightened. Some cheered, but women screamed and children cried. Who would bring a child to a hanging? Trice's body jerked, then twitched and then swayed before it hung still, only twisting with the twisting of the rope.

Tom left as the deputies held the body and loosened the noose, bitterly regretting that he had stopped to watch. After finding water for Strider he rode out of town quickly, not wanting to meet anyone who had witnessed the execution. It seemed appropriate that the skies darkened. Soon he was in the middle of a downpour, his umbrella, hat, and raincoat affording meager protection. The hard rain left him cold and soaked, but he rode until nightfall. A farmer offered him dinner and a bed for the night, which Tom gratefully accepted—not the first time he had availed himself of Illinois hospitality. However, the day marked the acquisition of two maladies that had plagued him ever since—his cold and his nightmare.

He dreamed of the hooded figure on the platform. The condemned lifts his head heavenward, then drops through the trap door. The body jerks, swings, and twitches, until death stills its movement. Men in black come for the body and one begins to remove the hood. No, Tom screams, don't remove the hood, but they can't hear him. A man removes the hood. The face of the corpse is the face of his father.

Tom awoke that horrible night, gasping and sweating. There was darkness and he didn't know where he was. He was in a bed, in a little room. Strider was hitched outside. Why had he watched the hanging? He had to find Ben. He coughed repeatedly, seized by an uncontrollable fit. He put his hand over his mouth to muffle the sound and hoped he wasn't waking anyone. He didn't fall back asleep.

He had left the farm early the next morning with a saddlebag full of food, a bottle of cough elixir from the farmer's wife, and renewed determination to find Ben. Every night since then he had dreamed the same nightmare. It had propelled him on his fruitless journey over the Illinois countryside. Each quizzical look, each shake of the head, had eroded his hope, but he wasn't going to quit until his father's court of inquiry. He yearned for Jessica. His one-month leave of absence from the railroad was up. He didn't know if he'd still have a job when he returned to Wyoming, but he owed his father his best effort. He owed his father much more than that.

Today he would ride east to Beardstown. He had to cross the Illinois River to get to Springfield for the November 1 rendezvous in two days, and there was a steel drawbridge at Beardstown. He hoped that if he hadn't found Ben by then, one of the other men would have, but if they hadn't, he would keep searching.

He rode towards the sun on a rutted earthen road that cut through corn and wheat fields and an occasional pasture with grazing cattle and sheep. Strider, bought in Quincy, was muddy brown with white markings. He was what Jessica would call a worker—short on speed, long on endurance. He plodded, but with food and water and a little rest he was good for the daylight hours. Tom saw few people on the road or in the fields, many already harvested. To those he did see he made his usual query and received his usual response. The sun hit the point in the sky that marked the middle of the morning. About twenty yards off the road, Tom came upon a young Negro girl and a younger boy he assumed was her brother. They were playing a game with a stick and a hoop, raising a small cloud of dust. Both children were dressed in makeshift outfits that appeared to be nothing more than modified burlap produce sacks. They played in a patch of dirt before a weathered hut no bigger than a tool shed.

"Excuse me," Tom said as he rode up to the children. "Are your parents here?"

The little boy stared at him and stepped back. Surprisingly, the little girl took a couple of steps towards him. She looked about nine or ten years old.

"They's not here," she said. "They's in the field. Why you want to see them, Mister?"

"I'm looking for someone and they might know where he is."

"Who you looking for?"

"An old man named Ben."

"Booker's grandpappy's name is Ben."

"We ain't supposed to talk to strangers," the little boy said.

"He was a slave," the girl said, ignoring her brother.

Tom felt a jolt of excitement for the first time on his journey. "Who's Booker?"

"He's my friend who lives up the way." The girl pointed east.

"Does he live with his grandfather?"

"His grandpappy lives somewhere else."

"Do you know where?"

"No. Pappy might."

"Can you take me to your Pappy?"

The girl's eyes widened. "No, sir, can't do that. We's not supposed to talk to strangers. Supposed to run inside. Pappy will whup me."

"I won't get you in trouble. I'll tell your Pappy you ran inside, and I went after you and made you talk to me. It's very important that I talk to your Pappy."

The girl stared at him. "What's your horse's name?"

"Strider."

"Can we ride Strider?"

"Uh, sure."

"I'll show you the way. Let me on the horse."

"What's your name?"

"I'm Sally and my brother's Josh."

Tom dismounted. Sally slipped her foot into the stirrup and got on the horse unaided. Tom hoisted Josh and put him in front of her on the saddle. "Hold on to the horn." He mounted the horse, sitting behind the children.

"Through the fields, that way," Sally said, pointing. "It ain't far."

It took less than ten minutes to reach a field where a group of Negroes were clearing corn stalks. They looked up from their work and a man and woman came running up to them.

"Sally, what's you doing on that horse with that man?" the woman said angrily.

"They ran inside when they saw me, but I talked to them through the door," Tom said.

"He's looking for Booker's grandpappy," Sally said.

Tom dismounted and helped the children down.

"What's you want with Booker's grandpa?" the man said. He was taller than Tom, in his late twenties. Sweat glistened on his muscular arms and broad shoulders.

"I'm not sure he's even the right man. Is his name Ben and was he a slave?"

"I ain't saying nothing til you tell me why you want to know."

Tom looked at the man and woman, the first lead he'd had after more than a month of searching. The way Negroes were treated by whites, he couldn't blame them for their suspicions. His father's letters about what had happened during the Civil War had been in the strictest confidence, but if this man knew where Ben was, he had to win his trust.

"If this Ben is the right man, my father once saved his life. My father was a soldier for the North in the Civil War. He and some other men got lost in a swamp in Mississippi. An escaping slave named Ben helped them find their way back. Ben got hurt and one of the men my father was with wanted to shoot him. My father wouldn't shoot Ben. Instead..." Tom took a deep breath. "Instead he killed the man who wanted to shoot Ben. The men made their way back. For his help, my father helped arrange for Ben to be put on a boat that took him to Quincy.

"Now the army wants to know what happened forty years ago in Mississippi. If I find Ben, he can tell his story and it will help my father. Otherwise, my father might have to stand trial for killing the man who wanted to kill Ben. That's why I have to find him."

From the way the man and woman looked at each other, Tom knew they knew something. Some of the other field hands had wandered over. The man scowled and barked, "Y'all get back to work. This ain't none of your business," and they walked away.

"Ben's the one," the man said quietly. "He was a slave down in Mississippi. Everybody knows his story about how he got out of

Mississippi special, on a boat with soldiers. Never heard 'bout a man getting killed, but I can see why he never said nothing 'bout it."

"Did he have a scar on his left cheek and a notch on his right ear?"

"Yep."

"Did he have a lot of scars on his back?"

"Don't know 'bout that."

"Do you know where he is?"

"He used to live here, but now he's with his boy, Willie Bowers, outside Macomb, up in McDonough County. You go east on the road you came in on for a few miles. Take the road that crosses north. It goes all the way to Macomb. You go by Littleton and Industry. They built a railroad down from Macomb—the road follows the track. Willie's on this side of Macomb, in a house by a field near a little stream. You might have to ask for him. I lived up there a spell, so tell 'em Sam Parker sent you and folks will treat you friendlier. You can get up there by nightfall, 'less your horse is slower than molasses."

Tom withdrew a ten-dollar gold piece from his pocket and handed it to Parker. "Thank you. Take this. You may have saved my father's life."

Parker took the gold piece. "Ain't seen Ben for years. He was getting on, might not be alive."

"That's what I have to find out. Thank you for helping me." Tom mounted Strider, waved at the Negro family, and rode back towards the road. Now that he had a destination and a purpose, Strider's plod was no longer satisfactory. However, when he urged the horse on, he got only a brief spurt forward before Strider settled back to his accustomed pace. Jessica could have coaxed more speed from him. The feeling that he was racing time, that every second counted, prodded him, but not his horse.

Tom found the northern road to Macomb. At noon he came to the village of Littleton. He watered Strider, bought some cheese and dried meat, and went to the train station to check the schedule. The next train to Macomb wouldn't leave until the following morning, so he set off with Strider. The town of Industry was fifteen miles away and Macomb was eight miles beyond.

The skies opened two miles south of Industry. Man and horse were soaked by the time they reached the town. Tom decided to wait out the storm. He went into a saloon and changed his clothes in the washroom, sat at the bar, and ordered a beer and a plate of steak and beans. Two other men at the bar argued politics and took no notice of him. Impatience, and his annoyed realization that Strider would make slower progress on the muddy road after the rain, left him in no mood to talk.

The rain stopped as Tom wiped his plate with a piece of bread. He paid the bartender, left the saloon, unhitched Strider, threw a sack with his wet clothes in a saddlebag, and mounted the horse for the final leg of the day's journey. The mud slowed Strider, but although he wasn't fast, he was strong, and they made better speed than Tom had thought they would.

Tom knew they were close to Macomb when he started seeing people on horses and in carts on the road. It was getting dark. Macomb was larger than Industry or Littleton. A sign read: *Welcome to Macomb, County Seat of McDonough County.* He looked for Negroes on the road and approached one man walking towards town.

"Excuse me."

The man looked up. Something wasn't right with his eyes—they went off in different directions. He was in his early fifties, his black hair tinged with white. His stolid expression registered no change. The one eye that gazed at Tom did so with complete indifference.

"I'm looking for Willie Bowers and his father."

That man turned and continued walking.

"I was told by Sam Parker, who used to live in Macomb, that they lived here."

The man kept walking. Tom would have to get his information from somebody else. He came upon four Negroes, two men and two women, in their twenties, walking towards him. They were talking and laughing. He was encouraged; perhaps they would be more forthcoming.

"Excuse me," he said. "I'm looking for Willie Bowers and his father, Ben."

The talking and laughter stopped. None of the four answered him. They nervously shifted their feet and looked at the ground.

"I was sent by a friend of theirs, Sam Parker, who used to live here in Macomb. I mean them no harm. Ben can help me and I intend to pay him well for doing so."

There was a long silence before one of the men spoke. "Sir, Willie and Ben, the whole family, they's killed in a fire at their house last month."

Tom felt short of breath and dizzy, as if he would fall from Strider. Ben was dead. "How," he gasped. "I mean…I mean the fire. Was it an accident?"

The other man shook his head. "Weren't no accident. Sheriff said it was, but it weren't. Me and my brother snuck over there that night. You could smell the kerosene. Somebody set that fire, but nobody knows who."

Tom hung his head as his tears flowed. Ben was dead. Hope was dead.

Chapter 24

Tribunal

Where was Daniel?

Eleanor sat up in bed. The first rays of dawn had yet to poke through the bedroom window. She and Daniel had gone to bed very late and she had only slept, lightly, for a few hours. She was surprised she had slept at all; Daniel probably hadn't. She stepped onto the carpeted floor, went to the closet, fumbled in the dark for her slippers and robe, and opened the bedroom door. Down the hall, a crack of light came from under the door of Daniel's study. When she entered, he was in his green plaid flannel pajamas and slippers, sitting in his desk chair, leaning back and staring contemplatively. He held a cup of coffee over a saucer. On his desk was the silver coffee service. It had another cup and saucer. Had he been expecting her?

He motioned towards a chair in front of his desk. "Good morning, dearest. Coffee?"

She nodded and he poured her coffee. It was still steaming and she smelled it as she sat in the chair. She wanted to ask him about the issue that had kept them up so late the previous night, but something about his manner deterred her. Instead, she glanced at the clock across the room—4:14—and said, "What finds you up so early?"

"Going off to fight was the biggest mistake I ever made," he said distantly. "It would have been even if this Pomeroy business had never happened." He shook his head. "I don't think I gave it an hour's thought. There was a war, men were signing up, soldiering seemed more interesting than shoveling coal, and I signed up."

Daniel voiced regret as often as politicians kept their promises. But he was doing so now, the morning of his court of inquiry. Some part of the war still raged within him, like some part of the childhood of which he never spoke. "You fought for your country, to preserve the Union," she said, wanting him to talk.

"Will Farrows once said, 'You don't fight for your country, you fight for your government.' Lincoln threw Will's father in jail for opposing the war. You ought to have an idea about what kind of government you're risking your life for, but I didn't even think about it until after I met Will. Lincoln was after power, just like the rest of 'em. He wanted a war, for the power. He tore up the Constitution, gave us greenbacks, an income tax, and the transcontinental railroad fiasco. That's the man I fought for, that Will died for. Neither one of us should have joined up."

He said it as if he were examining a business decision gone awry. He could do that—dispassionately analyze something, anything, including his own actions, regardless of the circumstances or turmoil around him. After many years, Eleanor had concluded that it wasn't that he suppressed his emotions, but rather that he couldn't suppress his mind. Everything had to be analyzed and the appropriate conclusions filed in that unfathomably complex mind. It had left her in awe on more than one occasion. Today, on the morning of his court of inquiry, his life hanging in the balance, it was simply eerie.

Or perhaps it wasn't. Perhaps he had made his fateful decision and come to terms with it.

"Back then, you weren't as wise as you are now," she said. "The war was fought and the slaves were freed. You helped free a slave, and now you have to decide what you're going to say to the court of inquiry." There it was—the issue that had kept them up last night, many nights.

Daniel put his head back in his chair and stared at the ceiling. "That is the question, isn't it?"

Eleanor sighed. "Yes, dearest."

He stood, placed his hands on his desk and stared at her. "I'm going to tell the truth."

Hadn't she known that was what he'd do? He couldn't lie. Mr. Kincaid had said the army prosecutors' cross-examination would be relentless. Under that pressure it would be difficult to maintain consistency. Clinging to a false denial would be risky, precarious.

"You'll be admitting the charge against you. Ben's dead. Riley's dead. Will Farrows is dead. There's nobody to support your story. They've got Landers and Culpepper. Mr. Kincaid wants you to deny everything." This was what she had done since they had received the army summons—shut out the fear, the doubt, and the ever-present worry. Force herself to think, always think. Go to the meetings with the attorney, ask questions, take notes, keep track of details, play devil's advocate, understand the law—that was how she helped her Daniel.

"I can't lie. For me, it would be more dangerous than telling the truth."

"No," she said softly. "You can't lie." She inhaled deeply. "Are you prepared to...?" She couldn't say it. "To face the consequences?"

He came from behind the desk and stood before her, taking her hands in his. "I suppose you don't really know until you stand on the gallows, but I don't think I'm afraid to die. I'm only afraid for you, for the family."

She stared silently at him for a long time. "I understand," she whispered.

Daniel was annoyed, but not surprised, by the horde of reporters and onlookers that greeted his family's carriage as it arrived at Fort Hamilton, in Brooklyn, on the Narrows across from Staten Island. Months of lurid headlines and breathless stories about the army's court of inquiry meant that the title of New York's most obscure millionaire had passed to someone else. Fortunately, soldiers in dress blue uniforms faced each other in two lines, forming a walkway and an impenetrable barrier. All the journalistic pack could do was shout questions, which were ignored, as Daniel, Eleanor, John, Constance, and her fiancé, Heinrich Larsen, entered the almost three-quarters-of-a-century-old granite fortress, foreboding and dank.

Inside, Tom and Jessica, Laura and Michael Palos, and Alexander and his wife, Hanna, stood talking in a hallway with Aldus Kincaid. Their conversation stopped and they looked at Daniel and Eleanor. Alexander wore his usual stolid expression. Laura and Jessica came up to Eleanor and Laura took her hand. Tom had come to New York from Illinois and Jessica had arrived from Wyoming two days ago. Tom would follow Daniel on the witness stand. The only good news in the whole affair was that E. H. Harriman, president of the Union Pacific, had decided that Tom still had his regional supervisor's job with the railroad.

"Are there cannons here?" John said.

"Yes, there are," said Kincaid. "This fort guards the harbor." He turned to Daniel and Eleanor. "Mr. and Mrs. Durand, I was explaining today's procedure to your family. We'll be in a large hearing room. Family and friends are allowed, but newspapermen will be excluded. I wouldn't think this would go more than a couple of days, and we might even finish today. I need to confer privately with you now. One of the soldiers will show everyone else to the hearing room."

Kincaid led them to a conference room with a gleaming maple table surrounded by eight leather chairs. Daniel guessed the room was used for officers' meetings. Like Daniel, Kincaid wore a well-tailored black suit. Eleanor wore a dark blue dress that was, aside from her mourning attire, the most somber dress in her wardrobe. They sat at the table.

"Have you decided?" Kincaid said.

"I'm going to tell my story."

"Do you agree with this, Mrs. Durand?" Eleanor took Daniel's hand and nodded. "It's much the riskier course, but it's what I expected." Kincaid removed a timepiece from his vest pocket. "The hearing begins in ten minutes. Would you prefer to stay here until then?"

Daniel shook his head. "No, let's go to the hearing room. I want to see Landers and Culpepper. They're going to lie under oath today, and I want to look 'em in the eye."

Daniel was surprised the hearing room was packed, every chair occupied, people standing at the back of the room. Woodbury must have closed up shop and given everyone the day off—most of the Durand & Woodbury payroll was there. He saw Jack Pyburn, a clerk, and Solomon Raskind, a runner. Woodbury and the Pirate sat with the other traders. Benjamin Keane and Jakob Gottman, sitting next to each other, both smiled bravely and nodded at him. This was his other family. It had a family's jealousies and antagonisms, but also a family's cohesive love and support, defending its own. Daniel's eyes moistened. He took Eleanor's hand as they walked down the aisle in the hearing room.

Daniel was about to take his seat when he saw three men he hadn't seen in over forty years—Bart Landers, Steve Culpepper, and Richard Pomeroy—seated in the gallery behind a table where the two army attorneys sat, on the opposite side of the room. The decades hadn't been kind to them. Pomeroy, glowering at Daniel, leaned back in his chair with his arms folded over an ample belly. Greasy strands of Lander's gray-and-black hair were slicked over a dome gleaming in the light. He fidgeted with the knot of his tie. Culpepper looked as if he were trying to fold his lanky body into his chair, legs pulled in, arms crossed, shoulders hunched as he rocked back and forth. Landers and Culpepper glanced at him, but neither could hold his eye.

Daniel felt his stomach tighten as he sat between Eleanor and Kincaid at a plain table. Three military officers sat above him on an elevated judicial bench. To their left was a witness chair, although it had no railing around it like those in courtrooms. To their right an officer sat at a small table with several tablets and fountain pens. He would make a record of the proceedings. A soldier stood to the far right, by the wall.

The middle officer behind the bench banged a gavel and the hearing room fell silent. He was short and thick, with an unyielding face, prominent chin, cropped brown hair flecked with gray, and direct brown eyes. "This court of inquiry, in the matter of the death of Lieutenant Cyrus Lawrence Pomeroy, is hereby convened. I'm Colonel Cosgrove. To my left is Colonel Meyers, and to my right is Lieutenant Colonel Flint. The purpose of this hearing is to determine if a court-martial is warranted for Mr. Daniel Durand, Private

Durand at the time in question. After opening statements, Judge Advocates Sterling and Monaghan will present the army's case. Mr. Kincaid will present Mr. Durand's case. The judge advocates may present rebuttal evidence, followed by closing arguments.

"This proceeding is less formal than a court-martial and is not bound by traditional evidentiary rules. We are aware of those rules and their functions, but we want to see and hear all the evidence. I would advise counsel to use objections sparingly, if at all." Colonel Cosgrove glanced towards the army's table. "Who will present the army's opening statement?"

One of the judge advocates stood. "I will, sir."

"You may proceed, Judge Advocate Sterling."

Sterling was a scholarly looking fellow, tall and lanky, in his early forties, with a thin face, neat blond hair, and wire-rimmed glasses that magnified his pale blue eyes. He positioned himself so that he could address both the judges and the gallery.

"Thank you, Colonel Cosgrove. The foundation of an army is strict discipline. During battle, officers issue orders that may not be approved of, or understood, by the soldiers who must obey them." Sterling's voice was icily precise. "However, without unquestioning obedience down the chain of command, an army cannot fight. A soldier who murders his commanding officer has committed the most heinous crime possible in an army, for that crime undermines its foundation. That is why it is a capital offense.

"We will present evidence that demonstrates a prima facie case that Mr. Daniel Durand murdered his commanding officer, Lieutenant Cyrus Lawrence Pomeroy, during the Civil War, then engaged in a continuing conspiracy to keep the crime a secret and should be bound over for a court-martial. Two contemporaneous witnesses will testify against him, and we will present physical evidence uncovered at great effort by Lieutenant Pomeroy's cousin and comrade at arms, Richard Pomeroy. We cannot permit the passage of the years or the prominence of the accused prevent adjudication of this matter. Thank you, sirs."

Cosgrove turned towards Daniel's attorney. "Mr. Kincaid?"

Kincaid stood and stepped from behind the table. "Thank you, Colonel Cosgrove," he said, in the respectful manner that a Southern accent seemed to convey. "While killing one's commanding officer is a crime under the Articles of War, so too is the murder of an innocent civilian. Mr. Durand was faced with a terrible choice. He could allow the deliberate murder of an innocent civilian, or he could stop the man who would commit that murder. He had to make his choice in an instant, a heartbeat." Kincaid paused. The hearing room was silent. "The testimony of Mr. Durand and the corroborating evidence presented by his son, Mr. Thomas Durand, will demonstrate conclusively that he made the correct decision. Thank you, sirs."

There was a rush of whispered murmurs—Kincaid had acknowledged that Daniel had killed his commanding officer. Daniel took a deep breath. The die was cast.

Judge Advocate Monaghan stood. He was older and bulkier than Sterling, with a beefy face, tight mouth, red hair, and hard blue eyes. His stood with his feet wide apart—a fighter's stance. Daniel guessed he had probably grown up in a tough Irish neighborhood.

"The army calls Mr. Steven Culpepper," he said in a raspy brogue.

Culpepper stood and walked with a noticeable hitch to the witness chair. The officer standing at the far right approached him with a Bible. Culpepper placed his hand on it.

"Do you swear to tell the truth, the whole truth, and nothing but the truth, so help you God?"

"I do." Culpepper sat in the witness chair and in response to Monaghan's prompt, stated his name, address, and occupation, a bricklayer.

"Mr. Culpepper," Monaghan said. "Please recount, to the best of your recollection, the events leading to the death of Lieutenant Pomeroy. I may interrupt with questions."

"It was just after Christmas, in 1862." Culpepper's voice wavered. His words whistled through the gap in his front teeth, just as they had during the war. "The 48th Ohio—that's our regiment—was part of General Sherman's army. General Sherman wanted to take Vicksburg. Vicksburg is in Mississippi, on the river. Up north of Vicksburg is some hills, the Walnut Hills. We was going to go through the swamp below those hills and attack the Confederates."

Culpepper glanced nervously around the hearing room. "With all due respect to General Sherman, it wasn't a very good plan. The Rebs were up above, in the Chickasaw Bluffs, with big guns and sharpshooters, and they just picked us off. Everyone was running round, trying to get away from the guns. Me and Danny, Danny's friend Will Farrows, and Bart Landers and Lieutenant Pomeroy ran off together back into the swamp. Before long we was dead lost."

"Was Lieutenant Pomeroy the ranking officer?" Monaghan said.

"Yes, sir, the rest of us was just privates. Now Lieutenant Pomeroy, he tried to lead us back to our camp upriver at Johnson's plantation, but Danny and Farrows, seems like they argued with him every step of the way." Culpepper cast a sidelong glance at Daniel. "Those two, they always acted like they was better than anyone else."

"Had there been any incidents between either Mr. Durand or Mr. Farrows and Lieutenant Pomeroy before this?"

"There was, at Shiloh. We was pinned down by Rebs who was up top of a little rise. Lieutenant Pomeroy ordered us to directly attack them, but Danny and Will lit off in a different direction. That's the way they were."

"Continue your account at Walnut Hills."

"We wandered around for the rest of that afternoon and on into the evening. That swamp, you couldn't tell if you was coming or going, it all looked alike. Lieutenant Pomeroy found us a sheltered place under an overhanging little hill. Danny and the lieutenant argued about whether to light a fire. The lieutenant thought it was dangerous, but he finally allowed it. We had something to eat from our rations and went to sleep. It rained that night.

"The next morning we was all tired and wet and hungry. The ground was muddy, and we had to wade through considerable swamp. Danny and the lieutenant kept arguing about which way to go. Later, early afternoon, we heard rifle fire. Not a lot, just a skirmish. Lieutenant Pomeroy wanted to go towards the fire, but Danny wanted to go the other way. He was scared.

"They started shouting at each other—they was both really hot. Finally the lieutenant shouted, 'We're going this way and that's an order,' and he pointed the way with his sword. You could see Danny's madder than a stirred up hornets' nest. So when the lieutenant starts marching off in his direction, Danny raises his rifle at him. Will shouts, 'No, Danny!" and then the lieutenant turns back around. That's when Danny shot him, right in the forehead."

A murmur ran through the hearing room. Daniel gripped the table but kept his face expressionless. Culpepper was making him look like an insubordinate coward. Eleanor rested her hand on his forearm. He had wondered what kind of story Culpepper and Landers would concoct—their affidavits had been vague on many details. He hadn't imagined they'd drop the most important parts of the story— Culpepper's wounded leg and their rescue by Ben.

"What happened after Mr. Durand shot Lieutenant Pomeroy?"

"Will took over. Danny was kind of in a fog. We dragged the body to a place where the swamp was deep and we dumped it there.

Will said that if anybody found the body they'd think he'd been killed in a skirmish. He said we had to keep quiet and if we didn't, there'd be hell to pay."

"Did you understand that to be a threat?"

"Yes, sir."

"Did you keep quiet?"

"Yes, sir. We made it back to Johnson's plantation, and I didn't say a word to anybody about what happened, not for over forty years."

"Why did you step forward now?

Culpepper pointed at Richard Pomeroy. "Mr. Pomeroy was putting together an investigation and he contacted me. I wanted to clear my conscience. When a man gets older, he wants to clear his conscience."

"I have no further questions at this time." Monaghan sat down.

Kincaid stood and stepped towards Culpepper. "Mr. Culpepper, before the battle at Walnut Hills, there was an incident at Shiloh. You said you were pinned down below a little rise and Lieutenant Pomeroy ordered a direct attack on the Rebel position. Correct?"

"Yes."

"You said that Mr. Durand and Mr. Farrows took off in a different direction. What route did they take? Did any other men follow them?"

"They went away from the rise to a group of trees. They stopped behind the trees, then came up the other side of the rise, with Danny and Farrows leading the way. They surprised the Rebs."

"How do you know all this, if they came up the other side of the rise?"

"Uh, I was with them."

"You were with them! In contravention of Lieutenant Pomeroy's order. Why?"

"Well, the Rebs had the direct route covered pretty good."

"How do you know that?"

"Because of the earlier group."

"You didn't mention an earlier group. What happened to the earlier group?"

"Uh, some of them got shot."

"Had Lieutenant Pomeroy ordered them to take the direct line of attack?"

"Yes."

"You say some of them got shot. How big a group was it, and how many got shot?"

Culpepper glanced towards the judge advocates' table. "Uh, it was maybe twelve, fifteen men." He looked down. "I'd say most of them were shot."

"But Lieutenant Pomeroy ordered your group to take the same line of attack?"

"Yes."

"Mr. Durand and Mr. Farrow took a different way and you followed them?"

"Yes."

"Did you take the Confederate position?"

"Yes."

"Why didn't Lieutenant Pomeroy lead the attack, if he was the commanding officer?"

"I don't know, sir."

"Is it fair to say that Lieutenant Pomeroy and Private Durand didn't like each other?"

"Yes."

Kincaid stepped away from the witness. "Were you wounded during your service?"

"Yes, sir."

"What was the nature of your wound?"

"A minié or a piece of shrapnel went through the upper part of my right leg."

"Would that be in the front or the back of your leg?"

"The front, sir."

"At what battle did you sustain your wound?"

"Shiloh."

"I see. Were you wounded at Walnut Hills?"

"No."

"The group that got separated—who was in it?"

"Me, Durand, Farrows, the lieutenant, and Bart Landers."

"At any time during your group's separation were you joined by anyone else?"

"No."

"I remind you, Mr. Culpepper, that you are under oath, and lying under oath is perjury, a criminal offense. Were you joined at any time by anyone else?"

"No."

"Were you wounded at Shiloh before or after you followed Durand and Farrows up the rise?"

"Huh? Oh, uh, before…I mean after."

"So it was after you took the rise?"

"Uh, yes."

"Did you seek treatment for your wound?"

"No."

"Why?"

"I was afraid they'd cut off my leg."

"Didn't your wound fester? Wasn't it common with such wounds for rot to set in?"

"Uh, yes, but one of the men had some medicine that seemed to fix it up."

"Do you remember the name of this miracle cure?"

"I'm sorry, I don't."

"Do you remember the name of the soldier who gave it to you?"

Culpepper looked up to the ceiling. "Uh, it was Jake Blanchard."

"I'll venture a guess that Blanchard died during the war."

"As a matter of fact, he did. Some sort of fever."

"Mr. Culpepper, you said you stepped forward now, after all these years, to clear your conscience. Did Mr. Pomeroy offer you money to testify?"

"Just money for expenses."

"Are you a wealthy man, Mr. Culpepper?"

"No, not by a stretch."

"Were you worried that if you came forward, you yourself might be charged, since from your own testimony you could plausibly be said to be an accomplice?"

"Uh, yes I was. But Mr. Pomeroy and his lawyer, Mr. Tutweiler, worked out a deal with the army. I wouldn't be charged if I testified against Mr. Durand."

"You and Mr. Landers both reside in Cleveland. Did you two have any contact before now?"

"No."

"I have no further questions at this time."

Daniel glanced towards Pomeroy, who was whispering something to a man next to him, perhaps Tutweiler, his lawyer. Culpepper returned to his seat in the gallery.

Monaghan stood. "The army calls Mr. Bartholomew Landers."

Landers stood, walked to the witness chair, sat down, and shifted his position several times. The oath was administered. He recited his name and address and only gave as his occupation that he was a laborer. He did not look towards Daniel.

"Mr. Landers," Monaghan said. "Mr. Culpepper has testified that you were with the group that was separated and lost during the Walnut Hills battle. Is that correct?"

"Yes, sir."

"From the time this group was separated until the time you returned to Johnson's plantation, does your memory of events differ from Mr. Culpepper's testimony?"

"No, sir."

"Mr. Durand and Lieutenant Pomeroy quarreled frequently?"

"Yes, sir."

"On the second day, they argued about whether they should move towards the rifle fire?"

"Yes, sir. It was like Steve said. Lieutenant Pomeroy said we would go in the direction of the rifle fire and he said it was an order. When he walked away, Danny raised his rifle and Will shouted, 'Don't do it, Danny!' and when the lieutenant turned around Danny shot him dead."

"Did you help dispose of the body and agree not to say anything about the murder?"

"Yes, sir."

"Why are you testifying now?"

Landers shifted in his chair. "Same as Steve. Mr. Pomeroy contacted me. At first I wasn't going to testify, but Mr. Pomeroy convinced me that it was the right thing to do. I had another reason." For the first time, Landers looked at Daniel. "About ten years ago I wrote to Danny. Seeing as how he had become a big banker, I asked him for a loan. He never wrote back, not even to tell me that he wouldn't give me the loan. I was mad about that."

Daniel stared hard at Landers, who turned away. He had never received such a letter. Landers' story was almost certainly a fabrication.

"I have no further questions." Monaghan returned to the army table.

"How much was the loan for?" Kincaid asked before he even stood up.

"Uh, a hundred dollars."

"What was it for?" Kincaid stood and advanced towards Landers.

"What was it for?" Landers said.

"Yes, for what were you going to use the money? Or did you just write a letter to a man you hadn't seen for thirty years and ask him to lend you one hundred dollars?"

"Uh, it was to help out a friend of mine, Doug Crandall. He was having hard times."

"How admirable. If Mr. Crandall didn't pay you back, would you have still paid Mr. Durand?"

"Yes."

"So not only were you to derive no personal benefit from the loan, other than that of helping a friend, but you also would have assumed the risk of nonpayment from Mr. Crandall?"

"Yes, I guess so."

"Is Mr. Crandall still with us?"

"No, he died a few years back."

"Let's go back to Walnut Hills. According to your story, when Mr. Durand raised his rifle towards Lieutenant Pomeroy, what did Will Farrows shout?"

"He shouted, 'Don't do it, Danny!'"

"Mr. Culpepper said he shouted, 'No, Danny!'"

"That's not my recollection."

"I see. Do you have the same agreement with the judge advocates as Mr. Culpepper regarding receiving immunity for your testimony?"

"Yes."

"And monetary arrangements regarding expenses?"

"Yes."

"I have no further questions." Kincaid returned to the defense table.

Judge Advocate Sterling stood. "The army calls Mr. Richard Pomeroy."

Pomeroy stepped to the witness chair, took the oath, and stated his name, address, and occupation, a foundry foreman. Bulky during the war, he had run to fat. His red hair was thinning and he no longer had the ornate mustache he'd had during the war. He scowled at Daniel.

"Mr. Pomeroy, were you with the 70th Ohio regiment?" Sterling said.

"Yes, sir, I was a sergeant."

"When did you first meet Mr. Durand?"

"At a card game."

"What is your relation to Lieutenant Cyrus Pomeroy?"

"He's my cousin."

"What happened to you at the battle of Walnut Hills?"

"Our regiment got cut up. The Rebels were up on the bluff, firing down on us. We returned fire, but that was mostly wasted. When it became evident that we were outgunned, my main concern was making an orderly retreat. I helped a couple of wounded soldiers, but we had to leave many of our wounded and dead behind. I made it back to base camp about mid-afternoon."

"When did you become aware that your cousin was missing?"

"Around nightfall. I started asking around and nobody knew where he was. I got worried. Cyrus was more like a brother than a cousin. Finally one soldier told me that he thought he had seen Cyrus running from heavy shelling towards the swamp with Privates Durand and Farrows."

"Did Lieutenant Pomeroy, Mr. Durand, or Mr. Farrows return that day?"

"No."

"Did you see your cousin alive again?"

"No."

"What about Mr. Durand and Mr. Farrows?"

Pomeroy glanced at Daniel. "I heard that they came back the next day, with Private Culpepper and Private Landers. I saw them that night. They were around a campfire with some other men. I said that someone had seen Cyrus retreating with Durand and Farrows. Durand said he never saw Cyrus, and Farrows said he might have been in a group that was behind them."

"What did you do then?"

"I left, but I was mad. I thought they were lying to me—just something about the way they answered me. And Farrows looked over at Culpepper and Landers."

"Did you voice your suspicions to anybody?"

"No, but I vowed to myself that I'd get to the bottom of all this someday. We left Walnut Hills a few days later, but I never forgot what happened."

"Why did you wait so long?"

"I got married after the war and started a family in Cincinnati. I was working and didn't have the time for it. Then about twenty years ago there was a bad panic, business went sour, and my family lost a lot of money. We had to close the steel mill my father owned, where I worked. I went to work at a foundry. I saved my money and invested it. It took a long time, but I made enough over the years that I could start thinking about retirement. Last year I decided I needed to do the one thing I had always wanted to do."

"How did you proceed?"

"I hired a man, Kocher, to track down Durand, Culpepper, Landers, and Farrows."

"What is Kocher's background?"

"He's an investigator."

"And he located the men?"

"Three of them. Farrows died at Vicksburg."

"And you contacted Culpepper and Landers?"

Pomeroy testified how he had found out the "truth" of what had happened at Walnut Hills. He had convinced Culpepper and Landers to testify against Daniel in return for immunity. Pomeroy had gone back to Walnut Hills.

"What did you and the local workmen find in the swamp?"

"We found Cyrus's sword with his engraved initials—CLP. Nearby, about a yard away, we found a skeleton. The skull had a hole through the forehead and was shattered in the back. We found a rifle, but we couldn't identify it as Cyrus's, although it probably was."

Sterling went to the judge advocates' table and lifted a brown canvas bag from the floor to the table. He removed a sword and a sheaf of papers and placed the sword before Pomeroy. "Is this the sword you found?"

"Yes."

Sterling went to the bench and placed the sword and the sheaf of papers before the officers. "Here is the sword, sirs, and a report from the Warren County, Mississippi, coroner, describing the skeletal remains found by Mr. Pomeroy, and the basis for his conclusion that they are the remains of Lieutenant Pomeroy."

The officers flipped through the report and inspected the sword. Daniel remembered Lieutenant Pomeroy grandiosely waving that sword as an extension of his arm.

Pomeroy described how he had contacted the army with his evidence and pressed it to pursue an investigation and court-martial against Daniel. Pomeroy's attorney, Tutweiler, had arranged for the agreement that gave Culpepper and Landers immunity from prosecution.

"What's the ultimate goal of your efforts, Mr. Pomeroy?"

Pomeroy turned and stared at Daniel. "I want to see Mr. Durand stand trial before a court-martial for the murder of my cousin."

"I have no further questions."

Daniel quickly wrote out a note on his pad and slid it to Kincaid. *This is a lie from beginning to end. Pomeroy doesn't have the tenacity or strength of character to pursue this investigation to avenge his cousin. Somebody is paying him and they're behind all this.* Kincaid glanced at the note and slid the pad back to Daniel. He showed it to Eleanor, who nodded in agreement.

Kincaid stood and stepped towards Pomeroy. "Mr. Pomeroy, your investigation appears to be an expensive endeavor. You've hired a lawyer and a private investigator. You're paying Mr. Culpepper's and Mr. Lander's expenses. How many men did you hire to help you dig up that swamp in Mississippi?"

"Maybe a dozen, fifteen. It varied."

"How long did it take you to unearth the sword and the skeleton?"

"Almost a month."

"How much did you pay the men?"

"I hired a local man, Mr. Slydell, to oversee things. He got five dollars a day. The nig—the local Negroes I paid a dollar a day."

"This was last summer?"

"Yes."

"How much have you expended so far?"

"About a thousand dollars."

"How big an area is the swamp?"

"I don't know the exact size. It's large."

"So you spent a thousand dollars and dug up this large swamp in the summer heat and humidity on the remote chance you'd find evidence that might avenge your cousin?"

"Yes, sir, I did." Pomeroy sounded offended.

"You said you had made some money on investments?"

"Yes."

"Which investments?"

"Two companies, mostly, Industrial Bearings and Fasteners and Magnusson Railcar. They're both Cincinnati firms I knew through my dealings with them."

"Which stock brokerage firm handled your business?"

"Crenshaw and Branson. They're a Cincinnati firm, with correspondents here in New York."

"Could you produce records from that firm?"

"Yes, sir, I can."

"Let's go back to the Civil War. Had you met Mr. Durand before Walnut Hills?"

"Yes, at a card game."

"What card game did you play?"

"Poker."

"Did you win?"

"I don't recall."

"Did Mr. Durand win?"

"Again, I don't recall. It was just one card game among many."

"Did you ask Mr. Durand to lend you money after the game?"

"No."

"After playing cards with him, did you like or dislike him?"

Pomeroy said nothing for several seconds. "I disliked him. I asked my cousin about him, and he didn't like him, either."

Robert Gore

"When you started your investigation, all you had was a suspicion that Durand, Farrows, Culpepper, and Landers were somehow responsible for your cousin's death. Is that correct?"

"Yes."

"But you had no idea who might have actually killed your cousin?"

"No."

"Which of those men did you contact first?"

"Mr. Culpepper."

"Why did he disclose what had happened to you? After all, by his own account, if a crime were committed, he was an accessory to it."

"Mr. Tutweiler offered him immunity."

"How could he do so? Before you heard his story, you had no idea that it wasn't Culpepper who killed your cousin."

There was a long silence before Pomeroy answered. "We had informed the army of our investigation and we had reached an agreement that anyone who testified against the man who killed Cyrus would receive immunity for their testimony."

"But we have a chicken and an egg problem, Mr. Pomeroy. You don't know if it was Culpepper who killed your cousin until you hear his story, so you can't offer him immunity, but he won't tell his story until he receives immunity. How did you get around that?"

"We showed him the document verifying our agreement with the army."

"So in effect you told him that if he said he was not the one who killed your cousin, that it was someone else, he wouldn't get in trouble. And lo and behold, he told you he was not the one who killed your cousin, that it was in fact Mr. Durand?"

"Uh, that's correct."

"Did you offer the same proposition to Mr. Landers?"

"Yes."

656

"And he verified Mr. Culpepper's story?"

"Yes, he did."

"How long after you talked to Mr. Culpepper did you talk to Mr. Landers?"

"About two weeks."

"Did Mr. Landers say whether or not he had talked to Mr. Culpepper in the interim?"

"He said he had not."

"But they both lived in Cleveland, so it's conceivable that they did?"

"I suppose."

"Did you ever contact Mr. Durand and tell him of your arrangement with the army and offer him immunity for his testimony if he was not the one who killed your cousin?"

"No."

"Why not?"

"Because I had the same story from Mr. Landers and Mr. Culpepper."

"But they both had an incentive to point the finger away from themselves, and they could have contacted each other, or some third party could have contacted both of them, so that they got their stories straight. Isn't that correct?"

"I suppose."

"It was Mr. Durand whom you were after all along, wasn't it?"

"No, that's not right."

"Then in the interest of fairness, why didn't you contact him?"

This silence was painfully long. "It didn't occur to me."

"And you had heard what you wanted to hear. I have no further questions."

"The army has no further witnesses," Sterling said.

"We'll adjourn ninety minutes for lunch," Colonel Cosgrove said.

Daniel, Eleanor, and Kincaid returned to the room where they had conferred before the hearing began. "My opening statement may have been a mistake," Kincaid said, stroking his mustache. "I intimated that we would offer an affirmative defense, but we could have left the strategy open until after we heard their witnesses' testimony. They've been well prepared, but it unravels at the seams, especially at the end with Pomeroy."

"When you asked him about contacting Culpepper and then Landers," Eleanor said, "you implied that a third party could have been in communication with both of them."

"Yes, it's all I could get away with, but that's the ghost in the room—the unseen hand pulling these people's strings. Mr. Durand, the first time we met, I asked you about your enemies. As you said in your note, someone paid Pomeroy a lot of money to dig up that swamp. A sixty-year-old man doesn't root around a Mississippi bog in the heat and humidity looking for one body among hundreds, forty years after the fact, on a quest for justice. His story was hogwash. And someone put that story in Culpepper's and Landers' mouths. My pre-hearing motion to keep Landers out of the courtroom during Culpepper's testimony was denied, but it didn't matter; they were going to tell the same story. However, I'm not sure that we wouldn't have been better off having you not testify and me paint the picture with my closing statement."

"You didn't make a mistake," Daniel said. "Whoever is behind all this has put in an impressive effort, but their stories didn't stitch together. However, I—"

"Daniel," Eleanor said, "when this is over, we have to find out who's pulling the strings. They want to destroy you, to destroy us, our family, and they won't stop with this if they're not successful. I don't care what you have to do, we have to find out."

Daniel nodded. She was right, but first he had to get through this ordeal...and perhaps a court-martial. "Mr. Kincaid, I made up my mind to testify and I still think it's the right thing to do. I'll be telling the truth and the truth doesn't unravel."

"I couldn't agree with you more, but I worry about two things. You're going to be admitting that you killed your commanding officer. It was justified, but the army doesn't cotton to soldiers killing their commanding officers. I also worry about that hand pulling the strings. I stayed away from the cozy arrangement Pomeroy's attorney, Tutweiler, seems to have with the army, being able to offer immunity. It wouldn't be good tactics to suggest army impropriety at an army hearing. But officers' badges of rank don't render them impervious to influence or bribes. That unseen hand might have its thumb on the scale of justice."

"Do you promise to tell the truth, the whole truth, and nothing but the truth, so help you God?"

Daniel stood at the front of the hearing room with his hand on the Bible. "Yes, I do." He took his seat in the witness chair feeling as if he were back on a battlefield. Then it had been load your rifle, find a target, ignore the miniés, pull the trigger, then repeat the routine, over and over. Today, it was tell the truth, slowly and clearly, the whole truth and nothing but the truth, without hesitation or equivocation. He swallowed—his mouth was dry—and took a deep breath.

Kincaid stepped towards him. "State your name, address, and occupation."

"Daniel Durand, eighty-eight 52nd Street, here in New York. I'm the managing partner of Durand & Woodbury."

"Mr. Durand. when did you first meet Lieutenant Pomeroy?"

"Not long after I volunteered for the army, in February of 1862."

"What was your impression of Pomeroy?"

"He was pompous. I didn't like him."

"When did you first see him in battle?"

"At Shiloh."

"Mr. Culpepper mentioned an incident at Shiloh, in which you supposedly disobeyed an order from Lieutenant Pomeroy. Please explain what happened."

"We got pinned down by a Confederate unit at the top of a small hill. There were about thirty of us, including Lieutenant Pomeroy. He ordered half the men to directly attack the hill. They were all shot before they made it halfway up the hill. Then Pomeroy ordered the rest of us to take the same route up the hill. It was lunacy. We were all certain to get killed, just like the first group. So Will and I took a different route where we could loop around more towards the side of the hill, under cover of some trees. The rest of the men followed. Nobody wanted to get killed."

"Did that include Mr. Culpepper or Mr. Landers?"

"Culpepper, but I don't think Landers was part of our group."

"Was Lieutenant Pomeroy with you?"

"No, he stayed behind."

"Did you take the hill?"

"We surprised the Confederates and after some hand-to-hand fighting, they retreated. That's when Pomeroy came up, waving his sword as if he had led the charge. After that, I despised him and did my best to stay away from him."

"Were there any other incidents with the lieutenant that day?"

"No."

"And the history books tell us that the Union repelled the Confederate advance. Was it after this battle that you met the lieutenant's cousin, Richard Pomeroy?"

"Yes. I played cards with him and a group of men in a Memphis tavern. Richard Pomeroy was a sergeant. He wasn't a very good player and he drank. He lost quite a bit of money. After the game, on the way back to Fort Pickering, where we were stationed, he asked me to lend him five dollars. I didn't want to lend it to him, but I didn't have much of a choice. He was an officer and I was a private."

"Did he pay you back?"

"No. I decided he was cut from the same cloth as his cousin, so I stayed away from him, too."

"Did you have other significant encounters with either Lieutenant Pomeroy or Sergeant Pomeroy from that time until the incidents at Walnut Hills?"

"No."

"Please tell us what happened at Walnut Hills."

Daniel told his story. He, Farrows, Landers, Culpepper, and Lieutenant Pomeroy, fleeing Confederate shelling, had gotten separated from the rest of the fighting force and then lost in the swamp below Walnut Hills. For the first time the hearing room heard that Culpepper had received his wound at Walnut Hills, not Shiloh, and about the escaping slave, Ben.

"After Ben accosted you, did you tell Lieutenant Pomeroy about him?" Kincaid asked.

"Yes. He and Pomeroy came to an agreement. Ben knew the swamp and would lead us back to Johnson's plantation if Pomeroy would get him on a boat north up the Mississippi."

"Lieutenant Pomeroy promised to do that?"

"Yes, as an officer and a gentleman."

"Did you then start back, with Ben leading the way?"

"Culpepper's leg was wounded and he was having trouble walking. In that swamp, even small cuts would puff up and fill with pus. Ben had some sort of salve he said his mother cooked up. It smelled terrible and we had to hold Culpepper down and keep him quiet when Ben put it on, but it worked. Steve's wound didn't seem to trouble him as much as it had and he could walk more easily. It didn't puff up, and he was able to sleep that night. It rained, but Ben found us a little hollow under a hill and we didn't get too wet."

"What happened the next day?"

"Ben caught a catfish and some crawfish, which they eat in that part of the country, and cooked us breakfast. Then we set out for Johnson's plantation. Ben knew where he was going and we made good progress, although we had to stop every so often and let Culpepper rest. About noon we came to a swampy place. Ben said we could cross it since the water was only waist-deep. We had stayed out of any deep water because of Steve's leg. Ben said it would take an extra hour to go around the swamp, and he could carry Steve across. Ben put Steve on his shoulders and we were almost across when Ben stumbled and wrenched his knee, but he didn't drop Steve. Ben's knee was swelling up when he got to the other side. He said he needed some help to walk the rest of the way.

"I offered to help Ben, but about that time we heard rifle fire close by. Pomeroy panicked. He said we'd have to leave Ben—it would slow us up too much to bring him. I said I wouldn't leave Ben there. Pomeroy ordered me to leave Ben and I said I wouldn't. He asked me if I was disobeying an order and I said that I was. He said we'd have to shoot Ben, that's what you did with horses and Negroes—he said 'niggers'—when they pulled up lame. He ordered me to shoot Ben and threatened to bring me up on charges if I didn't. He was furious, shouting at me."

"Did you comply with that order?"

"No. I said I wouldn't do it. Then Pomeroy said he would, and he pointed his rifle at him."

"What did you do?"

Daniel was suddenly struck by the silence in the room. He had never heard so many people so quiet. He glanced at Eleanor. Her expression grave, she nodded as if to say: do what you must. "I shot him…before he could shoot Ben. I shot him in the head and killed him."

There were gasps and murmurs. Cosgrove tapped his gavel.

"What happened after that?"

"I was in a daze. Will, Steve, and Bart threw Pomeroy's body and rifle in the swamp and we made it to the road to Johnson's plantation. Will said we had to get our story straight. We agreed to say we hadn't seen Pomeroy and that he wasn't with us."

"That's what you told everybody, including Sergeant Pomeroy, when you got back to Johnson's plantation?"

"Yes."

"To the best of your knowledge, did everyone stick to that agreement?"

"I'm not sure. Will and I had a friend, Corporal Mike Riley, and he said something to me once—that he was glad I had killed Lieutenant Pomeroy. I don't know if he guessed what had happened, or if one of the other men told him. I asked, but he wouldn't say."

"Is Mr. Riley still alive?"

"Objection," Monaghan shouted, standing. "Irrelevant."

"It's relevant," Kincaid said. "He could be a corroborating witness."

"Overruled." Colonel Cosgrove said.

"Riley was a policeman in Cincinnati and was recently shot and killed," Daniel said. "Nobody has been apprehended or charged." This set off new murmuring.

"Why did you feel that you couldn't disclose the truth?"

"A court-martial back then wouldn't be like this, with lawyers and a fair chance to tell your story. Killing your commanding officer was the worst thing you could do, a capital offense. That's all the officers hearing our case would have cared about—that I admitted killing my commanding officer, and that Will, Steve, and Bart helped cover it up. They wouldn't have cared about why I killed Pomeroy, just that I had done so and that the other men helped hide the truth."

"Did you tell anybody the truth?"

"Not until I received the summons to this hearing. I told Eleanor and some other people who are close to me."

"Did Ben receive passage on a boat up the Mississippi River?"

"Yes, he did."

"Did you ever receive a letter from Mr. Landers asking for a loan?"

"No."

"I have no further questions."

Daniel glanced at Monaghan and Sterling, huddled together, hashing out their strategy of cross-examination. Monaghan stood and approached Daniel. Daniel felt a stab of apprehension.

"Mr. Durand, you, William Farrows, Mr. Culpepper, Mr. Landers, and Lieutenant Pomeroy were separated from your regiment at Walnut Hills and got lost in the swamp. You said Mr. Culpepper was wounded in the leg, is that correct?"

"Yes."

"And you say you were accosted by an escaping slave named Ben, who subsequently helped you back to Johnson's plantation. Is that correct?"

"Yes."

"You're not presenting Ben as a witness?"

"No, he's dead."

"By your account this Ben, if he existed at all, was in the middle of the unpleasantness between you and Lieutenant Pomeroy. What were you thinking when you shot the lieutenant?"

"I was thinking that at the first sign of trouble Pomeroy was going to kill Ben, who had kept up his end of the bargain and who had been helpful at every turn. He was panicking and I had to make a choice between him and Ben."

"But you had to make that choice instantaneously?"

"Yes."

"How could all that run through your head? Didn't you just act out of your admitted antipathy towards Lieutenant Pomeroy?"

"No. If I had had time for a fully reasoned deliberation on the matter, I still would have done exactly what I did. I've never regretted it. It's true I didn't like Pomeroy, but he was in the wrong and he was going to kill the man who was in the right. I had to stop him."

"But you didn't think that military justice would comport with your idea of justice?"

"No."

"So you've hidden what you did for all these years?"

"Yes. I don't like hiding the truth, but let me tell you something, Mr. Monaghan. If Pomeroy had killed Ben, I wouldn't have had to hide anything. Nobody would have inquired about the death of a slave, and even if the truth had come to light, nobody would have cared. There was a great deal of prejudice towards Negroes within the Union and the army, even though we were fighting to free them. If I had let Pomeroy kill Ben and then gone along with it, I would have gotten away with it, but I wouldn't have been able to live with myself. I'd rather have done what I did and hidden the truth, have it disclosed, stand for a court-martial and then on the gallows, if that's to be my fate, than not to have pulled the trigger that day. I have no remorse."

It seemed to Daniel that everyone in the room stared at him. Except Eleanor—her eyes were closed, her face skewed in a tormented grimace.

"I have no further questions," Monaghan said gruffly, returning to his table.

Daniel stood and returned to the defense table. Eleanor squeezed his hand, but her expression was grave.

"Mr. Thomas Durand," Kincaid said, standing.

Tom, sitting between Jessica and Laura, stood and made his way to the front of the hearing room. He took the oath and Kincaid began his questioning.

"Mr. Durand, state your occupation and place of residence."

"I'm a regional supervisor for the Union Pacific railroad in Cheyenne, Wyoming."

"Please describe your efforts to uncover evidence related to the incident in question."

"I went to Memphis, Tennessee, two months ago and received permission from Matthew Bainbridge, the owner of a warehouse, to go through shipping records stored there. The records went back to the Civil War. Several men from the Terrance Stoddard Detective Agency, including Mr. Stoddard, a couple of local men, and I searched the warehouse. Boxes were stacked to the ceiling and we had to sort through more than forty years of records."

Kincaid walked to the defense table and picked up a piece of cardboard with a yellowed document on top of it. He carried it to Tom.

"Did you find this document in that warehouse?"

"Yes." Kincaid took the manifest from Tom and put it before the officers, who studied it for several minutes. He showed it to the army lawyers. Finally he returned it to Tom.

"Would you please read to the court the relevant sections of this document?"

"At the top it says *Passenger Manifest, The Henry McAllister.* It's dated January 13, 1863. At the bottom here is a notation, *Ben, Negro, Sp. Ord. Gen. W.T. Sherman, dest. Quincy, Ill.*"

"What did you do after you found this manifest?" Kincaid asked.

"Mr. Stoddard and his men and I went to Quincy. We made inquiries there, and fanned out over the surrounding countryside. We guessed that Ben might have gone to work on a farm somewhere, but we didn't know. Finally, after a few weeks, I met a Negro man, Sam Parker, who knew about Ben. He said that Ben had been a slave—"

"Objection," Monaghan said. "Hearsay."

"We're not going to produce everyone Tom talked to in Illinois for a court of inquiry," Kincaid said. "But we can if further proceedings make it necessary."

"Overruled," Colonel Cosgrove said.

"Continue, Mr. Durand."

"Sam Parker said that Ben had helped some lost soldiers during the Civil War, and that he had been put on a troop transport to Quincy. My father had written me that Ben had a scar on his left cheek and a notch on his right ear. Mr. Parker said this Ben had such a scar and the notched ear. He said Ben had gone to live with his son, Willie Bowers, near Macomb, Illinois. So I rode to Macomb."

"Did you find Ben?"

"No. A local Negro man told me that Ben had died with his family in a fire about a month before. I asked him if the fire had been an accident. He said—"

"Objection," Monaghan shouted. "Hearsay and relevance. This answer will be speculative and may be prejudicial."

"Overruled."

"The man told me that the local police said it was an accident, but that he had gone to the scene of the fire and smelled kerosene. He said the fire had been set, although he didn't know by whom."

"The man that you talked to, did you find out his name?"

"Yes, Isaiah Daniels."

"No further questions."

Monaghan stood and advanced towards the witness box. "Mr. Durand, you can't conclusively state that the Ben on that manifest is the same Ben who allegedly helped your father?"

"No."

"Nor can you conclusively state that the Ben whom Sam Parker told you about in Illinois is the same Ben that was on that manifest?"

"No."

"No further questions."

Tom returned to his seat. Kincaid stood and said, "We have no other witnesses."

"We'll take a short recess and then hear closing arguments," Colonel Cosgrove said.

"On one point there is agreement," Judge Advocate Sterling said, beginning his closing argument, facing the three officers. "Mr. Daniel Durand shot and killed his commanding officer, Lieutenant Cyrus Pomeroy, at Walnut Hills, Mississippi. However, we've heard contradictory accounts of the circumstances of that shooting. We've heard the corroborating accounts of Mr. Culpepper and Mr. Landers that Mr. Durand and Lieutenant Pomeroy argued about the direction their group should take to return to Johnson's plantation, and that when ordered to go one direction, Mr. Durand refused and shot the lieutenant. Absent from those corroborating accounts is any mention of a supposed escaping slave named Ben, who serves as the linchpin for Mr. Durand's attempted defense of his actions.

"Our burden is not to prove to a certainty that Mr. Durand's un-corroborated account of events is false, although we believe that task is imminently feasible, but to establish a prima facie case against Mr. Durand, and to demonstrate that there are issues of law and fact that can only be decided by a court-martial. Keep in mind that Mr. Kincaid didn't put a dent in the corroborating accounts of Mr. Culpepper and Mr. Landers, or in Mr. Pomeroy's account of his quest to uncover the truth about the murder of his cousin.

"Let's assume, hypothetically against the weight of the evidence, that Mr. Durand's story is the correct one. Then the question becomes: Was Mr. Durand's shooting of Lieutenant Pomeroy, his commanding officer, justified under military law? That, I would suggest, is a question best addressed in a court-martial, with its procedural protections for the accused and the full range of evidentiary safeguards that would require the defense to substantiate its witnesses' stories, especially that of Mr. Thomas Durand concerning the people from whom he allegedly received information in Illinois. Not because of any limitations of those who hear the evidence, but because of the limitations of a court of inquiry, a court-martial is the best forum to adjudicate the questions of both fact and law that this case presents. Thank you, sirs."

The brevity of Sterling's closing argument surprised Daniel, who had met too many attorneys who were paid by the word. How would Kincaid respond?

Kincaid looked over a tablet containing his notes, stood, and approached the officers. "The judge advocate is saying wait until next time and then we'll show you that Mr. Durand's story is false, because they haven't made any such demonstration during this hearing. The assertion was made that Culpepper's, Landers', and Pomeroy's stories are not dented, which is wrong. Mr. Durand's testimony, on the other hand, is untouched, pristine. During the noon recess, Mr. Durand told me that 'the truth doesn't unravel,' and Mr. Monaghan's cross-examination couldn't pick a stitch.

"However, we are told that Mr. Durand's testimony was uncorroborated. Mr. Durand said that an escaping slave, Ben, helped his wayward group back to Johnson's plantation, among other things cooking them breakfast and administering some sort of home-brewed but effective salve to Mr. Culpepper's wounded leg. Ben made a deal with Lieutenant Pomeroy, which the lieutenant breached, and Daniel shot Pomeroy to prevent him from shooting Ben. They returned to camp and Daniel and Will Farrows kept their end of the bargain, seeing that Ben was put on a boat north. Tom Durand produced a manifest with Ben's name and destination on it and a note—by special order of General Sherman. That's corroboration. Tom journeyed to Illinois and against all odds found Sam Parker, who knew a Ben, a former slave. This Ben helped some Union soldiers and was put on a boat north from Mississippi. What's that if not corroborative? The judge advocates have made no attempt to refute this corroboration. Yes, if there is a court-martial, we'll have to produce Sam Parker and Isaiah Daniels, the man who told Tom that Ben had died under mysterious circumstances in a fire. We will produce both if necessary, assuming they're able to avoid the untimely and unnatural deaths that recently befell Ben and another potential corroborating witness, Mike Riley."

The courtroom rustled with the mention of those "untimely and unnatural deaths."

"The judge advocates claim that Culpepper's and Landers' stories corroborate each other, and the evidence uncovered by Richard Pomeroy further corroborates their stories. Richard Pomeroy's evidence is entirely consistent with Mr. Durand's testimony, so it adds nothing to these proceedings. As for Culpepper and Landers, their stories do, for the most part, match. However, recall that Culpepper said Will Farrows shouted, 'No, Danny!' and Landers said it was, 'Don't do it Danny!' Given the immediacy and drama of the circumstances, it seems odd that they should have differing memories on this point. Recall also that Culpepper claimed he received his leg wound at Shiloh, but had trouble remembering if it was before or after his regiment charged the hill, couldn't remember the miracle nostrum that had prevented the leg from rotting, and had obtained it from a man who died during the war. In similar vein, Landers claimed to have asked Mr. Durand for a loan, but he seemed to stumble over the purpose of the loan, then said it was for an acquaintance, also conveniently dead, and made the implausible assertion he would have acted as surety for the loan. Maybe Culpepper and Landers can claim that their stories didn't unravel, but they were certainly fraying at the edges.

"This leaves the judge advocates with the argument that this proceeding cannot evaluate whether Mr. Durand had legal justification for shooting Pomeroy. Mr. Durand said he despised the lieutenant. From what we've heard, the lieutenant was a despicable man. At Shiloh, according to both Mr. Durand and Mr. Culpepper, Pomeroy ordered a second group into a line of fire that had already cut down a prior group while he stayed safely back. Only after Mr. Durand and Mr. Farrows wisely disobeyed Pomeroy's order and led a charge, which included Mr. Culpepper, that took the Confederate position did Pomeroy follow. At Walnut Hills, at the first sign of trouble, Pomeroy reneged on an agreement he had made with Ben. He panicked, ordered Mr. Durand to shoot Ben, and prepared to shoot Ben himself when Mr. Durand refused.

"If Mr. Durand had allowed Pomeroy to shoot Ben and participated in a subsequent cover-up, he could have been brought before a hearing like this one as a coconspirator in the brutal murder of an innocent civilian. Mr. Durand had to make an instantaneous choice between two actions, either of which could be construed as a crime. Does Judge Advocate Sterling seriously mean to suggest that the three officers impanelled to hear this case cannot make the correct decision—that in a fleeting instant of time Mr. Durand chose the morally commendable and legally justified course? I respectfully submit, sirs, that you have both the power and the duty to make that decision. Thank you."

Daniel turned to Eleanor, his expression asking: What do you think?

"That was good. He's given me a little hope," she said. The look on her face said she wasn't convinced.

Daniel glanced at the three officers. They didn't look as if they relished their decision.

"At this time," Colonel Cosgrove said, "the court of inquiry will adjourn while Colonel Meyers, Lieutenant Colonel Flint, and I confer. All parties and their attorneys please remain in an area from which you can be summoned and return to this hearing room within ten minutes. Everyone is reminded that rules of decorum still apply." The officers rose and exited through a door behind the bench.

Daniel stood to stretch his legs. He removed his watch from his vest pocket: 6:58, three minutes later than the last time he had checked, over two and a half hours since the hearing had adjourned. How late would the officers go before they quit and carried over until tomorrow? Last night was rough; tonight would be excruciating if he didn't know his fate.

After the adjournment there had been an excited cacophony and a stream of friends and family approaching Daniel and Eleanor, expressing support and optimism that the officers would decide for Daniel. As time wore on, the cacophony diminished and eventually a pall settled over the hearing room. What seemed like a cut-and-dried decision was perhaps not so cut and dried after all. Daniel had asked Kincaid what the lengthy deliberations might mean, and the attorney had shrugged. Now he sat at the table, reading and scribbling notes.

There was one thing Daniel had meant to do but had not. He approached Tom and Jessica. Tom needed some good meals—this ordeal had cost him pounds, among other things. Daniel had called E. H. Harriman, whom he knew from the railroad man's days as the head of a New York brokerage, and thanked him for allowing Tom to keep his job with the Union Pacific. A brilliant businessman, Harriman knew he had to hang on to his best employees. Harriman hadn't changed, gruffly acknowledging the thanks and expressing hope that Daniel would win his case in a conversation that lasted less than two minutes.

"Tommy," Daniel said. "No matter how things turn out, I'll always be grateful for what you did. We wouldn't have a chance at all if you hadn't found that manifest and discovered what happened to Ben. I'm proud of you, what you've become, and you, Jessica. Thank you. This couldn't have been easy in your condition."

"Thank you, Mr. Durand," Jessica said softly, her eyes glistening.

Tom stood and put his hand on Daniel's shoulder. "We're going to win, Father."

Daniel saw a soldier approach the judge advocates, tell them something, then walk over to Kincaid and tell him something. The officers must have reached some sort of decision. Daniel hoped it wasn't a decision to call it a day. He hurried over to Kincaid.

"Colonel Cosgrove will announce the decision in ten minutes," Kincaid said.

Never had ten minutes been so interminably long. Daniel couldn't still his churning stomach, couldn't sit, couldn't stand, couldn't hear what was said to him, couldn't speak more than a word or two, couldn't hold Eleanor's hand when she tried to squeeze his, and couldn't impose any type of order on the jumble of his thoughts. Finally the door behind the bench opened and the three officers entered and took their seats. The hearing room went silent.

"Mr. Durand, would you please stand?"

Daniel stood and felt his legs tremble. Somebody had said that courage wasn't an absence of fear, but rather a willingness to confront it. He held himself military straight and tall and stared directly at Cosgrove.

"Mr. Durand, it is the judgment of this court of inquiry that no further proceedings are necessary. There will be no court-martial unless and until further evidence comes to light in this case. It is the finding of this court that the killing of Lieutenant Pomeroy was justified as a defense of innocent life. Case dismissed."

Daniel had to restrain himself from leaping into the air. Eleanor's arms were around him and they were kissing and squeezing each other as tightly as they could. All semblance of decorum dissolved as the hearing room erupted into cheers and stamping feet. There were loud whistles from Woodbury—Daniel had heard the same whistles after trading coups. People packed in on Daniel and Eleanor. Keane was pounding him on the back. Tommy, Alexander, Palos, and a string of men from Durand & Woodbury pumped his hand. Gottman shouted, "*Mazel tov!*" repeatedly, others joining in. Constance and Laura were crying, hugging Eleanor, and tears came to Daniel's eyes. Only Eleanor knew him, really knew him to the core, but even as a quiet, sometimes remote father, friend, colleague, or boss, he realized how much he meant to those gathered around him. Joy! Joy! Joy! The truth was finally out—he had nothing to hide.

The reporter had called Will's office from Brooklyn with the news of his father's exoneration. Overcome by emotions, not all of which he could identify, the first thing Will had said was, "I'm glad, I'm happy he won. If he killed this Pomeroy…well, if he killed him, then he had a damn good reason." Then Will had realized that everything he had just said would be quoted in the newspaper and certain parties might not be happy with that quote. "I mean, I'm happy that the process has run its course and that it's over. I'm happy for my father's sake that he won't have to stand for a court-martial." He had hung up without another word, surprised at himself. He was rarely rude to reporters. They were too important to his career.

Now he sat at his favorite bar, twirling his whiskey and ice in the glass. Why had he told the reporter he was happy with the decision? There were two reasons, one admirable, the other less so. His anger at his father for firing him had not turned into something more malignant—he didn't hate him. What he did feel towards him was too complicated to sort out, but he didn't hate him. What was the not-so-admirable reason? If his father had lost, then gone on to an adverse court-martial verdict, it would have meant military prison or execution. Will knew he didn't have the strength to face that consequence of a chain of events he had played such a large part in starting. Mixed with happiness for his father was relief for himself.

Sylvia hated his father, had from the beginning. Why? Was that too complicated to sort out? Perhaps it was too simple. Father, in Sylvia's eyes a peasant, refused to doff his hat for the would-be monarchs of the world, and Sylvia was a would-be monarch. She despised humanity, so she would rule it. That attitude, rife among the British aristocracy, was less tenable in democratic America. Daniel Durand, like so many of his countrymen in this nation of refugees from oppression, refused to grant the self-anointed high and mighty what they considered their due. His father wouldn't even take them seriously, which might ultimately be a mistake. Politically, Will would play up to the crowd and take what he could get from it—that was the game. Unlike his wife, however, he had no delusion that the crowd would yield him the whip hand. Memories of, and escapes from, the corruption and evil of absolute power were still too recent and deep, the love of liberty too strong. Someday that would change, but long after he and Sylvia were laid to rest.

Will finished his drink. It was only his second, usually just the start of a good night's work. Tonight he was going home. He was going to tell Sylvia what he'd said to the reporter rather than endure the explosion tomorrow when she read it. He put a dollar on the bar, took his coat from the stand, buttoned it, and stepped out into the cold November night. No need to summon a hack. The bar wasn't far from the Durand residence and the chill was bracing over a short distance.

Sylvia rushed up to Will in the entryway as he unbuttoned his coat. She appeared uncharacteristically disheveled, a strand or two of hair out of place.

"He won," she said.

Will stared at her face. He supposed she was still beautiful, but she had to spend more time at her dressing table in the morning than she used to. No amount of cosmetics could eliminate the way the corners of her mouth turned down, an expression of perpetual petulance. "So he did."

"Have you talked to the newspaper men?"

"Just one, Cox at the *Post*."

"What did you say?"

Will took a deep breath. "I told him I was glad Father had won. I said that if Father killed the man, he had a damn good reason for doing so."

"You said that?"

"I did."

"Don't you realize that was the worst thing you could have said? To publicly support him after what he's done to you! Do you realize what you've said?"

"I do."

"You fool! You absolute imbecile! I wish I had married a man, a man who has the courage to do what he must to advance his own cause, not an irresolute eunuch!"

The back of his hand slapped across her face, hard. It was the first time he had hit her, although he had wanted to do so on other occasions.

She stared at him, stunned, as blood trickled from the corner of her mouth. "If you ever strike me again, I will take the children to England and you shan't see us. I will ruin you, I promise."

"You needn't worry. I won't lay a finger on you again...ever." He opened the door and was met by a chill blast. Better than the chill inside. He slammed the door as he stepped into the night.

Tim Harkness had received the call several hours ago from Micah Baldwin, in Brooklyn, informing him of the court of inquiry's decision. For the fourth time, Daniel Durand had bested the Winfields. Micah had one of the officers who had heard the case in his back pocket. He had two corroborating witnesses and Lieutenant Cyrus

Pomeroy's sword and skull. Two potentially adverse witnesses had met untimely demises. Still they had lost.

They had lost because Durand had told the truth. If he had taken the stand and denied everything, or if he'd refused to testify, the case would have gone to a court-martial. Instead, he had told the truth. There might be a power outside the usual calculations of money, politics, public opinion, and corruption. Grandfather always said that you learned more from your failures than your successes. This case's adverse outcome alerted Tim to the potential threat of this previously unaccounted-for power, something to remember as he exercised conventional power, the family's stock in trade.

Soon he would exercise that power unencumbered. He listened to the small gasps coming from the bed in the great master bedroom of his grandfather, Curtis Winfield. How ironic that he would never know he had been defeated an intolerable fourth time. Yesterday, Grandmother had found him slumped over, his head on his desk. The doctors said he had suffered a stroke and that he might not be able to speak or move if he regained consciousness. Now that pos-sibility was fading—he wouldn't last the night. His frail body was shutting down after eighty years of vaulting ambition and ceaseless work, of unsentimental assessment of kin, allies, and enemies, of pragmatic caution, cynical manipulation, all manner of corruption, and unforgiving ruthlessness in the service of money and, more im-portantly, power.

Tim did not maintain his vigil out of love. Sometimes he admired his grandfather, occasionally he feared him, always he learned from him, but love was not an identifiable emotion in their relation-ship—going either way—by Tim's own unsentimental assessment. Somewhere in his quest for the Winfield empire he had, like his grandfather, discarded love. People served or hindered one's pur-poses; that was all. He stayed, listening to the labored breathing, because Grandfather had taught him that he couldn't be too careful. The possibility was remote, but if he awoke and Tim wasn't there, Uncle Prescott, Uncle Harrison, or Uncle Archer might be, with a codicil to the will for a confused old man to sign before he slipped back to the netherworld. The prize was only hours away. Why take chances?

Tim's eyes narrowed and the corners of his mouth tightened. He rarely flashed the smile that had made the debutantes swoon. That smile had served its purpose—he had married one of them. Those he charmed never knew of the ruthless calculation that dominated his thoughts. Conventional power rested on a willingness to use violence. As he had discarded love, so too had Tim discarded any qualms about violence, helping his grandfather plan the murders of the police sergeant and the former slave. He could not have refused to help with the nefarious deeds, not without rejecting his legacy.

But he was going to reject, or at least suspend, part of his inheritance from his grandfather: the vendetta against Daniel Durand. This last design had been elegant, too elegant—complications always carried risk—and it had failed. Durand had the money to uncover the truth about who was behind the court of inquiry, and if he did, the risk to Tim was clear. Fortunately, his grandfather always put several layers of operatives between him and those who carried out his darker schemes, and he had done so in this case. A layer or two could disappear if Durand's inquiries got too close to the truth of Tim's complicity in the policeman's and the slave's murders.

Durand might discover, to his own satisfaction, the Winfield role in the court of inquiry, but other than the murders there was nothing illegal about that role. Durand had to know that a courtroom-worthy proof of Winfield complicity in those murders would pose a dauntingly difficult challenge and would run head-on into the Winfields' wealth, influence, and power. Durand was too smart to tilt at windmills. Tim was willing to wager that he'd call it a draw if there were no further provocations. A more cold-blooded consideration would also give Durand pause. The Winfields had Will, a hostage as it were. If the elder Durand still felt anything for Will, and he probably did, concern for his son's welfare would stay his hand.

Sometimes truces were necessary to win the ultimate fight. The Winfield enterprise had grown so large and powerful that it could no longer remain hidden from public view. It would only weaken itself if it pursued every slight, if it didn't wisely pick its battles. There would always be the sub rosa, but dark tactics had to be used sparingly and only when they were unavoidable. The empire would grow, but it could no longer thrive in obscurity as it had under Curtis Winfield. Pursuing a decades-old vendetta against a family whose wealth, if not power, matched the Winfields' would be an irrational waste of money and energy and could expose the family to new dangers. There would be no fifth round with Mr. Daniel Durand... unless there was a new provocation.

Chapter 25

Vox Populi

The report sitting on Daniel's desk had cost him ten thousand dollars—two thousand dollars a page—a bargain. The author of the report, Mr. Terrance Stoddard of the Stoddard Detective Agency, sat in Daniel's office. Daniel had read the report, twice, more astonished and enraged with the rereading. Eleanor had said they had to find out who was behind the army's prosecution. Now that he had the answer, he wasn't sure if he could share his knowledge with her.

"How did you get this information?" Daniel said.

"The key was Pomeroy's brokerage in Cincinnati, Crenshaw and Branson," Stoddard said. Most people wouldn't like the stout, red-haired ex-policeman. He was abrupt, uninterested in personalities, and obsessed with detail—all virtues in a detective, by Daniel's reckoning. "During the court of inquiry Pomeroy mentioned its correspondents in New York. That firm is Hanover and Wells. I had to spread some cash, but I found out one of its partners is a Winfield front."

Winfield! The name had jumped from the first page when Daniel had begun his hurried read of Stoddard's report. Daniel had "stolen" Eleanor from Archer Winfield. He and Mr. Keane had sold their bank at an inflated price to Eleanor's father, Phillip Haverford, who he later discovered had the Winfields' backing. He had been unaware of any further clashes with the secretive empire. However, Stoddard's report detailed how Durand & Woodbury had helped thwart a massive bear raid and short sale of the stock of Hill's St. Paul Railroad, which, unknown to Daniel, had been masterminded by the Winfields. The report mentioned the late Curtis Winfield's penchant for brutally punishing his enemies.

Will's name jumped from the second page. After Daniel had fired Will, Harvard classmate and Bovinity chum Timothy Harkness brought him into the Winfield fold. Will's connection to the Winfields was a closely kept secret.

Daniel had never forgotten an incident when he had visited Will at Harvard. Will had mentioned a professor named Pomeroy and had intently watched his reaction, which might have betrayed some surprise, Daniel couldn't recall. What he did remember was that his reaction was important to his son. Will was the only possible link between the name Pomeroy and the Winfields. How had he obtained that name? The report didn't say, but he must have given it to the them. With their money and Curtis Winfield's passion for vengeance, they had uncovered its significance.

"So my son was complicit in a plot that could have led to my execution?" It was difficult to ask the question. He felt sick to his stomach. Will had betrayed him.

"That's what it looks like, and it almost succeeded. The Winfields needed one more vote for a court-martial, but they didn't get it. Of course, you might have prevailed at a court-martial."

Or he might not have. His son had been involved in a scheme that could have put him on the gallows.

Eleanor had pressed him repeatedly to find out who had been behind the court of inquiry. If she were to question the veracity of

Stoddard's report or try to exonerate Will, he couldn't trust his own reaction. Disclosure would have to wait.

The short one pushed the door open. A dagger of cold air cut through the boy. A path through the snow led to the privy. Stinging tears came to his eyes. The tall one pushed him and he fell into the snow. The wind from the frozen lake whipped through the yard and swirled the deep drifts. He stood up, but sunk into the snow. The short one grabbed the pail of water and came towards him. His teeth chattered. He was shaking so hard his whole body hurt.

"No!" he screamed. "No! No!"

The cascade of water poured down upon him. For a moment there was no pain, then it came—a freeze from inside his body that spread outwards. His teeth clattered wildly, uncontrollably, and tears rolled down his cheeks. Wracking coughs welled up from deep within his chest and snot gushed from his nose. Stumbling through the snow he ran to the door and found it shut tight.

"Oh, let me in! Please let me in!" he cried, shaking the handle.

The door remained shut. They were going to let him die out here. He was going to die. He trembled and his teeth banged together. He couldn't feel his toes. He tried wiggling them, but they wouldn't wiggle. "Let me in!"

Finally a dark crack opened and he stumbled inside.

Daniel awoke from his recurring dream. He stared into the blackness of the night. Two mating cats yowled. His son wanted him dead.

Will sat in the great library of the Winfield estate on the Hudson. He had never seen anything like it—two-story-high bookcases, bearskin rugs, a giant stone fireplace, and above an imposing oak desk and rosewood humidor, an English country landscape. Floor-to-ceiling windows framed a real landscape of manicured lawns and hedges on lush rolling hills, statuary, fountains, and riding trails, and in the distance, the Hudson River winding its way through stately pines. In the center of the room, Will, Tim Harkness, his uncles, Prescott and Harrison Winfield, and Micah Baldwin, the Winfields' attorney, sat on expansive, brown leather couches arranged around a handcrafted oak table. Arresting as the room and furnishings were, Will's gaze kept returning to Tim.

His classmate from Harvard had always drawn people to him. Still strikingly handsome, gray touches in his blond hair added distinction. He sipped a whiskey and smoked a cigar, but there was no trace of dissipation in his appearance. He must have exercised regularly—boxing, rowing, maybe tennis— he had put perhaps five pounds on his athletic frame since his Harvard days. Caesar was tall; so were Washington and Lincoln. Tim was six and a half feet, the height of command. That word defined Tim—command. He summoned affability, curiosity, or intelligence as required, showing only that facet of his personality he wanted seen. Easy lay the head that wore the Winfield crown, Will marveled—Tim had been born to his inheritance. His uncles and Baldwin accepted Tim's birthright, deferring to their junior of at least twenty years.

"It's time you moved from Albany to Washington," Tim boomed, grinning. "How does 'Representative Durand' sound?"

"I'm honored, but only if you think that's the best way for me to continue humbly serving the interests of the people of New York," Will said, smiling.

"To hell with the people of New York, how about our interests? We've got four in the House, but we can always use more. You can't have too much influence. Play your cards right and you'll find yourself in the Senate."

"But first you have to win this election," Harrison said flatly. The easy conviviality that had won the corpulent elder statesman fourteen elections to the House of Representatives vanished inside the Winfield sanctum. "Campbell won't have any significant opposition in the primary. He's not to be taken lightly, but you'll defeat him. You'll get President Roosevelt's and the important newspapers' endorsements. Publicly I'll express the usual party line support, no more. My work will be behind the scenes in the House. I'll get you on the right committees."

"I wasn't sure, Will, how your statement to the papers would play after the decision in your father's court of inquiry," Prescott said. "Micah and I both thought it seemed hasty, an ill-considered reaction. Fortunately, your star is in ascendance and the public liked seeing the estranged son of a plutocrat publicly expressing support for his vindicated father. It gives you a certain nobility and largeness of character."

Will stared at Prescott. The Winfields were maintaining the fiction that they'd had nothing to do with the prosecution against his father, even extracting benefit from Will's publicly expressed satisfaction that their effort had failed. They did so because Will could win elections. Not just anybody could win elections. Will liked the sound of Representative Durand, and Senator Durand even more. President Durand? It wouldn't happen without the Winfields. Marriages of mutual necessity could be strong, unlike those founded on always-fleeting romance.

"No more ill-considered reactions, Durand!" Tim waved his finger menacingly but flashed his winning smile. "We think before we

talk to the papers and we keep our nose clean during the campaign—
no scandals! Don't tarnish your luster."

The morning of April 18, 1906, Tom noticed that he hadn't received the usual batch of telegrams from Union Pacific's San
Francisco office. He went to the telegraph wire room to see if someone had forgotten to bring them to him.

"No, Mr. Durand, we didn't forget," replied Jed Farley, one of the
operators. "For some reason San Francisco is late today. Wait a minute, here's one coming in from Monterey. Good God!" He handed
the telegram to Tom.

MAJOR EARTHQUAKE BAY AREA STOP DAMAGE
MASSIVE LOSS OF LIFE STOP COMMUNICATIONS
IMPAIRED ALL TRAINS STOPPED MULTIPLE AFTER-
SHOCKS

"Send word to New York," Tom said. "See which of our telegraph lines are still operational to Northern California. Bring me
every dispatch you receive. I'll be upstairs."

Tom hurried back to his office, his mind racing. Damage massive, loss of life—San Francisco would need medical supplies, food,
and water. Shelter would have to be found for those whose homes
had been destroyed, hospitals for the injured, morgues for the dead.
How bad was the damage? If gas lines broke there could be fires,
maybe civil unrest. How long would the aftershocks last? The city
would have to be rebuilt. It would need lumber, bricks, and cement.
Railroad and telegraph lines had to be repaired.

Within an hour the Union Pacific's private telegraph wire in Cheyenne erupted with a flood of telegrams from E. H. Harriman in New York to Tom, the Rocky Mountain regional manager.

RESTORE COMMUNICATIONS BAY AREA SPARE NO EXPENSE
DIVERT ALL TRAINS IN SURROUNDING AREAS STOP SUPPLIES INTO SF SURVIVORS OUT NO CHARGE COOPERATE WITH GOVERNMENT AND MILITARY

Later, after midnight, a messenger brought Tom a telegram in his office, where he was still at work.

LEAVE NY AM FOR SF ARRIVE CHEY TWO DAYS STOP YOU STAY IN CHEY TO COORDINATE REGIONAL RESPONSE BUT EVERY MAN THAT CAN BE SPARED TO SF

For the next two days Tom improvised and directed while following telegraphed orders from Harriman, en route from New York. He guzzled strong coffee, and when he was too exhausted to continue working he grabbed quick naps on a cot in his office. He went home once, on the second day, to hastily shower, shave, change clothes, and have dinner with Jessica and their one-year-old daughter, Elizabeth. Harriman's express pulled into Cheyenne late that night.

Edward Henry Harriman was a nondescript little man with a bushy mustache, wire-rimmed glasses, and a face nobody would remember, but who, once he opened his mouth, nobody ever forgot. A dynamo of concentrated energy, his brain was a lightning-fast machine that left behind those not giving him their full attention, with no opportunity to catch up. He jumped from the train when it stopped and hurried up to Tom, standing on the platform.

"Evening, Durand. How many men are you sending to San Francisco?"

"Fourteen, including three mechanics and my assistant, Mike Griswold."

"You can spare the mechanics?"

"Some of the others have volunteered for double shifts."

"Everyone ready to go?"

"They're waiting in the station."

"Has the telegraph line been reconnected with Calvin?" E. E. Calvin was the Northern California regional manager.

"This afternoon. The dispatches are in my office if you want to read them."

"No time. Give me the long and short of it."

"Two lines have been repaired into San Francisco for supplies. Our riverboats are also bringing in supplies. The army is handling distribution, over fifty tons so far. We're buying food, tools, and medicine all over the peninsula and East Bay, but everybody's running out."

Harriman motioned towards the train. "Twenty cars' full."

Tom nodded. "You'll be pulling another twelve from here. Calvin says the UP's ferried over thirty thousand people from San Francisco to Oakland. He converted the Ferry Building into a relief center. It wasn't damaged in the quake."

"So far. How bad are the aftershocks?"

"Still frequent, still severe."

"How many dead?'

"Government officials are saying a few hundred. Calvin says they're lying so as not to frighten people. He says it's in the thousands, with well over a hundred thousand homeless. We've opened our own information bureaus in San Francisco and the company hospital to all the injured the staff can handle. However, there are multiple fires and Calvin had to evacuate one of our car barns outside the city due to fire danger, so the bureaus and hospital are day-to-day."

"Have we lost any people?"

"Three dead and at least twenty missing. Calvin hasn't said how many are homeless."

"How are our customers responding to your diversion of trains?"

"No complaints, yet. Everyone understands the situation. However, that won't last—they can't keep their freight in storage forever."

"Sort it out, but raise rates to separate the necessity shippers from the matter-of-convenience ones. We need all the cars we can get to the Bay Area. I have to draft wires to New York, Denver, and Calvin. I'll use your office, and I'd be grateful if you'd bring me the largest mug of coffee you can get your hands on and something to eat. Let me know when my train's ready to go."

The train departed within an hour. Tom stayed at the station until he couldn't keep his bleary eyes open. Realizing that sleep in his comfortable bed would do him more good than tossing and turning on the cot in his office, he went home, but was back in his office at six the next morning. Such was to be his routine for the next two months as the full dimensions of the horror in San Francisco unfolded: 80 percent—twenty-five thousand—of the city's buildings destroyed by the quake, aftershocks, or fire; widespread damage in cities around the Bay Area; at least three thousand dead and thousands more injured; San Francisco's parks and beaches covered with makeshift tents for the homeless; business in the West Coast's center of commerce brought to a virtual halt. Tom had only been to San Francisco once, for his honeymoon with Jessica. Its streets, packed with people from all over the world—hustling, bustling, sharp-eyed, sharp-elbowed—reminded him of New York. The thought of this great city in charred ruins felt like the death of a not-well-known but still-admired acquaintance.

Tom's assistant, Mike Griswold, was the last of the men sent from Cheyenne to return from the Bay Area. Both E. E. Calvin and E. H. Harriman confirmed via telegrams what Tom knew when he had asked Griswold to go: that he was invaluable and had a bright future at the Union Pacific. Tom met him as he stepped off the train. Griswold was taller and stockier than Tom, ten years younger, with sweeping blond hair, blue eyes, a broad, open face, and a quick smile. He carried himself well, but today it took an effort for him to stand tall and keep his shoulders square. His eyelids hung and he looked like Tom felt—that given the opportunity he would collapse on a bed and sleep for fifteen or twenty hours.

"It was bad," Tom said.

"The devil can't cook up much worse in hell." Griswold shook his head. "I never want to see anything like that again."

"You can tell me about it later, after you've got some sleep and a couple of good meals. I'd like to give you tomorrow off, but I've got to have you back. We've been swamped and it's not going to let up until things get better in the Bay Area."

Griswold nodded. "I understand." He started to walk away, but then turned back towards Tom. "You know, Mr. Durand, bad as things were, there was another side to it, too. I never got used to the aftershocks. There was one, and I guess I have must have looked scared to death, because a man put his hand on my shoulder, kind of reassurance. He was standing next to a heap of rubble that he told me had been his store. His name was Ross Desmond. He asked me to help him move a big wooden beam and we got it moved. Out of his pocket he took a drawing—he already had plans for his new store. A lot of bank vaults were melted shut in the fires, so money is real short. Mr. Harriman had said to extend Union Pacific credit where it seemed prudent, so I asked him if he needed a loan. He said he already had a loan from Mr. Giannini of the Bank of Italy. Seems this gentleman had set up his bank outside his house in San Mateo and was lending people money on a signature and a handshake.

"Mr. Desmond said he didn't much like bankers, but he would move heaven and earth to pay back Mr. Giannini. Then he said his store was all he had left. By the way he said it, I knew he had lost his family. There are so many people who have lost so much, but they're like Mr. Desmond—picking themselves up, dusting off, and starting all over. They're pulling together, helping each other out. That's the part I'll try to remember. It'll take a few years, but San Francisco will be back, stronger than ever."

There had been moments in her marriage that Eleanor wished she could capture forever. This was one of them. The warm sun beamed on Daniel, reflecting off a shiny spot on his forehead, and a gentle sea breeze blew through his thinning hair as he reclined, eyes closed, on a lounge chair on the deck of the yacht. Like Edison and electricity, her husband had harnessed an elemental force, a tension, but his came from within. Only in repose did the tension ebb. There were none of the wrinkles on his forehead from deep concentration; the lids were closed over eyes that scanned, probed, or narrowed into an intently focused stare; and his mouth—generally shut, yielding hints of either smiles or frowns recognizable only to people who knew him well—was opened slightly as he napped. This was an image she wished she could enshrine.

Daniel hadn't realized it yet, but it was time for him to retire. Of course he had earned his relaxation long ago, but relaxation was going to be momentary with him—the tension would always be there. But the source of that tension, his mind, was pulling him away from business, in a direction he hadn't fully recognized. He had always had an intellectual bent, but he was reading more and, it seemed to Eleanor, thinking more deeply than he ever had before. When they talked, he was increasingly analytical and philosophical. As he absorbed his many and growing number of volumes that had now spilled over from his library to bookcases elsewhere in their home, a reordering and consolidation was occurring in his mind, almost as if it was teaching itself to think in a different way.

Eleanor had never suggested to Daniel that he retire; he would have to reach that conclusion on his own. After Constance's marriage only John remained at home, and with his mental limitations it appeared that's where he would stay. However, he spent his days working at a flower shop and didn't require her full-time attention. She had her friends, but she had no use for the gilded society to which the Durands' wealth would have afforded entrée, the playpen for so many New York matrons. She wanted to watch her grandchildren grow up, read some of the books Daniel read, and accompany him on his mental journeys.

Looking through a travel magazine one day, she had realized she wanted to take other journeys as well. Since the Civil War, the country had been transformed. Forty years had seen more progress than centuries before. Factories and mass production, railroads, mining, logging, farming, petroleum extraction and refining, elevators and skyscrapers, electricity and light, telegraphs, ticker tapes and telephones, chemistry, medicine, laboratories and science, and now these new inventions, the horseless carriage and the aeroplane—the list of endeavors that had either been invented or improved beyond recognition was mind-boggling, and the average American, if not too busy to even notice, took it for granted that it would continue. Eleanor darkly suspected that like a meteor in the night sky, the brilliance would burn itself out, or, more likely, be snuffed out. She wanted to take in this unprecedented explosion of human creativity while it was occurring.

Her other dark thought about this progress was recognition of the absence of one half of the human race from much of it. She had never regretted the path she had chosen, but she had often wondered if she might not have taken a different one had she had the freedom to do so. Someday social custom, prejudice, and the law itself would change for women. She held on to the hope that she'd be around to see it.

She had suggested to Daniel that they start taking trips. So as not to shock him, she first proposed shorter sojourns, long weekends and the like. One of her first suggestions had been Cape Cod; it was beautiful in the summer and they had never been there. To her delight, Daniel said he knew several Boston bankers and they might be able to rent a cottage. Not only had they secured a cottage—actually a villa—one banker had thrown in his yacht. Daniel had always scorned yachts as expensive affectations, his view probably colored by his antipathy towards J. P. Morgan, but once he got aboard this one, he had allowed that there might be something to them, after all, especially since the crew did all the work.

Daniel had paced the decks for an hour, settled down to sip iced tea with Eleanor and read, and now he was asleep. Eleanor left him to his nap and walked to the bow. The air was tangy with salt spray and the breeze tugged at her wide-brimmed white hat. The shore was no longer visible, but from the position of the afternoon sun to their left she could tell they were going north. She closed her eyes and tilted her head, feeling the sun and wind on her face.

"Excuse me, Mrs. Durand."

It was Captain Medford. Eleanor turned around. "Yes, Captain?"

"It's time to turn back. I don't like the look of those clouds." He pointed east, where dark clouds loomed on the horizon.

"That's fine. It's been a lovely cruise."

Within an hour they had docked at Hyannis Harbor. Eleanor and Daniel debarked and strolled through the village of Hyannis. Something caught her eye on a side street.

"Daniel, look at the sign in front of that art gallery."

The sign read: *See the Remarkable Work of Mrs. Arabella Thompson! Meet the Artist! Exhibit June 6 through June 10.*

"Daniel, you don't suppose that's Arabella, the woman Will courted at Harvard? She was an artist, and according to Will, a very good one."

"Arabella is not that common a name. There's one way to find out."

When Eleanor saw a painting in the window of the gallery—a seascape of exquisite detail and consummate skill—she had an intuition that this was indeed the same Arabella.

They entered a spacious, well-lit gallery. Paintings hung from a series of moveable partitions. Eleanor gazed at a portrait of a wizened old woman that seemed to capture a lifetime of unremitting endurance and toil. She moved on to one of a young girl with a cat on her lap, girl and pet staring at each other in such a way as to suggest that they were confederates against a world that had treated neither of them very well, lifting the painting above the usual banality of such work. A lighthouse on a rocky outcropping, standing above the crashing waves below, portrayed solitary strength. There were no two paintings of the same subject. In each painting the artist had extracted and conveyed an essential quality or meaning. Eleanor noticed discreet tags with a handwritten *Sold* by many of them. She saw a knot of people towards the back of the gallery.

Several people walked away from the group as she moved towards it and Eleanor glimpsed the center of attention. It was Arabella, who recognized Eleanor and walked towards her.

"You?"

"Yes."

"Of course." It was one of those rare times where everything was as it should be. That Arabella would be painting and selling her work at an exhibition in an exclusive gallery was unquestionably logical and right; it was the thought that she couldn't that was absurd beyond consideration. If Arabella were her own daughter Eleanor wouldn't have felt more proudly elated, overcome by a surge that expressed itself in two words: *at last*.

Arabella embraced her. "Mrs. Durand, how good to see you! I hoped I would see you again."

"Please, it's Eleanor. This is absolutely amazing—your work. I knew you were an artist and Will said you were good, but I had no idea that you were great. Your paintings…I just stand and gape. I'm in awe."

"Thank you."

Undoubtedly Arabella had received compliments and said "thank you" thousands of times, but it seemed to Eleanor that the way she said it now both acknowledged her achievement and conveyed that it was significant to her that Eleanor had done so.

"You were Arabella Brewster, now you're Arabella Thompson. You must have married?"

"Yes, to Brandon Thompson. He stayed at our cottage with the children. He's a mathematics professor at the Massachusetts Institute of Technology."

"So you have a family, children?"

"Three boys and a girl."

"Where do you find the time?"

"To paint? Or to be a wife and mother?" Arabella smiled. "I have to paint—it's as essential to me as breathing. I didn't think I would meet a man who understood that, but I did. It's been a struggle at times, but our circumstances have allowed us to have nannies. Our children have done well. It's good for them to see their mother with a career, especially Cynthia, my daughter."

"Extraordinary." When Will had brought Arabella home to New York, Eleanor had liked her, realizing she heard a different drummer. She had found the courage to blaze her own trail and if no one else followed, so be it. This gallery was as natural a setting for her as Daniel's office or study was for him. This was how things were going to change. A woman would decide that painting, or medicine or science or finance, was as essential to her as breathing, she'd set off on her chosen path, struggle but eventually triumph, and clear the way for other women to follow. Someday nobody would think it unusual for women to pursue their dreams.

Daniel approached them. "Arabella! Eleanor thought it was you when she saw the sign. It's a delight to see you again." Arabella extended her hand and Daniel shook it. "I can't tell you how much I admire and enjoy your work. If the lighthouse hasn't sold, I'll buy it."

Arabella looked at Daniel as if she were appraising him for a portrait. "Yes," she said softly. "You would like that one. It hasn't sold, probably because it's the most expensive one."

Daniel smiled. "Cost no object."

"I'll be happy knowing you have that painting. It's one of my favorites. You'll need to talk to Mr. Hoover, the manager, to arrange the sale. There's something else I want you two to have. It's back in my studio. I'll have to fetch it. It's not far. Do you have a few minutes?"

"We're on vacation," Eleanor said. "We're in no hurry."

While Arabella went to her studio and Daniel arranged the purchase of the lighthouse painting, Eleanor wandered through the gallery. It wasn't correct to say that she liked art, or literature or music for that matter. It happened perhaps one time in a thousand, maybe less. She would see a painting or sculpture, read a book, or hear a piece of music to which she responded. Like was too trivial a word for the profound emotions evoked by the works she cherished—revered—and it certainly didn't apply to the vast body of artistic creation that left her indifferent. Not every one of Arabella's paintings inspired her reverence, but there were several before which she stood enthralled, aware only of the painting. While gazing at one, a city street scene throbbing with exuberant energy (and that was also, regrettably, tagged *Sold*), she was tapped on the shoulder. She turned to see Arabella, holding a canvas covered with a cloth, and Daniel.

"I suppose I could have sent this to you," Arabella said. "But I always had this feeling that I would see you again." She removed the cloth to reveal a portrait of Will from his Harvard days.

Eleanor gasped. Arabella had caught the soul, the enigmatic essence of her son. How in the world had she done it? What was it about this painting? "You…you painted his mouth after you visited us in New York, didn't you?"

Arabella's eyes widened. "How do you know that?"

"I'm…I'm not sure. It's the way it goes crooked; that's exactly the way it used to go…when he had a secret. It gave him away. You would have seen it after New York, but not before."

"I was angry after New York. I wanted to paint the mouth—"

"The mouth of someone who doesn't always tell the truth." Eleanor knew that was what Arabella would have said. "We haven't seen Will and his family for five years."

"I read he's running for the House of Representatives. He'll do well in Washington."

If Daniel had said that, the sardonic undertone would have been savagely damning. Coming from Arabella, it was matter-of-fact.

"Yes, he'll do well in Washington," Eleanor said in sad agreement.

The *New York Daily Chronicle*'s majority owner and editor, Mr. Harold Needham, and a reporter, Mr. Allen Hayes, sat in Daniel's office at Durand & Woodbury. During a financial panic, Daniel had extended funds to Needham in exchange for 10 percent of the equity and the *Daily Chronicle* had survived. Daniel occasionally saw Needham at business functions, but apart from a tour of the newspaper's offices and printing facilities, he had never had any contact with the employees, nor had he exercised any control over what the paper published.

"I'm not printing a scandal sheet, Mr. Durand," Needham said. He was in his mid-fifties, of ample girth, with a bushy handlebar mustache and a gleaming dome. "This story came looking for us; we didn't go looking for it."

"Miss Tyler approached me a few months ago," Hayes said. He was about ten years younger and seventy-five pounds thinner than Needham. The most memorable feature of his nondescript face was the prominent wart on his chin, with which he frequently fiddled. "She said she had an affair with your son while she was working in a dance hall, about four years ago. Women claiming to have affairs with prominent men are a dime a dozen in this city, so my inclination was to tell her to get lost. But she had her boy, named Sam, with her. He's four years old and damn if he isn't the spitting image of Will Durand. She's also got a photograph of her and Mr. Durand, and a letter she claims is from him, in which he promises to send her twenty-five dollars a month to support the boy in exchange for her keeping quiet about the whole thing. She let me read the letter, but she wouldn't let me have it. I got a hold of something Mr. Durand had handwritten—a letter to a constituent—and it sure looks like the same handwriting. I found the owner of the dance hall, an Anthony Mancini, and he said that Mr. Durand had spent time with Miss Tyler. He thought it was three or four years ago."

"If Miss Tyler agreed to keep quiet, why did she approach you?" Daniel said.

Hayes rubbed the wart on his chin. "She said Mr. Durand had quit sending her money. She sent him letters, but he didn't answer. So she decided to go to the newspapers. She's honest about it—she wants to ruin his chances in the election."

"With the corroboration we have, I have no qualms about running this story," Needham said. "If we don't print it, she'll go somewhere else, and an affair that produces a bastard son is certainly newsworthy when it concerns an up-and-coming politician. However, since he's your son, Mr. Durand, I wanted to check with you before we ran it. It will cause him a great deal of embarrassment and it could cost him the election."

Daniel's initial shock and pain at the revelation in the Stoddard report had metastasized into a red-hot rage. Was he going to worry about Will's embarrassment, about the problems this newspaper article would cause with his witch of a wife, or the ruination of his political career? His son had tried to kill him. "That's Will's problem, not mine," he said evenly. "I've never interfered with how you run your paper and I'm not going to start now. As a minority owner I have no right to do so. Make your decision as if Will and I were unrelated."

"Then I'm going to run the story."

"So be it."

That night, Daniel and Eleanor had their usual coffee after dinner in the sitting room.

"This is hard to believe," Daniel said, "but we have a grandson we didn't know about."

"What are you talking about?"

He told her about his meeting with Mr. Needham and the newspaper's story.

"So…so we really do have this grandson?" she stammered.

"Yes."

"Oh Will, poor Will. He's so unhappy with Sylvia. I knew he'd find someone else." She shook her head. "But in a dance hall...this will be the end of his political career, Daniel. It's all he has." She felt a plunging sensation in her stomach and tears coming to her eyes.

She looked at him and he returned her gaze, but didn't speak.

"You could hold the story up," she said desperately. "This Tyler lady wants money, she needs money. We could give her money, enough to rear her son, enough for her comfort, if she'd keep quiet. Or maybe she doesn't want to rear him—we could. He's our grandson. Maybe we could at least see him."

"I won't hold up that story. Needham would have, but I told him I was only a minority owner with no right to exercise control over the stories he published. I told him to proceed as if I had no ownership interest in the paper at all. What he publishes is his decision, not mine, and he's decided to publish this story.

"As for Will…" The anger in Daniel's voice was unmistakable. "I don't give a damn about his political career. He's another worthless politician as far as I'm concerned and I most assuredly have no interest in seeing, supporting, or rearing his bastard!"

One thought took shape amidst Eleanor's roiling emotions: her husband must blame her son for the attempt to convict and potentially execute him. That was the only thing that could be behind his reaction.

"I said no scandals!" Tim Harkness slammed the *New York Daily Chronicle* on the conference room table. "We had this damn election won and now this, Durand! What were you thinking? Why did you stop paying this Miss Tyler?"

Will, Tim, Prescott and Harrison Winfield, and Micah Baldwin sat in a small conference room of a bank in which the Winfields had a controlling interest. The joyless room was a far cry from cigars and drinks at the Winfield estate on the Hudson. It had no windows—against prying eyes, and, it seemed to Will, no air. Outside the room the bank itself was deserted; it was a Sunday afternoon.

He had never thought his dalliance would threaten his political career. Almost everyone in his line of work had something going on the side. He and Pamela had both known it would someday end and he thought he could keep it at that. Then there was the baby and the ceaseless, escalating demands for money and it hadn't ended, hadn't gone away. Like an imbecile, one day he had refused and hoped, hoped that somehow nothing bad would come of it. Now the truth was out. Tim's blue eyes were icy and penetrating as he'd never seen them before. His Harvard pal, he realized as if it were a new thought, was one of the most powerful men in America. Will's career and future were in jeopardy, and he was afraid as he'd never been afraid before.

"It started out as support for the boy," Will said. "But she kept asking for more. It turned into blackmail."

"So he's yours?"

"Yes. I didn't think she'd actually go to the newspapers."

"But you ran that risk. How foolish! You idiot!"

"Why didn't you tell us about this?" Prescott Winfield said.

"I was afraid you'd withdraw your support."

"I can't tell you how many times people have tried to blackmail me," Representative Harrison Winfield said. "It's an occupational hazard. The problem now is that it's much easier to deal with threats before they're carried out than afterward."

"If you had told us beforehand, there are things we could have done," Baldwin said. "Money changes hands, people disappear—we're not without recourse in this sort of affair. Now that it's hit the papers it's much trickier."

"Can we extricate ourselves from this mess?" Tim said. Will knew his political career hung on one thread—Harkness hated to concede, hated to lose, at anything. Will realized that even if they pulled this one out, his stock within the Winfield organization had fallen, and it might take a considerable time before he regained his former favor with Tim.

"I've found out an interesting fact," Baldwin said. He rubbed his hands together and Will thought of a praying—or was it a prey-ing?—mantis. "Will, did you know your father is a minority share-holder in the *Daily Chronicle?*"

"No." Will kept his face expressionless, but he felt a crushing sense of betrayal and loss. His father had used his paper for a hatchet job on him. This was the final abandonment.

"That's interesting," Prescott said thoughtfully. "Daniel Durand pays back his son with a story like this, after his son, notwithstand-ing a rift with his father, publicly expressed support for him when he was exonerated. It looks like the son is ready to forgive and forget, but the father is animated by less noble motives."

"What if the story weren't true?" Tim said. "Will hasn't publicly acknowledged that the child is his. Have you admitted this to anyone else, Will?"

Will shook his head.

"Well, that's one thing you've done right. Sure, the child looks like you, but that's coincidence. There are lots of blue-eyed, blond-haired kids out there. If Miss Tyler wants money, Micah, perhaps she can be induced to recant, to one of our newspapers."

"Not recant," Baldwin said. "That would smell like a payoff. I think it will be better if there's a story behind her original story. One that puts Daniel Durand in an entirely different, and unfavorable, light."

"The enmity of a father towards his son that drives him to put out a false story," Harrison said. "And consider the political angle. Here you have Will Durand, a man of the people, a supporter of President Roosevelt. Like our president, this son of privilege realizes that privilege owes a duty to the public and the country. Daniel Durand is a hidebound reactionary who's opposed antitrust and railroad regulation and every other progressive measure. He'll stop at nothing, even persecuting his enlightened son, to oppose progress and the will of the people."

"The public's attention is fleeting and its favor fickle," Prescott said. "The key is to shift the spotlight from the accused to the accuser. Will has to continue to strenuously deny the allegation and we've got to get to Miss Tyler, fast."

Harrison nodded. "This could work."

"It has to work," Tim said. "Micah, you handle Miss Tyler. We've put too much into you, Will, and we're too damn close to winning this election to let it go now." Tim stared directly at him with that hard, severe look. "Listen to me, Durand, because I'm only going to say this once. Lie to your wife, lie to your children, lie to your constituents, lie to your God, but never lie to me. If we salvage this situation and you win the election, don't ever think, no matter how far you go, that you're bigger than me. You're not. Understood?"

Will nodded, the dog in obedience to his master.

"Good." Tim smiled, the old charm instantly summoned. "Round up your wife and children and go somewhere public this afternoon, so the world can see the Durand family standing by their husband and father. We'll communicate with you in the usual way."

It was a dismissal, but Will was grateful, almost overjoyed. He had expected much worse. At the very least he had thought his political career was over. As he left the conference room he felt a glimmer of hope for the first time since the story broke in the *Daily Chronicle*.

Eleanor liked to spend Sunday mornings reading the newspapers. Daniel read them less frequently than he used to, sometimes ignoring them altogether, preferring to settle into his library with weightier tomes. Two Sundays after the *Daily Chronicle*'s scoop about Will, Eleanor dropped a paper, the *Metropolitan Examiner*, in his lap, opened to an article headlined: "Tyler Changes Story."

> *Miss Pamela Tyler, who has accused congressional candidate Mr. William Durand of fathering her child, now says her story was "in error." She claims that the newspaper in which the story first appeared, the* New York Daily Chronicle, *approached her based on a rumored dalliance with Mr. Durand. Although she has a four-year-old son, born out of wedlock, who has blue eyes and blond hair similar to Mr. Durand's, she now maintains that Mr. Durand was not the father and that she did not have "relations" with him. She said she was in a "condition of destitution" and received a large payment from the* Chronicle *for her story.*
>
> *The* Examiner *has learned that Durand's father, Mr. Daniel Durand, is part owner of the* Daily Chronicle. *William and Daniel Durand have been estranged since the younger Durand left the Durand & Woodbury partnership in 1901. An Army court*

of inquiry recently dismissed charges against Daniel Durand in connection with an incident during the Civil War....

Eleanor watched Daniel's face as he read the article. His jaw tightened and his eyes narrowed. He finished the article and tossed the paper on the table.

"This is garbage, pure garbage. I would guess that Miss Tyler's money problems are over. She must have been paid to change her story. Needham and Hayes said she came to them. If it happened this other way they both ought to lose their jobs. This makes it sound like I went after Will. It was the way I told you. Needham had a story. He thought it was newsworthy and wanted to run it. I told him it was his decision and he ran the story. That's all there was to it."

Eleanor shook her head. "Daniel, I feel terrible that you're subjected to this. Everyone who knows you will believe you, but most people in this city will go the other way. It's too sensational—wealthy but spiteful Wall Street banker tries to destroy his public-servant son. That's the angle on the editorial page." She picked up the paper, turned to the editorial page, and handed it to him.

The Examiner *has made no secret of its support for Will Durand. His record in Albany has impressed us and we have endorsed his campaign for the House of Representatives. He shares President Roosevelt's progressive vision, a vision much more in tune with the needs of the country than that of his father, Mr. Daniel Durand. The elder Durand's mossback view of government is that it should provide courts, police, a military, and nothing else. Unlike others who have made their fortune in this great country, he feels no obligation to give back to the public. Charitable works are conspicuously absent from his "illustrious" record....*

Unfortunately, Daniel Durand has been unable to keep his political differences with his son on a higher plane of reasoned discourse. He has stooped to the lowest kind of subterfuge to destroy Will Durand's political career. The Examiner *calls on all citizens to ignore this attempt to manufacture scandal and to consider Will Durand on his record and his political philosophy. A fair-minded evaluation yields only one conclusion: Will Durand will best serve the interests of New York in Washington. The* Examiner *proudly reiterates its endorsement of Mr. Durand.*

Daniel tossed the paper back on the table, leaned back in his chair, and stared up at the ceiling. "How would they know whether I give money to charities? I don't advertise it when I do. And how would they know my political philosophy?"

"You never kept it from Will. He could have written this editorial. You've either walked into a trap or your son has managed to turn the tables on you. You once said the average intelligence of a crowd is the intelligence of its stupidest member divided by twice the number of people in the crowd. Vox populi, Daniel. You strayed too close to the mud hole and you've been splattered. You might want to deny it once and then maintain a dignified silence. Let the mud dry—then you can brush it off." She pointed at the newspaper. "The voice of the people. Will's going to win his election."

"You sound like you're happy about it."

Eleanor felt a surge of anger like that she had felt at Aldus Kincaid's office when Daniel had suggested that Will might be behind the plot to expose his shooting of Pomeroy. "Don't tell me you don't want to see him lose!" she said, her voice rising. "It's a question of principle! You 'can't interfere' with your editor's decision? What bilge! You think Will was behind the court of inquiry and you want to pay him back. That's why you let that story go!"

Daniel sprung from his chair. "He *was* behind it! And you're damn right, someone who tries to put a noose around my neck doesn't get my vote or an editorial endorsement!" He walked to his desk, opened a drawer, took out several papers from the bottom of a stack, and handed them to Eleanor. "Read this."

Eleanor looked at the top page. *Stoddard Detective Agency. Prepared for Mr. Daniel Durand. Confidential.* She felt an ominous foreboding, quite certain she didn't want to turn the page, but compelled to know what the report said. She began to read.

She gasped the first time she saw the name Winfield. It was stunning, unbelievable, that her rejection of Archer Winfield over forty years ago had set all this in motion. Daniel had found himself in Curtis Winfield's crosshairs. Will had thrown his lot in with this family and they were behind the court of inquiry—that was clear from the report. But had Will been involved with the court of inquiry too?

She threw the report on the table, scattering its pages. "Why didn't you show me this when you got it?"

"Because I didn't trust myself. I find it a little difficult to get used to the fact that my son tried to have me killed."

"And because you didn't trust me, did you? Here you have your smoking gun in black and white. You thought your irrational wife, with her irrational devotion to her son, wouldn't accept the 'truth.' That's part of it too, isn't it, Daniel?"

"Yes."

"Well, call me crazy, but I don't accept it! I will never believe that Will tried to kill you, not unless I hear it from him! And I can't believe that you'd believe it!" She stormed from the library, slamming the door. She stood in the hallway and trembled. She had never been so angry.

The pain knifed through Tom's stomach and then spread out through his lower digestive tract. He wiped the sweat from his upper lip. None of his endless trips to the bathroom eased the pain for very long. Last night's dinner, at the restaurant in the New Willard Hotel—one of Washington's finest—wasn't responsible for his malady. It was the coming day's ordeal.

How do you not lie, but not tell the truth?

The first time he had appeared before the panel of examiners from the Interstate Commerce Commission, in his innocence, or stupidity, he had not thought he needed a lawyer, and he couldn't understand why Thackeray, the corporate attorney from New York, had been there. During his tenure as Rocky Mountain regional manager, the region had shown marked improvement in load factors, on-time percentages, rates of return, operating efficiency, and safety. He had done many things right, with no major mistakes, and he had thought that would carry the day. He was soon disabused of that quaintly naïve notion.

The examiners randomly probed decisions he had made, many so inconsequential he couldn't remember them. They were wholly uninterested in the business rationales for those decisions. When he said he had lowered a rate to undercut a rival, the examiners looked at him as blue bloods would if he belched at a dinner party. Thackeray glared. When he said that he had raised a rate so the railroad could make more money, their jaws dropped in horror, acolytes witnessing the desecration of their sect's most sacred relic. Telling the truth was implicitly forbidden, but as the examiners had informed him at the beginning of the hearing, telling a lie would open him up to a charge of perjury. How do you not lie, but not tell the truth?

Like acolytes, the examiners had their own mystical incantations, unintelligible to the uninitiated. "Common carrier," "fair pricing," "competitive equity," "regulatory compliance," and the ultimate talisman, "the public interest," were frequently invoked, but never defined. Thackeray tried to translate Tom's answers into this vague lexicon, but he grew visibly frustrated at his obtuse client. After the session was over, Thackeray administered a severe tongue-lashing, vowing to "prepare" Tom the next time he came to Washington.

Tom had arrived the previous morning and spent the afternoon with the attorney, learning the new rules, the new language, and the supreme commandment of regulatory hearings: regardless of how little the commission's officials knew about railroading, they were entitled to a deference bordering on obsequience. He had to hold his tongue no matter how idiotic their questions. These men, Thackeray stressed repeatedly, could have just as much of an effect—up or down—on the railroad's profits as a mother lode, a big accident, or a bumper crop. Tom had listened intently and nodded when asked if he understood and would he do what was required. That night his stomach had rebelled.

He couldn't do it.

He sat on his bed with his head in his hands as the morning sun peeked through the curtains. He couldn't do it. He didn't know what he was going to do, but he couldn't play Thackeray's game.

He showered, shaved, and dressed. His stomach felt a little better, but he didn't want to risk eating breakfast. The inquisition was at nine o'clock, an hour and a half away. He'd take a walk, see some sights and clear his head.

He walked from the hotel towards the White House, two blocks west. There were only a few carriages on Pennsylvania Avenue.

He thought of two people—Bill James and Mario.

What would Bill James do? He couldn't imagine his mentor, the legendary Cheyenne yardmaster, at this kind of hearing. Straight-shooting James wouldn't tolerate the foolishness. He simply wouldn't be here, even if the fate of the railroad depended on it.

Then there was Mario. What if he had bravely stood up and announced that he wouldn't kill Filipino civilians? He would have been tossed into a military stockade. The government ran over people like a locomotive ran over a squirrel on the track. Having met the demands of his conscience, Mario would still be alive, but he would still be in that stockade, too. For the most part, Daniel Durand and Bill James' generation had been able to ignore the government, but things were changing. Bill James had his way with the Union Pacific because he was smarter and more competent than everyone else, but that meant nothing at all with the government. Mario couldn't tolerate its evil. James wouldn't have tolerated its foolishness, and like Mario, he would have wound up dead on the track.

At nine o'clock, Tom sat down at one end of a table in a small conference room with Mr. Thackeray opposite three men from the Interstate Commerce Commission. Thackeray was in his late fifties or early sixties, of medium height and build, his gray-and-black hair slicked back. Gold-rimmed glasses rested on his large, hooked nose, the most prominent feature of his thin, sharply defined face. His impassive, lusterless blue eyes didn't miss a thing. His lips were generally pursed, although they could form a smile when professionally necessary. He was the consummate corporate attorney, a polished negotiator and conciliator who had made a fortune at a Wall Street firm and then had found that his decades of contacts, especially those established with his cronies who had migrated to Washington, were a prized commodity for businessmen like E. H. Harriman, compelled to "do business" with the government. Tom didn't like him and would have taken a bet at short odds that he had neither convictions nor friends.

"Are you ready to testify, Mr. Durand?" Thackeray said.

"No."

Thackeray frowned.

One of the men from the commission, in his mid-fifties with a drooping mustache, cleared his throat. "Gentlemen, I'm Mr. Morris, and my associates are Mr. Grimes and Mr. Peterson. As our request for your appearance noted, we're interested in the Union Pacific's rate decisions in the Rocky Mountain region after the San Francisco earthquake. Mr. Durand, you were the official with direct responsibility for those decisions?"

"Subject to approval from headquarters in New York, yes."

"Within three weeks of the earthquake, your region published rate hikes of ten to twenty percent. What was the rationale for that?"

"After the earthquake there was a surge in demand for commodities and supplies in the Bay Area. It sucked up every train we had in our region. I had to raise rates to bring demand in alignment with what we could supply. I wanted to raise them more, and in fact we raised them several times after that first increase."

Thackeray had instructed him that the only acceptable regulatory justification for increased rates was increased costs. The attorney glared at him—there had been no mention of costs.

"You were aware that those increases fueled anger among the public against your railroad?" Peterson asked. He looked as if he was only a few years out of college.

"Which public, Mr. Peterson?"

"Excuse me?"

"Which members of the public?"

"Why, those who had to pay the higher rates."

"Even at the higher rates we couldn't supply enough trains. We had to turn down business from many of our regular shippers. They would have paid much higher rates—they were livid that we didn't have the trains. Aren't they members of the public? And their customers as well?"

"Mr. Durand," Grimes replied, "you must understand that your railroad is invested with a public interest, and you must take due account of that interest."

"Which public? And what interest? One public may be interested in lower fares, at least until we can't supply the trains, and another public may be interested in shipping at higher rates, if it can get the trains. Of which public and which interest am I supposed to take due account?"

How do you not lie, but not tell the truth? You ask a question. There was a long, stony silence.

"Mr. Durand," Mr. Morris said. "We have the figures. You don't deny that during this time your region achieved a higher than average rate of return?"

Mr. Thackeray had instructed him to stress that this higher return would be temporary, although it was his job to permanently elevate the rate of return.

"No, I don't deny that we achieved a rate of return that was higher than our average."

"You would also concede that the Union Pacific has consistently maintained shipping rates that are lower than your competitors', even after you raised them?"

"Yes, we have, even as we've achieved that higher rate of return."

"Are you aware that such a practice could be construed as predatory pricing?"

Tom remembered his father telling him how Rockefeller had built Standard Oil, relentlessly achieving efficiencies that drove the price of kerosene from eighty cents to a few pennies a gallon while garnering legendary profits. Now that kind of competitive efficiency was suspect.

"When I was here in August, didn't you say that rates that matched our competitors' could be evidence of collusion?" Tom said.

"I may have said something to that effect."

"Under the antitrust law, can't rates that are higher than those which normally prevail be evidence of monopoly power?"

"That is…wait a minute, I know where you're going with this." Morris said, eluding checkmate.

"If our rates are low, we're predators, if they're the same we're colluders, and if they're higher we're monopolists. Which one should we pick?"

"Mr. Durand," Mr. Grimes said. "We're not here to tell you how to run your railroad."

"But the railroad can be subject to civil and criminal penalties if you don't like what we do after the fact, and so can I."

"It's not arbitrary, Mr. Durand," Grimes said. "We have procedures and regulations."

"Where in your procedures and regulations does it tell me at what level to set rates?"

"Let's turn to the issue of service availability in Denver," Mr. Morris said.

The session continued for a little over two hours, the men from the commission making Tom explain and justify decisions while disavowing any intent to tell anyone at Union Pacific how to run the railroad; Tom stifling his anger, answering questions with questions; the commission men changing subjects when confronted with the inexplicable; Mr. Thackeray clenching his teeth, breaking two pencils.

"Mr. Durand and Mr. Thackeray, you understand why we're here," Mr. Morris said, glancing at a clock on the wall. "The Commission protects the public's interest in our common carriers. We will report our findings and administrative determinations and make them available to you. Union Pacific business practices will continue to be an ongoing concern of the commission, and I must say that today, I don't think all of our concerns were adequately addressed. Thank you."

They filed out of the conference room. Neither Tom nor Mr. Thackeray said anything until they had walked out of the building.

"We'll probably be cited and fined," Mr. Thackeray said angrily. "That's not how we went over it yesterday, Mr. Durand."

Tom shook his head. "No, it's not."

"Don't you understand? The rules of the game have changed. This is the future of railroading. Whether it makes sense or not, you recite the necessary incantations. The Union Pacific has to show it's willing to play by the new rules. Politically we're hanging by a thread, what with Roosevelt making an issue of the Imperial Valley."

Another corporation had diverted water from the Colorado River into the Imperial Valley in Southern California for irrigation. The idea had worked until the Colorado had changed course, flooding the region. To protect its Southern Pacific line into the valley, the Union Pacific had tried and failed to tame the renegade river through a costly series of dams and levees.

"After the quake, we did more to put San Francisco back together than anyone, at enormous expense," Tom said evenly. "Roosevelt never said a word. Now we get blamed for the Imperial Valley because we can't clean up someone else's mess. We get no credit for the things we do right and blamed for things other people do wrong. We come to Washington to justify our decisions by standards that nobody can define to officials who don't know horsepower from horseshit. I understand one thing, Mr. Thackeray. Whatever this new game is, the railroad won't win. The government holds all the cards. If this is the future of railroading, it may not be mine."

"They're not going to like your attitude in New York."

"I'm sure they won't." It was what Bill James would have said. Tom turned and walked away. It was what Bill James would have done, and hang whether or not he got run over.

Chapter 26

Capitalist

Jessica knew it was coming. Ever since Tom's second trip to Washington, she had expected some sort of explosion. He had been tied up in knots after that trip. His love of railroading and the Union Pacific was colliding with the regulators in Washington, who were making him justify his decisions according to contradictory standards, and with the executives in New York, who were telling him that he had to do so, in the best interests of the railroad. He had exercised a relatively free hand as regional manager, but now his decisions were often overridden by New York for reasons he found incomprehensible. The Interstate Commerce Commission hadn't "invited" him back to Washington, but it had hauled many Union Pacific executives, including Harriman himself, before an investigative committee. Tom read the sensationalized newspaper accounts of the hearings with a temple-throbbing fury he somehow managed to contain. His passion and joy for his work were ebbing, and Jessica took it as a portent when he sold their Union Pacific stock. All she could do was encourage him to talk.

There was no explosion—it was more like a snowflake that triggers an avalanche. One day after work Tom was reading the newspaper at the kitchen table while she cooked dinner. The aroma from the bread in the oven filled the kitchen. Their three-year-old daughter, Elizabeth, played with her toys in the parlor.

"He's contemptible," Tom said softly, setting the paper on the table.

"Who?" Jessica said as she seasoned a stew.

"Roosevelt. He's blaming Harriman for the stock market's drop."

"Harriman probably owns more railroad shares than anyone in the country, save Morgan and Rockefeller. Why would he want to see their price go down? It would cost him millions."

"It would. Roosevelt takes on the two best railroads. He brings his first antitrust case against Hill and he hauls Harriman before his commission. He signs the Hepburn Act so he can regulate railroad rates. Surprise, surprise, investors figure out that the best days for the railroads are behind them. They sell, just like I did, and it leads the rest of the market down. How many politicians take the blame when they screw things up? Roosevelt points his finger at Harriman to divert attention from what he's done. Roosevelt doesn't know a thing about business. He couldn't make money if he owned the only cathouse in a mining camp."

"Tom, your language—Elizabeth can hear you. Nobody's going to believe Roosevelt."

"You give people too much credit. Somebody elected him. This paper is lapping it up."

Jessica removed a loaf of bread from the oven and set it on the stove. "Poor Mr. Harriman."

"Mr. Mahl was out here from New York the other day. He said Harriman looks terrible. He's losing weight and he's in pain, although he tries to hide it. Roosevelt's going to kill him."

She turned away from the stove and looked directly at him. "Tom, what are you going to do?"

He looked past her. "You know what bothers me the most about all this?"

She shook her head.

"Not one businessman is standing up and saying, 'What you're doing is wrong.' They're too scared. Harriman tangled with Roosevelt and everybody sees what's happened to him. The system has changed and we're not going back. The government started with the railroads because that's the biggest, most profitable industry. They don't go after the bad lines—the corrupt ones that buy the politicians and live off subsidies and favors. They go after the two best roads, the ones that don't need any of that. Not because they did anything wrong, but because of everything they did right. Nobody stands up to defend them. They all just spout this 'public interest' nonsense that jackass Thackeray tried to put over on me in Washington. They figure they can accommodate themselves to the government, and maybe they can, for a while, but the government will always win. Someday there's going to be hell to pay."

She sat down at the table with Tom. "What are you going to do?"

He sighed and his eyes glistened. "If capital—the smart money—is getting out of the railroads, can labor be far behind?"

He had struggled with this dilemma for months and she knew how hard it was for him to say what he was saying. She put her hand on his arm. "Not the smart labor."

Alexander and Daniel were in Daniel's office early, before many of Durand & Woodbury's employees had arrived for work. Financial markets were queasy, everybody was busy putting out fires, and once the workday began it would be difficult to have a serious discussion. As Daniel looked at Alexander across the desk, he could see, from the knit of his brow, that his quiet son, the one he knew the least, meant to have some sort of serious discussion.

"You wanted to speak with me," Daniel said.

"It's about Tommy." Alexander shook his head. "I'm never going to get used to calling him Tom. Now that he's resigned from the railroad and will be working here, there are some things I want to say."

"Does it bother you that I didn't ask you before I talked with him about it?"

"No, why should you? You've never consulted with me before you've hired other men and that's not my place. Tommy…Tom is quite capable and I have no doubt he'll do well here. I just want to warn you."

"About?"

"I know he's your favorite. Now that I've got three of my own, I know there's always a favorite. Tom is smart and ambitious and he's got something special, a spark, but if you bring him in and put him before everyone else, that would be a big mistake. It would be wrong."

Daniel's eyes narrowed, but he said nothing.

"I've never been jealous of Tom. Will always was, it hurt him that he wasn't your favorite, although he was Mother's. Tommy's smarter than me. He might even be as smart as you. You say the hardest thing to find in business is imagination and Tom's got plenty. I don't, usually. It's not the way I think. You're going to retire soon."

"What makes you say that?"

"You're not as involved. You're pulling away. I don't know exactly what's going on between you and Mother and it's none of my business, but I hope you'll get that patched up. It would be a shame for you two to spend your golden years at odds with each other. When you leave for good, you want a son to run the firm. If Tom's on board, you can do that. I couldn't run this place. In time he prob-ably could."

Daniel pondered his second son. To dispute his assessments that he wasn't his father's favorite, that he didn't have his brother's imagination, or that he wasn't capable of running the firm would have been an exercise in wasted words. Yet that he had reached these unsentimental conclusions bespoke strength, a lack of self-delusion. That strength was the part of Alexander's character Daniel knew the best and appreciated the most. There was no pretense or prevarication in him, but he revealed what he was thinking on his own terms. Such revelations were seldom, if ever, driven solely by a desire to impart his thoughts. He always had his purpose. Daniel was beginning to see the purpose of this conversation.

"So you don't mind Tommy working here, but you don't think he should be elevated to some sort of leadership position?"

"No, I don't, not if it's your decision. E. H. Harriman is no fool, and if Tommy weren't top notch he wouldn't have promoted him the way he did. Tommy may end up running the firm, but he has to prove himself first, to the partners who will be here after you're gone. We'll make the decision. When you step down, Benjamin Keane should be the managing partner."

"I've talked it over with George. That's the current line of suc-cession—Benjamin Keane will be the managing partner. You've al-ways thought of the best interests of the firm and your partners; I'm not surprised you reached the same conclusion. Nothing changes if Tom starts working here. He has to prove himself and he has to be chosen to advance by the partners he works with. You'll show him the ropes."

Alexander rarely smiled, but Daniel thought he detected one. Alexander stood to leave.

"Alexander, why don't you bring the family over for dinner Saturday? It's been a while."

"I'd like that. I'll check with Hanna. Thank you, Father."

J. P. Morgan glowered at Daniel, because Morgan glowered at everyone. During this crisis, he did so to impart a fear greater than the panic seizing Wall Street and induce the men with the money to part with it and underwrite a rescue of the financial system. Daniel felt no particular fear. He had been through enough panics to see them for what they were—opportunities. The key to a panic was to "panic" before everyone else; sell while prices were high and sell more than one actually had, that is, sell short. That had been Woodbury and the Pirate's strategy since a partners' meeting several months ago. The past two weeks, while Broad and Wall Streets were jammed with anxious speculators and investors as prices crashed inside the Stock Exchange; while long lines of depositors hoping to withdraw their money stretched outside banks and trust companies; while Secretary of the Treasury Cortelyou hustled to New York to confer with the captains of finance; while President Roosevelt, re-turning from a trip shooting the furry and feathered in Louisiana, tried to quell the panic by publicly praising "those conservative and substantial businessmen" whom he had recently lambasted as "malefactors of great wealth"; Durand & Woodbury bought in stock to cover its shorts and Daniel added to his vast holdings.

Daniel stared through a cloud of cigar smoke at Morgan's nose—it was impossible not to stare. Morgan suffered from rhinophyma, which, as the name of the disease implied, left his nose deformed—hugely swollen, bright red and purple, overlaid with a prominent tracing of veins. His sycophants said the force of his personality so quickly overwhelmed that one soon forgot the nose. Everyone else stared at it.

"Mr. Durand, is Durand & Woodbury good for two million?" Morgan said.

The short-term loan market that greased the workings of Wall Street was broken and Morgan was trying to fix it. The traders who made the markets in stocks faced ruinous interest rates of as much as 100 percent trying to finance their positions. One man's ruinous rate was another man's opportunity. Durand & Woodbury was flush. It had taken many conferences among financiers and government officials and hours poring over documents and accounts by their underlings, but there were glimmers at the end of the tunnel. Notwithstanding the idiocies of its politicians, the American economy had, in a few decades, become the world's biggest and most innovative, a strapping youth who didn't yet know his own power. America had eclipsed England, not that the British or Anglophile Morgan would admit it. By Daniel's estimation there was nothing fundamentally wrong with the dynamic economy, merely a shortage of cash. Talk of a central bank and an income tax bothered him, but as long as the country stayed on the gold standard and incomes remained untaxed, the economy would remain essentially sound.

Daniel's gaze absently wandered around the study of the Pierpont Morgan Library. Its opulent décor—a wooden ceiling antiqued with coats of arms, stained glass panels set into the windows, red damask wall covering, kneeling angels holding candelabra—offended his austere sensibilities, but then, most of what New York's wealthy surrounded themselves with did. He was grateful for Eleanor's selective, elegant tastes.

"Mr. Durand, is Durand & Woodbury good for two million?" Morgan asked again.

"Durand & Woodbury is good for five million."

Morgan raised his eyebrows. The true wealth of Durand & Woodbury was one of Wall Street's better kept secrets, although Morgan was too well connected not to see beyond the discreet profile it presented to the world. He and Daniel had not liked each other since their first meeting aboard Morgan's yacht; perhaps he was surprised that Daniel would now come to his aid. Their animus was irrelevant to Daniel—money was money and Durand & Woodbury would be lending at a high interest rate against strong stocks and money-good bonds as collateral.

"Mr. Caldwell," Morgan said. "Are you good for one million?"

"Yes."

He had to go around the table twice, but Morgan got his contributions from the bankers. Wall Street would have enough money to function. The emergency meeting adjourned so another emergency meeting—this one to rescue several tottering trust companies—could be convened. Daniel would help save Wall Street at plump interest rates, but the trust companies were a less remunerative mission of mercy he would leave to others. He left the study and stepped into the vaulted foyer of the famous library's rotunda.

Morgan, too busy to be much of a reader, had commissioned the library in 1902, and prominent Italianate Renaissance architect Charles Follen McKim designed it and supervised construction. As every newspaper at the time had breathlessly reported, among its twenty thousand rare and valuable volumes were one of the world's great collections of medieval and Renaissance illuminated manuscripts, two Gutenberg Bibles, and first editions of *City of God* and *Paradise Lost*. The rotunda was an eclectic riot of angel statues, purple columns, biblical ceiling murals, and historical and literary paintings from Homer to King Arthur to Dante and seemingly everything in between. The bankers milling about were neither contemplating the artwork nor perusing the volumes. They smoked cigars whose ends they had chewed to tatters, huddled in nervous groups engaged in muffled conversations, or paced the marble floor.

Benjamin Keane, Tom, and Alexander approached Daniel.

"What's the ante?" Keane said.

Daniel held up five fingers and Keane nodded. "Let's get out of here," Daniel said.

"We can't," Alexander said. "Morgan's locked the front door. Nobody leaves until the trust company situation gets worked out."

Daniel shook his head. "If I thought it would get me to bed quicker, I'd go back in there and write a check for a million. Morgan and his melodrama—this is ridiculous."

"What's he like?" Tom said.

Daniel chuckled. "A bundle of contradictions. Makes darn sure you know that he doesn't care what you think of him, but you'd better be impressed by his books and his art and his yachts. He's supposed to be the symbol of capitalism, but he actually distrusts it—too much change too quickly, too wild for his tastes. He's more interested in power than money and likes big, well-ordered cartels that he controls. That's the key to him, control—he has to have control. Good luck. It's an enormous strain. Nobody will replace him after he's gone—nobody can ride this bronco. As it is, he's hanging on for dear life."

A voice rose above the hushed tones. "This whole sorry crisis shows what I've been saying for years! This country needs a central bank. If we had one, we wouldn't be in this mess."

They turned towards the speaker. "Who's that?" Tom whispered to Keane.

Keane shook his head. "Maybe one of Morgan's men. They're all for a central bank."

"That's what we need," Daniel said. "A central bank will solve all our problems."

The speaker, a tall man with a pompadour of silver hair and a flowing silver mustache, heard Daniel and turned towards him. "Sir, you do not support the establishment of a central bank?"

"No, it will only make our problems worse."

"Don't you find it intolerable that the government has to go hat in hand when the country encounters financial difficulties?"

"The government has to go to the people with money when it wants money. It would be intolerable to give the government the ability to manufacture it."

"Many in Washington are extremely dissatisfied with the current state of affairs. I believe after this crisis that you'll be standing against the tide."

"I'm sure you're right about that. It won't be the first time."

"Good evening, sir." The speaker turned back to the group to which he had been speaking.

"You really think we'll have a central bank?" Alexander said.

"The roar grows louder with every panic."

The four Durand & Woodbury men continued their discussion for the better part of an hour. Finally the door to the study opened and a group of bedraggled bankers emerged. Morgan stepped into the foyer. "Gentlemen, we have reached an agreement on the trust companies. Good evening."

The front door was unlocked and the men streamed outside to Madison Avenue. As Daniel stepped into the frosty autumn night air, a feeling seized him. There was no other way to put it—he was bored and had been bored, stale, throughout the crisis. He had always done what he wanted. For the first time since Thomas Keane had hired him in Cleveland, he wanted to do something besides banking. "It's time to quit."

"I should say so," Thomas Keane's son replied, removing his watch from its vest pocket. "It's after three."

Daniel stopped walking and the other men did too. "No, I mean it's time for me to quit…at Durand & Woodbury."

Keane and Daniel's sons stared at him. They had to have known this day was coming—Alexander had said as much to Daniel—but there was no hiding either their surprise or their apprehension. They were the future of Durand & Woodbury.

Eleanor lounged on a sofa in the sitting room, reading the newspaper. Daniel had come in very late the previous evening and was still asleep. She had a pot of coffee waiting for him when he came down. She was trying—they were both trying—to return things between them to what they had been. It was wrenching. After so many years in which, except for Will, she and Daniel had agreed on all the important things, that one exception had erupted with such volcanic fury. There had been tension and fights for weeks. Finally the emotions diminished to something less raw and the fights became discussions. They had recognized that neither one was going to accept the other's view. Daniel believed that Will had tried to kill him; Eleanor didn't. Some diseases were cured and some you learned to live with. Their unsatisfactory modus vivendi had to serve as the basis for salving severely abraded feelings, but they both wanted to make the effort.

Eleanor checked the public events section of the newspaper. She liked to take her grandchildren—Laura and Michael's two sons and two daughters, Alexander and Hanna's daughter and two sons, Jessica and Tom's daughter and son, and Constance and Heinrich's son—to exhibits and activities. This weekend there was an exhibit of European Impressionists and a show of the new automobiles. The girls would favor the paintings, the boys the automobiles. They'd all go to both—it was good for them.

Daniel entered the sitting room in his bathrobe, yawning. Eleanor poured him a cup of coffee. He sat next to her on the couch and sipped his coffee.

"What time did you come in?"

"Around four this morning.

"Do we still have a financial system?"

Daniel chuckled. "For all the newspaper histrionics and Morgan's dramatics you'd think the fate of the world was at stake. Rescues were stitched together and I think the worst is behind us. Wall Street still stands."

"Nice alliteration for someone who just got up. Are you going to the office?"

"Later. An interesting thing happened last night."

"What?"

"After we saved the world, I realized that I hadn't had the same enthusiasm, the same relish, for this panic as I've had in the past. I was meeting with big names in government and finance, huge sums of money were at stake, the firm made a killing, and I bought a lot of stock, but it all seemed like old hat. I was tired, but this feeling went way beyond that. I thought to myself, if this doesn't get your juices going, it's time to do something else. I thought you'd be the first I'd tell I was going to retire, but I blurted it out to Tom, Alexander, and Benjamin—'it's time to quit.'"

Although she had expected it for some time, it was still a shock to hear him say it. "So you're going to retire?"

"Yes, I am. I think I can."

"Now that Tom's at the firm?"

"That's part of it, although I wasn't planning on staying until they carried me out. Sooner or later it has to move on without me, with or without Tom."

"I've thought you were going to retire for the last year or two, but I didn't say anything. It had to be your decision."

Daniel nodded. "I'll keep my hand in a little bit, but it's time to do something else. I have many books I want to read, or reread. I may even do some writing. We wanted to spend time together, travel. Maybe things between us can…"

"Heal?"

"I was going to say, 'get better,' but let's be ambitious. Who knows how much time we have."

She took his hand and squeezed it. "I'm glad you're retiring."

The Honorable William Durand, Republican Representative from the state of New York, stood in the well of the House of Representatives and cleared his throat. Few of his fellow representatives looked up from their reading or conversations. Those who knew Durand liked him well enough, but they weren't going to pay much attention to a speech from a freshman representative.

"Nobody likes a blowhard," Harrison Winfield had told Will, "although the place is crawling with them. They'll pretend to listen to you because they're waiting for their turn to talk. Play it safe. See which way the wind is blowing before you take a stand, and if possible, get on record taking the opposite side, too—it keeps everybody happy. Remember, the only thing anybody is interested in is what you can do for them, and until you've been there awhile you can't do much. Keep the speeches simple and brief. That will earn you some gratitude, if nothing else."

"Esteemed Representatives," Will said. "I stand before you because I believe that the recent panic demonstrates that it's long past time that the United States had a reserve bank. While I in no way believe that our financial difficulties amounted to crucifixion on a 'Cross of Gold,' the plain truth of the matter is that a severe shortage of ready money almost brought down our financial system and economy. Many other nations have discovered the advantages of reserve banking, and now the United States must adopt this progressive innovation as well.

"In a financial panic money is scare, which forces the interest rate, or price of money, upward, and by necessitating the sale of assets, forces their price downward. For many years, leading financiers have called for a more elastic money supply and a central bank, a lender of last resort." Will smiled. "Leading financiers," perhaps, but not his father. "Such a bank would prevent the distress sale of assets and the economic hardship attendant on financial contraction.

"Today I announce my support for Senator Aldrich and Representative Vreeland's legislation, which would establish a National Monetary Commission to study the currency issue and suggest proposals for a reserve bank and other banking reforms. Serious men of goodwill shall differ on the details of a reserve bank. However, that should not stop us from establishing this institution, now that its necessity has once again been so painfully demonstrated. I add my name as a cosponsor to the Aldrich-Vreeland Bill in the House of Representatives. Thank you."

Will stepped down. Most of the representatives hadn't bothered to look up. The central bank issue was a marker—unlike most issues, he had to make his early support clear. Rockefeller and most of the other big industrialists, Morgan, Baker, and most of the other big bankers supported a central bank. Usually a freshman representative's view on anything wouldn't amount to spit to his colleagues, but it meant more since he was the son of one of the few—and certainly the most prominent—New York bankers who publicly opposed a central bank.

Daniel stood on the elevated dais at the front of one of Delmonico's banquet rooms and looked through the cigar smoke at the applauding assemblage. It could have been a much bigger crowd, requiring an even larger room, if Daniel had invited all the prominent men with whom he had done business to his retirement dinner, but that was not what he wanted. He wanted to say goodbye to Durand & Woodbury his way, with no outsiders. He glanced at Eleanor and she smiled supportively. She knew how difficult this would be for him.

"Thank you," Daniel said as the clapping subsided. "I'll keep my remarks brief—"

"That's a surprise!" Woodbury shouted. The room erupted in laughter. Daniel's laconicism was legendary.

Daniel smiled and waited for the laughter to die down. There was a serious matter to be addressed. His profession, the firm's business, and the firm itself were under attack from all quarters after the recent panic.

"The love of money is supposedly the root of evil. What could be more evil than the profession devoted to money? It has stood condemned since Jesus drove the moneychangers from the temple.

"At the heart of capitalism is capital. When one produces more than one consumes and saves the surplus, that surplus is capital. Long ago a caveman, or more likely a cavewoman, saved a few seeds, planted and tended them, and in due time ate the result, while saving a few more seeds. It was the beginning of agriculture and civilization was on its way. Back then capital was a seed, today it's money, but at every step of progress someone consumed less than he or she produced and put the surplus to productive use.

"That productive use is the other half of capitalism. Someone has an invention, a new business, an idea, but the innovation requires capital, money. How do capital and innovation get together? That's the role of the banker. Those who produce more than they consume entrust capital to the banker, who must then decide on the most productive use of that capital. Neither saving nor innovation is evil—they're the foundations of human progress. How then can the intermediary function that joins them be evil? It's the essential linchpin of capitalism.

"Balzac wrote, 'Behind every great fortune lies a great crime.' Unfortunately, for most of human history, that statement has been correct. The savers and the innovators have had their labors plundered by their rulers or their priests. The kings acquired their fortunes through the outright theft of taxation or the stealth theft of debasement of the store of value. The holy men acquired theirs through blackmail—ostracism, damnation, and death awaited those who did not render unto the gods' representatives here on earth. You can bet that the day after Jesus drove the moneychangers from the temple the priests invited them back in, because without the 'contributions' they extracted from the moneychangers, who performed a useful and productive function, the priests couldn't survive.

"It's no wonder, then, that mankind's progress has been so haltingly slow. Slow, that is, until producers were offered a true 'square deal': you may keep what you produce, no one can take it from you, and your store of value will not be debased. The result? Since the founding of the United States and the enshrinement of the ideal of human liberty, and especially in the forty-five years since the emancipation of the Negro, man has progressed more than he has in all the centuries past.

"Those who embrace this square deal—the tired, the poor, the huddled masses yearning to breathe free who stream to our shores—are the true cream of humanity. Capitalism gives the cream its chance to rise. The rulers must seek the consent of the governed and religion must rely on the donations of its adherents. Millions of uncommon 'common' people are indeed rising, and many would-be rulers and high priests despise them for it. They're in the vanguard of the mounting hostility towards liberty, towards property and contract rights, towards gold and honest money, and, most passionately, towards the capitalism that's given those who want to make their own way a means to escape their poverty."

Daniel paused, looked out over the crowd, and took a deep breath. "I'm proud to call myself a banker and a capitalist, and I'm proud of the part Durand & Woodbury has played for thirty-five years in this unprecedented Industrial Revolution. We've helped Mr. Rockefeller and then Mr. Edison and Mr. Westinghouse light the country, and Mr. Hill and Mr. Harriman to span the continent. We've issued securities for countless entrepreneurs and supported and traded those securities in the aftermarket. In all this, we've performed the essential function of intermediating between savings and investment on the one hand and enterprise on the other. We've done so honorably and well, and we've been rewarded. I'm proud that Durand & Woodbury has prospered. We've earned every dime we've made!" The room erupted in applause. Daniel's eyes fixed on one of the firm's oldest partners. Now came the hard part.

"Jakob Gottman came to us early on from Cleveland, where I knew his grandfather, Isaak, and his grandfather's brother, Abram, who was very dear to me. He said he could sell, and I could see he had chutzpah." Daniel said the Yiddish term with relish. "Everyone knows there's a Jewish Wall Street and a *goyim* Wall Street. I asked Jakob why he chose Durand & Woodbury instead of a Jewish firm. He said he wanted to be successful banker, not a successful Jewish banker, and all he wanted was a chance. Well, Jakob got his chance, and boy, can he sell!"

There was laughter and a few "hear, hears."

"Jakob, you're a cornerstone of our firm."

Daniel gestured towards his son-in-law. "Michael Palos was the son of our firm's hostler way back when. Mr. Palos was fresh off the boat from Eastern Europe and I could barely understand his English, but he said he had 'very smart boy,' and maybe I 'want to talk to him.' Well, I did talk to him, and Michael was a very smart boy. He certainly didn't have to marry my daughter to make partner."

There was laughter and applause.

"'We don't care where you started from, only where you're going and how you get there' has become the unofficial motto of our firm. I'm proud that I have two sons in the firm and I know George is just as proud of his son, Richard. I hope we never have a policy against nepotism. We'd close the door to too many good men and women, and besides, we know things about our relatives that we could never find out in a job interview. But 'we don't care where you started from' takes on a new meaning when decisions have to be made about positions and promotions. We have to keep advancing the best people, regardless of where they came from. George and I have agreed on my successor, the best man for the position. Ladies and gentlemen, it's my privilege and pleasure to announce our new managing partner, Mr. Benjamin Keane. Benjamin, please stand up."

Keane stood to hearty applause and waved.

Daniel waited a long time, until the applause had died down and Benjamin had accepted his many congratulations. "Now I want to say a few words about my wife, my treasured, my beautiful and brilliant Eleanor. Without her, there would be no Durand & Woodbury and I wouldn't be standing before you today. It was Eleanor who urged me to leave Cleveland and go into business with George. Since then, I can't think of an important decision or development at the firm that I haven't discussed with her, and I can't think of a time when I haven't benefited from her wisdom. Someday Wall Street will have as many women as it does men and nobody will think anything of it. Eleanor could have been a banker. Instead she was the mother of our children. I'm confident that Alexander and Tom will continue to do credit to Durand & Woodbury, and one of the reasons is because Eleanor is their mother. She has given so much to them." Daniel looked towards Eleanor. "Dearest, thank you."

She smiled and nodded. This round of applause gave way to a standing ovation.

Again Daniel let the lengthy, noisy appreciation die of its own accord. "Thirty-five years ago, George and I started Durand & Woodbury. George, I'd like to congratulate you. Tonight is the first time in thirty-five years that I haven't seen a stain on your shirt." The room burst into laughter, Woodbury laughing the hardest of all. His slovenliness was as famous as Daniel's taciturnity. "How fortunate we were to start the firm when we did! George and I have had a front row seat on the world's greatest explosion of human ingenuity, industry, and creativity ever. We're living in an age of giants. It's been the excitement of dreams and aspirations, of self-interest, of raising money, investing, floating securities, watching George and the Pirate trade those securities through up and down markets, and ultimately watching the businesses we nurtured, including our own, take off that's kept me coming to work every day. Most days it didn't even feel like work."

He didn't want it to happen, he had hoped it wouldn't happen, but it was happening anyway. His eyes glistened. "Now it's time for more sedate pursuits," he said, his voice dropping. "I'm going to miss that excitement, but more than that I'm going to…" He had to stop. A tear trickled down his cheek and he sighed. "I'm going to miss you all more than you can know. I'll be by once in a while—you're not getting rid of me for good—and I'll still have my office, but there's nothing like the day-to-day. And George—my cofounder, my partner, my friend—you I'm going to miss the most. The humor, the quotes in Latin and Greek, the strategy sessions, the war whoops after big trades, even that rat's nest you call an office. This firm has been my life. I wouldn't change a single thing, and it all couldn't have happened without George." He stopped and took a long breath. "I think I'd better say thank you and good night."

As the room jumped to a standing ovation, George rushed to the dais, his shirttail fluttering from under his cummerbund. "*Te, canis, numquam putavi prius abiturum esse quam me!*"

Daniel looked at him quizzically.

"You dog! I never thought you'd leave before me!" He threw his arms around Daniel in a bear hug.

Chapter 27

Fools' Gold

Daniel sat in the small library at Durand & Woodbury he had
established several years before his retirement, at a table strewn
with papers and books. In a few weeks, after 1912 turned into 1913,
he would address a subcommittee of the House of Representatives'
Committee on Banking and Currency, which was considering legislation to establish a central bank, the Federal Reserve. He stood
virtually alone among New York bankers in his opposition to the
legislation, and he knew most of the representatives would be hostile to his position. His research had to be meticulous and his facts
accurate or the lawyers-turned-politicians on the committee would
crucify him with their cross-examination. The preparation reminded
him of the work he had done before the court of inquiry.

Anthony Keane, Benjamin's son and a clerk at the firm, poked
his head in the door. "Mr. Salisbury is here, sir."

"Thank you, Anthony."

Daniel walked to a conference room where Durand & Woodbury
partners met with important clients. He had never met Mr. Salisbury.
His initial contact had been a letter with a return address from
Salisbury & Markle, Threadneedle Street, London. Mr. Salisbury

had written that he wanted to discuss Daniel's upcoming testimony. Daniel investigated Salisbury & Markle, a merchant bank founded over sixty years ago by Salisbury's grandfather, before he answered the letter. Its client list included some of England's most respectable fortunes and it did business with the best European and American banking establishments. Its name had appeared on many of the same "tombstone" announcements of securities' distributions as Durand & Woodbury's. Beyond that, Daniel had discovered only that it shared Durand & Woodbury's penchant for discretion.

Keane ushered a man to the conference room who appeared every inch the proper London banker—tall, stocky but not fat, in his mid-fifties. He wore a black, perfectly cut Saville Row suit with a gold watch-chain across the vest, black Oxfords, and a blue tie with discreet yellow dots extending from under a high collar. Black-and-gray mutton-chop sideburns met his mustache and strands of hair stretched across his otherwise gleaming pate. Daniel guessed that he had left a bowler on the hat stand in the reception room.

"Mr. Salisbury, may I present Mr. Durand?" Keane said.

The men shook hands. "I'm pleased to meet you, Mr. Salisbury."

"How do you do?" His cultured accent confirmed Daniel's initial assessment.

"May I get you tea or coffee?" Keane asked.

"Tea—white with sugar."

They settled into high-backed leather chairs across from each other at a rectangular table of dark, gleaming rosewood. Keane left and returned with coffee and tea. He set a cup of tea before Salisbury and a cup of coffee before Daniel and left the room.

"Your letter said you wished to discuss my testimony on the Federal Reserve Act."

"Yes, I did. It's my understanding that you will testify against the legislation."

"I will."

"As it stands, you will be the only man of prominence within banking who will publicly oppose the Federal Reserve Act. I'd like to suggest that you reconsider your stance." Salisbury placidly sipped his tea.

"Why would I reconsider? All my research has strengthened my conviction that a reserve bank would be bad for the country."

"I'm sure you have your reasons, Mr. Durand." Salisbury's tone was dismissive—reasons were apparently irrelevant. "However, I wonder if you've fully considered the depth of support, both in this country and Europe, for the establishment of an American central bank. Your resistance will prove futile."

"If it's futile, why is anybody worried about it?"

"Despite the manifest advantages of central banking and a lengthy campaign to educate the public, there's historical antagonism among certain segments of your population. Although it's remote, there's a chance you might reawaken that antagonism."

"I hope so."

Salisbury set his saucer and teacup on the table. "I'm thinking of where your true interest lies," he said, his tone persuasive. "You can have your grand gesture, but this legislation will become law, and people, important people, will remember your opposition. Mr. Durand, you've been too successful, scaled too many heights, not to realize what that would mean."

Daniel smiled. "Mr. Salisbury, before I scaled all those heights, I grew up in Cleveland, among what you would call 'the lower classes.' When someone didn't like what you had to say, he didn't send you a letter on bonded letterhead written in the King's English, and he didn't pretend he was acting in your interest. He told you to shut up and you were in a fight if you didn't. Now we're in our nice clothes in a nice room and we use nice words in civilized tones, but we might as well be in a back alley in Cleveland. You're threatening me if I don't shut up."

"I haven't threatened you."

"You haven't? Who sent you?"

"I speak only on my own behalf."

"What about those important people of whom you spoke?"

"As I said, I speak only on my own behalf."

It was a lie and meant to be seen as such, but Daniel knew he would learn no more. He had no way to assess the threat. He suspected he couldn't completely disregard it, although it wouldn't stop him from testifying. "Good day, Mr. Salisbury."

Salisbury looked surprised as he realized the meeting had concluded. He stood. "Good day, Mr. Durand."

That afternoon, after Daniel had returned from the office, over coffee in the sitting room he told Eleanor of his meeting with Salisbury.

Eleanor leaned her head back on the back of the sofa. "There may be something quixotic about what you're doing. According to the newspapers the legislation is all but passed and signed into law. The chances of stopping it seem remote."

"It's a long shot, but even sure things don't pay off if the jockey doesn't get on the horse. What bothers me is the stampede. When everybody favors something, watch out! I may be tilting at windmills, but I can't let this go without challenging it. A reserve bank will be a disaster and I want my opposition on record. Someday people will look back and ask: 'Where did we go wrong?'"

"You have no idea who's behind this Salisbury?"

Daniel snorted. "'Important people,' but it seems that every important person on the planet thinks this country needs a central bank, so it could be anyone or everyone. Are you worried?"

"I don't worry about him any more than I do about your other enemies in high places." She smiled. "My father was the first and that didn't turn out too badly. I know you too well. Your meeting with Mr. Salisbury just made you more determined to give your testimony."

It had been twelve years since Eleanor had last seen her oldest son. Unable to sit still, she paced the floor of the Washington hotel suite, waiting for Will. She was nervous about seeing him and nervous that Daniel didn't know. Will's letter had said she could tell him, but only after the meeting. Undoubtedly, Will believed that Daniel wouldn't allow the reunion if he knew about it. Eleanor wasn't sure. He wouldn't like it, but he might not have stood in her way. Perhaps enough time had passed, or perhaps she would have met Will despite his opposition.

Daniel was meeting Representative McKinney, who was sponsoring his testimony before the subcommittee. He would be at the Capitol until his testimony that afternoon. What if something unexpected happened and he returned to the hotel? Eleanor shuddered.

Two soft knocks! She hurried across the sitting room to open the door. Will! She threw her arms around him. Tears rolled down her cheeks during their lengthy embrace. She squeezed him tightly, afraid to let go. He gently nudged her inside the room.

"Mother," he said, his voice shaky. He sighed. "It's so good to see you."

"Oh, Will, it's been too long." She wiped away her tears with a handkerchief and stepped back from him to perform a mother's inspection. He was forty-four now. She had seen his picture in the newspapers, but he looked better in person. There were white tinges in his hair, but it was still predominantly blond. A few lines on the handsome face, but he looked no heavier—he might even have lost weight—since the last time she saw him. His eyes were clear, not bloodshot—maybe he wasn't drinking as much. His black suit was impeccably tailored. He had always dressed well. "Representative Durand," she said softly.

He smiled, rueful, not exactly his old winning smile. "Shall we sit down?" They sat across from each other on two cream-colored sofas in the center of the room.

"Can I get you anything?"

He shook his head.

"Why did you want to see me, Will, after all this time? Does it have something to do with your father's testimony this afternoon?"

She expected him to flinch, as he always had when confronted with an uncomfortable question. Instead, he looked directly at her. "Yes, it does, in part, but only in part. I wanted to see you because I wanted to see you. After Father fired me, the most difficult part of the break was knowing that I wasn't going to see you. It was quite painful."

He had brought up the past—the firing—and acknowledged his own pain in a way that sought no pity. "How are your children?" Eleanor asked. "Are they here, in Washington? I wish I could see them."

"Gwendolyn is sixteen. She's beautiful, already breaking hearts. Roger is thirteen, smart, energetic, into everything—like Tommy. Henry is eight and he's quiet, like Laura and Alexander. They're back in New York, with Sylvia."

Eleanor let her raised eyebrows ask the question: And how is Lady Sylvia?

"It's a marriage in name only, Mother." His voice was oddly unemotional.

Will's penchant for evasiveness had always distressed Eleanor. Yet she found this straightforward admission discomfiting. "Then why do you stay together?"

"We're both still attached to my political career. Sylvia wants to be the First Lady."

"Do you want to be the president?"

"I'm not sure, which may in itself disqualify me. A man has to be consumed with the desire for it."

Eleanor stared at her son. "You've changed, Will."

"Yes, I have, although probably not enough."

An odd thing to say. "What did you want to tell me about your father's testimony?"

"If there's any way in your power, persuade him not to give it."

"Why?"

"I can't overemphasize how important this reserve bank legislation is for those who want it passed. The reserve bank and the income tax—they've been laying the groundwork for years. They got the tax and now the reserve bank looks like it will pass. They don't want anything to go wrong. Father is testifying on a Friday afternoon to a lame duck committee. Some of the representatives will have already gone back to their districts. By the time he's finished it will be well past the reporters' filing deadlines, if any bother to attend. Their stories about the testimony, if there are any, will be buried on tomorrow's back pages. They've controlled for virtually every contingency, but they're still worried. Father's unpredictable and sometimes the smallest of sparks can turn into a raging fire. He could give the opposition new energy."

"Who is the 'they' to whom you keep referring?"

"Very important people—in business, finance, the government."

"The Winfields?"

Will was visibly taken aback.

"Your father and I know about the Winfields, Will."

"Nobody knows about the Winfields," he stammered.

"We also know they were behind the court of inquiry."

Will was too stunned to speak. He slumped and his face drained of all color. "That means…that means he must think I was behind it. That I tried to put him in prison, or…"

"Or put him on the gallows," Eleanor said quietly.

Wills eyes widened. "That's not what happened, Mother. That's not how it happened."

"Then what did happen?"

Will took a long, deep breath. "Do you remember when I took that trip out to Minnesota with Father, to see Mr. Hill and his railroad?"

Eleanor nodded.

"We were out on the prairie and Mr. Hill had a little party. Father drank wine, more than he should have. That night, when we were asleep in our tent, I woke up and he was talking in his sleep. You've told me he's not the soundest of sleepers. Anyway, he said the name 'Pomeroy,' and I could see that the name upset him. I never told Father that I had heard that name, but I remembered it. When I got to Harvard, by coincidence there was a professor there named Pomeroy. I don't think he was related to Father's Pomeroy, he just happened to have the same last name. Father visited me at Harvard and I mentioned that professor to him, to see how he would react to his name. He reacted, although he tried to hide it."

"You didn't know it was the name of the man he had killed during the war?"

"No."

"How did the Winfields get that name?"

"I told it to Tim Harkness, my friend at Harvard who's now the head of the family. I went to him after Father fired me and he launched my political career. Tim, Harrison Winfield—that's Tim's uncle, he's a representative—and I had a reception with President Roosevelt. Tim and I were on the train ride back from Washington. We had been drinking quite a bit, celebrating, and I told him that I didn't know why, but the name Pomeroy was very important to my father. To this day, Tim has never said that they put together the investigation that led to the court of inquiry. But I know they did, because they had that name—Pomeroy. I never would have given it to them had I known. I was mad at Father, but I couldn't kill him." He shook his head vigorously. "No, no, no. You've got to believe that."

For the first time since she had read the Stoddard Detective Agency report she knew to a certainty, not an almost or a virtual certainty, but to an actual certainty, that Will had not been behind the court of inquiry. There had always been a niggling doubt, but Will's startled reaction, his face draining color, what he had just said, rang true—it wasn't an act. "I believe you."

Will leaned forward on the sofa, rested his elbows on his knees, hung his head, and ran his fingers through his hair. "Oh God. Good God. I wish I could tell Father. No wonder he dug up Pamela Tyler and tried to derail me before the election."

"He didn't dig her up, a reporter on a newspaper in which he owns stock did, although he didn't hold up the story and he could have. What is the story? That Tyler lady said she had your child and then she said she didn't. Did you and the Winfields set Daniel up, or was she telling the truth the first time and got paid off to change her story?"

743

"She was telling the truth the first time. She had my child. The Winfields paid her a king's ransom to change her story."

Eleanor felt an excited stab of curiosity. "What happened to her, and to your son?"

"I don't know. I don't know at all. Obviously, after the story changed—that she hadn't had my son—the Winfields weren't going to take any chances. It would look odd indeed if I were to somehow get in contact with this woman who supposedly didn't have my son. They probably sent her and the boy packing somewhere. I have no idea where. I don't even know if they're still alive."

A chill seized her. Will's last statement reawakened a dark realization she'd had after reading the Stoddard report, but that she had submerged in the conflict with Daniel about Will's role in the court of inquiry. "Will, the policeman, Riley—Daniel's friend during the war—and Ben, the escaping slave...and his family. The Winfields must have had them murdered. How can you stay with them?"

He stared at her. "You answered your own question." His voice was barely above a whisper.

"Oh God, no! You're in danger?"

"I'm trying to extricate myself, but I may be in too deep." His voice wavered.

Eleanor sat next to Will and took his hand. They said nothing for a long time.

"Do the Winfields know you're here?"

He shook his head. "No, although they wouldn't have objected if I had explained that I wanted to persuade you to persuade Father to change his mind. Just like everyone else, they're for this reserve bank, but I didn't want to taint my motivation with that. I wanted to warn you, because I think Father's position is dangerous. It may come tomorrow or it may come years from now, but there will be retribution."

744

"What kind of retribution? From whom?"

"I can't say because I don't know, and there's no reason why I'll find out. You read the papers and you know who supports it. They've carefully stage-managed this whole thing."

"I'm not even sure I'll have time to talk to him before his testimony. I'd have to tell him why I was worried, and about our meeting here. I'm sorry, Will, but once he knew it was coming from you, I'm sure he'd dismiss it."

Will nodded. "I understand why, after what you've told me."

"He received another warning and he ignored it."

"Another warning?"

"From a Mr. Salisbury, a British banker he had never met before."

Will shook his head. "Never heard of him, but Father should have taken it more seriously." He pulled his watch from his vest pocket. "I have to be getting back." He said it with a note of finality that suggested he had an appointment that couldn't be missed.

"Can we get together again, before another twelve years have passed?"

Will pondered. "Occasionally, but I have to be careful. It will have to be discreet and it will have to be in New York. You and Father have been Sylvia's sworn enemies since the firing. She would make life very difficult if she found out I had seen you."

"Can I see my grandchildren?"

"No. It would be too hard to arrange without Sylvia finding out."

"I see," Eleanor said, crushed. At least she might be able to see Will.

They stood and walked to the door. She threw her arms around him and they embraced. When they separated, she looked him in the eye. She had never felt more like his mother.

"Will, it's never too late. You don't have to stay on this path you're on."

Will's wistful smile seemed to capture a lifetime of regret. "You mean perhaps I haven't sold my soul, I've only pawned it?"

Eleanor bowed her head, overwhelmed that he could say such a thing.

"I wish I could believe that, Mother. Maybe I do believe it, but I'll have a devil of a time redeeming the token." He took both her hands and squeezed them. "Goodbye. I'll see you in New York."

Tears streamed down her face as he turned and walked down the hall. She was afraid for him in a way she had never been afraid for her other children or for Daniel, even before his court of inquiry. What had his pursuit of power cost her son?

Daniel sat at a table in a committee hearing room of the House of Representatives. The drafts crisscrossing the room carried the winter cold of February. There were few spectators in the gallery. Daniel glanced at Eleanor, who sat with Tom and Alexander, but she was staring in a different direction. Although she had wished him well, she had seemed preoccupied when they met briefly in the hall outside the hearing room.

Members of the subcommittee of the House Committee on Banking and Currency strolled to their seats, signs denoting the representative, at an elevated, semicircular panel at the front of the room. They chatted with each other. Nine representatives sat down. The chair for Representative Bulkley of Ohio remained empty. The chairman of the subcommittee, Representative Carter Glass, from Virginia, banged his gavel.

"The hearing in consideration of House Bill 7837, for the establishment of a federal reserve bank and the furnishing of an elastic currency, shall now come to order. The subcommittee will hear the testimony of Mr. Daniel Durand, from the firm of Durand & Woodbury, of New York." Chairman Glass's accent had an unmistakable Virginia lilt that reminded Daniel of Aldus Kincaid, his attorney for the court of inquiry. A dapper gentleman in his mid-fifties, Glass had prominent ears and a nose that filled a larger proportion of his face than the average nose filled of the average face.

"Thank you, Mr. Chairman, and thank you, members of the committee," Daniel said. "This legislation is still in its early stages and the details of the reserve system are the subjects of dispute. However, before everyone is enmeshed in them, it's time to consider not just the purported benefits but also the real dangers of central banking and government-created money, or an elastic currency, if you will, and to ask if this supposed innovation is in the best interests of our country." He glanced at his notes.

"A persistent misnomer is the term 'bank deposit,' which is not a deposit at all. If I take an item to a warehouse and pay a fee to deposit it for safekeeping, when I exercise my contractual rights and claim it, the owner of the warehouse must give it back to me. The owner can't lend it out, use it to secure a loan, or give it to another depositor to satisfy his claim. On the other hand, when I put my money in a bank, the banker can lend or invest it, use those loans and investments as collateral to borrow money, or use my funds to pay creditors or other depositors. I haven't deposited my money in the same sense that I deposited the item at the warehouse.

"My deposit is actually a loan and I'm an unsecured creditor of the bank. Much of the instability of the present system stems from a fiction. The respectable bank is housed in a neoclassical fortress and prominently displays a sturdy vault, to convince the depositor his money is safe. In fact, almost all his money leaves the bank in search of a return higher than the interest the bank pays him. Only a small portion is held in reserve to meet depositor withdrawals, although all depositors are told they can withdraw their money on demand.

"The bank has made a promise that it can't always keep. Business and financial cycles are as immutable as human nature. When famine follows feast and fear replaces greed, the demand for money inevitably increases. The banker faces his worst nightmare—a run on the bank. Banks with sufficient reserves or borrowing power survive. Those without them go bankrupt."

Daniel looked up at the representatives. Only a couple appeared interested.

"When faced with the danger of these inevitable bank runs, bankers clamor for a lender of last resort, a central bank. If only the banks could take their loans and investments and pledge them as collateral for ready money from a central bank. It's an alluring prospect—put out the fire and repay the loan when conditions improve—but where does the central bank get its money?

"Freely convertible paper money is anchored to the quantity of available gold and silver—it's not elastic. The only elastic money is that which can be derived from thin air. That's the key to understanding the support from both the bankers and the government for central banking. A banker doesn't care if the money he uses to satisfy his obligation to his depositor was printed up that morning. All he cares is that he can obtain it by borrowing from the central bank against his bank's collateral. There's a more subtle point. When a central bank stands ready to lend in a panic, bankers can relax during more normal times. They reduce the amount of money they keep on ready reserve and lend out the new excess. They make riskier loans to increase their profits. A central bank has been touted as a means of reducing risk, but it will actually increase it.

"For the government, money from thin air is the philosopher's stone. The alchemy of central banking is a much easier way to obtain money than either taxation, which must be approved by the voters or the legislative branch, or borrowing, which has the troublesome requirement that the money be repaid. Every dollar the central bank creates finds its way into the banking system, funding factories, mortgages, purchases of goods and services, and jobs, all of which make people more inclined to reelect their elected officials.

"This prosperity proves illusory. More money pursuing the same amount of goods and services pushes prices up, thus devaluing the money people already have. While the government realizes a short-term benefit from the new money, it comes at the expense of its citizens, who hold a depreciating currency. For politicians, the best part of money creation is that it's a hidden tax. Most people have no idea the central bank is picking their pockets. Since debts are repaid in depreciating currency, debtors, including the government, gain at the expense of creditors."

Daniel paused and surveyed the representatives. Most of them looked as if they wished they were somewhere else. One representative's barely concealed contempt seemed to say: of course, you fool, that's why we want to do it. Was it possible to hold politicians in too low an esteem?

"Historically, government money creation follows a dreary progression. A government wants more money than it's able to borrow or take from its citizens. It first debases the money already outstanding. Precious-metal coins are alloyed with or replaced by baser metals. If paper currency is convertible into precious metal, the exchange ratio is increased. As Gresham noted in 1558, bad money drives out the good. People separate the wheat from the chaff—they use the paper currency and hoard the coins. The government then enacts a legal tender law, forcing people to accept the paper currency at a government-mandated value. To keep its precious metal, the government curtails and eventually prohibits conversion of the paper money.

"The government creates money until its value falls to its cost of production, close to zero. Like the opium addict who must continuously increase the amount he uses to achieve the same delirium, the government must produce an ever-increasing amount of money to achieve the same illusory prosperity. Since the store of value has become elastically indeterminate, production declines while speculation increases. Since debtors win and creditors lose, savings vanish and debt increases. Eventually this house of cards collapses and illusory prosperity is replaced by very real depression, bankruptcy, and ruin.

"Washington Irving captured this progression in his book *The Great Mississippi Bubble*, written in 1830 about events in 1720. He noted that 'every now and then the world is visited by one of those delusive seasons when the "credit system," as it is called, expands to full luxuriance....the broad way to certain and sudden wealth lies plain and open.' The inevitable result? 'A panic succeeds, and the whole superstructure built upon credit and reared by speculation crumbles to the ground, leaving scarce a wreck behind.'" Daniel looked up from his notes. "Gentlemen, I believe that you know where this legislation will lead. Adam Smith said, 'There is a great deal of ruin in a nation.' After the greatest explosion of industrial and technological progress in history, there is much ruin in our nation. It will come several generations in the future, when everyone here is safely dead and gone, but if we start down this path our wealth will make our ruin no less inevitable. Is that the legacy you want? I implore you to halt this rush to central banking and government-created money, not out of a fear of the unknown, but from a clear-eyed appraisal of a known and unbroken record of failure. Thank you."

"Thank you, Mr. Durand," murmured Chairman Glass. "Allow us a moment to get our notes in order and we'll open the floor to questions from the members."

Several of the members stood to stretch their legs while legislative aides refreshed coffee cups and water glasses. Daniel glanced at Eleanor and she smiled, but there was something wrong with her smile. He'd find out what it was soon enough, for now he had to put it out of his mind.

The subcommittee members settled into their chairs. Chairman Glass cleared his throat. "Mr. Durand, how would you address the manifest problems of the current system, especially that of bank runs, without a central bank?" Glass was a strong supporter of the legislation.

"I'd start by calling a deposit what it is—an unsecured loan to a speculative enterprise known as a bank, which the depositor, or more correctly the creditor, may or may not be able to withdraw when he desires. Contractual recognition of that reality would allow the bank to curtail or stop withdrawals during a panic without going out of business. It would put a brake on the panic. Solvent banks would have time to call in loans and investments and arrange financing. Insolvent ones would fail and incompetent bankers would be put out of business. Bankers would have to pay for this privilege of limiting withdrawals with a higher rate of interest on deposits. Safety-minded depositors would gravitate towards banks that maintained a higher percentage of reserves."

"Wouldn't that have the effect of constricting the general credit?"

"It would. Banks would be paying depositors more and maintaining higher reserves; they'd have less to lend and invest. Lending and investing would be for productive activities that produce a return that liquidates the loan. With fewer loans and investments of better quality outstanding, the system as a whole would be far less prone to instability. Overall, credit would expand in line with the productive capacity of the economy. As Mr. Irving noted, expansion beyond that capacity leads to ruin—you can't consume more than you produce."

"Mr. Glass, may I?" asked Representative Korbly, from Indiana. Glass nodded.

"Mr. Durand, what about the depositor who wants absolute safety and the assurance he'll always have access to his money? Your way would leave him out in the cold."

"Mr. Korbly, there's no such thing as absolute safety, under either the current system or the proposed reserve system. The closest a bank customer could get to absolute safety would be a fortress bank that takes his money and locks it in a strong vault. Reject this legislation and I'll capitalize such a bank with a million dollars. I'll put a vault with a six-inch steel door in a building with walls the thickness of a castle and I'll guarantee depositors—who will be depositors, not creditors—access to their money in person during banking hours or by drafts drawn on their account. Nothing is free, of course; they'll have to pay for safety. I'll charge the fees necessary for my bank to turn a profit, since I won't be lending or investing depositors' funds."

"Your bank would be a rather boring business."

"That kind of banking should be boring. People with money who want more risk can speculate in our stock and bond markets, or they can invest their money with intermediaries such as Durand & Woodbury, which they understand to be a speculative enterprise."

"Why couldn't you open your fortress bank if we passed this legislation?"

"Because I would be in competition with the U.S. government. When the government becomes the lender of last resort, everyone becomes less vigilant about where they leave their money. The government can print, borrow, and now, with the income tax, take money to support the banking system. Why worry about safety?"

"Excuse me, Mr. Korbly." The speaker was Representative Taylor, from Alabama. His fleshy jowls jiggled when he talked. "Why do our nation's strongest banks support this legislation, Mr. Durand?" he said in a thick Southern accent.

"If the only function the central bank performed was as a lender of last resort, the strong banks would fight this legislation as a prop for their weakest competitors. However, that function will allow all banks to hold less in reserve, which will allow them to lend more and make more money. An elastic money supply puts more money in the system, which leads to more lending and profits, for a while. The regulation that goes with this legislation will make it harder for new entrants into banking. Less competition means more profits. The Pujo subcommittee just concluded its investigation of the so-called money trust. Cartels and monopolies are difficult, if not impossible, to maintain without the aid of the government. This legislation enshrines a money trust—a banking cartel. That's why the large banks support it."

"Why do you say an elastic money supply allows more lending and profits only for 'a while'?" said Representative Vreeland, from New York. Daniel found it curious that he ignored his assertion that the legislation would enshrine a cartel and instead seemed concerned that the new law's profits for banks might only be temporary.

"Because dishonest money sets a country on the road to bankruptcy, and when the government goes bankrupt it takes its banking cartel with it."

"You talk of dishonest money and debasement. You are aware that all the reserve bank assets will be backed forty percent by gold?" said Representative Talbott, from Maryland.

"I don't believe for a moment the assurances that there is no intent to debase the currency or prohibit its exchange for gold. I heard the same thing as a soldier during the Civil War, but the government printed so many greenbacks that our thirteen-dollars-a-month pay became virtually worthless. Soldiers played poker and other games of chance, trying to attain a living 'wage.'

"Debasement by the government is inevitable because the government benefits from it. That forty percent reserve requirement can be changed with new legislation. It will shrink until it vanishes. I draw no comfort from a promise that supports a promise the government won't keep. Eventually, government-created money won't be convertible into real money—gold." Daniel took a deep breath. He had just called the representatives liars and thieves.

"Why do you speak of suspending convertibility? No such action is under consideration."

Daniel took out a double eagle—a twenty-dollar gold piece—and a twenty-dollar bill and laid them side by side on the table before him. He held up the gleaming coin. "For centuries gold has served as a store of value and a medium of exchange. An ounce of gold bought a man's suit in 1500, 1600, 1700, 1800, and now, in 1913. It takes real resources to find, mine, smelter, and mint gold. It's divisible, portable, storable, assayable, indestructible, and, I might add, beautiful." Daniel put the coin down and picked up the bill. "This is a twenty-dollar bill. It can be torn to shreds and thrown to the wind. Its cost of production is virtually nothing. It depends for its value not on any intrinsic quality, but on the willingness of people to accept it as payment and the promise of politicians not to print too many of them. That promise has been broken every time it's been made. Mr. Talbott, the law says they must be regarded as equivalent. I'll offer you a choice. Which would you prefer?"

There was no answer.

"If this legislation becomes law, this piece of paper will buy less in ten years than this coin. Gold has been called an anachronistic relic, but you can't fool all the people all the time. Depreciating paper will be exchanged for gold. The government will have to mandate acceptance of its counterfeit money and the number of dollars necessary for conversion to a stated amount of real money will steadily increase. Eventually convertibility will be suspended so the government doesn't lose all its gold."

"Mr. Durand, you're a wealthy Wall Street banker." The speaker was Representative Moore, from Texas. "Your point of view represents a certain segment of the moneyed class. A reserve bank and a less astringent currency will promote economic stability, which will help farmers and wage earners, the people who have not shared your good fortune."

"On one point I cannot argue, Mr. Moore. Depreciation devalues debt, so if a farmer or wage earner is in debt, he can pay it off with devalued money. If, however, he's a saver, his savings are devalued. That's one of many pernicious results of elastic money—it encourages debt at the expense of saving. Wages will buy less every year. What the government gains from monetary debasement, the wage earner loses. Adjustments to his wage won't keep up with money inflation. As for promoting economic stability, look at the railroads. Every line upon which the government has laid its 'benevolent' hand has come to ruin. You want to make it responsible for the entire economy? The Wall Street moneyed class will have a field day with elastic money and financial instability. It's your average wage-earning American who will be hurt the most."

"Mr. Durand," Representative Korbly said. "I find your opposition to this progressive innovation old-fashioned and reactionary. You'd put a straightjacket on the government."

"The Chinese invented paper money around the year 900. By the turn of the millennium they had invented inflation. There's nothing innovative about governments debasing their currencies. They've been doing it for centuries with the same ruinous result. Honest recognition that a deposit is a loan and privately issued money backed by gold would be true innovations. The straightjacket you dislike is the idea of limited government, which was the Founding Fathers' idea."

"This is a banking issue, not some question of fundamental liberty," Korbly said.

"Gentlemen, since the end of the Civil War, this country has approached the golden pinnacle of human liberty. Our people have enjoyed more freedom than any people have before. They've worked in their chosen occupations; kept what they earned in money of certain value; saved, invested, innovated, and taken risks; voluntarily exchanged the fruits of their efforts; said and wrote what they wanted, traveled where and when they wanted, worshipped the way they wanted, lived where they wanted, associated with whom they wanted, and voted for their leaders. In short, they've pursued their own happiness, for the most part unhindered by a government conceived to secure their liberty.

"The result has been an unprecedented explosion of knowledge, technology, enterprise, and creativity. Capitalism—the economics of free people—has lifted millions from poverty, made America rich, and been a beacon for ambitious immigrants from all over the earth. The forty-eight years since the Civil War haven't been without their blemishes, their ups and downs, but I challenge you to find a comparable period in history when a nation has enjoyed the progress, prosperity, and peace that ours has.

"Take the path you are proposing and these last forty-eight years will far surpass the next forty-eight. You say this isn't a question of fundamental liberty. The income tax amendment gives the government first claim on the labor of every producer in the country. This reserve bank and elastic currency mean that the value of what they're allowed to keep will be determined by political whim, not the objective reality of the value of gold. What liberties are more fundamental than to keep what you earn, and to keep it in a store of objective value? With two strokes the government that was almost our servant will have become our master, and the golden pinnacle will recede into the mist. It's cold, trivial comfort that you'll leave us with some of our rights. We'll be free to complain about our slavery and to elect the leaders who will perpetuate it. As the utopian dream dissolves into nightmare reality, those rights will be eliminated as well."

Daniel paused and looked up at the representatives. "Allow me to give you and your successors a warning. Someday a hoodwinked, enslaved, bankrupted people will realize who is responsible for its ruin. When the slaves revolt, they will seek the blood of their masters. Thank you."

The only sound in the room was Daniel gathering his notes. He stood and walked back to Eleanor, Tom, and Alexander, who were all staring at him, wide-eyed. They rose and walked with him out of the committee room.

In the hall, Tom said, "You were the one to stand up and say, 'this is wrong,' but I can't believe there won't be hell to pay."

Beyond congratulating Daniel on his appearance before the subcommittee, Eleanor said nothing, not wanting their automobile's driver, an innocuous-looking fellow, to hear what she had to say.

When they returned to their hotel room and Daniel had closed the door, she could contain herself no longer. "I saw Will this morning."

Daniel's eyes widened. "Will. I knew something had happened. Where did you see him?"

"Right here, in this room. Daniel, he wasn't behind the court of inquiry. He had the name Pomeroy and he knew it was important to you, but he didn't know why. He gave the name to the Winfields, to Tim Harkness, and they discovered what happened during the war. The Winfields have never even told Will that they were behind the investigation, but he knows they were."

"How did Will get the name Pomeroy?"

Eleanor's words came in a torrent—rapids rushing over rocks, shooting through channels, sometimes swirling backwards—as she told her husband of her conversation with their son. Daniel listened, but as usual gave little clue to what he was thinking.

"If you had seen his face when I told him we knew about the Winfields, that they were behind the court of inquiry. He went white as a sheet when he realized that you thought he was behind it. It wasn't an act—he couldn't fake that. He had no idea where the name Pomeroy would lead."

Daniel was silent for a long time as he weighed what she had said. He took a deep breath. "It sounds plausible. You don't know how much I want to believe him. But dearest, if he's telling the truth, he's in way over his head."

He was alone in the kitchen. Coal embers glowed in the stove and he curled up on the floor, trying to catch their meager warmth. Shivering violently, he realized he had to get out of his wet clothes and find more warmth. Each movement provoked a shivering fit, but

he made his way out of the kitchen, up the stairs, and to the bedroom. The door creaked as he opened it. He heard boys scurrying towards him from their beds. One of the older boys helped him take off his partially frozen nightclothes, and another boy wrapped him in a blanket. There were no blankets to spare so someone was making a big sacrifice, sleeping in the cold. Many hands rubbed him, trying to warm him. Finally his shivering stopped and he could feel his toes and fingers. He fell into a troubled sleep wedged between two boys.

I've got to get out of here. That was his last waking thought and his first thought the next morning. It wasn't as if he were in a jail. Boys had left the orphanage before—bad boys, or boys the fathers thought were bad. If they wanted you to leave, the fathers would make your life miserable until you did. They wanted him to leave.

He was absent when the boys formed their usual line for the morning's prayers. From the privy where he hid, he heard the bell tolling and knew that everyone would be entering the chapel. No one saw him as he headed the opposite direction, out the back gate, which was kept open during the day. Over his thin coat he wore a blanket he had stolen that morning from a supply closet for the fathers. A simple escape, but as soon as he was on the frozen streets of Cleveland a safe distance from the orphanage, he felt a surge of joyous elation. He had no money, nothing but his clothes and blanket; he'd have to find a job at low wages; he had no place to go, no parents, no relatives, no friends; he didn't even know his birthday or who had given him his name. But there would be no more of the orphanage and people he hated telling him what to do. No more fathers and their cruelty. No more questions answered with a hickory switch. No more food a dog wouldn't eat. He had nothing and he had everything—he was free!

For the first time Daniel awoke gently from his recurring dream. He felt something akin to the elation he had felt as a child upon his escape—stronger than an echo although not the original. He glanced at Eleanor, reached over, and brushed her hand with his. Exhausted from the day, she was in a deep slumber. "Freedom," he whispered as he fell back asleep.

After he awoke and dressed the next morning, Daniel went to a newsstand outside the hotel, bought the morning editions of the local papers and scanned through them. There was no mention of his testimony before the subcommittee.

Chapter 28

The End of Innocence

Eleanor was having breakfast with her youngest son, John, now thirty-five. The day began early at Mr. Ameche's shop where John worked. Flower venders acquired new inventory every day, before regular business hours. John didn't have to accompany Mr. Ameche on his trips to the wholesalers', where the proprietor inspected the flowers, haggled over price, and arranged deliveries to his shop. However, he had to be at the shop when the flowers arrived as the sun poked above the East River. They had to be stored and arranged for the day's stream of customers making their purchases—to woo a lover or grace a dinner table or, sadly, place before a headstone. That business had increased with America's entry into the European war.

"Mr. Ameche's smart," John said as he chewed on a strip of bacon. He was husky to Eleanor, chubby to everyone else, and liked to eat. "He's set things up so if a customer wants to put flowers on a grave regular-like, every month or so, they fill out a card and we'll have what they want. Or if the customer wants, we deliver it to the grave."

"That is smart," Eleanor said. Not hungry at this hour and still in her dressing gown, she sat at the kitchen table sipping coffee as John ate.

"There's this pretty woman, Mrs. Turner. She'll be coming in today because it's Wednesday. She comes in every Wednesday to get a bouquet of white carnations and one red rose. Mr. Turner died fighting in France on a Wednesday. I don't know what she does with the bouquet. She has these real sad, dark eyes. It makes me sad to see her. She always smiles at me, but even her smile is sad. Do you think Father would want to go ice skating with me this Sunday?"

"I think he would, but you'll have to ask him. Look at the time, John. You have to go." John liked to talk and time frequently got away from him.

John finished the last forkfuls of eggs and wiped his mouth with his sleeve. He gulped down a glass of milk. Mrs. Elmwood, the maid, entered carrying a paper bag, muttering under her breath. She grumbled every day about having to fix John his early breakfast and lunch.

John took his lunch and walked with Eleanor to the front door. Several inches over six feet, he bowed his head for her to kiss him. "Goodbye, Mother."

"Goodbye. Have a good day at the shop."

He opened the door and walked down the steps. He waved and Eleanor watched as he lumbered away. How ironic that Will had called him Little John when he was boy—now he was over two hundred pounds. She was always a little anxious when he left.

Eleanor had bought flowers for years from Mr. Ameche, an Italian immigrant whose shop was one of the best in New York. John loved flowers and often went with her. One day as she was paying her bill and John was wandering around the shop, Mr. Ameche said, in his thick accent, "John have a job? I use him here, in the shop."

"He has certain difficulties."

"I know what he can do. I know what people can do. John loves the flowers, he understands the flowers. He work in my shop. Don't tell me what people can't do, Mrs. Durand. Who thinks a poor boy from San Severo, who don't go to school, would own such a nice shop?"

Or that a Cleveland orphan would become one of the richest men on Wall Street? This was America! Mr. Ameche, a short, wiry man in his mid-fifties with slicked-back salt-and-pepper hair and a bushy mustache, stared at her, awaiting her answer.

"Why don't you talk with John?"

Mr. Ameche talked with John and offered him a job at two dollars a day. He got more out of him than a succession of tutors and specialists ever had. John couldn't handle the money, but he made deliveries, waited on customers, trimmed and arranged flowers, and helped keep the shop spotless. Undoubtedly the proudest moment in his life was when he received a raise, to two dollars and fifty cents a day.

The job had been nothing but good for John, but Eleanor still felt a tug of anxiety when he left for work. He was sweetly gullible in a city that ran the gamut of human motives, from the sublime to the dark. He didn't comprehend the latter and never would.

There was a chill in the air—it felt like snow today. Perhaps that was adding to her usual anxiety. She shut the door and glanced at the coat stand. John hadn't taken his gloves or his hat and she hadn't reminded him.

The snow came down in thick flurries. Daniel looked up from his book. This was quite a storm. His old war wounds in his leg and shoulder ached as they usually did when it got cold. He got up and put another log on the fire. The older he got the more he appreciated warm fires.

Eleanor opened the door to his library, an envelope in her hand. "Look at this." She handed him the envelope.

It was addressed to John. The return address was from the United States Army. Daniel shuddered, remembering the letter he had received from the army, ordering him to appear before the court of inquiry. He started to open the letter.

"Don't. John doesn't get many letters. He'll be disappointed if he doesn't get to open this one."

"But it could be a draft notice." Last year, one month after America's entry into the war in Europe, President Wilson had signed a law authorizing conscription, requiring all men between the ages of twenty-one to thirty-one to register for the draft. A month ago, the upper age had been raised to forty-five and John had registered.

Eleanor looked horrified. "A draft notice? John can't be a soldier!"

"You'd be surprised. I remember the men who were drafted during the Civil War. They were a bad lot. They dragged some of them from prisons and asylums."

Eleanor's forehead furrowed in worry. "Maybe we should open it." She shook her head. "No, we'll wait."

John came in twenty minutes later. Eleanor and Daniel anxiously greeted him at the door. He smiled as he took off a snow-covered hat. "I forgot my hat. Mr. Ameche loaned me one of his." He set the hat on the coat stand.

"John," Eleanor said. "You got a letter." She handed it to him.

He looked at the letter. "The United States Army," he read the return address. He tore open the envelope, removed the letter, unfolded it and began reading aloud in his slow way, maddeningly slow now, tripping over or mangling the longer words.

Greetings, Mr. Durand,

> *You are hereby inducted into the United States Army. You are ordered to report to the Induction Center at 1252 East 38th Street, New York, on February 19, 1918, at 10:00 A.M., for a physical examination.*

Selective Service Board, New York
Office of the Provost Marshall General
The War Department

John looked up from the letter. "Does this mean I'm going to be a soldier?"

Eleanor and Daniel glanced at each other, not sure what to say.

"It means..." Daniel said slowly, "it means that you must report to the army, and the army will decide if you're going to be a soldier."

"But I don't want to be a soldier! I want to work in the flower shop with Mr. Ameche."

Daniel sighed. "I'm afraid you don't have a choice. The government needs soldiers." He felt the rage rising within. He had been adamantly against the United States' entry into the war. "The best advice George Washington ever gave was to stay out of European wars," he had said after the declaration of war. "They've been slaughtering each other for centuries over there, why the hell should we get involved?" He recalled Devereux's warnings against an American empire and wars. When there had been no groundswell of volunteers, he took it as indication that the men who would actually have to fight—as opposed to the idiots who waved flags for every war—saw no danger to their country and wouldn't support the war with their lives. The draft further infuriated him, and now his son was caught in its deadly net.

"John," he said. "There's a possibility that the army might decide they don't need you to be a soldier. We'll have to go to the induction center in two weeks."

"I don't want to be a soldier."

Eleanor rested her hand on his shoulder. "There may be something we can do."

John took the letter and walked away, mumbling disconsolately.

When he was out of earshot, Eleanor said, "I don't care what you have to do, whom you have to bribe, John can't go into the army. He can't be a soldier!"

"I know, I know. We'll do everything we can." Daniel would pull every string that could be pulled, but he wondered if it would do any good. That John would receive a draft notice so soon after the age of eligibility had been raised struck him as more than just an unlucky coincidence. There was Daniel's well-known contempt for politicians and his long list of prominent enemies. There were the warnings from the English banker and from Will before he testified against the Federal Reserve. Was this retribution?

For years Daniel had been content to ignore the politicians. They had favors to exchange for discreet "contributions" of money, share certificates, or other valuable consideration, but since they didn't produce anything, only took from someone else, their largess was stolen property. However, the politicians hadn't ignored Daniel. They knew who would or wouldn't ply their corrupt trade and they seemed to share a special animus against the latter. As Daniel feared, doors were closed against him, with invariably polite expressions of regret, in both Albany and Washington.

Eleanor listened to Daniel's accounts of futile overtures with mounting frustration. One evening she said, "Maybe Will can do something. I'm going to write him."

She wrote Representative Durand, but his response was another account of futility.

Of course John shouldn't be in the army, but believe me, Mother, I've exhausted all avenues of inquiry. It's now illegal to hire substitutes and I'm told that everyone is very sensitive to the appearance of those who are wealthy or influential being able to avoid service. I'm very sorry and quite concerned, but I've been stymied at every turn.

John kept his appointment at the induction center and was pronounced physically fit for military service after a perfunctory examination. The clerk who processed John's paperwork was unmoved by Daniel and Eleanor's entreaties.

"His capabilities will be accessed at Camp Sherman," the clerk said flatly.

"There'll be thousands of men there," Eleanor said bitterly. "How will he be assessed?"

"He'll be assessed." It was a dismissal, without recourse.

Two weeks later Daniel and Eleanor said goodbye to John at Grand Central Station before he boarded a troop transport for Camp Sherman, in Ohio. Daniel threw his arms around him, hugging him for a long time. When he stepped away Eleanor took her turn.

Several army officials yelled, "Attention! Time to board!"

Eleanor and John stepped apart, their eyes brimming with tears. "You mustn't let the other men see you cry, John," Eleanor said, wiping his eyes with a handkerchief. "You'll be brave?"

John nodded without enthusiasm. "I don't want to be a soldier."

"John, listen to the officers and do as they say," Daniel said. "You'll be fine. We'll write to you and you write to us. We'll be thinking of you. We love you, son."

"All aboard!"

Confusion and fear were etched on John's face as he made his final wave before he disappeared into the railcar. Eleanor buried her head in Daniel's shoulder and sobbed. Daniel knew that John's parting look would haunt him until the end of his days, especially if he didn't come back.

After Daniel retired, the day-to-day flow of events, even that concerning business, was less important than his books and his contemplation. However, once John left for basic training, Daniel again made the newspapers his first reading. He followed each battle of the war he despised, learned the names of the European villages, rivers, valleys, forests, and fields where the insane carnage of trench warfare attrition progressed in meters per week, and tallied the casualty figures claiming the prime of European and now American manhood. He clung to one hope as the Allies repelled a German advance that got within artillery distance of Paris and adopted new tactics, pushing the Germans back across France. Their progress was now marked in kilometers per day. Perhaps they would move fast enough and far enough to force a German surrender before John had to fight. In Germany, people were marching against the war and their economy was in ruins. German capitulation was John's best chance of surviving the war.

John had reached Camp Sherman and an army functionary pronounced him fit for service. He wrote home once a week in his virtually illegible scrawl, fully decipherable only by Eleanor. He worked in the camp bakery, helping bake each day's thousands of loaves. The physical training was rigorous. He reported that he was *not nearly as fat as I used to be. You'd be proud.* Daniel and Eleanor were proud, and heartened when John wrote that *Fred likes me and stops the men from teasing me. He was a football player.*

One day Eleanor entered Daniel's library, her face streaked with tears. "He's shipping out next Tuesday. We won't even see him."

She sobbed. He wrapped his arms around her. "The war will be over soon. He'll come back. Maybe that fellow Fred will be with him." He didn't hear much hope in his voice.

Eleanor must not have, either. She continued to sob.

John's feet hurt. He had been walking for six hours and his boots, which had never fit right, rubbed several spots on his feet so raw they bled. Sergeant Howler said they were making good progress, but they wouldn't stop until nightfall, several hours away. It was best not to complain. The sergeant gave latrine duty to complainers—John had found out the hard way. He hoped they'd at least stop for a rest soon.

They were marching through what had been a farmer's field. Ahead loomed a forest. "Company C, fall out!" an officer yelled. John lined up with Company C. "You are to proceed ahead off the right flank to the woods," the officer ordered. "There may be a Kraut emplacement in there. Find and destroy it."

"Durand, Kelleher, Mason, Danby, Grange, and Sutter, front and center," Sergeant Howler shouted. The men called stepped forward. John wondered why he had been called. This was the second time in a row. Howler didn't like him. "You six will be out front."

The men exchanged nervous glances.

"Let's move," Howler yelled.

The little group trotted forward. "I'm more afraid of Howler than the Krauts," one of the men muttered when they were out of the sergeant's earshot.

"Well, we know who's on his list," muttered another. "'Better to lose a few men on reconnaissance than an entire company,'" he mocked. "Not so good if you're one of the few."

"Step gently, there might be mines."

"Fan out. John, don't stay so close to me," Sutter said.

John wanted to stay close to Sutter because he was scared and because Sutter wasn't mean to him. The other men moved away from each other so he had to as well. He crouched down with his rifle in the ready position, like the other men, and tentatively advanced forward.

Each step he took he thought of the land mines, but nothing exploded under his or the other men's feet. They were getting closer to the forest. Maybe there were no Germans in there. He looked back. The two companies were slowly moving forward, about fifty yards behind. He turned back towards the woods.

The last thing John saw were the flashes from a barrage of machine guns.

The scream that came from downstairs, followed by a piercing cry, could only mean one thing. With an armistice in sight, John wasn't coming back. Daniel flew down the stairs, almost falling, to the entryway. Eleanor was slumped on the floor in a heap, wailing. Mrs. Elmwood was crouched over her, a hand on her shoulder, tears streaming. The letter that Daniel knew contained the worst news any mother or father could receive lay crumpled on the floor. Daniel picked it up and read through his tears.

October 4, 1918

United States Army

> *With deep regret I inform you that your son, John Durand, has died in service to his country. The United States recognizes John's bravery and your great sacrifice, and extends its condolences on your loss. May John be committed to God's hands.*

Sincerely,

Sergeant Wallace Thurgood
U.S. Army Chaplain

"They murdered him!" Eleanor screamed. "He never should have been there!" Her body shuddered, wracked with despair and rage.

Daniel knelt on the floor and held her very close, his tears mingling with hers. This was retribution. This was murder.

Daniel, Tom, Alexander, John's two brother-in-laws—Michael Palos and Heinrich Larsen—and Mr. Ameche served as John's pallbearers. They stood outside the front doors of Alexander's church. He had arranged the funeral service. The large crowd had tied up traffic and the pallbearers had paused to give the late arrivals a chance to enter.

They bore their burden through the front doors and again paused in the vestibule before the doors to the nave. From inside, Daniel could hear the strains of "How Great Thou Art." It had taken six weeks for John's body to be returned from Europe. For the first time,

Daniel had felt the weight of his years. He had always been tough, resilient, but this loss was a dagger through part of him that couldn't be protected.

It was the death of a son. Thirty-five years ago he and Eleanor had experienced, for the sixth time, that ever-new miracle when two people create and nurture new life. They had worried about John's difficulties, tried to protect him from the world's indifference and cruelty, thrilled when he surmounted obstacles, exulted in his triumphs, and loved him as they loved all their children, in a way differently, and perhaps more profoundly, than the way they loved each other. Now he was gone.

It was the death of an innocent. John didn't understand the evil men did in pursuit of territory and treasure, vengeance and power. He wanted to work in Mr. Ameche's flower shop, amidst the dazzling color and floral beauty, to bestow small joys, to see a smile on a customer's face. Placing him amidst the horror of war was an act of barbaric ruthlessness. Daniel had never conceived such retribution possible. It was the death of innocence itself.

The hymn ended and the doors opened for the pallbearers. They carried John solemnly down the center aisle. The church was full. Daniel saw people from Durand & Woodbury and their families, but he also saw many people he didn't know, testament to the ever-expanding web of friendships of his children and their families. The pallbearers reached the chancel and placed the coffin on its bier.

Daniel turned to go to his seat in the front pew with the other members of the family and was brought up short. At the other end of the aisle, apparently arriving late and trying to find a seat, was Will, with a young lady and two young men who, Daniel suddenly realized, were his grandchildren. Will and Daniel stared at each other for a timeless moment. Daniel motioned with his hand, beckoning the son he hadn't seen for seventeen years.

Will and his children walked slowly up the aisle. The children stopped at the end of the pews but Will came forward to the coffin. His eyes brimmed with tears. He stared at the coffin.

"Little John," he whispered. He turned towards his father.

Daniel looked at the coffin. "I've lost a son." He turned towards Will. "I've found a son." They embraced.

"Come sit with your family." Daniel gestured towards the front pew. Eleanor rose from her seat. Tears streaming down her face, she came up quickly to Will and embraced him. Daniel had worried about her since they had received word of John's death. That morning she had said, "Today will be difficult, Daniel—no, it will be impossible. Eventually I'll be better, but even though it's been six weeks it seems like that letter came just yesterday." Time would do its work and the pain and rage would subside, but nothing could be as restorative as a reunion with Will and her grandchildren.

As the people in the church realized what was happening they murmured, abridging the usual funeral decorum. Daniel waved Gwendolyn, Roger, and Henry over and room was quickly made for Will and his children after a series of embraces. Everyone settled in and a proper silence descended over the church.

"We are gathered to commemorate the life of John Walter Durand," intoned the preacher, the Reverend Harold Stratton. His magnificent baritone filled the church. "John died serving his country in Flanders."

Daniel had spent his abbreviated childhood in an orphanage run by a religious order. Attendance at daily chapel had been mandatory. The orphanage had not been a happy experience and had fixed his attitude towards religion, although later in life he refined his visceral rejection with a more philosophical critique. Since childhood, except for occasional weddings and funerals, he had not attended church services. John had not gone to church, either, but Daniel had allowed Alexander to give his younger brother a religious commemoration. As the service progressed, he was glad he had done so.

Rev. Stratton demonstrated a subtle sensitivity to the situation. There were no concessions to the sad necessity for war, no tributes to John's bravery, no expressions from a grateful country for his and his family's sacrifice. Rather, the theme was the essential goodness that was John. The hymns, the prayers, the Bible readings, and the short sermon emphasized the simplicity of virtue, shorn of the worldly, that salvation required, the equality of all before God's eyes, and his special solicitude for the meek, the humble, the downtrodden, for John and for all those the world would rather forget.

Alexander gave John's eulogy. He recounted John's difficulties in performing tasks that other children took for granted, his triumph when he finally learned to read. When he talked of John's special relationship as a child with his oldest brother, Will cried. When he talked of John's love of his work at the flower shop, Mr. Ameche sobbed. Eleanor wept during the entire eulogy. Daniel often joined her.

"John died in a battle he shouldn't have been fighting. We must never forget the injustice that took John from his flower shop and dropped him into the horrors and evils of this just-concluded war. Fighting such injustice is a battle we all must fight, but foremost in our thoughts must be our memories of John, our love for him. We know he's at peace with God, for the innocent shall know peace everlasting. Thank you."

As Alexander stepped away from the pulpit, Daniel leaned over and whispered in Eleanor's ear, "The last thing Alexander said—'for the innocent shall know peace everlasting'—that should be John's epitaph."

Eleanor nodded.

After the funeral, after the graveside service, after friends had squeezed into the Durands' brownstone for a reception and then departed, Eleanor beheld a scene she had hoped for for years. They were heartbroken and angry and numb, but all of her children—with the tragic exception of John—and their spouses—with the not-tragic exception of Sylvia—were in the sitting room after dinner, drinking their tea or coffee, talking. The younger grandchildren were upstairs. Gwendolyn, Roger, and Henry had gone for a walk in the park across the street. Nobody had asked Will about Sylvia's absence.

Eleanor had been to enough funerals to know that there was a time afterwards when the black cloud of grief lifted and the mourners realized that they were with people to whom they were closely tied, people they hadn't seen in some time, who were raising families and pursuing careers, whose lives they were interested in, with whom they wanted to share not just their deepest emotions, but the latest developments and latest thoughts. It was an alleviation of the pain, for the human mind and heart, the human spirit, couldn't remain in pain. It didn't mean that the deceased was forgotten or the pain was over, but it was a respite that humans craved and required.

"It's sad that it took a funeral to get us all back together," Laura said. She sat with her husband, Michael Palos, and Will on a sofa. "But it's good to see you, Will. Did I hear you say you're getting out of politics?"

Will nodded. "I am."

"Why?"

Will took a deep breath. "I've done things in politics I'm not proud of. I don't want to be associated with the Winfields anymore."

An uncomfortable silence settled over the room at the mention of the Winfields. Eleanor glanced at Daniel. He asked the question that only he could ask.

"Do you think they had anything to do with John's death?"

Eleanor gave Will credit for looking directly at his father when he answered.

"I don't know. I've been trying to break with them for several years, but the thought that they might be behind John is the straw that broke this camel's back. I won't be with them anymore."

"Can you do that?" Tom asked. "Aren't you afraid they might arrange some sort of 'accident' for you?"

Eleanor shuddered.

"They don't know what papers I've saved, what names might get revealed, upon my death. I'd no longer be worried about saving my own skin and I could hurt them—badly. If I'm alive and we keep things on reasonably good terms, they have my instinct for self-preservation working in their favor. I might be able to extricate myself, or I might not, but I have to try."

"It sounds dangerous," Alexander said.

"It will be."

The uncomfortable pall again settled over the room.

"What if the Winfields weren't behind John's death?" Jessica said. "What if this Mr. Salisbury who warned Mr. Durand about testifying wasn't connected to them, and was acting on behalf of someone else?"

"Father, have you contacted Salisbury since John's death?" Tom said.

"He died last year, apparently after eating tainted fish at a London restaurant. Mr. Stoddard says he could have been poisoned. I've also made inquiries concerning John's conscription, but with the government it's like shooting a bullet into a wad of cotton so thick it stops the bullet. I'm coming away with very little."

"If the Winfields weren't behind Salisbury, then whoever was is presumably responsible for John's death," Will said. "It was somebody who supported the central bank legislation, feared opposition, and had enough influence in the government to get John drafted. That could be the Winfields, but it could be many other people, too."

"One thing I did find out," Daniel said. "John was one of the first, if not the first, thirty-five-year-olds to be drafted."

"With everybody supporting the law, why were they so worried about Mr. Durand's testimony against it?" Michael Palos said.

"I recently reread your testimony in the Congressional Record," Will said, turnings towards Daniel. "I had thought they wanted to stop you because they were worried you would arouse the opposition. That was part of it, but I think they had another motive. As long as nobody said that what they were doing was wrong, they could pose as benefactors. If their scheme failed, they could say they were motivated by the best of intentions, and while the execution of the plan may have been flawed, there was nothing wrong with its design or intent. That's much harder to say if someone is on record saying before inception that it won't work and questioning your motives."

"Then what they really want is power," Laura said.

"That's it," Will said. "They don't care if things turn out badly for the country, as long as they're the ones running it into the ground."

"That's sick," Alexander said.

"It's pathological."

Eleanor winced. Will was speaking from personal experience. Would he be able to "extricate" himself?

"So there's no crime they won't commit," Tom said. "When a man ignores your warning and speaks his mind, you murder his most vulnerable son."

Hanna, Alexander's wife, wept softly and dabbed her eyes with her handkerchief.

Painful as it was, Eleanor thought, it was necessary for the family to come together, to try to understand John's brutal death. The family was solace and safety in a world much more threatening than it had appeared until recently. Will was back, reconciled, a changed man. What had prompted the change? An assurance given to a constituent that he'd vote their way, shortly after an assurance to another constituent that he wouldn't? An ugly hangover, the previous night's drinking unable to vanquish doubts about necessary evils and little white lies? A look of admiration from one of his children, a look he knew he didn't deserve? One day she'd ask.

"So now you know what you're up against, if you choose to fight," Daniel said.

The room went quiet. Implicit in that statement was acknowledgment that the fight would last longer than Daniel.

"What do mean, what we're up against?" asked Heinrich Larsen, Constance's husband. The Norwegian's voice had a trace of an accent, but his English was excellent.

"What I said before the subcommittee. Our government's walking down the path of corruption and ruin. It's claiming your money at the point of a gun, and what they don't get that way they debase. By my definition, that's a criminal enterprise. Like any criminal, those running the government will protect their racket. Things will get worse."

"How do you fight it?"

"On the plain of reason and persuasion—that's the last battlefield they want. They'll make every effort to shut you up or drag you down. Time is your most certain ally. Their path inevitably leads to failure. The only government that will last is the one that safeguards the liberty of its people."

A shrill burst of angry argument came from upstairs. Alexander looked at his watch. "It's getting late. I'm sure the children are tired. Time to get them home to bed."

Eleanor felt a weariness accumulated over six weeks of sorrow and grief. Today had been the longest, most draining day. Hanna, Jessica, Laura, and Constance went upstairs to summon the children. Suddenly, everyone seemed to be yawning.

As the family progressed from the sitting room to the entry and outside, on the front stairs, there were teary farewells, long embraces, and promises to get together more often. Tommy and Heinrich carried sleeping children in their arms. Only Will lingered. His children were visible in the streetlight as they emerged from the park across the street.

"Bring everybody over for dinner," Daniel said, presumably leaving it to Will to determine if the invitation included Sylvia.

Will nodded as Gwendolyn, Roger, and Henry came up the stairs. Will's daughter, twenty-two, was strikingly beautiful, with her mother's dark hair and Will's blue eyes. Will had told Eleanor that she would probably be engaged to a lawyer, the son of a prominent industrialist, sometime soon. Roger, nineteen, was a student at Columbia, and Henry attended Concord Academy, the same preparatory school Will, Alexander, and Tom had attended. The boys looked alike in the way only two siblings could, with their father's blond hair and their mother's finely honed features. Their governesses had done a good job—all three were polite and respectful.

Will embraced Eleanor. "At least some good came of it."

"Call us, Will."

Will and his children descended the stairs to their car. They waved as they rode away.

Eleanor turned to Daniel. "Did Will tell you that he and Sylvia have separated?"

He shook his head.

"They don't have Will's political career to hold them together any more. She's going back to England."

"Good things often emerge from bad."

"Yes, they do." A solitary tear made its way down her cheek. The family was finally a family again.

Chapter 29

A Place of Peace

The black Packard motored up the narrow road and stopped at an inviting bower. The front door opened and Roger, Will's oldest son, slid out from the driver's seat. He opened the passenger door and offered his hand to his grandmother. Eleanor took it and stepped from the car. He asked, as he always did, if she wanted him to come with her. She shook her head, as she always did. No, she would prefer to be by herself.

She stood tall, her poise and confidence undiminished. There were not many strands of golden hair left among the snowy white, but there were only a few lines on her face. Now, even more than when she was younger, her face suggested aristocracy—the regally high forehead and cheekbones, the delicately fine nose and chin. The captivating blue eyes hadn't lost their ever-changing sparkle of intelligence, curiosity, and wit. She wore a simple blue dress, one of Daniel's favorites.

She walked up a gently sloping path until she reached a granite bench that faced out on a valley and a river. The view was magnificent. Behind her was another scene of beauty and she turned to admire it. Stately pine and fir stood in a semicircular ring, a kind of

natural cathedral, around a little meadow of tall grass and pink tril-
lium, purple asters, white lilies of the valley, buttercups, and gold-
enrod. On a weekend sojourn with Eleanor, Daniel had found this
place a few years ago, only an hour's drive outside the city. He liked
it so much that he had bought it from the landowner for three times
what it was worth. They had visited it frequently, sometimes pic-
nicking with children and grandchildren. This quiet, lovely bower
offered restoration and rejuvenation.

Once, Daniel had said, "This is where I'd like to be…" Eleanor
had completed his sentence in her own mind. In front of the granite
bench were two headstones. She sat on the bench and read the in-
scriptions.

JOHN WALTER DURAND
JUNE 12, 1883–SEPTEMBER 29, 1918
FOR THE INNOCENT SHALL KNOW PEACE EVERLASTING

And:

DANIEL DURAND
SPRING 1844—JANUARY 24, 1920

Father and son were together in this place of peace. That was a
consolation. Another was the absence of a headstone for Will. He
had managed to "extricate" himself from the Winfields and was now
a professor at a small college in New England.

Sweet, simple John should have known peace at the flower shop
for all his days. His death had been a crime and a tragedy the family
had survived, but that had left its residue of bitterness, cynicism, and
distrust. He had died in the dubiously named War to End All Wars,
but Eleanor thought of him as a casualty of the battle Alexander had

spoken of, the battle against the injustice of power that had slipped its legitimate bonds.

Daniel's life had been anything but peaceful. Starting with nothing but a name given to him by someone he never knew, he had fled an orphanage, began working when he was eight years old, fought in the Civil War, killed his commanding officer to save the life of an escaping slave, had his best friend die in his arms, taught himself banking, married the bank president's daughter over the determined opposition of the bank president, moved to New York, founded a firm that grew into one of Wall Street's preeminent banks, financed the giants of American industry, fired his son, built one of the country's largest fortunes, risked a death sentence to tell the truth about what he had done in the war, and stood up for his convictions, ignoring a warning and a tidal wave of public opinion and testifying against a central bank, suffering terrible retribution. There hadn't been many moments of peace in his life, but wasn't that true of the lives of all great men?

He had never tried to find out the date of his birth and so never had a birthday party. However, every September the fourth a cake was baked and the family had a little celebration. September the fourth was what Daniel called Job Day—the anniversary of the day Thomas Keane had offered him the position that launched his career in banking. It was just like Daniel that he didn't celebrate the day everyone else did, but celebrated his own private holiday instead. In all her years with him, she had never heard him compare himself to anyone else. He simply didn't think that way. He had his own standards and they were the only ones he cared about.

He also had his anchors. He never forgot the orphanage and the streets of Cleveland. Trading and investing served up regular reminders of fallibility. Nothing punctured pomposity as quickly and as ruthlessly as children. He hadn't moved the family from the brownstone on 52nd Street—it was big enough, who needed a mansion? She had been his sturdiest anchor. While women were regarded as second-class citizens in business and politics, she had refused to be a second-class citizen in her own marriage. She had questioned him, challenged him, argued with him, and, when all else failed, turned her mordant wit on him.

Daniel had been a risk. From the night they'd discussed Shakespeare on the balcony, she had sensed his unpredictability. He would be dangerous—that was what had excited her, aroused her. Like all great drama, all great art, all greatness, there was a tension to him. When he touched her face with his hand and kissed her; when he led her to the bedroom and closed the door, took off his clothes, and stood before her; when gentle caresses gave way to passionate, insistent intensity and their bodies merged, every sensation, emotion, instinct, and thought within her responded to that tension, that driving force, within him. After their youthful fire had mellowed to a warm glow, she still felt it when he looked at her, when he spoke to her, when they touched.

She had once asked George Woodbury the secret to trading stocks. His answer: "Timing." That was one of the secrets to Daniel's life— timing. He had been a giant and had been fortunate enough to live during one of those rare times when humanity made room for its giants, giving them the freedom they must have. Daniel's age had been one of scientists, inventors, engineers, entrepreneurs, executives, and capitalists. The coming age, with its inevitable decline, would be one of politicians, bureaucrats, social workers, and generals. While countless volumes had been written about the Civil War, the Spanish-American War, and what was now called the Great War, Eleanor had been unable to find one good history of the Industrial Revolution. Unprecedented progress, peace, and prosperity didn't capture the popular imagination the way war and carnage did. She made no apologies for wanting to revisit the past, or for expressing happiness that she wouldn't be around for the future.

Many of the giants—Hill, Carnegie, Harriman, and Durand—were gone. Nineteen thirteen, the year of the income tax and the Federal Reserve, had marked the passing of their era. Now their names were on plaques at museums, libraries, opera houses, universities, statues, and monuments, but the intoxicating spirit of unfettered freedom, unlimited possibilities, unbounded confidence, and buoyant optimism of their era was gone. Nobody had recognized it at the time. Only a perceptive few had noted it after its passing. Would it ever return?

Daniel had given money to institutions he deemed worthy, but he had donated anonymously and never allowed his name on a plaque. In a way it was odd that there was no epitaph on his headstone, but in a way it was fitting. The Pirate had said it best, taking Eleanor's hands at Daniel's funeral. "Mrs. Durand, there wasn't ever anybody like him and there won't be nobody like him again."

That inelegant statement probably would have made the best epitaph, but even it was not up to the daunting task of summing up the life of Daniel Durand. His family had combed through the quote books and some had made their own tries at composition, but it had proven impossible to find a pithy sentence or combination of sentences that captured what he was and what he had meant to them. There wasn't ever anybody like him and there won't be nobody like him again.

Eleanor closed her eyes and leaned her head back against the bench. The wind rustled through the trees and the sun warmed her face. She didn't know if she'd see Daniel again. She had lived her life with him, borne his children, raised their family with him, and loved him as deeply as a woman could love a man. He was part of her, she was part of him, and that was all that mattered.

She stood and took a last look at her son's headstone and then Daniel's, without a date of birth or an epitaph. The discreet sign at Durand & Woodbury was the one plaque his name was on, and it was only his last name at that.

Starting down the path, she smiled. She had thought of an epitaph: Memories Last Longer Than Monuments.